$27.50

9/3/0?

Middlesex

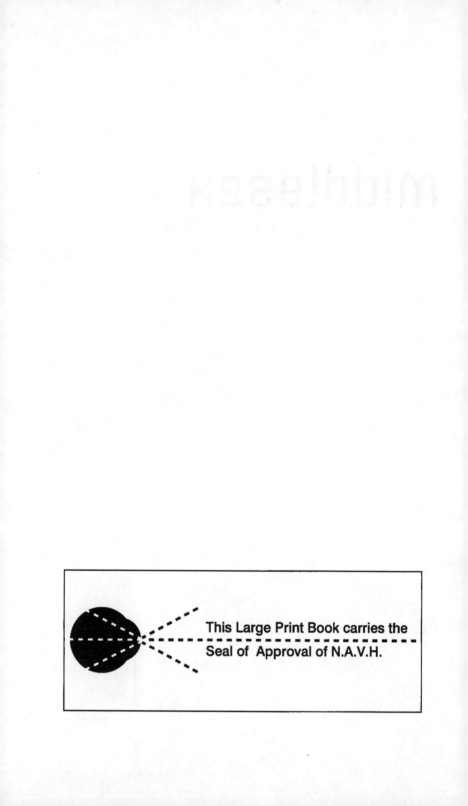

This Large Print Book carries the
Seal of Approval of N.A.V.H.

Middlesex

꧁꧂

Jeffrey Eugenides

Thorndike Press • Waterville, Maine

Published in 2003 by arrangement with Farrar, Straus and Giroux, LLC.

Thorndike Press® Large Print Basic.

The tree indicium is a trademark of Thorndike Press.

The text of this Large Print edition is unabridged. Other aspects of the book may vary from the original edition.

Set in 16 pt. Plantin by Elena Picard.

Printed in the United States on permanent paper.

Library of Congress Cataloging-in-Publication Data

Eugenides, Jeffrey.
    Middlesex / Jeffrey Eugenides.
        p. cm.
    ISBN 0-7862-5700-8 (lg. print : hc : alk. paper)
    1. Greek Americans — Fiction. 2. Grosse Pointe (Mich.)
— Fiction. 3. Detroit (Mich.) — Fiction. 4. Gender
identity — Fiction. 5. Hermaphroditism — Fiction.
6. Teenagers — Fiction. 7. Large type books. I. Title.
PS3555.U4M53 2003
    813'.54—dc21   2003053016

For Yama, Who Comes
from a Different Gene Pool Entirely

As the Founder/CEO of NAVH, the only national health agency solely devoted to those who, although not totally blind, have an eye disease which could lead to serious visual impairment, I am pleased to recognize Thorndike Press* as one of the leading publishers in the large print field.

Founded in 1954 in San Francisco to prepare large print textbooks for partially seeing children, NAVH became the pioneer and standard setting agency in the preparation of large type.

Today, those publishers who meet our standards carry the prestigious "Seal of Approval" indicating high quality large print. We are delighted that Thorndike Press is one of the publishers whose titles meet these standards. We are also pleased to recognize the significant contribution Thorndike Press is making in this important and growing field.

Lorraine H. Marchi, L.H.D.
Founder/CEO
NAVH

* Thorndike Press encompasses the following imprints: Thorndike, Wheeler, Walker and Large Pr int Press.

The author would like to thank the Whiting Younger Writers' Awards, the John Simon Guggenheim Foundation, the National Endowment for the Arts, the Deutscher Akademischer Austauschdienst, the American Academy in Berlin, the MacDowell Colony, Yaddo, Helen Papanikolas, and Milton Karafilis, for their help and support. In addition, the author would like to cite the following works from which he drew information crucial in the writing of *Middlesex*: *The Smyrna Affair* by Marjorie Housepian Dobkin; "Wrestling with Death: Greek Immigrant Funeral Customs in Utah" by Helen Z. Papanikolas; *An Original Man* by Claude Andrew Clegg III; *The Black Muslims in America* by C. Eric Lincoln; *Venuses Penuses: Sexology, Sexosophy, and Exigency Theory* by Dr. John Money; *Third Sex, Third Gender: Beyond Sexual Dimorphism in Culture and History*, edited by Gilbert Herdt; *Hermaphrodites and the Medical Invention of Sex* by Alice Domurat Dreger; "Androgens and the Evolution of Male Gender Identity

Among Male Pseudo-hermaphrodites with 5-alpha-reductase Deficiency" by Julianne Imperato-McGinley, M.D., Ralph E. Peterson, M.D., Teofilo Gautier, M.D., and Erasmo Sturla, M.D.; and *Hermaphrodites with Attitude*, the newspaper published by the Intersex Society of North America.

Contents

Book One

The Silver Spoon

꧁꧂

I was born twice: first, as a baby girl, on a remarkably smogless Detroit day in January of 1960; and then again, as a teenage boy, in an emergency room near Petoskey, Michigan, in August of 1974. Specialized readers may have come across me in Dr. Peter Luce's study, "Gender Identity in 5-Alpha-Reductase Pseudohermaphrodites," published in the *Journal of Pediatric Endocrinology* in 1975. Or maybe you've seen my photograph in chapter sixteen of the now sadly outdated *Genetics and Heredity*. That's me on page 578, standing naked beside a height chart with a black box covering my eyes.

My birth certificate lists my name as Calliope Helen Stephanides. My most recent driver's license (from the Federal Republic of Germany) records my first name simply as Cal. I'm a former field hockey goalie, long-standing member of the Save-the-Manatee Foundation, rare attendant at the Greek Orthodox liturgy, and, for most of my adult life, an employee of the U.S.

State Department. Like Tiresias, I was first one thing and then the other. I've been ridiculed by classmates, guinea-pigged by doctors, palpated by specialists, and researched by the March of Dimes. A redheaded girl from Grosse Pointe fell in love with me, not knowing what I was. (Her brother liked me, too.) An army tank led me into urban battle once; a swimming pool turned me into myth; I've left my body in order to occupy others — and all this happened before I turned sixteen.

But now, at the age of forty-one, I feel another birth coming on. After decades of neglect, I find myself thinking about departed great-aunts and -uncles, long-lost grandfathers, unknown fifth cousins, or, in the case of an inbred family like mine, all those things in one. And so before it's too late I want to get it down for good: this roller-coaster ride of a single gene through time. Sing now, O Muse, of the recessive mutation on my fifth chromosome! Sing how it bloomed two and a half centuries ago on the slopes of Mount Olympus, while the goats bleated and the olives dropped. Sing how it passed down through nine generations, gathering invisibly within the polluted pool of the Stephanides family. And sing how Providence, in the guise of a massacre, sent the gene flying again; how it blew like a seed across the sea to America, where it drifted through our industrial rains until it fell to earth in the fertile soil of my mother's own midwestern womb.

Sorry if I get a little Homeric at times. That's genetic, too.

Three months before I was born, in the aftermath of one of our elaborate Sunday dinners, my grandmother Desdemona Stephanides ordered my brother to get her silkworm box. Chapter Eleven had been heading toward the kitchen for a second helping of rice pudding when she blocked his way. At fifty-seven, with her short, squat figure and intimidating hairnet, my grandmother was perfectly designed for blocking people's paths. Behind her in the kitchen, the day's large female contingent had congregated, laughing and whispering. Intrigued, Chapter Eleven leaned sideways to see what was going on, but Desdemona reached out and firmly pinched his cheek. Having regained his attention, she sketched a rectangle in the air and pointed at the ceiling. Then, through her ill-fitting dentures, she said, "Go for *yia yia*, dolly *mou*."

Chapter Eleven knew what to do. He ran across the hall into the living room. On all fours he scrambled up the formal staircase to the second floor. He raced past the bedrooms along the upstairs corridor. At the far end was a nearly invisible door, wallpapered over like the entrance to a secret passageway. Chapter Eleven located the tiny doorknob level with his head and, using all his strength, pulled it open. Another set of stairs lay behind it. For a long moment my brother stared hesitantly into the darkness above, before climbing, very slowly now, up to the attic where my grandparents lived.

In sneakers he passed beneath the twelve damply newspapered birdcages suspended from the rafters. With a brave face he immersed himself in the sour odor of the parakeets, and in my grandparents' own particular aroma, a mixture of mothballs and hashish. He negotiated his way past my grandfather's book-piled desk and his collection of rebetika records. Finally, bumping into the leather ottoman and the circular coffee table made of brass, he found my grandparents' bed and, under it, the silkworm box.

Carved from olivewood, a little bigger than a shoe box, it had a tin lid perforated by tiny airholes and inset with the icon of an unrecognizable saint. The saint's face had been rubbed off, but the fingers of his right hand were raised to bless a short, purple, terrifically self-confident-looking mulberry tree. After gazing awhile at this vivid botanical presence, Chapter Eleven pulled the box from under the bed and opened it. Inside were the two wedding crowns made from rope and, coiled like snakes, the two long braids of hair, each tied with a crumbling black ribbon. He poked one of the braids with his index finger. Just then a parakeet squawked, making my brother jump, and he closed the box, tucked it under his arm, and carried it downstairs to Desdemona.

She was still waiting in the doorway. Taking the silkworm box out of his hands, she turned back into the kitchen. At this point Chapter Eleven was granted a view of the room, where all the women now fell silent. They moved aside to let Desdemona pass and there, in the middle of the linoleum, was my mother. Tessie Stephanides was leaning back in a kitchen chair, pinned beneath the immense, drum-tight globe of her pregnant belly. She had a happy, helpless expression on her face, which was flushed and hot. Desdemona set the silkworm box on the kitchen table and opened the lid. She reached under the wedding crowns and the hair braids to come up with something Chapter Eleven hadn't seen: a silver spoon. She tied a piece of string to the spoon's handle. Then, stooping forward, she dangled the spoon over my mother's swollen belly. And, by extension, over me.

Up until now Desdemona had had a perfect record: twenty-three correct guesses. She'd known that Tessie was going to be Tessie. She'd predicted the sex of my brother and of all the babies of her friends at church. The only children whose genders she hadn't divined were her own, because it was bad luck for a mother to plumb the mysteries of her own womb. Fearlessly, however, she plumbed my mother's. After some initial hesitation, the spoon swung north to south, which meant that I was going to be a boy.

Splay-legged in the chair, my mother tried to smile. She didn't want a boy. She had one already. In fact, she was so certain I was going to be a girl that she'd picked out only one name for me: Calliope. But when my grandmother shouted in Greek, "A boy!" the cry went around the room, and out into the hall, and across the hall into the living room where the men were arguing politics. And my mother, hearing it repeated so many times, began to believe it might be true.

As soon as the cry reached my father, however, he marched into the kitchen to tell his mother that, this time at least, her spoon was wrong. "And how you know so much?" Desdemona asked him. To which he replied what many Americans of his generation would have:

"It's science, Ma."

★ ★ ★

Ever since they had decided to have another child — the diner was doing well and Chapter Eleven was long out of diapers — Milton and Tessie had been in agreement that they wanted a daughter. Chapter Eleven had just turned five years old. He'd recently found a dead bird in the yard, bringing it into the house to show his mother. He liked shooting things, hammering things, smashing things, and wrestling with his father. In such a masculine household, Tessie had begun to feel like the odd woman out and saw herself in ten years' time imprisoned in a world of hubcaps and hernias. My mother pictured a daughter as a counterinsurgent: a fellow lover of lapdogs, a seconder of proposals to attend the Ice Capades. In the spring of 1959, when discussions of my fertilization got under way, my mother couldn't foresee that women would soon be burning their brassieres by the thousand. Hers were padded, stiff, fire-retardant. As much as Tessie loved her son, she knew there were certain things she'd be able to share only with a daughter.

On his morning drive to work, my father had been seeing visions of an irresistibly sweet, dark-eyed little girl. She sat on the seat beside him — mostly during stoplights — directing questions at his patient, all-knowing ear. "What do you call that thing, Daddy?" "That? That's the Cadillac seal." "What's the Cadillac seal?" "Well, a long time ago, there was a French explorer named Cadillac, and he was the one who discovered Detroit. And that seal was his family seal, from France." "What's France?" "France is a country in Europe." "What's Europe?" "It's a continent, which is like a great big piece of land, way, way bigger than a country. But Cadillacs don't come from Europe anymore, *kukla*. They come from right here in the good old U.S.A." The light turned green and he drove on. But my prototype lingered. She was there at the next light and the next. So pleasant was her company that my father, a man loaded with initiative, decided to see what he could do to turn his vision into reality.

Thus: for some time now, in the living room where the men discussed politics, they had also been discussing the velocity of sperm. Peter Tatakis, "Uncle Pete," as we called him, was a leading member of the debating society that formed every week on our black love seats. A lifelong bachelor, he had no family in America and so had become attached to ours. Every Sunday he arrived in his wine-dark Buick, a tall, prune-faced, sad-seeming man with an incongruously vital head of wavy hair.

He was not interested in children. A proponent of the Great Books series — which he had read twice — Uncle Pete was engaged with serious thought and Italian opera. He had a passion, in history, for Edward Gibbon, and, in literature, for the journals of Madame de Staël. He liked to quote that witty lady's opinion on the German language, which held that German wasn't good for conversation because you had to wait to the end of the sentence for the verb, and so couldn't interrupt. Uncle Pete had wanted to become a doctor, but the "catastrophe" had ended that dream. In the United States, he'd put himself through two years of chiropractic school, and now ran a small office in Birmingham with a human skeleton he was still paying for in installments. In those days, chiropractors had a somewhat dubious reputation. People didn't come to Uncle Pete to free up their kundalini. He cracked necks, straightened spines, and made custom arch supports out of foam rubber. Still, he was the closest thing to a doctor we had in the house on those Sunday afternoons. As a young man he'd had half his stomach surgically removed, and now after dinner always drank a Pepsi-Cola to help digest his meal. The soft drink had been named for the digestive enzyme pepsin, he sagely told us, and so was suited to the task.

It was this kind of knowledge that led my father to trust what Uncle Pete said when it came to the reproductive timetable. His head on a throw pillow, his shoes off, *Madama Butterfly* softly playing on my parents' stereo, Uncle Pete explained that, under the microscope, sperm carrying male chromosomes had been observed to swim faster than those carrying female chromosomes. This assertion generated immediate merriment among the restaurant owners and fur finishers assembled in our living room. My father, however, adopted the pose of his favorite piece of sculpture, *The Thinker*, a miniature of which sat across the room on the telephone table. Though the topic had been brought up in the open-forum atmosphere of those postprandial Sundays, it was clear that, notwithstanding the impersonal tone of the discussion, the sperm they were talking about was my father's. Uncle Pete made it clear: to have a girl baby, a couple should "have sexual congress twenty-four hours prior to ovulation." That way, the swift male sperm would rush in and die off. The female sperm, sluggish but more reliable, would arrive just as the egg dropped.

My father had trouble persuading my mother to go along with the scheme. Tessie Zizmo had been a virgin when she married Milton Stephanides at the age of twenty-two. Their engagement, which coincided with the Second World War, had been a chaste affair. My mother was proud of the way she'd managed to simultaneously kindle and snuff my father's flame, keeping him at a low burn for the duration of a global cataclysm. This hadn't been all that difficult, however, since she was in Detroit and Milton was in Annapolis at the U.S. Naval Academy. For more than a year Tessie lit candles at the Greek church for her fiancé, while Milton gazed at her photographs pinned over his bunk. He liked to pose Tessie in the manner of the movie magazines, standing sideways, one high heel raised on a step, an expanse of black stocking visible. My mother looks surprisingly pliable in those old snapshots, as though she liked nothing better than to have her man in uniform arrange her against the porches and lampposts of their humble neighborhood.

She didn't surrender until after Japan had. Then, from their wedding night onward (according to what my brother told my covered ears), my parents made love regularly and enjoyably. When it came to having children, however, my mother had her own ideas. It was her belief that an embryo could sense the amount of love with which it had been created. For this reason, my father's suggestion didn't sit well with her.

"What do you think this is, Milt, the Olympics?"

"We were just speaking theoretically," said my father.

"What does Uncle Pete know about having babies?"

"He read this particular article in *Scientific American*," Milton said. And to bolster his case: "He's a subscriber."

"Listen, if my back went out, I'd go to Uncle Pete. If I had flat feet like you do, I'd go. But that's it."

"This has all been verified. Under the microscope. The male sperms are faster."

"I bet they're stupider, too."

"Go on. Malign the male sperms all you want. Feel free. We don't want a male sperm. What we want is a good old, slow, reliable female sperm."

"Even if it's true, it's still ridiculous. I can't just do it like clockwork, Milt."

"It'll be harder on me than you."

"I don't want to hear it."

"I thought you wanted a daughter."

"I do."

"Well," said my father, "this is how we can get one."

Tessie laughed the suggestion off. But behind her sarcasm was a serious moral reservation. To tamper with something as mysterious and miraculous as the birth of a child was an act of hubris. In the first place, Tessie didn't believe you could do it. Even if you could, she didn't believe you should try.

Of course, a narrator in my position (prefetal at the time) can't be entirely sure about any of this. I can only explain the scientific mania that overtook my father during that spring of '59 as a symptom of the belief in progress that was infecting everyone back then. Remember, *Sputnik* had been launched only two years earlier. Polio, which had kept my parents quarantined indoors during the summers of their childhood, had been conquered by the Salk vaccine. People had no idea that viruses were cleverer than human beings, and thought they'd soon be a thing of the past. In that optimistic, postwar America, which I caught the tail end of, everybody was the master of his own destiny, so it only followed that my father would try to be the master of his.

A few days after he had broached his plan to Tessie, Milton came home one evening with a present. It was a jewelry box tied with a ribbon.

"What's this for?" Tessie asked suspiciously.

"What do you mean, what is it for?"

"It's not my birthday. It's not our anniversary. So why are you giving me a present?"

"Do I have to have a reason to give you a present? Go on. Open it."

Tessie crumpled up one corner of her mouth, unconvinced. But it was difficult to hold a jewelry box in your hand without opening it. So finally she slipped off the ribbon and snapped the box open.

Inside, on black velvet, was a thermometer.

"A thermometer," said my mother.

"That's not just any thermometer," said Milton. "I had to go to three different pharmacies to find one of these."

"A luxury model, huh?"

"That's right," said Milton. "That's what you call a basal thermometer. It reads the temperature down to *a tenth of a degree*." He raised his eyebrows. "Normal thermometers only read every two tenths. This one does it every tenth. Try it out. Put it in your mouth."

"I don't have a fever," said Tessie.

"This isn't about a fever. You use it to find out what your base temperature is. It's more accurate and precise than a regular fever-type thermometer."

"Next time bring me a necklace."

But Milton persisted: "Your body temperature's changing all the time, Tess. You may not notice, but it is. You're in constant flux, temperature-wise. Say, for instance" — a little cough — "you happen to be ovulating. Then your temperature goes up. Six tenths of a degree, in most case scenarios. Now," my father went on, gaining steam, not noticing that his wife was frowning, "if we were to implement the system we talked about the other day — just for instance, say — what you'd do is, *first,* establish your *base temperature.* It might not be ninety-eight point six. Everybody's a little different. That's another thing I learned from Uncle Pete. Anyway, once you established your *base temperature,* then you'd look for that six-tenths-degree rise. And that's when, if we were to go through with this, that's when we'd know to, you know, mix the cocktail."

My mother said nothing. She only put the thermometer into the box, closed it, and handed it back to her husband.

"Okay," he said. "Fine. Suit yourself. We may get another boy. Number two. If that's the way you want it, that's the way it'll be."

"I'm not so sure we're going to have anything at the moment," replied my mother.

Meanwhile, in the greenroom to the world, I waited. Not even a gleam in my father's eye yet (he was staring gloomily at the thermometer case in his lap). Now my mother gets up from the so-called love seat. She heads for the stairway, holding a hand to her forehead, and the likelihood of my ever coming to be seems more and more remote. Now my father gets up to make his rounds, turning out lights, locking doors. As he climbs the stairway, there's hope for me again. The timing of the thing had to be just so in order for me to become the person I am. Delay the act by an hour and you change the gene selection. My conception was still weeks away, but already my parents had begun their slow collision into each other. In our upstairs hallway, the Acropolis night-light is burning, a gift from Jackie Halas, who owns a souvenir shop. My mother is at her vanity when my father enters the bedroom. With two fingers she rubs Noxzema into her face, wiping it off with a tissue. My father had only to say an affectionate word and she would have forgiven him. Not me but somebody like me might have been made that night. An infinite number of possible selves crowded the threshold, me among them but with no guaranteed ticket, the hours moving slowly, the planets in the heavens circling at their usual pace, weather coming into it, too, because my mother was afraid of thunderstorms and would have cuddled against my father had it rained that night. But, no, clear skies held out, as did my parents' stubbornness. The bedroom light went out. They stayed on their own sides of the bed. At last, from my mother, "Night." And from my father, "See you in the morning." The moments that led up to me fell into place as though decreed. Which, I guess, is why I think about them so much.

The following Sunday, my mother took Desdemona and my brother to church. My father never went along, having become an apostate at the age of eight over the exorbitant price of votive candles. Likewise, my grandfather preferred to spend his mornings working on a modern Greek translation of the "restored" poems of Sappho. For the next seven years, despite repeated strokes, my grandfather worked at a small desk, piecing together the legendary fragments into a larger mosaic, adding a stanza here, a coda there, soldering an anapest or an iamb. In the evenings he played his bordello music and smoked a hookah pipe.

In 1959, Assumption Greek Orthodox Church was located on Charlevoix. It was there that I would be baptized less than a year later and would be brought up in the Orthodox faith. Assumption, with its revolving chief priests, each sent to us via the Patriarchate in Constantinople, each arriving in the full beard of his authority, the embroidered vestments of his sanctity, but each wearying after a time — six months was the rule — because of the squabbling of the congregation, the personal attacks on the way he sang, the constant need to shush the parishioners who treated the church like the bleachers at Tiger Stadium, and, finally, the effort of delivering a sermon each week twice, first in Greek and then again in English. Assumption, with its spirited coffee hours, its bad foundation and roof leaks, its strenuous ethnic festivals, its catechism classes where our heritage was briefly kept alive in us before being allowed to die in the great diaspora. Tessie and company advanced down the central aisle, past the sand-filled trays of votive candles. Above, as big as a float in the Macy's Thanksgiving Day Parade, was the Christ Pantocrator. He curved across the dome like space itself. Unlike the suffering, earthbound Christs depicted at eye level on the church walls, our Christ Pantocrator was clearly transcendent, all-powerful, heaven-bestriding. He was reaching down to the apostles above the altar to present the four rolled-up sheepskins of the Gospels. And my mother, who tried all her life to believe in God without ever quite succeeding, looked up at him for guidance.

The Christ Pantocrator's eyes flickered in the dim light. They seemed to suck Tessie upward. Through the swirling incense, the Savior's eyes glowed like televisions flashing scenes of recent events . . .

First there was Desdemona the week before, giving advice to her daughter-in-law. "Why you want more children, Tessie?" she had asked with studied nonchalance. Bending to look in the oven, hiding the alarm on her face (an alarm that would go unexplained for another sixteen years), Desdemona waved the idea away. "More children, more trouble . . ."

Next there was Dr. Philobosian, our elderly family physician. With ancient diplomas behind him, the old doctor gave his verdict. "Nonsense. Male sperm swim faster? Listen. The first person who saw sperm under a microscope was Leeuwenhoek. Do you know what they looked like to him? Like worms . . ."

And then Desdemona was back, taking a different angle: "God decides what baby is. Not you . . ."

These scenes ran through my mother's mind during the interminable Sunday service. The congregation stood and sat. In the front pew, my cousins, Socrates, Plato, Aristotle, and Cleopatra, fidgeted. Father Mike emerged from behind the icon screen and swung his censer. My mother tried to pray, but it was no use. She barely survived until coffee hour.

From the tender age of twelve, my mother had been unable to start her day without the aid of at least two cups of immoderately strong, tar-black, unsweetened coffee, a taste for which she had picked up from the tugboat captains and zooty bachelors who filled the boardinghouse where she had grown up. As a high school girl, standing five foot one inch tall, she had sat next to auto workers at the corner diner, having coffee before her first class. While they scanned the racing forms, Tessie finished her civics homework. Now, in the church basement, she told Chapter Eleven to run off and play with the other children while she got a cup of coffee to restore herself.

She was on her second cup when a soft, womanly voice sighed in her ear. "Good morning, Tessie." It was her brother-in-law, Father Michael Antoniou.

"Hi, Father Mike. Beautiful service today," Tessie said, and immediately regretted it. Father Mike was the assistant priest at Assumption. When the last priest had left, harangued back to Athens after a mere three months, the family had hoped that Father Mike might be promoted. But in the end another new, foreign-born priest, Father Gregorios, had been given the post. Aunt Zo, who never missed a chance to lament her marriage, had said at dinner in her comedienne's voice, "My husband. Always the bridesmaid and never the bride."

By complimenting the service, Tessie hadn't intended to compliment Father Greg. The situation was made still more delicate by the fact that, years ago, Tessie and Michael Antoniou had been engaged to be married. Now she was married to Milton and Father Mike was married to Milton's sister. Tessie had come down to clear her head and have her coffee and already the day was getting out of hand.

Father Mike didn't appear to notice the slight, however. He stood smiling, his eyes gentle above the roaring waterfall of his beard. A sweet-natured man, Father Mike was popular with church widows. They liked to crowd around him, offering him cookies and bathing in his beatific essence. Part of this essence came from Father Mike's perfect contentment at being only five foot four. His shortness had a charitable aspect to it, as though he had given away his height. He seemed to have forgiven Tessie for breaking off their engagement years ago, but it was always there in the air between them, like the talcum powder that sometimes puffed out of his clerical collar.

Smiling, carefully holding his coffee cup and saucer, Father Mike asked, "So, Tessie, how are things at home?"

My mother knew, of course, that as a weekly Sunday guest at our house, Father Mike was fully informed about the thermometer scheme. Looking in his eyes, she thought she detected a glint of amusement.

"You're coming over to the house today," she said carelessly. "You can see for yourself."

"I'm looking forward to it," said Father Mike. "We always have such interesting discussions at your house."

Tessie examined Father Mike's eyes again but now they seemed full of genuine warmth. And then something happened to take her attention away from Father Mike completely.

Across the room, Chapter Eleven had stood on a chair to reach the tap of the coffee urn. He was trying to fill a coffee cup, but once he got the tap open he couldn't get it closed. Scalding coffee poured out across the table. The hot liquid splattered a girl who was standing nearby. The girl jumped back. Her mouth opened, but no sound came out. With great speed my mother ran across the room and whisked the girl into the ladies' room.

No one remembers the girl's name. She didn't belong to any of the regular parishioners. She wasn't even Greek. She appeared at church that one day and never again, and seems to have existed for the sole purpose of changing my mother's mind. In the bathroom the girl held her steaming shirt away from her body while Tessie brought damp towels. "Are you okay, honey? Did you get burned?"

"He's very clumsy, that boy," the girl said.

"He can be. He gets into everything."

"Boys can be very obstreperous."

Tessie smiled. "You have quite a vocabulary."

At this compliment the girl broke into a big smile. " 'Obstreperous' is my favorite word. My brother is very obstreperous. Last month my favorite word was 'turgid.' But you can't use 'turgid' that much. Not that many things are turgid, when you think about it."

"You're right about that," said Tessie, laughing. "But obstreperous is all over the place."

"I couldn't agree with you more," said the girl.

Two weeks later. Easter Sunday, 1959. Our religion's adherence to the Julian calendar has once again left us out of sync with the neighborhood. Two Sundays ago, my brother watched as the other kids on

35

the block hunted multicolored eggs in nearby bushes. He saw his friends eating the heads off chocolate bunnies and tossing handfuls of jelly beans into cavity-rich mouths. (Standing at the window, my brother wanted more than anything to believe in an American God who got resurrected on the right day.) Only yesterday was Chapter Eleven finally allowed to dye his own eggs, and then only in one color: red. All over the house red eggs gleam in lengthening, solstice rays. Red eggs fill bowls on the dining room table. They hang from string pouches over doorways. They crowd the mantel and are baked into loaves of cruciform *tsoureki*.

But now it is late afternoon; dinner is over. And my brother is smiling. Because now comes the one part of Greek Easter he prefers to egg hunts and jelly beans: the egg-cracking game. Everyone gathers around the dining table. Biting his lip, Chapter Eleven selects an egg from the bowl, studies it, returns it. He selects another. "This looks like a good one," Milton says, choosing his own egg. "Built like a Brinks truck." Milton holds his egg up. Chapter Eleven prepares to attack. When suddenly my mother taps my father on the back.

"Just a minute, Tessie. We're cracking eggs here."

She taps him harder.

"What?"

"My temperature." She pauses. "It's up six tenths."

She has been using the thermometer. This is the first my father has heard of it.

"Now?" my father whispers. "Jesus, Tessie, are you sure?"

"No, I'm not sure. You told me to watch for any rise in my temperature and I'm telling you I'm up six tenths of a degree." And, lowering her voice, "Plus it's been thirteen days since my last you know what."

"Come on, Dad," Chapter Eleven pleads.

"Time out," Milton says. He puts his egg in the ashtray. "That's my egg. Nobody touch it until I come back."

Upstairs, in the master bedroom, my parents accomplish the act. A child's natural decorum makes me refrain from imagining the scene in much detail. Only this: when they're done, as if topping off the tank, my father says, "That should do it." It turns out he's right. In May, Tessie learns she's pregnant, and the waiting begins.

By six weeks, I have eyes and ears. By seven, nostrils, even lips. My genitals begin to form. Fetal hormones, taking chromosomal cues, inhibit Müllerian structures, promote Wolffian ducts. My twenty-three paired chromosomes have linked up and crossed over, spinning their roulette wheel, as my *papou* puts his hand on my mother's belly and says, "Lucky two!" Arrayed in their regiments, my genes carry out their orders. All except two, a pair of miscreants — or revolutionaries, depending on your view — hiding out on chromosome number 5. Together, they siphon off an enzyme, which stops the production of a certain hormone, which complicates my life.

In the living room, the men have stopped talking about politics and instead lay bets on whether Milt's new kid will be a boy or a girl. My father is confident. Twenty-four hours after the deed, my mother's body temperature rose another two tenths, confirming ovulation. By then the male sperm had given up, exhausted. The female sperm, like tortoises, won the race. (At which point Tessie handed Milton the thermometer and told him she never wanted to see it again.)

All this led up to the day Desdemona dangled a utensil over my mother's belly. The sonogram didn't exist at the time; the spoon was the next best thing. Desdemona crouched. The kitchen grew silent. The other women bit their lower lips, watching, waiting. For the first minute, the spoon didn't move at all. Desdemona's hand shook and, after long seconds had passed, Aunt Lina steadied it. The spoon twirled; I kicked; my mother cried out. And then, slowly, moved by a wind no one felt, in that unearthly Ouija-board way, the silver spoon began to move, to swing, at first in a small circle but each orbit growing gradually more elliptical until the path flattened into a straight line pointing from oven to banquette. North to south, in other words. Desdemona cried, *"Koros!"* And the room erupted with shouts of *"Koros, koros."*

That night, my father said, "Twenty-three in a row means she's bound for a fall. This time, she's wrong. Trust me."

"I don't mind if it's a boy," my mother said. "I really don't. As long as it's healthy, ten fingers, ten toes."

"What's this 'it.' That's my daughter you're talking about."

I was born a week after New Year's, on January 8, 1960. In the waiting room, supplied only with pink-ribboned cigars, my father cried out, "Bingo!" I was a girl. Nineteen inches long. Seven pounds four ounces.

That same January 8, my grandfather suffered the first of his thirteen strokes. Awakened by my parents rushing off to the hospital, he'd gotten out of bed and gone downstairs to make himself a cup of coffee. An hour later, Desdemona found him lying on the kitchen floor. Though his mental faculties remained intact, that morning, as I let out my first cry at Women's Hospital, my *papou* lost the ability to speak. According to Desdemona, my grandfather collapsed right after overturning his coffee cup to read his fortune in the grounds.

When he heard the news of my sex, Uncle Pete refused to accept any congratulations. There was no magic involved. "Besides," he joked, "Milt did all the work." Desdemona became grim. Her American-born son had been proven right and, with this fresh defeat, the old country, in which she still tried to live despite its being four thousand miles and thirty-eight years away, receded one more notch. My arrival marked the end of her baby-guessing and the start of her husband's long decline. Though the silkworm box reappeared now and then, the spoon was no longer among its treasures.

I was extracted, spanked, and hosed off, in that order. They wrapped me in a blanket and put me on display among six other infants, four boys, two girls, all of them, unlike me, correctly tagged. This can't be true but I remember it: sparks slowly filling a dark screen.

Someone had switched on my eyes.

Matchmaking

When this story goes out into the world, I may become the most famous hermaphrodite in history. There have been others before me. Alexina Barbin attended a girls' boarding school in France before becoming Abel. She left behind an autobiography, which Michel Foucault discovered in the archives of the French Department of Public Hygiene. (Her memoirs, which end shortly before her suicide, make unsatisfactory reading, and it was after finishing them years ago that I first got the idea to write my own.) Gottlieb Göttlich, born in 1798, lived as Marie Rosine until the age of thirty-three. One day abdominal pains sent Marie to the doctor. The physician checked for a hernia and found undescended testicles instead. From then on, Marie donned men's clothes, took the name of Gottlieb, and made a fortune traveling around Europe, exhibiting himself to medical men.

As far as the doctors are concerned, I'm even better than Gottlieb. To the extent that fetal hormones affect brain chemistry and histology, I've got a male brain. But I was raised as a girl. If you were going to devise an experiment to measure the relative influences of nature versus nurture, you couldn't come up with anything better than my life. During my time at the Clinic nearly three decades ago, Dr. Luce ran me through a barrage of tests. I was given the Benton Visual Retention Test and the Bender Visual-Motor Gestalt Test. My verbal IQ was measured, and lots of other things, too. Luce even analyzed my prose style to see if I wrote in a linear, masculine way, or in a circular, feminine one.

All I know is this: despite my androgenized brain, there's an innate feminine circularity in the story I have to tell. In any genetic history, I'm the final clause in a periodic sentence, and that sentence begins a long time ago, in another language, and you have to read it from the beginning to get to the end, which is my arrival.

And so now, having been born, I'm going to rewind the film, so that my pink blanket flies off, my crib scoots across the floor as my umbilical cord reattaches, and I cry out as I'm sucked back between my mother's legs. She gets really fat again. Then back some more as a spoon stops swinging and a thermometer goes back into its velvet case. *Sputnik* chases its rocket trail back to the launching pad and polio stalks the land. There's a quick shot of my father as a twenty-year-old clarinetist, playing an Artie Shaw number into the phone, and then he's in church, age eight, being scandalized by the price of candles; and next my grandfather is untaping his first U.S. dollar bill over a cash register in 1931. Then we're out of America completely; we're in the middle of the ocean, the sound track sounding funny in reverse. A steamship appears, and up on deck a lifeboat is curiously rocking; but then the boat docks, stern first, and we're up on dry land again, where the film unspools, back at the beginning . . .

⚜

In the late summer of 1922, my grandmother Desdemona Stephanides wasn't predicting births but deaths, specifically, her own. She was in her silkworm cocoonery, high on the slope of Mount Olympus in Asia Minor, when her heart, without warning, missed a beat. It was a distinct sensation: she felt her heart stop and squeeze into a ball. Then, as she stiffened, it began to race, thumping against her ribs. She let out a small, astonished cry. Her twenty thousand silkworms, sensitive to human emotion, stopped spinning cocoons. Squinting in the dim light, my grandmother looked down to see the front of her tunic visibly fluttering; and in that instant,

43

as she recognized the insurrection inside her, Desdemona became what she'd remain for the rest of her life: a sick person imprisoned in a healthy body. Nevertheless, unable to believe in her own endurance, despite her already quieting heart, she stepped out of the cocoonery to take a last look at the world she wouldn't be leaving for another fifty-eight years.

The view was impressive. A thousand feet below lay the old Ottoman capital of Bursa, like a backgammon board spread out across the valley's green felt. Red diamonds of roof tile fit into diamonds of whitewash. Here and there, the sultans' tombs were stacked up like bright chips. Back in 1922, automobile traffic didn't clog the streets. Ski lifts didn't cut swaths into the mountain's pine forests. Metallurgic and textile plants didn't ring the city, filling the air with smog. Bursa looked — at least from a thousand feet up — pretty much as it had for the past six centuries, a holy city, necropolis of the Ottomans and center of the silk trade, its quiet, declining streets abloom with minarets and cypress trees. The tiles of the Green Mosque had turned blue with age, but that was about it. Desdemona Stephanides, however, kibitzing from afar, gazed down on the board and saw what the players had missed.

To psychoanalyze my grandmother's heart palpitations: they were the manifestations of grief. Her parents were dead — killed in the recent war with the Turks. The Greek Army, encouraged by the Allied Nations, had invaded western Turkey in 1919, reclaiming the ancient Greek territory in Asia Minor. After years of living apart up on the mountain, the people of Bithynios, my grandmother's village, had emerged into the safety of the *Megale Idea* — the Big Idea, the dream of Greater Greece. It was now Greek troops who occupied Bursa. A Greek flag flew over the former Ottoman palace. The Turks and their leader, Mustafa Kemal, had retreated to Angora in the east. For the first time in their lives the Greeks of Asia Minor were out from under Turkish rule. No longer were the giaours ("infidel dogs") forbidden to wear bright clothing or ride horses or use saddles. Never again, as in the last centuries, would Ottoman officials arrive in the village every year, carting off the strongest boys to serve in the Janissaries. Now, when the village men took silk to market in Bursa, they were free Greeks, in a free Greek city.

Desdemona, however, mourning her parents, was still imprisoned by the past. And so she stood on the mountain, looking down at the emancipated city, and felt cheated by her inability to feel happy like

45

everybody else. Years later, in her widow-hood, when she'd spend a decade in bed trying with great vitality to die, she would finally agree that those two years between wars a half century earlier had been the only decent time in her life; but by then everyone she'd known would be dead and she could only tell it to the television.

For the greater part of an hour Des-demona had been trying to ignore her fore-boding by working in the cocoonery. She'd come out the back door of the house, through the sweet-smelling grape arbor, and across the terraced yard into the low, thatch-roofed hut. The acrid, larval smell inside didn't bother her. The silkworm cocoonery was my grandmother's own per-sonal, reeking oasis. All around her, in a firmament, soft white silkworms clung to bundled mulberry twigs. Desdemona watched them spinning cocoons, moving their heads as though to music. As she watched, she forgot about the world out-side, its changes and convulsions, its ter-rible new music (which is about to be sung in a moment). Instead she heard her mother, Euphrosyne Stephanides, speaking in this very cocoonery years ago, eluci-dating the mysteries of silkworms — "To have good silk, you have to be pure," she used to tell her daughter. "The silkworms know everything. You can always tell what somebody is up to by the way their silk looks" — and so on, Euphrosyne giving examples — "Maria Poulos, who's always lifting her skirt for everyone? Have you seen her cocoons? A stain for every man. You should look next time" — Desdemona only eleven or twelve and believing every word, so that now, as a young woman of twenty-one, she still couldn't entirely disbelieve her mother's morality tales, and examined the cocoon constellations for a sign of her own impurity (the dreams she'd been having!). She looked for other things, too, because her mother also maintained that silkworms reacted to historical atrocities. After every massacre, even in a village fifty miles away, the silkworms' filaments turned the color of blood — "I've seen them bleed like the feet of Christos Himself," Euphrosyne again, and her daughter, years later, remembering, squinting in the weak light to see if any cocoons had turned red. She pulled out a tray and shook it; she pulled out another; and it was right then that she felt her heart stop, squeeze into a ball, and begin punching her from inside. She dropped the tray, saw her tunic flutter from interior force, and understood that her heart operated on its own instructions, that she had no control over it or, indeed, over anything else.

So my *yia yia*, suffering the first of her

imaginary diseases, stood looking down at Bursa, as though she might spot a visible confirmation of her invisible dread. And then it came from inside the house, by means of sound: her brother, Eleutherios ("Lefty") Stephanides, had begun to sing. In badly pronounced, meaningless English:

"Ev'ry morning, ev'ry evening, ain't we got fun," Lefty sang, standing before their bedroom mirror as he did every afternoon about this time, fastening the new celluloid collar to the new white shirt, squeezing a dollop of hair pomade (smelling of limes) into his palm and rubbing it into his new Valentino haircut. And continuing: "In the meantime, in-between time, ain't we got fun." The lyrics meant nothing to him, either, but the melody was enough. It spoke to Lefty of jazz-age frivolity, gin cocktails, cigarette girls; it made him slick his hair back with panache . . . while, out in the yard, Desdemona heard the singing and reacted differently. For her, the song conjured only the disreputable bars her brother went to down in the city, those hash dens where they played rebetika and American music and where there were loose women who sang . . . as Lefty put on his new striped suit and folded the red pocket handkerchief that matched his red necktie . . . and she felt funny inside, especially her stomach, which was roiled by complicated emotions, sadness, anger, and something else she couldn't name that hurt most of all. "The rent's unpaid, dear, we haven't a car," Lefty crooned in the sweet tenor I would later inherit; and beneath the music Desdemona now heard her mother's voice again, Euphrosyne Stephanides' last words spoken just before she died from a bullet wound, "Take care of Lefty. Promise me. Find him a wife!" . . . and Desdemona, through her tears, replying, "I promise. I promise!" . . . these voices all speaking at once in Desdemona's head as she crossed the yard to go into the house. She came through the small kitchen where she had dinner cooking (for one) and marched straight into the bedroom she shared with her brother. He was still singing — "Not much money, Oh! but honey" — fixing his cuff links, parting his hair; but then he looked up and saw his sister — "Ain't we got" — and pianissimo now — "fun" — fell silent.

For a moment, the mirror held their two faces. At twenty-one, long before ill-fitting dentures and self-imposed invalidism, my grandmother was something of a beauty. She wore her black hair in long braids pinned up under her kerchief. These braids were not delicate like a little girl's but heavy and womanly, possessing a natural

49

power, like a beaver's tail. Years, seasons, and various weather had gone into the braids; and when she undid them at night they fell to her waist. At present, black silk ribbons were tied around the braids, too, making them even more imposing, if you got to see them, which few people did. What was on view for general consumption was Desdemona's face: her large, sorrowful eyes, her pale, candlelit complexion. I should also mention, with the vestigial pang of a once flat-chested girl, Desdemona's voluptuous figure. Her body was a constant embarrassment to her. It was always announcing itself in ways she didn't sanction. In church when she knelt, in the yard when she beat rugs, beneath the peach tree when she picked fruit, Desdemona's feminine elaborations escaped the constraints of her drab, confining clothes. Above the jiggling of her body, her kerchief-framed face remained apart, looking slightly scandalized at what her breasts and hips were up to.

Eleutherios was taller and skinnier. In photographs from the time he looks like the underworld figures he idolized, the thin mustachioed thieves and gamblers who filled the seaside bars of Athens and Constantinople. His nose was aquiline, his eyes sharp, the overall impression of his face hawk-like. When he smiled, however, you saw the softness in his eyes, which made it clear that Lefty was in fact no gangster but the pampered, bookish son of comfortably well-off parents.

That summer afternoon in 1922, Desdemona wasn't looking at her brother's face. Instead her eyes moved to the suit coat, to the gleaming hair, to the striped trousers, as she tried to figure out what had happened to him these past few months.

Lefty was one year younger than Desdemona and she often wondered how she'd survived those first twelve months without him. For as long as she could remember he'd always been on the other side of the goat's-hair blanket that separated their beds. Behind the *kelimi* he performed puppet shows, turning his hands into the clever, hunchbacked Karaghiozis who always outwitted the Turks. In the dark he made up rhymes and sang songs, and one of the reasons she hated his new American music was that he sang it exclusively to himself. Desdemona had always loved her brother as only a sister growing up on a mountain could love a brother: he was the whole entertainment, her best friend and confidant, her co-discoverer of short cuts and monks' cells. Early on, the emotional sympathy she'd felt with Lefty had been so absolute that she'd sometimes forgotten they were separate people. As kids they'd scrabbled down the terraced mountainside like a four-legged, two-headed creature. She was accustomed to their Siamese shadow springing up against the white-washed house at evening, and whenever she encountered her solitary outline, it seemed cut in half.

Peacetime seemed to be changing everything. Lefty had taken advantage of the new freedoms. In the last month he'd gone down to Bursa a total of seventeen times. On three occasions he'd stayed overnight in the Cocoon Inn across from the Mosque of Sultan Ouhan. He'd left one morning dressed in boots, knee socks, breeches, *doulamas,* and vest and come back the following evening in a striped suit, with a silk scarf tucked into his collar like an opera singer and a black derby on his head. There were other changes. He'd begun to teach himself French from a small, plum-colored phrase book. He'd picked up affected gestures, putting his hands in his pockets and rattling change, for instance, or doffing his cap. When Desdemona did the laundry, she found scraps of paper in Lefty's pockets, covered with mathematical figures. His clothes smelled musky, smoky, and sometimes sweet.

Now, in the mirror, their joined faces couldn't hide the fact of their growing separation. And my grandmother, whose constitutional gloom had broken out into full cardiac thunder, looked at her brother, as she once had her own shadow, and felt that something was missing.

"So where are you going all dressed up?"

"Where do you think I'm going? To the Koza Han. To sell cocoons."

"You went yesterday."

"It's the season."

With a tortoiseshell comb Lefty parted his hair on the right, adding pomade to an unruly curl that refused to stay flat.

Desdemona came closer. She picked up the pomade and sniffed it. It wasn't the smell on his clothes. "What else do you do down there?"

"Nothing."

"You stay all night sometimes."

"It's a long trip. By the time I walk there, it's late."

"What are you smoking in those bars?"

"Whatever's in the hookah. It's not polite to ask."

"If Mother and Father knew you were smoking and drinking like this . . ." She trailed off.

"They don't know, do they?" said Lefty. "So I'm safe." His light tone was unconvincing. Lefty acted as though he had recovered from their parents' deaths, but Desdemona saw through this. She smiled grimly at her brother and, without comment, held out her fist. Automatically, while still admiring himself in the mirror, Lefty made a fist, too. They counted, "One, two, three . . . shoot!"

"Rock crushes snake. I win," said Desdemona. "So tell me."

"Tell you what?"

"Tell me what's so interesting in Bursa."

Lefty combed his hair forward again and parted it on the left. He swiveled his head back and forth in the mirror. "Which looks better? Left or right?"

"Let me see." Desdemona raised her hand delicately to Lefty's hair — and mussed it.

"Hey!"

"What do you want in Bursa?"

"Leave me alone."

"Tell me!"

"You want to know?" Lefty said, exasperated with his sister now. "What do you think I want?" He spoke with pent-up force. "I want a woman."

Desdemona gripped her belly, patted her heart. She took two steps backward and from this vantage point examined her brother anew. The idea that Lefty, who shared her eyes and eyebrows, who slept in the bed beside hers, could be possessed by such a desire had never occurred to Desdemona before. Though physically mature, Desdemona's body was still a stranger to its owner. At night, in their bedroom, she'd seen her sleeping brother press against his rope mattress as though angry with it. As a child she'd come upon him in the cocoonery, innocently rubbing against a wooden post. But none of this had made an impression. "What are you doing?" she'd asked Lefty, eight or nine at the time, and gripping the post, moving his knees up and down. With a steady, deter-mined voice, he'd answered, "I'm trying to get that feeling."

"What feeling?"

"You know" — grunting, puffing, pumping knees — "that *feeling.*"

But she didn't know. It was still years before Desdemona, cutting cucumbers, would lean against the corner of the kitchen table and, without realizing it, would lean in a little harder, and after that would find herself taking up that position every day, the table corner snug between her legs. Now, preparing her brother's meals, she sometimes struck up her old ac-quaintance with the dining table, but she wasn't conscious of it. It was her body that did it, with the cunning and silence of bodies everywhere.

Her brother's trips to the city were dif-ferent. He knew what he was looking for, apparently; he was in full communication with his body. His mind and body had become one entity, thinking one thought, bent on one obsession, and for the first time ever Desdemona couldn't read that thought. All she knew was that it had nothing to do with her.

It made her mad. Also, I suspect, a little jealous. Wasn't she his best friend? Hadn't they always told each other everything? Didn't she do everything for him, cook, sew, and keep house as their mother used to? Wasn't she the one who had been taking care of the silkworms single-handedly so that he, her smart little brother, could take lessons from the priest, learning ancient Greek? Hadn't she been the one to say, "You take care of the books, I'll take care of the cocoonery. All you have to do is sell the cocoons at the market." And when he had started lingering down in the city, had she complained? Had she mentioned the scraps of paper, or his red eyes, or the musky-sweet smell on his clothes? Desdemona had a suspicion that her dreamy brother had become a hashish smoker. Where there was rebetika music there was always hashish. Lefty was dealing with the loss of their parents in the only way he could, by disappearing in a cloud of hash smoke while listening to the absolutely saddest music in the world. Desdemona understood all this and so had said nothing. But now she saw that her brother was trying to escape his grief in a way she hadn't expected; and she was no longer content to be quiet.

"You want a woman?" Desdemona asked in an incredulous voice. "What kind of woman? A Turkish woman?"

Lefty said nothing. After his outburst he had resumed combing his hair.

"Maybe you want a harem girl. Is that right? You think I don't know about those types of loose girls, those *poutanes?* Yes, I do. I'm not so stupid. You like a fat girl shaking her belly in your face? With a jewel in her fat belly? You want one of those? Let me tell you something. Do you know why those Turkish girls cover their faces? You think it's because of religion? No. It's because otherwise no one can stand to look at them!"

And now she shouted, "Shame on you, Eleutherios! What's the matter with you? Why don't you get a girl from the village?"

It was at this point that Lefty, who was now brushing off his jacket, called his sister's attention to something she was overlooking. "Maybe you haven't noticed," he said, "but there aren't any girls in this village."

Which, in fact, was pretty much the case. Bithynios had never been a big village, but in 1922 it was smaller than ever. People had begun leaving in 1913, when the phylloxera blight ruined the currants. They had continued to leave during the Balkan Wars. Lefty and Desdemona's cousin, Sourmelina, had gone to America and was living now in a place called Detroit. Built along a gentle slope of the mountain, Bithynios wasn't a precarious, cliffside sort of place. It was an elegant, or at least harmonious, cluster of yellow stucco houses with red roofs. The grandest houses, of which there were two, had *çikma,* enclosed bay windows that hung out over the street. The poorest houses, of which there were many, were essentially one-room kitchens. And then there were houses like Desdemona and Lefty's, with an overstuffed parlor, two bedrooms, a kitchen, and a backyard privy with a European toilet. There were no shops in Bithynios, no post office or bank, only a church and one taverna. For shopping you had to go into Bursa, walking first and then taking the horse-drawn streetcar.

In 1922 there were barely a hundred people living in the village. Fewer than half of those were women. Of forty-seven women, twenty-one were old ladies. Another twenty were middle-aged wives. Three were young mothers, each with a daughter in diapers. One was his sister. That left two marriageable girls. Whom Desdemona now rushed to nominate.

"What do you mean there aren't any girls? What about Lucille Kafkalis? She's a nice girl. Or Victoria Pappas?"

"Lucille smells," Lefty answered reasonably. "She bathes maybe once a year. On her name day. And Victoria?" He ran a finger over his upper lip. "Victoria has a mustache bigger than mine. I don't want to share a razor with my wife." With that, he put down his clothing brush and put on his jacket. "Don't wait up," he said, and left the bedroom.

"Go!" Desdemona called after him. "See what I care. Just remember. When your Turkish wife takes off her mask, don't come running back to the village!"

But Lefty was gone. His footsteps faded away. Desdemona felt the mysterious poison rising in her blood again. She paid no attention. "I don't like eating alone!" she shouted, to no one.

The wind from the valley had picked up, as it did every afternoon. It blew through the open windows of the house. It rattled the latch on her hope chest and her father's old worry beads lying on top. Desdemona picked the beads up. She began to slip them one by one through her fingers, exactly as her father had done, and her grandfather, and her great-grandfather, performing a family legacy of precise, codified, thorough worrying. As the beads clicked together, Desdemona gave herself up to them. What was the matter with God? Why had He taken her parents and left her to worry about her brother? What was she supposed to do with him? "Smoking, drinking, and now worse! And where does he get the money for all his foolishness? From my cocoons, that's how!" Each bead slipping through her fingers was another resentment recorded and released. Desdemona, with her sad eyes, her face of a girl forced to grow up too fast, worried with her beads like all the Stephanides men before and after her (right down to me, if I count).

She went to the window and put her head out, heard the wind rustling in the pine trees and the white birch. She kept counting her worry beads and, little by little, they did their job. She felt better. She decided to go on with her life. Lefty wouldn't come back tonight. Who cared? Who needed him anyway? It would be easier for her if he never came back. But she owed it to her mother to see that he didn't catch some shameful disease or, worse, run off with a Turkish girl. The beads continued to drop, one by one, through Desdemona's hands. But she was no longer counting her pains. Instead, the beads now summoned to her mind images in a magazine hidden in their father's old desk. One bead was a hairstyle. The next bead was a silk slip. The next was a black brassiere. My grandmother had begun to matchmake.

Lefty, meanwhile, carrying a sack of cocoons, was on his way down the mountain. When he reached the city, he came down Kapali Carsi Caddesi, turned at Borsa Sokak, and soon was passing through the arch into the courtyard of the Koza Han. Inside, around the aquamarine fountain, hundreds of stiff, waist-high sacks foamed over with silkworm cocoons. Men crowded everywhere, either selling or buying. They had been shouting since the opening bell at ten that morning and their voices were hoarse. "Good price! Good quality!" Lefty squeezed through the narrow paths between the cocoons, holding his own sack. He had never had any interest in the family livelihood. He couldn't judge silkworm cocoons by feeling or sniffing them as his sister could. The only reason he brought the cocoons to market was that women were not allowed. The jostling, the bumping of porters and sidestepping of sacks made him tense. He thought how nice it would be if everyone would just stop moving a moment, if they would stand still to admire the luminosity of the cocoons in the evening light; but of course no one ever did. They went on yelling and thrusting cocoons in one another's faces and lying and haggling. Lefty's father had loved market season at the Koza Han, but the mercantile impulse hadn't been passed down to his son.

Near the covered portico Lefty saw a merchant he knew. He presented his sack. The merchant reached deep into it and brought out a cocoon. He dipped it into a bowl of water and then examined it. Then he dipped it into a cup of wine.

"I need to make organzine from these. They're not strong enough."

Lefty didn't believe this. Desdemona's silk was always the best. He knew that he was supposed to shout, to act offended, to pretend to take his business elsewhere. But he had gotten such a late start; the closing bell was about to sound. His father had always told him not to bring cocoons late in the day because then you had to sell them at a discount. Lefty's skin prickled under his new suit. He wanted the transaction to be over. He was filled with embarrassment: embarrassment for the human race, its preoccupation with money, its love of swindle. Without protest he accepted the man's price. As soon as the deal was completed he hurried out of the Koza Han to attend to his real business in town.

It wasn't what Desdemona thought.

Watch closely: Lefty, setting his derby at a rakish angle, walks down the sloping streets of Bursa. When he passes a coffee kiosk, however, he doesn't go in. The proprietor hails him, but Lefty only waves. In the next street he passes a window behind whose shutters female voices call out, but he pays no attention, following the meandering streets past fruit sellers and restaurants until he reaches another street where he enters a church. More precisely: a former mosque, with minaret torn down and Koranic inscriptions plastered over to provide a fresh canvas for the Christian saints that are, even now, being painted on the interior. Lefty hands a coin to the old lady selling candles, lights one, stands it upright in sand. He takes a seat in a back pew. And in the same way my mother will later pray for guidance over my conception, Lefty Stephanides, my great-uncle (among other things) gazes up at the unfinished Christ Pantocrator on the ceiling. His prayer begins with words he learned as a child, *Kyrie eleison, Kyrie eleison, I am not worthy to come before Thy throne,* but soon it veers off, becoming personal with *I don't know why I feel this way, it's not natural . . .* and then turning a little accusatory, praying *You made me this way, I didn't ask to think things like . . .* but getting abject finally with *Give me strength, Christos, don't let me be this way, if she even knew* . . . eyes squeezed shut, hands bending the derby's brim, the words drifting up with the incense toward a Christ-in-progress.

He prayed for five minutes. Then came out, replaced his hat on his head, and rattled the change in his pockets. He climbed back up the sloping streets and, this time (his heart unburdened), stopped at all the places he'd resisted on his way down. He stepped into a kiosk for coffee and a smoke. He went to a café for a glass of ouzo. The backgammon players shouted, "Hey, Valentino, how about a game?" He let himself get cajoled into playing, just one, then lost and had to go double or nothing. (The calculations Desdemona found in Lefty's pants pockets were gambling debts.) The night wore on. The ouzo kept flowing. The musicians arrived and the rebetika began. They played songs about lust, death, prison, and life on the street. "At the hash den on the seashore, where I'd go every day," Lefty sang along, "Every morning, bright and early, to chase the blues away; I ran into two harem girls sitting on the sand; Quite stoned the poor things were, and they were really looking grand." Meanwhile, the hookah was being filled. By midnight, Lefty came floating back onto the streets.

An alley descends, turns, dead-ends. A

door opens. A face smiles, beckoning. The next thing Lefty knows, he's sharing a sofa with three Greek soldiers, looking across at seven plump, perfumed women sharing two sofas opposite. (A phonograph plays the hit song that's playing everywhere: "Ev'ry morning, ev'ry evening . . .") And now his recent prayer is forgotten completely because as the madam says, "Anyone you like, sweetheart," Lefty's eyes pass over the blond, blue-eyed Circassian, and the Armenian girl suggestively eating a peach, and the Mongolian with the bangs; his eyes keep scanning to fix on a quiet girl at the end of the far couch, a sad-eyed girl with perfect skin and black hair in braids. ("There's a scabbard for every dagger," the madam says in Turkish as the whores laugh.) Unconscious of the workings of his attraction, Lefty stands up, smooths his jacket, holds out his hand toward his choice . . . and only as she leads him up the stairs does a voice in his head point out how this girl comes up to exactly where . . . and isn't her profile just like . . . but now they've reached the room with its unclean sheets, its blood-colored oil lamp, its smell of rose water and dirty feet. In the intoxication of his young senses Lefty doesn't pay attention to the growing similarities the girl's disrobing reveals. His eyes take in the large breasts, the slim waist, the hair cascading down to the defenseless coccyx; but Lefty doesn't make connections. The girl fills a hookah for him. Soon he drifts off, no longer hearing the voice in his head. In the soft hashish dream of the ensuing hours, he loses sense of who he is and who he's with. The limbs of the prostitute become those of another woman. A few times he calls out a name, but by then he is too stoned to notice. Only later, showing him out, does the girl bring him back to reality. "By the way, I'm Irini. We don't have a Desdemona here."

The next morning he awoke at the Cocoon Inn, awash in recriminations. He left the city and climbed back up the mountain to Bithynios. His pockets (empty) made no sound. Hung over and feverish, Lefty told himself that his sister was right: it was time for him to get married. He would marry Lucille, or Victoria. He would have children and stop going down to Bursa and little by little he'd change; he'd get older; everything he felt now would fade into memory and then into nothing. He nodded his head; he fixed his hat.

Back in Bithynios, Desdemona was giving those two beginners finishing lessons. While Lefty was still sleeping it off at the Cocoon Inn, she invited Lucille Kafkalis and Victoria Pappas over to the house. The girls were even younger than Desdemona, still living at home with their parents. They looked up to Desdemona as the mistress of her own home. Envious of her beauty, they gazed admiringly at her; flattered by her attentions, they confided in her; and when she began to give them advice on their looks, they listened. She told Lucille to wash more regularly and suggested she use vinegar under her arms as an antiperspirant. She sent Victoria to a Turkish woman who specialized in removing unwanted hair. Over the next week, Desdemona taught the girls everything she'd learned from the only beauty magazine she'd ever seen, a tattered catalogue called *Lingerie Parisienne*. The catalogue had belonged to her father. It contained thirty-two pages of photographs showing models wearing brassieres, corsets, garter belts, and stockings. At night, when everyone was sleeping, her father used to take it out of the bottom drawer of his desk. Now Desdemona studied the catalogue in secret, memorizing the pictures so that she could re-create them later.

She told Lucille and Victoria to stop by every afternoon. They walked into the house, swaying their hips as instructed, and passed through the grape arbor where Lefty liked to read. They wore a different dress each time. They also changed their hairstyles, walks, jewelry, and mannerisms. Under Desdemona's direction, the two drab girls multiplied themselves into a small city of women, each with a signature laugh, a personal gemstone, a favorite song she hummed. After two weeks, Desdemona went out to the grape arbor one afternoon and asked her brother, "What are you doing here? Why aren't you down in Bursa? I thought you'd have found a nice Turkish girl to marry by now. Or do they all have mustaches like Victoria's?"

"Funny you should mention that," Lefty said. "Have you noticed? Vicky doesn't have a mustache anymore. And do you know what else?" — getting up now, smiling — "even Lucille's starting to smell okay. Every time she comes over, I smell flowers." (He was lying, of course. Neither girl looked or smelled more appealing to him than before. His enthusiasm was only his way of giving in to the inevitable: an arranged marriage, domesticity, children — the complete disaster.) He came up close to Desdemona. "You were right," he said. "The most beautiful girls in the world are right here in this village."

She looked shyly back up into his eyes. "You think so?"

"Sometimes you don't even notice what's right under your nose."

They stood gazing at each other, as

Desdemona's stomach began to feel funny again. And to explain the sensation I have to tell you another story. In his presidential address at the annual convention of the Society for the Scientific Study of Sexuality in 1968 (held that year in Mazatlán among lots of suggestive piñatas), Dr. Luce introduced the concept of "periphescence." The word itself means nothing; Luce made it up to avoid any etymological associations. The state of periphescence, however, is well known. It denotes the first fever of human pair bonding. It causes giddiness, elation, a tickling on the chest wall, the urge to climb a balcony on the rope of the beloved's hair. Periphescence denotes the initial drugged and happy bedtime where you sniff your lover like a scented poppy for hours running. (It lasts, Luce explained, up to two years — tops.) The ancients would have explained what Desdemona was feeling as the workings of Eros. Now expert opinion would put it down to brain chemistry and evolution. Still, I have to insist: to Desdemona periphescence felt like a lake of warmth flooding up from her abdomen and across her chest. It spread like the 180-proof, fiery flood of a mint-green Finnish liqueur. With the pumping of two efficient glands in her neck, it heated her face. And then the warmth got other ideas and started spreading into places a girl like Desdemona didn't allow it to go, and she broke off the stare and turned away. She walked to the window, leaving the periphescence behind, and the breeze from the valley cooled her down. "I will speak to the girls' parents," she said, trying to sound like her mother. "Then you must go pay court."

The next night, the moon, like Turkey's future flag, was a crescent. Down in Bursa the Greek troops scrounged for food, caroused, and shot up another mosque. In Angora, Mustafa Kemal let it be printed in the newspaper that he would be holding a tea at Chankaya while in actuality he'd left for his headquarters in the field. With his men, he drank the last raki he'd take until the battle was over. Under cover of night, Turkish troops moved not north toward Eskiş ehir, as everyone expected, but to the heavily fortified city of Afyon in the south. At Eskiş ehir, Turkish troops lit campfires to exaggerate their strength. A small diversionary force feinted northward toward Bursa. And, amid these deployments, Lefty Stephanides, carrying two corsages, stepped out the front door of his house and began walking to the house where Victoria Pappas lived.

It was an event on the level of a birth or a death. Each of the nearly hundred citizens of Bithynios had heard about Lefty's upcoming visits, and the old widows, the married women, and the young mothers, as well as the old men, were waiting to see which girl he would choose. Because of the small population, the old courting rituals had nearly ceased. This lack of romantic possibility had created a vicious cycle. No one to love: no love. No love: no babies. No babies: no one to love.

Victoria Pappas stood half in and half out of the light, the shading across her body exactly that of the photograph on page 8 of *Lingerie Parisienne*. Desdemona (costume lady, stage manager, and director all in one) had pinned up Victoria's hair, letting ringlets fall over her forehead and warning her to keep her biggish nose in shadow. Perfumed, depilated, moist with emollients, wearing kohl around her eyes, Victoria let Lefty look upon her. She felt the heat of his gaze, heard his heavy breathing, heard him try to speak twice — small squeaks from a dry throat — and then she heard his feet coming toward her, and she turned, making the face Desdemona had taught her; but she was so distracted by the effort to pout her lips like the French lingerie model that she didn't realize the footsteps weren't approaching but retreating; and she turned to see that Lefty Stephanides, the only eligible bachelor in town, had taken off . . .

. . . Meanwhile, back at home, Desdemona opened her hope chest. She reached in and pulled out her own corset. Her mother had given it to her years ago in expectation of her wedding night, saying, "I hope you fill this out someday." Now, before the bedroom mirror, Desdemona held the strange, complicated garment against herself. Down went her knee socks, her gray underwear. Off came her high-waisted skirt, her high-collared tunic. She shook off her kerchief and unbraided her hair so that it fell over her bare shoulders. The corset was made of white silk. As she put it on, Desdemona felt as though she were spinning her own cocoon, awaiting metamorphosis.

But when she looked in the mirror again, she caught herself. It was no use. She would never get married. Lefty would come back tonight having chosen a bride, and then he would bring her home to live with them. Desdemona would stay where she was, clicking her beads and growing even older than she already felt. A dog howled. Someone in the village kicked over a bundle of sticks and cursed. And my grandmother wept silently because she was going to spend the rest of her days counting worries that never went away . . .

. . . While in the meantime Lucille Kafkalis was standing exactly as she'd been told, half in and half out of the light, wearing a white hat sashed with glass cherries, a mantilla over bare shoulders, a bright green, décolleté dress, and high heels, in which she didn't move for fear of falling. Her fat mother waddled in, grinning and shouting, "Here he comes! Even one minute he couldn't stay with Victoria!" . . .

. . . Already he could smell the vinegar. Lefty had just entered the low doorway of the Kafkalis house. Lucille's father welcomed him, then said, "We'll leave you two alone. To get acquainted." The parents left. It was dim in the room. Lefty turned . . . and dropped another corsage.

What Desdemona hadn't anticipated: her brother, too, had pored over the pages of *Lingerie Parisienne*. In fact, he'd done it from the time he turned twelve to the time he turned fourteen, when he discovered the real loot: ten postcard-sized photographs, hidden in an old suitcase, showing "Sermin, Girl of the Pleasure Dome," in which a bored, pear-shaped twenty-five-year-old assumed a variety of positions on the tasseled pillows of a staged seraglio. Finding her in the toiletries pocket was like rubbing a genie's lamp. Up she swirled in a plume of shining dust: wearing nothing but a pair of Arabian Nights slippers and a sash around her waist (flash); lying languidly on a tiger skin, fondling a scimitar (flash); and bathing, lattice-lit, at a marble hammam. Those ten sepia-toned photographs were what had started Lefty's fascination with the city. But he had never entirely forgotten his first loves in *Lingerie Parisienne*. He could summon them in his imagination at will. When he had seen Victoria Pappas looking like page 8, what had struck Lefty most acutely was the distance between her and his boyhood ideal. He tried to imagine himself married to Victoria, living with her, but every image that came to mind had a gaping emptiness at the center, the lack of the person he loved more and knew better than any other. And so he had fled from Victoria Pappas to come down the street and find Lucille Kafkalis, just as disappointingly, failing to live up to page 22 . . .

. . . And now it happens. Desdemona, weeping, takes off the corset, folds it back up, and returns it to the hope chest. She throws herself on the bed, Lefty's bed, to continue crying. The pillow smells of his lime pomade and she breathes it in, sobbing . . .

. . . until, drugged by weeping's opiates, she falls asleep. She dreams the dream she's been having lately. In the dream everything's the way it used to be. She and Lefty are children again (except they have

74

adult bodies). They're lying in the same bed (except now it's their parents' bed). They shift their limbs in sleep (and it feels extremely nice, how they shift, and the bed is wet) . . . at which point Desdemona wakes up, as usual. Her face is hot. Her stomach feels funny, way deep down, and she can almost name the feeling now . . .

. . . As I sit here in my Aeron chair, thinking E. O. Wilson thoughts. Was it love or reproduction? Chance or destiny? Crime or nature at work? Maybe the gene contained an override, ensuring its expression, which would explain Desdemona's tears and Lefty's taste in prostitutes; not fondness, not emotional sympathy; only the need for this new thing to enter the world and hence the heart's rigged game. But I can't explain it, any more than Desdemona or Lefty could have, any more than each one of us, falling in love, can separate the hormonal from what feels divine, and maybe I cling to the God business out of some altruism hard-wired to preserve the species; I can't say. I try to go back in my mind to a time before genetics, before everyone was in the habit of saying about everything, "It's in the genes." A time before our present freedom, and so much freer! Desdemona had no idea what was happening. She didn't envision her insides as a vast computer code, all 1s and 0s, an infinity of sequences, any one of which might contain a bug. Now we know we carry this map of ourselves around. Even as we stand on the street corner, it dictates our destiny. It brings onto our faces the same wrinkles and age spots our parents had. It makes us sniff in idiosyncratic, recognizable family ways. Genes embedded so deep they control our eye muscles, so that two sisters have that same way of blinking, and boy twins dribble in unison. I feel myself sometimes, in anxious moods, playing with the cartilage of my nose exactly as my brother does. Our throats and voice boxes, formed from the same instructions, press air out in similar tones and decibels. And this can be extrapolated backward in time, so that when I speak, Desdemona speaks, too. She's writing these words now. Desdemona, who had no idea of the army inside her, carrying out its million orders, or of the one soldier who disobeyed, going AWOL . . .

. . . Running like Lefty away from Lucille Kafkalis and back to his sister. She heard his feet hurrying as she was refastening her skirt. She wiped her eyes with her kerchief and put a smile on as he came through the door.

"So, which one did you choose?"

Lefty said nothing, inspecting his sister. He hadn't shared a bedroom with her all his life not to be able to tell when she'd been crying. Her hair was loose, covering most of her face, but the eyes that looked up at him were brimming with feeling. "Neither one," he said.

At that Desdemona felt tremendous happiness. But she said, "What's the matter with you? You have to choose."

"Those girls look like a couple of whores."

"Lefty!"

"It's true."

"You don't want to marry them?"

"No."

"You have to." She held out her fist. "If I win, you marry Lucille."

Lefty, who could never resist a bet, made a fist himself. "One, two, three . . . shoot!

"Ax breaks rock," Lefty said. "I win."

"Again," said Desdemona. "This time, if I win, you marry Vicky. One, two, three . . ."

"Snake swallows ax. I win again! So long to Vicky."

"Then who will you marry?"

"I don't know" — taking her hands and looking down at her. "How about you?"

"Too bad I'm your sister."

"You're not only my sister. You're my third cousin, too. Third cousins can marry."

"You're crazy, Lefty."

"This way will be easier. We won't have to rearrange the house."

Joking but not joking, Desdemona and Lefty embraced. At first they just hugged in the standard way, but after ten seconds the hug began to change; certain positions of the hands and strokings of the fingers weren't the usual displays of sibling affection, and these things constituted a language of their own, announced a whole new message in the silent room. Lefty began waltzing Desdemona around, European-style; he waltzed her outside, across the yard, over to the cocoonery, and back under the grape arbor, and she laughed and covered her mouth with her hand. "You're a good dancer, cousin," she said, and her heart jumped again, making her think she might die right then and there in Lefty's arms, but of course she didn't; they danced on. And let's not forget where they were dancing, in Bithynios, that mountain village where cousins sometimes married third cousins and everyone was somehow related; so that as they danced, they started holding each other more tightly, stopped joking, and then just danced together, as a man and a woman, in lonely and pressing circumstances, might sometimes do.

And in the middle of this, before anything had been said outright or any decisions made (before fire would make those decisions for them), right then, mid-waltz, they heard explosions in the distance, and looked down to see, in firelight, the Greek Army in full retreat.

An Immodest Proposal

꧁ঌ

Descended from Asia Minor Greeks, born in America, I live in Europe now. Specifically, in the Schöneberg district of Berlin. The Foreign Service is split into two parts, the diplomatic corps and the cultural staff. The ambassador and his aides conduct foreign policy from the newly opened, extensively barricaded embassy on Neustädtische Kirchstrasse. Our department (in charge of readings, lectures, and concerts) operates out of the colorful concrete box of Amerika Haus.

This morning I took the train to work as usual. The U-Bahn carried me gently west from Kleistpark to Berliner Strasse and then, after a switch, northward toward Zoologischer Garten. Stations of the former West Berlin passed one after another. Most were last remodeled in the seventies and have the colors of suburban kitchens from my childhood: avocado, cinnamon, sunflower yellow. At Spichernstrasse the train halted to conduct an exchange of bodies. Out on the platform a street musician played a teary Slavic melody on an accordion. Wing tips gleaming, my hair still damp, I was flipping through the *Frankfurter Allgemeine* when she rolled her unthinkable bicycle in.

You used to be able to tell a person's nationality by the face. Immigration ended that. Next you discerned nationality via the footwear. Globalization ended that. Those Finnish seal puppies, those German flounders — you don't see them much anymore. Only Nikes, on Basque, on Dutch, on Siberian feet.

The bicyclist was Asian, at least genetically. Her black hair was cut in a shag. She was wearing a short olive green windbreaker, flared black ski pants, and a pair of maroon Campers resembling bowling shoes. The basket of her bike contained a camera bag.

I had a hunch she was American. It was the retro bike. Chrome and turquoise, it had fenders as wide as a Chevrolet's, tires as thick as a wheelbarrow's, and appeared to weigh at least a hundred pounds. An expatriate's whim, that bike. I was about to use it as a pretext for starting a conversation when the train stopped again. The bicyclist looked up. Her hair fell away from her beautiful, hooded face and, for a moment, our eyes met. The placidity of her countenance along with the smoothness of her skin made her face appear like a mask, with living, human eyes behind it. These eyes now darted away from mine as she grasped the handlebars of her bike and pushed her great two-wheeler off the train and toward the elevators. The U-Bahn resumed, but I was no longer reading. I sat in my seat, in a state of voluptuous agitation, of agitated voluptuousness, until my stop. Then I staggered out.

Unbuttoning my suit jacket, I took a cigar from the inner pocket of my coat. From a still smaller pocket I took out my cigar cutter and matches. Though it wasn't after dinner, I lit the cigar — a Davidoff Grand Cru No. 3 — and stood smoking, trying to calm myself. The cigars, the double-breasted suits — they're a little too much. I'm well aware of that. But I need them. They make me feel better. After what I've been through, some overcompensation is to be expected. In my bespoke suit, my checked shirt, I smoked my medium-fat cigar until the fire in my blood subsided.

Something you should understand: I'm not androgynous in the least. 5-alpha-reductase deficiency syndrome allows for normal biosynthesis and peripheral action of testosterone, in utero, neonatally, and at puberty. In other words, I operate in society as a man. I use the men's room. Never the urinals, always the stalls. In the men's locker room at my gym I even shower, albeit discreetly. I possess all the secondary sex characteristics of a normal man except one: my inability to synthesize dihydrotestosterone has made me immune to baldness. I've lived more than half my life as a male, and by now everything comes naturally. When Calliope surfaces, she does so like a childhood speech impediment. Suddenly there she is again, doing a hair flip, or checking her nails. It's a little like being possessed. Callie rises up inside me, wearing my skin like a loose robe. She sticks her little hands into the baggy sleeves of my arms. She inserts her chimp's feet through the trousers of my legs. On the sidewalk I'll feel her girlish walk take over, and the movement brings back a kind of emotion, a desolate and gossipy sympathy for the girls I see coming home from school. This continues for a few more steps. Calliope's hair tickles the back of my throat. I feel her press tentatively on my chest — that old nervous habit of hers — to see if anything is happening there. The sick fluid of adolescent despair that runs through her veins overflows again into mine. But then, just as suddenly, she is leaving, shrinking and melting away inside me, and when I turn to see my reflection in a window there's this: a forty-one-year-old man with longish, wavy hair, a thin mustache, and a goatee. A kind of modern Musketeer.

But that's enough about me for now. I have to pick up where explosions interrupted me yesterday. After all, neither Cal nor Calliope could have come into existence without what happened next.

⚜

"I told you!" Desdemona cried at the top of her lungs. "I told you all this good luck would be bad! This is how they liberate us? Only the Greeks could be so stupid!"

By the morning after the waltz, you see, Desdemona's forebodings had been borne out. The *Megale Idea* had come to an end. The Turks had captured Afyon. The Greek Army, beaten, was fleeing toward the sea. In retreat, it was setting fire to everything in its path. Desdemona and Lefty, in dawn's light, stood on the mountainside and surveyed the devastation. Black smoke rose for miles across the valley. Every village, every field, every tree was aflame.

"We can't stay here," Lefty said. "The Turks will want revenge."

"Since when did they need a reason?"

"We'll go to America. We can live with Sourmelina."

"It won't be nice in America," Desdemona insisted, shaking her head. "You shouldn't believe Lina's letters. She exaggerates."

"As long as we're together we'll be okay."

84

He looked at her, in the way of the night before, and Desdemona blushed. He tried to put his arm around her, but she stopped him. "Look."

Down below, the smoke had thinned momentarily. They could see the roads now, clogged with refugees: a river of carts, wagons, water buffalo, mules, and people hurrying out of the city.

"Where can we get a boat? In Constantinople?"

"We'll go to Smyrna," said Lefty. "Everyone says Smyrna's the safest way." Desdemona was quiet for a moment, trying to fathom this new reality. Voices rumbled in the other houses as people cursed the Greeks, the Turks, and started packing. Suddenly, with resolve: "I'll bring my silkworm box. And some eggs. So we can make money."

Lefty took hold of her elbow and shook her arm playfully. "They don't farm silk in America."

"They wear clothes, don't they? Or do they go around naked? If they wear clothes, they need silk. And they can buy it from me."

"Okay, whatever you want. Just hurry."

Eleutherios and Desdemona Stephanides left Bithynios on August 31, 1922. They left on foot, carrying two suitcases packed with clothes, toiletries, Desdemona's dream book and worry beads, and two of Lefty's texts of Ancient Greek. Under her arm Desdemona also carried her silkworm box containing a few hundred silkworm eggs wrapped in a white cloth. The scraps of paper in Lefty's pockets now recorded not gambling debts but forwarding addresses in Athens or Astoria. Over a single week, the hundred or so remaining citizens of Bithynios packed their belongings and set out for mainland Greece, most en route to America. (A diaspora which should have prevented my existence, but didn't.)

Before leaving, Desdemona walked out into the yard and crossed herself in the Orthodox fashion, leading with the thumb. She said her goodbyes: to the powdery, rotting smell of the cocoonery and to the mulberry trees lined along the wall, to the steps she'd never have to climb again and to this feeling of living above the world, too. She went inside the cocoonery to look at her silkworms for the last time. They had all stopped spinning. She reached up, plucked a cocoon from a mulberry twig, and put it in her tunic pocket.

On September 6, 1922, General Hajienestis, Commander in Chief of the Greek forces in Asia Minor, awoke with the impression that his legs were made of glass. Afraid to get out of bed, he sent the barber away, forgoing his morning shave. In the afternoon he declined to go ashore to enjoy his usual lemon ice on the Smyrna waterfront. Instead he lay on his back, still and alert, ordering his aides — who came and went with dispatches from the front — not to slam the door or stomp their feet. This was one of the commander's more lucid, productive days. When the Turkish Army had attacked Afyon two weeks earlier, Hajienestis had believed that he was dead and that the ripples of light reflecting on his cabin walls were the pyrotechnics of heaven.

At two o'clock, his second-in-command tiptoed into the general's cabin to speak in a whisper: "Sir, I am awaiting your orders for a counterattack, sir."

"Do you hear how they squeak?"

"Sir?"

"My legs. My thin, vitreous legs."

"Sir, I am aware the general is having trouble with his legs, but I submit, with all due respect, sir" — a little louder than a whisper now — "this is not a time to concentrate on such matters."

"You think this is some kind of joke, don't you, lieutenant? But if your legs were made of glass, you'd understand. I can't go into shore. That's exactly what Kemal is banking on! To have me stand up and shatter my legs to pieces."

"These are the latest reports, General."
His second-in-command held a sheet of
paper over Hajienestis' face. " 'The
Turkish cavalry has been sighted one hun-
dred miles east of Smyrna,' " he read.
" 'The refugee population is now 180,000.'
That's an increase of 30,000 people since
yesterday."

"I didn't know death would be like this,
lieutenant. I feel close to you. I'm gone.
I've taken that trip to Hades, yet I can
still see you. Listen to me. Death is not
the end. This is what I've discovered. We
remain, we persist. The dead see that I'm
one of them. They're all around me. You
can't see them, but they're here. Mothers
with children, old women — everyone's
here. Tell the cook to bring me my
lunch."

Outside, the famous harbor was full of
ships. Merchant vessels were tied up to a
long quay alongside barges and wooden
caiques. Farther out, the Allied warships
lay at anchor. The sight of them, for the
Greek and Armenian citizens of Smyrna
(and the thousands and thousands of
Greek refugees), was reassuring, and whenever a rumor circulated — yesterday an Armenian newspaper had claimed that the
Allies, eager to make amends for their support of the Greek invasion, were planning
to hand the city over to the victorious

Turks — the citizens looked out at the French destroyers and British battleships, still on hand to protect European commercial interests in Smyrna, and their fears were calmed.

Dr. Nishan Philobosian had set off for the harbor that afternoon seeking just such reassurance. He kissed his wife, Toukhie, and his daughters, Rose and Anita, goodbye; he slapped his sons, Karekin and Stepan, on the back, pointing at the chessboard and saying with mock gravity, "Don't move those pieces." He locked the front door behind him, testing it with his shoulder, and started down Suyane Street, past the closed shops and shuttered windows of the Armenian Quarter. He stopped outside Berberian's bakery, wondering whether Charles Berberian had taken his family out of the city or whether they were hiding upstairs like the Philobosians. For five days now they'd been under self-imprisonment, Dr. Philobosian and his sons playing endless games of chess, Rose and Anita looking at a copy of *Photoplay* he'd picked up for them on a recent visit to the American suburb of Paradise, Toukhie cooking day and night because eating was the only thing that relieved the anxiety. The bakery door showed only a sign that said **OPEN SOON** and a portrait — which made Philobosian wince — of Kemal, the

Turkish leader resolute in astrakhan cap and fur collar, his blue eyes piercing beneath the crossed sabers of his eyebrows. Dr. Philobosian turned away from the face and moved on, rehearsing all the arguments against putting up Kemal's portrait like that. For one thing — as he'd been telling his wife all week — the European powers would never let the Turks enter the city. Second, if they did, the presence of the warships in the harbor would restrain the Turks from looting. Even during the massacres of 1915 the Armenians of Smyrna had been safe. And finally — for his own family, at least — there was the letter he was on his way to retrieve from his office. So reasoning, he continued down the hill, reaching the European Quarter. Here the houses grew more prosperous. On either side of the street rose two-story villas with flowering balconies and high, armored walls. Dr. Philobosian had never been invited into these villas socially, but he often made house calls to attend the Levantine girls living inside; girls of eighteen or nineteen who awaited him in the "water palaces" of the courtyards, lying languidly on daybeds amid a profusion of fruit trees; girls whose desperate need to find European husbands gave them a scandalous amount of freedom, cause itself for Smyrna's reputation as being exceptionally kind to military officers, and responsible for the fever blushes the girls betrayed on the mornings of Dr. Philobosian's visits, as well as for the nature of their complaints, which ran from the ankle twisted on the dance floor to more intimate scrapes higher up. All of which the girls showed no modesty about, throwing open silk peignoirs to say, "It's all red, Doctor. Do something. I have to be at the *Casin* by eleven." These girls all gone now, taken out of the city by their parents after the first fighting weeks ago, off in Paris and London — where the Season was beginning — the houses quiet as Dr. Philobosian passed by, the crisis receding from his mind at the thought of all those loosened robes. But then he turned the corner, reaching the quay, and the emergency came back to him.

From one end of the harbor to the other, Greek soldiers, exhausted, cadaverous, unclean, limped toward the embarkation point at Chesme, southwest of the city, awaiting evacuation. Their tattered uniforms were black with soot from the villages they'd burned in retreat. Only a week before, the waterfront's elegant open-air cafés had been filled with naval officers and diplomats; now the quay was a holding pen. The first refugees had come with carpets and armchairs, radios, Victrolas, lampstands, dressers, spreading them out before the harbor, under the open sky. The more recent arrivals turned up with only a sack or a suitcase. Amid this confusion, porters darted everywhere, loading boats with tobacco, figs, frankincense, silk, and mohair. The warehouses were being emptied before the Turks arrived.

Dr. Philobosian spotted a refugee picking through chicken bones and potato peels in a heap of garbage. It was a young man in a well-tailored but dirty suit. Even from a distance, Dr. Philobosian's medical eye noticed the cut on the young man's hand and the pallor of malnutrition. But when the refugee looked up, the doctor saw only a blank for a face; he was indistinguishable from any of the refugees swarming the quay. Nevertheless, staring into this blankness, the doctor called, "Are you sick?"

"I haven't eaten for three days," said the young man.

The doctor sighed. "Come with me."

He led the refugee down back streets to his office. He ushered him inside and brought gauze, antiseptic, and tape from a medical cabinet, and examined the hand.

The wound was on the man's thumb, where the nail was missing.

"How did this happen?"

"First the Greeks invaded," the refugee said. "Then the Turks invaded back. My hand got in the way."

Dr. Philobosian said nothing as he cleaned the wound. "I'll have to pay you with a check, Doctor," the refugee said. "I hope you don't mind. I don't have a lot of money on me at the moment."

Dr. Philobosian reached into his pocket. "I have a little. Go on. Take it."

The refugee hesitated only a moment. "Thank you, Doctor. I'll repay you as soon as I get to the United States. Please give me your address."

"Be careful what you drink," Dr. Philobosian ignored the request. "Boil water, if you can. God willing, some ships may come soon."

The refugee nodded. "You're Armenian, Doctor?"

"Yes."

"And you're not leaving?"

"Smyrna is my home."

"Good luck, then. And God bless you."

"You too." And with that Dr. Philobosian led him out. He watched the refugee walk off. It's hopeless, he thought. He'll be dead in a week. If not typhus, something else. But it wasn't his concern. Reaching inside a typewriter, he extracted a thick wad of money from beneath the ribbon. He rummaged through drawers until he found, inside his medical diploma, a faded typewritten letter: "This letter is to certify that Nishan Philobosian, M.D., did, on April 3, 1919, treat Mustafa Kemal Pasha for diverticulitis. Dr. Philobosian is respectfully recommended by Kemal Pasha to the esteem, confidence, and protection of all persons to whom he may present this letter." The bearer of this letter now folded it and tucked it into his pocket.

By then the refugee was buying bread at a bakery on the quay. Where now, as he turns away, hiding the warm loaf under his grimy suit, the sunlight off the water brightens his face and his identity fills itself in: the aquiline nose, the hawk-like expression, the softness appearing in the brown eyes.

For the first time since reaching Smyrna, Lefty Stephanides was smiling. On his previous forays he'd brought back only a single rotten peach and six olives, which he'd encouraged Desdemona to swallow, pits and all, to fill herself up. Now, carrying the sesame-seeded *chureki,* he squeezed back into the crowd. He skirted the edges of open-air living rooms (where families sat listening to silent radios) and stepped over bodies he hoped were sleeping. He was feeling encouraged by another development, too. Just that morning word had spread that Greece was sending a fleet of ships to evacuate refugees. Lefty looked out at the Aegean. Having lived on a mountain for twenty years, he'd never seen the sea before. Somewhere over the water was America and their cousin Sourmelina. He smelled the sea air, the warm bread, the antiseptic from his bandaged thumb, and then he saw her — Desdemona, sitting on the suitcase where he'd left her — and felt even happier.

Lefty couldn't pinpoint the moment he'd begun to have thoughts about his sister. At first he'd just been curious to see what a real woman's breasts looked like. It didn't matter that they were his sister's. He tried to *forget* that they were his sister's. Behind the hanging *kelimi* that separated their beds, he saw Desdemona's silhouette as she undressed. It was just a body; it could have been anyone's, or Lefty liked to pretend so. "What are you doing over there?" Desdemona asked, undressing. "Why are you so quiet?"

"I'm reading."

"What are you reading?"

"The Bible."

"Oh, sure. You never read the Bible."

Soon he'd found himself picturing his sister after the lights went out. She'd invaded his fantasies, but Lefty resisted. He went down to the city instead, in search of naked women he wasn't related to.

But since the night of their waltz, he'd stopped resisting. Because of the messages of Desdemona's fingers, because their parents were dead and their village destroyed, because no one in Smyrna knew who they were, and because of the way Desdemona looked right now, sitting on a suitcase.

And Desdemona? What did she feel? Fear foremost, and worry, punctuated by unprecedented explosions of joy. She had never rested her head in a man's lap before while riding in an oxcart. She'd never slept like spoons, encircled by a man's arms; she'd never experienced a man getting hard against her spine while trying to talk as though nothing were happening. "Only fifty more miles," Lefty had said one night on the arduous journey to Smyrna. "Maybe we'll be lucky tomorrow and get a ride. And when we get to Smyrna, we'll get a boat to Athens" — his voice tight, funny-sounding, a few tones higher than normal — "and from Athens we'll get a boat to America. Sound good? Okay. I think that's good."

What am I doing? Desdemona thought. He's my brother! She looked at the other refugees on the quay, expecting to see them shaking their fingers, saying, "Shame on you!" But they only showed her lifeless faces, empty eyes. Nobody knew. Nobody cared. Then she heard her brother's excited voice, as he lowered the bread before her face. "Behold. Manna from heaven."

Desdemona glanced up at him. Her mouth filled with saliva as Lefty broke the *chureki* in two. But her face remained sad. "I don't see any boats coming," she said.

"They're coming. Don't worry. Eat." Lefty sat down on the suitcase beside her. Their shoulders touched. Desdemona moved away.

"What's the matter?"

"Nothing."

"Every time I sit down you move away." He looked at Desdemona, puzzled, but then his expression softened and he put his arm around her. She stiffened.

"Okay, have it your way." He stood up again.

"Where are you going?"

"To find more food."

"Don't go," Desdemona pleaded. "I'm sorry. I don't like sitting here all alone."

But Lefty had stormed off. He left the quay and wandered the city streets, muttering to himself. He was angry with Desdemona for rebuffing him and he was angry at himself for being angry at her, because he knew she was right. But he didn't stay angry long. It wasn't in his nature. He was tired, half-starved, he had a sore throat, a wounded hand, but for all that Lefty was still twenty years old, on his first real trip away from home, and alert to the newness of things. When you got away from the quay you could almost forget that there was a crisis on. Back here there were fancy shops and high-toned bars, still operating. He came down the Rue de France and found himself at the Sporting Club. Despite the emergency, two foreign consuls were playing tennis on the grass courts out back. In fading light they moved back and forth, swatting the ball while a dark-skinned boy in a white jacket held a tray of gin and tonics courtside. Lefty kept walking. He came to a square with a fountain and washed his face. A breeze came up, bringing the smell of jasmine all the way in from Bournabat. And while Lefty stops to breathe it in, I'd like to take this opportunity to resuscitate — for purely elegiac reasons and only for a paragraph — that city which disappeared, once and for all, in 1922.

Smyrna endures today in a few rebetika songs and a stanza from *The Waste Land*:

> *Mr. Eugenides, the Smyrna merchant*
> *Unshaven, with a pocketful of currants*
> *C.i.f. London: documents at sight,*
> *Asked me in demotic French*
> *To luncheon at the Cannon Street Hotel*
> *Followed by a weekend at the Metropole.*

Everything you need to know about Smyrna is contained in that. The merchant is rich, and so was Smyrna. His proposal was seductive, and so was Smyrna, the most cosmopolitan city in the Near East. Among its reputed founders were, first, the Amazons (which goes nicely with my theme), and second, Tantalus himself. Homer was born there, and Aristotle Onassis. In Smyrna, East and West, opera and *politakia*, violin and *zourna*, piano and *daouli* blended as tastefully as did the rose petals and honey in the local pastries.

Lefty started walking again and soon came to the Smyrna *Casin*. Potted palms flanked a grand entrance, but the doors stood wide open. He stepped inside. No one stopped him. There was no one around. He followed a red carpet to the second floor and into the gaming room. The craps table was unoccupied. Nobody was at the roulette wheel. In the far corner, however, a group of men were playing cards. They glanced up at Lefty but then returned to their game, ignoring his dirty clothes. That was when he realized that the gamblers weren't regular club members; they were refugees like him. Each had wandered through the open door in hopes of winning money to buy passage out of Smyrna. Lefty approached the table. A card player asked, "You in?"

"I'm in."

He didn't understand the rules. He'd

never played poker before, only backgammon, and for the first half hour he lost again and again. Eventually, though, Lefty began to understand the difference between five-card draw and seven-card stud, and gradually the balance of payments around the table began to shift. "Three of these," Lefty said, showing three aces, and the men started to grumble. They watched his dealing more closely, mistaking his clumsiness for a cardsharp's sleight of hand. Lefty began to enjoy himself, and after winning a big pot cried, "Ouzo all around!" But when nothing happened, he looked up and saw again how truly deserted the *Casin* was, and the sight brought home to him the high stakes they were playing for. Life. They were playing for their lives, and now, as he examined his fellow gamblers, and saw perspiration beading their brows and smelled their sour breath, Lefty Stephanides, showing far more restraint than he would four decades later when he played the Detroit numbers, stood up and said, "I'm folding."

They nearly killed him. Lefty's pockets bulged with winnings, and the men insisted he couldn't leave without giving them a chance to win some of it back. He bent over to scratch his leg, insisting, "I can go out any time I want." One of the men grabbed him by his soiled lapels, and Lefty added, "And I don't want to yet." He sat down, scratching his other leg, and thereafter started losing again and again. When all his money was gone, Lefty got up and said with disgusted anger, "Can I leave now?" The men said sure, leave, laughing as they dealt the next hand. Lefty walked stiffly, dejectedly, out of the *Casin*. In the entrance, between the potted palms, he bent down to collect the money he'd stashed in his ripe-smelling socks.

Back at the quay, he sought out Desdemona. "Look what I found," he said, flashing his money. "Somebody must have dropped it. Now we can get a ship."

Desdemona screamed and hugged him. She kissed him right on the lips. Then she pulled back, blushing, and turned to the water. "Listen," she said, "those British are playing music again."

She was referring to the service band on the *Iron Duke*. Every night, as officers dined, the band began playing on the ship's deck. Strains of Vivaldi and Brahms floated out over the water. Over brandy, Major Arthur Maxwell of His Majesty's Marines and his subordinates passed around binoculars to observe the situation ashore.

"Jolly crowded, what?"

"Looks like Victoria Station on Christmas Eve, sir."

"Look at those poor wretches. Left to fend for themselves. When word gets out about the Greek commissioner's leaving, it's going to be pandemonium."

"Will we be evacuating refugees, sir?"

"Our orders are to protect British property and citizens."

"But, surely, sir, if the Turks arrive and there's a massacre . . ."

"There's nothing we can do about it, Phillips. I've spent years in the Near East. The one lesson I've learned is that there is nothing you can do with these people. Nothing at all! The Turks are the best of the lot. The Armenian I liken to the Jew. Deficient moral and intellectual character. As for the Greeks, well, look at them. They've burned down the whole country and now they swarm in here crying for help. Nice cigar, what?"

"Awfully good, sir."

"Smyrna tobacco. Finest in the world. Brings a tear to my eyes, Phillips, the thought of all that tobacco lying in those warehouses out there."

"Perhaps we could send a detail to save the tobacco, sir."

"Do I detect a note of sarcasm, Phillips?"

"Faintly, sir, faintly."

"Good Lord, Phillips, I'm not heartless. I wish we could help these people. But we can't. It's not our war."

"Are you certain of that, sir?"

"What do you mean?"

"We might have supported the Greek forces. Seeing as we sent them in."

"They were dying to be sent in! Venizelos and his bunch. I don't think you fathom the complexity of the situation. We have interests here in Turkey. We must proceed with the utmost care. We cannot let ourselves get caught up in these Byzantine struggles."

"I see, sir. More cognac, sir?"

"Yes, thank you."

"It's a beautiful city, though, isn't it?"

"Quite. You are aware of what Strabo said of Smyrna, are you not? He called Smyrna the finest city in Asia. That was back in the time of Augustus. It's lasted that long. Take a good look, Phillips. Take a good long look."

By September 7, 1922, every Greek in Smyrna, including Lefty Stephanides, is wearing a fez in order to pass as a Turk. The last Greek soldiers are being evacuated at Chesme. The Turkish Army is only thirty miles away — and no ships arrive from Athens to evacuate the refugees.

Lefty, newly moneyed and befezzed,

makes his way through the maroon-capped crowd at the quay. He crosses tram tracks and heads uphill. He finds a steamship office. Inside, a clerk is bending over passenger lists. Lefty takes out his winnings and says, "Two seats to Athens!"

The head remains down. "Deck or cabin?"

"Deck."

"Fifteen hundred drachmas."

"No, not cabin," Lefty says, "deck will be fine."

"That is deck."

"Fifteen hundred? I don't have fifteen hundred. It was five hundred yesterday."

"That was yesterday."

On September 8, 1922, General Hajienestis, in his cabin, sits up in bed, rubs first his right leg and then his left, raps his knuckles against them, and stands up. He goes above deck, walking with great dignity, much as he will later proceed to his death in Athens when he is executed for losing the war.

On the quay, the Greek civil governor, Aristedes Sterghiades, boards a launch to take him out of the city. The crowd hoots and jeers, shaking fists. General Hajienestis takes the scene in calmly. The crowd obscures the waterfront, his favorite café. All he can see is the marquee of the movie theater at which, ten days earlier, he'd been to see *Le Tango de la Mort*. Briefly — and possibly this is another hallucination — he smells the fresh jasmine of Bournabat. He breathes this in. The launch reaches the ship and Sterghiades, ashen-faced, climbs aboard.

And then General Hajienestis gives his only military order of the past few weeks: "Up anchors. Reverse engines. Full steam ahead."

On shore, Lefty and Desdemona watched the Greek fleet leaving. The crowd surged toward the water, raised its four hundred thousand hands, and shouted. And then it fell silent. Not one mouth uttered a sound as the realization came home that their own country had deserted them, that Smyrna now had no government, that there was nothing between them and the advancing Turks.

(And did I mention how in summer the streets of Smyrna were lined with baskets of rose petals? And how everyone in the city could speak French, Italian, Greek, Turkish, English, and Dutch? And did I tell you about the famous figs, brought in by camel caravan and dumped onto the ground, huge piles of pulpy fruit lying in the dirt, with dirty women steeping them in salt water and children squatting to defecate behind the clusters? Did I mention how the reek of the fig women mixed with pleasanter smells of almond trees, mimosa, laurel, and peach, and how everybody wore masks on Mardi Gras and had elaborate dinners on the decks of frigates? I want to mention these things because they all happened in that city that was no place exactly, that was part of no country because it was all countries, and because now if you go there you'll see modern high-rises, amnesiac boulevards, teeming sweatshops, a NATO headquarters, and a sign that says Izmir . . .)

Five cars, bedecked with olive branches, burst the city gates. Cavalry gallop fender to fender. The cars roar past the covered bazaar, through cheering throngs in the Turkish Quarter where every streetlamp, door, and window streams red cloth. By Ottoman law, Turks must occupy a city's highest ground, so the convoy is high above the city now, heading down. Soon the five cars pass through the deserted sections where houses have been abandoned or where families hide. Anita Philobosian peeks out to see the beautiful, leaf-covered vehicles approaching, the sight so arresting she starts to unfasten the shutters before her mother pulls her away . . . and there are other faces pressed to slats, Armenian, Bulgarian, and Greek eyes peeking out of hideaways and attics to get a look at the conqueror and divine his intentions; but the cars move too fast, and the sun on the cavalry's raised sabers blinds the eyes, and then the cars are gone, reaching the quay, where horses charge into the crowd and refugees scream and scatter.

In the backseat of the last car sits Mustafa Kemal. He is lean from battle. His blue eyes flash. He hasn't had a drink in over two weeks. (The "diverticulitis" Dr. Philobosian had treated the pasha for was just a cover-up. Kemal, champion of Westernization and the secular Turkish state, would remain true to those principles to the end, dying at fifty-seven of cirrhosis of the liver.)

And as he passes he turns and looks into the crowd, as a young woman stands up from a suitcase. Blue eyes pierce brown. Two seconds. Not even two. Then Kemal looks away; the convoy is gone.

And now it is all a matter of wind. 1 a.m., Wednesday, September 13, 1922. Lefty and Desdemona have been in the city seven nights now. The smell of jasmine has turned to kerosene. Around the Armenian Quarter barricades have been erected. Turkish troops block the exits from the quay. But the wind remains blowing in the wrong direction. Around midnight, how-

ever, it shifts. It begins blowing southwest-
erly, that is, away from the Turkish heights
and toward the harbor.

In the blackness, torches gather. Three
Turkish soldiers stand in a tailor shop.
Their torches illuminate bolts of cloth and
suits on hangers. Then, as the light grows,
the tailor himself becomes visible. He is
sitting at his sewing machine, right shoe
still on the foot treadle. The light grows
brighter still to reveal his face, the gaping
eye sockets, the beard torn out in bloody
patches.

All over the Armenian Quarter fires
bloom. Like a million fireflies, sparks fly
across the dark city, inseminating every
place they land with a germ of fire. At his
house on Suyane Street, Dr. Philobosian
hangs a wet carpet over the balcony, then
hurries back inside the dark house and
closes the shutters. But the blaze penetrates the room, lighting it up in stripes:
Toukhie's panicked eyes; Anita's forehead,
wrapped with a silver ribbon like Clara
Bow's in *Photoplay*; Rose's bare neck;
Stepan's and Karekin's dark, downcast
heads.

By firelight Dr. Philobosian reads for the
fifth time that night " '. . . is respectfully
recommended . . . to the esteem, confidence, and protection . . .' You hear that?
'Protection . . .' "

Across the street Mrs. Bidzikian sings the climactic three notes of the "Queen of the Night" aria from *The Magic Flute*. The music sounds so strange amid the other noises — of doors crashing in, people screaming, girls crying out — that they all look up. Mrs. Bidzikian repeats the B flat, D, and F two more times, as though practicing the aria, and then her voice hits a note none of them has ever heard before, and they realize that Mrs. Bidzikian hasn't been singing an aria at all.

"Rose, get my bag."

"Nishan, no," his wife objects. "If they see you come out, they'll know we're hiding."

"No one will see."

The flames first registered to Desdemona as lights on the ships' hulls. Orange brushstrokes flickered above the waterline of the U.S.S. *Litchfield* and the French steamer *Pierre Loti*. Then the water brightened, as though a school of phosphorescent fish had entered the harbor.

Lefty's head rested on her shoulder. She checked to see if he was asleep. "Lefty. Lefty?" When he didn't respond, she kissed the top of his head. Then the sirens went off.

She sees not one fire but many. There are twenty orange dots on the hill above. And they have an unnatural persistence, these fires. As soon as the fire department puts out one blaze, another erupts somewhere else. They start in hay carts and trash bins; they follow kerosene trails down the center of streets; they turn corners; they enter bashed-in doorways. One fire penetrates Berberian's bakery, making quick work of the bread racks and pastry carts. It burns through to the living quarters and climbs the front staircase where, halfway up, it meets Charles Berberian himself, who tries to smother it with a blanket. But the fire dodges him and races up into the house. From there it sweeps across an Oriental rug, marches out to the back porch, leaps nimbly up onto a laundry line, and tightrope-walks across to the house behind. It climbs in the window and pauses, as if shocked by its good fortune: because everything in this house is just made to burn, too — the damask sofa with its long fringe, the mahogany end tables and chintz lampshades. The heat pulls down wallpaper in sheets; and this is happening not only in this apartment but in ten or fifteen others, then twenty or twenty-five, each house setting fire to its neighbor until entire blocks are burning. The smell of things burning that aren't meant to burn wafts across the city: shoe polish, rat poison, toothpaste, piano strings, hernia trusses, baby cribs, Indian clubs. And hair and skin. By this time, hair and skin. On the quay, Lefty and Desdemona stand up along with everyone else, with people too stunned to react, or still half-asleep, or sick with typhus and cholera, or exhausted beyond caring. And then, suddenly, all the fires on the hillside form one great wall of fire stretching across the city and — it's inevitable now — start moving down toward them.

(And now I remember something else: my father, Milton Stephanides, in robe and slippers, bending over to light a fire on Christmas morning. Only once a year did the need to dispose of a mountain of wrapping paper and cardboard packaging overrule Desdemona's objections to using our fireplace. "Ma," Milton would warn her, "I'm going to burn up some of this garbage now." To which Desdemona would cry, *"Mana!"* and grab her cane. At the hearth, my father would pull a long match from the hexagonal box. But Desdemona would already be moving away, heading for the safety of the kitchen, where the oven was electric. "Your *yia yia* doesn't like fires," my father would tell us. And, lighting the match, he would hold it to paper covered with elves and Santas as flames leapt up, and we ignorant, American children went crazy throwing paper, boxes, and ribbons into the blaze.)

Dr. Philobosian stepped out into the street, looked both ways, and ran straight across through the door opposite. He climbed to the landing, where he could see the top of Mrs. Bidzikian's head from behind as she sat in the living room. He ran to her, telling her not to worry, it was Dr. Philobosian from across the street. Mrs. Bidzikian seemed to nod, but her head didn't come back up. Dr. Philobosian knelt beside her. Touching her neck, he felt a weak pulse. Gently he pulled her out of the chair and laid her on the floor. As he did so, he heard footsteps on the stairway. He hurried across the room and hid behind the drapes just as the soldiers stormed in.

For fifteen minutes, they ransacked the apartment, taking whatever the first band had left. They dumped out drawers and slit open sofas and clothing, looking for jewelry or money hidden inside. After they were gone, Dr. Philobosian waited a full five minutes before stepping out from behind the drapes. Mrs. Bidzikian's pulse had stopped. He spread his handkerchief over her face and made the sign of the cross over her body. Then he picked up his doctor's bag and hurried down the stairs again.

The heat precedes the fire. Figs heaped

along the quay, not loaded in time, begin to bake, bubbling and oozing juice. The sweetness mixes with the smell of smoke. Desdemona and Lefty stand as close to the water as possible, along with everyone else. There is no escape. Turkish soldiers remain at the barricades. People pray, raise their arms, pleading to ships in the harbor. Searchlights sweep across the water, lighting up people swimming, drowning.

"We're going to die, Lefty."

"No we're not. We're going to get out of here." But Lefty doesn't believe this. As he looks up at the flames, he is certain, too, that they are going to die. And this certainty inspires him to say something he would never have said otherwise, something he would never even have thought. "We're going to get out of here. And then you're going to marry me."

"We should never have left. We should have stayed in Bithynios."

As the fire approaches, the doors of the French consulate open. A marine garrison forms two lines stretching across the quay to the harbor. The Tricolor descends. From the consulate's doors people emerge, men in cream-colored suits and women in straw hats, walking arm in arm to a waiting launch. Over the Marines' crossed rifles, Lefty sees fresh powder on the women's faces, lit cigars in the men's mouths. One woman holds a small poodle under her arm. Another woman trips, breaking her heel, and is consoled by her husband. After the launch has motored away, an official turns to the crowd.

"French citizens only will be evacuated. We will begin processing visas immediately."

When they hear knocking, they jump. Stepan goes to the window and looks down. "It must be Father."

"Go. Let him in! Quick!" Toukhie says.

Karekin vaults down the stairs two at a time. At the door he stops, collects himself, and quietly unbolts the door. At first, when he pulls it open, he sees nothing. Then there's a soft hiss, followed by a ripping noise. The noise sounds as though it has nothing to do with him until suddenly a shirt button pops off and clatters against the door. Karekin looks down as all at once his mouth fills with a warm fluid. He feels himself being lifted off his feet, the sensation bringing back to him childhood memories of being whisked into the air by his father, and he says, "Dad, my button," before he is lifted high enough to make out the steel bayonet puncturing his sternum. The fire's reflection leads along the gun barrel, over the sight and hammer, to the soldier's ecstatic face.

The fire bore down on the crowd at the quay. The roof of the American consulate caught. Flames climbed the movie theater, scorching the marquee. The crowd inched back from the heat. But Lefty, sensing his opportunity, was undeterred.

"Nobody will know," he said. "Who's to know? There's nobody left but us."

"It's not right."

Roofs crashed, people screamed, as Lefty put his lips to his sister's ear. "You promised you'd find me a nice Greek girl. Well. You're it."

On one side a man jumped into the water, trying to drown himself; on the other, a woman was giving birth, as her husband shielded her with his coat. *"Kaymaste! Kaymaste!"* people shouted. "We're burning! We're burning!" Desdemona pointed, at the fire, at everything. "It's too late, Lefty. It doesn't matter now."

"But if we lived? You'd marry me then?"

A nod. That was all. And Lefty was gone, running toward the flames.

On a black screen, a binocular-shaped template of vision sweeps back and forth, taking in the distant refugees. They scream without sound. They hold out their arms, beseeching.

"They're going to cook the poor wretches alive."

"Permission to retrieve a swimmer, sir."

"Negative, Phillips. Once we take one aboard we'll have to take them all."

"It's a girl, sir."

"How old?"

"Looks to be about ten or eleven."

Major Arthur Maxwell lowers his binoculars. A triangular knot of muscle tenses in his jaw and disappears.

"Have a look at her, sir."

"We mustn't be swayed by emotions here, Phillips. There are greater things at stake."

"Have a look at her, sir."

The wings of Major Maxwell's nose flare as he looks at Captain Phillips. Then, slapping one hand against his thigh, he moves to the side of the ship.

The searchlight sweeps across the water, lighting up its own circle of vision. The water looks odd under the beam, a colorless broth littered with a variety of objects: a bright orange; a man's fedora with a brim of excrement; bits of paper like torn letters. And then, amid this inert matter, she appears, holding on to the ship's line, a girl in a pink dress the water darkens to red, hair plastered to her small skull. Her eyes make no appeal, staring up. Her sharp feet kick every so often, like fins.

Rifle fire from shore hits the water around her. She pays no attention.

"Turn off the searchlight."

The light goes off and the firing stops. Major Maxwell looks at his watch. "It is now 2115 hours. I am going to my cabin, Phillips. I will stay there until 0700 hours. Should a refugee be taken aboard during that period, it would not come to my attention. Is that understood?"

"Understood, sir."

It didn't occur to Dr. Philobosian that the twisted body he stepped over in the street belonged to his younger son. He noticed only that his front door was open. In the foyer, he stopped to listen. There was only silence. Slowly, still holding his doctor's bag, he climbed the stairs. All the lamps were on now. The living room was bright. Toukhie was sitting on the sofa, waiting for him. Her head had fallen backward as though in hilarity, the angle opening the wound so that a section of windpipe gleamed. Stepan sat slumped at the dining table, his right hand, which held the letter of protection, nailed down with a steak knife. Dr. Philobosian took a step and slipped, then noticed a trail of blood leading down the hallway. He followed the trail into the master bedroom, where he found his two daughters. They were both naked, lying on their backs. Three of their four breasts had been cut off. Rose's hand reached out toward her sister as though to adjust the silver ribbon across her forehead.

The line was long and moved slowly. Lefty had time to go over his vocabulary. He reviewed his grammar, taking quick peeks at the phrase book. He studied "Lesson 1: Greetings," and by the time he reached the official at the table, he was ready.

"Name?"

"Eleutherios Stephanides."

"Place of birth?"

"Paris."

The official looked up. "Passport."

"Everything was destroyed in the fire! I lost all my papers!" Lefty puckered his lips and expelled air, as he'd seen Frenchmen do. "Look at what I'm wearing. I lost all my good suits."

The official smiled wryly and stamped the papers. "Pass."

"I have my wife with me."

"I suppose she was born in Paris, too."

"Of course."

"Her name?"

"Desdemona."

"Desdemona Stephanides?"

"That's right. Same as mine."

When he returned with the visas, Desdemona wasn't alone. A man sat beside her on the suitcase. "He tried to throw himself in the water. I caught him just in time." Dazed, bloody, a shining bandage wrapping one hand, the man kept repeating, "They couldn't read. They were illiterate!" Lefty checked to see where the man was bleeding but couldn't find a wound. He unwrapped the man's bandage, a silver ribbon, and tossed it away. "They couldn't read my letter," the man said, looking at Lefty, who recognized his face.

"You again?" the French official said.

"My cousin," said Lefty, in execrable French. The man stamped a visa and handed it to him.

A motor launch took them out to the ship. Lefty kept hold of Dr. Philobosian, who was still threatening to drown himself. Desdemona opened her silkworm box and unwrapped the white cloth to check on her eggs. In the hideous water, bodies floated past. Some were alive, calling out. A searchlight revealed a boy halfway up the anchor chain of a battleship. Sailors dumped oil on him and he slipped back into the water.

On the deck of the *Jean Bart*, the three new French citizens looked back at the burning city, ablaze from end to end. The fire would continue for the next three days, the flames visible for fifty miles. At sea, sailors would mistake the rising smoke for a gigantic mountain range. In the country they were heading for, America, the burning of Smyrna made the front pages for a day or two, before being bumped off by the Hall-Mills murder case (the body of Hall, a Protestant minister, had been found with that of Miss Mills, an attractive choir member) and the opening of the World Series. Admiral Mark Bristol of the U.S. Navy, concerned about damage to American-Turkish relations, cabled a press release in which he stated that "it is impossible to estimate the number of deaths due to killings, fire, and execution, but the total probably does not exceed 2,000." The American consul, George Horton, had a larger estimate. Of the 400,000 Ottoman Christians in Smyrna before the fire, 190,000 were unaccounted for by October 1. Horton halved that number and estimated the dead at 100,000.

The anchors surged up out of the water. The deck rumbled underfoot as the destroyer's engines were thrown into reverse. Desdemona and Lefty watched Asia Minor recede.

As they passed the *Iron Duke*, the British military service band started into a waltz.

The Silk Road

According to an ancient Chinese legend, one day in the year 2640 B.C., Princess Si Ling-chi was sitting under a mulberry tree when a silkworm cocoon fell into her teacup. When she tried to remove it, she noticed that the cocoon had begun to unravel in the hot liquid. She handed the loose end to her maidservant and told her to walk. The servant went out of the princess's chamber, and into the palace courtyard, and through the palace gates, and out of the Forbidden City, and into the countryside a half mile away before the cocoon ran out. (In the West, this legend would slowly mutate over three millennia, until it became the story of a physicist and an apple. Either way, the meanings are the same: great discoveries, whether of silk or of gravity, are always windfalls. They happen to people loafing under trees.)

I feel a little like that Chinese princess, whose discovery gave Desdemona her livelihood. Like her I unravel my story, and the longer the thread, the less there is left to tell.

Retrace the filament and you go back to the cocoon's beginning in a tiny knot, a first tentative loop. And following my story's thread back to where I left off, I see the *Jean Bart* dock in Athens. I see my grandparents on land again, making preparations for another voyage. Passports are placed into hands, vaccinations administered to upper arms. Another ship materializes at the dock, the *Giulia*. A foghorn sounds.

And look: from the deck of the *Giulia* something else unwinds now. Something multicolored, spinning itself out over the waters of Piraeus.

It was the custom in those days for passengers leaving for America to bring balls of yarn on deck. Relatives on the pier held the loose ends. As the *Giulia* blew its horn and moved away from the dock, a few hundred strings of yarn stretched across the water. People shouted farewells, waved furiously, held up babies for last looks they wouldn't remember. Propellers churned; handkerchiefs fluttered, and, up on deck, the balls of yarn began to spin. Red, yellow, blue, green, they untangled toward the pier, slowly at first, one revolution every ten seconds, then faster and faster as the boat picked up speed. Passengers held the yarn as long as possible, maintaining the connection to the faces disappearing onshore. But finally, one by one, the balls ran out. The strings of yarn flew free, rising on the breeze.

From two separate locations on the *Giulia*'s deck, Lefty and Desdemona — and I can say it now, finally, my grandparents — watched the airy blanket float away. Desdemona was standing between two air manifolds shaped like giant tubas. At midships Lefty slouched in a brace of bachelors. In the last three hours they hadn't seen each other. That morning, they'd had coffee together in a café near the harbor after which, like professional spies, they'd picked up their separate suitcases — Desdemona keeping her silkworm box — and had departed in different directions. My grandmother was carrying falsified documents. Her passport, which the Greek government had granted under the condition that she leave the country immediately, bore her mother's maiden name, Aristos, instead of Stephanides. She'd presented this passport along with her boarding card at the top of the *Giulia*'s gangway. Then she'd gone aft, as planned, for the send-off.

At the shipping channel, the foghorn sounded again, as the boat came around to the west and picked up more speed. Dirndls, kerchiefs, and suit coats flapped in the breeze. A few hats flew off heads, to shouts and laughter. Yarn drift-netted the sky, barely visible now. People watched as long as they could. Desdemona was one of the first to go below. Lefty lingered on deck for another half hour. This, too, was part of the plan.

For the first day at sea, they didn't speak to each other. They came up on deck at the appointed mealtimes and stood in separate lines. After eating, Lefty joined the men smoking at the rail while Desdemona hunched on deck with the women and children, staying out of the wind. "You have someone meeting you?" the women asked. "A fiancé?"

"No. Just my cousin in Detroit."

"Traveling all by yourself?" the men asked Lefty.

"That's right. Free and easy."

At night, they descended to their respective compartments. In separate bunks of seaweed wrapped in burlap, with life vests doubling as pillows, they tried to sleep, to get used to the motion of the ship, and to tolerate the smells. Passengers had brought on board all manner of spices and sweetmeats, tinned sardines, octopus in wine sauce, legs of lamb preserved with garlic cloves. In those days you could identify a person's nationality by smell. Lying on her back with eyes closed, Desdemona could detect the telltale oniony aroma of a Hungarian woman on her right, and the raw-meat smell of an Armenian on her left.

(And they, in turn, could peg Desdemona as a Hellene by her aroma of garlic and yogurt.) Lefty's annoyances were auditory as well as olfactory. To one side was a man named Callas with a snore like a miniature foghorn itself; on the other was Dr. Philobosian, who wept in his sleep. Ever since leaving Smyrna the doctor had been beside himself with grief. Racked, gut-socked, he lay curled up in his coat, blue around the eye sockets. He ate almost nothing. He refused to go up on deck to get fresh air. On the few occasions he did go, he threatened to throw himself overboard.

In Athens, Dr. Philobosian had told them to leave him alone. He refused to discuss plans about the future and said that he had no family anywhere. "My family's gone. They murdered them."

"Poor man," Desdemona said. "He doesn't want to live."

"We have to help him," Lefty insisted. "He gave me money. He bandaged my hand. Nobody else cared about us. We'll take him with us." While they waited for their cousin to wire money, Lefty tried to console the doctor and finally convinced him to come with them to Detroit. "Wherever's far away," said Dr. Philobosian. But now on the boat he talked only of death.

The voyage was supposed to take from twelve to fourteen days. Lefty and Desdemona had the schedule all worked out. On the second day at sea, directly after dinner, Lefty made a tour of the ship. He picked his way among the bodies sprawled across the steerage deck. He passed the stairway to the pilothouse and squeezed past the extra cargo, crates of Kalamata olives and olive oil, sea sponges from Kos. He proceeded forward, running his hand along the green tarps of the lifeboats, until he met the chain separating steerage from third class. In its heyday, the *Giulia* had been part of the Austro-Hungarian Line. Boasting modern conveniences (*"lumina electrica, ventilatie et comfortu cel mai mare"*), it had traveled once a month between Trieste and New York. Now the electric lights worked only in first class, and even then sporadically. The iron rails were rusted. Smoke from the stack had soiled the Greek flag. The boat smelled of old mop buckets and a history of nausea. Lefty didn't have his sea legs yet. He kept falling against the railing. He stood at the chain for an appropriate amount of time, then crossed to port and returned aft. Desdemona, as arranged, was standing alone at the rail. As Lefty passed, he smiled and nodded. She nodded coldly and looked back out to sea.

On the third day, Lefty took another after-dinner stroll. He walked forward, crossed to port, and headed aft. He smiled at Desdemona and nodded again. This time, Desdemona smiled back. Rejoining his fellow smokers, Lefty inquired if any of them might happen to know the name of that young woman traveling alone.

On the fourth day out, Lefty stopped and introduced himself.

"So far the weather's been good."

"I hope it stays that way."

"You're traveling alone?"

"Yes."

"I am, too. Where are you going to in America?"

"Detroit."

"What a coincidence! I'm going to Detroit, too."

They stood chatting for another few minutes. Then Desdemona excused herself and went down below.

Rumors of the budding romance spread quickly through the ship. To pass the time, everybody was soon discussing how the tall young Greek with the elegant bearing had become enamored of the dark beauty who was never seen anywhere without her carved olivewood box. "They're both traveling alone," people said. "And they both have relatives in Detroit."

"I don't think they're right for each other."

"Why not?"

"He's a higher class than she is. It'll never work."

"He seems to like her, though."

"He's on a boat in the middle of the ocean! What else does he have to do?"

On the fifth day, Lefty and Desdemona took a stroll on deck together. On the sixth day, he presented his arm and she took it.

"I introduced them!" one man boasted. City girls sniffed. "She wears her hair in braids. She looks like a peasant."

My grandfather, on the whole, came in for better treatment. He was said to have been a silk merchant from Smyrna who'd lost his fortune in the fire; a son of King Constantine I by a French mistress; a spy for the Kaiser during the Great War. Lefty never discouraged any speculation. He seized the opportunity of transatlantic travel to reinvent himself. He wrapped a ratty blanket over his shoulders like an opera cape. Aware that whatever happened now would become the truth, that whatever he seemed to be would become what he was — already an American, in other words — he waited for Desdemona to come up on deck. When she did, he adjusted his wrap, nodded to his shipmates, and sauntered across the deck to pay his respects.

"He's smitten!"

"I don't think so. Type like that, he's just out for a little fun. That girl better watch it or she'll have more than that box to carry around."

My grandparents enjoyed their simulated courtship. When people were within earshot, they engaged in first- or second-date conversations, making up past histories for themselves. "So," Lefty would ask, "do you have any siblings?"

"I had a brother," Desdemona replied wistfully. "He ran off with a Turkish girl. My father disowned him."

"That's very strict. I think love breaks all taboos. Don't you?"

Alone, they told each other, "I think it's working. No one suspects."

Each time Lefty encountered Desdemona on deck, he pretended he'd only recently met her. He walked up, made small talk, commented on the beauty of the sunset, and then, gallantly, segued into the beauty of her face. Desdemona played her part, too. She was standoffish at first. She withdrew her arm whenever he made an off-color joke. She told him that her mother had warned her about men like him. They passed the voyage playing out this imaginary flirtation and, little by little, they began to believe it. They fabricated memories, improvised fate. (Why did they do it? Why did they go to all that trouble?

Couldn't they have said they were already engaged? Or that their marriage had been arranged years earlier? Yes, of course they could have. But it wasn't the other travelers they were trying to fool; it was themselves.)

Traveling made it easier. Sailing across the ocean among half a thousand perfect strangers conveyed an anonymity in which my grandparents could re-create themselves. The driving spirit on the *Giulia* was self-transformation. Staring out to sea, tobacco farmers imagined themselves as race car drivers, silk dyers as Wall Street tycoons, millinery girls as fan dancers in the *Ziegfeld Follies*. Gray ocean stretched in all directions. Europe and Asia Minor were dead behind them. Ahead lay America and new horizons.

On the eighth day at sea, Lefty Stephanides, grandly, on one knee, in full view of six hundred and sixty-three steerage passengers, proposed to Desdemona Aristos while she sat on a docking cleat. Young women held their breath. Married men nudged bachelors: "Pay attention and you'll learn something." My grandmother, displaying a theatrical flair akin to her hypochondria, registered complex emotions: surprise; initial delight; second thoughts; prudent near refusal; and then, to the applause already starting up, dizzy acceptance.

130

★ ★ ★

The ceremony took place on deck. In lieu of a wedding dress, Desdemona wore a borrowed silk shawl over her head. Captain Kontoulis loaned Lefty a necktie spotted with gravy stains. "Keep your coat buttoned and nobody will notice," he said. For *stephana*, my grandparents had wedding crowns woven with rope. Flowers weren't available at sea and so the *koumbaros*, a guy named Pelos serving as best man, switched the king's hempen crown to the queen's head, the queen's to the king's, and back again.

Bride and bridegroom performed the Dance of Isaiah. Hip to hip, arms interwoven to hold hands, Desdemona and Lefty circumambulated the captain, once, twice, and then again, spinning the cocoon of their life together. No patriarchal linearity here. We Greeks get married in circles, to impress upon ourselves the essential matrimonial facts: that to be happy you have to find variety in repetition; that to go forward you have to come back where you began.

Or, in my grandparents' case, the circling worked like this: as they paced around the deck the first time, Lefty and Desdemona were still brother and sister. The second time, they were bride and bridegroom. And the third, they were husband and wife.

131

★ ★ ★

The night of my grandparents' wedding,
the sun set directly before the ship's bow,
pointing the way to New York. The moon
rose, casting a silver stripe over the ocean.
On his nightly tour of the deck, Captain
Kontoulis descended from the pilothouse
and marched forward. The wind had
picked up. The *Giulia* pitched in high seas.
As the deck tilted back and forth, Captain
Kontoulis didn't stumble once, and was
even able to light one of the Indonesian
cigarettes he favored, dipping his cap's
braided brim to cut the wind. In his not
terribly clean uniform, wearing knee-high
Cretan boots, Captain Kontoulis scruti-
nized running lights, stacked deck chairs,
lifeboats. The *Giulia* was alone on the vast
Atlantic, hatches battened down against
swells crashing over the side. The decks
were empty except for two first-class passengers, American businessmen sharing a
nightcap under lap blankets. "From what I
hear, Tilden doesn't just play tennis with
his protégés, if you get my drift." "You're
kidding." "Lets them drink from the loving
cup." Captain Kontoulis, understanding
none of this, nodded as he passed . . .

Inside one of the lifeboats, Desdemona
was saying, "Don't look." She was lying on
her back. There was no goat's-hair blanket
between them, so Lefty covered his eyes

with his hands, peeking through his fingers. A single pinhole in the tarp leaked moonlight, which slowly filled the lifeboat. Lefty had seen Desdemona undress many times, but usually as no more than a shadow and never in moonlight. She had never curled onto her back like this, lifting her feet to take off her shoes. He watched and, as she pulled down her skirt and lifted her tunic, was struck by how different his sister looked, in moonlight, in a lifeboat. She *glowed*. She gave off white light. He blinked behind his hands. The moonlight kept rising; it covered his neck, it reached his eyes until he understood: Desdemona was wearing a corset. That was the other thing she'd brought along: the white cloth enfolding her silkworm eggs was nothing other than Desdemona's wedding corset. She thought she'd never wear it, but here it was. Brassiere cups pointed up at the canvas roof. Whalebone slats squeezed her waist. The corset's skirt dropped garters attached to nothing because my grandmother owned no stockings. In the lifeboat, the corset absorbed all available moonlight, with the odd result that Desdemona's face, head, and arms disappeared. She looked like Winged Victory, tumbled on her back, being carted off to a conqueror's museum. All that was missing was the wings.

Lefty took off his shoes and socks, as grit

rained down. When he removed his underwear, the lifeboat filled with a mushroomy smell. He was ashamed momentarily, but Desdemona didn't seem to mind.

She was distracted by her own mixed feelings. The corset, of course, reminded Desdemona of her mother, and suddenly the wrongness of what they were doing assailed her. Until now she had been keeping it at bay. She had had no time to dwell on it in the chaos of the last days.

Lefty, too, was conflicted. Though he had been tortured by thoughts of Desdemona, he was glad for the darkness of the lifeboat, glad, in particular, that he couldn't see her face. For months Lefty had slept with whores who resembled Desdemona, but now he found it easier to pretend that she was a stranger.

The corset seemed to possess its own sets of hands. One was softly rubbing her between the legs. Two more cupped her breasts, one, two, three hands pressing and caressing her; and in the lingerie Desdemona saw herself through new eyes, her thin waist, her plump thighs; she felt beautiful, desirable, most of all: not herself. She lifted her feet, rested her calves on the oarlocks. She spread her legs. She opened her arms for Lefty, who twisted around, chafing his knees and elbows, dislodging oars, nearly setting off a flare, until finally he fell into her softness, swooning. For the first time Desdemona tasted the flavor of his mouth, and the only sisterly thing she did during their lovemaking was to come up for air, once, to say, "Bad boy. You've done this before." But Lefty only kept repeating, "Not like this, not like this . . ."

And I was wrong before, I take it back. Underneath Desdemona, beating time against the boards and lifting her up: a pair of wings.

"Lefty!" Desdemona now, breathlessly. "I think I felt it."

"Felt what?"

"You know. That *feeling*."

"Newlyweds," Captain Kontoulis said, watching the lifeboat rock. "Oh, to be young again."

After Princess Si Ling-chi — whom I find myself picturing as the imperial version of the bicyclist I saw on the U-Bahn the other day; I can't stop thinking about her for some reason, I keep looking for her every morning — after Princess Si Ling-chi discovered silk, her nation kept it a secret for three thousand one hundred and ninety years. Anyone who attempted to smuggle silkworm eggs out of China faced punishment of death. My family might never have become silk farmers if it hadn't been for the Emperor Justinian, who, according to

135

Procopius, persuaded two missionaries to risk it. In A.D. 550, the missionaries snuck silkworm eggs out of China in the swallowed condom of the time: a hollow staff. They also brought the seeds of the mulberry tree. As a result, Byzantium became a center for sericulture. Mulberry trees flourished on Turkish hillsides. Silkworms ate the leaves. Fourteen hundred years later, the descendants of those first stolen eggs filled my grandmother's silkworm box on the *Giulia*.

I'm the descendant of a smuggling operation, too. Without their knowing, my grandparents, on their way to America, were each carrying a single mutated gene on the fifth chromosome. It wasn't a recent mutation. According to Dr. Luce, the gene first appeared in my bloodline sometime around 1750, in the body of one Penelope Evangelatos, my great-grandmother to the ninth power. She passed it on to her son Petras, who passed it on to his two daughters, who passed it on to three of their five children, and so on and so on. Being recessive, its expression would have been fitful. Sporadic heredity is what the geneticists call it. A trait that goes underground for decades only to reappear when everyone has forgotten about it. That was how it went in Bithynios. Every so often a hermaphrodite was born, a seeming girl who, in growing up, proved otherwise.

For the next six nights, under various meteorological conditions, my grandparents trysted in the lifeboat. Desdemona's guilt flared up during the day, when she sat on deck wondering if she and Lefty were to blame for everything, but by nighttime she felt lonely and wanted to escape the cabin and so stole back to the lifeboat and her new husband.

Their honeymoon proceeded in reverse. Instead of getting to know each other, becoming familiar with likes and dislikes, ticklish spots, pet peeves, Desdemona and Lefty tried to defamiliarize themselves with each other. In the spirit of their shipboard con game, they continued to spin out false histories for themselves, inventing brothers and sisters with plausible names, cousins with moral shortcomings, in-laws with facial tics. They took turns reciting Homeric genealogies, full of falsifications and borrowings from real life, and sometimes they fought over this or that favorite real uncle or aunt, and had to bargain like casting directors. Gradually, as the nights passed, these fictional relatives began to crystallize in their minds. They'd quiz each other on obscure connections, Lefty asking, "Who's your second cousin Yiannis married to?" And Desdemona replying,

"That's easy. Athena. With the limp."
(And am I wrong to think that my obsession with family relations started right
there in the lifeboat? Didn't my mother
quiz me on uncles and aunts and cousins,
too? She never quizzed my brother, because he was in charge of snow shovels and
tractors, whereas I was supposed to provide the feminine glue that keeps families
together, writing thank-you notes and remembering everybody's birthdays and
name days. Listen, I've heard the following
genealogy come out of my mother's mouth:
"That's your cousin Melia. She's Uncle
Mike's sister Lucille's brother-in-law
Stathis's daughter. You know Stathis the
mailman, who's not too swift? Melia's his
third child, after his boys Mike and
Johnny. You should know her. Melia! She's
your cousin-in-law by marriage!")

And here I am now, sketching it all out
for you, dutifully oozing feminine glue, but
also with a dull pain in my chest, because I
realize that genealogies tell you nothing.
Tessie knew who was related to whom but
she had no idea who her own husband
was, or what her in-laws were to each
other; the whole thing a fiction created in
the lifeboat where my grandparents made
up their lives.

Sexually, things were simple for them.
Dr. Peter Luce, the great sexologist, can

cite astonishing statistics asserting that oral sex didn't exist between married couples prior to 1950. My grandparents' lovemaking was pleasurable but unvarying. Every night Desdemona would disrobe down to her corset and Lefty would press its clasps and hooks, searching for the secret combination that sprung the locked garment open. The corset was all they needed in terms of an aphrodisiac, and it remained for my grandfather the singular erotic emblem of his life. The corset made Desdemona new again. As I said, Lefty had glimpsed his sister naked before, but the corset had the odd power of making her seem somehow more naked; it turned her into a forbidding, armored creature with a soft inside he had to hunt for. When the tumblers clicked, it popped open; Lefty crawled on top of Desdemona and the two of them hardly even moved; the ocean swells did the work for them.

Their periphescence existed simultaneously with a less passionate stage of pair bonding. Sex could give way, at any moment, to coziness. So, after making love, they lay staring up through the pulled-back tarp at the night sky passing overhead and got down to the business of life. "Maybe Lina's husband can give me a job," Lefty said. "He's got his own business, right?"

"I don't know what he does. Lina never gives me a straight answer."

"After we save some money, I can open a casino. Some gambling, a bar, maybe a floor show. And potted palms everywhere."

"You should go to college. Become a professor like Mother and Father wanted. And we have to build a cocoonery, remember."

"Forget the silkworms. I'm talking roulette, rebetika, drinking, dancing. Maybe I'll sell some hash on the side."

"They won't let you smoke hashish in America."

"Who says?"

And Desdemona announced with certitude:

"It's not that kind of country."

They spent what remained of their honeymoon on deck, learning how to finagle their way through Ellis Island. It wasn't so easy anymore. The Immigration Restriction League had been formed in 1894. On the floor of the U.S. Senate, Henry Cabot Lodge thumped a copy of *On the Origin of Species*, warning that the influx of inferior peoples from southern and eastern Europe threatened "the very fabric of our race." The Immigration Act of 1917 barred thirty-three kinds of undesirables from entering the United States, and so, in 1922, on the deck of the *Giulia*, passengers discussed how to escape the categories. In nervous cram sessions, illiterates learned to pretend to read; bigamists to admit to only one wife; anarchists to deny having read Proudhon; heart patients to simulate vigor; epileptics to deny their fits; and carriers of hereditary diseases to neglect mentioning them. My grandparents, unaware of their genetic mutation, concentrated on the more blatant disqualifications. Another category of restriction: "persons convicted of a crime or misdemeanor involving moral turpitude." And a subset of this group: "Incestuous relations."

They avoided passengers who seemed to be suffering from trachoma or favus. They fled anyone with a hacking cough. Occasionally, for reassurance, Lefty took out the certificate that declared:

ELEUTHERIOS STEPHANIDES
HAS BEEN VACCINATED AND
UNLOUSED
AND IS PASSED AS VERMIN-FREE THIS DATE
SEPT. 23, 1922
DISINFECTION MARITIME PIRAEUS

Literate, married to only one person (albeit a sibling), democratically inclined, mentally stable, and authoritatively deloused, my grandparents saw no reason why they would have trouble getting through. They each had the requisite twenty-five dollars apiece. They also had a sponsor: their cousin Sourmelina. Just the year before, the Quota Act had reduced the annual numbers of southern and eastern European immigrants from 783,000 to 155,000. It was nearly impossible to get into the country without either a sponsor or stunning professional recommendations. To help their own chances, Lefty put away his French phrase book and began memorizing four lines of the King James New Testament. The *Giulia* was full of inside sources familiar with the English literacy test. Different nationalities were asked to translate different bits of Scripture. For Greeks, it was Matthew 19:12: "For there are some eunuchs, which were so born from their mother's womb: and there are some eunuchs, which were made eunuchs of men: and there be eunuchs, which have made themselves eunuchs for the kingdom of heaven's sake."

"Eunuchs?" Desdemona quailed. "Who told you this?"

"This is a passage from the Bible."

"What Bible? Not the Greek Bible. Go ask somebody else what's on that test."

But Lefty showed her the Greek at the top of the card and the English below. He repeated the passage word by word, making her memorize it, whether or not she understood it.

"We didn't have enough eunuchs in Turkey? Now we have to talk about them at Ellis Island?"

"The Americans let in everyone," Lefty joked. "Eunuchs included."

"They should let us speak Greek if they're so accepting," Desdemona grumbled.

Summer was abandoning the ocean. One night it grew too cold in the lifeboat to crack the corset's combination. Instead they huddled under blankets, talking.

"Is Sourmelina meeting us in New York?" Desdemona asked.

"No. We have to take a train to Detroit."

"Why can't she meet us?"

"It's too far."

"Just as well. She wouldn't be on time anyway."

The ceaseless sea wind made the tarp's edges flap. Frost formed on the lifeboat's gunwales. They could see the top of the *Giulia*'s smokestack, the smoke itself discernible only as a starless patch of night sky. (Though they didn't know it, that striped, canted smokestack was already informing them about their new home; it was whispering about River Rouge and the Uniroyal plant, and the Seven Sisters and

Two Brothers, but they didn't listen; they wrinkled up their noses and ducked down in the lifeboat away from the smoke.)

And if the smell of industry didn't insist on entering my story already, if Desdemona and Lefty, who grew up on a pine-scented mountain and who could never get used to the polluted air of Detroit, hadn't ducked down in the lifeboat, then they might have detected a new aroma wafting in on the brisk sea air: a humid odor of mud and wet bark. Land. New York. America.

"What are we going to tell Sourmelina about us?"

"She'll understand."

"Will she keep quiet?"

"There are a few things she'd rather her husband didn't know about her."

"You mean Helen?"

"I didn't say a thing," said Lefty.

They fell asleep after that, waking to sunlight, and a face staring down at them.

"Did you have a good sleep?" Captain Kontoulis said. "Maybe I could get you a blanket?"

"I'm sorry," Lefty said. "We won't do it again."

"You won't get the chance," said the captain and, to prove his point, pulled the lifeboat's tarp completely away. Desdemona and Lefty sat up. In the distance, lit by the rising sun, was the skyline of New York. It wasn't the right shape for a city — no domes, no minarets — and it took them a minute to process the tall geometric forms. Mist curled off the bay. A million pink windowpanes glittered. Closer, crowned with her own sunrays and dressed like a classical Greek, the Statue of Liberty welcomed them.

"How do you like that?" Captain Kontoulis asked.

"I've seen enough torches to last the rest of my life," said Lefty.

But Desdemona, for once, was more optimistic. "At least it's a woman," she said. "Maybe here people won't be killing each other every single day."

Book Two

Henry Ford's English-Language Melting Pot

❦

> Everyone who builds a factory
> builds a temple.
> — Calvin Coolidge

Detroit was always made of wheels. Long before the Big Three and the nickname "Motor City"; before the auto factories and the freighters and the pink, chemical nights; before anyone had necked in a Thunderbird or spooned in a Model T; previous to the day a young Henry Ford knocked down his workshop wall because, in devising his "quadricycle," he'd thought of everything but how to get the damn thing out; and nearly a century prior to the cold March night, in 1896, when Charles King tiller-steered his horseless carriage down St. Antoine, along Jefferson, and up Woodward Avenue (where the two-stroke engine promptly quit); way, way back, when the city was just a piece of stolen Indian land located on the strait from which it got its name, a fort fought over by the British and French until, wearing them out, it fell into the hands of the Americans; way back then, before cars and cloverleaves, Detroit was made of wheels.

I am nine years old and holding my father's meaty, sweaty hand. We are standing at a window on the top floor of the Pontchartrain Hotel. I have come downtown for our annual lunch date. I am wearing a miniskirt and fuchsia tights. A white patent leather purse hangs on a long strap from my shoulder.

The fogged window has spots on it. We are way up high. I'm going to order shrimp scampi in a minute.

The reason for my father's hand perspiration: he's afraid of heights. Two days ago, when he offered to take me wherever I wanted, I called out in my piping voice, "Top of the Pontch!" High above the city, amid the business lunchers and power brokers, was where I wanted to be. And Milton has been true to his promise. Despite racing pulse he has allowed the maître d' to give us a table next to the window; so that now here we are — as a tuxedoed waiter pulls out my chair — and my father, too frightened to sit, begins a history lesson instead.

What's the reason for studying history? To understand the present or avoid it? Milton, olive complexion turning a shade pale, only says, "Look. See the wheel?"

And now I squint. Oblivious, at nine, to the prospect of crow's-feet, I gaze out over downtown, down to the streets where my father is indicating (though not looking). And there it is: half a hubcap of city plaza, with the spokes of Bagley, Washington, Woodward, Broadway, and Madison radiating from it.

That's all that remains of the famous Woodward Plan. Drawn up in 1807 by the hard-drinking, eponymous judge. (Two years earlier, in 1805, the city had burned to the ground, the timber houses and ribbon farms of the settlement founded by Cadillac in 1701 going up in the span of three hours. And, in 1969, with my sharp vision, I can read the traces of that fire on the city's flag a half mile away in Grand Circus Park: *Speramus meliora; resurget cineribus.* "We hope for better things; it will rise from the ashes.")

Judge Woodward envisioned the new Detroit as an urban Arcadia of interlocking hexagons. Each wheel was to be separate yet united, in accordance with the young nation's federalism, as well as classically symmetrical, in accordance with Jeffersonian aesthetics. This dream never quite

151

came to be. Planning is for the world's great cities, for Paris, London, and Rome, for cities dedicated, at some level, to culture. Detroit, on the other hand, was an American city and therefore dedicated to money, and so design had given way to expediency. Since 1818, the city had spread out along the river, warehouse by warehouse, factory by factory. Judge Woodward's wheels had been squashed, bisected, pressed into the usual rectangles.

Or seen another way (from a rooftop restaurant): the wheels hadn't vanished at all, they'd only changed form. By 1900 Detroit was the leading manufacturer of carriages and wagons. By 1922, when my grandparents arrived, Detroit made other spinning things, too: marine engines, bicycles, handrolled cigars. And yes, finally: cars.

All this was visible from the train. Approaching along the shore of the Detroit River, Lefty and Desdemona watched their new home take shape. They saw farmland give way to fenced lots and cobblestone streets. The sky darkened with smoke. Buildings flew by, brick warehouses painted in pragmatic Bookman white: WRIGHT AND KAY CO. . . . J. H. BLACK & SONS . . . DETROIT STOVE WORKS. Out on the water, squat, tar-colored barges dragged along, and people popped up on the streets, workmen in grimy overalls, clerks thumbing suspenders, the signs of eateries and boardinghouses appearing next: **We Serve Stroh's Temperance Beer . . . Make This Your Home Meals 15 cents . . .**

. . . As these new sights flooded my grandparents' brains, they jostled with images from the day before. Ellis Island, rising like a Doge's Palace on the water. The Baggage Room stacked to the ceiling with luggage. They'd been herded up a stairway to the Registry Room. Pinned with numbers from the *Giulia*'s manifest, they'd filed past a line of health inspectors who'd looked in their eyes and ears, rubbed their scalps, and flipped their eyelids inside out with buttonhooks. One doctor, noticing inflammation under Dr. Philobosian's eyelids, had stopped the examination and chalked an **X** on his coat. He was led out of line. My grandparents hadn't seen him again. "He must have caught something on the boat," Desdemona said. "Or his eyes were red from all that crying." Meanwhile, chalk continued to do its work all around them. It marked a **Pg** on the belly of a pregnant woman. It scrawled an **H** over an old man's failing heart. It diagnosed the **C** of conjunctivitis, the **F** of favus, and the **T** of trachoma. But, no matter how well trained, medical eyes couldn't spot a recessive mutation hiding out on a fifth chromosome. Fingers couldn't feel it. Buttonhooks couldn't bring it to light . . .

Now, on the train, my grandparents were tagged not with manifest numbers but with destination cards: "To the Conductor: Please show bearer where to change and where to get off, as this person does not speak English. Bearer is bound to: Grand Trunk Sta. Detroit." They sat next to each other in unreserved seats. Lefty faced the window, looking out with excitement. Desdemona stared down at her silkworm box, her cheeks crimson with the shame and fury she'd been suffering for the last thirty-six hours.

"That's the last time anyone cuts my hair," she said.

"You look fine," said Lefty, not looking. "You look like an *Amerikanidha*."

"I don't want to look like an *Amerikanidha*."

In the concessions area at Ellis Island, Lefty had cajoled Desdemona to step into a tent run by the YWCA. She'd gone in, shawled and kerchiefed, and had emerged fifteen minutes later in a drop-waisted dress and a floppy hat shaped like a chamber pot. Rage flamed beneath her new face powder. As part of the makeover, the YWCA ladies had cut off Desdemona's immigrant braids.

Obsessively, in the way a person worries

a rip deep in a pocket, she now reached up under the floppy hat to feel her denuded scalp for the thirtieth or fortieth time. "That's the last haircut," she said again. (She was true to this vow. From that day on, Desdemona grew her hair out like Lady Godiva, keeping it under a net in an enormous mass and washing it every Friday; and only after Lefty died did she ever cut it, giving it to Sophie Sassoon, who sold it for two hundred and fifty dollars to a wigmaker who made five separate wigs out of it, one of which, she claimed, was later bought by Betty Ford, post White House and rehab, so that we got to see it on television once, during Richard Nixon's funeral, my grandmother's hair, sitting on the ex-President's wife's head.)

But there was another reason for my grandmother's unhappiness. She opened the silkworm box in her lap. Inside were her two braids, still tied with the ribbons of mourning, but otherwise the box was empty. After carrying her silkworm eggs all the way from Bithynios, Desdemona had been forced to dump them out at Ellis Island. Silkworm eggs appeared on a list of parasites.

Lefty remained glued to the window. All the way from Hoboken he'd gazed out at the marvelous sights: electric trams pulling pink faces up Albany's hills; factories glowing like volcanoes in the Buffalo night. Once, waking as the train pulled through a city at dawn, Lefty had mistaken a pillared bank for the Parthenon, and thought he was in Athens again.

Now the Detroit River sped past and the city loomed. Lefty stared out at the motor cars parked like giant beetles at the curbsides. Smokestacks rose everywhere, cannons bombarding the atmosphere. There were red brick stacks and tall silver ones, stacks in regimental rows or all alone puffing meditatively away, a forest of smokestacks that dimmed the sunlight and then, all of a sudden, blocked it out completely. Everything went black: they'd entered the train station.

Grand Trunk Station, now a ruin of spectacular dimensions, was then the city's attempt to one-up New York. Its base was a mammoth marble neoclassical museum, complete with Corinthian pillars and carved entablature. From this temple rose a thirteen-story office building. Lefty, who'd been observing all the ways Greece had been handed down to America, arrived now at where the transmission stopped. In other words: the future. He stepped off to meet it. Desdemona, having no alternative, followed.

But just imagine it in those days! Grand Trunk! Telephones in a hundred shipping

156

offices ringing away, still a relatively new sound; and merchandise being sent east and west; passengers arriving and departing, having coffee in the Palm Court or getting their shoes shined, the wing tips of banking, the cap toes of parts supply, the saddle shoes of rum-running. Grand Trunk, with its vaulted ceilings of Guastavino tilework, its chandeliers, its floors of Welsh quarry stone. There was a six-chair barbershop, where civic leaders were mummified in hot towels; and bathtubs for rent; and elevator banks lit by translucent egg-shaped marble lamps.

Leaving Desdemona behind a pillar, Lefty searched through the mob in the station for the cousin who was meeting their train. Sourmelina Zizmo, née Papadiamandopoulos, was my grandparents' cousin and hence my first cousin twice removed. I knew her as a colorful, older woman. Sourmelina of the precarious cigarette ash. Sourmelina of the indigo bathwater. Sourmelina of the Theosophical Society brunches. She wore satin gloves up to the elbow and mothered a long line of smelly dachshunds with tearstained eyes. Footstools populated her house, allowing the short-legged creatures access to sofas and chaise longues. In 1922, however, Sourmelina was only twenty-eight. Picking her out of this crowd at Grand Trunk is as difficult for me as identifying guests in my parents' wedding album, where all the faces wear the disguise of youth. Lefty had a different problem. He paced the concourse, looking for the cousin he'd grown up with, a sharp-nosed girl with the grinning mouth of a comedy mask. Sun slanted in from the skylights above. He squinted, examining the passing women, until finally she called out to him, "Over here, cousin. Don't you recognize me? I'm the irresistible one."

"Lina, is that you?"

"I'm not in the village anymore."

In the five years since leaving Turkey, Sourmelina had managed to erase just about everything identifiably Greek about her, from her hair, which she dyed to a rich chestnut and now wore bobbed and marcelled, to her accent, which had migrated far enough west to sound vaguely "European," to her reading material (*Collier's*, *Harper's*), to her favorite foods (lobster thermidor, peanut butter), and finally to her clothes. She wore a short green flapper dress fringed at the hemline. Her shoes were a matching green satin with sequined toes and delicate ankle straps. A black feather boa was wrapped around her shoulders, and on her head was a cloche hat that dangled onyx pendants over her plucked eyebrows.

For the next few seconds she gave Lefty

the full benefit of her sleek, American pose, but it was still Lina inside there (under the cloche) and soon her Greek enthusiasm bubbled out. She spread her arms wide. "Kiss me hello, cousin."

They embraced. Lina pressed a rouged cheek against his neck. Then she pulled back to examine him and, dissolving into laughter, cupped her hand over his nose. "It's still you. I'd know this nose anywhere." Her laugh completed its follow-through, as her shoulders went up and down, and then she was on to the next thing. "So, where is she? Where is this new bride of yours? Your telegram didn't even give a name. What? Is she hiding?"

"She's . . . in the bathroom."

"She must be a beauty. You got married fast enough. Which did you do first, introduce yourself or propose?"

"I think I proposed."

"What does she look like?"

"She looks . . . like you."

"Oh, darling, not that good surely."

Sourmelina brought her cigarette holder to her lips and inhaled, scanning the crowd. "Poor Desdemona! Her brother falls in love and leaves her behind in New York. How is she?"

"She's fine."

"Why didn't she come with you? She's not jealous of your new wife, is she?"

"No, nothing like that."

She clutched his arm. "We read about the fire. *Terrible!* I was so worried until I got your letter. The Turks started it. I know it. Of course, my husband doesn't agree."

"He doesn't?"

"One suggestion, since you'll be living with us? Don't talk politics with my husband."

"All right."

"And the village?" Sourmelina inquired.

"Everybody left the *horeo*, Lina. There's nothing now."

"If I didn't hate that place, maybe I'd shed two tears."

"Lina, there's something I have to explain to you . . ."

But Sourmelina was looking away, tapping her foot. "Maybe she fell in."

". . . Something about Desdemona and me . . ."

"Yes?"

". . . My wife . . . Desdemona . . ."

"Was I right? They don't get along?"

"No . . . Desdemona . . . my wife . . ."

"Yes?"

"Same person." He gave the signal. Desdemona stepped from behind the pillar.

"Hello, Lina," my grandmother said. "We're married. Don't tell."

And that was how it came out, for the

next-to-last time. Blurted out by my *yia yia*, beneath the echoing roof of Grand Trunk, toward Sourmelina's cloche-covered ears. The confession hovered in the air a moment, before floating away with the smoke rising from her cigarette. Desdemona took her husband's arm.

My grandparents had every reason to believe that Sourmelina would keep their secret. She'd come to America with a secret of her own, a secret that would be guarded by our family until Sourmelina died in 1979, whereupon, like everyone's secrets, it was posthumously declassified, so that people began to speak of "Sourmelina's girlfriends." A secret kept, in other words, only by the loosest definition, so that now — as I get ready to leak the information myself — I feel only a slight twinge of filial guilt.

Sourmelina's secret (as Aunt Zo put it): "Lina was one of those women they named the island after."

As a girl in the *horeo*, Sourmelina had been caught in compromising circumstances with a few female friends. "Not many," she told me herself, years later, "two or three. People think if you like girls, you like every single one. I was always picky. And there wasn't much to pick from." For a while she'd struggled against her predisposition. "I went to church. It didn't help. In those days that was the best place to meet a girlfriend. In church! All of us praying to be different." When Sourmelina was caught not with another girl but with a full-grown woman, a mother of two children, a scandal arose. Sourmelina's parents tried to arrange her marriage but found no takers. Husbands were hard enough to come by in Bithynios without the added liability of an uninterested, defective bride.

Her father had then done what Greek fathers of unmarriageable girls did in those days: he wrote to America. The United States abounded with dollar bills, baseball sluggers, raccoon coats, diamond jewelry — and lonely, immigrant bachelors. With a photograph of the prospective bride and a considerable dowry, her father had come up with one.

Jimmy Zizmo (shortened from Zisimopoulos) had come to America in 1907 at the age of thirty. The family didn't know much about him except that he was a hard bargainer. In a series of letters to Sourmelina's father, Zizmo had negotiated the amount of the dowry in the formal language of a barrister, even going so far as to demand a bank check before the wedding day. The photograph Sourmelina received showed a tall, handsome man with a virile mustache, holding a pistol in one hand and a bottle of liquor in the other. When she stepped off the train at Grand Trunk two months later, however, the short man who greeted her was clean-shaven, with a sour expression and a laborer's dark complexion. Such a discrepancy might have disappointed a normal bride, but Sourmelina didn't care one way or another.

Sourmelina had written often, describing her new life in America, but she concentrated on the new fashions, or her Aeriola Jr., the radio she spent hours each day listening to, wearing earphones and manipulating the dial, stopping every so often to clean off the carbon dust that built up on the crystal. She never mentioned anything connected to what Desdemona referred to as "the bed," and so her cousins were forced to read between the lines of those aerograms, trying to see, in a description of a Sunday drive through Belle Isle, whether the face of the husband at the wheel was happy or unsatisfied; or inferring, from a passage about Sourmelina's latest hairstyle — something called "cootie garages" — whether Zizmo was ever allowed to muss it up.

This same Sourmelina, full of her own secrets, now took in her new co-conspirators. "Married? You mean sleeping-together married?"

Lefty managed, "Yes."

Sourmelina noticed her ash for the first time, and flicked it. "Just my luck. Soon as I leave the village, things get interesting."

But Desdemona couldn't abide such irony. She grabbed Sourmelina's hands and pleaded, "You have to promise never to tell. We'll live, we'll die, and that will be the end of it."

"I won't tell."

"People can't even know I'm your cousin."

"I won't tell anyone."

"What about your husband?"

"He thinks I'm picking up my cousin and his new wife."

"You won't say anything to him?"

"That'll be easy." Lina laughed. "He doesn't listen to me."

Sourmelina insisted on getting a porter to carry their suitcases to the car, a black-and-tan Packard. She tipped him and climbed behind the wheel, attracting looks. A woman driving was still a scandalous sight in 1922. After resting her cigarette holder on the dashboard, she pulled out the choke, waited the requisite five seconds, and pressed the ignition button. The car's tin bonnet shuddered to life. The leather seats began to vibrate and Desdemona took hold of her husband's arm. Up front, Sourmelina took off her satin-strap high heels to drive barefoot. She put the car into gear and, without checking traffic, lurched off down Michigan Avenue toward Cadillac Square. My grandparents' eyes glazed over at the sheer activity, streetcars rumbling, bells clanging, and the monochrome traffic swerving in and out. In those days downtown Detroit was filled with shoppers and businessmen. Outside Hudson's Department Store the crowd was ten thick, jostling to get in the newfangled revolving doors. Lina pointed out the sights: **the Café Frontenac . . . the Family Theatre . . .** and the enormous electric signs: **Ralston . . . Wait & Bond Blackstone Mild 10¢ Cigar.** Above, a thirty-foot boy spread **Meadow Gold Butter** on a ten-foot slice of bread. One building had a row of giant oil lamps over the entrance to promote a sale on until October 31. It was all swirl and hubbub, Desdemona lying against the backseat, already suffering the anxiety that modern conveniences would induce in her over the years, cars mainly, but toasters, too, lawn sprinklers and escalators; while Lefty grinned and shook his head. Skyscrapers were going up everywhere, and movie palaces and hotels. The twenties saw the construction of nearly all Detroit's great buildings, the Penobscot Building and the second Buhl Building colored like an Indian belt, the New Union Trust Building, the Cadillac Tower, the Fisher Building with its gilded roof. To my grandparents Detroit was like one big Koza Han during cocoon season. What they didn't see were the workers sleeping on the streets because of the housing shortage, and the ghetto just to the east, a thirty-square-block area bounded by Leland, Macomb, Hastings, and Brush streets, teeming with the city's African Americans, who weren't allowed to live anywhere else. They didn't see, in short, the seeds of the city's destruction — its second destruction — because they were part of it, too, all these people coming from everywhere to cash in on Henry Ford's five-dollar-a-day promise.

The East Side of Detroit was a quiet neighborhood of single-family homes, shaded by cathedral elms. The house on Hurlbut Street Lina drove them to was a modest, two-story building of root-beer-colored brick. My grandparents gaped at it from the car, unable to move, until suddenly the front door opened and someone stepped out.

Jimmy Zizmo was so many things I don't know where to begin. Amateur herbalist; antisuffragist; big-game hunter; ex-con; drug pusher; teetotaler — take your pick. He was forty-five years old, nearly twice as old as his wife. Standing on the dim porch, he wore an inexpensive suit and a shirt with a pointy collar that had lost most of its starch. His frizzy black hair gave him the wild look of the bachelor he'd been for so many years, and this impression was heightened by his face, which was rumpled like an unmade bed. His eyebrows, however, were as seductively arched as a nautch girl's, his eyelashes so thick he might have been wearing mascara. But my grandmother didn't notice any of that. She was fixated on something else.

"An Arab?" Desdemona asked as soon as she was alone with her cousin in the kitchen. "Is that why you didn't tell us about him in your letters?"

"He's not an Arab. He's from the Black Sea."

"This is the *sala*," Zizmo was meanwhile explaining to Lefty as he showed him around the house.

"Pontian!" Desdemona gasped with horror, while also examining the icebox. "He's not Muslim, is he?"

"Not everybody from the Pontus converted," Lina scoffed. "What do you think, a Greek takes a swim in the Black Sea and turns into a Muslim?"

"But does he have Turkish blood?" She lowered her voice. "Is that why he's so dark?"

"I don't know and I don't care."

"You're free to stay as long as you like" — Zizmo was now leading Lefty upstairs — "but there are a few house rules. First, I'm a vegetarian. If your wife wants to cook meat, she has to use separate pots and dishes. Also, no whiskey. Do you drink?"

"Sometimes."

"No drinking. Go to a speakeasy if you want to drink. I don't want any trouble with the police. Now, about the rent. You just got married?"

"Yes."

"What kind of dowry did you get?"

"Dowry?"

"Yes. How much?"

"But did you know he was so old?" Desdemona whispered downstairs as she inspected the oven.

"At least he's not my brother."

"Quiet! Don't even joke."

"I didn't get a dowry," answered Lefty. "We met on the boat over."

"No dowry!" Zizmo stopped on the stairs to look back at Lefty with astonishment. "Why did you get married, then?"

"We fell in love," Lefty said. He'd never announced it to a stranger before, and it made him feel happy and frightened all at once.

"If you don't get paid, don't get married," Zizmo said. "That's why I waited so

long. I was holding out for the right price."
He winked.

"Lina mentioned you have your own business now," Lefty said with sudden interest, following Zizmo into the bathroom. "What kind of business is it?"

"Me? I'm an importer."

"I don't know of what," Sourmelina answered in the kitchen. "An importer. All I know is he brings home money."

"But how can you marry somebody you don't know anything about?"

"To get out of that country, Des, I would have married a cripple."

"I have some experience with importing," Lefty managed to get in as Zizmo demonstrated the plumbing. "Back in Bursa. In the silk industry."

"Your portion of the rent is twenty dollars." Zizmo didn't take the hint. He pulled the chain, unleashing a flood of water.

"As far as I'm concerned," Lina was continuing downstairs, "when it comes to husbands, the older the better." She opened the pantry door. "A young husband would be after me all the time. It would be too much of a strain."

"Shame on you, Lina." But Desdemona was laughing now, despite herself. It was wonderful to see her old cousin again, a little piece of Bithynios still intact. The dark pantry, full of figs, almonds, walnuts, halvah, and dried apricots, made her feel better, too.

"But where can I get the rent?" Lefty finally blurted out as they headed back downstairs. "I don't have any money left. Where can I work?"

"Not a problem." Zizmo waved his hand. "I'll speak to a few people." They came through the *sala* again. Zizmo stopped and looked significantly down. "You haven't complimented my zebra skin rug."

"It's very nice."

"I brought it back from Africa. Shot it myself."

"You've been to Africa?"

"I've been all over."

Like everybody else in town, they squeezed in together. Desdemona and Lefty slept in a bedroom directly above Zizmo and Lina's, and the first few nights my grandmother climbed out of bed to put her ear to the floor. "Nothing," she said, "I told you."

"Come back to bed," Lefty scolded. "That's their business."

"What business? That's what I'm telling you. They aren't having any business."

While in the bedroom below, Zizmo was discussing the new boarders upstairs. "What a romantic! Meets a girl on the boat and marries her. No dowry."

"Some people marry for love."

"Marriage is for housekeeping and for children. Which reminds me."

"Please, Jimmy, not tonight."

"Then when? Five years we've been married and no children. You're always sick, tired, this, that. Have you been taking the castor oil?"

"Yes."

"And the magnesium?"

"Yes."

"Good. We have to reduce your bile. If the mother has too much bile, the child will lack vigor and disobey his parents."

"Good night, *kyrie*."

"Good night, *kyria*."

Before the week was out, all my grandparents' questions about Sourmelina's marriage had been answered. Because of his age, Jimmy Zizmo treated his young bride more like a daughter than a wife. He was always telling her what she could and couldn't do, howling over the price and necklines of her outfits, telling her to go to bed, to get up, to speak, to keep silent. He refused to give her the car keys until she cajoled him with kisses and caresses. His nutritional quackery even led him to monitor her regularity like a doctor, and some of their biggest fights came as a result of his interrogating Lina about her stools. As for sexual relations, they had happened, but not recently. For the last five months Lina had complained of imaginary ailments, preferring her husband's herbal cures to his amatory attentions. Zizmo, in turn, harbored vaguely yogic beliefs about the mental benefits of semen retention, and so was disposed to wait until his wife's vitality returned. The house was sex-segregated like the houses in the *patridha,* the old country, men in the *sala,* women in the kitchen. Two spheres with separate concerns, duties, even — the evolutionary biologists might say — thought patterns. Lefty and Desdemona, accustomed to living in their own house, were forced to adapt to their new landlord's ways. Besides, my grandfather needed a job.

In those days there were a lot of car companies to work for. There was Chalmers, Metzger, Brush, Columbia, and Flanders. There was Hupp, Paige, Hudson, Krit, Saxon, Liberty, Rickenbacker, and Dodge. Jimmy Zizmo, however, had connections at Ford.

"I'm a supplier," he said.

"Of what?"

"Assorted fuels."

They were in the Packard again, vibrating on thin tires. A light mist was falling. Lefty squinted through the fogged windshield. Little by little, as they approached along Michigan Avenue, he began to be aware of a monolith looming in the distance, a building like a gigantic church organ, pipes running into the sky.

There was also a smell: the same smell that would drift upriver, years later, to find me in my bed or in the field hockey goal. Like my own, similarly beaked nose at those times, my grandfather's nose went on alert. His nostrils flared. He inhaled. At first the smell was recognizable, part of the organic realm of bad eggs and manure. But after a few seconds the smell's chemical properties seared his nostrils, and he covered his nose with his handkerchief.

Zizmo laughed. "Don't worry. You'll get used to it."

"No, I won't."

"Do you want to know the secret?"

"What?"

"Don't breathe."

When they reached the factory, Zizmo took him into the Personnel Department.

"How long has he lived in Detroit?" the manager asked.

"Six months."

"Can you verify that?"

Zizmo now spoke in a low tone. "I could drop the necessary documents by your house."

The personnel manager looked both

ways. "Old Log Cabin?"

"Only the best."

The chief jutted out his lower lip, examining my grandfather. "How's his English?"

"Not as good as mine. But he learns fast."

"He'll have to take the course and pass the test. Otherwise he's out."

"It's a deal. Now, if you'll write down your home address, we can schedule a delivery. Would Monday evening, say around eight-thirty, be suitable?"

"Come around to the back door."

My grandfather's short employ at the Ford Motor Company marked the only time any Stephanides has ever worked in the automobile industry. Instead of cars, we would become manufacturers of hamburger platters and Greek salads, industrialists of spanakopita and grilled cheese sandwiches, technocrats of rice pudding and banana cream pie. Our assembly line was the grill; our heavy machinery, the soda fountain. Still, those twenty-five weeks gave us a personal connection to that massive, forbidding, awe-inspiring complex we saw from the highway, that controlled Vesuvius of chutes, tubes, ladders, catwalks, fire, and smoke known, like a plague or a monarch, only by a color: "the Rouge."

On his first day of work, Lefty came into

the kitchen modeling his new overalls. He spread his flannel-shirted arms and snapped his fingers, dancing in work boots, and Desdemona laughed and shut the kitchen door so as not to wake up Lina. Lefty ate his breakfast of prunes and yogurt, reading a Greek newspaper a few days old. Desdemona packed his Greek lunch of feta, olives, and bread in a new American container: a brown paper bag. At the back door, when he turned to kiss her she stepped back, anxious that people might see. But then she remembered that they were married now. They lived in a place called Michigan, where the birds seemed to come in only one color, and where no one knew them. Desdemona stepped forward again to meet her husband's lips. Their first kiss in the great American outdoors, on the back porch, near a cherry tree losing its leaves. A brief flare of happiness went off inside her and hung, raining sparks, until Lefty disappeared around the front of the house.

My grandfather's good mood accompanied him all the way to the trolley stop. Other workers were already waiting, loose-kneed, smoking cigarettes and joking. Lefty noticed their metal lunch pails and, embarrassed by his paper sack, held it behind him. The streetcar showed up first as a hum in the soles of his boots. Then it appeared against the rising sun, Apollo's own chariot, only electrified. Inside, men stood in groups arranged by language. Faces scrubbed for work still had soot inside the ears, deep black. The streetcar sped off again. Soon the jovial mood dissipated and the languages fell silent. Near downtown, a few blacks boarded the car, standing outside on the runners, holding on to the roof.

And then the Rouge appeared against the sky, rising out of the smoke it generated. At first all that was visible was the tops of the eight main smokestacks. Each gave birth to its own dark cloud. The clouds plumed upward and merged into a general pall that hung over the landscape, sending a shadow that ran along the trolley tracks; and Lefty understood that the men's silence was a recognition of this shadow, of its inevitable approach each morning. As it came on, the men turned their backs so that only Lefty saw the light leave the sky as the shadow enveloped the streetcar and the men's faces turned gray and one of the *mavros* on the runners spat blood onto the roadside. The smell seeped into the streetcar next, first the bearable eggs and manure, then the unbearable chemical taint, and Lefty looked at the other men to see if they registered it, but they didn't, though they continued to breathe. The doors opened and they all filed out.

Through the hanging smoke, Lefty saw other streetcars letting off other workers, hundreds and hundreds of gray figures trudging across the paved courtyard toward the factory gates. Trucks were driving past, and Lefty let himself be taken along with the flow of the next shift, fifty, sixty, seventy thousand men hurrying last cigarettes or getting in final words — because as they approached the factory they'd begun to speak again, not because they had anything to say but because beyond those doors language wasn't allowed. The main building, a fortress of dark brick, was seven stories high, the smokestacks seventeen. Running off it were two chutes topped by water towers. These led to observation decks and to adjoining refineries studded with less impressive stacks. It was like a grove of trees, as if the Rouge's eight main smokestacks had sown seeds to the wind, and now ten or twenty or fifty smaller trunks were sprouting up in the infertile soil around the plant. Lefty could see the train tracks now, the huge silos along the river, the giant spice box of coal, coke, and iron ore, and the catwalks stretching overhead like giant spiders. Before he was sucked in the door, he glimpsed a freighter and a bit of the river French explorers named for its reddish color, long before the water turned orange from runoff or ever caught on fire.

Historical fact: people stopped being human in 1913. That was the year Henry Ford put his cars on rollers and made his workers adopt the speed of the assembly line. At first, workers rebelled. They quit in droves, unable to accustom their bodies to the new pace of the age. Since then, however, the adaptation has been passed down: we've all inherited it to some degree, so that we plug right into joysticks and remotes, to repetitive motions of a hundred kinds.

But in 1922 it was still a new thing to be a machine.

On the factory floor, my grandfather was trained for his job in seventeen minutes. Part of the new production method's genius was its division of labor into unskilled tasks. That way you could hire anyone. And fire anyone. The foreman showed Lefty how to take a bearing from the conveyor, grind it on a lathe, and replace it. Holding a stopwatch, he timed the new employee's attempts. Then, nodding once, he led Lefty to his position on the Line. On the left stood a man named Wierzbicki; on the right, a man named O'Malley. For a moment, they are three men, waiting together. Then the whistle blows.

Every fourteen seconds Wierzbicki reams a bearing and Stephanides grinds a bearing and O'Malley attaches a bearing to a camshaft. This camshaft travels away on a conveyor, curling around the factory, through its clouds of metal dust, its acid fogs, until another worker fifty yards on reaches up and removes the camshaft, fitting it onto the engine block (twenty seconds). Simultaneously, other men are unhooking parts from adjacent conveyors — the carburetor, the distributor, the intake manifold — and connecting them to the engine block. Above their bent heads, huge spindles pound steam-powered fists. No one says a word. Wierzbicki reams a bearing and Stephanides grinds a bearing and O'Malley attaches a bearing to a camshaft. The camshaft circles around the floor until a hand reaches up to take it down and attach it to the engine block, growing increasingly eccentric now with swooshes of pipe and the plumage of fan blades. Wierzbicki reams a bearing and Stephanides grinds a bearing and O'Malley attaches a bearing to a camshaft. While other workers screw in the air filter (seventeen seconds) and attach the starter motor (twenty-six seconds) and put on the flywheel. At which point the engine is finished and the last man sends it soaring away . . .

Except that he isn't the last man. There are other men below hauling the engine in, as a chassis rolls out to meet it. These men attach the engine to the transmission (twenty-five seconds). Wierzbicki reams a bearing and Stephanides grinds a bearing and O'Malley attaches a bearing to a camshaft. My grandfather sees only the bearing in front of him, his hands removing it, grinding it, and putting it back as another appears. The conveyor over his head extends back to the men who stamp out the bearings and load ingots into the furnaces; it goes back to the Foundry where the Negroes work, goggled against the infernal light and heat. They feed iron ore into the Blast Oven and pour molten steel into core molds from ladles. They pour at just the right rate — too quickly and the molds will explode; too slowly and the steel will harden. They can't stop even to pick the burning bits of metal from their arms. Sometimes the foreman does it; sometimes not. The Foundry is the deepest recess of the Rouge, its molten core, but the Line goes back farther than that. It extends outside to the hills of coal and coke; it goes to the river where freighters dock to unload the ore, at which point the Line becomes the river itself, snaking up to the north woods until it reaches its source, which is the earth itself, the limestone and sandstone therein; and then the Line leads back again, out of substrata to river to freighters and finally to the cranes, shovels, and furnaces where it is turned into molten steel and poured into molds, cooling and hardening into car parts — the gears, drive shafts, and fuel tanks of 1922 Model T's. Wierzbicki reams a bearing and Stephanides grinds a bearing and O'Malley attaches a bearing to a camshaft. Above and behind, at various angles, workers pack sand into core molds, or hammer plugs into molds, or put casting boxes into the cupola furnace. The Line isn't a single line but many, diverging and intersecting. Other workers stamp out body parts (fifty seconds), bump them (forty-two seconds), and weld the pieces together (one minute and ten seconds). Wierzbicki reams a bearing and Stephanides grinds a bearing and O'Malley attaches a bearing to a camshaft. The camshaft flies around the factory until a man unhooks it, attaches it to the engine block, growing eccentric now with fan blades, pipes, and spark plugs. And then the engine is finished. A man sends it dropping down onto a chassis rolling out to meet it, as three other workers remove a car body from the oven, its black finish baked to a shine in which they can see their own faces, and they recognize themselves, momentarily, before they drop the body onto the chassis rolling out to meet it. A man jumps into the front seat (three seconds), turns the ignition (two seconds), and drives the automobile away.

★ ★ ★

By day, no words; by night, hundreds. Every evening at quitting time my exhausted grandfather would come out of the factory and tramp across to an adjacent building housing the Ford English School. He sat in a desk with his workbook open in front of him. The desk felt as though it were vibrating across the floor at the Line's 1.2 miles per hour. He looked up at the English alphabet in a frieze on the classroom walls. In rows around him, men sat over identical workbooks. Hair stiff from dried sweat, eyes red from metal dust, hands raw, they recited with the obedience of choirboys:

"Employees should use plenty of soap and water in the home.

"Nothing makes for right living so much as cleanliness.

"Do not spit on the floor of the home.

"Do not allow any flies in the house.

"The most advanced people are the cleanest."

Sometimes the English lessons continued on the job. One week, after a lecture by the foreman on increasing productivity, Lefty speeded up his work, grinding a bearing every twelve seconds instead of fourteen. Returning from the lavatory later, he found the word "RAT" written on the side of his lathe. The belt was cut. By the

182

time he found a new belt in the equipment bin, a horn sounded. The Line had stopped.

"What the hell's the matter with you?" the foreman shouted at him. "Every time we shut down the line, we lose money. If it happens again, you're out. Understand?"

"Yes, sir."

"Okay! Let her go!"

And the Line started up again. After the foreman had gone, O'Malley looked both ways and leaned over to whisper, "Don't try to be a speed king. You understand? We all have to work faster that way."

Desdemona stayed home and cooked. Without silkworms to tend or mulberry trees to pick, without neighbors to gossip with or goats to milk, my grandmother filled her time with food. While Lefty ground bearings nonstop, Desdemona built pastitsio, moussaka and galactoboureko. She coated the kitchen table with flour and, using a bleached broomstick, rolled out paper-thin sheets of dough. The sheets came off her assembly line, one after another. They filled the kitchen. They covered the living room, where she'd laid bedsheets over the furniture. Desdemona went up and down the line, adding walnuts, butter, honey, spinach, cheese, adding more layers of dough, then more butter, before forging the assembled concoctions in the oven. At the Rouge, workers collapsed from heat and fatigue, while on Hurlbut my grandmother did a double shift. She got up in the morning to fix breakfast and pack a lunch for her husband, then marinated a leg of lamb with wine and garlic. In the afternoon she made her own sausages, spiced with fennel, and hung them over the heating pipes in the basement. At three o'clock she started dinner, and only when it was cooking did she take a break, sitting at the kitchen table to consult her dream book on the meaning of her previous night's dreams. No fewer than three pots simmered on the stove at all times. Occasionally, Jimmy Zizmo brought home a few of his business associates, hulking men with thick, ham-like heads stuffed into their fedoras. Desdemona served them meals at all hours of the day. Then they were off again, into the city. Desdemona cleaned up.

The only thing she refused to do was the shopping. American stores confused her. She found the produce depressing. Even many years later, seeing a Kroger's McIntosh in our suburban kitchen, she would hold it up to ridicule, saying, "This is nothing. This we fed to goats." To step into a local market was to miss the savor of the peaches, figs, and winter chestnuts of

Bursa. Already, in her first months in America, Desdemona was suffering "the homesickness that has no cure." So, after working at the plant and attending English class, Lefty was the one to pick up the lamb and vegetables, the spices and honey.

And so they lived . . . one month . . . three . . . five. They suffered through their first Michigan winter. A January night, just past 1 a.m. Desdemona Stephanides asleep, wearing her hated YWCA hat against the wind blowing through the thin walls. A radiator sighing, clanking. By candlelight, Lefty finishes his homework, notebook propped on knees, pencil in hand. And from the wall: rustling. He looks up to see a pair of red eyes shining out from a hole in the baseboard. He writes R-A-T before throwing his pencil at the vermin. Desdemona sleeps on. He brushes her hair. He says, in English, "Hello, sweetheart." The new country and its language have helped to push the past a little further behind. The sleeping form next to him is less and less his sister every night and more and more his wife. The statute of limitations ticks itself out, day by day, all memory of the crime being washed away. (But what humans forget, cells remember. The body, that elephant . . .)

Spring arrived, 1923. My grandfather, accustomed to the multifarious conjugations of ancient Greek verbs, had found English, for all its incoherence, a relatively simple tongue to master. Once he had swallowed a good portion of the English vocabulary, he began to taste the familiar ingredients, the Greek seasoning in the roots, prefixes, and suffixes. A pageant was planned to celebrate the Ford English School graduation. As a top student, Lefty was asked to take part.

"What kind of pageant?" Desdemona asked.

"I can't tell you. It's a surprise. But you have to sew me some clothes."

"What kind?"

"Like from the *patridha*."

It was a Wednesday evening. Lefty and Zizmo were in the *sala* when suddenly Lina came in to listen to "The Ronnie Ronnette Hour." Zizmo gave her a disapproving look, but she escaped behind her head-phones.

"She thinks she's one of these *Ameri-kanidhes*," Zizmo said to Lefty. "Look. See? She even crosses her legs."

"This is America," Lefty said. "We're all *Amerikanidhes* now."

"This is not America," Zizmo countered. "This is my house. We don't live like the *Amerikanidhes* in here. Your wife under-stands. Do you see her in the *sala* showing her legs and listening to the radio?"

Someone knocked at the door. Zizmo, who had an inexplicable aversion to un-announced guests, jumped up and reached under his coat. He motioned for Lefty not to move. Lina, noticing something, took off her earphones. The knock came again. *"Kyrie,"* Lina said, "if they were going to kill you, would they knock?"

"Who's going to kill!" Desdemona said, rushing in from the kitchen.

"Just a way of speaking," said Lina, who knew more about her husband's importing concern that she'd been letting on. She glided to the door and opened it.

Two men stood on the welcome mat. They wore gray suits, striped ties, black brogues. They had short sideburns. They carried matching briefcases. When they removed their hats, they revealed identical chestnut hair, neatly parted in the center. Zizmo took his hand out of his coat.

"We're from the Ford Sociological Department," the tall one said. "Is Mr. Stephanides at home?"

"Yes?" Lefty said.

"Mr. Stephanides, let me tell you why we're here."

"Management has foreseen," the short one seamlessly continued, "that five dollars a day in the hands of some men might work a tremendous handicap along the paths of rectitude and right living and

187

might make of them a menace to society in general."

"So it was established by Mr. Ford" — the taller one again took over — "that no man is to receive the money who cannot use it advisedly and conservatively."

"Also" — the short one again — "that where a man seems to qualify under the plan and later develops weaknesses, that it is within the province of the company to take away his share of the profits until such time as he can rehabilitate himself. May we come in?"

Once across the threshold, they separated. The tall one took a pad from his briefcase. "I'm going to ask you a few questions, if you don't mind. Do you drink, Mr. Stephanides?"

"No, he doesn't," Zizmo answered for him.

"And who are you, may I ask?"

"My name is Zizmo."

"Are you a boarder here?"

"This is my house."

"So Mr. and Mrs. Stephanides are the boarders?"

"That's right."

"Won't do. Won't do," said the tall one. "We encourage our employees to obtain mortgages."

"He's working on it," Zizmo said.

Meanwhile, the short one had entered the

kitchen. He was lifting lids off pots, opening the oven door, peering into the garbage can. Desdemona started to object, but Lina checked her with a glance. (And notice how Desdemona's nose has begun to twitch. For two days now, her sense of smell has been incredibly acute. Foods are beginning to smell funny to her, feta cheese like dirty socks, olives like goat droppings.)

"How often do you bathe, Mr. Stephanides?" the tall one asked.

"Every day, sir."

"How often do you brush your teeth?"

"Every day, sir."

"What do you use?"

"Baking soda."

Now the short one was climbing the stairs. He invaded my grandparents' bedroom and inspected the linens. He stepped into the bathroom and examined the toilet seat.

"From now on, use this," the tall one said. "It's a dentifrice. Here's a new toothbrush."

Disconcerted, my grandfather took the items. "We come from Bursa," he explained. "It's a big city."

"Brush along the gum lines. Up on the bottoms and down on the tops. Two minutes morning and night. Let's see. Give it a try."

"We are civilized people."

"Do I understand you to be refusing hygiene instruction?"

"Listen to me," Zizmo said. "The Greeks built the Parthenon and the Egyptians built the pyramids back when the Anglo-Saxons were still dressing in animal skins."

The tall one took a long look at Zizmo and made a note on his pad.

"Like this?" my grandfather said. Grinning hideously, he moved the toothbrush up and down in his dry mouth.

"That's right. Fine."

The short one now reappeared from upstairs. He flipped open his pad and began: "Item one. Garbage can in kitchen has no lid. Item two. Housefly on kitchen table. Item three. Too much garlic in food. Causes indigestion."

(And now Desdemona locates the culprit: the short man's hair. The smell of brilliantine on it makes her nauseous.)

"Very considerate of you to come here and take an interest in your employee's health," Zizmo said. "We wouldn't want anybody to get sick, now, would we? Might slow down production."

"I'm going to pretend I didn't hear that," said the tall one. "Seeing as you are not an official employee of the Ford Motor Company. However" — turning back to my grandfather — "I should advise you,

Mr. Stephanides, that in my report I am going to make a note of your social relations. I'm going to recommend that you and Mrs. Stephanides move into your own home as soon as it is financially feasible."

"And may I ask what your occupation is, sir?" the short one wanted to know.

"I'm in shipping," Zizmo said.

"Nice of you gentlemen to stop by," Lina moved in. "But if you'll excuse us, we're just about to have dinner. We have to go to church tonight. And, of course, Lefty has to be in bed by nine to get rest. He likes to be fresh in the morning."

"That's fine. Fine."

Together, they put on their hats and left.

And so we come to the weeks leading up to the graduation pageant. To Desdemona sewing a *palikari* vest, embroidering it with red, white, and blue thread. To Lefty getting off work one Friday evening and crossing over Miller Road to be paid from the armored truck. To Lefty again, the night of the pageant, taking the streetcar to Cadillac Square and walking into Gold's Clothes. Jimmy Zizmo meets him there to help him pick out a suit.

"It's almost summer. How about something cream-colored? With a yellow silk necktie?"

"No. The English teacher told us. Blue or gray only."

"They want to turn you into a Protestant. Resist!"

"I'll take the blue suit, please, thank you," Lefty says in his best English.

(And here, too, the shop owner seems to owe Zizmo a favor. He gives them a 20 percent discount.)

Meanwhile, on Hurlbut, Father Stylianopoulos, head priest of Assumption Greek Orthodox Church, has finally come over to bless the house. Desdemona watches the priest nervously as he drinks the glass of Metaxa she has offered him. When she and Lefty became members of his congregation, the old priest had asked, as a formality, if they had received an Orthodox wedding. Desdemona had replied in the affirmative. She had grown up believing that priests could tell whether someone was telling the truth or not, but Father Stylianopoulos had only nodded and written their names into the church register. Now he sets down his glass. He stands and recites the blessing, shaking holy water on the threshold. Before he's finished, however, Desdemona's nose begins acting up again. She can smell what the priest had for lunch. She can detect the aroma under his arms as he makes the sign of the cross. At the door, letting him out, she holds her breath. "Thank you, Father. Thank you." Stylianopoulos goes on his way. But it's no use. As soon as she inhales again, she can smell the fertilized flower beds and Mrs. Czeslawski boiling cabbage next door and what she swears must be an open jar of mustard somewhere, all these scents gone wayward on her, as she puts a hand to her stomach.

Right then the bedroom door swings open. Sourmelina steps out. Powder and rouge cover one side of her face; the other side, bare, looks green. "Do you smell something?" she asks.

"Yes. I smell everything."

"Oh my God."

"What is it?"

"I didn't think this would happen to me. To you maybe. But not to me."

And now we are in the Detroit Light Guard Armory, later that night, 7:00 p.m. An assembled audience of two thousand settles down as the house lights dim. Prominent business leaders greet each other with handshakes. Jimmy Zizmo, in a new cream-colored suit with yellow necktie, crosses his legs, jiggling one saddle shoe. Lina and Desdemona hold hands, joined in a mysterious union.

The curtain parts to gasps and scattered applause. A painted flat shows a steamship, two huge smokestacks, and a swath of deck and railing. A gangway extends into the stage's other focal point: a giant gray cauldron emblazoned with the words FORD ENGLISH SCHOOL MELTING POT. A European folk melody begins to play. Suddenly a lone figure appears on the gangway. Dressed in a Balkan costume of vest, ballooning trousers, and high leather boots, the immigrant carries his possessions bundled on a stick. He looks around with apprehension and then descends into the melting pot.

"What propaganda," Zizmo murmurs in his seat.

Lina shushes him.

Now SYRIA descends into the pot. Then ITALY. POLAND. NORWAY. PALESTINE. And finally: GREECE.

"Look, it's Lefty!"

Wearing embroidered *palikari* vest, puffy-sleeved *poukamiso*, and pleated *foustanella* skirt, my grandfather bestrides the gangway. He pauses a moment to look out at the audience, but the bright lights blind him. He can't see my grandmother looking back, bursting with her secret. GERMANY taps him on the back. "*Macht schnell.* Excuse me. Go fastly."

In the front row, Henry Ford nods with approval, enjoying the show. Mrs. Ford tries to whisper in his ear, but he waves her off. His blue seagull's eyes dart from face to face as the English instructors appear onstage next. They carry long spoons, which they insert into the pot. The lights turn red and flicker as the instructors stir. Steam rises over the stage.

Inside the cauldron, men are packed together, throwing off immigrant costumes, putting on suits. Limbs are tangling up, feet stepping on feet. Lefty says, "Pardon me, excuse me," feeling thoroughly American as he pulls on his blue wool trousers and jacket. In his mouth: thirty-two teeth brushed in the American manner. His underarms: liberally sprinkled with American deodorant. And now spoons are descending from above, men are churning around and around . . .

. . . as two men, short and tall, stand in the wings, holding a piece of paper . . .

. . . and out in the audience my grandmother has a stunned look on her face . . .

. . . and the melting pot boils over. Red lights brighten. The orchestra launches into "Yankee Doodle." One by one, the Ford English School graduates rise from the cauldron. Dressed in blue and gray suits, they climb out, waving American flags, to thunderous applause.

The curtain had barely come down before the men from the Sociological Department approached.

"I pass the final exam," my grandfather told them. "Ninety-three percent! And today I open savings account."

"That sounds fine," the tall one said.

"But unfortunately, it's too late," said the short one. He took a slip from his pocket, a color well known in Detroit: pink.

"We did some checking on your landlord. This so-called Jimmy Zizmo. He's got a police record."

"I don't know anything," my grandfather said. "I'm sure is a mistake. He is a nice man. Works hard."

"I'm sorry, Mr. Stephanides. But you can understand that Mr. Ford can't have workers maintaining such associations. You don't need to come down to the plant on Monday."

As my grandfather struggled to absorb this news, the short one leaned in. "I hope you learn a lesson from this. Mixing with the wrong crowd can sink you. You seem like a nice guy, Mr. Stephanides. You really do. We wish you the best of luck in the future."

A few minutes later, Lefty came out to meet his wife. He was surprised when, in front of everyone, she hugged him, refusing to let go.

"You liked the pageant?"

"It's not that."

"What is it?"

Desdemona looked into her husband's eyes. But it was Sourmelina who explained it all. "Your wife and I?" she said in plain English. "We're both knocked up."

Minotaurs

Which is something I'll never have much to do with. Like most hermaphrodites but by no means all, I can't have children. That's one of the reasons why I've never married. It's one of the reasons, aside from shame, why I decided to join the Foreign Service. I've never wanted to stay in one place. After I started living as a male, my mother and I moved away from Michigan and I've been moving ever since. In another year or two I'll leave Berlin, to be posted somewhere else. I'll be sad to go. This once-divided city reminds me of myself. My struggle for unification, for *Einheit*. Coming from a city still cut in half by racial hatred, I feel hopeful here in Berlin.

A word on my shame. I don't condone it. I'm trying my best to get over it. The intersex movement aims to put an end to infant genital reconfiguration surgery. The first step in that struggle is to convince the world — and pediatric endocrinologists in particular — that hermaphroditic genitals are not diseased. One out of every two thousand babies is born with ambiguous genitalia. In the United States, with a population of two hundred and seventy-five million, that comes to one hundred and thirty-seven thousand intersexuals alive today.

But we hermaphrodites are people like everybody else. And I happen not to be a political person. I don't like groups. Though I'm a member of the Intersex Society of North America, I have never taken part in its demonstrations. I live my own life and nurse my own wounds. It's not the best way to live. But it's the way I am.

The most famous hermaphrodite in history? Me? It felt good to write that, but I've got a long way to go. I'm closeted at work, revealing myself only to a few friends. At cocktail receptions, when I find myself standing next to the former ambassador (also a native of Detroit), we talk about the Tigers. Only a few people here in Berlin know my secret. I tell more people than I used to, but I'm not at all consistent. Some nights I tell people I've just met. In other cases I keep silent forever.

That goes especially for women I'm attracted to. When I meet someone I like and who seems to like me, I retreat. There are lots of nights out in Berlin when, emboldened by a good-value Rioja, I forget my physical predicament and allow myself to hope. The tailored suit comes off. The Thomas Pink shirt, too. My dates can't fail to be impressed by my physical condition. (Under the armor of my double-breasted suits is another of gym-built muscle.) But the final protection, my roomy, my discreet boxer shorts, these I do not remove. Ever. Instead I leave, making excuses. I leave and never call them again. Just like a guy.

And soon enough I am at it again. I am trying once more, toeing the line. I saw my bicyclist again this morning. This time I found out her name: Julie. Julie Kikuchi. Raised in northern California, graduate of the Rhode Island School of Design, and currently in Berlin on a grant from the Künstlerhaus Bethanien. But more important, right now: my date for Friday night.

It's just a first date. It won't come to anything. No reason to mention my peculiarities, my wandering in the maze these many years, shut away from sight. And from love, too.

꧁ꦿ꧂

The Simultaneous Fertilization had occurred in the early morning hours of March 24, 1923, in separate, vertical bedrooms, after a night out at the theater. My grandfather, not knowing he was soon to be fired, had splurged on four tickets to *The Minotaur*, playing at the Family. At first Desdemona had refused to go. She disapproved of theater in general, especially vaudeville, but in the end, unable to resist the Hellenic theme, she had put on a new pair of stockings, and a black dress and overcoat, and made her way with the others down the sidewalk and into the terrifying Packard.

When the curtain rose at the Family Theater, my relatives expected to get the whole story. How Minos, King of Crete, failed to sacrifice a white bull to Poseidon. How Poseidon, enraged, caused Minos's wife Pasiphaë to be smitten with love for a bull. How the child of that union, Asterius, came out with a bull's head attached to a human body. And then Daedalus, the maze, etc. As soon as the footlights came on, however, the production's nontraditional emphasis became clear. Because now they pranced onstage: the chorus girls. Dressed in silver halters, robed in see-through shifts, they danced, reciting strophes that didn't scan to the eerie piping of flutes. The Minotaur appeared, an actor wearing a papier-mâché bull's head. Lacking any sense of classical psychology, the actor played his half-human character as pure movie monster. He growled; drums pounded; chorus girls screamed and fled. The Minotaur pursued, and of course he caught them, each one, and devoured her bloodily, and dragged her pale, defenseless body deeper into the maze. And the curtain came down.

In the eighteenth row my grandmother gave her critical opinion. "It's like the paintings in the museum," she said. "Just an excuse to show people with no clothes."

She insisted on leaving before Act II. At home, getting ready for bed, the four theatergoers went about their nightly routines. Desdemona washed out her stockings, lit the vigil lamp in the hallway. Zizmo drank a glass of the papaya juice he touted as beneficial for the digestion. Lefty neatly hung up his suit, pinching each trouser crease, while Sourmelina removed her makeup with cold cream and went to bed. The four of them, moving in their individual orbits, pretended that the play had had no effect on them. But now Jimmy Zizmo was turning off his bedroom light. Now he was climbing into his single bed — to find it occupied! Sourmelina, dreaming of chorus girls, had sleepwalked across the throw rug. Murmuring strophes, she climbed on top of her stand-in husband. ("You see?" Zizmo said in the dark. "No more bile. It's the castor oil.") Upstairs, Desdemona might have heard something through the floor if she hadn't been pretending to be asleep. Against her will, the play had aroused her, too. The Minotaur's savage, muscular thighs. The suggestive sprawl of his victims. Ashamed of her excitement, she gave no outward sign. She switched off the lamp. She told her husband good night. She yawned (also theatrical) and turned her back. While Lefty stole up from behind.

Freeze the action. A momentous night, this, for all involved (including me). I want to record the positions (Lefty dorsal, Lina couchant) and the circumstances (night's amnesty) and the direct cause (a play about a hybrid monster). Parents are supposed to pass down physical traits to their children, but it's my belief that all sorts of other things get passed down, too: motifs, scenarios, even fates. Wouldn't I also sneak up on a girl pretending to be asleep? And wouldn't there also be a play involved, and somebody dying onstage?

Leaving these genealogical questions aside, I return to the biological facts. Like college girls sharing a dorm room, Desdemona and Lina were both synchronized in their menstrual cycles. That night was day fourteen. No thermometer verified this, but a few weeks later the symptoms of nausea and hypersensitive noses did. "Whoever named it morning sickness was a man," Lina declared. "He was just home in the morning to notice." The nausea kept no schedule; it owned no watch. They were sick in the afternoon, in the middle of the night. Pregnancy was a boat in a storm and they couldn't get off. And so they lashed themselves to the masts of their beds and rode out the squall. Everything they came in contact with, the bedsheets, the pillows, the air itself, began to turn on them. Their husbands' breath became intolerable, and when they weren't too sick to move, they were waving their arms, gesturing to the men to keep away.

Pregnancy humbled the husbands. After an initial rush of male pride, they quickly recognized the minor role that nature had assigned them in the drama of reproduction, and quietly withdrew into a baffled reserve, catalysts to an explosion they couldn't explain. While their wives grandly suffered in the bedrooms, Zizmo and Lefty retreated to the *sala* to listen to music, or drove to a coffee house in Greektown where no one would be offended by their smell. They played backgammon and talked politics, and no one spoke about women because in the coffee house everyone was a bachelor, no matter how old he was or how many children he'd given a wife who preferred their company to his. The talk was always the same, of the Turks and their brutality, of Venizelos and his mistakes, of King Constantine and his return, and of the unavenged crime of Smyrna burned.

"And does anybody care? No!"

"It's like what Bérenger said to Clemenceau: 'He who owns the oil owns the world.' "

"Those damn Turks! Murderers and rapists!"

"They desecrated the Hagia Sophia and now they destroyed Smyrna!"

But here Zizmo spoke up: "Stop bellyaching. The war was the Greeks' fault."

"What!"

"Who invaded who?" asked Zizmo.

"The Turks invaded. In 1453."

"The Greeks can't even run their own country. Why do they need another?"

At this point, men stood up, chairs were knocked over. "Who the hell are you, Zizmo? Goddamned Pontian! Turk-sympathizer!"

"I sympathize with the truth," shouted Zizmo. "There's no evidence the Turks started that fire. The Greeks did it to blame it on the Turks."

Lefty stepped between the men, preventing a fight. After that, Zizmo kept his political opinions to himself. He sat morosely drinking coffee, reading an odd assortment of magazines or pamphlets speculating on space travel and ancient civilizations. He chewed his lemon peels and told Lefty to do so, too. Together, they settled into the random camaraderie of

men on the outskirts of a birth. Like all ex-
pectant fathers, their thoughts turned to
money.

My grandfather had never told Jimmy
the reason for his dismissal from Ford, but
Zizmo had a good idea why it might have
happened. And so, a few weeks later, he
made what restitution he could.
"Just act like we're going for a drive."
"Okay."
"If we get stopped, don't say anything."
"Okay."
"This is a better job than the Rouge. Believe me. Five dollars a day is nothing. And
here you can eat all the garlic you want."
They are in the Packard, passing the
amusement grounds of Electric Park. It's
foggy out, and late — just past 3 a.m. To
be honest, the amusement grounds should
be closed at this hour, but, for my own
purposes, tonight Electric Park is open all
night, and the fog suddenly lifts, all so that
my grandfather can look out the window
and see a roller coaster streaking down the
track. A moment of cheap symbolism only,
and then I have to bow to the strict rules
of realism, which is to say: they can't see a
thing. Spring fog foams over the ramparts
of the newly opened Belle Isle Bridge. The
yellow globes of streetlamps glow, aureoled
in the mist.

"Lot of traffic for this late," Lefty marvels.

"Yes," says Zizmo. "It's very popular at night."

The bridge lifts them gently above the river and sets them back down on the other side. Belle Isle, a paramecium-shaped island in the Detroit River, lies less than half a mile from the Canadian shore. By day, the park is full of picnickers and strollers. Fishermen line its muddy banks. Church groups hold tent meetings. Come dark, however, the island takes on an offshore atmosphere of relaxed morals. Lovers park in secluded lookouts. Cars roll over the bridge on shadowy missions. Zizmo drives through the gloom, past the octagonal gazebos and the monument of the Civil War Hero, and into the woods where the Ottawa once held their summer camp. Fog wipes the windshield. Birch trees shed parchment beneath an ink-black sky.

Missing from most cars in the 1920s: rearview mirrors. "Steer," Zizmo keeps saying, and turns around to see if they're being followed. In this fashion, trading the wheel, they weave along Central Avenue and The Strand, circling the island three times, until Zizmo is satisfied. At the northeastern end, he pulls the car over, facing Canada.

"Why are we stopping?"

"Wait and see."

Zizmo turns the headlights on and off three times. He gets out of the car. So does Lefty. They stand in the darkness amid river sounds, waves lapping, freighters blowing foghorns. Then there's another sound: a distant hum. "You have an office?" my grandfather asks. "A warehouse?" "This is my office." Zizmo waves his hands through the air. He points to the Packard. "And that's my warehouse." The hum is getting louder now; Lefty squints through the fog. "I used to work for the railroad." Zizmo takes a dried apricot out of his pocket and eats it. "Out West in Utah. Broke my back. Then I got smart." But the hum has almost reached them; Zizmo is opening the trunk. And now, in the fog, an outboard appears, a sleek craft with two men aboard. They cut the engine as the boat glides into the reeds. Zizmo hands an envelope to one man. The other whisks the tarp off the boat's stern. In moonlight, neatly stacked, twelve wooden crates gleam.

"Now I run a railroad of my own," says Zizmo. "Start unloading."

The precise nature of Jimmy Zizmo's importing business was thus revealed. He didn't deal in dried apricots from Syria, halvah from Turkey, and honey from Lebanon. He imported Hiram Walker's whiskey from Ontario, beer from Quebec, and rum from Barbados by way of the St. Lawrence River. A teetotaler himself, he made his living buying and selling liquor. "If these *Amerikani* are all drunks, what can I do?" he justified, driving away minutes later.

"You should have told me!" Lefty shouted, enraged. "If we get caught, I won't get my citizenship. They'll send me back to Greece."

"What choice do you have? You have a better job? And don't forget. You and I, we have babies on the way."

So began my grandfather's life of crime. For the next eight months he worked in Zizmo's rum-running operation, observing its odd hours, getting up in the middle of the night and having dinner at dawn. He adopted the slang of the illegal trade, increasing his English vocabulary fourfold. He learned to call liquor "hooch," "bingo," "squirrel dew," and "monkey swill." He referred to drinking establishments as "boozeries," "doggeries," "rumholes," and "schooners." He learned the locations of blind pigs all over the city, the funeral parlors that filled bodies not with embalming fluid but with gin, the churches that offered something more than sacramental wine, and the barbershops whose Barbicide jars contained "blue ruin." Lefty grew familiar with the shoreline of the Detroit

River, its screened inlets and secret landings. He could identify police outboards at a distance of a quarter mile. Rum-running was a tricky business. The major bootlegging was controlled by the Purple Gang and the Mafia. In their beneficence they allowed a certain amount of amateur smuggling to go on — the day trips to Canada, the fishing boats out for a midnight cruise. Women took the ferry to Windsor with gallon flasks under their dresses. As long as such smuggling didn't cut into the main business, the gangs allowed it. But Zizmo was far exceeding the limit.

They went out five to six times a week. The Packard's trunk could fit four cases of liquor, its commodious, curtained backseat eight more. Zizmo respected neither rules nor territories. "As soon as they voted in Prohibition, I went to the library and looked at a map," he said, explaining how he'd gotten into the business. "There they were, Canada and Michigan, almost kissing. So I bought a ticket to Detroit. When I got here, I was broke. I went to see a marriage broker in Greektown. The reason I let Lina drive this car? She paid for it." He smiled with satisfaction, but then followed his thoughts a little further and his face darkened. "I don't approve of women driving, mind you. And now they get to vote!" He grumbled to himself. "Remember that play we saw? All women are like that. Given the chance, they'd all fornicate with a bull."

"Those are just stories, Jimmy," said Lefty. "You can't take them literally."

"Why not?" Zizmo continued. "Women aren't like us. They have carnal natures. The best thing to do with them is to shut them up in a maze."

"What are you talking about?"

Zizmo smiled. "Pregnancy."

It was like a maze. Desdemona kept turning this way and that, left side, right side, trying to find a comfortable position. Without leaving her bed, she wandered the dark corridors of pregnancy, stumbling over the bones of women who had passed this way before her. For starters, her mother, Euphrosyne (whom she was suddenly beginning to resemble), her grandmothers, her great-aunts, and all the women before them stretching back into prehistory right back to Eve, on whose womb the curse had been laid. Desdemona came into a physical knowledge of these women, shared their pains and sighs, their fear and protectiveness, their outrage, their expectation. Like them she put a hand to her belly, supporting the world; she felt omnipotent and proud; and then a muscle in her back spasmed.

I give you now the entire pregnancy in

211

time lapse. Desdemona, at eight weeks, lies on her back, bedcovers drawn up to her armpits. The light at the window flickers with the change of day and night. Her body jerks; she's on her side, her belly; the covers change shape. A wool blanket appears and disappears. Food trays fly to the bedside table, then jump away before returning. But throughout the mad dance of inanimate objects the continuity of Desdemona's shifting body remains at center. Her breasts inflate. Her nipples darken. At fourteen weeks her face begins to grow plump, so that for the first time I can recognize the *yia yia* of my childhood. At twenty weeks a mysterious line starts drawing itself down from her navel. Her belly rises like Jiffy Pop. At thirty weeks her skin thins, and her hair gets thicker. Her complexion, pale with nausea at first, grows less so until there it is: a glow. The bigger she gets, the more stationary. She stops lying on her stomach. Motionless, she swells toward the camera. The window's strobe effect continues. At thirty-six weeks she cocoons herself in bedsheets. The sheets go up and down, revealing her face, exhausted, euphoric, resigned, impatient. Her eyes open. She cries out.

Lina wrapped her legs in putties to prevent varicose veins. Worried that her breath was bad, she kept a tin of mints beside her bed. She weighed herself each morning, biting her lower lip. She enjoyed her new buxom figure but fretted about the consequences. "My breasts will never be the same. I know it. After this, just flaps. Like in the *National Geographic*." Pregnancy made her feel too much like an animal. It was embarrassing to be so publicly colonized. Her face felt on fire during hormone surges. She perspired; her makeup ran. The entire process was a holdover from more primitive stages of development. It linked her with the lower forms of life. She thought of queen bees spewing eggs. She thought of the collie next door, digging its hole in the backyard last spring.

The only escape was radio. She wore her earphones in bed, on the couch, in the bathtub. During the summer she carried her Aeriola Jr. outside and sat under the cherry tree. Filling her head with music, she escaped her body.

On a third-trimester October morning, a cab pulled up outside 3467 Hurlbut Street and a tall, slender figure climbed out. He checked the address against a piece of paper, collected his things — umbrella and suitcase — and paid the driver. He took off his hat and stared into it as though reading instructions along the lining. Then he put the hat back on and walked up onto the porch.

Desdemona and Lina both heard the knocking. They met at the front door.

When they opened it, the man looked from belly to belly.

"I'm just in time," he said.

It was Dr. Philobosian. Clear-eyed, clean-shaven, recovered from his grief. "I saved your address." They invited him in and he told his story. He had indeed contracted the eye disease favus on the *Giulia*. But his medical license had saved him from being sent back to Greece; America needed physicians. Dr. Philobosian had stayed a month in the hospital at Ellis Island, after which, with sponsorship from the Armenian Relief Agency, he had been admitted into the country. For the last eleven months he'd been living in New York, on the Lower East Side. "Grinding lenses for an optometrist." Recently he'd managed to retrieve some assets from Turkey and had come to the Midwest. "I'm going to open a practice here. New York has too many doctors already."

He stayed for dinner. The women's delicate conditions didn't excuse them from domestic duties. On swollen legs they carried out dishes of lamb and rice, okra in tomato sauce, Greek salad, rice pudding. Afterward, Desdemona brewed Greek coffee, serving it in demitasse cups with the brown foam, the *lakia*, on top. Dr. Philobosian remarked to the seated husbands, "Hundred-to-one odds. Are you sure it happened on the same night?"

"Yes," Sourmelina replied, smoking at the table. "There must have been a full moon."

"It usually takes a woman five or six months to get pregnant," the doctor went on. "To have you two do it on the same night — a-hundred-to-one odds!"

"Hundred-to-one?" Zizmo looked across the table at Sourmelina, who looked away.

"Hundred-to-one at least," assured the doctor.

"It's all the Minotaur's fault," Lefty joked.

"Don't talk about that play," Desdemona scolded.

"Why are you looking at me like that?" asked Lina.

"I can't look at you?" asked her husband.

Sourmelina let out an exasperated sigh and wiped her mouth with her napkin. There was a strained silence. Dr. Philobosian, pouring himself another glass of wine, rushed in.

"Birth is a fascinating subject. Take deformities, for instance. People used to think they were caused by maternal imagination. During the conjugal act, whatever the mother happened to look at or think about would affect the child. There's a story in Damascene about a woman who had a picture of John the Baptist over her bed. Wearing the traditional hair shirt. In the throes of passion, the poor woman happened to glance up at this portrait. Nine months later, her baby was born — furry as a bear!" The doctor laughed, enjoying himself, sipping more wine.

"That can't happen, can it?" Desdemona, suddenly alarmed, wanted to know.

But Dr. Philobosian was on a roll. "There's another story about a woman who touched a toad while making love. Her baby came out with pop eyes and covered with warts."

"This is in a book you read?" Desdemona's voice was tight.

"Paré's *On Monsters and Marvels* has most of this. The Church got into it, too. In his *Embryological Sacra*, Cangiamilla recommended intra-uterine baptisms. Suppose you were worried that you might be carrying a monstrous baby. Well, there was a cure for that. You simply filled a syringe with holy water and baptized the infant before it was born."

"Don't worry, Desdemona," Lefty said, seeing how anxious she looked. "Doctors don't think that anymore."

"Of course not," said Dr. Philobosian.

"All this nonsense comes from the Dark Ages. We know now that most birth deformities result from the consanguinity of the parents."

"From the what?" asked Desdemona.

"From families intermarrying."

Desdemona went white.

"Causes all kinds of problems. Imbecility. Hemophilia. Look at the Romanovs. Look at any royal family. Mutants, all of them."

"I don't remember what I was thinking that night," Desdemona said later while washing the dishes.

"I do," said Lina. "Third one from the right. With the red hair."

"I had my eyes closed."

"Then don't worry."

Desdemona turned on the water to cover their voices. "And what about the other thing? The con . . . the con . . ."

"The consanguinity?"

"Yes. How do you know if the baby has that?"

"You don't know until it's born."

"*Mana!*"

"Why do you think the Church doesn't let brothers and sisters get married? Even first cousins have to get permission from a bishop."

"I thought it was because . . ." and she

trailed off, having no answer.

"Don't worry," Lina said. "These doctors exaggerate. If families marrying each other was so bad, we'd all have six arms and no legs."

But Desdemona did worry. She thought back to Bithynios, trying to remember how many children had been born with something wrong with them. Melia Salakas had a daughter with a piece missing from the middle of her face. Her brother, Yiorgos, had been eight years old his whole life. Were there any babies with hair shirts? Any frog babies? Desdemona recalled her mother telling stories about strange infants born in the village. They came every few generations, babies who were sick in some way, Desdemona couldn't remember how exactly — her mother had been vague. Every so often these babies appeared, and they always met with tragic ends: they killed themselves, they ran off and became circus performers, they were seen years later in Bursa, begging or prostituting themselves. Lying alone in bed at night, with Lefty out working, Desdemona tried to recall the details of these stories, but it was too long ago and now Euphrosyne Stephanides was dead and there was no one to ask. She thought back to the night she'd gotten pregnant and tried to reconstruct events. She turned on her side. She made a pillow stand in for Lefty, pressing it against her back. She looked around the room. There were no pictures on the walls. She hadn't been touching any toads. "What did I see?" she asked herself. "Only the wall."

But she wasn't the only one tormented by anxieties. Recklessly now, and with an official disclaimer as to the veracity of what I'm about to tell you — because, of all the actors in my midwestern Epidaurus, the one wearing the biggest mask is Jimmy Zizmo — I'll try to give you a glimpse into his emotions that last trimester. Was he excited about becoming a father? Did he bring home nutritive roots and brew homeopathic teas? No, he wasn't, he didn't. After Dr. Philobosian came to dinner that night, Jimmy Zizmo began to change. Maybe it was what the doctor had said regarding the synchronous pregnancies. A-hundred-to-one odds. Maybe it was this stray bit of information that was responsible for Zizmo's increasing moodiness, his suspicious glances at his pregnant wife. Maybe he was doubting the likelihood that a single act of intercourse in a five-month dry spell would result in a successful pregnancy. Was Zizmo examining his young wife and feeling old? Tricked?

In the late autumn of 1923, minotaurs haunted my family. To Desdemona they came in the form of children who couldn't stop bleeding, or who were covered with fur. Zizmo's monster was the well-known one with green eyes. It stared out of the river's darkness while he waited onshore for a shipment of liquor. It leapt up from the roadside to confront him through the Packard's windshield. It rolled over in bed when he got home before sunrise: a green-eyed monster lying next to his young, inscrutable wife, but then Zizmo would blink and the monster would disappear.

When the women were eight months pregnant, the first snow fell. Lefty and Zizmo wore gloves and mufflers as they waited on the shore of Belle Isle. Nevertheless, despite his insulation, my grandfather was shivering. Twice in the last month they'd had close calls with the police. Sick with jealous suspicions, Zizmo had been erratic, forgetting to schedule rendezvous, choosing drop-off points with insufficient preparation. Worse, the Purple Gang was consolidating its hold on the city's rum-running. It was only a matter of time before they ran afoul of it.

Meanwhile, back on Hurlbut, a spoon was swinging. Sourmelina, legs bandaged, lay back in her boudoir as Desdemona performed the first of the many prognostications that would end with me.

"Tell me it's a girl."

"You don't want a girl. Girls are too much trouble. You have to worry about them going with the boys. You have to get a dowry and find a husband —"

"They don't have dowries in America, Desdemona."

The spoon began to move.

"If it's a boy, I'll kill you."

"A daughter you'll fight with."

"A daughter I can talk to."

"A son you will love."

The spoon's arc increased.

"It's . . . it's . . ."

"What?"

"Start saving money."

"Yes?"

"Lock the windows."

"Is it? Is it really?"

"Get ready to fight."

"You mean it's a . . ."

"Yes. A girl. Definitely."

"Oh, thank God."

. . . And a walk-in closet being cleaned out. And the walls being painted white to serve as a nursery. Two identical cribs arrive from Hudson's. My grandmother sets them up in the nursery, then hangs a blanket between them in case her child is a boy. Out in the hall, she stops before the vigil light to pray to the All-Holy: "Please don't let my baby be this thing a hemophiliac. Lefty and I didn't know what we were doing. Please, I swear I will never have another baby. Just this one."

Thirty-three weeks. Thirty-four. In uterine swimming pools, babies perform half-gainers, flipping over headfirst. But Sourmelina and Desdemona, so synchronized in their pregnancies, diverged at the end. On December 17, while listening to a radio play, Sourmelina removed her earphones and announced that she was having pains. Three hours later, Dr. Philobosian delivered a girl, as Desdemona predicted. The baby weighed only four pounds three ounces and had to be kept in an incubator for a week. "See?" Lina said to Desdemona, gazing at the baby through the glass. "Dr. Phil was wrong. Look. Her hair's black. Not red."

Jimmy Zizmo approached the incubator next. He removed his hat and bent very close to squint. And did he wince? Did the baby's pale complexion confirm his doubts? Or provide answers? As to why a wife might complain of aches and pains? Or why she might be conveniently cured, in order to prove his paternity? (Whatever his doubts, the child was his. Sourmelina's complexion had merely stolen the show. Genetics, a crapshoot, entirely.)

All I know is this: shortly after Zizmo

saw his daughter, he came up with his final scheme. A week later, he told Lefty, "Get ready. We have business tonight."

And now the mansions along the lake are lit with Christmas lights. The great snow-covered lawn of Rose Terrace, the Dodge mansion, boasts a forty-foot Christmas tree trucked in from the Upper Peninsula. Elves race around the pine in miniature Dodge sedans. Santa is chauffeured by a reindeer in a cap. (Rudolph hasn't been created yet, so the reindeer's nose is black.) Outside the mansion's gates, a black-and-tan Packard passes by. The driver looks straight ahead. The passenger gazes out at the enormous house.

Jimmy Zizmo is driving slowly because of the chains on the tires. They've come out along E. Jefferson, past Electric Park and the Belle Isle Bridge. They've continued through Detroit's East Side, following Jefferson Avenue. (And now we're here, my neck of the woods: Grosse Pointe. Here's the Starks' house, where Clementine Stark and I will "practice" kissing the summer before third grade. And there's the Baker & Inglis School for Girls, high on its hill over the lake.) My grandfather is well aware that Zizmo hasn't come to Grosse Pointe to admire the big houses. Anxiously, he waits to see what Zizmo has in mind. Not far from Rose Terrace, the lakefront opens up, black, empty, and frozen solid. Near the bank the ice piles up in chunks. Zizmo follows the shoreline until he comes to a gap in the road where boats launch in summer. He turns in to it and stops.

"We're going over the ice?" my grandfather says.

"Easiest way to Canada at the moment."

"Are you sure it will hold?"

In response to my grandfather's question, Zizmo only opens his door: to facilitate escape. Lefty follows suit. The Packard's front wheels drop onto ice. It feels as if the entire frozen lake shifts. A high-pitched noise follows, as when teeth bear down on ice cubes. After a few seconds, this stops. The rear wheels drop. The ice settles.

My grandfather, who hasn't prayed since he was in Bursa, has the impulse to give it another go. Lake St. Clair is controlled by the Purple Gang. It provides no trees to hide behind, no side roads to sneak down. He bites his thumb where the nail is missing.

Without a moon, they see only what the insectile headlamps illuminate: fifteen feet of granular, ice-blue surface, crisscrossed by tire tracks. Vortices of snow whirl up in front of them. Zizmo wipes the fogged windshield with his shirt sleeve. "Keep a lookout for dark ice."

"Why?"

"That means it's thin."

It's not long before the first patch appears. Where shoals rise, lapping water weakens the ice. Zizmo steers around it. Soon, however, another patch appears and he has to go in the other direction. Right. Left. Right. The Packard snakes along, following the tire tracks of other rumrunners. Occasionally an ice house blocks their path and they have to back up, return the way they came. Now to the right, now the left, now backward, now forward, moving into the darkness over ice as smooth as marble. Zizmo leans over the wheel, squinting toward where the beams die out. My grandfather holds his door open, listening for the sound of the ice groaning . . .

. . . But now, over the engine noise, another noise starts up. Across town on this very same night, my grandmother is having a nightmare. She's in a lifeboat aboard the *Giulia*. Captain Kontoulis kneels between her legs, removing her wedding corset. He unlaces it, pulls it open, while puffing on a clove cigarette. Desdemona, filled with embarrassment at her sudden nakedness, looks down at the object of the captain's fascination: a heavy ship's rope disappears inside her. "Heave ho!" Captain Kontoulis shouts, and Lefty appears, looking concerned. He takes the end of the rope and begins pulling. And then:

Pain. Dream pain, real but not real, just the neurons firing. Deep inside Desdemona, a water balloon explodes. Warmth gushes against her thighs as blood fills the lifeboat. Lefty gives a tug on the rope, then another. Blood spatters the captain's face, but he lowers his brim and weathers it. Desdemona cries out, the lifeboat rocks, and then there's a popping sound and she feels a sick sensation, as if she's being torn in two, and there, on the end of the rope, is her child, a little knot of muscle, bruise-colored, and she looks to find the arms and cannot, and she looks to find the legs and cannot, and then the tiny head lifts and she looks into her baby's face, a single crescent of teeth opening and closing, no eyes, no mouth, only teeth, flapping open and shut . . .

Desdemona bolts awake. It's a moment before she realizes that her actual, real-life bed is soaked through. Her water has broken . . .

. . . while out on the ice the Packard's headlamps brighten with each acceleration, as more juice flows from the battery. They're in the shipping lane now, equidistant from both shores. The sky a great black bowl above them, pierced with celestial fires. They can't remember the way they came now, how many turns they took, where the bad ice is. The frozen terrain is scrawled with tire tracks leading in every possible direction. They pass the carcasses of old jalopies, front ends fallen through the ice, doors riddled with bullet holes. There are axles lying about, and hubcaps, and a few spare tires. In the darkness and whirling snow, my grandfather's eyes play tricks on him. Twice he thinks he sees a phalanx of cars approaching. The cars toy with them, appearing now in front, now to the side, now behind, coming and going so quickly he can't be sure if he saw them at all. And there is another smell in the Packard now, above leather and whiskey, a stringent, metallic smell overpowering my grandfather's deodorant: fear. It's right then that Zizmo, in a calm voice, says, "Something I always wondered about. Why don't you ever tell anyone that Lina is your cousin?"

The question, coming out of the blue, takes my grandfather off guard. "We don't keep it a secret."

"No?" says Zizmo. "I've never heard you mention it."

"Where we come from, everybody is a cousin," Lefty tries to joke. Then: "How much farther do we have to go?"

"Other side of the shipping lane. We're still on the American side."

"How are you going to find them out here?"

"We'll find them. You want me to speed up?" Without waiting for a reply, Zizmo steps on the accelerator.

"That's okay. Go slow."

"Something else I always wanted to know," Zizmo says, accelerating.

"Jimmy, be safe."

"Why did Lina have to leave the village to get married?"

"You're going too fast. I don't have time to check the ice."

"Answer me."

"Why did she leave? There was no one to marry. She wanted to come to America."

"Is that what she wanted?" He accelerates again.

"Jimmy. Slow down!"

But Zizmo pushes the pedal to the floor. And shouts, "Is it you!"

"What are you talking about?"

"Is it you!" Zizmo roars again, and now the engine is whining, the ice is whizzing by underneath the car. "Who is it!" he demands to know. "Tell me! Who is it?" . . .

. . . But before my grandfather can come up with an answer, another memory comes careening across the ice. It is a Sunday night during my childhood and my father is taking me to the movies at the Detroit

Yacht Club. We ascend the red-carpeted stairs, passing silver sailing trophies and the oil portrait of the hydroplane racer Gar Wood. On the second floor, we enter the auditorium. Wooden folding chairs are set up before a movie screen. And now the lights have been switched off and the clanking projector shoots out a beam of light, showing a million dust motes in the air.

The only way my father could think of to instill in me a sense of my heritage was to take me to dubbed Italian versions of the ancient Greek myths. And so, every week, we saw Hercules slaying the Nemean lion, or stealing the girdle of the Amazons ("That's some girdle, eh, Callie?"), or being thrown gratuitously into snake pits without textual support. But our favorite was the Minotaur . . .

. . . On the screen an actor in a bad wig appears. "That's Theseus," Milton explains. "He's got this ball of string his girlfriend gave him, see. And he's using it to find his way back out of the maze."

Now Theseus enters the Labyrinth. His torch lights up stone walls made of cardboard. Bones and skulls litter his path. Bloodstains darken the fake rock. Without taking my eyes from the screen, I hold out my hand. My father reaches into the pocket of his blazer to find a butterscotch candy. As he gives it to me, he whispers, "Here comes the Minotaur!" And I shiver with fear and delight.

Academic to me then, the sad fate of the creature. Asterius, through no fault of his own, born a monster. The poisoned fruit of betrayal, a thing of shame hidden away; I don't understand any of that at eight. I'm just rooting for Theseus . . .

. . . as my grandmother, in 1923, prepares to meet the creature hidden in her womb. Holding her belly, she sits in the backseat of the taxi, while Lina, up front, tells the driver to hurry. Desdemona breathes in and out, like a runner pacing herself, and Lina says, "I'm not even mad at you for waking me up. I was going to the hospital in the morning anyway. They're letting me take the baby home." But Desdemona isn't listening. She opens her prepacked suitcase, feeling among nightgown and slippers for her worry beads. Amber like congealed honey, cracked by heat, they've gotten her through massacres, a refugee march, and a burning city, and she clicks them as the taxi rattles over the dark streets, trying to outrace her contractions . . .

. . . as Zizmo races the Packard over the ice. The speedometer needle rises. The engine thunders. Tire chains rooster-tail snow. The Packard hurtles into the darkness, skidding on patches, fishtailing. "Did you two have it all planned?" he shouts. "Have Lina marry an American citizen so she could sponsor you?"

"What are you talking about?" my grandfather tries to reason. "When you and Lina got married, I didn't even know I was coming to America. Please slow down."

"Was that the plan? Find a husband and then move into his house!"

The never-failing conceit of Minotaur movies. The monster always approaches from the direction you least expect. Likewise, out on Lake St. Clair, my grandfather has been looking out for the Purple Gang, when in reality the monster is right next to him, at the wheel of the car. In the wind from the open door, Zizmo's frizzy hair streams back like a mane. His head is lowered, his nostrils flared. His eyes shine with fury.

"Who is it!"

"Jimmy! Turn around! The ice! You're not looking at the ice."

"I won't stop unless you tell me."

"There's nothing to tell. Lina's a good girl. A good wife to you. I swear!"

But the Packard hurtles on. My grandfather flattens himself against his seat.

"What about the baby, Jimmy? Think about your daughter."

"Who says it's mine?"

"Of course it's yours."

"I never should have married that girl."

Lefty doesn't have time to argue the point. Without answering any more questions, he rolls out the open door, free of the car. The wind hits him like a solid force, knocking him back against the rear fender. He watches as his muffler, in slow motion, winds itself around the Packard's back wheel. He feels it tighten like a noose, but then the scarf comes loose from his neck, and time speeds up again as Lefty is thrown clear of the auto. He covers his face as he hits the ice, skidding a great distance. When he looks up again, he sees the Packard, still going. It's impossible to tell if Zizmo is trying to turn, to brake. Lefty stands up, nothing broken, and watches as Zizmo hurtles crazily on into the darkness . . . sixty yards . . . eighty . . . a hundred . . . until suddenly another sound is heard. Above the engine roar comes a loud crack, followed by a scintillation spreading underfoot, as the Packard hits a dark patch on the frozen lake.

Just like ice, lives crack, too. Personalities. Identities. Jimmy Zizmo, crouching over the Packard's wheel, has already changed past understanding. Right here is where the trail goes cold. I can take you this far and no further. Maybe it was a jealous rage. Or maybe he was just figuring his options. Weighing a dowry against the expense of raising a family. Guessing that it couldn't go on forever, this boom time of Prohibition.

And there's one further possibility: he might have been faking the whole thing.

But there's no time for these ruminations. Because the ice is screaming. Zizmo's front wheels crash through the surface. The Packard, as gracefully as an elephant standing on its front legs, flips up onto its grille. There's a moment where the headlamps illuminate the ice and water below, like a swimming pool, but then the hood crashes through and, with a shower of sparks, everything goes dark.

At Women's Hospital, Desdemona was in labor for six hours. Dr. Philobosian delivered the baby, whose sex was revealed in the usual manner: by spreading the legs apart and looking. "Congratulations. A son."

Desdemona, with great relief, cried out, "The only hair is on his head."

Lefty arrived at the hospital soon thereafter. He had walked back to shore and hitched a ride on a milk truck home. Now he stood at the window of the nursery, his armpits still rank with fear, his right cheek roughened by his fall on the ice and his lower lip swollen. Just that morning, fortuitously, Lina's baby had gained enough weight to leave the incubator. The nurses held up both children. The boy was named Miltiades after the great Athenian general, but would be known as Milton, after the great English poet. The girl, who would grow up without a father, was named Theodora, after the scandalous empress of Byzantium whom Sourmelina admired. She would later get an American nickname, too.

But there was something else I wanted to mention about those babies. Something impossible to see with the naked eye. Look closer. There. That's right:

One mutation apiece.

Marriage on Ice

⚜

Jimmy Zizmo's funeral was held thirteen days later by permission of the bishop in Chicago. For nearly two weeks the family stayed at home, polluted by death, greeting the occasional visitor who came to pay respects. Black cloths covered the mirrors. Black streamers draped the doors. Because a person should never show vanity in the presence of death, Lefty stopped shaving and by the day of the funeral had grown nearly a full beard.

The failure of the police to recover the body had caused the delay. On the day after the accident, two detectives had gone out to inspect the scene. The ice had refrozen during the night and a few inches of new snow had fallen. The detectives trudged back and forth, searching for tire tracks, but after a half hour gave up. They accepted Lefty's story that Zizmo had gone ice-fishing and might have been drinking. One detective assured Lefty that bodies often turned up in the spring, remarkably preserved because of the freezing water.

The family went ahead with their grief. Father Stylianopoulos brought the case to the attention of the bishop, who granted the request to give Zizmo an Orthodox funeral, provided an interment ceremony be held at the graveside if the body were later found. Lefty took care of the funeral arrangements. He picked out a casket, chose a plot, ordered a headstone, and paid for the death notices in the newspaper. In those days Greek immigrants were beginning to use funeral parlors, but Sourmelina insisted that the viewing be held at home. For over a week mourners arrived into the darkened *sala,* where the window shades had been drawn and the scent of flowers hung heavy in the air. Zizmo's shadowy business associates made visits, as well as people from the speakeasies he supplied and a few of Lina's friends. After giving the widow their condolences, they crossed the living room to stand before the open coffin. Inside, resting on a pillow, was a framed photograph of Jimmy Zizmo. The picture showed Zizmo in three-quarters profile, gazing up toward the celestial glow of studio lighting. Sourmelina had cut the ribbon between their wedding crowns and placed her husband's inside the coffin, too.

Sourmelina's anguish at her husband's death far exceeded her affection for him in life. For ten hours over two days she keened over Jimmy Zizmo's empty coffin, reciting the *mirologhia*. In the best histrionic village style, Sourmelina unleashed soaring arias in which she lamented the death of her husband and castigated him for dying. When she was finished with Zizmo she railed at God for taking him so soon, and bemoaned the fate of her newborn daughter. "You are to blame! It is all your fault!" she cried. "What reason was there for you to die? You have left me a widow! You have left your child on the streets!" She nursed the baby as she keened and every so often held her up so that Zizmo and God could see what they had done. The older immigrants, hearing Lina's rage, found themselves returning to their childhood in Greece, to memories of their own grandparents' or parents' funerals, and everyone agreed that such a display of grief would guarantee Jimmy Zizmo's soul eternal peace.

In accordance with Church law, the funeral was held on a weekday. Father Stylianopoulos, wearing a tall *kalimafkion* on his head and a large pectoral cross, came to the house at ten in the morning. After a prayer was said, Sourmelina brought the priest a candle burning on a plate. She blew it out, the smoke rose and dispersed, and Father Stylianopoulos broke the candle in two. After that, everyone filed outside to begin the procession to the church. Lefty had rented a limousine for the day, and opened the door for his wife and cousin. When he got in himself, he gave a small wave to the man who had been chosen to stay behind, blocking the doorway to keep Zizmo's spirit from re-entering the house. This man was Peter Tatakis, the future chiropractor. Following tradition, Uncle Pete guarded the doorway for more than two hours, until the service at the church was over.

The ceremony contained the full funeral liturgy, omitting only the final portion where the congregation is asked to give the deceased a final kiss. Instead, Sourmelina passed by the casket and kissed the wedding crown, followed by Desdemona and Lefty. Assumption Church, which at that time operated out of a small storefront on Hart Street, was still less than a quarter full. Jimmy and Lina had not been regular churchgoers. Most of the mourners were old widows for whom funerals were a form of entertainment. At last the pallbearers brought the casket outside for the funeral photograph. The participants clustered around it, the simple Hart Street church in the background. Father Stylianopoulos took his position at the head of the casket. The casket itself was reopened to show the photo of Jimmy Zizmo resting against the pleated satin. Flags were held over the coffin, the Greek flag on one side, the American flag on the other. No one smiled for the flash. Afterward, the funeral procession continued to Forest Lawn Cemetery on Van Dyke, where the casket was put in storage until spring. There was still a possibility that the body might materialize with the spring thaw.

Despite the performance of all the necessary rites, the family remained aware that Jimmy Zizmo's soul wasn't at rest. After death, the souls of the Orthodox do not wing their way directly to heaven. They prefer to linger on earth and annoy the living. For the next forty days, whenever my grandmother misplaced her dream book or her worry beads, she blamed Zizmo's spirit. He haunted the house, making fresh milk curdle and stealing the bathroom soap. As the mourning period drew to an end, Desdemona and Sourmelina prepared the *kolyvo*. It was like a wedding cake, made in three blindingly white tiers. A fence surrounded the top layer, from which grew fir trees made of green gelatin. There was a pond of blue jelly, and Zizmo's name was spelled out in silver-coated dragées. On the fortieth day after the funeral, another church ceremony was held, after which everyone returned to Hurlbut Street. They gathered around the *kolyvo,* which was sprinkled with the powdered sugar of the afterlife and mixed with the immortal seeds of pomegranates. As soon as they ate the cake, they could all feel it: Jimmy Zizmo's soul was leaving the earth and entering heaven, where it couldn't bother them anymore. At the height of the festivities, Sourmelina caused a scandal when she returned from her room wearing a bright orange dress.

"What are you doing?" Desdemona whispered. "A widow wears black for the rest of her life."

"Forty days is enough," said Lina, and went on eating.

Only then could the babies be baptized. The next Saturday, Desdemona, seized with conflicting emotions, watched as the children's godfathers held them above the baptismal font at Assumption. As she entered the church, my grandmother had felt an intense pride. People crowded around, trying to get a look at her new baby, who had the miraculous power of turning even the oldest women into young mothers again. During the rite itself, Father Stylianopoulos clipped a lock of Milton's hair and dropped it into the water. He chrismed the sign of the cross on the baby's forehead. He submerged the infant under the water. But as Milton was cleansed of original sin, Desdemona remained cognizant of her iniquity. Silently, she repeated her vow never to have another child.

"Lina," she began a few days later, blushing.

"What?"

"Nothing."

"Not nothing. Something. What?"

"I was wondering. How do you . . . if you don't want . . ." And she blurted it out: "How do you keep from getting pregnant?"

Lina gave a low laugh. "That's not something I have to worry about anymore."

"But do you know how? Is there a way?"

"My mother always said as long as you're nursing, you can't get pregnant. I don't know if it's true, but that's what she said."

"But after that, what then?"

"Simple. Don't sleep with your husband."

At present, it was possible. Since the birth of the baby, my grandparents had taken a hiatus from lovemaking. Desdemona was up half the night breast-feeding. She was always exhausted. In addition, her perineum had torn during the delivery and was still healing. Lefty politely kept himself from starting anything amorous, but after the second month he began to come over to her side of the bed. Desdemona held him off as long as she could. "It's too soon," she said. "We don't want another baby."

"Why not? Milton needs a brother."

"You're hurting me."

"I'll be gentle. Come here."

"No, please, not tonight."

"What? Are you turning into Sourmelina? Once a year is enough?"

"Quiet. You'll wake the baby."

"I don't care if I wake the baby."

"Don't shout. Okay. Here. I'm ready."

But five minutes later: "What's the matter?"

"Nothing."

"Don't tell me nothing. It's like being with a statue."

"Oh, Lefty!" And she burst into sobs.

Lefty comforted her and apologized, but as he turned over to go to sleep he felt himself being enclosed in the loneliness of fatherhood. With the birth of his son, Eleutherios Stephanides saw his future and continuing diminishment in the eyes of his wife, and as he buried his face in his pillow, he understood the complaint of fathers everywhere who lived like boarders in their own homes. He felt a mad jealousy toward his infant son, whose cries were the only sounds Desdemona seemed to hear, whose little body was the recipient of unending ministrations and caresses, and who had muscled his own father aside in Desdemona's affections by a seemingly divine subterfuge, a god taking the form of a piglet in order to suckle at a woman's breast. Over the next weeks and months, Lefty watched from the Siberia of his side of the bed as this mother-infant love affair blossomed. He saw his wife scrunch her face up against the baby's to make cooing noises; he marveled at her complete lack of disgust toward the infant's bodily processes, the tenderness with which she cleaned up and powdered the baby's bottom, rubbing with circular motions and even once, to Lefty's shock, spreading the tiny buttocks to daub the rosebud between with petroleum jelly.

From then on, my grandparents' relationship began to change. Up until Milton's birth, Lefty and Desdemona had enjoyed an unusually close and egalitarian marriage for its time. But as Lefty began to feel left out, he retaliated with tradition. He stopped calling his wife *kukla*, which meant "doll," and began calling her *kyria*, which meant "Madame." He reinstituted sex segregation in the house, reserving the *sala* for his male companions and banishing Desdemona to the kitchen. He began to give orders. "*Kyria*, my dinner." Or: "*Kyria*, bring the drinks!" In this he acted like his contemporaries and no one noticed anything out of the ordinary except Sourmelina. But even she couldn't entirely throw off the chains of the village, and when Lefty had his male friends over to the house to smoke cigars and sing kleftic songs, she retreated to her bedroom.

Shut up in the isolation of paternity, Lefty Stephanides concentrated on finding a safer way to make a living. He wrote to the Atlantis Publishing Company in New York, offering his services as a translator, but received in return only a letter thanking him for his interest, along with a catalogue. He gave the catalogue to Desdemona, who ordered a new dream book. Wearing his blue Protestant suit, Lefty visited the local universities and colleges in person to inquire about the possibility of becoming a Greek instructor. But there were few positions, and all were filled. My grandfather lacked the necessary classics degree; he hadn't even graduated from university. Though he learned to speak a fluent, somewhat eccentric English, his written command of the language was mediocre at best. With a wife and child to support, there was no thought of his returning to school. Despite these obstacles or maybe because of them, during the forty-day mourning period Lefty had set up a study for himself in the living room and returned to his scholarly pursuits. Obstinately, and for sheer escape, he spent hours translating Homer and Mimnermos into English. He used beautiful, much too expensive Milanese notebooks and wrote with a fountain pen filled with emerald ink. In the evenings, other young immigrant men came over, bringing bootleg whiskey, and they all drank and played backgammon. Sometimes Desdemona smelled the familiar musky-sweet scent seeping under the door.

During the daytime, if he felt cooped up, Lefty pulled his new fedora low on his forehead and left the house to think. He walked down to Waterworks Park, amazed that the Americans had built such a palace to house plumbing filters and intake valves. He went down to the river and stood among the dry-docked boats. German shepherds, chained in ice-whitened yards, snarled at him. He peeked into the windows of bait shops closed for the winter. During one of these walks he passed a demolished apartment building. The façade had been torn down, revealing the inner rooms like a dollhouse. Lefty saw the brightly tiled kitchens and bathrooms hanging in midair, half-enclosed spaces whose rich colors reminded him of the sultans' tombs, and he had an idea.

The next morning he climbed down into

the basement on Hurlbut and went to work. He removed Desdemona's spiced sausages from the heating pipes. He swept up the cobwebs and laid a rug over the dirt floor. He brought down Jimmy Zizmo's zebra skin from upstairs and tacked it on the wall. In front of the sink he built a small bar out of discarded lumber and covered it with scavenged tiles: blue-and-white arabesques; Neapolitan checkerboard; red heraldic dragons; and local, earth-tone Pewabics. For tables, he upended cable reels and spread them with cloths. He tented bedsheets overhead, hiding the pipes. From his old connections in the rum-running business he rented a slot machine and ordered a week's supply of beer and whiskey. And on a cold Friday night in February of 1924, he opened for business.

The Zebra Room was a neighborhood place with irregular hours. Whenever Lefty was open for business he put an icon of St. George in the living room window, facing the street. Patrons came around back, giving a coded knock — a long and two shorts followed by two longs — on the basement door. Then they descended out of the America of factory work and tyrannical foremen into an Arcadian grotto of forgetfulness. My grandfather put the Victrola in the corner. He set out braided sesame *koulouria* on the bar. He greeted people with the exuberance they expected from a foreigner and he flirted with the ladies. Behind the bar a stained glass window of liquor bottles glowed: the blues of English gin, the deep reds of claret and Madeira, the tawny browns of scotch and bourbon. A hanging lamp spun on its chain, speckling the zebra skin with light and making the customers feel even drunker than they were. Occasionally someone would stand up from his chair and begin to twitch and snap his fingers to the strange music, while his companions laughed.

Down in that basement speakeasy, my grandfather acquired the attributes of the barkeep he would be for the rest of his life. He channeled his intellectual powers into the science of mixology. He learned how to serve the evening rush one-man-band style, pouring whiskeys with his right hand while filling beer steins with his left, as he pushed out coasters with his elbow and pumped the keg with his foot. For fourteen to sixteen hours a day he worked in that sumptuously decorated hole in the ground and never stopped moving the entire time. If he wasn't pouring drinks, he was refilling the *koulouria* trays. If he wasn't rolling out a new beer keg, he was placing hard-boiled eggs in a wire hamper. He kept his body busy so that his mind wouldn't have a chance to think: about the growing coldness of his wife, or the way their crime pursued them. Lefty had dreamed of opening a casino, and the Zebra Room was as close as he ever came to it. There was no gambling, no potted palms, but there was rebetika and, on many nights, hashish. Only in 1958, when he had stepped from behind the bar of another Zebra Room, would my grandfather have the leisure to remember his youthful dreams of roulette wheels. Then, trying to make up for lost time, he would ruin himself, and finally silence his voice in my life forever.

Desdemona and Sourmelina remained upstairs, raising the children. Practically speaking, this meant that Desdemona got them out of bed in the morning, fed them, washed their faces, and changed their diapers before bringing them in to Sourmelina, who by then was receiving visitors, still smelling of the cucumber slices she put over her eyelids at night. At the sight of Theodora, Sourmelina spread her arms and crooned, *"Chryso fili!"* — snatching her golden girl from Desdemona and covering her face with kisses. For the rest of the morning, drinking coffee, Lina amused herself by applying kohl to little Theodora's eyelashes. When odors arose, she handed the baby back, saying, "Something happened."

It was Sourmelina's belief that the soul didn't enter the body until a child started speaking. She let Desdemona worry about the diaper rashes and whooping coughs, the earaches and nosebleeds. Whenever company came over for Sunday dinner, however, Sourmelina greeted them with the overdressed baby pinned to her shoulder, the perfect accessory. Sourmelina was bad with babies but terrific with teenagers. She was there for your first crushes and heartbreaks, your party dresses and spins at sophisticated states like anomie. And so, in those early years, Milton and Theodora grew up together in the traditional Stephanides way. As once a *kelimi* had separated a brother and sister, now a wool blanket separated second cousins. As once a double shadow had leapt up against a mountainside, now a similarly conjoined shadow moved across the back porch of the house on Hurlbut.

They grew. At one, they shared the same bathwater. At two, the same crayons. At three, Milton sat in a toy airplane while Theodora spun the propeller. But the East Side of Detroit wasn't a small mountain village. There were lots of kids to play with. And so when he turned four, Milton renounced his cousin's companionship, preferring to play with neighborhood boys. Theodora didn't care. By then she had another cousin to play with.

Desdemona had done everything she could to fulfill her promise of never having another child. She nursed Milton until he was three. She continued to rebuff Lefty's advances. But it was impossible to do so every night. There were times when the guilt she felt for marrying Lefty conflicted with the guilt she felt for not satisfying him. There were times when Lefty's need seemed so desperate, so pitiful, that she couldn't resist giving in to him. And there were times when she, too, needed physical comfort and release. It happened no more than a handful of times each year, though more often in the summer months. Occasionally Desdemona had too much wine on somebody's name day, and then it also happened. And on a hot night in July of 1927 it significantly happened, and the result was a daughter: Zoë Helen Stephanides, my Aunt Zo.

From the moment she learned that she was pregnant, my grandmother was again tormented by fears that the baby would suffer a hideous birth defect. In the Orthodox Church, even the children of closely related godparents were kept from marrying, on the grounds that this amounted to spiritual incest. What was that compared with this? This was much worse! So Desdemona agonized, unable to sleep at night as the new baby grew inside her. That she had promised the Panaghia, the All-Holy Virgin, that she would never have another child only made Desdemona feel more certain that the hand of judgment would now fall heavy on her head. But once again her anxieties were for naught. The following spring, on April 27, 1928, Zoë Stephanides was born, a large, healthy girl with the squarish head of her grandmother, a powerful cry, and nothing at all the matter with her.

Milton had little interest in his new sister. He preferred shooting his slingshot with his friends. Theodora was just the opposite. She was enthralled with Zoë. She carried the new baby around with her like a new doll. Their lifelong friendship, which would suffer many strains, began from day one, with Theodora pretending to be Zoë's mother.

The arrival of another baby made the house on Hurlbut feel crowded. Sourmelina decided to move out. She found a job in a florist's shop, leaving Lefty and Desdemona to assume the mortgage on the house. In the fall of that same year, Sourmelina and Theodora took up residence nearby in the O'Toole Boardinghouse, right behind Hurlbut on Cadillac Boulevard. The backs of the two houses faced each other and Lina and Theodora

251

were still close enough to visit nearly every day.

On Thursday, October 24, 1929, on Wall Street in New York City, men in finely tailored suits began jumping from the windows of the city's famous sky-scrapers. Their lemming-like despair seemed far away from Hurlbut Street, but little by little the dark cloud passed over the nation, moving in the opposite direction to the weather, until it reached the Midwest. The Depression made itself known to Lefty by a growing number of empty barstools. After nearly six years of operating at full ca-pacity, there began to be slow periods, nights when the place was only two-thirds full, or just half. Nothing deterred the stoic alcoholics from their calling. Despite the international banking conspiracy (un-masked by Father Coughlin on the radio), these stalwarts presented themselves for duty whenever St. George galloped in the window. But the social drinkers and family men stopped showing up. By March of 1930, only half as many patrons gave the secret dactylic-spondaic knock on the base-ment door. Business picked up during the summer. "Don't worry," Lefty told Desdemona. "President Herbert Hoover is taking care of things. The worst is over." They skated along through the next year and a half, but by 1932 only a few customers were coming in each day. Lefty extended credit, discounted drinks, but it was no use. Soon he couldn't pay for shipments of liquor. One day two men came in and repossessed the slot machine.

"It was terrible. Terrible!" Desdemona still cried fifty years later, describing those years. Throughout my childhood the slightest mention of the Depression would set my *yia yia* off into a full cycle of wailing and breast-clutching. (Even once when the subject was "manic depression.") She would go limp in her chair, squeezing her face in both hands like the figure in Munch's *The Scream* — and then would do so: "*Mana!* The Depression! So terrible you no can believe! Everybody they no have work. I remember the marches for the hunger, all the people they are marching in the street, a million people, one after one, one after one, to go to tell Mr. Henry Ford to open the factory. Then we have in the alley one night a noise was terrible. The people they are killing rats, plam plam plam, with sticks, to go to eat the rats. Oh my God! And Lefty he was no working in the factory then. He only having, you know, the speakeasy, where the people they use to come to drink. But in the Depression was in the middle another bad time, economy very bad, and nobody they have money to drink. They no can eat, how they can drink? So soon *papou* and *yia yia* we no have money. And *then*" — hand to heart — "then they make me go to work for those *mavros*. Black people! Oh my God!"

It happened like this. One night, my grandfather got into bed with my grandmother to find that she wasn't alone. Milton, eight years old now, was snuggled up against her side. On her other side was Zoë, who was only four. Lefty, exhausted from work, looked down at the spectacle of this menagerie. He loved the sight of his sleeping children. Despite the problems of his marriage, he could never blame his son or daughter for them. At the same time, he rarely saw them. In order to make enough money he had to keep the speakeasy open sixteen, sometimes eighteen, hours a day. He worked seven days a week. To support his family he had to be exiled from them. In the mornings when he was around the house, his children treated him like a familiar relative, an uncle maybe, but not a father.

And then there was the problem of the bar ladies. Serving drinks day and night, in a dim grotto, he had many opportunities to meet women drinking with their friends or even alone. My grandfather was thirty years old in 1932. He had filled out and become a man; he was charming, friendly, always well dressed — and still in his physical prime. Upstairs his wife was too frightened to have sex, but down in the Zebra Room women gave Lefty bold, hot looks. Now, as my grandfather gazed down at the three sleeping figures in the bed, his head contained all these things at once: love for his children, love for his wife, along with frustration with his marriage, and boyish, unmarried-feeling excitement around the bar ladies. He bent his face close to Zoë's. Her hair was still wet from the bath, and richly fragrant. He took his fatherly delights while at the same time he remained a man apart. Lefty knew that all the things in his head couldn't hold together. And so after gazing on the beauty of his children's faces, he lifted them out of the bed and carried them back to their own room. He returned and got into bed beside his sleeping wife. Gently, he began stroking her, moving his hand up under her nightgown. And suddenly Desdemona's eyes opened.

"What are you doing!"

"What do you think I'm doing?"

"I'm sleeping."

"I'm waking you up."

"Shame on you." My grandmother pushed him away. And Lefty relented. He rolled angrily away from her. There was a long silence before he spoke.

"I don't get anything from you. I work all the time and I get nothing."

"You think I don't work? I have two children to take care of."

"If you were a normal wife, it might be worth it for me to be working all the time."

"If you were a normal husband, you would help with the children."

"How can I help you? You don't even understand what it takes to make money in this country. You think I'm having a good time down there?"

"You play music, you drink. I can hear the music in the kitchen."

"That's my job. That's why the people come. And if they don't come, we can't pay our bills. The whole thing rests on me. That's what you don't understand. I work all day and night and then when I come to bed I can't even sleep. There's no room!"

"Milton had a nightmare."

"I'm having a nightmare every day."

He switched the light on and, in its glow, Desdemona saw her husband's face screwed up with a malice she'd never seen before. It was no longer Lefty's face, no longer that of her brother or her husband. It was the face of someone new, a stranger she was living with.

And this terrible new face delivered an ultimatum:

"Tomorrow morning," Lefty spat, "you're going to go get a job."

The next day, when Lina came over for lunch, Desdemona asked her to read the newspaper for her.

"How can I work? I don't even know English."

"You know a little."

"We should have gone to Greece. In Greece a husband wouldn't make his wife go out and get a job."

"Don't worry," Lina said, holding up the recycled newsprint. "There aren't any." The 1932 *Detroit Times* classifieds, advertised to a population of four million, ran to just over one column. Sourmelina squinted, looking for something appropriate.

"Waitress," Lina read.

"No."

"Why not?"

"Men would flirt with me."

"You don't like to flirt?"

"Read," Desdemona said.

"Tool and dye," said Lina.

My grandmother frowned. "What is that?"

"I don't know."

"Like dyeing fabric?"

"Maybe."

"Go on," said Desdemona.

"Cigar roller," Lina continued.

"I don't like smoke."

"Housemaid."

"Lina, please. I can't be a maid for somebody."

"Silk worker."

"What?"

"Silk worker. That's all it says. And an address."

"Silk worker? I'm a silk worker. I know everything."

"Then congratulations, you have a job. If it's not gone by the time you get there."

An hour later, dressed for job hunting, my grandmother reluctantly left the house. Sourmelina had tried to persuade her to borrow a dress with a low neckline. "Wear this and no one will notice what kind of English you speak," she said. But Desdemona set out for the streetcar in one of her plain dresses, gray with brown polka dots. Her shoes, hat, and handbag were each a brown that almost matched.

Though preferable to automobiles, streetcars didn't appeal to Desdemona either. She had trouble telling the lines apart. The fitful, ghost-powered trolleys were always making unexpected turns, shuttling her off into unknown parts of the city. When the first trolley stopped, she shouted at the conductor, "Downtown?" He nodded. She boarded, flipped down a seat, and took from her purse the address

Lina had written out. When the conductor passed by, she showed it to him.

"Hastings Street? That what you want?"

"Yes. Hastings Street."

"Stay on this car to Gratiot. Then take the Gratiot car downtown. Get off at Hastings."

At the mention of Gratiot, Desdemona felt relieved. She and Lefty took the Gratiot line to Greektown. Now everything made sense. *So, they don't make silk in Detroit?* she triumphantly asked her absent husband. *That's how much you know.* The streetcar picked up speed. The storefronts of Mack Avenue passed by, more than a few closed up, windows soaped over. Desdemona pressed her face to the glass, but now, because she was alone, she had a few more words to say to Lefty. *If those policemen at Ellis Island hadn't taken my silkworms, I could set up a cocoonery in the backyard. I wouldn't have to get a job. We could make a lot of money. I told you so.* Passengers' clothes, still dressy in those days, nevertheless showed wear and tear: hats gone unblocked for months, hemlines and cuffs frayed, neckties and lapels gravy-stained. On the curb a man held up a hand-painted sign: WORK-iS-WHAT-I-WANT-AND-NOT-CHARiTY-WHO-WiLL-HELP-ME-GET-A-JOB.-7 YEARS-IN-DETROIT. NO-MONEy.-SENT-AWAY-

FURNISH-BEST-OF-REFERENCES. *Look at that poor man.* Mana! *He looks like a refugee. Might as well be Smyrna, this city. What's the difference?* The streetcar labored on, moving away from the landmarks she knew, the greengrocer's, the movie theater, the fire hydrants and neighborhood newspaper stands. Her village eyes, which could differentiate between trees and bushes at a glance, glazed over at the signage along the route, the meaningless roman letters swirling into one another and the ragged billboards showing American faces with the skin peeling off, faces without eyes, or with no mouth, or with nothing but a nose. When she recognized Gratiot's diagonal swath, she stood up and called out in a ringing voice: "Sonnamabiche!" She had no idea what this English word meant. She had heard Sourmelina employ it whenever she missed her stop. As usual, it worked. The driver braked the streetcar and the passengers moved quickly aside to let her off. They seemed surprised when she smiled and thanked them.

On the Gratiot streetcar she told the conductor, "Please, I want Hastings Street."

"Hastings? You sure?"

She showed him the address and said it louder: *"Hastings Street."*

"Okay. I'll let you know."

The streetcar made for Greektown. Desdemona checked her reflection in the window and fixed her hat. Since her pregnancies she had put on weight, thickened in the waist, but her skin and hair were still beautiful and she was still an attractive woman. After looking at herself, she returned her attention to the passing scenery. What else would my grandmother have seen on the streets of Detroit in 1932? She would have seen men in floppy caps selling apples on corners. She would have seen cigar rollers stepping outside windowless factories for fresh air, their faces stained a permanent brown from tobacco dust. She would have seen workers handing out pro-union pamphlets while Pinkerton detectives tailed them. In alleyways, she might have seen union-busting goons working over those same pamphleteers. She would have seen policemen, on foot and horseback, 60 percent of whom were secretly members of the white Protestant Order of the Black Legion, who had their own methods for disposing of blacks, Communists, and Catholics. "But come on, Cal," I hear my mother's voice, "don't you have anything nice to say?" Okay, all right. Detroit in 1932 was known as "The City of Trees." More trees per square mile here than any other city in the country. To shop, you had Kern's and Hudson's. On Woodward Avenue the auto magnates had built the beautiful Detroit Institute of Arts, where, that very minute while Desdemona rode to her job interview, a Mexican artist named Diego Rivera was working on his own new commission: a mural depicting the new mythology of the automobile industry. On scaffolding he sat on a folding chair, sketching the great work: the four androgynous races of humankind on the upper panels, gazing down on the River Rouge assembly line, where auto workers labored, their bodies harmonized with effort. Various smaller panels showed the "germ cell" of an infant wrapped in a plant bulb, the wonder and dread of medicine, the indigenous fruits and grains of Michigan; and way over in one corner Henry Ford himself, gray-faced and tight-assed, going over the books.

The trolley passed McDougal, Jos. Campau, and Chene, and then, with a little shiver, it crossed Hastings Street. At that moment every passenger, all of whom were white, performed a talismanic gesture. Men patted wallets, women refastened purses. The driver pulled the lever that closed the rear door. Desdemona, noticing all this, looked out to see that the streetcar had entered the Black Bottom ghetto.

There was no roadblock, no fence. The streetcar didn't so much as pause as it crossed the invisible barrier, but at the same time in the length of a block the world was different. The light seemed to change, growing gray as it filtered through laundry lines. The gloom of front porches and apartments without electricity seeped out into the streets, and the thundercloud of poverty that hung over the neighborhood directed attention downward toward the clarity of forlorn, shadowless objects: red bricks crumbling off a stoop, piles of trash and ham bones, used tires, crushed pinwheels from last year's fair, someone's old lost shoe. The derelict quiet lasted only a moment before Black Bottom erupted from all its alleys and doorways. *Look at all the children! So many!* Suddenly children were running alongside the streetcar, waving and shouting. They played chicken with it, jumping in front of the tracks. Others climbed onto the back. Desdemona put a hand to her throat. *Why do they have so many children? What's the matter with these people? The mavro women should nurse their babies longer. Somebody should tell them.* Now in the alleys she saw men washing themselves at open faucets. Half-dressed women jutted out hips on second-story porches. Desdemona looked in awe and terror at all the faces filling the windows, all the bodies filling the streets, nearly a half million people squeezed into twenty-five square blocks. Ever since World War I when E. I. Weiss, manager of the Packard Motor Company, had brought, by his own report, the first "load of niggers" to the city, here in Black Bottom was where the establishment had thought to keep them. All kinds of professions now crowded in together, foundry workers and lawyers, maids and carpenters, doctors and hoodlums, but most people, this being 1932, were unemployed. Still, more and more were coming every year, every month, seeking jobs in the North. They slept on every couch in every house. They built shacks in the yards. They camped on roofs. (This state of affairs couldn't last, of course. Over the years, Black Bottom, for all the whites' attempts to contain it — and because of the inexorable laws of poverty and racism — would slowly spread, street by street, neighborhood by neighborhood, until the so-called ghetto would become the entire city itself, and by the 1970s, in the no-tax-base, white-flight, murder-capital Detroit of the Coleman Young administration, black people could finally live wherever they wanted to . . .)

But now, back in 1932, something odd was happening. The streetcar was slowing down. In the middle of Black Bottom, it was stopping and — unheard of! — opening its doors. Passengers fidgeted. The conductor tapped Desdemona on the shoulder. "Lady, this is it. Hastings."

"Hastings Street?" She didn't believe him. She showed him the address again. He pointed out the door.

"Silk factory here?" she asked the conductor.

"No telling what's here. Not my neighborhood."

And so my grandmother stepped off onto Hastings Street. The streetcar pulled away, as white faces looked back at her, a woman thrown overboard. She started walking. Gripping her purse, she hurried down Hastings as though she knew where she was going. She kept her eyes fixed straight ahead. Children jumped rope on the sidewalk. At a third-story window a man tore up a piece of paper and shouted, "From now on, you can send my mail to Paris, postman." Front porches were full of living room furniture, old couches and armchairs, people playing checkers, arguing, waving fingers, and breaking into laughter. *Always laughing,* these mavros. *Laughing, laughing, as though everything is funny. What is so funny, tell me? And what is — oh my God! — a man doing his business in the street! I won't look.* She passed the yard of a junk artist: the Seven Wonders of the World made in bottle caps. An ancient drunk in a colorful sombrero moved in slow motion, sucking his toothless maw and holding out a hand for spare change. *But what can they do? They don't have any plumbing. No sewers, terrible, terrible.* She walked by a barbershop where men were getting their hair straightened, wearing shower caps like women. Across the street young men were calling out to her:

"Baby, you got so many curves you make a car crash!"

"You must be a doughnut, baby, 'cause you make my jelly roll!"

Laughter erupted behind her as she hurried on. Farther and farther in, past streets she didn't know the names of. The smell of unfamiliar food in the air now, fish caught from the nearby river, pig knuckles, hominy grits, fried baloney, black-eyed peas. But also many houses where nothing was cooking, where no one was laughing or even talking, dark rooms full of weary faces and scroungy dogs. It was from a porch like this that somebody finally spoke. A woman, thank God.

"You lost?"

Desdemona took in the soft, molded face. "I am looking for factory. Silk factory."

"No factories around here. If there was they'd be closed."

Desdemona handed her the address.

The lady pointed across the street. "You there."

And turning, what did Desdemona see? Did she see a brown brick building known until recently as McPherson Hall? A place rented out for political meetings, weddings, or demonstrations by the occasional traveling clairvoyant? Did she notice the ornamental touches around the entrance, the Roman urns spilling granite fruit, the harlequin marble? Or did her eyes focus instead on the two young black men standing at attention outside the front door? Did she notice their impeccable suits, one the light blue of a globe's watery portions, the other the pale lavender of French pastilles? Certainly she must have noticed their military bearing, the high polish of their shoes, their vivid neckties. She must have felt the contrast between the young men's confident air and that of the downtrodden neighborhood, but whatever she felt at that moment, her complex reaction has come down to me as a single, shocked realization.

Fezzes. They were wearing fezzes. The soft, maroon, flat-topped headgear of my grandparents' former tormentors. The hats named for the city in Morocco where the blood-colored dye came from, and which (on the heads of soldiers) had chased my grandparents out of Turkey, staining the earth a dark maroon. Now here they were again, in Detroit, on the heads of two handsome young Negroes. (And fezzes will appear once more in my story, on the day of a funeral, but the coincidence, being the kind of thing only real life can come up with, is too good to give away right now.)

Tentatively, Desdemona crossed the street. She told the men she'd come about the ad. One nodded. "You have to go around back," he said. Politely, he led her down an alley and into the well-swept backyard. At that moment, as at a discreet signal, the back door swung open and Desdemona received her second shock. Two women in chadors appeared. They looked, to my grandmother, like devout Muslims from Bursa, except for the color of their garments. They weren't black. They were white. The chadors started at their chins and hung all the way to their ankles. White headscarves covered their hair. They wore no veils, but as they came forward, Desdemona saw brown school oxfords on their feet.

Fezzes, chadors, and next this: a mosque. Inside, the former McPherson Hall had been redecorated according to a Moorish theme. The attendants led Desdemona over geometric tilework. They took her past thick, fringed draperies that shut out the light. There was no sound but the swishing of the women's robes and, from far off, what sounded like a voice speaking or praying. Finally, they showed her into an office where a woman was hanging a picture.

"I'm Sister Wanda," the woman said, without turning around. "Supreme Captain, Temple No. 1." She wore another sort of chador entirely, with piping and epaulettes. The picture she was hanging showed a flying saucer hovering over the skyline of New York. It was shooting out rays.

"You come about the job?"

"Yes. I am silk worker. Have lot experience. Farming the silk, making the cocoonery, weaving the . . ."

Sister Wanda swiveled around. She scanned Desdemona's face. "We got a problem. What you is?"

"I'm Greek."

"Greek, huh. That's a kind of white, isn't it? You born in Greece?"

"No. From Turkey. We come from Turkey. My husband and me, too."

"Turkey! Why didn't you say so? Turkey's a Muslim country. You a Muslim?"

"No, Greek. Greek Church."

"But you born in Turkey."

"*Ne.*"

"What?"

"Yes."

"And your people come from Turkey?"

"Yes."

"So you probably mixed up a little bit, right? You not all white."

Desdemona hesitated.

"See, I'm trying to see how we can work it," Sister Wanda went on. "Minister Fard, who come to us from the Holy City of Mecca, he always be impressing on us the importance of self-reliance. Can't rely on no white man no more. Got to do for ourself, understand?" She lowered her voice. "Problem is, nobody worth a toot come for the ad. People come in here, they *say* they know silk, but they don't know nothing. Just hoping to get hired and fired. Get a day's pay." She narrowed her eyes. "That what you planning?"

"No. I want only hire. No fire."

"But what you is? Greek, Turkish, or what?"

Again Desdemona hesitated. She thought about her children. She imagined coming home to them without any food. And then she swallowed hard. "Everybody mixed. Turks, Greeks, same same."

"That's what I wanted to hear." Sister Wanda smiled broadly. "Minister Fard, he mixed, too. Let me show you what we need."

She led Desdemona down a long, wainscoted corridor, through a telephone operator's office, and into another darker hallway. At the far end heavy drapes blocked off the main lobby. Two young guards stood at attention. "You come to work for us, few things you should know. Never, ever, go through them curtains. Main temple in there, where Minister Fard deliver his sermons. You stay back here in the women's quarters. Best cover your hair, too. That hat shows your ears, which be an enticement."

Desdemona instinctively touched her ears, looking back at the guards. Their expressions remained impassive. She turned back, following the Supreme Captain.

"Let me show you the operation we got going," Sister Wanda said. "We got everything. All we need is a little, you know, know-how." She started up the stairs and Desdemona followed.

(It's a long stairway, three flights up, and Sister Wanda has bad knees, so it will take some time for them to reach the top. Leave them there, climbing, while I explain what my grandmother had gotten herself into.)

"Sometime in the summer of 1930, an amiable but faintly mysterious peddler suddenly appeared in the black ghetto of Detroit." (I'm quoting from C. Eric Lincoln's *The Black Muslims of America*.) "He was thought to be an Arab, although his racial and national identity remain undocumented. He was welcomed into homes of culture-hungry African-Americans who

271

were eager to purchase his silks and artifacts, which he claimed were those worn by black people in their homeland across the sea . . . His customers were so anxious to learn of their own past and the country from which they came that the peddler soon began holding meetings from house to house throughout the community.

"At first, the 'prophet,' as he came to be known, confined his teachings to a recitation of his experiences in foreign lands, admonitions against certain foods, and suggestions for improving listeners' physical health. He was kind, friendly, unassuming and patient."

"Having aroused the interests of his host" (we move now to *An Original Man* by Claude Andrew Clegg III), "[the peddler] would then deliver his sales pitch on the history and future of African-Americans. The tactic worked well, and eventually he honed it to the point that meetings of curious blacks were held in private homes. Later, public halls were rented for his orations, and an organizational structure for his 'Nation of Islam' began to take shape in the midst of poverty-stricken Detroit."

The peddler had many names. Sometimes he called himself Mr. Farrad Mohammad, or Mr. F. Mohammad Ali. Other times he referred to himself as Fred

Dodd, Professor Ford, Wallace Ford, W. D. Ford, Wali Farrad, Wardell Fard, or W. D. Fard. He had just as many origins. People claimed he was a black Jamaican whose father was a Syrian Muslim. One rumor maintained that he was a Palestinian Arab who had fomented racial unrest in India, South Africa, and London before moving to Detroit. There was a story that he was the son of rich parents from the tribe of Koreish, the Prophet Muhammad's own tribe, while FBI records stated that Fard was born in either New Zealand or Portland, Oregon, to either Hawaiian or British and Polynesian parents.

One thing is clear: by 1932, Fard had established Temple No. 1 in Detroit. It was the back stairs of this temple that Desdemona found herself climbing.

"We sell the silks right from the temple," Sister Wanda explained above. "Make the clothes ourself according to Minister Fard's own designs. From clothes our forefathers wore in Africa. Used to be we just ordered the fabric and sewed up the clothes ourself. But with this Depression, fabric getting harder and harder to come by. So Minister Fard he had one of his revelations. Come to me one morning and said, 'We must own the means and ends of sericulture itself.' That how he talk. Eloquent? Man could talk a dog off a meat truck."

Climbing, Desdemona was beginning to make sense of things. The fancy suits of the men outside. The redecoration within. Sister Wanda reached the landing — "In here our training class" — and threw open the door. Desdemona stepped up and saw them.

Twenty-three teenage girls, in bright chadors and head scarves, sewing clothes. They didn't so much as look up from their labor as the Supreme Captain brought in the stranger. Heads bent, mouths fanning straight pins, hem-covered oxfords working unseen treadles, they continued production. "This be our Muslim Girls Training and General Civilization Class. See how good and proper they are? Don't say a word unless you do. 'Islam' means submission. You know that? But getting back to why I run the ad. We running low on fabric. Everybody out of business seems like."

She led Desdemona across the room. A wooden box full of dirt lay open.

"So what we did was, we ordered these silkworms from a company. You know, mail order? We got more on the way. Problem is, they don't seem to like it here in Detroit. Don't blame 'em myself. They keep dying on us, and when they do? Ooowhee, what a stink! My sweet Jes—" She caught herself. "Just an expression. I was brought up Sanctified. Listen, what you say your name was?"

"Desdemona."

"Listen, Des, before I became Supreme Captain, I did hair and nails. Not no farmer's daughter, understand? This thumb look green to you? Help me out. What do these silkworm fellas like? How we get them to, you know, silkify?"

"It hard work."

"We don't mind."

"It take money."

"We got plenty."

Desdemona picked up a shriveled worm, barely alive. She cooed to it in Greek.

"Listen up now, little sisters," Sister Wanda said, and, as one, the girls stopped sewing, crossed hands in laps, and looked up attentively. "This the new lady gonna teach us how to make silk. She a mulatto like Minister Fard and she gonna bring us back the knowledge of the lost art of our people. So we can do for ourself."

Twenty-three pairs of eyes fell on Desdemona. She gathered courage. She translated what she wanted to say into English and went over it twice before she spoke. "To make good silk," she then pronounced, beginning her lessons to the Muslim Girls Training and General Civilization Class, "you have to be pure."

"We trying, Des. Praise Allah. We trying."

Tricknology

❧

That was how my grandmother came to work for the Nation of Islam. Like a cleaning lady working in Grosse Pointe, she came and went by the back door. Instead of a hat, she wore a head scarf to conceal her irresistible ears. She never spoke above a whisper. She never asked questions or complained. Having grown up in a country ruled by others, she found it all familiar. The fezzes, the prayer rugs, the crescent moons: it was a little like going home.

For the residents of Black Bottom it was like traveling to another planet. The temple's front doors, in a sweet reversal of most American entrances, let blacks in and kept whites out. The former paintings in the lobby — landscapes aglow with Manifest Destiny, scenes of Indians being slaughtered — had been carted down to the basement. In their place were depictions of African history: a prince and princess strolling beside a crystal river; a conclave of black scholars debating in an outdoor forum.

People came to Temple No. 1 to hear Fard's lectures. They also came to shop. In the old cloakroom, Sister Wanda displayed the garments that the Prophet said were "the same kind that the Negro people use in their home in the East." She rippled the iridescent fabrics under the lights as converts stepped up to pay. Women exchanged the maids' uniforms of subservience for the white chadors of emancipation. Men replaced the overalls of oppression with the silk suits of dignity. The temple's cash register overflowed. In lean times, the mosque was flush. Ford was closing factories but, at 3408 Hastings Street, Fard was open for business.

Desdemona saw little of all this up on the third floor. She spent her mornings teaching in the classroom and her afternoons in the Silk Room, where the uncut fabrics were stored. One morning she brought in her silkworm box for show-and-tell. She passed the box around, telling the story of its travels, how her grandfather had carved it from olivewood and how it had survived a fire, and she managed to do all this without saying anything derogatory about the students' co-religionists. In fact, the girls were so sweet and friendly that Desdemona remembered what it had been like in the times when the Greeks and Turks used to get along.

Nevertheless: black people were still new to my *yia yia*. She was shocked by various discoveries: "Inside the hands," she informed her husband, "the *mavros* are white like us." Or: "The *mavros* don't have scars, only bumps." Or: "Do you know how the *mavro* men shave? With a powder! I saw it in the store window." In the streets of Black Bottom, Desdemona was appalled at the way people lived. "Nobody sweeps up. Garbage on the porches and nobody sweeps it. Terrible." But at the temple things were different. The men worked hard and didn't drink. The girls were clean and modest.

"This Mr. Fard is doing something right," she said at Sunday dinner.

"Please," Sourmelina dismissed this, "we left veils back in Turkey."

But Desdemona shook her head. "These American girls could use a veil or two."

The Prophet himself remained veiled to Desdemona. Fard was like a god: present everywhere and visible nowhere. His glow lingered in the eyes of people leaving a lecture. He expressed himself in the dietary laws, which favored native African foods — the yam, the cassava — and prohibited the consumption of swine. Every so often Desdemona saw Fard's car — a brand-new Chrysler coupe — parked in front of the temple. It always looked freshly washed and waxed, its chrome grille polished. But she never saw Fard at the wheel.

"How do you expect to see him if he's God?" Lefty asked with amusement one night as they were going to bed. Desdemona lay smiling, as though tickled by her first week's pay hidden under the mattress. "I'll have to have a vision," she said.

Her first project at Temple No. 1 was to convert the outhouse into a cocoonery. Calling upon the Fruit of Islam, as the military wing of the Nation was known, she stood by while the young men pulled out the wooden commode from the rickety shack. They covered the cesspool with dirt and removed old pinup calendars from the walls, averting their eyes as they threw the offending material in the trash. They installed shelves and perforated the ceiling for ventilation. Despite their efforts, a bad smell lingered. "Just wait," Desdemona told them. "Compared to silkworms, this is nothing."

Upstairs, the Muslim Girls Training and General Civilization Class wove feeding trays. Desdemona tried to save the initial batch of silkworms. She kept them warm under electric lightbulbs and sang Greek songs to them, but the silkworms weren't fooled. Hatching from their black eggs, they detected the dry, indoor air and the false sun of the lightbulbs, and began to shrivel up. "Got more on the way," Sister Wanda said, brushing off this setback. "Be here directly."

The days passed. Desdemona became accustomed to the pale palms of Negro hands. She got used to using the back door and to not speaking until spoken to. When she wasn't teaching the girls, she waited upstairs in the Silk Room.

The Silk Room: a description is in order. (So much happened in that fifteen-by-twenty-foot space: God spoke; my grandmother renounced her race; creation was explained; and that's just for starters.) It was a small, low-ceilinged room, with a cutting table at one end. Bolts of silk leaned against the walls. The plushness extended floor to ceiling, like the inside of a jewelry box. Fabric was getting harder to come by, but Sister Wanda had stockpiled quite a bit.

Sometimes the silks seemed to be dancing. Stirred by air currents of a mysterious origin, the fabrics flapped up and floated around the room. Desdemona would have to catch the cloth and roll it back up.

And one day, in the middle of a ghostly pas de deux — a green silk leading as Desdemona backpedaled — she heard a voice.

"I was born in the holy city of Mecca, on February 17, 1877."

At first she thought someone had come into the room. But when she turned, no one was there.

"My father was Alphonso, an ebony-hued man of the tribe of Shabazz. My mother's name was Baby Gee. She was a Caucasian, a devil."

A what? Desdemona couldn't quite hear. Or determine the location of the voice. It seemed to be coming from the floor now. "My father met her in the hills of East Asia. He saw potential in her. He led her in the righteous ways until she became a holy Muslim."

It wasn't what the voice was saying that intrigued Desdemona — she didn't catch what it was saying. It was the sound of the voice, a deep bass that set her breastbone humming. She let go of the dancing silk. She lowered her kerchiefed head to listen. And when the voice started up again, she searched through bolts of silk for its source. "Why did my father marry a Caucasian devil? Because he knew that his son was destined to spread the word to the lost portion of the tribe of Shabazz." Three, four, five bolts, and there it was: a heating grate. And the voice was louder now. "Therefore, he felt that I, his son, should have a skin color that would allow

281

me to deal with both white and black people justly and righteously. So I am here, a mulatto, like Musa before me, who brought the commandments to the Jews."

From the depths of the building the Prophet's voice rose. It began in the auditorium three floors below. It filtered down through the trapdoor in the stage out of which, at the old tobacconist conventions, the Rondega girl used to pop, clad in nothing but a cigar ribbon. The voice reverberated in the crawl space that led to the wings, whereupon it entered a heating vent and circulated around the building, growing distorted and echoey, until it rushed hotly out the grate at which Desdemona now crouched. "My education, as well as the royal blood that runs in my veins, might have led me to seek a position of power. But I heard my uncle weeping, brothers. I heard my uncle in America weeping."

She could make out a faint accent now. She waited for more, but there was only silence. Furnace smell blew into her face. She bent lower, listening. But the next voice she heard was Sister Wanda's on the landing: "Yoo-hoo! Des! We ready for you."

And she tore herself away.

My grandmother was the only white

person who ever heard W. D. Fard sermonize, and she understood less than half of what he said. It was a result of the heating vent's bad acoustics, her own imperfect English, and the fact that she kept lifting her head to hear if anyone was coming. Desdemona knew that it was forbidden for her to listen to Fard's lectures. The last thing she wanted was to jeopardize her new job. But there was no other place for her to go.

Every day, at one o'clock, the grate began to rumble. At first she heard the noise of people coming into the auditorium. This was followed by chanting. She rolled extra bolts of silk in front of the grate to muffle the sound. She moved her chair to the far corner of the Silk Room. But nothing helped.

"Perhaps you recall, in our last lecture, how I told you about the deportation of the moon?"

"No, I don't," said Desdemona.

"Sixty trillion years ago a god-scientist dug a hole through the earth, filled it with dynamite and blew the earth in two. The smaller of these two pieces became the moon. Do you recall that?"

My grandmother clamped her hands over her ears; on her face was a look of refusal. But through her lips a question slipped out: "Somebody blew up the earth? Who?"

"Today I want to tell you about another god-scientist. An evil scientist. By the name of Yacub."

And now her fingers spread apart, letting the voice reach her ears . . .

"Yacub lived eighty-four hundred years ago in the present twenty-five-thousand-year-cycle of history. He was possessed, this Yacub, of an unusually large cranium. A smart man. A brilliant man. One of the preeminent scholars of the Nation of Islam. This was a man who discovered the secrets of magnetism when he was only six years old. He was playing with two pieces of steel and he held them together and discovered that scientific formula: magnetism."

Like a magnet itself, the voice worked on Desdemona. Now it was pulling her hands down to her sides. It was making her lean forward in her chair . . .

"But Yacub wasn't content with magnetism. With his large cranium he had other great ideas. And so one day Yacub thought to himself that if he could create a race of people completely different from the original people — genetically different — that race could come to dominate the black nation through tricknology."

. . . And when leaning wasn't enough, she moved closer. Walking across the room, moving silk bolts aside, she knelt

284

down before the grate, as Fard continued his explanation: **"Every black man is made of two germs: a black germ and a brown germ. And so Yacub convinced fifty-nine thousand nine hundred and ninety-nine Muslims to emigrate to the island of Pelan. The island of Pelan is in the Aegean. You will find it today on European maps, under a false name. To this island Yacub brought his fifty-nine thousand nine hundred and ninety-nine Muslims. and there he commenced his grafting."**

She could hear other things now. Fard's footsteps as he paced the stage. The squeaking of chairs as his listeners bent forward, hanging on his every word.

"In his laboratories on Pelan, Yacub kept all original black people from reproducing. If a black woman gave birth to a child, that child was killed. Yacub only let brown babies live. He only let brown-skinned people mate."

"Terrible," Desdemona said, up on the third floor. "Terrible, this Yacub person."

"You have heard of the Darwinian theory of natural selection? This was unnatural selection. By his scientific grafting Yacub produced the first yellow and red people. But he didn't stop there. He went on mating the light-skinned offspring of those people. Over many, many years he

genetically changed the black man, one generation at a time, making him paler and weaker, diluting his righteousness and morality, turning him into the paths of evil. And then, my brothers, one day Yacub was done. One day Yacub was finished with his work. And what had his wickedness created? As I have told you before: like can only come from like. Yacub had created the white man! Born of lies. Born of homicide. A race of blue-eyed devils."

Outside, the Muslim Girls Training and General Civilization Class installed silkworm trays. They worked in silence, daydreaming of various things. Ruby James was thinking about how handsome John 2X had looked that morning, and wondered if they would get married someday. Darlene Wood was beginning to get miffed because all the brothers had gotten rid of their slave names but Minister Fard hadn't gotten around to the girls yet, so here she was, still Darlene Wood. Lily Hale was thinking almost entirely about the spit curl hairdo she had hidden up under her headscarf and how tonight she was going to stick her head out her bedroom window, pretending to check the weather, so that Lubbock T. Hass next door could see. Betty Smith was thinking, *Praise Allah Praise Allah Praise Allah.* Millie Little wanted gum.

While upstairs, her face hot from the air rushing out of the vent, Desdemona resisted this new twist in the story line. "Devils? All white people?" She snorted. She got up from the floor, dusting herself off. "Enough. I'm not going to listen to this crazy person anymore. I work. They pay me. That's it."

But the next morning, she was back at the temple. At one o'clock the voice began speaking, and again my grandmother paid attention:

"Now let us make a physiological comparison between the white race and the original people. White bones, anatomically speaking, are more fragile. White blood is thinner. Whites possess roughly one-third the physical strength of blacks. Who can deny this? What does the evidence of your own eyes suggest?"

Desdemona argued with the voice. She ridiculed Fard's pronouncements. But as the days passed, my grandmother found herself obediently spreading out silk before the heating vent to cushion her knees. She knelt forward, putting her ear to the grate, her forehead nearly touching the floor. "He's just a charlatan," she said. "Taking everyone's money." Still, she didn't move. In a moment, the heating system rumbled with the latest revelations.

What was happening to Desdemona?

Was she, always so receptive to a deep priestly voice, coming under the influence of Fard's disembodied one? Or was she just, after ten years in the city, finally becoming a Detroiter, meaning that she saw everything in terms of black and white?

There's one last possibility. Could it be that my grandmother's sense of guilt, that sodden, malarial dread that swamped her insides almost seasonally — could this incurable virus have opened her up to Fard's appeal? Plagued by a sense of sin, did she feel that Fard's accusations had weight? Did she take his racial denunciations personally?

One night she asked Lefty, "Do you think anything is wrong with the children?"

"No. They're fine."

"How do you know?"

"Look at them."

"What's the matter with us? How could we do what we did?"

"Nothing's the matter with us."

"No, Lefty. We" — she started to cry — "we are not good people."

"The children are fine. We're happy. That's all in the past now."

But Desdemona threw herself onto the bed. "Why did I listen to you?" she sobbed. "Why didn't I jump into the water like everybody else!"

My grandfather tried to embrace her, but

she shrugged him off. "Don't touch me!"

"Des, please . . ."

"I wish I had died in the fire! I swear to you! I wish I had died in Smyrna!"

She began to watch her children closely. So far, aside from one scare — at five, Milton had nearly died from a mastoid infection — they had both been healthy. When they cut themselves, their blood congealed. Milton got good marks at school, Zoë above average. But Desdemona wasn't reassured by any of this. She kept waiting for something to happen, some disease, some abnormality, fearing that the punishment for her crime was going to be taken out in the most devastating way possible: not on her own soul but in the bodies of her children.

I can feel how the house changed in the months leading to 1933. A coldness passing through its root-beer-colored bricks, invading its rooms and blowing out the vigil light burning in the hall. A cold wind that fluttered the pages of Desdemona's dream book, which she consulted for interpretations to increasingly nightmarish dreams. Dreams of the germs of infants bubbling, dividing. Of hideous creatures growing up from pale foam. Now she avoided all love-making, even in the summer, even after three glasses of wine on somebody's name day. After a while, Lefty stopped persisting. My grandparents, once so inseparable, had drifted apart. When Desdemona went off to Temple No. 1 in the morning, Lefty was asleep, having kept the speakeasy open all night. He disappeared into the basement before she returned home.

Following this cold wind, which kept blowing through the Indian summer of 1932, I sail down the basement stairs to find my grandfather, one morning, counting money. Shut out of his wife's affections, Lefty Stephanides concentrated on work. His business, however, had gone through some changes. Responding to the fall-off in customers at the speakeasy, my grandfather had diversified.

It is a Tuesday, just past eight o'clock. Desdemona has left for work. And in the front window, a hand is removing the icon of St. George from view. At the curb, an old Daimler pulls up. Lefty hurries outside and gets into the backseat.

My grandfather's new business associates: in the front seat sits Mabel Reese, twenty-six years old, from Kentucky, face rouged, hair giving off a burnt smell from the morning's curling iron. "Back in Paducah," she is telling the driver, "there's this deaf man who's got a camera. He just goes up and down the river, taking pictures. He takes the darndest things."

"So do I," responds the driver. "But mine make money." Maurice Plantagenet, his Kodak box camera sitting in the backseat beside Lefty, smiles at Mabel and drives out Jefferson Avenue. Plantagenet has found these pre-WPA years inimical to his artistic inclinations. As they head toward Belle Isle he delivers a disquisition on the history of photography, how Nicéphore Niepce invented it, and how Daguerre got all the credit. He describes the first photograph ever taken of a human being, a Paris street scene done with an exposure so long that none of the fast-moving pedestrians showed up except for a lone figure who had stopped to get his shoes shined. "I want to get in the history books myself. But I don't think this is the right route, exactly."

On Belle Isle, Plantagenet pilots the Daimler along Central Avenue. Instead of heading toward The Strand, however, he takes a small turnoff down a dirt road that dead-ends. He parks and they all get out. Plantagenet sets up his camera in favorable light, while Lefty attends to the automobile. With his handkerchief he polishes the spoked hubcaps and the headlamps; he kicks mud off the running board, cleans the windows and windshield. Plantagenet says, "The maestro is ready."

Mabel Reese takes off her coat. Underneath she is wearing only a corset and garter belt. "Where do you want me?"

"Stretch out over the hood."

"Like this?"

"Yeah. Good. Face against the hood. Now spread your legs just a bit."

"Like this?"

"Yeah. Now turn your head and look back at the camera. Okay, smile. Like I'm your boyfriend."

That was how it went every week. Plantagenet took the photographs. My grandfather provided the models. The girls weren't hard to find. They came into the speakeasy every night. They needed money like everybody else. Plantagenet sold the photos to a distributor downtown and gave Lefty a percentage of the take. The formula was straightforward: women in lingerie lounging in cars. The scantily dressed girls curled up in the backseat, or bared breasts in the front, or fixed flat tires, bending way over. Usually there was one girl, but sometimes there were two. Plantagenet teased out all the harmonies, between a buttock's curve and a fender's, between corset and upholstery pleats, between garter belts and fan belts. It was my grandfather's idea. Remembering his father's old hidden treasure, "Sermin, Girl of the Pleasure Dome," he'd had a vision for updating an old ideal. The days of the harem were over. Bring on the era of the backseat! Automobiles were the new pleasure domes. They turned the common man into a sultan of the open road. Plantagenet's photographs suggested picnics in out-of-the-way places. The girls napped on running boards, or dipped to get a tire iron out of the trunk. In the middle of the Depression, when people had no money for food, men found money for Plantagenet's auto-erotica. The photographs provided Lefty with a steady side income. He began to save money, in fact, which later brought about his next opportunity.

Every now and then at flea markets, or in the occasional photography book, I come across one of Plantagenet's old pictures, usually erroneously ascribed to the twenties because of the Daimler. Sold during the Depression for a nickel, they now fetch upward of six hundred dollars. Plantagenet's "artistic" work has all been forgotten, but his erotic studies of women and automobiles remain popular. He got into the history books on his day off, when he thought he was compromising himself. Going through the bins, I look at his women, their engineered hosiery, their uneven smiles. I gaze into those faces my grandfather gazed into, years ago, and I ask myself: Why did Lefty stop searching for his sister's face and start searching for others, for blondes with thin lips, for gun molls with provocative rumps? Was his interest in these models merely pecuniary? Did the cold wind blowing through the house lead him to seek warmth in other places? Or had guilt begun to infect him, too, so that to distract himself from the thing he'd done he ended up with these Mabels and Lucies and Doloreses?

Unable to answer these questions, I return now to Temple No. 1, where new converts are consulting compasses. Tear-shaped, white with black numbers, the compasses have a drawing of the Kaaba stone at the center. Still hazy about the actual requirements of their new faith, these men pray at no prescribed times. But at least they've got these compasses, bought from the same good sister who sells the clothes. The men revolve, one step at a time, until compass needles point to 34, the number coding for Detroit. They consult the rim's arrow to determine the direction of Mecca.

"Let us move now to craniometry. What is craniometry? It is the scientific measurement of the brain, of what is called by the medical community 'gray matter.' The brain of the average white man weighs six ounces. The brain of the average black man weighs seven ounces and one half." Fard lacks the fire of a Baptist preacher, the deep-gut oratory, but to his audience of disaffected Christians (and one Orthodox believer) this turns out to be an advantage. They're tired of the holy-rolling, the shouting and brow-mopping, the raspy breathing. They're tired of slave religion, by which the White Man convinces the Black that servitude is holy.

"But there is one thing at which the white race excelled the original people. By destiny, and by their own genetic programming, the white race excelled at tricknology. Do I have to tell you this? This is what you already know. Through tricknology the Europeans brought the original people from Mecca and other parts of East Asia. In 1555 a slave trader named John Hawkins brought the first members of the tribe of Shabazz to the shores of this country. 1555. The name of the ship? *Jesus.* This is in the history books. You can go to the Detroit Public Library and look this up.

"What happened to the first generation of original people in America? The white man murdered them. Through tricknology. He murdered them so that their children would grow up with no knowledge of their own people, of where they came from. The descendants of those children, the descendants of those poor orphans — that is who you are. You here in this room. And all the so-called Negroes in the ghettos of America. I have come here to tell you who you are. You are the lost members of the tribe of Shabazz."

And riding through Black Bottom didn't help. Desdemona realized now why there was so much trash in the streets: the city didn't pick it up. White landlords let their apartment buildings fall into disrepair while they continued to raise the rents. One day Desdemona saw a white shop clerk refuse to take change from a Negro customer. "Just leave it on the counter," she said. *Didn't want to touch the lady's hand!* And in those guilt-ridden days, her mind crammed with Fard's theories, my grandmother started to see his point. There were blue-eyed devils all over town. The Greeks had an old saying, too: "Red beard and blue eyes portend the Devil." My grandmother's eyes were brown, but that didn't make her feel any better. If anybody was a devil it was her. There was nothing she could do to change the way things were. But she could make sure that it didn't happen again. She went to see Dr. Philobosian.

"That's a very extreme measure, Desdemona," the doctor told her.

"I want to make sure."

"But you're still a young woman."

"No, Dr. Phil, I'm not," my grandmother said in a weary voice. "I'm eighty-four hundred years old."

On November 21, 1932, the *Detroit Times* ran the following headline: "Altar Scene of Human Sacrifice." The story followed: "One hundred followers of a negro cult leader, who is held for human sacrifice on a crude altar in his home, were being rounded up today by police for questioning. The self-styled king of the Order of Islam is Robert Harris, 44, of 1429 Dubois Ave. The victim, whom he admits bludgeoning with a car axle and stabbing with a silver knife through the heart, was James J. Smith, 40, negro roomer in the Harris home." This Harris, who came to be known as the "voodoo slayer," had hung around Temple No. 1. Just possibly, he had read Fard's "Lost Found Muslim Lessons No. 1 and 2," including the passage: **"All Muslims will murder the devil because they know he is a snake and also if he be allowed to live, he would sting someone else."** Harris had then founded his own order. He had gone looking for a (white) devil but, finding one hard to come by in his neighborhood, had settled for a devil closer at hand.

Three days later, Fard was arrested. Under interrogation, he insisted that he had never commanded anyone to sacrifice a human being. He claimed that he was the "supreme being on earth." (At least, that was what he said during his first interrogation. The second time he was arrested, months later, he "admitted," according to the police, that the Nation of Islam was nothing but "a racket." He had invented the prophecies and the cosmologies "to get all the money he could.") Whatever the truth of the matter, the upshot was this: in exchange for having the charges dropped, Fard agreed to leave Detroit once and for all.

And so we come to May 1933. And to Desdemona, saying goodbye to the Muslim Girls Training and General Civilization Class. Head scarves frame faces streaked with tears. The girls file by, kissing Desdemona on both cheeks. (My grandmother will miss the girls. She has grown very fond of them.) "My mother used to tell me in bad times silkworms no can spin," she says. "Make bad silk. Make bad cocoons." The girls accept this truth and examine the newly hatched worms for signs of despair.

In the Silk Room, all the shelves are empty. Fard Muhammad has transferred power to a new leader. Brother Karriem, the former Elijah Poole, is now Elijah Muhammad, Supreme Minister of the Nation of Islam. Elijah Muhammad has a different vision for the Nation's economic future. From now on, it will be real estate, not clothing.

And now Desdemona is descending the stairs on her way out. She reaches the first floor and turns to look back at the lobby. For the first time ever, the Fruit of Islam do not guard the lobby entrance. The drapes hang open. Desdemona knows she should keep going out the back door, but she has nothing to lose now, and so ventures toward the front. She approaches the double doors and pushes her way into the sanctum sanctorum.

For the first fifteen seconds, she stands still, as her idea of the room switches places with reality. She had imagined a soaring dome, a richly colored Ezine carpet, but the room is just a simple auditorium. A small stage at one end, folding chairs stacked along the walls. She absorbs all this quietly. And then, once more, there is a voice:

"Hello, Desdemona."

On the empty stage, the Prophet, the Mahdi, Fard Muhammad, stands behind the podium. He is barely more than a silhouette, slender and elegant, wearing a fedora that shadows his face.

"You're not supposed to be in here," he says. "But I guess today it's all right."

Desdemona, her heart in her throat,

manages to ask, "How you know my name?"

"Haven't you heard? I know everything."

Coming through the heating vent, Fard Muhammad's deep voice had made her solar plexus vibrate. Now, closer up, it penetrates her entire body. The rumble spreads down her arms until her fingers are tingling.

"How's Lefty?"

This question rocks Desdemona back on her heels. She is speechless. She is thinking many things at once, first of all, how can Fard know her husband's name, did she tell Sister Wanda? . . . and, second, if it's true he knows everything, then the rest must be true, too, about the blue-eyed devils and the evil scientist and the Mother Plane from Japan that will come to destroy the world and take the Muslims away. Dread seizes her, while at the same time she is remembering something, asking where she has heard that voice before . . .

Now Fard Muhammad steps from behind the podium. He crosses the stage and descends to the main floor. He approaches Desdemona while continuing to display his omniscience.

"Still running the speakeasy? Those days are numbered. Lefty better find something else to do." Fedora tilted to one side, suit neatly buttoned, face in shadow, the Mahdi

300

approaches her. She wants to flee but cannot. "And how are the children?" Fard asks. "Milton must be what now, eight?"

He is only ten feet away. As Desdemona's heart madly thumps, Fard Muhammad removes his hat to reveal his face. And the Prophet smiles.

Surely you've guessed by now. That's right: Jimmy Zizmo.

"*Mana!*"

"Hello, Desdemona."

"You!"

"Who else?"

She stares, wide-eyed. "We thought you died, Jimmy! In the car. In the lake."

"Jimmy did."

"But you are Jimmy." Having said this, Desdemona becomes aware of the repercussions and begins to scold. "Why you leave your wife and child? What's the matter with you?"

"My only responsibility is to my people."

"What people? The *mavros?*"

"The Original People." She cannot tell if he is serious or not.

"Why you don't like white people? Why you call them devils?"

"Look at the evidence. This city. This country. Don't you agree?"

"Every place has devils."

"That house on Hurlbut, especially."

There is a pause, after which Desdemona

cautiously asks, "How you mean?"

Fard, or Zizmo, is smiling again. "Much that is hidden has been revealed to me."

"What is hidden?"

"My so-called wife Sourmelina is a woman of, let us say, unnatural appetites. And you and Lefty? Do you think you fooled me?"

"Please, Jimmy."

"Don't call me that. That isn't my name."

"What you mean? You are my brother-in-law."

"You don't know me!" he shouts. "You never knew me!" Then, composing himself: "You never knew who I was or where I came from." With that, the Mahdi walks past my grandmother, through the lobby and double doors, and out of our lives.

This last part Desdemona didn't see. But it's well documented. First, Fard Muhammad shook hands with the Fruit of Islam. The young men fought back tears as he said farewell. He then moved through the crowd outside Temple No. 1 to his Chrysler coupe parked at the curb. He stepped up on the running board. Afterward, every single person would insist that the Mahdi had maintained personal eye contact the entire time. Women were openly weeping now, pleading for him not to go. Fard Muhammad removed his hat and held it to his chest. He looked down kindly and said,

"Don't worry. I am with you." He raised the hat in a gesture that took in the entire neighborhood, the ghetto with its shanty-town porches, unpaved streets, and disconsolate laundry. "I will be back to you in the near future to lead you out of this hell." Then Fard Muhammad got into the Chrysler, turned the ignition, and with a final, reassuring smile, motored away.

Fard Muhammad was never seen again in Detroit. He went into occultation like the Twelfth Imam of the Shiites. One report places him on an ocean liner bound for London in 1934. According to the Chicago newspapers in 1959, W. D. Fard was a "Turkish-born Nazi agent" and ended up working for Hitler in World War II. A conspiracy theory holds that the police or the FBI were involved in his death. It's anybody's guess. Fard Muhammad, my maternal grandfather, returned to the nowhere from which he'd come.

As for Desdemona, her meeting with Fard may have contributed to the drastic decision she made around the same time. Not long after the Prophet's disappearance, my grandmother underwent a fairly novel medical procedure. A surgeon made two incisions below her navel. Stretching open the tissue and muscle to expose the circuitry of the fallopian tubes, he tied each in a bow, and there were no more children.

Clarinet Serenade

We had our date. I picked Julie up at her studio in Kreuzberg. I wanted to see her work, but she wouldn't let me. And so we went to dinner at a place called Austria.

Austria is like a hunting lodge. The walls are covered with mounted deer horns, maybe fifty or sixty sets. These horns look comically small, as though they come from animals you could kill with your bare hands. The restaurant is dark, warm, woody, and comfortable. Anybody who wouldn't like it is someone I wouldn't like. Julie liked it.

"Since you won't show me your work," I said as we sat down, "can you at least tell me what it is?"

"Photography."

"You probably don't want to tell me of what."

"Let's have a drink first."

Julie Kikuchi is thirty-six. She looks twenty-six. She is short without being small. She is irreverent without being crude. She used to see a therapist but stopped. Her right hand is partly arthritic, from an elevator accident. This makes it painful to hold a camera for a long period. "I need an assistant," she told me. "Or a new hand." Her fingernails are not particularly clean. In fact they are the dirtiest fingernails I have ever seen on such a lovely, wonderful-smelling person.

Breasts have the same effect on me as on anyone with my testosterone level.

I translated the menu for Julie and we ordered. Out came the platters of boiled beef, the bowls of gravy and red cabbage, the knödels as big as softballs. We talked about Berlin and the differences between European countries. Julie told me a Barcelona story of getting locked in the Parque Güell with her boyfriend after visiting hours. Here it comes, I thought. The first ex-boyfriend had been summoned. Soon the rest would follow. They would file around the table, presenting their deficiencies, telling of their addictions, their cheating hearts. After that, I would be called on to present my own ragged gallery. And here is where my first dates generally go wrong. I lack sufficient data. I don't have it in quite the bulk a man of my years should have. Women sense this and a strange, questioning look comes into their eyes. And already I am retreating from them, before dessert has been served . . .

But that didn't happen with Julie. The boyfriend popped up in Barcelona and then was gone. None followed. This was surely not because there weren't any. This was because Julie isn't husband-hunting. So she didn't have to interview me for the job.

I like Julie Kikuchi. I like her a lot.

And so I have my usual questions. What does she want from? How would she react if? Should I tell her that? No. Too soon. We haven't even kissed. And right now, I've got another romance to concentrate on.

❧

We open on a summer evening in 1944. Theodora Zizmo, whom everyone now calls Tessie, is painting her toenails. She sits on a daybed at the O'Toole Boardinghouse, her feet propped up on a pillow, a pillow of cotton between each toe. The room is full of wilting flowers and her mother's various messes: lidless cosmetics, discarded hose, Theosophy books, and a box of chocolates, also lidless, full of empty paper wrappings and a few tooth-scarred, rejected creams. Over where Tessie is, it's neater. Pens and pencils stand upright in cups. Between brass book-ends, each a miniature bust of Shakespeare, are the novels she collects at yard sales.

Tessie Zizmo's twenty-year-old feet: size four and a half, pale, blue-veined, the red toenails fanning out like suns on a peacock's tail. She examines them sternly, going down the line, just as a gnat, attracted by the lotion perfuming her legs, lands on her big toenail and gets stuck. "Oh, shoot," Tessie says. "Darn bugs." She sets to work again, picking the gnat off, reapplying polish.

On this evening in the middle of World War II, a serenade is about to begin. It's minutes away. If you listen closely you can hear a window scraping open, a fresh reed being inserted into a woodwind's mouthpiece. The music which started everything and on which, you could say, my entire existence depended, is on its way. But before the tune launches into full volume, let me fill you in on what has happened these last eleven years.

Prohibition has ended, for one thing. In 1933, by ratification of all the states, the Twenty-first Amendment repealed the Eighteenth. At the American Legion Convention in Detroit, Julius Stroh removed the bung from a Gilded Keg of Stroh's Bohemian beer. President Roosevelt was photographed sipping a cocktail at the White House. And on Hurlbut Street, my grandfather, Lefty Stephanides, took down the zebra skin, dismantled his underground speakeasy, and emerged once again into the upper atmosphere.

With the money he'd saved from the auto-erotica, he put a down payment on a building on Pingree Street, just off West Grand Boulevard. The above-ground Zebra Room was a bar & grill, set in the middle of a busy commercial strip. The neighboring businesses were still there when I was a kid. I can dimly remember them: A. A. Laurie's optometrist's shop with its neon sign in the shape of a pair of eyeglasses; New Yorker Clothes, in whose front window I saw my first naked mannequins, dancing a murderous tango. Then there was Value Meats, Hagermoser's Fresh Fish, and the Fine-Cut Barber Shop. On the corner was our place, a narrow single-story building with a wooden zebra's head projecting over the sidewalk. At night, blinking red neon outlined the muzzle, neck, and ears.

The clientele were mainly auto workers. They came in after their shifts. They came in, quite often, *before* their shifts. Lefty opened the bar at eight in the morning, and by eight-thirty the barstools were filled with men dulling themselves before reporting to work. As he filled their shells with beer, Lefty learned what was going on in the city outside. In 1935 his patrons had celebrated the forming of the United Auto

Workers. Two years later, they cursed the armed guards from Ford who had beat up their leader, Walter Reuther, in the "Battle of the Overpass." My grandfather took no sides in these discussions. His job was to listen, nod, refill, smile. He said nothing in 1943 when talk at the bar turned ugly. On a Sunday in August, fistfights had broken out between blacks and whites on Belle Isle. "Some nigger raped a white woman," one customer said. "Now all those niggers are going to pay. You wait and see." By Monday morning a race riot was under way. But when a group of men came in, boasting of having beaten a Negro to death, my grandfather refused to serve them.

"Why don't you go back to your own country?" one of them shouted.

"This is my country," Lefty said, and to prove it, he did a very American thing: he reached under the counter and produced a pistol.

These conflicts lie in the past now — as Tessie paints her toenails — overshadowed by a much bigger conflict. All over Detroit in 1944, automobile factories have been re-tooled. At Willow Run, B-24s roll off the assembly line instead of Ford sedans. Over at Chrysler, they're making tanks. The industrialists have finally found a cure for the stalled economy: war. The Motor City, which hasn't been dubbed Motown yet, becomes for a time the "Arsenal of Democracy." And in the boardinghouse on Cadillac Boulevard, Tessie Zizmo paints her toenails and hears the sound of a clarinet.

Artie Shaw's big hit "Begin the Beguine" floats on the humid air. It freezes squirrels on telephone lines, who cock their heads alertly to listen. It rustles the leaves of apple trees and sets a rooster on a weather vane spinning. With its fast beat and swirling melody, "Begin the Beguine" rises over the victory gardens and the lawn furniture, the bramble-choked fences and porch swings; it hops the fence into the backyard of the O'Toole Boardinghouse, stepping around the mostly male tenants' recreational activities — a lawn-bowling swath, some forgotten croquet mallets — and then the song climbs the ragged ivy along the brick facing, past windows where bachelors snooze, scratch their beards, or, in the case of Mr. Danelikov, formulate chess problems; up and up it soars, Artie Shaw's best and most beloved recording from back in '39, which you can still hear playing from radios all over the city, music so fresh and lively it seems to ensure the purity of the American cause and the Allies' eventual triumph; but now here it is, finally, coming through Theodora's window, as she fans her toes to dry them. And, hearing it, my mother turns toward the window and smiles.

The source of the music was none other than a Brylcreemed Orpheus who lived directly behind her. Milton Stephanides, a twenty-year-old college student, stood at his own bedroom window, dexterously fingering his clarinet. He was wearing a Boy Scout uniform. Chin lifted, elbows out, right knee keeping time within khaki trousers, he unleashed his love song on the summer day, playing with an ardor that had burned out completely by the time I found that fuzz-clogged woodwind in our attic twenty-five years later. Milton had been third clarinet in the Southeastern High School orchestra. For school concerts he had to play Schubert, Beethoven, and Mozart, but now that he had graduated, he was free to play whatever he liked, which was swing. He styled himself after Artie Shaw. He copied Shaw's exuberant, off-balance stance, as if being blown backward by the force of his own playing. Now, at the window, he flourished his stick with Shaw's precise, calligraphic dips and circles. He looked along the length of the shining black instrument, sighting on the house two backyards away, and especially on the pale, timid, excited face at the third-floor window. Tree branches and telephone lines obscured his view, but he could make out the long dark hair that shone like his clarinet itself.

She didn't wave. She made no sign — other than smile — that she heard him at all. In neighboring yards people continued what they were doing, oblivious to the serenade. They watered lawns or filled bird feeders; young kids chased butterflies. When Milton got to the end of the song, he lowered his instrument and leaned out the window, grinning. Then he started again, from the beginning.

Downstairs, entertaining company, Desdemona heard her son's clarinet and, as if orchestrating a harmony, let out a long sigh. For the last forty-five minutes Gus and Georgia Vasilakis and their daughter Gaia had been sitting in the living room. It was Sunday afternoon. On the coffee table a dish of rose jelly reflected light from the sparkling glasses of wine the adults were drinking. Gaia nursed a glass of lukewarm Vernor's ginger ale. An open tin of butter cookies sat on the table.

"What do you think about that, Gaia?" her father teased her. "Milton's got flat feet. Does that sour the deal for you?"

"Daddeee," said Gaia, embarrassed.

"Better to have flat feet than to be knocked off your feet forever," said Lefty.

"That's right," agreed Georgia Vasilakis.

"You're lucky they wouldn't take Milton. I don't think it's any kind of dishonor at all. I don't know what I'd do if I had to send a son off to war."

Every so often during this conversation, Desdemona had patted Gaia Vasilakis on the knee and said, "Miltie he is coming. Soon." She had been saying it since her guests arrived. She had been saying it every Sunday for the past month and a half, and not only to Gaia Vasilakis. She had said it to Jeanie Diamond, whose parents had brought her last Sunday, and she had said it to Vicky Logathetis, who'd come the week before that.

Desdemona had just turned forty-three and, in the manner of women of her generation, she was practically an old woman. Gray had infiltrated her hair. She'd begun to wear rimless gold eyeglasses that magnified her eyes, making her look even more perpetually dismayed than she already was. Her tendency to worry (which the swing music upstairs had aggravated of late) had brought back her heart palpitations. They were a daily occurrence with her now. Within the surround of this worrying, however, Desdemona remained a bundle of activity, always cooking, cleaning, doting on her children and the children of others, always shrieking at the top of her lungs, full of noise and life.

Despite my grandmother's corrective lenses, the world remained out of focus. Desdemona didn't understand what the fighting was all about. At Smyrna the Japanese had been the only country to send ships to rescue refugees. My grandmother maintained a lifelong sense of gratitude. When people brought up the sneak attack on Pearl Harbor, she said, "Don't tell me about an island in the middle of the ocean. This country isn't big enough they have to have all the islands, too?" The Statue of Liberty's gender changed nothing. It was the same here as everywhere: men and their wars. Fortunately, Milton had been turned down by the Army. Instead of going off to war he was going to night school and helping out at the bar during the day. The only uniform he wore was that of the Boy Scouts, where he was a troop leader. Every so often he took his scouts camping up north.

After five more minutes, when Milton still had not materialized, Desdemona excused herself and climbed the stairs. She stopped outside Milton's bedroom, frowning at the music coming from inside. Then, without knocking, she entered.

In front of the window, clarinet erect, Milton played on, oblivious. His hips swayed in an indecent fashion and his lips glistened as brightly as his hair. Desdemona marched across the room and slammed the window shut.

"Come, Miltie," she commanded. "Gaia is downstairs."

"I'm practicing."

"Practice later." She was squinting out the window at the O'Toole Boardinghouse across the yard. At the third-floor window she thought she saw a head duck down, but she couldn't be sure.

"Why you always play by the window?"

"I get hot."

Desdemona was alarmed. "How you mean hot?"

"From playing."

She snorted. "Come. Gaia brought you cookies."

For some time now my grandmother had suspected the growing intimacy between Milton and Tessie. She noted the attention Milton paid to Tessie whenever Tessie came over for dinner with Sourmelina. Growing up, Zoë had always been Tessie's best friend and playmate. But now it was Milton whom Tessie sat in the porch swing with. Desdemona had asked Zoë, "Why you no go out with Tessie no more?" And Zoë, in a slightly bitter tone, had replied, "She's busy."

This was what brought on the return of my grandmother's heart palpitations. After everything she had done to atone for her crime, after she had turned her marriage into an arctic wasteland and allowed a surgeon to tie her fallopian tubes, consanguinity wasn't finished with her. And so, horrified, my grandmother had resumed an activity at which she had tried her hand once before, with decidedly mixed results. Desdemona was matchmaking again.

From Sunday to Sunday, as in the house in Bithynios, a parade of marriageable girls came through the front door of Hurlbut. The only difference was that in this case they weren't the same two girls multiplied over and over. In Detroit, Desdemona had a large pool to choose from. There were girls with squeaky voices or soft altos, plump girls and thin ones, babyish girls who wore heart lockets and girls who were old before their time and worked as secretaries in insurance firms. There was Sophie Georgopoulos, who walked funny ever since stepping on hot coals during a camping trip, and there was Mathilda Livanos, supremely bored in the way of beautiful girls, who'd shown no interest in Milton and hadn't even washed her hair. Week after week, aided or coerced by their parents, they came, and week after week Milton Stephanides excused himself to go up to his bedroom and play his clarinet out the window.

316

Now, with Desdemona riding herd behind, he came down to see Gaia Vasilakis. She was sitting between her parents on the overstuffed sea-foam-green sofa, a large girl herself, wearing a white crinoline dress with a ruffled hem and puffed sleeves. Her short white socks had ruffles, too. They reminded Milton of the lace cover over the bathroom trashcan.

"Boy, those are a lot of badges," Gus Vasilakis said.

"Milton needed one more badge and he could have been an Eagle Scout," Lefty said.

"Which one is that?"

"Swimming," said Milton. "I can't swim for beans."

"I'm not a very good swimmer either," Gaia said, smiling.

"Have a cookie, Miltie," Desdemona urged.

Milton looked down at the tin and took a cookie.

"Gaia made them," Desdemona said. "How you like it?"

Milton chewed, meditatively. After a moment, he held up the Boy Scout salute. "I cannot tell a lie," he said. "This cookie is lousy."

Is there anything as incredible as the love story of your own parents? Anything as

317

hard to grasp as the fact that those two over-the-hill players, permanently on the disabled list, were once in the starting lineup? It's impossible to imagine my father, who in my experience was aroused mainly by the lowering of interest rates, suffering the acute, adolescent passions of the flesh. Milton lying on his bed, dreaming about my mother in the same way I would later dream about the Obscure Object. Milton writing love letters and even, after reading Marvell's "To His Coy Mistress" at night school, love *poems*. Milton mixing Elizabethan metaphysics with the rhyming styles of Edgar Bergen:

> *You're just as amazing, Tessie Zizmo*
> *as some new mechanical gizmo*
> *a GE exec might give a pal*
> *you're a World's Fair kind of gal . . .*

Even looking back through a daughter's forgiving eye, I have to admit: my father was never good-looking. At eighteen, he was alarmingly, consumptively skinny. Blemishes dotted his face. Beneath his doleful eyes the skin was already darkening in pouches. His chin was weak, his nose overdeveloped, his Brylcreemed hair as massive and gleaming as a Jell-O mold. Milton, however, was aware of none of these physical deficits. He possessed a flinty self-confidence that protected him like a shell from the world's assaults.

Theodora's physical appeal was more obvious. She had inherited Sourmelina's beauty on a smaller scale. She was only five foot one, thin-waisted and small-busted, with a long, swanlike neck supporting her pretty, heart-shaped face. If Sourmelina had always been a European kind of American, a sort of Marlene Dietrich, then Tessie was the fully Americanized daughter Dietrich might have had. Her mainstream, even countrified, looks extended to the slight gap between her teeth and her turned-up nose. Traits often skip a generation. I look much more typically Greek than my mother does. Somehow Tessie had become a partial product of the South. She said things like "shucks" and "golly." Working every day at the florist's shop, Lina had left Tessie in the care of an assortment of older women, many of them Scotch Irish ladies from Kentucky, and in this way a twang had gotten into Tessie's speech. Compared with Zoë's strong, mannish features, Tessie had so-called all-American looks, and this was certainly part of what attracted my father.

Sourmelina's salary at the florist's shop was not high. Mother and daughter were forced to economize. At secondhand shops,

Sourmelina gravitated to Vegas showgirl outfits. Tessie picked out sensible clothes. Back at O'Toole's, she mended wool skirts and hand-washed blouses; she de-pilled sweaters and polished used saddle shoes. But the faint thrift-store smell never quite left her clothes. (It would attach to me years later when I went on the road.) The smell went along with her fatherlessness, and with growing up poor.

Jimmy Zizmo: all that remained of him was what he'd left on Tessie's body. Her frame was delicate like his, her hair, though silken, was black like his. When she didn't wash it enough, it got oily, and, sniffing her pillow, she would think, "Maybe this is what my dad smelled like." She got canker sores in wintertime (against which Zizmo had taken vitamin C). But Tessie was fair-skinned and burned easily in the sun.

Ever since Milton could remember, Tessie had been in the house, wearing the stiff, churchy outfits her mother found so amusing. "Look at the two of us," Lina would say. "Like a Chinese menu. Sweet and sour." Tessie didn't like it when Lina talked this way. She didn't think she was sour; only proper. She wished that her mother would act more proper herself. When Lina drank too much, Tessie was the one who took her home, undressed her, and put her to bed. Because Lina was an exhibitionist, Tessie had become a voyeur. Because Lina was loud, Tessie had turned out quiet. She played an instrument, too: the accordion. It sat in its case under her bed. Every so often she took it out, throwing the strap over her shoulders to keep the huge, many-keyed, wheezing instrument off the ground. The accordion seemed nearly as big as she was and she played it dutifully, badly, and always with the suggestion of a carnival sadness.

As little children Milton and Tessie had shared the same bedroom and bathtub, but that was long ago. Up until recently, Milton thought of Tessie as his prim cousin. Whenever one of his friends expressed interest in her, Milton told them to give up the idea. "That's honey from the icebox," he said, as Artie Shaw might have. "Cold sweets don't spread."

And then one day Milton came home with some new reeds from the music store. He hung his coat and hat on the pegs in the foyer, took out the reeds, and balled the paper bag up in his fist. Stepping into the living room, he took a set shot. The paper sailed across the room, hit the rim of the trashcan, and bounced out. At which point a voice said, "You better stick to music."

Milton looked to see who it was. He saw

321

who it was. But who it was was no longer who it had been.

Theodora was lying on the couch, reading. She had on a spring dress, a pattern of red flowers. Her feet were bare and that was when Milton saw them: the red toenails. Milton had never suspected that Theodora was the kind of girl who would paint her toenails. The red nails made her look womanly while the rest of her — the thin pale arms, the fragile neck — remained as girlish as always. "I'm watching the roast," she explained.

"Where's my mom?"

"She went out."

"She went out? She never goes out."

"She did today."

"Where's my sister?"

"4-H." Tessie looked at the black case he was holding. "That your clarinet?"

"Yeah."

"Play something for me."

Milton set his instrument case down on the sofa. As he opened it and took out his clarinet, he remained aware of the nakedness of Tessie's legs. He inserted the mouthpiece and limbered up his fingers, running them up and down the keys. And then, at the mercy of an overwhelming impulse, he bent forward, pressing the flaring end of the clarinet to Tessie's bare knee, and blew a long note.

She squealed, moving her knee away.

"That was a D flat," Milton said. "You want to hear a D sharp?"

Tessie still had her hand over her buzzing knee. The vibration of the clarinet had sent a shiver all the way up her thigh. She felt funny, as though she were about to laugh, but she didn't laugh. She was staring at her cousin, thinking, "Will you just look at him smiling away? Still got pimples but thinks he's the cat's meow. Where does he get it?"

"All right," she answered at last.

"Okay," said Milton. "D sharp. Here goes."

That first day it was Tessie's knees. The following Sunday, Milton came up from behind and played his clarinet against the back of Tessie's neck. The sound was muffled. Wisps of her hair flew up. Tessie screamed, but not long. "Yeah, dad," said Milton, standing behind her.

And so it began. He played "Begin the Beguine" against Tessie's collarbone. He played "Moonface" against her smooth cheeks. Pressing the clarinet right up against the red toenails that had so dazzled him, he played "It Goes to Your Feet." With a secrecy they didn't acknowledge, Milton and Tessie drifted off to quiet parts of the house, and there, lifting her skirt a little, or removing a sock, or once, when nobody was home, pulling up her blouse to expose her lower back, Tessie allowed Milton to press his clarinet to her skin and fill her body with music. At first it only tickled her. But after a while the notes spread deeper into her body. She felt the vibrations penetrate her muscles, pulsing in waves, until they rattled her bones and made her inner organs hum.

Milton played his instrument with the same fingers he used for the Boy Scout salute, but his thoughts were anything but wholesome. Breathing hard, bent over Tessie with trembling concentration, he moved the clarinet in circles, like a snake charmer. And Tessie was a cobra, mesmerized, tamed, ravished by the sound. Finally, one afternoon when they were all alone, Tessie, his proper cousin, lay down on her back. She crossed one arm over her face. "Where should I play?" whispered Milton, his mouth feeling too dry to play anything. Tessie undid a button on her blouse and in a strangled voice said, "My stomach."

"I don't know a song about a stomach," Milton ventured.

"My ribs, then."

"I don't know any songs about ribs."

"My sternum?"

"Nobody ever wrote a song about a sternum, Tess."

She undid more buttons, her eyes closed. And in barely a whisper: "How about this?"

"That one I know," said Milton.

When he couldn't play against Tessie's skin, Milton opened the window of his bedroom and serenaded her from afar. Sometimes he called the boardinghouse and asked Mrs. O'Toole if he could speak with Theodora. "Minute," Mrs. O'Toole said, and shouted up the stairs, "Phone for Zizmo!" Milton heard the sound of feet running down the stairs and then Tessie's voice saying hello. And he began playing his clarinet into the phone.

(Years later, my mother would recall the days when she was wooed by clarinet. "Your father couldn't play very well. Two or three songs. That was it." "Whaddya mean?" Milton would protest. "I had a whole repertoire." He'd begin to whistle "Begin the Beguine," warbling the melody to evoke a clarinet's vibrato and fingering the air. "Why don't you serenade me anymore?" Tessie would ask. But Milton had something else on his mind: "Whatever happened to that old clarinet of mine?" And then Tessie: "How should I know? You expect me to keep track of everything?" "Is it down in the basement?" "Maybe I threw it out!" "You threw it out!

325

What the hell did you do that for!" "What are you going to do, Milt, practice up? You couldn't play the darn thing back then.")

All love serenades must come to an end. But in 1944, there was no stop to the music. By July, when the telephone rang at the O'Toole Boardinghouse, there was sometimes another kind of love song issuing from the earpiece: *"Kyrie eleison, Kyrie eleison."* A soft voice, nearly as feminine as Tessie's own, cooing into a phone a few blocks away. The singing continued for a minute at least. And then Michael Antoniou would ask, "How was that?"

"That was swell," my mother said.

"It was?"

"Just like in church. You could have fooled me."

Which brings me to the final complication in that overplotted year. Worried about what Milton and Tessie were getting up to, my grandmother wasn't only trying to marry Milton off to somebody else. By that summer she had a husband picked out for Tessie, too.

Michael Antoniou — Father Mike, as he would come to be known in our family — was at that time a seminarian at the Greek Orthodox Holy Cross Theological School out in Pomfret, Connecticut. Back home for the summer, he had been paying a lot of attention to Tessie Zizmo. In 1933, Assumption Church had moved out of its quarters in the storefront on Hart Street. Now the congregation had a real church, on Vernor Highway just off Beniteau. The church was made of yellow brick. It wore three dove-gray domes, like caps, and had a basement for socializing. During coffee hour, Michael Antoniou told Tessie what it was like out at Holy Cross and educated her about the lesser-known aspects of Greek Orthodoxy. He told her about the monks of Mount Athos, who in their zeal for purity banned not only women from their island monastery but the females of every other species, too. There were no female birds on Mount Athos, no female snakes, no female dogs or cats. "A little too strict for me," Michael Antoniou said, smiling meaningfully at Tessie. "I just want to be a parish priest. Married with kids." My mother wasn't surprised that he showed interest in her. Being short herself, she was used to short guys asking her to dance. She didn't like being chosen by virtue of her height, but Michael Antoniou was persistent. And he might not have been pursuing her because she was the only girl shorter than he was. He might have been responding to the need in Tessie's eyes, her desperate yearning to believe that there was something instead of nothing.

Desdemona seized her opportunity. "Mikey is good Greek boy, nice boy," she said to Tessie. "And going to be a priest!" And to Michael Antoniou: "Tessie is small but she is strong. How many plates you think she can carry, Father Mike?" "I'm not a father yet, Mrs. Stephanides." "Please, how many?" "Six?" "That all you think? Six?" And now holding up two hands: "Ten! Ten plates Tessie can carry. Never break a thing."

She began inviting Michael Antoniou over for Sunday dinner. The presence of the seminarian inhibited Tessie, who no longer wandered upstairs for private swing sessions. Milton, growing surly at this new development, threw barbs across the dinner table. "I guess it must be a lot harder to be a priest over here in America, huh?"

"How do you mean?" Michael Antoniou asked.

"I just mean that over in the old country people aren't too well educated," Milton said. "They'll believe whatever stories the priests tell them. Here it's different. You can go to college and learn to think for yourself."

"The Church doesn't want people not to think," Michael replied without taking offense. "The Church believes that thinking will take a person only so far. Where thinking ends, revelation begins."

"Chrysostomos!" Desdemona exclaimed. "Father Mike, you have a mouth of gold."

But Milton persisted, "I'd say where thinking ends, stupidity begins."

"That's how people live, Milt" — Michael Antoniou again, still kindly, gently — "by telling stories. What's the first thing a kid says when he learns how to talk? 'Tell me a story.' That's how we understand who we are, where we come from. Stories are everything. And what story does the Church have to tell? That's easy. It's the greatest story ever told."

My mother, listening to this debate, couldn't fail to notice the stark contrasts between her two suitors. On one side, faith; on the other, skepticism. On one side, kindness; on the other, hostility. An admittedly short though pleasant-looking young man against a scrawny, pimply, 4-F boy with circles under his eyes like a hungry wolf. Michael Antoniou hadn't so much as tried to kiss Tessie, whereas Milton had led her astray with a woodwind. D flats and A sharps licking at her like so many tongues of flame, here behind the knee, up here on the neck, right below the navel . . . the inventory filled her with shame. Later that afternoon, Milton cornered her. "I got a new song for you, Tess. Just learned it today." But Tessie told him, "Get away." "Why? What's the matter?"

"It's . . . it's . . ." — she tried to think of the most damning pronouncement — "It's not nice!" "That's not what you said last week." Milton waved the clarinet, adjusting the reed with a wink, until Tessie, finally: "I don't want to do that anymore! Do you understand? Leave me alone!"

Every Saturday for the remainder of the summer, Michael Antoniou came by O'Toole's to pick Tessie up. Taking her purse as they walked along, he swung it by its strap, pretending it was a censer. "You have to do it just right," he told her. "If you don't swing it hard enough, the chain buckles and the embers fall out." On their way down the street, my mother tried to ignore her embarrassment at being seen in public with a man swinging a purse. At the drugstore soda fountain, she watched him tuck a napkin into his shirt collar before eating his sundae. Instead of popping the cherry into his mouth as Milton would have done, Michael Antoniou always offered it to her. Later, seeing her home, he squeezed her hand and looked sincerely into her eyes. "Thank you for another enjoyable afternoon. See you in church tomorrow." Then he walked away, folding his hands behind his back. Practicing how to walk like a priest, too.

After he was gone, Tessie went inside and climbed the stairs to her room. She lay

down on her daybed to read. One afternoon, unable to concentrate, she stopped
reading and put the book over her face.
Just then, outside, a clarinet began to play.
Tessie listened for a while, without
moving. Finally, her hand rose to take the
book off her face. It never got there, however. The hand waved in the air, as if con-
ducting the music, and then, sensibly,
resignedly, desperately, it slammed the
window shut.

"Bravo!" Desdemona shouted into the
phone a few days later. Then, holding the
mouthpiece to her chest: "Mikey Antoniou
just proposed to Tessie! They're engaged!
They are going to get married as soon as
Mikey he finishes the seminary."

"Don't look too excited," Zoë told her
brother.

"Why don't you shut up?"

"Don't get sore at me," she said, blind
to the future. "I'm not marrying him.
You'd have to shoot me first."

"If she wants to marry a priest," Milton
said, "let her marry a priest. The hell with
her." His face turned red and he bolted
from the table and fled up the stairs.

But why did my mother do it? She could
never explain. The reasons people marry
the people they do are not always evident
to those involved. So I can only speculate.
Maybe my mother, having grown up

331

without a father, was trying to marry one. It's possible, too, that her decision was a practical one. She'd asked Milton what he wanted to do with his life once. "I was thinking of maybe taking over my dad's bar." On top of all the other oppositions, there may have been this final one: bartender, priest.

Impossible to imagine my father weeping from a broken heart. Impossible to imagine him refusing to eat. Impossible, also, to imagine him calling the boardinghouse again and again until finally Mrs. O'Toole said, "Listen, sugar. She don't want to talk to you. Get it?" "Yeah" — Milton swallowing hard — "I got it." "Plenty of other fish in the sea." Impossible to imagine any of these things, but they are, in fact, what happened.

Maybe Mrs. O'Toole's maritime metaphor had given him an idea. A week after Tessie became engaged, on a steamy Tuesday morning, Milton put his clarinet away for good and went down to Cadillac Square to exchange his Boy Scout uniform for another.

"Well, I did it," he told the family at dinner that night. "I enlisted."

"In the Army!" Desdemona said, horrified.

"What did you do that for?" said Zoë. "The war's almost over. Hitler's finished."

"I don't know about Hitler. It's Hirohito I've got to worry about. I joined the Navy. Not the Army."

"What about your feet?" Desdemona cried.

"They didn't ask about my feet."

My grandfather, who had sat through the clarinet serenades as he sat through everything, aware of their significance but unconvinced of the wisdom of getting involved, now glared at his son. "You're a very stupid young man, do you know that? You think this is some kind of game?"

"No, sir."

"This is a war. You think it is some kind of fun, a war? Some kind of big joke to play on your parents?"

"No, sir."

"You will see what kind of a big joke it is."

"The Navy!" Desdemona meanwhile continued to moan. "What if your boat it sinks?"

"You see what you do?" Lefty shook his head. "You're going to make your mother sick worrying so much."

"I'll be okay," said Milton.

Looking at his son, Lefty now saw a painful sight: himself twenty years earlier, full of stupid, cocky optimism. There was nothing to do with the spike of fear that shot through him but to speak out in anger. "Okay, then. Go to the Navy," said Lefty. "But you know what you forgot, Mr. almost Eagle Scout?" He pointed at Milton's chest. "You forgot you never win a badge for swimming."

News of the World

❧⋆❧

I waited three days before calling Julie again. It was ten o'clock at night and she was still in her studio working. She hadn't eaten, so I suggested we get something. I said I'd come by and pick her up.

This time, she let me in. Her studio was a mess, frightening in its chaos, but after the first few steps I forgot about all that. My attention was arrested by what I saw on the walls. Five or six large test prints were tacked up, each one showing the industrial landscape of a chemical plant. Julie had shot the factory from a crane, so that the effect for the viewer was of floating just above the snaking pipes and smokestacks.

"Okay, that's enough," she said, pushing me toward the door.

"Hold on," I said. "I love factories. I'm from Detroit. This is like an Ansel Adams for me."

"Now you've seen it," she said, shooing me out, pleased, uncomfortable, smiling, stubborn.

"I've got a Bernd and Hilla Becher in my

living room," I boasted.

"You've got a Bernd and Hilla Becher?" She stopped pushing me.

"It's an old cement factory."

"Okay, all right," said Julie, relenting. "I do factories. That's what I do. Factories. These are the I. G. Farben plant." She winced. "I'm worried it's the typical thing for an American to do over here."

"Holocaust industry, you mean?"

"I haven't read that book, but yeah."

"If you've always done factories, I think it's different," I told her. "Then you're not just glomming on. If factories are your subject, how could you *not* do I. G. Farben."

"You think it's okay?"

I pointed to the test prints. "These are great."

We fell silent, looking at each other, and without thinking I leaned forward and kissed Julie lightly on the lips.

When the kiss was over she opened her eyes very wide. "I thought you were gay when we met," she said.

"Must have been the suit."

"My gay-dar went off completely." Julie was shaking her head. "I'm always suspicious, being the last stop."

"The last what?"

"Haven't you ever heard of that? Asian chicks are the last stop. If a guy's in the closet, he goes for an Asian because their bodies are more like boys'."

"Your body's not like a boy's," I said.

This embarrassed Julie. She looked away.

"You've had a lot of closeted gay guys go after you?" I asked her.

"Twice in college, three times in graduate school," answered Julie.

There was no other response to this but to kiss her again.

❧

To resume my parents' story, I need to bring up a very embarrassing memory for a Greek American: Michael Dukakis on his tank. Do you remember that? The single image that doomed our hopes of getting a Greek into the White House: Dukakis, wearing an oversize army helmet, bouncing along on top of an M41 Walker Bulldog. Trying to look presidential but looking instead like a little boy on an amusement park ride. (Every time a Greek gets near the Oval Office something goes wrong. First it was Agnew with the tax evasion and then it was Dukakis with the tank.) Before Dukakis climbed up on that armored vehicle, before he took off his J. Press suit and put on those army fatigues, we all felt — I speak for my fellow Greek Americans, whether they want me to or not — a sense of exultation. This man was the Democratic nominee for President of the United States! He was from Massachusetts, like the Kennedys! He practiced a religion even stranger than Catholicism, but no one was bringing it up. This was 1988. Maybe the time had finally come when anyone — or at least not the same old someones — could be President. Behold the banners at the Democratic Convention! Look at the bumper stickers on all the Volvos. "Dukakis." A name with more than two vowels in it running for President! The last time that had happened was Eisenhower (who looked good on a tank). Generally speaking, Americans like their presidents to have no more than two vowels. Truman. Johnson. Nixon. Clinton. If they have more than two vowels (Reagan), they can have no more than two syllables. Even better is one syllable and one vowel: Bush. Had to do that twice. Why did Mario Cuomo decide against running for President? What conclusion did he come to as he withdrew to think the matter through? Unlike Michael Dukakis, who was from academic Massachusetts, Mario Cuomo was from New York and knew what was what. Cuomo knew he'd never win. Too liberal for the moment, certainly. But also: too many vowels.

On top of a tank, Michael Dukakis rode toward a bank of photographers and into the political sunset. Painful as the image is to recall, I bring it up for a reason. More than anything, that was what my newly enlisted father, Seaman 2nd Class Milton Stephanides, looked like as he bounced in a landing craft off the California coast in the fall of 1944. Like Dukakis, Milton was mostly helmet. Like Dukakis's, Milton's chin strap looked as though it had been fastened by his mother. Like Dukakis's, Milton's expression betrayed a creeping awareness of error. Milton, too, couldn't get off his moving vehicle. He, too, was riding toward extinction. The only difference was the absence of photographers because it was the middle of the night.

A month after joining the United States Navy, Milton found himself stationed at Coronado naval base in San Diego. He was a member of the Amphibious Forces, whose job it was to transport troops to the Far East and assist their storming of beaches. It was Milton's job — luckily so far only in maneuvers — to lower the landing craft off the side of the transport ship. For over a month, six days a week, ten hours a day, that's what he'd been doing — lowering boats full of men into various sea conditions.

When he wasn't lowering landing craft, he was in one himself. Three or four nights a week, they had to practice night landings. These were extremely tricky. The coast around Coronado was treacherous. The inexperienced pilots had trouble steering toward the diff lights, which marked the beaches, and often brought the boats to shore on the rocks.

Though the army helmet obscured Milton's present vision, it gave him a pretty good picture of the future. The helmet weighed as much as a bowling ball. It was as thick as the hood of a car. You put it over your head, like a hat, but it was nothing like a hat. In contact with the skull, an army helmet transmitted images directly into the brain. These were of objects the helmet was designed to keep out. Bullets, for instance. And shrapnel. The helmet closed off the mind for contemplation of these essential realities.

And if you were a person like my father, you began to think about how you could escape such realities. After a single week of drills, Milton realized that he had made a terrible mistake joining the Navy. Battle could be only slightly less dangerous than this preparation for it. Every night someone got injured. Waves slammed guys up against the boats. Guys fell and got swept underneath. The week before, a kid from Omaha had drowned.

During the day they trained, playing football on the beach in army boots to build up their legs, and then at night they had the drills. Exhausted, seasick, Milton stood packed in like a sardine, shouldering a heavy pack. He had always wanted to be an American and now he got to see what his fellow Americans were like. In close quarters he suffered their backwoods lubricity and knucklehead talk. They were in the boats for hours together, getting slammed around, getting wet. They got to bed at three or four in the morning. Then the sun came up and it was time to do it all over again.

Why had he joined the Navy? For revenge, for escape. He wanted to get back at Tessie and he wanted to forget her. Neither had worked. The dullness of military life, the endless repetition of duties, the standing in line to eat, to use the bathroom, to shave, served as no distraction at all. Standing in line all day brought on the very thoughts Milton wanted to avoid, of a clarinet imprint, like a ring of fire, on Tessie's flushed thigh. Or of Vandenbrock, the kid from Omaha who'd drowned: his battered face, the seawater leaking through his busted teeth.

All around Milton in the boat now guys were already getting sick. Ten minutes in the swells and sailors were bending over and regurgitating the beef stew and instant mashed potatoes of that evening's dinner onto the ridged metal floor. This provoked no comment. The vomit, which was an eerie blue color in the moonlight, had its own wave action, sloshing back and forth over everybody's boots. Milton lifted his face, trying to get a whiff of fresh air.

The boat pitched and rolled. It fell off waves and came crashing down, the hull shuddering. They were getting close to shore, where the surf picked up. The other men readjusted their packs and got ready for the make-believe assault, and Seaman Stephanides abandoned the solitude of his helmet.

"Saw it in the library," the sailor beside him was saying to another. "On the bulletin board."

"What kind of test?"

"Some kind of admittance exam. For Annapolis."

"Yeah, right, they're gonna let a couple of guys like us into Annapolis."

"Doesn't matter if they let us in or not. Deal is, whoever takes the test gets excused from drills."

"What did you say about a test?" Milton asked, butting in.

The sailor looked around to see if anyone else had heard. "Keep quiet about it. If we all sign up, it won't work."

"When is it?"

But before the sailor could answer there was a loud, grinding sound: they had hit the rocks again. The sudden stop knocked everyone forward. Helmets rang against one another; noses broke. Sailors fell into a pile and the front hatch fell away. Water was streaming into the boat now and the lieutenant was yelling. Milton, along with everyone else, leapt into the confusion — the black rocks, the sucking undertow, the Mexican beer bottles, the startled crabs.

Back in Detroit, also in the dark, my mother was at the movies. Michael Antoniou, her fiancé, had returned to Holy Cross and now she had her Saturdays free. On the screen of the Esquire theater, numerals flashed . . . 5 . . . 4 . . . 3 . . . and a newsreel began. Muted trumpets blared. An announcer began giving war reports. It had been the same announcer throughout the war, so that by now Tessie felt she knew him; he was almost family. Week after week he had informed her about Monty and the Brits driving Rommel's tanks out of North Africa and the American troops liberating Algeria and landing in Sicily. Munching popcorn, Tessie had watched as the months and years passed. The newsreels followed an itinerary. At first they'd concentrated on Europe. There were tanks rolling through tiny villages and French girls waving handkerchiefs from balconies. The French girls didn't look like they'd been through a war; they wore pretty, ruffled skirts, white ankle socks, and silk scarves. None of the men wore berets, which surprised Tessie. She'd always wanted to go to Europe, not to Greece so much, but to France or Italy. As she watched these newsreels, what Tessie noticed wasn't the bombed-out buildings but the sidewalk cafés, the fountains, the self-composed, urbane little dogs.

Two Saturdays ago, she'd seen Antwerp and Brussels liberated by the Allies. Now, as attention turned toward Japan, the scenery was changing. Palm trees cropped up in the newsreels, and tropical islands. This afternoon the screen gave the date "October 1944" and the announcer announced, *As American troops prepare for the final invasion of the Pacific, General Douglas MacArthur, vowing to make good on his promise of "I shall return," surveys his troops.* The footage showed sailors standing at attention on deck, or dropping artillery shells into guns, or horsing around on a beach, waving to the folks back home. And out in the audience my mother found herself doing a crazy thing. She was looking for Milton's face.

He was her second cousin, wasn't he? It was only natural she should worry about him. They had also been, not in love exactly, but in something more immature, a kind of infatuation or crush. Nothing like

344

what she had with Michael. Tessie sat up in her seat. She adjusted her purse in her lap. She sat up like a young lady who was engaged to be married. But after the newsreel ended and the movie began, she forgot about being an adult. She sank down in her seat and put her feet up over the seat in front.

Maybe it wasn't a very good movie that day, or maybe she'd seen too many movies lately — she'd gone for the last eight straight days — but whatever the reason, Tessie couldn't concentrate. She kept thinking that if something happened to Milton, if he was wounded or, God forbid, if he didn't come back — she would be somehow to blame. She hadn't told him to enlist in the Navy. If he'd asked her, she would have told him not to. But she knew he'd done it because of her. It was a little like *Into the Sands*, with Claude Barron, which she'd seen a couple of weeks ago. In that picture Claude Barron enlists in the Foreign Legion because Rita Carrol marries another guy. The other guy turns out to be a cheater and drinker, and so Rita Carrol leaves him and travels out to the desert where Claude Barron is fighting the Arabs. By the time Rita Carrol gets there he's in the hospital, wounded, or not a hospital really but just a tent, and she tells him she loves him and Claude Barron says,

"I went into the desert to forget about you. But the sand was the color of your hair. The desert sky was the color of your eyes. There was nowhere I could go that wouldn't be you." And then he dies. Tessie cried buckets. Her mascara ran, staining the collar of her blouse something awful.

Drilling at night and going to Saturday matinees, jumping into the sea and sliding down in movie seats, worrying and regretting and hoping and trying to forget — nevertheless, to be perfectly honest, mostly what people did during the war was write letters. In support of my personal belief that real life doesn't live up to writing about it, the members of my family seem to have spent most of their time that year engaged in correspondence. From Holy Cross, Michael Antoniou wrote twice a week to his fiancée. His letters arrived in light blue envelopes embossed with the head of Patriarch Benjamin in the upper left-hand corner, and on the stationery inside, his handwriting, like his voice, was feminine and neat. "Most likely, the first place they'll send us after my ordination will be somewhere in Greece. There's going to be a lot of rebuilding to do now that the Nazis have left."

At her desk beneath the Shakespeare bookends, Tessie wrote back faithfully, if not entirely truthfully. Most of her daily activities didn't seem virtuous enough to tell a seminarian-fiancé. And so she began to invent a more appropriate life for herself. "This morning Zo and I went down to volunteer at the Red Cross," wrote my mother, who had spent the entire day at the Fox Theater, eating nonpareils. "They had us cut up old bedsheets into strips for bandages. You should see the blister I've got on my thumb. It's a real whopper." She didn't start out with these wholesale fictions. At first Tessie had given an honest accounting of her days. But in one letter Michael Antoniou had said, "Movies are fine as entertainment, but with the war I wonder if they're the best way to spend your time." After that, Tessie started making things up. She rationalized her lying by telling herself that this was her last year of freedom. By next summer she'd be a priest's wife, living somewhere in Greece. To mitigate her dishonesty, she deflected all honor from herself, filling her letters with praise for Zoë. "She works six days a week but on Sundays gets up bright and early to take Mrs. Tsontakis to church — poor thing's ninety-three and can barely walk. That's Zoë. Always thinking of others."

Meanwhile, Desdemona and Milton were

writing to each other, too. Before going off to war, my father had promised his mother that he'd finally become literate in Greek. Now, from California, lying on his bunk in the evenings, so sore he could barely move, Milton consulted a Greek-English dictionary to piece together reports on his navy life. No matter how hard he concentrated, however, by the time his letters arrived at Hurlbut Street something had been lost in translation.

"What kind of paper this is?" Desdemona asked her husband, holding up a letter that resembled Swiss cheese. Like mice, military censors had nibbled at Milton's letters before Desdemona got to digest them. They bit off any mention of the word "invasion," any reference to "San Diego" or "Coronado." They chewed through whole paragraphs describing the naval base, the destroyers and submarines docked at the pier. Since the censors' Greek was even worse than Milton's, they often made mistakes, lopping off endearments, x's and o's.

Despite the gaps in Milton's missives (syntactical and physical), my grandmother registered the danger of his situation. In his badly penned sigmas and deltas she spied the shaking hand of her son's growing anxiety. Over his grammatical mistakes she detected the note of fear in his voice. The stationery itself frightened her because it already looked blown to bits.

Seaman Stephanides, however, was doing his best to prevent injury. On a Wednesday morning, he reported to the base library to take the admittance exam for the U.S. Naval Academy. Over the next five hours, every time he looked up from his test paper, he saw his shipmates doing calisthenics in the hot sun. He couldn't help smiling. While his buddies were baking out there, Milton was sitting under a ceiling fan, working out a mathematical proof. While they were forced to run up and down the sandy gridiron, Milton was reading a paragraph by someone named Carlyle and answering the questions that followed. And tonight, when they would be getting creamed against the rocks, he would be snug in his bunk, fast asleep.

By the time the early months of 1945 rolled in, everyone was looking for exemptions from duty. My mother hid from charitable works by going to the movies. My father ducked maneuvers by taking a test. But when it came to exemptions, my grandmother sought one from nothing less than heaven itself.

One Sunday in March, she arrived at Assumption before the Divine Liturgy had started. Going into a niche, she approached the icon of St. Christopher and proposed a deal. "Please, St. Christopher," Desdemona kissed her fingertips and touched them to the saint's forehead, "if you keep Miltie safe in the war, I will make him promise to go back to Bithynios and fix the church." She looked up at St. Christopher, the martyr of Asia Minor. "If the Turks destroyed it, Miltie will build it again. If it only needs painting, he'll paint." St. Christopher was a giant. He held a staff and forded a rushing river. On his back was the Christ Child, the heaviest baby in history because he had the world in his hands. What better saint to protect her own son, in peril on the sea? In the shadowy, lamplit space, Desdemona prayed. She moved her lips, spelling out the conditions. "I would also like, if possible, St. Christopher, if Miltie he could be excused from the training. He tells me it is very dangerous. He's writing to me in Greek now, too, St. Christopher. Not too good but okay. I also make him promise to put in the church new pews. Also, if you like, some carpets." She lapsed into silence, closing her eyelids. She crossed herself numerous times, waiting for an answer. Then her spine suddenly straightened. She opened her eyes, nodded, smiled. She kissed her fingertips and touched them to the saint's picture, and she hurried home to write Milton the good news.

"Yeah, sure," my father said when he got the letter. "St. Christopher to the rescue." He slipped the letter into his Greek-English dictionary and carried both to the incinerator behind the Quonset hut. (That was the end of my father's Greek lessons. Though he continued to speak Greek to his parents, Milton never succeeded in writing it, and as he got older he began to forget what even the simplest words meant. In the end he couldn't say much more than Chapter Eleven or me, which was almost nothing at all.)

Milton's sarcasm was understandable under the circumstances. Only the day before, his C.O. had given Milton a new assignment in the upcoming invasion. The news, like all bad news, hadn't registered at first. It was as if the C.O.'s words, the actual syllables he addressed to Milton, had been scrambled by the boys over in Intelligence. Milton had saluted and walked out. He'd continued down to the beach still unaffected, the bad news acting with a kind of discretion, allowing him these last few peaceful, deluded moments. He watched the sunset. He admired a neutral Switzerland of seals out on the rocks. He took off his boots to feel the sand against his feet, as if the world were a place he was only beginning to live in instead of somewhere he would soon be leaving. But then the fissures appeared. A split in the top of his skull, through which the bad news hissingly poured; a groove in his knees, which buckled, and suddenly Milton couldn't keep it out any longer.

Thirty-eight seconds. That was the news.

"Stephanides, we're switching you over to signalman. Report to Building B at 0700 hours tomorrow morning. Dismissed." That was what the C.O. had said. Only that. And it was no surprise, really. As the invasion neared, there had been a sudden rash of injuries to signalmen. Signalmen had been chopping off fingers doing KP duty. Signalmen had been shooting themselves in the feet while cleaning their guns. In the nighttime drills, signalmen lustily flung themselves onto the rocks.

Thirty-eight seconds was the life expectancy of a signalman. When the landing took place, Seaman Stephanides would stand in the front of the boat. He would operate a sort of lantern, flashing signals in Morse code. This lantern would be bright, clearly visible to enemy positions onshore. That was what he was thinking about as he stood on the beach with his boots off. He was thinking that he would never take over his father's bar. He was thinking that he would never see Tessie again. Instead, a few weeks from now, he would stand up in a boat, exposed to hostile fire, holding a bright light. For a little while, at least.

Not included in the News of the World: a shot of my father's AKA transport ship leaving Coronado naval base, heading west. At the Esquire Theater, holding her feet off the sticky floor, Tessie Zizmo watches as white arrows arc across the Pacific. *The U.S. Naval Twelfth Fleet forges ahead on its invasion of the Pacific,* the announcer says. *Final destination: Japan.* One arrow starts out in Australia, moving through New Guinea toward the Philippines. Another arrow shoots out from the Solomon Islands and another from the Marianas. Tessie has never heard of these places before. But now the arrows continue on, advancing toward other islands she's never heard of — Iwo Jima, Okinawa — each flagged with the Rising Sun. The arrows converge from three directions on Japan, which is just a bunch of islands itself. As Tessie is getting the geography straight, the newsreel breaks into filmed footage. A hand cranks an alarm bell; sailors jump out of bunks, double-time it up stairways, assuming battle stations. And then there he is — Milton — running across the deck of the ship! Tessie recognizes his skinny chest, his raccoon eyes. She forgets about the floor and puts her feet down. In the newsreel the destroyer's guns fire without sound and, half a world away, amid the elegance of an old-fashioned cinema, Tessie Zizmo feels the recoils. The theater is about half-full, mostly with young women like her. They, too, are snacking on candies for emotional reasons; they, too, are searching the grainy newsreel for the faces of fiancés. The air smells of Tootsie Pops and perfume and of the cigarette the usher is smoking in the lobby. Most of the time the war is an abstract event, happening somewhere else. Only here, for four or five minutes, squeezed between the cartoon and the feature, does it become concrete. Maybe the blurring of identity, the mob release, has an effect on Tessie, inspiring the kind of hysteria Sinatra does. Whatever the reason, in the bedroom light of the movie theater Tessie Zizmo allows herself to remember things she's been trying to forget: a clarinet nosing its way up her bare leg like an invading force itself, tracing an arrow to her own island empire, an empire which, she realizes at that moment, she is giving up to the wrong man. While the flickering beam of the movie projector slants through the darkness over her head, Tessie admits to herself that she doesn't want to marry Michael Antoniou. She doesn't want to be a priest's wife or move to Greece. As she gazes at Milton in the newsreel, her eyes fill with tears and she says out loud, "There was nowhere I could go that wouldn't be you."

And while people shush her, the sailor in the newsreel approaches the camera — and Tessie realizes that it isn't Milton. It doesn't matter, however. She has seen what she has seen. She gets up to leave.

On Hurlbut Street that same afternoon, Desdemona was lying in bed. She had been there for the last three days, ever since the mailman had delivered another letter from Milton. The letter wasn't in Greek but English and Lefty had to translate:

Dear folks,
   This is the last letter I'll be able to send you. (Sorry for not writing in the native tongue, ma, but I'm a little busy at the moment.) The brass won't let me say much about what's going on, but I just wanted to drop you this note to tell you not to worry about me. I'm headed to a safe place. Keep the bar in good shape, Pop. This war'll be over some day and I want in on the family business. Tell Zo to stay out of my room.
                     Love and laughs,
                     Milt

Unlike the previous letters, this one arrived intact. Not a single hole anywhere.

At first this had cheered Desdemona until she realized what it implied. There was no need for secrecy anymore. The invasion was already under way.

At that point, Desdemona stood up from the kitchen table and, with a look of triumphant desolation, made a grave pronouncement:

"God has brought the judgment down on us that we deserve," she said.

She went into the living room, where she straightened a sofa cushion in passing, and climbed the stairs to the bedroom. There she undressed and put on her nightgown, even though it was only ten in the morning. And then, for the first time since being pregnant with Zoë and the last time before climbing in forever twenty-five years later, my grandmother took to her bed.

For three days she had stayed there, getting up only to go to the bathroom. My grandfather had tried in vain to coax her out. When he left for work the third morning, he had brought up some food, a dish of white beans in tomato sauce and bread.

The meal was still lying untouched on the bedside table when there came a knock at the front door. Desdemona did not get up to answer it but only pulled a pillow over her face. Despite this muffling, she heard the knocking continue. A little later, the front door opened, and finally footsteps made their way up the stairs and into her room.

"Aunt Des?" Tessie said.

Desdemona did not move.

"I've got something to tell you," Tessie continued. "I wanted you to be the first to know."

The figure in the bed remained motionless. Still, the alertness that had seized Desdemona's body told Tessie that she was awake and listening. Tessie took a breath and announced, "I'm going to call off the wedding."

There was a silence. Slowly Desdemona pulled the pillow off her face. She reached for her glasses on the bedside table, put them on, and sat up in bed. "You don't want to marry Mikey?"

"No."

"Mikey is a good Greek boy."

"I know he is. But I don't love him. I love Milton."

Tessie expected Desdemona to react with shock or outrage, but to her surprise my grandmother barely seemed to register the confession. "You don't know this, but Milton asked me to marry him a while ago. I said no. Now I'm going to write him and say yes."

Desdemona gave a little shrug. "You can write what you want, honey *mou*. Miltie he won't get it."

"It's not illegal or anything. First cousins can marry even. We're only second cousins. Milton went and looked up all the statutes."

Once again Desdemona shrugged. Drained by worry, abandoned by St. Christopher, she stopped fighting an eventuality that had never been fated in the first place. "If you and Miltie want to get married, you have my blessing," she said. Then, having given her benediction, she settled back into her pillows and closed her eyes to the pain of living. "And may God grant that you never have a child who dies in the ocean."

In my family, the funeral meats have always furnished the wedding tables. My grandmother agreed to marry my grandfather because she never thought she'd live to see the wedding. And my grandmother blessed my parents' marriage, after vigorously plotting against it, only because she didn't think Milton would survive to the end of the week.

At sea, my father didn't think so either. Standing at the bow of the transport ship, he stared out over the water at his fast-approaching end. He wasn't tempted to pray or to settle his accounts with God. He perceived the infinite before him but didn't warm it up with human wishing. The infinite was as vast and cold as the ocean spreading around the ship, and in all that emptiness what Milton felt most acutely was the reality of his own buzzing mind. Somewhere out over the water was the bullet that would end his life. Maybe it was already loaded in the Japanese gun from which it would be fired; maybe it was in an ammunition roll. He was twenty-one, oily-skinned, prominent about the Adam's apple. It occurred to him that he had been stupid to run off to war because of a girl, but then he took this back, because it wasn't just some girl; it was Theodora. As her face appeared in Milton's mind, a sailor tapped him on the back.

"Who do you know in Washington?"

He handed my father a transfer, effective immediately. He was to report to the Naval Academy at Annapolis. On the admissions test, Milton had scored a ninety-eight.

Every Greek drama needs a deus ex machina. Mine comes in the form of the bosun's chair that picked my father off the deck of the AKA transport ship and whisked him through the air to deposit him on the deck of a destroyer heading back to the U.S. mainland. From San Francisco he traveled by elegant Pullman car to Annapolis, where he was enrolled as a cadet.

"I tell you St. Christopher get you out of

the war," Desdemona exulted when he called home with the news.

"He sure did."

"Now you have to fix the church."

"What?"

"The church. You have to fix it."

"Sure, sure," Naval Cadet Stephanides said, and maybe he even intended to. He was grateful to be alive and to have his future back. But with one thing or another, Milton would put off his trip to Bithynios. Within a year's time he was married; later, he was a father. The war ended. He graduated from Annapolis and served in the Korean War. Eventually he returned to Detroit and went into the family business. From time to time Desdemona would remind her son about his outstanding obligation to St. Christopher, but my father always found an excuse for not fulfilling it. His procrastination would have disastrous effects, if you believe in that sort of thing, which, some days, when the old Greek blood is running high, I do.

My parents were married in June of 1946. In a show of generosity, Michael Antoniou attended the wedding. An ordained priest now, he presented a dignified, benevolent figure, but by the second hour of the reception it was clear he was crushed. He drank too much champagne at dinner and, when the band began playing, sought out the next best thing to the bride: the bridesmaid, Zoë Stephanides.

Zoë looked down at him — about a foot. He asked her to dance. The next thing she knew, they had started off across the ballroom floor.

"Tessie told me a lot about you in her letters," said Michael Antoniou.

"Nothing too bad, I hope."

"Just the opposite. She told me what a good Christian you are."

His long robe concealed his small feet, making it difficult for Zoë to follow. Nearby, Tessie was dancing with Milton in his white naval uniform. As the couples passed each other, Zoë glared comically at Tessie and mouthed the words, "I'm going to kill you." But then Milton twirled Tessie around and the two rivals came face-to-face.

"Hey there, Mike," said Milton cordially.

"It's Father Mike now," said the vanquished suitor.

"Got a promotion, eh? Congratulations. I guess I can trust you with my sister."

He danced away with Tessie, who looked back in silent apology. Zoë, who knew how infuriating her brother could be, felt sorry for Father Mike. She suggested they get some wedding cake.

Ex Ovo Omnia

❦

So, to recap: Sourmelina Zizmo (née Papadiamandopoulos) wasn't only my first cousin twice removed. She was also my grandmother. My father was his own mother's (and father's) nephew. In addition to being my grandparents, Desdemona and Lefty were my great-aunt and -uncle. My parents would be my second cousins once removed and Chapter Eleven would be my third cousin as well as my brother. The Stephanides family tree, diagrammed in Dr. Luce's "Autosomal Transmission of Recessive Traits," goes into more detail than I think you would care to know about. I've concentrated only on the gene's last few transmissions. And now we're almost there. In honor of Miss Barrie, my eighth-grade Latin teacher, I'd like to call attention to the quotation above: *ex ovo omnia*. Getting to my feet (as we did whenever Miss Barrie entered the room), I hear her ask, "Infants? Can any of you translate this little snippet and give its provenance?"

I raise my hand.

"Calliope, our muse, will start us off."

"It's from Ovid. *Metamorphoses*. The story of creation."

"Stunning. And can you render it into English for us?"

"Everything comes out of an egg."

"Did you hear that, infants? This classroom, your bright faces, even dear old Cicero on my desk — they all came out of an egg!"

❧

Among the arcana Dr. Philobosian imparted to the dinner table over the years (aside from the monstrous effects of maternal imagination) was the seventeenth-century theory of Preformation. The Preformationists, with their roller-coaster names — Spallazani, Swammerdam, Leeuwenhoek — believed that all of humankind had existed in miniature since Creation, in either the semen of Adam or the ovary of Eve, each person tucked inside the next like a Russian nesting doll. It all started when Jan Swammerdam used a scalpel to peel away the outer layers of a certain insect. What kind? Well . . . a member of the phylum Arthropoda. Latin name? Okay, then: *Bombyx mori*. The insect Swammerdam used in his experiments back in 1669 was nothing other than a silkworm. Before an audience of intellectuals, Swammerdam cut away the skin of the silkworm to reveal what appeared to be a tiny model of the future moth inside, from proboscis to antennae to folded wings. The theory of Preformation was born.

In the same way, I like to imagine my brother and me, floating together since the world's beginning on our raft of eggs. Each inside a transparent membrane, each slotted for his or her (in my case both) hour of birth. There's Chapter Eleven, always so pasty, and bald by the age of twenty-three, so that he makes a perfect homunculus. His pronounced cranium indicates his future deftness with mathematics and mechanical things. His unhealthy pallor suggests his coming Crohn's disease. Right next to him, there's me, his sometime sister, my face already a conundrum, flashing like a lenticular decal between two images: the dark-eyed, pretty little girl I used to be; and the severe, aquiline-nosed, Roman-coinish person I am today. And so we drifted, the two of us, since the world began, awaiting our cues and observing the passing show.

For instance: Milton Stephanides graduating from Annapolis in 1949. His white hat flying up into the air. He and Tessie were stationed at Pearl Harbor, where they lived in austere marital housing and where my mother, at twenty-five, got a terrible sunburn and was never seen in a bathing suit again. In 1951 they were transferred to Norfolk, Virginia, at which point Chapter Eleven's egg sac next door to mine began to vibrate. Nevertheless, he stuck around to watch the Korean conflict, where Ensign Stephanides served on a submarine chaser. We watched Milton's adult character forming during those years, taking on the no-nonsense attributes of our future father. The U.S. Navy was responsible for the precision with which Milton Stephanides ever after parted his hair, his habit of polishing his belt buckle with his shirt sleeve, his "yes, sir"s and "shipshape"s, and his insistence on making us synchronize our watches at the mall. Under the brass eagle and fasces of his ensign's cap, Milton Stephanides left the Boy Scouts behind. The Navy gave him his love of sailing and his aversion to waiting in lines. Even then his politics were being formed, his anti-communism, his distrust of the Russians. Ports of call in Africa and Southeast Asia were already forging his beliefs about racial IQ levels. From the social snubs of his commanding officers, he was picking up his hatred of Eastern liberals and the Ivy League at the same time as he was falling in love with Brooks Brothers clothing. His taste for tasseled loafers and seersucker shorts was seeping into him. We knew all this about our father before we were born and then we forgot it and had to learn it all over again. When the Korean War ended in 1953, Milton was stationed again in Norfolk. And in March of 1954, as my father weighed his future, Chapter Eleven, with a little wave of farewell to me, raised his arms and traveled down the waterslide into the world.

And I was all alone.

Events in the years before my birth: after dancing with Zoë at my parents' wedding, Father Mike pursued her doggedly for the next two and a half years. Zoë didn't like the idea of marrying someone either so religious or so diminutive. Father Mike proposed to her three times and in each case she refused, waiting for someone better to come along. But no one did. Finally, feeling that she had no alternative (and coaxed by Desdemona, who still thought it was a wonderful thing to marry a priest), Zoë gave in. In 1949, she married Father Mike and soon they went off to live in Greece. There she would give birth to four children, my cousins, and remain for the next eight years.

In Detroit, in 1950, the Black Bottom ghetto was bulldozed to put in a freeway. The Nation of Islam, now headquartered at Temple No. 2 in Chicago, got a new minister by the name of Malcolm X. During the winter of 1954, Desdemona first began to talk of retiring to Florida someday. "They have a city in Florida you know what it is called? New Smyrna Beach!" In 1956, the last streetcar stopped running in Detroit and the Packard plant closed. And that same year, Milton Stephanides, tired of military life, left the Navy and returned home to pursue an old dream.

"Do something else," Lefty Stephanides told his son. They were in the Zebra Room, drinking coffee. "You go to the Naval Academy to be a bartender?"

"I don't want to be a bartender. I want to run a restaurant. A whole chain. This is a good place to start."

Lefty shook his head. He leaned back and spread his arms, taking in the whole bar. "This is no place to start anything," he said.

He had a point. Despite my grandfather's assiduous drink-refilling and counter-wiping, the bar on Pingree Street had lost its luster. The old zebra skin, which he still had on the wall, had dried out and cracked. Cigarette smoke had dirtied the diamond shapes of the tin ceiling. Over the years the Zebra Room had absorbed the exhalations of its auto worker patrons. The place smelled of their beer and hair tonic, their punch-clock misery, their frayed nerves, their trade unionism. The neighborhood was also changing. When my grandfather had opened the bar in 1933, the area had been white and middle-class. Now it was becoming poorer, and predominantly black. In the inevitable chain of cause and effect, as soon as the first black family had moved onto the block, the white neighbors immediately put their houses up for sale. The oversupply of houses depressed the real estate prices, which allowed poorer people to move in, and with poverty came crime, and with crime came more moving vans.

"Business isn't so good anymore," Lefty said. "If you want to open a bar, try Greektown. Or Birmingham."

My father waved these objections aside. "Bar business isn't so good maybe," he said. "That's because there's too many bars around here. Too much competition. What this neighborhood needs is a decent diner."

Hercules Hot Dogs™, which at its height would boast sixty-six locations throughout Michigan, Ohio, and southeastern Florida — each restaurant identified by the distinctive "Pillars of Hercules" out front — could be said to have begun on the snowy February morning in 1956 when my father arrived at the Zebra Room to begin renovations. The first thing he did was to remove the sagging venetian blinds from the front windows to let in more light. He painted the interior a bright white. With a G.I. business loan, he had the bar remodeled into a diner counter and had a small kitchen installed. Workmen put red vinyl booths along the far wall and reupholstered the old barstools with Zizmo's zebra skin. One morning two deliverymen carried a jukebox in the front door. And while hammers pounded and sawdust filled the air, Milton acquainted himself with the papers and deeds Lefty had haphazardly kept in a cigar box beneath the register.

"What the hell is this?" he asked his father. "You've got three insurance policies on this place."

"You can never have too much insurance," Lefty said. "Sometimes the companies don't pay. Better to be sure."

"Sure? Each one of these is for more than this place is worth. We're paying on all these? That's a waste of money."

Up until this point, Lefty had let his son make whatever changes he wanted. But now he stood firm. "Listen to me, Milton. You haven't lived through a fire. You don't know what happens. Sometimes in a fire the insurance company burns down, too. Then what can you do?"

"But three —"

"We need three," insisted Lefty.

"Just humor him," Tessie told Milton later that night. "Your parents have been through a lot."

"Sure they've been through a lot. But we're the ones who have to keep paying these premiums." Nevertheless, he did as his wife said and maintained all three policies.

The Zebra Room I remember as a kid: it was full of artificial flowers, yellow tulips, red roses, dwarf trees bearing wax apples. Plastic daisies sprouted from teapots; daffodils erupted from ceramic cows. Photos of Artie Shaw and Bing Crosby adorned the wall, next to hand-painted signs that said ENJOY A NICE LIME RICKEY! and OUR FRENCH TOAST IS THE TOAST OF THE TOWN! There were photos of Milton putting a finishing-touch cherry on a milk shake or kissing someone's baby like the mayor. There were photographs of actual mayors, Miriani and Cavanaugh. The great right fielder Al Kaline, who stopped in on his way to practice at Tiger Stadium, had autographed his own head shot: "To my pal Milt, great eggs!" When a Greek Orthodox church in Flint burned down, Milton drove up and salvaged one of the surviving stained glass windows. He hung it on the wall over the booths. Athena olive oil tins lined the front window next to a bust of Donizetti. Everything was hodgepodge: grandmotherly lamps stood next to El Greco reproductions; bull's horns hung from the neck of an Aphrodite statuette. Above the coffeemaker an assortment of figurines marched along the shelf: Paul Bunyan and Babe the Blue Ox, Mickey Mouse, Zeus, and Felix the Cat.

My grandfather, trying to be of help, drove off one day and returned with a stack of fifty plates.

"I already ordered plates," said Milton. "From a restaurant supply place. They're only charging us 10 percent down."

"You don't want these?" Lefty looked disappointed. "Okay. I'll take them back."

"Hey, Pop," his son called after him. "Why don't you take the day off? I can handle things here."

"You don't need help?"

"Go home. Have Ma make you lunch."

Lefty did as he was told. But as he drove down West Grand Boulevard, feeling unneeded, he passed Rubsamen Medical Supply — a store with dirty windows and a neon sign that blinked even in the day — and felt the stirrings of old temptation.

The following Monday, Milton opened the new diner. He opened it at six in the morning, with a newly hired staff of two, Eleni Papanikolas, in a waitress uniform purchased at her own expense, and her husband, Jimmy, as short-order cook. "Remember, Eleni, you mostly work for tips," Milton pep-talked. "So smile."

"At who?" asked Eleni. For despite the red carnations in bud vases gracing each booth, despite the zebra-striped menus, matchbooks, and napkins, the Zebra Room itself was empty.

"Smart-ass," Milton said, grinning. Eleni's ribbing didn't bother him. He'd worked it all out. He'd found a need and filled it.

In the interest of time, I offer you now a stock capitalist montage. We see Milton greeting his first customers. We see Eleni serving them scrambled eggs. We see Milton and Eleni standing back, biting their lips. But now the customers are smiling and nodding! Eleni runs to refill their coffee. Next Milton, in different clothes, is greeting more customers; and Jimmy the cook is cracking eggs one-handed; and Lefty is looking left out. "Give me two fried whiskey down!" Milton shouts, showing off his new lingo. "Dry white, 68, hold the ice!" Close-up of the cash register ringing open and closed; of Milton's hands counting money; of Lefty putting on his hat and leaving unnoticed. Then more eggs; eggs being cracked, fried, flipped, and scrambled; eggs arriving in cartons through the back door and coming out on plates through the front hatch;

fluffy heaps of scrambled eggs in gleaming yellow Technicolor; and the cash register banging open again; and money piling up. Until, finally, we see Milton and Tessie, dressed in their best, following a real estate agent through a big house.

The neighborhood of Indian Village lay just twelve blocks west of Hurlbut, but it was a different world altogether. The four grand streets of Burns, Iroquois, Seminole, and Adams (even in Indian Village the White Man had taken half the names) were lined with stately houses built in eclectic styles. Red-brick Georgian rose next to English Tudor, which gave onto French Provincial. The houses in Indian Village had big yards, important walkways, picturesquely oxidizing cupolas, lawn jockeys (whose days were numbered), and burglar alarms (whose popularity was only just beginning). My grandfather remained silent, however, as he toured his son's impressive new home. "How do you like the size of this living room?" Milton was asking him. "Here, sit down. Make yourself comfortable. Tessie and I want you and Ma to feel like this is your house, too. Now that you're retired —"
"What do you mean retired?"
"Okay, semiretired. Now that you can take it a little bit easy, you'll be able to do

all the things you always wanted to do. Look, in here's the library. You want to come over and work on your translations, you can do it right here. How about that table? Big enough for you? And the shelves are built right into the wall."

Pushed out of the daily operations at the Zebra Room, my grandfather began to spend his days driving around the city. He drove downtown to the Public Library to read the foreign newspapers. Afterward, he stopped to play backgammon at a coffee house in Greektown. At fifty-four, Lefty Stephanides was still in good shape. He walked three miles a day for exercise. He ate sensibly and had less of a belly than his son. Nevertheless, time was making its inevitable depredations. Lefty had to wear bifocals now. He had a touch of bursitis in his shoulder. His clothes had gone out of style, so that he looked like an extra in a gangster movie. One day, appraising himself with severity in the bathroom mirror, Lefty realized that he had become one of those older men who slicked their hair back in allegiance to an era no one could remember. Depressed by this fact, Lefty gathered up his books. He drove over to Seminole, intending to use the library, but when he got to the house he kept on going. With a wild look in his eyes, he headed instead for Rubsamen Medical Supply.

Once you've visited the underworld, you never forget the way back. Forever after, you're able to spot the red light in the upstairs window or the champagne glass on the door that doesn't open until midnight. For years now, driving past Rubsamen Medical Supply, my grandfather had noticed the unchanging window display of hernia truss, neck brace, and crutches. He'd seen the desperate, crazily hopeful faces of the Negro men and women who went in and out without buying a thing. My grandfather recognized that desperation and knew that now, in his forced retirement, this was the place for him. Roulette wheels spun behind Lefty's eyes as he sped toward the West Side. The clicking of backgammon dice filled his ears as he pressed the accelerator. His blood grew hot with an old excitement, a quickening of the pulse he hadn't felt since descending the mountain to explore the back streets of Bursa. He parked at the curb and hurried inside. He walked past the startled customers (who weren't used to seeing white people); he strode past the props of aspirin bottles, corn plasters, and laxatives, and went up to the pharmacist's window in the rear.

"Can I help you?" the pharmacist asked.

"Twenty-two," said Lefty.

"You got it."

Trying to reclaim the drama of his gambling days, my grandfather started playing the West Side numbers. He started small. Little bets of two or three dollars. After a few weeks, to recoup his losses, he went up to ten bucks. Every day he wagered a piece of the new profits from the restaurant. One day he won and so went double or nothing the next, and lost. Amid hot-water bottles and enema bags, he placed his bets. Surrounded by cough medicine and cold sore ointment, he started playing a "gig," meaning three numbers at once. As they had in Bursa, his pockets filled up with scraps of paper. He wrote out lists of the numbers he played along with the dates, so as not to repeat any. He played Milton's birthday, Desdemona's birthday, the date of Greek Independence minus the last digit, the year of the burning of Smyrna. Desdemona, finding the scraps in the wash, thought they had to do with the new restaurant. "My husband the millionaire," she said, dreaming of Florida retirement.

For the first time ever, Lefty consulted Desdemona's dream book, in the hope of calculating a winning number on the abacus of his unconscious. He became alert to the integers that appeared in his dreams. Many of the Negroes who frequented Rubsamen's Medical Supply noticed my grandfather's preoccupation with the dream book, and after he won for two weeks in a row, word spread. This led to the only contribution Greeks have ever made to African American culture (aside from the wearing of gold medallions) as the blacks of Detroit began to buy dream books themselves. The Atlantis Publishing Company translated the books into English and shipped them to major cities all over America. For a short time elderly colored women began to hold the same superstitions my grandmother did, believing, for instance, that a running rabbit meant you were coming into money or that a black bird on a telephone line augured that somebody was about to die.

"Taking that money to the bank?" Milton asked, seeing his father empty the cash register.

"Yes, to the bank." And Lefty did go to the bank. He went to withdraw money from his savings account, in order to continue his steady assault on all nine hundred and ninety-nine possible permutations of a three-digit variable. Whenever he lost, he felt awful. He wanted to stop. He wanted to go home and confess to Desdemona. The only antidote to this feeling, however, was the prospect of winning the next day. It's possible that a hint of self-destructiveness played a part in my grandfather's numbers-playing. Full of survivor's guilt, he was surrendering himself to the random forces of the universe, trying to punish himself for still being alive. But, mostly, gambling just filled his empty days.

I alone, from the private box of my primordial egg, saw what was going on. Milton was too busy running the diner to notice. Tessie was too busy taking care of Chapter Eleven to notice. Sourmelina might have noticed something, but she didn't make many appearances at our house during those years. In 1953, at a Theosophical Society meeting, Aunt Lina had met a woman named Mrs. Evelyn Watson. Mrs. Watson had been attracted to the Theosophical Society by the hope of contacting her deceased husband, but soon lost interest in communicating with the spirit world in favor of whispering with Sourmelina in the flesh. With shocking speed, Aunt Lina had quit her job at the florist's shop and moved down to the Southwest with Mrs. Watson. Every Christmas since, she sent my parents a gift box containing hot sauce, a flowering cactus, and a photograph of Mrs. Watson and herself in front of some national monument. (One surviving photo shows the couple in an Anasazi ceremonial cave at Bandelier, Mrs. Watson looking as wisely lined as Georgia O'Keeffe while Lina, in a tremendous sunhat, descends a ladder into a kiva.)

As for Desdemona, during the mid-to-late fifties she was experiencing a brief and completely uncharacteristic spell of contentment. Her son had returned unhurt from another war. (St. Christopher had kept his word during the "police action" in Korea and Milton hadn't been so much as fired on.) Her daughter-in-law's pregnancy had caused the usual anxiety, of course, but Chapter Eleven had been born healthy. The restaurant was doing well. Every week family and friends gathered at Milton's new house in Indian Village for Sunday dinner. One day Desdemona received a brochure from the New Smyrna Beach Chamber of Commerce, which she had sent away for. It didn't look like Smyrna at all, but at least it was sunny, and there were fruit stands.

Meanwhile, my grandfather was feeling lucky. Having played at least one number every day for a little over two years, he had now bet on every number from 1 to 740. Only 259 numbers to go to reach 999! Then what? What else? — start over. Bank tellers handed rolls of money to Lefty, which he in turn handed to the pharmacist behind the window. He played 741, 742, and 743. He played 744, 745, and 746. And then one morning the bank teller informed Lefty that there weren't sufficient funds in his account to make a withdrawal.

The teller showed him his balance: $13.26. My grandfather thanked the teller. He crossed the bank lobby, adjusting his tie. He felt suddenly dizzy. The gambling fever he'd had for twenty-six months broke, sending a last wave of heat over his skin, and suddenly his entire body was dripping wet. Mopping his brow, Lefty walked out of the bank into his penniless old age.

The earsplitting cry my grandmother let out when she learned of the disaster cannot be done justice in print. The shriek went on and on, as she tore her hair and rent her garments and collapsed onto the floor. **"How will we eat!"** Desdemona wailed, staggering around the kitchen. **"Where will we live!"** She spread her arms, appealing to God, then beat on her chest, and finally took hold of her left sleeve and ripped it off. **"What kind of husband are you to do this to your wife who cooked and cleaned for you and gave you children and never complained!"** Now she tore off her right sleeve. **"Didn't I tell you not to gamble? Didn't I?"** She started on her dress proper now. She took the hem in her hands, as ancient Near Eastern ululations issued from her throat. **"Ouloulouloulouloulou! Ouloulouloulouloulou!"** My grandfather watched in astonishment as his modest wife shredded her clothing before his eyes, the skirt of the dress, the waist, the bosom, the neckline. With a final rip, the dress split in two and Desdemona lay on the linoleum, exposing to the world the misery of her underwear, her overburdened underwire brassiere, her gloomy underpants, and the frantic girdle whose stays she was even now popping as she approached the summit of her dishevelment. But at last she stopped. Before she was completely naked, Desdemona fell back as though depleted. She pulled off her hairnet and her hair spilled out to cover her and she closed her eyes, spent. In the next moment, she said in a practical tone, "Now we have to move in with Milton."

Three weeks later, in October 1958, my grandparents moved out of Hurlbut, one year before they would have paid off the mortgage. Over a warm Indian summer weekend, my father and dishonored grandfather carried furniture outside for the yard sale, the sea-foam-green sofa and armchairs, which still looked brand-new beneath plastic slipcovers, the kitchen table, the bookcases. Lamps were set out on the grass along with Milton's old Boy Scout manuals, Zoë's dolls and tap shoes, a framed photograph of Patriarch Athenagoras, and a closetful of Lefty's suits, which my grandmother forced him to sell as punishment. Hair safely restored beneath her hairnet, Desdemona glowered around the yard, submerged in a despair too deep for tears. She examined each object, sighing audibly before affixing a price tag, and scolded her husband for trying to carry things too heavy for him. "Do you think you're young? Let Milton do it. You're an old man." Under one arm she held the silkworm box, which wasn't for sale. When she saw the portrait of the Patriarch, she gasped in horror. "We don't have bad luck enough you want to sell the Patriarch?"

She snatched it up and carried it inside. For the rest of the day she remained in the kitchen, unable to watch the miscellaneous horde of yard sale scavengers pick over her personal possessions. There were weekend antiquers from the suburbs who brought their dogs along, and families down on their luck who roped chairs to the roofs of battered cars, and discriminating male couples who turned everything over to search for trademarks on the bottom. Desdemona would have felt no more ashamed had she herself been for sale, displayed naked on the green sofa, a price tag hanging from her foot. When everything had been sold or given away, Milton drove my grandparents' remaining belongings in a rented truck the twelve blocks to Seminole.

In order to give them privacy, my grandparents were offered the attic. Risking injury, my father and Jimmy Papanikolas carried everything up the secret stairway behind the wallpapered door. Up into the peaked space they carted my grandparents' disassembled bed, the leather ottoman, the brass coffee table, and Lefty's rebetika records. Trying to make up with his wife, my grandfather brought home the first of the many parakeets my grandparents would have over the years, and gradually, living on top of us all, Desdemona and Lefty made their next-to-last home together. For the next nine years, Desdemona complained of the cramped quarters and of the pain in her legs when she descended the stairs; but every time my father offered to move her downstairs, she refused. In my opinion, she enjoyed the attic because the vertigo of living up there reminded her of Mount Olympus. The dormer window provided a good view (not of sultans' tombs but of the Edison factory), and when she left the window open, the wind blew through as it used to do in Bithynios. Up in the attic, Desdemona and Lefty came back to where they started.

As does my story.

Because now Chapter Eleven, my five-year-old brother, and Jimmy Papanikolas are each holding a red egg. Dyed the color of the blood of Christ, more eggs fill a bowl on the dining room table. Red eggs are lined along the mantel. They hang in string pouches over doorways.

Zeus liberated all living things from an egg. *Ex ovo omnia.* The white flew up to become the sky, the yolk descended into earth. And on Greek Easter, we still play the egg-cracking game. Jimmy Papanikolas holds his egg out, passive, as Chapter Eleven rams his egg against it. Always only one egg cracks. "I win!" shouts Chapter Eleven. Now Milton selects an egg from the bowl. "This looks like a good one. Built like a Brinks truck." He holds it out. Chapter Eleven prepares to ram it. But before anything happens, my mother taps my father on the back. She has a thermometer in her mouth.

As dinner dishes are cleared from the table downstairs, my parents ascend hand in hand to their bedroom. As Desdemona cracks her egg against Lefty's, my parents shuck off a strict minimum of clothing. As Sourmelina, back from New Mexico for the holidays, plays the egg game with Mrs. Watson, my father lets out a small groan, rolls sideways off my mother, and declares, "That should do it."

The bedroom grows still. Inside my mother, a billion sperm swim upstream, males in the lead. They carry not only instructions about eye color, height, nose shape, enzyme production, microphage re-

384

sistance, but a story, too. Against a black background they swim, a long white silken thread spinning itself out. The thread began on a day two hundred and fifty years ago, when the biology gods, for their own amusement, monkeyed with a gene on a baby's fifth chromosome. That baby passed the mutation on to her son, who passed it on to his two daughters, who passed it on to three of their children (my great-great-greats, etc.), until finally it ended up in the bodies of my grandparents. Hitching a ride, the gene descended a mountain and left a village behind. It got trapped in a burning city and escaped, speaking bad French. Crossing the ocean, it faked a romance, circled a ship's deck, and made love in a lifeboat. It had its braids cut off. It took a train to Detroit and moved into a house on Hurlbut; it consulted dream books and opened an underground speakeasy; it got a job at Temple No. 1 . . . And then the gene moved on again, into new bodies . . . It joined the Boy Scouts and painted its toenails red; it played "Begin the Beguine" out the back window; it went off to war and stayed at home, watching newsreels; it took an entrance exam; posed like the movie magazines; received a death sentence and made a deal with St. Christopher; it dated a future priest and broke off an engagement; it was saved by a bosun's chair . . . always moving ahead, rushing along, only a few more curves left in the track now, Annapolis and a submarine chaser . . . until the biology gods knew this was their time, this was what they'd been waiting for, and as a spoon swung and a *yia yia* worried, my destiny fell into place . . . On March 20, 1954, Chapter Eleven arrived and the biology gods shook their heads, nope, sorry . . . But there was still time, everything was in place, the roller coaster was in free fall and there was no stopping it now, my father was seeing visions of little girls and my mother was praying to a Christ Pantocrator she didn't entirely believe in, until finally — right this minute! — on Greek Easter, 1959, it's about to happen. The gene is about to meet its twin.

As sperm meets egg, I feel a jolt. There's a loud sound, a sonic boom as my world cracks. I feel myself shift, already losing bits of my prenatal omniscience, tumbling toward the blank slate of personhood. (With the shred of all-knowingness I have left, I see my grandfather, Lefty Stephanides, on the night of my birth nine months from now, turning a demitasse cup upside down on a saucer. I see his coffee grounds forming a sign as pain explodes in his temple and he topples to the floor.) Again the sperm rams my capsule; and I realize I can't put it off any longer. The lease on my terrific little apartment is finally up and I'm being evicted. So I raise one fist (male-typically) and begin to beat on the walls of my eggshell until it cracks. Then, slippery as a yolk, I dive headfirst into the world.

"I'm sorry, little baby girl," my mother said in bed, touching her belly and already speaking to me. "I wanted it to be more romantic."

"You want romantic?" said my father. "Where's my clarinet?"

Book Three

Home Movies

My eyes, switched on at last, saw the following: a nurse reaching out to take me from the doctor; my mother's triumphant face, as big as Mount Rushmore, as she watched me heading for my first bath. (I said it was impossible, but still I remember it.) Also other things, material and immaterial: the relentless glare of OR lights; white shoes squeaking over white floors; a housefly contaminating gauze; and all around me, up and down the halls of Women's Hospital, individual dramas under way. I could sense the happiness of couples holding first babies and the fortitude of Catholics accepting their ninth. I could feel one young mother's disappointment at the reappearance of her husband's weak chin on the face of her newborn daughter, and a new father's terror as he calculated the tuition for triplets. On the floors above Delivery, in flowerless rooms, women lay recovering from hysterectomies and mastectomies. Teenage girls with burst ovarian cysts nodded out on morphine. It was all around me from the beginning, the weight of female suffering, with its biblical justification and vanishing acts.

The nurse who cleaned me up was named Rosalee. She was a pretty, long-faced woman from the Tennessee mountains. After suctioning the mucus from my nostrils, she gave me a shot of vitamin K to coagulate my blood. Inbreeding is common in Appalachia, as are genetic deformities, but Nurse Rosalee noticed nothing unusual about me. She was concerned about a purple splotch on my cheek, thinking it was a port-wine stain. It turned out to be placenta, and washed off. Nurse Rosalee carried me back to Dr. Philobosian for an anatomical exam. She placed me down on the table but kept one hand on me for security's sake. She'd noticed the doctor's hand tremor during the delivery.

In 1960, Dr. Nishan Philobosian was seventy-four. He had a camel's head, drooping on its neck, with all the activity in the cheeks. White hair surrounded his otherwise bald head in a nimbus and plugged his big ears like cotton. His surgeon's eyeglasses had rectangular loupes attached.

He began with my neck, searching for cretinous folds. He counted my fingers and toes. He inspected my palate; he noted my Moro reflex without surprise. He checked my backside for a sacral tail. Then, putting me on my back again, he took hold of each of my curved legs and pulled them apart.

What did he see? The clean, saltwater mussel of the female genitalia. The area inflamed, swollen with hormones. That touch of the baboon all babies have. Dr. Philobosian would have had to pull the folds apart to see any better, but he didn't. Because right at that instant Nurse Rosalee (for whom the moment was also destiny) accidentally touched his arm. Dr. Phil looked up. Presbyopic, Armenian eyes met middle-aged, Appalachian ones. The gaze lingered, then broke away. Five minutes old, and already the themes of my life — chance and sex — announced themselves. Nurse Rosalee blushed. "Beautiful," Dr. Philobosian said, meaning me but looking at his assistant. "A beautiful, healthy girl."

On Seminole, the birth celebrations were tempered by the prospect of death.

Desdemona had found Lefty on our kitchen floor, lying next to his overturned coffee cup. She knelt beside him and pressed an ear to his chest. When she heard no heartbeat, she cried out his name. Her wail echoed off the kitchen's hard surfaces: the toaster, the oven, the refrigerator. Finally she collapsed on his chest. In the silence that followed, however, Desdemona felt a strange emotion rising inside her. It spread in the space between her panic and grief. It was like a gas inflating her. Soon her eyes snapped open as she recognized the emotion: it was happiness. Tears were running down her face, she was already berating God for taking her husband from her, but on the other side of these proper emotions was an altogether improper relief. The worst had happened. This was it: the worst thing. For the first time in her life my grandmother had nothing to worry about.

Emotions, in my experience, aren't covered by single words. I don't believe in "sadness," "joy," or "regret." Maybe the best proof that the language is patriarchal is that it oversimplifies feeling. I'd like to have at my disposal complicated hybrid emotions, Germanic train-car constructions like, say, "the happiness that attends disaster." Or: "the disappointment of sleeping with one's fantasy." I'd like to show how "intimations of mortality brought on by aging family members" connects with "the hatred of mirrors that begins in middle age." I'd like to have a word for "the sadness inspired by failing restaurants" as well as for "the excitement of getting a room with a minibar." I've never had the right words to describe my life, and now that I've entered my story, I need them more than ever. I can't just sit back and watch from a distance anymore. From here on in, everything I'll tell you is colored by the subjective experience of being part of events. Here's where my story splits, divides, undergoes meiosis. Already the world feels heavier, now I'm a part of it. I'm talking about bandages and sopped cotton, the smell of mildew in movie theaters, and of all the lousy cats and their stinking litter boxes, of rain on city streets when the dust comes up and the old Italian men take their folding chairs inside. Up until now it hasn't been my world. Not my America. But here we are, at last.

The happiness that attends disaster didn't possess Desdemona for long. A few seconds later she returned her head to her husband's chest — and heard his heart beating! Lefty was rushed to the hospital. Two days later he regained consciousness. His mind was clear, his memory intact. But when he tried to ask whether the baby was a boy or a girl, he found he was unable to speak.

According to Julie Kikuchi, beauty is always freakish. Yesterday, over strudel and coffee at Café Einstein, she tried to prove this to me. "Look at this model," she said, holding up a fashion magazine. "Look at her ears. They belong on a Martian." She started flipping pages. "Or look at the mouth on this one. You could put your whole head in it."

I was trying to get another cappuccino. The waiters in their Austrian uniforms ignored me, as they do everyone, and outside, the yellow lindens were dripping and weeping.

"Or what about Jackie O.?" said Julie, still advocating. "Her eyes were so wide-set they were basically on the sides of her head. She looked like a hammerhead."

I'm working up with the foregoing to a physical description of myself. Baby pictures of the infant Calliope show a variety of features on the freakish side. My parents, looking fondly down into my crib, got stuck on every one. (I sometimes think that it was the arresting, slightly disturbing quality of my face that distracted everyone's attention from the complications below.) Imagine my crib as a diorama in a museum. Press one button and my ears light up like two golden trumpets. Press another and my stark chin begins to glow. Another, and the high, ethereal cheekbones appear out of the darkness. So far the effect isn't promising. On the evidence of ears, chin, and cheekbones I might be a baby Kafka. But the next button illuminates my mouth and things begin to improve. The mouth is small but well shaped, kissable, musical. Then, in the middle of the map, comes the nose. It is nothing like the noses you see in classical Greek sculpture. Here is a nose that came to Asia Minor, like silk itself, from the East. In this case, the Middle East. The nose of the diorama baby already forms, if you look closely, an arabesque. Ears, nose, mouth, chin — now eyes. Not only are they widely set (like Jackie O.'s), they're big. Too big for a baby's face. Eyes like my grandmother's. Eyes as big and sad as the eyes in a Keane painting. Eyes rimmed with long, dark eyelashes my mother couldn't believe had formed inside her. How had her body worked in such detail? The complexion around these eyes: a pale olive. The hair: jet black. Now press all the buttons at once. Can you see me? All of me? Probably not. No one ever really has.

As a baby, even as a little girl, I possessed an awkward, extravagant beauty. No single feature was right in itself and yet, when they were taken all together, something captivating emerged. An inadvertent harmony. A changeableness, too, as if beneath my visible face there was another, having second thoughts.

Desdemona wasn't interested in my looks. She was concerned with the state of my soul. "The baby she is two months old," she said to my father in March. "Why you still no baptize her?" "I don't want her baptized," answered Milton. "It's a bunch of hocus-pocus." "Hokey pokey is it?" Desdemona now threatened him with an index finger. "You think Holy Tradition that the Church keep for two thousand years is hokey pokey?" And then she called on the Panaghia, using every one of her names. "All-Holy, immaculate, most blessed and glorified Lady, Mother of God and Ever-Virgin, do you hear what my son Milton is saying?" When my father still refused, Desdemona unleashed her secret weapon. She started fanning herself.

To anyone who never personally experienced it, it's difficult to describe the ominous, storm-gathering quality of my grandmother's fanning. Refusing to argue anymore with my father, she walked on swollen ankles into the sun room. She sat down in a cane chair by the window. The winter light, coming from the side, reddened the far, translucent wing of her nose. She picked up her cardboard fan. The front of the fan was emblazoned with the words "Turkish Atrocities." Below, in smaller print, were the specifics: the 1955 pogrom in Istanbul in which 15 Greeks were killed, 200 Greek women raped, 4,348 stores looted, 59 Orthodox churches destroyed, and even the graves of the Patriarchs desecrated. Desdemona had six atrocity fans. They were a collector's set.

Each year she sent a contribution to the Patriarchate in Constantinople, and a few weeks later a new fan arrived, making claims of genocide and, in one case, bearing a photograph of Patriarch Athenagoras in the ruins of a looted cathedral. Not appearing on Desdemona's particular fan that day, but denounced nonetheless, was the most recent crime, committed not by the Turks but by her own Greek son, who refused to give his daughter a proper Orthodox baptism. Desdemona's fanning wasn't a matter of moving the wrist back and forth; the agitation came from deep within her. It originated from the spot between her stomach and liver where she once told me the Holy Spirit resided. It issued from a place deeper than her own buried crime. Milton tried to take shelter behind his newspaper, but the fan-disturbed air rustled the newsprint. The force of Desdemona's fanning could be felt all over the house; it swirled dustballs on the stairs; it stirred the window shades; and, of course, since it was winter, it made everyone shiver. After a while the entire house seemed to be hyperventilating. The fanning even pursued Milton into his Oldsmobile, which began to make a soft hissing from the radiator.

In addition to the fanning, my grandmother appealed to family feeling. Father

Mike, her son-in-law and my very own uncle, was by this time back from his years in Greece and serving — in an assistant capacity — at Assumption Greek Orthodox Church.

"Please, Miltie," Desdemona said. "Think of Father Mike. They never give him top job at the church. You think if his own niece she no gets baptized it will look good? Think of your sister, Miltie. Poor Zoë! They no have much money."

Finally, in a sign that he was weakening, my father asked my mother, "What do they charge for a baptism these days?"

"They're free."

Milton's eyebrows lifted. But after a moment's consideration he nodded, confirmed in his suspicions. "Figures. They let you in for free. Then you gotta pay for the rest of your life."

By 1960, the Greek Orthodox congregation of Detroit's East Side had yet another new building to worship in. Assumption had moved from Vernor Highway to a new site on Charlevoix. The erection of the Charlevoix church had been an event of great excitement. From the humble beginnings of the storefront on Hart Street, to the respectable but by no means splashy domicile off Beniteau, Assumption was finally going to get a grand church building. Many construction firms bid for the job, but in the end it was decided to give it to "someone from the community," and that someone was Bart Skiotis.

The motives behind building the new church were twofold: to resurrect the ancient splendor of Byzantium and to show the world the financial wherewithal of the prospering Greek American community. No expense was spared. An icon painter from Crete was imported to render the iconography. He stayed for over a year, sleeping in the unfinished structure on a thin mat. A traditionalist, he refrained from meat, alcohol, and sweets, in order to purify his soul and receive divine inspiration. Even his paintbrush was by the book, made from the tip of a squirrel's tail. Slowly, over two years, our East Side Hagia Sophia went up, not far from the Ford Freeway. There was only one problem. Unlike the icon painter, Bart Skiotis had not worked with a pure heart. It turned out that he had used inferior materials, siphoning the remaining cash into his personal bank account. He laid the foundation incorrectly, so that it wasn't long before cracks began to branch over the walls, scarring the iconography. The ceiling leaked, too.

Within the substandard construction of the Charlevoix church, literally upon a shaky foundation, I was baptized into the

Orthodox faith; a faith that had existed long before Protestantism had anything to protest and before Catholicism called itself catholic; a faith that stretched back to the beginnings of Christianity, when it was Greek and not Latin, and which, without an Aquinas to reify it, had remained shrouded in the smoke of tradition and mystery whence it began. My godfather, Jimmy Papanikolas, took me from my father's arms. He presented me to Father Mike. Smiling, overjoyed to be center stage for once, Father Mike cut a lock of my hair and tossed it into the baptismal pool. (It was this part of the ritual, I later suspected, that was responsible for the fuzzy quality of our font's surfaces. Years and years of baby hair, stimulated by the life-giving water, had taken root and grown.) But now Father Mike was ready for the dunking. "The servant of God, Calliope Helen is baptized in the Name of the Father, Amen . . ." and he pushed me under for the first time. In the Orthodox Church, we don't go in for partial immersion; no sprinkling, no forehead dabbing for us. In order to be reborn, you have to be buried first, so under the water I went. My family looked on, my mother seized with anxiety (what if I inhaled?), my brother dropping a penny into the water when no one was looking, my grandmother stilling her fan for the first time in weeks. Father Mike pulled me up into the air again — "and of the Son, Amen" — and dunked me under once more. This time I opened my eyes. Chapter Eleven's penny, in freefall, glinted through the murk. Down it sank to the bottom where, I now noticed, lots of things were collected: other coins, for instance, hairpins, somebody's old Band-Aid. In the green, scummy, holy water, I felt at peace. Everything was silent. The sides of my neck tingled in the place where humans once had gills. I was dimly aware that this beginning was somehow indicative of the rest of my life. My family were around me; I was in the hands of God. But I was in my own, separate element, too, submerged in rare sensations, pushing evolution's envelope. This knowledge whizzed through my mind, and then Father Mike pulled me up again — "and of the Holy Spirit, Amen . . ." One more dunking to go. Down I went and back up again, into light and air. The three submersions had taken a while. In addition to being murky, the water was warm. By the third time up, therefore, I had indeed been reborn: as a fountain. From between my cherubic legs a stream of crystalline liquid shot into the air. Lit from the dome above, its yellow scintillance arrested everyone's attention. The stream rose in an arc. Propelled by a full bladder, it cleared the lip of the font. And before my *nouno* had time to react, it struck Father Mike right in the middle of the face.

Suppressed laughter from the pews, a few old ladies gasping in horror, then silence. Disgraced by his own partial immersion — and dabbing himself like a Protestant — Father Mike completed the ceremony. Taking the chrism on his fingertips, he anointed me, marking the sign of the Cross on the required places, first my forehead, then eyes, nostrils, mouth, ears, breast, hands, and feet. As he touched each place, he said, "The seal of the gift of the Holy Spirit." Finally he gave me my First Communion (with one exception: Father Mike didn't forgive me for my sin).

"That's my girl," Milton crowed on the way home. "Pissed on a priest."

"It was an accident," Tessie insisted, still hot with embarrassment. "Poor Father Mike! He'll never get over it."

"That went really *far*," marveled Chapter Eleven.

In all the commotion, no one wondered about the engineering involved.

Desdemona took my reverse baptism of her son-in-law as a bad omen. Already potentially responsible for her husband's stroke, I had now committed a sacrilege at my first liturgical opportunity. In addition, I had humiliated her by being born a girl. "Maybe you should try guessing the weather," Sourmelina teased her. My father rubbed it in: "So much for your spoon, Ma. It sort of pooped out on you." The truth was that in those days Desdemona was struggling against assimilationist pressures she couldn't resist. Though she had lived in America as an eternal exile, a visitor for forty years, certain bits of her adopted country had been seeping under the locked doors of her disapproval. After Lefty came home from the hospital, my father took a TV up to the attic to provide some entertainment. It was a small black-and-white Zenith, prone to vertical shift. Milton placed it on a bedside table and went back downstairs. The television remained, rumbling, glowing. Lefty adjusted his pillows to watch. Desdemona tried to do housework but found herself looking over at the screen more and more often. She still didn't like cars. She covered her ears whenever the vacuum cleaner was on. But the TV was somehow different. My grandmother took to television right away. It was the first and only thing about America she approved of. Sometimes she forgot to turn the set off and would awaken at 2 a.m. to hear "The Star-Spangled Banner" playing before the station signed off.

The television replaced the sound of conversation that was missing from my grandparents' lives. Desdemona watched all day long, scandalized by the love affairs on *As the World Turns*. She liked detergent commercials especially, anything with animated scrubbing bubbles or avenging suds.

Living on Seminole contributed to the cultural imperialism. On Sundays, instead of serving Metaxa, Milton fixed cocktails for his guests. "Drinks with the names of people," Desdemona complained to her mute husband back in the attic. "Tom Collins. Harvey Wall Bang. This is a drink! And they are listening to music on the, how you say, the hi-fi. Milton he puts this music, and they drink Tom Collins and sometimes they are, you know, dancing, one on one, men together with the women. Like wrestling."

What was I to Desdemona but another sign of the end of things? She tried not to look at me. She hid behind her fans. Then one day Tessie had to go out and Desdemona was forced to baby-sit. Warily, she entered my bedroom. Taking cautious steps, she approached my crib. Black-draped sexagenarian leaned down to examine pink-swaddled infant. Maybe something in my expression set off an alarm. Maybe she was already making the connections she would later make, between village babies and this suburban one, between old wives' tales and new endocrinology . . . Then again, maybe not. Because as she peered distrustfully over the rail of my crib, she saw my face — and blood intervened. Desdemona's worried expression hovered above my (similarly) perplexed one. Her mournful eyes gazed down at my (equally) large black orbs. Everything about us was the same. And so she picked me up and I did what grandchildren are supposed to do: I erased the years between us. I gave Desdemona back her original skin.

From then on, I was her favorite. Midmornings she would relieve my mother by taking me up to the attic. Lefty had regained most of his strength by this time. Despite his speech paralysis, my grandfather remained a vital person. He got up early every day, bathed, shaved, and put on a necktie to translate Attic Greek for two hours before breakfast. He no longer had aspirations to publish his translations but did the work because he liked it and because it kept his mind sharp. In order to communicate with the rest of the family, he kept a little chalkboard with him at all times. He wrote messages in words and personal hieroglyphics. Aware that he and Desdemona were a burden to my parents, Lefty was extremely helpful around the house, doing repairs, assisting with the cleaning, running errands. Every afternoon he took his three-mile walk, no matter the weather, and returned cheerful, his smile full of gold fillings. At night he listened to his rebetika records in the attic and smoked his hookah pipe. Whenever Chapter Eleven asked what was in the pipe, Lefty wrote on his chalkboard, "Turkish mud." My parents always believed it was an aromatic brand of tobacco. Where Lefty obtained the hash is anybody's guess. Out on his walks, probably. He still had lots of Greek and Lebanese contacts in the city.

From ten to noon every day my grandparents took care of me. Desdemona fed me my bottles and changed my diapers. She finger-combed my hair. When I got fussy, Lefty carried me around the room. Since he couldn't speak to me, he bounced me a lot and hummed to me, and touched his big, arching nose to my little, latent one. My grandfather was like a dignified, unpainted mime, and I was almost five before I realized that anything was wrong with him. When he tired of making faces, he carried me to the dormer window, where, together, from the opposite ends of life, we gazed down at our leafy neighborhood.

Soon I was walking. Animated by

brightly wrapped presents, I scampered into the frames of my father's home movies. On those first celluloid Christmases I look as overdressed as the Infanta. Starved for a daughter, Tessie went a little overboard in dressing me. Pink skirts, lace ruffles, Yuletide bows in my hair. I didn't like the clothes, or the prickly Christmas tree, and am usually shown bursting dramatically into tears . . .

Or it might have been my father's cinematography. Milton's camera came equipped with a rack of merciless floodlights. The brightness of those films gives them the quality of Gestapo interrogations. Holding up our presents, we all cringe, as though caught with contraband. Aside from their blinding brightness, there was another odd thing about Milton's home movies: like Hitchcock, he always appeared in them. The only way to check the amount of film left in the camera was by reading the counter inside the lens. In the middle of Christmas scenes or birthday parties there always came a moment when Milton's eye would fill the screen. So that now, as I quickly try to sketch my early years, what comes back most clearly is just that: the brown orb of my father's sleepy, bearish eye. A postmodern touch in our domestic cinema, pointing up artifice, calling attention to mechanics. (And bequeathing me my aesthetic.) Milton's eye regarded us. It blinked. An eye as big as the Christ Pantocrator's at church, it was better than any mosaic. It was a living eye, the cornea a little bloodshot, the eyelashes luxuriant, the skin underneath coffee-stained and pouchy. This eye would stare us down for as long as ten seconds. Finally the camera would pull away, still recording. We'd see the ceiling, the lighting fixture, the floor, and then us again: the Stephanides.

First of all, Lefty. Still dapper despite stroke damage, wearing a starched white shirt and glen-plaid trousers, he writes on his chalkboard and holds it up: *"Christos Anesti."* Desdemona sits across from him, her dentures making her look like a snapping turtle. My mother, in this home movie marked "Easter '62," is two years from turning forty. The crow's-feet around her eyes are another reason (aside from the floodlights) why she holds a hand over her face. In this gesture I see the emotional sympathy I've always felt with Tessie, the two of us never happier than when unobserved, people-watching. Behind her hand I can see the traces of the novel she stayed up reading the previous night. All the big words she had to look up in the dictionary crowd her tired head, waiting to show up in the letters she writes me today. Her

410

hand is also a refusal, her only way of getting back at a husband who has begun to disappear on her. (Milton came home every night; he didn't drink or womanize but, preoccupied with business worries, he began to leave a little more of himself at the diner each day, so that the man who returned to us seemed less and less present, a kind of robot who carved turkeys and filmed holidays but who wasn't really there at all.) Finally, of course, my mother's upraised hand is a kind of warning, too, a predecessor of the black box.

Chapter Eleven sprawls on the carpet, wolfing candy. Grandson of the two former silk farmers (with chalkboard and worry beads), he has never had to help in the cocoonery. He has never been to the Koza Han. Environment has already made its imprint on him. He has the tyrannical, self-absorbed look of American children . . .

And now two dogs come bounding into the frame. Rufus and Willis, our two boxers. Rufus sniffs my diaper and, with perfect comic timing, sits on me. He will later bite someone, and both dogs will be given away. My mother appears, shooing Rufus . . . and there I am again. I stand up and toddle toward the camera, smiling, trying out my wave . . .

I know this film well. "Easter '62" was

the home movie Dr. Luce talked my parents into giving him. This was the film he screened each year for his students at Cornell University Medical School. This was the thirty-five-second segment that, Luce insisted, proved out his theory that gender identity is established early on in life. This was the film Dr. Luce showed to me, to tell me who I was. And who was that? Look at the screen. My mother is handing me a baby doll. I take the baby and hug it to my chest. Putting a toy bottle to the baby's lips, I offer it milk.

My early childhood passed, on film and otherwise. I was brought up as a girl and had no doubts about this. My mother bathed me and taught me how to clean myself. From everything that happened later, I would guess that these instructions in feminine hygiene were rudimentary at best. I don't remember any direct allusions to my sexual apparatus. All was shrouded in a zone of privacy and fragility, where my mother never scrubbed me too hard. (Chapter Eleven's apparatus was called a "pitzi." But for what I had there was no word at all.) My father was even more squeamish. In the rare times he diapered me or gave me a bath, Milton studiously averted his eyes. "Did you wash her all over?" my mother would ask him, speaking obliquely as usual. "Not *all* over. That's your department."

It wouldn't have mattered anyway. 5-alpha-reductase deficiency syndrome is a skillful counterfeiter. Until I reached puberty and androgens flooded my bloodstream, the ways in which I differed from other little girls were hard to detect. My pediatrician never noticed anything unusual. And by the time I was five Tessie had started taking me to Dr. Phil — Dr. Phil with his failing eyesight and his cursory examinations.

On January 8, 1967, I turned seven years old. 1967 marked the end of many things in Detroit, but among these was my father's home movies. "Callie's 7th B-Day" was the last of Milton's Super 8s. The setting was our dining room, decorated with balloons. On my head sits the usual conical hat. Chapter Eleven, twelve years old, does not join the boys and girls at the table but instead stands back against the wall, drinking punch. The difference in our ages meant that my brother and I were never close growing up. When I was a baby Chapter Eleven was a kid, when I was a kid he was a teenager, and by the time I became a teenager he was an adult. At twelve, my brother liked nothing better than to cut golf balls in half to see what was inside. Usually, his vivisection of

413

Wilsons and Spaldings revealed cores consisting of extremely tightly bundled rubber bands. But sometimes there were surprises. In fact, if you look very closely at my brother in this home movie, you will notice a strange thing: his face, arms, shirt, and pants are covered by thousands of tiny white dots.

Just before my birthday party had started, Chapter Eleven had been down in his basement laboratory, using a hacksaw on a newfangled Titleist that advertised a "liquid center." The ball was held firmly in a vise as Chapter Eleven sawed. When he reached the center of the Titleist, there was a loud popping sound followed by a puff of smoke. The center of the ball was empty. Chapter Eleven was mystified. But when he emerged from the basement, we all saw the dots . . .

Back at the party, my birthday cake is coming out with its seven candles. My mother's silent lips are telling me to make a wish. What did I wish for at seven? I don't remember. In the film I lean forward and, Aeolian, blow the candles out. In a moment, they re-ignite. I blow them out again. Same thing happens. And then Chapter Eleven is laughing, entertained at last. That was how our home movies ended, with a prank on my birthday. With candles that had multiple lives.

The question remains: Why was this Milton's last movie? Can it be explained by the usual petering out of parents' enthusiasm for documenting their children on film? By the fact that Milton took hundreds of baby photographs of Chapter Eleven and no more than twenty or so of me? To answer these questions, I need to go behind the camera and see things through my father's eyes.

The reason Milton was disappearing on us: after ten years in business, the diner was no longer making a profit. Through the front window (over Athena olive oil tins) my father looked out day after day at the changes on Pingree Street. The white family who'd lived across the way, good customers once, had moved out. Now the house belonged to a colored man named Morrison. He came into the diner to buy cigarettes. He ordered coffee, asked for a million refills, and smoked. He never ordered any food. He didn't seem to have a job. Sometimes other people moved into his house, a young woman, maybe Morrison's daughter, with her kids. Then they were gone and it was just Morrison again. There was a tarp up on his roof with bricks around it, to cover a hole.

Just down the block an after-hours place had opened up. Its patrons urinated in the doorway of the diner on their way home.

Streetwalkers had started working Twelfth Street. The dry cleaner's on the next block over had been held up, the white owner severely beaten. A. A. Laurie, who ran the optometrist's shop next door, took down his eye chart from the wall as workers removed the neon eyeglasses out front. He was moving to a new shop in Southfield.

My father had considered doing the same.

"That whole neighborhood's going down the tubes," Jimmy Fioretos had advised one Sunday after dinner. "Get out while the getting's good."

And then Gus Panos, who had had a tracheotomy and spoke through a hole in his neck, hissing like a bellows: "Jimmy's right . . . sssss . . . You should move out to . . . ssss . . . Bloomfield Hills."

Uncle Pete had disagreed, making his usual case for integration and support for President Johnson's War on Poverty.

A few weeks later, Milton had had the business appraised and was met with a shock: the Zebra Room was worth less than when Lefty had acquired it in 1933. Milton had waited too long to sell it. The getting out was no longer good.

And so the Zebra Room remained on the corner of Pingree and Dexter, the swing music on the jukebox growing increasingly out of date, the celebrities and sports figures on the walls more and more unrecognizable. On Saturdays, my grandfather often took me for a ride in the car. We drove out to Belle Isle to look for deer and then stopped in for lunch at the family restaurant. At the diner we sat in a booth while Milton waited on us, pretending we were customers. He took Lefty's order and winked. "And what'll the Mrs. have?"

"I'm not the Mrs.!"

"You're not?"

I ordered my usual of a cheeseburger, milk shake, and lemon meringue pie for dessert. Opening the cash register, Milton gave me a stack of quarters to use in the jukebox. While I chose songs, I looked out the front window for my neighborhood friend. Most Saturdays he was installed on the corner, surrounded by other young men. Sometimes he stood on a broken chair or a cinder block while he orated. Always his arm was in the air, waving and gesticulating. But if he happened to see me, his raised fist would open up, and he would wave.

His name was Marius Wyxzewixard Challouehliczilczese Grimes. I was not allowed to speak to him. Milton considered Marius to be a troublemaker, a view in which many Zebra Room patrons, white and black both, concurred. I liked him, though. He called me "Little Queen of the

Nile." He said I looked like Cleopatra. "Cleopatra was Greek," he said. "Did you know that?" "No." "Yeah, she was. She was a Ptolemy. Big family back then. They were Greek Egyptians. I've got a little Egyptian blood in me, too. You and me are probably related." If he was standing on his broken chair, waiting for a crowd to form, he would talk to me. But if other people were there he would be too busy.

Marius Wyxzewixard Challouehliczilczese Grimes had been named after an Ethiopian nationalist, a contemporary of Fard Muhammad, in fact, back in the thirties. Marius had been an asthmatic child. He'd spent most of his childhood inside, reading the eclectic books in his mother's library. As a teenager he'd been beaten up a lot (he wore glasses, Marius did, and had a habit of mouth-breathing). But by the time I got to know him, Marius W. C. Grimes was coming into his manhood. He worked at a record store and was going to U. of D. Law School, nights. There was something happening in the country, in the black neighborhoods especially, that was conducive to the ascension of a brother like Marius to the corner soapbox. It was suddenly cool to know stuff, to expatiate on the causes of the Spanish Civil War. Ché Guevara had asthma, too. And Marius wore a beret. A black paramilitary beret with black glasses and a little fledgling soul patch. In beret and glasses Marius stood on the corner waking people up to things. "Zebra Room," he pointed a bony finger, "white-owned." Then the finger went down the block. "TV store, white-owned. Grocery store, white-owned. Bank . . ." Brothers looked around . . . "You got it. No bank. They don't give loans to black folks." Marius was planning to become a public advocate. As soon as he graduated from law school he was going to sue the city of Dearborn for housing discrimination. He was currently number three in his law school class. But now it was humid out, his childhood asthma acting up, and Marius was feeling unhappy and unwell when I came roller-skating by.

"Hi, Marius."

He did not vocally respond, a sign with him that he was in low spirits. But he nodded his head, which gave me the courage to continue.

"Why don't you get a better chair to stand on?"

"You don't like my chair?"

"It's all broken."

"This chair is an antique. That means it's supposed to be broken."

"Not that broken."

But Marius was squinting across the street at the Zebra Room.

"Let me ask you something, little Cleo."

"What?"

"How come there's always at least three big fat officers of the so-called peace sitting at the counter of your dad's place?"

"He gives them free coffee."

"And why do you think he does that?"

"I don't know."

"You don't know? Okay, I'll tell you. He's paying protection money. Your old man likes to keep the fuzz around because he's scared of us black folks."

"He is not," I said, suddenly defensive.

"You don't think so?"

"No."

"Okay, then, Queenie. You know best."

But Marius's accusation bothered me. After that, I began to watch my father more closely. I noticed how he always locked the car doors when we drove through the black neighborhood. I heard him in the living room on Sundays: "They don't take care of their properties. They let everything go to hell." The next week, when Lefty took me to the diner, I was more aware than ever of the broad backs of policemen at the counter. I heard them joking with my father. "Hey, Milt, you better start putting some soul food on the menu."

"Think so?" — my father, jovially — "Maybe a little collard greens?"

I snuck out, going to look for Marius. He was in his usual spot but sitting, not standing, and reading a book.

"Test tomorrow," he told me. "Gotta study."

"I'm in second grade," I said.

"Only second! I had you down for high school at least."

I gave him my most winning smile.

"Must be that Ptolemy blood. Just stay away from the Roman men, okay?"

"What?"

"Nothing, Little Queen. Just playing with you." He was laughing now, which he didn't do that often. His face opened up, bright.

And suddenly my father was shouting my name. "Callie!"

"What?"

"Get over here right now!"

Marius stood up awkwardly from his chair. "We were just talking," he said. "Smart little girl you got here."

"You stay away from her, you hear me?"

"Daddy!" I protested, appalled, embarrassed for my friend.

But Marius's voice was soft. "It's cool, little Cleo. Got this test and all. Go on back to your dad."

For the rest of that day Milton kept after me. "You are never, ever, to talk to strangers like that. What's the matter with you?"

"He's not a stranger. His name is Marius Wyxzewixard Challouehliczilczese Grimes."

"You hear me? You stay away from people like that."

Afterward, Milton told my grandfather to stop bringing me down to the diner for lunch. But I would come again, in just a few months, under my own power.

Opa!

❀❀❀

They always think it's the old-school, gentlemanly routine. The slowness of my advances. The leisurely pace of my incursions. (I've learned to make the first move by now, but not the second.)

I invited Julie Kikuchi to go away for the weekend. To Pomerania. The idea was to drive to Usedom, an island in the Baltic, and stay in an old resort once favored by Wilhelm II. I made a point to emphasize that we would have separate rooms.

Since it was the weekend, I tried to dress down. It isn't easy for me. I wore a camel-hair turtleneck, tweed blazer, and jeans. And a pair of handmade cordovans by Edward Green. This particular style is called the Dundee. They look dressy until you notice the Vibram soles. The leather is of a double thickness. The Dundee is a shoe designed for touring the landed estates, for tromping through mud while wearing a tie, with your spaniels trailing behind. I had to wait four months for these shoes. On the shoebox it says: "Edward Green: Master

423

Shoemakers to the Few." That's me exactly. The few.

I picked Julie up in a rented Mercedes, an unquiet diesel. She had made a bunch of tapes for the ride and had brought reading material: *The Guardian*, the last two issues of *Parkett*. We drove out the narrow, tree-lined roads to the northeast. We passed villages of thatch-roofed houses. The land grew marshier, inlets appeared, and soon we traveled over the bridge to the island.

Shall I get right to it? No, slowly, leisurely, that's the way. Let me first mention that it is October here in Germany. Though the weather was cool, the beach at Herringsdorf was dotted with quite a few diehard nudists. Primarily men, they lay walrus-like on towels or boisterously congregated in the striped *Strandkörbe,* the little beach huts.

From the elegant boardwalk surrounded by pine and birch trees, I looked out at these naturists and wondered what I always wonder: What is it like to feel free like that? I mean, my body is so much better than theirs. I'm the one with the well-defined biceps, the bulging pectorals, the burnished glutes. But I could never saunter around in public like that.

"Not exactly the cover of *Sunshine and Health*," said Julie.

"After a certain age, people should keep their clothes on," I said, or something like that. When in doubt I resort to mildly conservative or British-sounding pronouncements. I wasn't thinking about what I was saying. I had suddenly forgotten all about the nudists. Because I was looking at Julie now. She had pushed her silver DDR-era eyeglasses onto the top of her head so that she could take pictures of the distant sunbathers. The wind off the Baltic was making her hair fly around. "Your eyebrows are like little black caterpillars," I said. "Flatterer," said Julie, still shooting. I said nothing else. As one does the return of sun after winter, I stood still and accepted the warm glow of possibility, of feeling right in the company of this small, oddly fierce person with the inky hair and the lovely, unemphasized body.

Still, that night, and the night after, we slept in separate rooms.

My father forbade me to talk to Marius Grimes in April, a damp, cool-headed month in Michigan. By May the weather grew warm; June was hot and July hotter still. In the backyard of our house on Seminole, I jumped through the sprinkler in my bathing suit, a two-piece number, while Chapter Eleven picked dandelions to make dandelion wine.

During that summer, as the temperature climbed, Milton tried to come to grips with the predicament he found himself in. His vision had been to open not one restaurant but a chain. Now he realized that the first link in that chain, the Zebra Room, was a weak one, and he was thrown into doubt and confusion. For the first time in his life Milton Stephanides came up against a possibility he'd never entertained: failure. What was he going to do with the restaurant? Should he sell it for peanuts? What then? (For the time being, he decided to close the diner on Mondays and Tuesdays to cut payroll expenses.)

My father and mother didn't discuss the situation in front of us and slipped into Greek when discussing it with our grandparents. Chapter Eleven and I were left to figure out what was going on by the tone of a conversation that made no sense to us, and to be honest, we didn't pay much attention. We only knew that Milton was suddenly around the house during the day. Milton, whom we had rarely seen in sunlight before, was suddenly out in the backyard, reading the newspaper. We discovered what our father's legs looked like in short pants. We discovered what he looked like when he didn't shave. The first two days his face got sandpapery the way it always did on weekends. But now, instead of seizing my hand and rubbing it against his whiskers until I screamed, Milton no longer had the high spirits to torment me. He just sat on the patio as the beard, like a stain, like a fungus, spread.

Unconsciously Milton was adhering to the Greek custom of not shaving after a death in the family. Only in this case what had ended wasn't a life but a livelihood. The beard fattened up his already plump face. He didn't keep it trimmed or very clean. And because he didn't utter a word about his troubles, his beard began to express silently all the things he wouldn't allow himself to say. Its knots and whorls indicated his increasingly tangled thoughts. Its bitter odor released the ketones of stress. As summer progressed, the beard grew shaggy, *unmown,* and it was obvious that Milton was thinking about Pingree Street; he was going to seed the way Pingree Street was.

Lefty tried to comfort his son. "Be strong," he wrote. With a smile he copied out the warrior epitaph at Thermopylae: "Go tell the Spartans, stranger passing by/ that here obedient to their laws we lie." But Milton barely read the quote. His father's stroke had convinced him that Lefty was no longer at the top of his game. Mute, carrying his pitiful chalkboard around, lost in his restoration of Sappho,

Lefty had begun to seem old to his son. Milton found himself getting impatient or not paying attention. *Intimations of mortality brought on by aging family members,* that's what Milton felt, seeing his father sunk in desk light, jutting out a moist underlip, scanning a dead language.

Despite the Cold War secrecy, bits of information leaked out to us kids. The deepening threat to our finances made itself known in the form of a jagged wrinkle, like a lightning bolt, that flashed above the bridge of my mother's nose whenever I asked for something expensive in a toy store. Meat began appearing less often on our dinner table. Milton rationed electricity. If Chapter Eleven left a light on for more than a minute, he returned to total darkness. And to a voice in the darkness: "What did I tell you about kilowatts!" For a while we lived with a single lightbulb, which Milton carried from room to room. "This way I can keep track of how much power we're using," he said, screwing the bulb into the dining room fixture so that we could sit down to dinner. "I can't see my food," Tessie complained. "What do you mean?" said Milton. "This is what they call *ambiance.*" After dessert, Milton took a handkerchief out of his back pocket, unscrewed the hot lightbulb, and, tossing it like an unambitious juggler, conveyed it into the living room. We waited in darkness as he fumbled through the house, knocking into furniture. Finally there was a brownout in the distance and Milton cheerily called out, "Ready!"

He kept up a brave front. He hosed down the sidewalk outside the diner and kept the windows spotless. He continued to greet customers with a hearty "How's everything?" or a *"Yahsou, patriote!"* But the Zebra Room's swing music and old-time baseball players couldn't stop time. It was no longer 1940 but 1967. Specifically, the night of Sunday, July 23, 1967. And there was something lumpy under my father's pillow.

Behold my parents' bedroom: furnished entirely in Early American reproductions, it offers them connection (at discount prices) with the country's founding myths. Notice, for instance, the veneer headboard of the bed, made from "pure cherrywood," as Milton likes to say, just like the little tree George Washington chopped down. Direct your attention to the wallpaper with its Revolutionary War motif. A repeating pattern showing the famous trio of drummer boy, fife player, and lame old man. Throughout my earliest years on earth those bloodied figures marched around my parents' bedroom, here disappearing behind a "Monticello" dresser, there emerging from behind a "Mount Vernon" mirror, or sometimes having no place to go at all and being cut in half by a closet.

Forty-three years old now, my parents, on this historic night, lie sound asleep. Milton's snores make the bed rattle; also, the wall connecting to my room, where I'm asleep myself in a grownup bed. And something else is rattling beneath Milton's pillow, a potentially dangerous situation considering what the object is. Under my father's pillow is the .45 automatic he brought back from the war.

Chekhov's first rule of playwriting goes something like this: "If there's a gun on the wall in act one, scene one, you must fire the gun by act three, scene two." I can't help thinking about that storytelling precept as I contemplate the gun beneath my father's pillow. There it is. I can't take it away now that I've mentioned it. (It really was there that night.) And there are bullets in the gun and the safety is off . . .

Detroit, in the stifling summer of 1967, is bracing for race riots. Watts had exploded two summers earlier. Riots had broken out in Newark recently. In response to the national turmoil, the all-white Detroit police force has been raiding after-hours bars in the city's black neighborhoods. The idea is to make preemptive strikes against possible flashpoints. Usually, the police park their paddy wagons in back alleys and herd the patrons into the vehicles without anyone seeing. But tonight, for reasons that will never be explained, three police vehicles arrive at the Economy Printing Co. at 9125 Twelfth Street — three blocks from Pingree — and park at the curb. You might think this wouldn't matter at five in the morning, but you would be wrong. Because in 1967, Detroit's Twelfth Street is open all night.

For instance, as the police arrive, there are girls lined along the street, girls in miniskirts, thigh-highs, and halter tops. (The sea wrack Milton hoses from the sidewalk every morning includes the dead jellyfish of prophylactics and the occasional hermit crab of a lost high heel.) The girls stand at the curbs as cars cruise by. Key-lime Cadillacs, fire-red Toronados, wide-mouthed, trolling Lincolns, all in perfect shape. Chrome glints. Hubcaps shine. Not a single rust spot anywhere. (Which is something that always amazes Milton about black people, the contradiction between the perfection of their automobiles and the disrepair of their houses.) . . . But now the gleaming cars are slowing. Windows are rolling down and girls are bending to chat with the drivers. There are calls back and forth, the lifting of already minuscule skirts, and sometimes a flash of breast or an obscene gesture, the girls working it, laughing, high enough by 5 a.m. to be numb to the rawness between their legs and the residues of men no amount of perfume can get rid of. It isn't easy to keep yourself clean on the street, and by this hour each of those young women smells in the places that count like a very ripe, soft French cheese . . . They're numb, too, to thoughts of babies left at home, six-month-olds with bad colds lying in used cribs, sucking on pacifiers, and having a hard time breathing . . . numb to the lingering taste of semen in their mouths along with peppermint gum, most of these girls no more than eighteen, this curb on Twelfth Street their first real place of employment, the most the country has to offer in the way of a vocation. Where are they going to go from here? They're numb to that, too, except for a couple who have dreams of singing backup or opening up a hair shop . . . But this is all part of what happened that night, what's about to happen (the police are getting out of their cars now, they are breaking in the door of the blind pig) . . . as a window opens and someone yells, "It's the fuzz! Out the back way!" At the curb the girls recognize the cops because they have to do them for free. But something is different tonight, something is happening . . . the girls don't disappear as usual when the cops show up. They stand and watch as the clients of the blind pig are led out in handcuffs, and a few girls even begin to grumble . . . and now other doors are opening and cars are stopping and suddenly everyone is out on the street . . . people stream out of other blind pigs and from houses and from street corners and you can feel it in the air, the way the air has somehow been keeping score, and how at this moment in July of 1967 the tally of abuses has reached a point so that the imperative flies out from Watts and Newark to Twelfth Street in Detroit, as one girl shouts, "Get yo' hands offa them, motherfucking pigs!" . . . and then there are other shouts, and pushing, and a bottle just misses a policeman and shatters a squad car window behind . . . and back on Seminole my father is sleeping on a gun that has just been recommissioned, because the riots have begun . . .

At 6:23 a.m., the Princess telephone in my bedroom rang and I picked it up. It was Jimmy Fioretos, who in his panic mistook my voice for my mother's. "Tessie, tell Milt to get down to the restaurant. The coloreds are rioting!"

"Stephanides residence," I continued politely, as I'd been taught. "Callie speaking."

"Callie? Jesus. Honey, let me speak to your father?"

"Just one minute please." I put down the pink phone, walked into my parents' bedroom, and shook my father awake.

"It's Mr. Fioretos."

"Jimmy? Christ, what does he want?" He lifted his cheek, in which could be discerned the imprint of a gun barrel.

"He says somebody's rioting."

At which point, my father jumped out of bed. As though he still weighed one hundred and forty pounds instead of one ninety, Milton flipped gymnastically into the air and landed on his feet, completely unaware of both his nakedness and his dream-filled morning erection. (So it was that the Detroit riots will always be connected in my mind with my first sight of the aroused male genitalia. Even worse, they were my father's, and worst of all, he was reaching for a gun. Sometimes a cigar is not a cigar.) Tessie was up now, too, shouting at Milton not to go, and Milton was hopping on one foot, trying to put on his pants; and before long everybody was into it.

"I tell you this what happen!" Desdemona screamed at Milton as he ran down the stairs. "Do you fix the church for St. Christopher? No!"

"Leave it to the police, Milt," Tessie pleaded.

And Chapter Eleven: "When are you going to be back, Dad? You promised to take me to Radio Shack today."

And me, still squeezing my eyes shut to erase what I'd seen: "I think I'll go back to bed now."

The only person who didn't say something was Lefty, because in all the confusion he couldn't find his chalkboard.

Half-dressed, in shoes but no socks, in pants but no underpants, Milton Stephanides raced his Delta 88 through the early morning streets. All the way to Woodward nothing seemed amiss. The roads were clear. Everyone was still asleep. As he turned onto West Grand Boulevard, however, he saw a pillar of smoke rising into the air. Unlike all the other pillars of smoke issuing from the city's smokestacks, this pillar didn't disperse into the general smog. It hung low to the ground like a vengeful tornado. It churned and kept its fearsome shape, fed by what it consumed. The Oldsmobile was heading straight for it. Suddenly people appeared. People running. People carrying things. People laughing and looking over their shoulders while other people waved their hands, appealing for them to stop. Sirens wailed. A police car raced past. The officer at the wheel signaled Milton to turn back, but Milton did not obey.

And it was funny, because these were his streets. Milton had known them his whole life. Over there on Lincoln there used to be a fruit stand. Lefty used to stop there with Milton to buy cantaloupes, teaching Milton how to pick a sweet one by looking for tiny punctures left by bees. Over on Trumbull was where Mrs. Tsatsarakis lived. *Used to always ask me to bring up Vernors from the basement,* Milton thought to himself. *Couldn't climb stairs anymore.* On the corner of Sterling and Commonwealth was the old Masonic Temple, where one Saturday afternoon thirty-five years before, Milton had been runner-up in a spelling bee. A spelling bee! Two dozen kids in their best clothes concentrating as hard as they could to piece out "prestidigitation" one letter at a time. That's what used to happen in this neighborhood. Spelling bees! Now ten-year-olds were running in the streets, carrying bricks. They were throwing bricks through store windows, laughing and jumping, thinking it was some kind of game, some kind of holiday.

Milton looked away from the dancing children and saw the pillar of smoke right in front of him, blocking the street. There was a second or two when he could have turned back. But he didn't. He hit it dead on. The Oldsmobile's hood ornament disappeared first, then the front fenders and the roof. The taillights gleamed redly for a moment and then winked out.

In every chase scene we'd ever watched, the hero always climbed up to the roof. Strict realists in my family, we always objected: "Why do they always go up?" "Watch. He's going to climb the tower. See? I told you." But Hollywood knew more about human nature than we realized. Because, faced with this emergency, Tessie took Chapter Eleven and me up to the attic. Maybe it was a vestige of our arboreal past; we wanted to climb up and out of danger. Or maybe my mother felt safer there because of the door that blended in with the wallpaper. Whatever the reason, we took a suitcase full of food up to the attic and stayed there for three days, watching the city burn on my grandparents' small black-and-white. In housedress and sandals, Desdemona held her cardboard fan to her chest, shielding herself against the spectacle of life repeating itself. "Oh my God! Is like Smyrna! Look at the *mavros!* Like the Turks they are burning everything!"

It was hard to argue with the comparison. In Smyrna people had taken their furniture down to the waterfront; and on television now people were carrying furniture, too. Men were lugging brand-new sofas out of stores. Refrigerators were sailing along the avenues, as were stoves and dishwashers. And just like in Smyrna everyone seemed to have packed all their clothes. Women were wearing minks despite the July heat. Men were trying on new suits and running at the same time. "Smyrna! Smyrna! Smyrna!" Desdemona kept wailing, and I'd already heard so much about Smyrna in my seven years that I watched the screen closely to see what it had been like. But I didn't understand. Sure, buildings were burning, bodies were lying in the street, but the mood wasn't one of desperation. I'd never seen people so happy in my entire life. Men were playing instruments taken from a music store. Other men were handing whiskey bottles through a shattered window and passing them around. It looked more like a block party than it did a riot.

Up until that night, our neighborhood's basic feeling about our fellow Negro citizens could be summed up in something Tessie said after watching Sidney Poitier's performance in *To Sir with Love*, which opened a month before the riots. She said, "You see, they can speak perfectly normal if they want." That was how we felt. (Even me back then, I won't deny it, because we're all the children of our parents.) We were ready to accept the Negroes. We weren't prejudiced against them. We wanted to include them in our society *if they would only act normal!*

In their support for Johnson's Great Society, in their applause after *To Sir with Love,* our neighbors and relatives made clear their well-intentioned belief that the Negroes were fully capable of being just like white people — but then what was this? they asked themselves as they saw the pictures on television. What were those young men doing carrying a sofa down the street? Would Sidney Poitier ever take a sofa or a large kitchen appliance from a store without paying? Would he dance like that in front of a burning building? "No respect for private property whatsoever," cried Mr. Benz, who lived next door. And his wife Phyllis: "Where are they going to live if they burn down their own neighborhood?" Only Aunt Zo seemed to sympathize: "I don't know. If I was walking down the street and there was a mink coat just sitting there, I might take it." "Zoë!" Father Mike was shocked. "That's stealing!" "Oh, what isn't, when you come right down to it. This whole country's stolen."

For three days and two nights we waited in the attic to hear from Milton. The fires had knocked out phone service, and when my mother called the restaurant, all she got was a recorded message with an operator's voice.

For three days no one left the attic except Tessie, who hurried downstairs to get food from our emptying cupboards. We watched the death toll rise.

Day 1: Deaths 15
       Injuries 500
       Stores looted 1,000
       Fires 800
Day 2: Deaths 27
       Injuries 700
       Stores looted 1,500
       Fires 1,000
Day 3: Deaths 36
       Injuries 1,000
       Stores looted 1,700
       Fires 1,163

For three days we studied the photographs of the victims as they appeared on TV. Mrs. Sharon Stone, struck by a sniper's bullet as her car was stopped at a traffic light. Carl E. Smith, a fireman, killed by a sniper as he battled a blaze.

For three days we watched the politicians hesitate and argue: the Republican governor, George Romney, asking President Johnson to send in federal troops; and Johnson, a Democrat, saying he had an "inability" to do such a thing. (There was an election coming up in the fall. The worse the riots got, the worse Romney was going to do. And so before he sent in the paratroopers, President Johnson sent in Cyrus Vance to assess the situation. Nearly twenty-four hours passed before federal troops arrived. In the meantime the inexperienced National Guard was shooting up the town.)

For three days we didn't bathe or brush our teeth. For three days all the normal rituals of our life were suspended, while half-forgotten rituals, like praying, were renewed. Desdemona said the prayers in Greek as we gathered around her bed, and Tessie tried as usual to dispel her doubts and truly believe. The vigil light no longer contained oil but was an electric bulb.

For three days we received no word from Milton. When Tessie returned from her trips downstairs I began to detect, in addition to the traces of tears on her face, faint streaks of guilt. Death always makes people practical. So while Tessie had been on the first floor, foraging for food, she had also been searching in Milton's desk. She had read the terms of his life insurance policy. She had checked the balance in their retirement account. In the bathroom mirror she appraised her looks, wondering if she could attract another husband at her age. "I had you kids to think of," she confessed to me years later. "I was wondering what we'd do if your father didn't come back."

To live in America, until recently, meant to be far from war. Wars happened in Southeast Asian jungles. They happened in Middle Eastern deserts. They happened, as the old song has it, *over there.* But then why, peeking out the dormer window, did I see, on the morning after our second night in the attic, a tank rolling by our front lawn? A green army tank, all alone in the long shadows of morning, its enormous treads clanking against the asphalt. An armor-plated military vehicle encountering no greater obstacle than a lost roller skate. The tank rolled past the affluent homes, the gables and turrets, the porte cocheres. It stopped briefly at the stop sign. The gun turret looked both ways, like a driver's ed student, and then the tank went on its way.

What had happened: late Monday night, President Johnson, finally giving in to Governor Romney's request, had ordered in federal troops. General John L. Throckmorton set up the headquarters of the 101st Airborne at Southeastern High, where my parents had gone to school. Though the fiercest rioting was on the West Side, General Throckmorton chose to deploy his paratroopers on the East Side, calling this decision "an operational convenience." By early Tuesday morning the

442

paratroopers were moving in to quell the disturbance.

No one else was awake to see the tank rumble by. My grandparents were dozing in bed. Tessie and Chapter Eleven were curled on air mattresses on the floor. Even the parakeets were quiet. I remember looking at my brother's face peeking out of his sleeping bag. On the flannel lining, hunters shot at ducks. This masculine background served only to emphasize Chapter Eleven's lack of heroic qualities. Who was going to come to my father's aid? Who could my father rely on? Chapter Eleven with his Coke-bottle glasses? Lefty with his chalkboard and sixty-plus years? What I did next had no connection, I believe, with my chromosomal status. It did not result from the high-testosterone plasma levels in my blood. I did what any loving, loyal daughter would have done who had been raised on a diet of Hercules movies. In that instant, I decided to find my father, to save him, if necessary, or at least to tell him to come home.

Crossing myself in the Orthodox fashion, I stole down the attic stairs, closing the door behind me. In my bedroom I put on sneakers and my Amelia Earhart aviator's cap. Without waking anyone I let myself out the front door, ran to my bicycle parked at the side of the house, and pedaled away. After two blocks, I caught sight of the tank: it had stopped at a red light. The soldiers inside were busy looking at maps, trying to find the best route to the riots. They didn't notice the little girl in the aviator's cap stealing up on a banana bike. It was still dark out. The birds were beginning to sing. Summer smells of lawn and mulch filled the air, and suddenly I lost my nerve. The closer I got to the tank, the bigger it looked. I was frightened and wanted to run back home. But the light changed and the tank lurched forward. Standing up on my pedals, I sped after it.

Across town, in the lightless Zebra Room, my father was trying to stay awake. Barricaded behind the cash register, holding the revolver in one hand and a ham sandwich in the other, Milton looked out the front window to see what was happening in the street. Over the last two sleepless nights the circles under Milton's eyes had darkened steadily with each cup of coffee he drank. His eyelids hung at half mast, but his brow was damp with the perspiration of anxiety and vigilance. His stomach hurt. He needed to go to the bathroom in the worst way but didn't dare.

Outside, they were at it again: the snipers. It was almost 5 a.m. Each night, the sinking sun, like a ring on a window shade, pulled night down over the neighborhood. From wherever the snipers disappeared to during the hot day, they returned. They took up their positions. From the windows of condemned hotels, from fire escapes and balconies, from behind cars jacked up in front yards, they extended the barrels of their assorted guns. If you looked closely, if you were brave or reckless enough to stick your head out the window this time of night, you could see by the moon — that other pull ring, going up — hundreds of glinting guns, pointed down into the street, through which the soldiers were now advancing.

The only light inside the diner came from the red glow of the jukebox. It stood to one side of the front door, a Disco-Matic made of chrome, plastic, and colored glass. There was a small window through which you could watch the robotic changing of records. Through a circulatory system along the jukebox's edges trails of dark blue bubbles rose. Bubbles representing the effervescence of American life, of our postwar optimism, of our fizzy, imperial, carbonated drinks. Bubbles full of the hot air of American democracy, boiling up from the stacked vinyl platters inside. "Mama Don't Allow It" by Bunny Berigan maybe, or "Stardust" by Tommy Dorsey and his orchestra. But not tonight. Tonight

Milton had the jukebox off so that he could hear if anyone was trying to break in.

The cluttered walls of the restaurant took no notice of the rioting outside. Al Kaline still beamed from his frame. Paul Bunyan and Babe the Blue Ox continued on their trek below the daily special. The menu board itself still offered eggs, hash browns, seven kinds of pie. So far nothing had happened. Somewhat miraculously. Squatting at the front window yesterday, Milton had seen looters break into every store down the block. They looted the Jewish market, taking everything but the matzoh and the yahrzeit candles. With a sharp sense of style, they stripped Joel Moskowitz's shoe store of its higher-priced and more fashionable models, leaving only some orthopedic offerings and a few Florsheims. All that was left in Dyer's Appliance, as far as Milton could tell, was a rack of vacuum bags. What would they loot if they looted the diner? Would they take the stained glass window, which Milton himself had taken? Would they show interest in the photo of Ty Cobb snarling as he slid, spikes first, into second base? Maybe they'd rip the zebra skins off the barstools. They liked anything African, didn't they? Wasn't that the new vogue, or the old vogue that was new again? Hell, they could have the goddamned zebra skins. He'd put them out front as a peace offering.

But now Milton heard something. The doorknob, was it? He listened. For the last few hours he'd been hearing things. His eyes had been playing tricks on him, too. He crouched behind the counter, squinting into the darkness. His ears echoed the way seashells do. He heard the distant gunfire and the squawking sirens. He heard the hum of the refrigerator and the ticking of the clock. To all this was added the rush of his blood, roaring through the channels in his head. But no sound came from the doorway.

Milton relaxed. He took another bite of the sandwich. Gently, experimentally, he lowered his head onto the counter. *Just for a minute.* When he closed his eyes, the pleasure was immediate. Then the doorknob rattled again, and Milton jumped. He shook his head, trying to wake himself up. He put down the sandwich and tiptoed out from behind the counter, holding the gun.

He didn't intend to use it. The idea was to scare the looter off. If that didn't work, Milton was prepared to leave. The Oldsmobile was parked out back. He could be home in ten minutes. The knob rattled again. And without thinking Milton stepped toward the glass door and shouted, "I've got a gun!"

Except it wasn't the gun. It was the ham sandwich! Milton was threatening the looter with two pieces of toasted bread, a slice of meat, and some hot mustard. Nevertheless, because it was dark out, this worked. The looter outside the door held up his hands.

It was Morrison from across the street.

Milton stared at Morrison. Morrison stared back. And then my father said — this is what white people say in a situation like this, "Can I help you?"

Morrison squinted, disbelieving. "What you doing here, man? You crazy? Ain't safe for no white people down here." A shot rang out. Morrison flattened himself against the glass. "Ain't safe for nobody."

"I've gotta protect my property."

"You life ain't you property?" Morrison raised his eyebrows to indicate the unimpeachable logic of this statement. Then he dropped the superior expression altogether and coughed. "Listen, chief, long as you here, maybe you can help me out." He held up small change. "Came over for some cigarettes."

Milton's chin dipped, fattening his neck, and his eyebrows slanted in disbelief. In a dry voice he said, "Now'd be a good time to kick the habit."

Another shot rang out, this time closer. Morrison jumped, then smiled. "It sure *is*

448

bad for my health. And gettin' more dangerous all the time." Then he smiled broadly. "This'll be my last pack," he said, "swear to God." He dropped the change through the mail slot. "Parliaments." Milton looked down at the coins for a moment and then went and got the cigarettes.

"Got any matches?" Morrison said.

Milton slipped these through, too. As he did, the riots, his frayed nerves, the smell of fire in the air, and the audacity of this man Morrison dodging sniper fire for a pack of cigarettes all became too much for Milton. Suddenly he was waving his arms, indicating everything, and shouting through the door, "What's the matter with you people?"

Morrison took only a moment. "The matter with us," he said, "is you." And then he was gone.

"The matter with us is you." How many times did I hear that growing up? Delivered by Milton in his so-called black accent, delivered whenever any liberal pundit talked about the "culturally deprived" or the "underclass" or "empowerment zones," spoken out of the belief that this one statement, having been delivered to him while the blacks themselves burned down a significant portion of our beloved city, proved its own absurdity. As the years went on,

Milton used it as a shield against any opinions to the contrary, and finally it grew into a kind of mantra, the explanation for why the world was going to hell, applicable not only to African Americans but to feminists and homosexuals; and then of course he liked to use it on us, whenever we were late for dinner or wore clothes Tessie didn't approve of.

"The matter with us is you!" Morrison's words echoed in the street, but Milton didn't have time to concentrate on them. Because right then, like a creaky Godzilla in a Japanese movie, the first military tank lumbered into view. Soldiers stood on both sides, not cops now but National Guardsmen, camouflaged, helmeted, nervously holding rifles with bayonets. Pointing those rifles up at all the other rifles pointing down. There was a moment of relative silence, enough for Milton to hear the slamming of Morrison's screen door across the street. Then there was a pop, a sound like a toy gun, and suddenly the street lit up with a thousand bursts of fire . . .

I heard them, too, from a quarter mile away. Following the slow tank at a discreet distance, I had ridden my bike from Indian Village on the East Side all the way to the West. I tried to keep my bearings as best I could, but I was only seven and a half, and didn't know many street names. While passing through downtown, I recognized *The Spirit of Detroit*, the Marshall Fredericks statue that stood in front of the City-County Building. A few years earlier, a prankster had painted a trail of red footprints in the statue's size, leading across Woodward to rendezvous with a statue of a naked woman in front of the National Bank of Detroit. The footprints were still faintly visible as I pedaled past. The tank turned up Bush Street, and I followed it past Monroe and the lights of Greektown. On a normal day, the old Greek men of my grandfather's generation would have been arriving at the coffee houses to spend the day playing backgammon, but on the morning of July 25, 1967, the street was empty. At some point my tank had found others; in a line they now headed northwest. Soon downtown vanished and I didn't know where I was. Ducking aerodynamically over my handlebars, I pedaled furiously into the thick, oily exhaust of the moving column . . .

. . . while, back on Pingree Street, Milton is crouching behind the crenellated olive oil tins. Bullets fly from every darkened window along the block, from Frank's Pool Hall and the Crow Bar, from the bell tower of the African Episcopal Church, so many bullets they blur the air like rain, making the one working streetlamp look as if it's flickering out. Bullets pounding on armor and ricocheting off brickwork and tattooing the parked cars. Bullets ripping the legs right out from under a U.S. Postal Service mailbox, so that it falls over on its side like a drunk. Bullets obliterating the window of the veterinarian office and continuing on through the walls to reach the cages of the animals in back. The German shepherd that has been barking nonstop for three days and two nights finally shuts up. A cat twists in the air, letting out a scream, its blazing green eyes going out like a light. A real battle is under way now, a firefight, a little bit of Vietnam brought back home. But in this case the Vietcong are lying on Beautyrest mattresses. They are sitting in camping chairs and drinking malt liquor, a volunteer army facing off against the enlistees in the streets.

It's impossible to know who all these snipers were. But it's easy to understand why the police called them snipers. It's easy to understand why Mayor Jerome Cavanaugh called them snipers, and Governor George Romney, too. A sniper, by definition, acts alone. A sniper is cowardly, sneaky; he kills from a distance, unseen. It was convenient to call them snipers, because if they weren't snipers, then what were they? The governor didn't say it; the newspapers didn't say it; the history books still do not say it, but I, who watched the entire thing on my bike, saw it clearly: in Detroit, in July of 1967, what happened was nothing less than a guerrilla uprising.

The Second American Revolution.

And now the guardsmen are fighting back. When the riot first broke, the police, on the whole, acted with restraint. They moved off, trying to contain the disturbance. Likewise, the federal troops, the paratroopers of the 82nd Airborne and 101st, are battle-hardened veterans who know to use appropriate force. But the National Guard is a different story. Weekend warriors, they have been called from their homes into sudden battle. They are inexperienced, scared. They move through the streets, blasting away at anything they see. Sometimes they drive tanks right up onto front lawns. They drive onto people's porches and crash through the walls. The tank in front of the Zebra Room has stopped momentarily. Ten or so troops surround it, taking aim at a sniper on the fourth floor of the Beaumont Hotel. The sniper fires; the National Guardsmen fire back, and the man drops, his legs tangling on the fire escape. Directly thereafter, another light flashes across the street. Milton looks up to see Morrison in his living room, lighting a cigarette. Lighting a Parliament with the zebra-striped matches.

"No!" Milton shouts. "No!" . . . And Morrison, if he hears, just thinks it's another diatribe against smoking, but let's face it, he doesn't hear. He only lights his cigarette and, two seconds later, a bullet rips through the front of his skull and he crumples in a heap. And then the soldiers move on.

The street is empty again, silent. The machine guns and tanks begin ripping up the next block, or the block after that. Milton stands at the front door, looking across at the empty window where Morrison had stood. And the realization comes over him that the restaurant is safe. The soldiers have come and gone. The riot is over . . .

. . . Except that now someone else is advancing along the street. As the tanks disappear down Pingree, a new figure is approaching from the other direction. Somebody who lives in the neighborhood is rounding the corner and heading for the Zebra Room . . .

. . . following the line of tanks, I am no longer thinking about showing up my brother. The outbreak of so much shooting has taken me completely by surprise. I have looked through my father's World War II scrapbook many times; I have seen Vietnam on television; I have ingested countless movies about Ancient Rome or the battles of the Middle Ages. But none of it has prepared me for warfare in my own hometown. The street we are moving down is lined with leafy elms. Cars are parked at the curb. We pass lawns and porch furniture, bird feeders and birdbaths. As I look up at the canopy of elms, the sky is just beginning to grow light. Birds move among the branches, and squirrels, too. A kite is stuck up in one tree. Over a limb of another, someone's tennis shoes dangle with the laces knotted. Directly below these sneakers, I see a street sign. It is full of bullet holes, but I manage to read it: Pingree. All of a sudden I recognize where I am. There is Value Meats! And New Yorker Clothes. I am so happy to see them that for a moment I don't register that both places are on fire. Letting the tanks get away, I ride up a driveway and stop behind a tree. I get off my bike and peek across the street at the diner. The zebra head sign is still intact. The restaurant is not burning. At that moment, however, the figure that has been approaching the Zebra Room enters my field of vision. From thirty yards away I see him lift a bottle in his hand. He lights the rag hanging from the bottle's mouth and with a not terribly good arm flings the Molotov cocktail through the front window of the Zebra Room. And as flames erupt within the diner, the arsonist shouts in an ecstatic voice:

"*Opa,* motherfucker!"

I saw him only from the back. It was not yet fully light. Smoke rose from the adjacent burning buildings. Still, in the firelight, I thought I recognized the black beret of my friend Marius Wyxzewixard Challouehliczilczese Grimes before the figure ran off.

"*Opa!*" Inside the diner, my father heard the well-known cry of Greek waiters, and before he knew what was happening the place was going up like a flaming appetizer. The Zebra Room had become a *saganaki!* As the booths caught fire, Milton raced behind the counter to grab the fire extinguisher. Coming out again, he held the hose, like a lemon wedge wrapped in cheesecloth, over the flames, and prepared to squeeze . . .

. . . when suddenly he stopped. And now I recognize a familiar expression on my father's face, the expression he wore so often at the dinner table, the faraway look of a man who could never stop thinking about business. Success depends on adapting to new situations. And what situation was newer than this? Flames were climbing the walls; the photo of Jimmy Dorsey was curling up. And Milton was asking himself a few, pertinent questions. For instance:

How would he ever run a restaurant in this neighborhood again? And: What do you suppose the already depressed real estate prices would be tomorrow morning? Most important of all: How was it a crime? Did *he* start the riot? Did he throw the Molotov cocktail? Like Tessie, Milton's mind was searching the bottom drawer of his desk, in particular a fat envelope containing the three fire insurance policies from separate companies. He saw them in his mind's eye; he read the fire indemnity coverage, and added them up. The final sum, $500,000, blinded him to everything else. Half a million bucks! Milton looked around with wild, eager eyes. The French toast sign was in flames. The zebra-skin barstools were like a row of torches. And madly, he turned and hurried outside to the Oldsmobile . . .

Where he encountered me.

"Callie! What the hell are you doing here?"

"I came to help."

"What's the matter with you!" Milton shouted. But despite the anger in his voice he was down on his knees, hugging me. I wrapped my arms around his neck.

"The restaurant's burning down, Daddy."

"I know it is."

I began to cry.

"It's okay," my father told me, carrying me to the car. "Let's go home now. It's all over."

So was it a riot or a guerrilla uprising? Let me answer that question with other questions. After the riot was over, were, or were there not, caches of weapons found all over the neighborhood? And were these weapons, or were they not, AK-47s and machine guns? And why had General Throckmorton deployed his tanks on the East Side, miles from the rioting? Was that the kind of thing you did to subdue an un-organized gang of snipers? Or was it more in keeping with military strategy? Was it like establishing a front line in a war? Believe whatever you want. I was seven years old and followed a tank into battle and saw what I saw. It turned out that when it finally happened, the revolution wasn't televised. On TV they called it only a riot.

The following morning, as the smoke cleared, the city's flag could once again be seen. Remember the symbol on it? A phoenix rising from its ashes. And the words beneath? *Speramus meliora; resurget cineribus.* "We hope for better things; it will rise from the ashes."

Middlesex

❧

Shameful as it is to say, the riots were the best thing that ever happened to us. Overnight we went from being a family desperately trying to stay in the middle class to one with hopes of sneaking into the upper, or at least the upper-middle. The insurance money didn't amount to quite as much as Milton had anticipated. Two of the companies refused to pay the full amount, citing excessive insurance clauses. They paid only a quarter of their policies' value. Still, taken all together, the money was much more than the Zebra Room had been worth, and it allowed my parents to make some changes in our lives.

Of all my childhood memories, none has the magic, the pure dreaminess, of the night we heard a honk outside our house and looked out the window to see that a spaceship had landed in our driveway.

It had set down noiselessly next to my mother's station wagon. The front lights flashed. The back end gave off a red glow. For thirty seconds nothing more happened.

But then finally the window of the space-ship slowly retracted to reveal, instead of a Martian inside, Milton. He had shaved off his beard.

"Get your mother," he called, smiling. "We're going for a little ride."

Not a spaceship then, but close: a 1967 Cadillac Fleetwood, as intergalactic a car as Detroit ever produced. (The moon shot was only a year away.) It was as black as space itself and shaped like a rocket lying on its side. The long front end came to a point, like a nose cone, and from there the craft stretched back along the driveway in a long, beautiful, ominously perfect shape. There was a silver multi-chambered grille, as though to filter stardust. Chrome piping, like the housing for circuitry, led from con-ical yellow turn signals along the rounded sides of the car, all the way to the rear, where the vehicle flared propulsively into jet fins and rocket boosters.

Inside, the Cadillac was as plushly car-peted and softly lit as the bar at the Ritz. The armrests were equipped with ashtrays and cigarette lighters. The interior itself was black leather and gave off a strong new smell. It was like climbing into somebody's wallet.

We didn't move right away. We re-mained parked, as if it were enough just to sit in the car, as if now that we owned it, we could forget about our living room and stay in the driveway every night. Milton started the engine. Keeping the transmission in park, he showed us the marvels. He opened and closed the windows by pressing a button. He locked the doors by pressing another. He buzzed the front seat forward, then tilted it back until I could see the dandruff on his shoulders. By the time he put the car into gear we were all slightly giddy. We drove away down Seminole, past our neighbors' houses, already saying farewell to Indian Village. At the corner, Milton put the blinker on and it ticked, counting the seconds down to our eventual departure.

The '67 Fleetwood was my father's first Cadillac, but there were many more to come. Over the next seven years, Milton traded up almost every year, so it's possible for me to chart my life in relation to the styling features of his long line of Cadillacs. When tail fins disappeared, I was nine; when power antennas arrived, eleven. My emotional life accords with the designs, too. In the sixties, when Cadillacs were futuristically self-assured, I was also self-confident and forward-looking. In the gas-short seventies, however, when the manufacturer came out with the unfortunate Seville — a car that looked as though it had been rear-ended — I also felt misshapen. Pick a year and I'll tell you what car we had. 1970: the cola-colored Eldorado. 1971: the red sedan DeVille. 1972: the golden Fleetwood with the passenger sun visor that opened up into a starlet's dressing room mirror (in which Tessie checked her makeup and I my first blemishes). 1973: the long, black, dome-roofed Fleetwood that made other cars stop, thinking a funeral was passing. 1974: the canary-yellow, two-door "Florida Special" with white vinyl top, sunroof, and tan leather seats that my mother is still driving today, almost thirty years later.

But in 1967 it was the space-age Fleetwood. Once we got going the required speed, Milton said, "Okay. Now get a load of this." He flipped a switch under the dash. There was a hissing sound, like balloons inflating. Slowly, as if lifted on a magic carpet, the four of us rose to the upper reaches of the car's interior.

"That's what they call the 'Air-Ride.' Brand-new feature. Smooth, huh?"

"Is it some kind of hydraulic suspension system?" Chapter Eleven wanted to know.

"I think so."

"Maybe I won't have to use my pillow when I drive," said Tessie.

For a moment after that, none of us spoke. We were headed east, out of Detroit, literally floating on air.

Which brings me to the second part of our upward mobility. Shortly after the riots, like many other white Detroiters, my parents began looking for a house in the suburbs. The suburb they had their sights on was the affluent lakefront district of the auto magnates: Grosse Pointe.

It was much harder than they ever expected. In the Cadillac, scouting the five Grosse Pointes (the Park, the City, the Farms, the Woods, the Shores), my parents saw **FOR SALE** signs on many lawns. But when they stopped in at the realty offices and filled out applications, they found that the houses suddenly went off the market, or were sold, or doubled in price.

After two months of searching, Milton was down to his last real estate agent, a Miss Jane Marsh of Great Lakes Realty. He had her — and some growing suspicions.

"This property is rather eccentric," Miss Marsh is telling Milton one September afternoon as she leads him up the driveway. "It takes a buyer with a little vision." She opens the front door and leads him inside. "But it does have quite a pedigree. It was designed by Hudson Clark." She waits for recognition. "Of the Prairie School?"

Milton nods, dubiously. He swivels his head, looking over the place. He hadn't much cared for the picture Miss Marsh had shown him over at the office. Too boxy-looking. Too modern.

"I'm not sure my wife would go for this kind of thing, Miss Marsh."

"I'm afraid we don't have anything more *traditional* to show at the moment."

She leads him along a spare white hallway and down a small flight of open stairs. And now, as they step into the sunken living room, Miss Marsh's head begins to swivel, too. Smiling a polite smile that reveals a rabbity expanse of upper gum, she examines Milton's complexion, his hair, his shoes. She glances at his real estate application again.

"Stephanides. What kind of name is that?"

"It's Greek."

"Greek. How interesting."

More upper gum flashes as Miss Marsh makes a notation on her pad. Then she resumes the tour: "Sunken living room. Greenhouse adjoining the dining area. And, as you can see, the house is well supplied with windows."

"It pretty much *is* a window, Miss Marsh." Milton moves closer to the glass and examines the backyard. Meanwhile, a few feet behind, Miss Marsh examines Milton.

"May I ask what business you're in, Mr. Stephanides?"

"The restaurant business."

Another mark of pen on pad. "Can I tell you what churches we have in the area? What denomination are you?"

"I don't go in for that sort of thing. My wife takes the kids to the Greek church."

"She's a Grecian, too?"

"She's a Detroiter. We're both East Siders."

"And you need space for your two children, is that right?"

"Yes, ma'am. Plus we have my folks living with us, too."

"Oh, I see." And now pink gums disappear as Miss Marsh begins to add it all up. *Let's see. Southern Mediterranean. One point. Not in one of the professions. One point. Religion? Greek church. That's some kind of Catholic, isn't it? So there's another point there. And he has his parents living with him! Two more points! Which makes — five! Oh, that won't do. That won't do at all.*

To explain Miss Marsh's arithmetic: back in those days, the real estate agents in Grosse Pointe evaluated prospective buyers by something called the Point System. (Milton wasn't the only one who worried about the neighborhood going to hell.) No one spoke of it openly. Realtors only mentioned "community standards" and selling to "the right sort of people." Now that white flight had begun, the Point System

465

was more important than ever. You didn't want what was happening in Detroit to happen out here.

Discreetly, Miss Marsh now draws a tiny "5" next to "Stephanides" and circles it. As she does so, however, she feels something. A kind of regret. The Point System isn't her idea, after all. It was in place long before she came to Grosse Pointe from Wichita, where her father works as a butcher. But there is nothing she can do. Yes, Miss Marsh feels sorry. *I mean, really. Look at this house! Who's going to buy it if not an Italian or a Greek. I'll never be able to sell it. Never!*

Her client is still standing at the window, looking out.

"I do understand your preference for something more 'Old World,' Mr. Stephanides. We do get them from time to time. You just have to be patient. I've got your telephone number. I'll let you know if anything comes on the market."

Milton doesn't hear her. He is absorbed in the view. The house has a roof deck, plus a patio out back. And there are two other, smaller buildings beyond that.

"Tell me more about this Hudson Clark fella," he now asks.

"Clark? Well, to be honest, he's a minor figure."

"Prairie School, eh?"

466

"Hudson Clark was no Frank Lloyd Wright, if that's what you mean."

"What are these outbuildings I see here?"

"I wouldn't call them outbuildings, Mr. Stephanides. That's making it a bit grand. One's a bathhouse. Rather decrepit, I'm afraid. I'm not sure it even works. Behind that is the guest house. Which also needs a lot of work."

"Bathhouse? That's different." Milton turns away from the glass. He begins walking around the house, looking it over in a new light: the Stonehenge walls, the Klimt tilework, the open rooms. Everything is geometric and grid-like. Sunlight falls in beams through the many skylights. "Now that I'm in here," Milton says, "I sort of get the idea behind this place. The photo you showed me doesn't do it justice."

"Really, Mr. Stephanides, for a family such as yours, with young children, I'm not sure this is quite the best —"

Before she can finish, however, Milton holds up his hands in surrender. "You don't have to show me any more. Decrepit outbuildings or not, I'll take it."

There is a pause. Miss Marsh smiles with her double-decker gums. "That's wonderful, Mr. Stephanides," she says without enthusiasm. "Of course, it's all contingent on the approval of the loan."

But now it is Milton's turn to smile. For all the disavowals of its existence, the Point System is no secret. Harry Karras tried unsuccessfully to buy a house in Grosse Pointe the year before. Same thing happened to Pete Savidis. But no one is going to tell Milton Stephanides where to live. Not Miss Marsh and not a bunch of country club real estate guys, either.

"You don't have to bother with that," my father said, relishing the moment. "I'll pay cash."

Over the barrier of the Point System, my father managed to get us a house in Grosse Pointe. It was the only time in his life he paid for anything up front. But what about the other barriers? What about the fact that real estate agents had shown him only the least-desirable houses, in the areas closest to Detroit? Houses no one else wanted? And what about his inability to see anything except the grand gesture, and the fact that he bought the house without first consulting my mother? Well, for those problems there was no remedy.

On moving day we set off in two cars. Tessie, fighting tears, took Lefty and Desdemona in the family station wagon. Milton drove Chapter Eleven and me in the new Fleetwood. Along Jefferson, signs of the riots still remained, as did my unanswered questions. "What about the Boston

Tea Party?" I challenged my father from the backseat. "The colonists stole all that tea and dumped it into the harbor. That was the same thing as a riot."

"That wasn't the same at all," Milton answered back. "What the hell are they teaching you in that school of yours? With the Boston Tea Party the Americans were revolting against another country that was oppressing them."

"But it wasn't another country, Daddy. It was the same country. There wasn't even such a thing as the United States then."

"Let me ask you something. Where was King George when they dumped all that tea into the drink? Was he in Boston? Was he in America even? No. He was way the hell over there in England, eating crumpets."

The implacable black Cadillac powered along, bearing my father, brother, and me out of the war-torn city. We crossed over a thin canal which, like a moat, separated Detroit from Grosse Pointe. And then, before we had time to register the changes, we were at the house on Middlesex Boulevard.

The trees were what I noticed first. Two enormous weeping willows, like woolly mammoths, on either side of the property. Their vines hung over the driveway like streamers of sponge at a car wash. Above was the autumn sun. Passing through the willows' leaves, it turned them a phosphorescent green. It was as though, in the middle of the block's cool shade, a beacon had been switched on; and this impression was only strengthened by the house we'd now stopped in front of.

Middlesex! Did anybody ever live in a house as strange? As sci-fi? As futuristic and outdated at the same time? A house that was more like communism, better in theory than reality? The walls were pale yellow, made of octagonal stone blocks framed by redwood siding along the roofline. Plate glass windows ran along the front. Hudson Clark (whose name Milton would drop for years to come, despite the fact that no one ever recognized it) had designed Middlesex to harmonize with the natural surroundings. In this case, that meant the two weeping willow trees and the mulberry growing against the front of the house. Forgetting where he was (a conservative suburb) and what was on the other side of those trees (the Turnbulls and the Picketts), Clark followed the principles of Frank Lloyd Wright, banishing the Victorian vertical in favor of a midwestern horizontal, opening up the interior spaces, and bringing in a Japanese influence. Middlesex was a testament to theory uncompromised by practicality. For instance: Hudson Clark hadn't believed in doors. The concept of the door, of this thing that swung one way or the other, was outmoded. So on Middlesex we didn't have doors. Instead we had long, accordion-like barriers, made from sisal, that worked by a pneumatic pump located down in the basement. The concept of stairs in the traditional sense was also something the world no longer needed. Stairs represented a teleological view of the universe, of one thing leading to another, whereas now everyone knew that one thing didn't lead to another but often nowhere at all. So neither did our stairs. Oh, they went up, eventually. They took the persistent climber to the second floor, but on the way they took him lots of other places as well. There was a landing, for instance, overhung with a mobile. The stairway walls had peepholes and shelves cut into them. As you climbed, you could see the legs of someone passing along the hallway above. You could spy on someone down in the living room.

"Where are the closets?" Tessie asked as soon as we got inside.

"Closets?"

"The kitchen's a million miles away from the family room, Milt. Every time you want a snack you have to traipse all the way across the house."

"It'll give us some exercise."

"And how am I supposed to find curtains for those windows? They don't make curtains that big. Everyone can see right in!"

"Think of it this way. We can see right out."

But then there was a scream at the other end of the house:

"Mana!"

Against her better judgment, Desdemona had pressed a button on the wall. "What kind door this is?" she was shouting as we all came running. "It move by itself!"

"Hey, cool," said Chapter Eleven. "Try it, Cal. Put your head in the doorway. Yeah, like that . . ."

"Don't fool with that door, kids."

"I'm just testing the pressure."

"Ow!"

"What did I tell you? Birdbrain. Now get your sister out of the door."

"I'm trying. The button doesn't work."

"What do you mean it doesn't work?"

"Oh, this is wonderful, Milt. No closets, and now we have to call the fire department to get Callie out of the door."

"It's not designed to have someone's neck in it."

"Mana!"

"Can you breathe, honey?"

"Yeah, but it hurts."

"It's like that guy at Carlsbad Caverns," said Chapter Eleven. "He got stuck and they had to feed him for forty days and then he finally died."

"Stop wriggling, Callie. You're making it —"

"I'm *not* wriggling —"

"I can see Callie's underwear! I can see Callie's underwear!"

"Stop that right now."

"Here, Tessie, take Callie's leg. Okay, on three. A-one and a-two and a-three!"

We settled in, with our various misgivings. After the incident with the pneumatic door, Desdemona had a premonition that this house of modern conveniences (which was in fact nearly as old as she was) would be the last she would ever live in. She moved what remained of her and my grandfather's belongings into the guest house — the brass coffee table, the silkworm box, the portrait of Patriarch Athenagoras — but she could never get used to the skylight, which was like a hole in the roof, or the push-pedal faucet in the bathroom, or the box that spoke on the wall. (Every room on Middlesex was equipped with an intercom. Back when they had been installed in the 1940s — over thirty years after the house itself had been built in 1909 — the intercoms had probably all worked. But by 1967 you might speak into the kitchen intercom only to have your voice come out in the master bedroom. The speakers distorted our voices, so that we had to listen very closely to understand what was being said, like deciphering a child's first, garbled speech.)

Chapter Eleven tapped into the pneumatic system in the basement and spent hours sending a Ping-Pong ball around the house through a network of vacuum cleaner hoses. Tessie never stopped complaining about the lack of closet space and the impractical layout, but gradually, thanks to a touch of claustrophobia, she grew to appreciate Middlesex's glass walls.

Lefty cleaned them. Making himself useful as always, he took upon himself the Sisyphean task of keeping all those Modernist surfaces sparkling. With the same concentration he trained on the aorist tense of ancient Greek verbs — a tense so full of weariness it specified actions that might never be completed — Lefty now cleaned the huge picture windows, the fogged glass of the greenhouse, the sliding doors that led to the courtyard, and even the skylights. As he was Windexing the new house, however, Chapter Eleven and I were exploring it. Or, I should say, them. The meditative, pastel yellow cube that faced the street contained the main living quarters. Behind that lay a courtyard with a dry pool and a fragile dogwood leaning over in vain to see its reflection. Along the western edge of this courtyard, extending from the back of the kitchen, ran a white, translucent tunnel, something like the tubes that conduct football teams onto the field. This tunnel led to a small domed outbuilding — a sort of huge igloo — surrounded by a covered porch. Inside was a bathing pool (just warming up now, getting ready to play its part in my life). Behind the bathhouse was yet another courtyard, floored with smooth black stones. Along the eastern edge of this, to balance the tunnel, ran a portico lined with thin brown iron beams. The portico led up to the guest house, where no guests ever stayed: only Desdemona, for a short time with her husband and a long time alone.

But more important to a kid: Middlesex had lots of sneaker-sized ledges to walk along. It had deep, concrete window wells perfect for making into forts. It had sun decks and catwalks. Chapter Eleven and I climbed all over Middlesex. Lefty would wash the windows and, five minutes later, my brother and I would come along, leaning on the glass and leaving fingerprints. And seeing them, our tall, mute grandfather, who in another life might have been a professor but in this one was holding a wet rag and bucket, only smiled and washed the windows all over again.

Although he never said a word to me, I loved my Chaplinesque *papou*. His speechlessness seemed to be an act of refinement. It went with his elegant clothes, his shoes with woven vamps, the glaze of his hair. And yet he was not stiff at all but playful, even comedic. When he took me for rides in the car Lefty often pretended to fall asleep at the wheel. Suddenly his eyes would close and he would slump to one side. The car would continue on, unpiloted, drifting toward the curb. I laughed, screamed, pulled my hair and kicked my legs. At the last possible second, Lefty would spring awake, taking the wheel and averting disaster.

We didn't need to speak to each other. We understood each other without speaking. But then a terrible thing happened.

It is a Saturday morning a few weeks after our move to Middlesex. Lefty is taking me for a walk around the new neighborhood. The plan is to go down to the lake. Hand in hand we stroll across our new front lawn. Change is clinking in his trouser pocket, just below the level of my shoulders. I run my fingers over his thumb, fascinated by the missing nail, which Lefty has always told me a monkey bit off at the zoo.

Now we reach the sidewalk. The man who makes the sidewalks in Grosse Pointe has left his name in the cement: J. P. Steiger. There is also a crack, where ants are having a war. Now we are crossing the grass between the sidewalk and the street. And now we are at the curb.

I step down. Lefty doesn't. Instead, he drops, cleanly, six inches into the street. Still holding his hand, I laugh at him for being so clumsy. Lefty laughs, too. But he doesn't look at me. He keeps staring straight ahead into space. And, gazing up, I suddenly can see things about my grandfather I should be too young to see. I see fear in his eyes, and bewilderment, and, most astonishing of all, the fact that some adult worry is taking precedence over our walk together. The sun is in his eyes. His pupils contract. We remain at the curb, in its dust and leaf matter. Five seconds. Ten seconds. Long enough for Lefty to come face-to-face with the evidence of his own diminished faculties and for me to feel the onrush of my own growing ones.

What nobody knew: Lefty had had another stroke the week before. Already speechless, he now began to suffer spatial disorientation. Furniture advanced and retreated in the mechanical manner of a fun house. Like practical jokers, chairs offered themselves and then pulled away at the last moment. The diamonds of the back-gammon board undulated like player piano keys. Lefty told no one.

Because he no longer trusted himself to drive, Lefty started taking me on walks instead. (That was how we'd arrived at that curb, the curb he couldn't wake up and turn away from in time.) We went along Middlesex, the silent, old, foreign gentleman and his skinny granddaughter, a girl who talked enough for two, who babbled so fluently that her father the ex-clarinet man liked to joke she knew circular breathing. I was getting used to Grosse Pointe, to the genteel mothers in chiffon headscarves and to the dark, cypress-shrouded house where the one Jewish family lived (having also paid cash). Whereas my grandfather was getting used to a much more terrifying reality. Holding my hand to keep his balance, as trees and bushes made strange, sliding movements in his peripheral vision, Lefty was confronting the possibility that consciousness was a biological accident. Though he'd never been religious, he realized now that he'd always believed in the soul, in a force of personality that survived death. But as his mind continued to waver, to short-circuit, he finally arrived at the cold-eyed conclusion, so at odds with his youthful cheerfulness, that the brain was just an organ like any other and that when it failed he would be no more.

A seven-year-old girl can take only so many walks with her grandfather. I was the new kid on the block and wanted to make friends. From our roof deck I sometimes glimpsed a girl about my age who lived in the house behind us. She came out onto a small balcony in the evenings and tugged petals off flowers in the window box. In friskier moods, she performed lazy pirouettes, as though to the accompaniment of my own music box, which I always brought to the roof to keep me company. She had long, white-blond hair cut in bangs, and since I never saw her in the daytime, I decided she was an albino.

But I was wrong: because there she was one afternoon in sunshine, getting a ball that had flown onto our property. Her name was Clementine Stark. She wasn't an albino, just very pale, and allergic to hard-to-avoid items (grass, house dust). Her father was about to have a heart attack, and my memories of her now are tinged with a blue wash of misfortune that hadn't quite befallen her at the time. She was standing bare-legged in the jungly weeds that grew up between our houses. Her skin was already beginning to react to the grass cuttings stuck to the ball, whose sogginess was suddenly explained by the overweight Labrador who now limped into view.

Clementine Stark had a canopy bed moored like an imperial barge at one end of her sea-blue bedroom carpet. She had a collection of mounted poisonous-looking insects. She was a year older than me, hence worldly, and had been to Krakow once, which was in Poland. Because of her allergies, Clementine was kept indoors a lot. This led to our being inside together most of the time and to Clementine's teaching me how to kiss.

When I told my life story to Dr. Luce, the place where he invariably got interested was when I came to Clementine Stark. Luce didn't care about criminally smitten grandparents or silkworm boxes or serenading clarinets. To a certain extent, I understand. I even agree.

Clementine Stark invited me over to her house. Without even comparing it to Middlesex, it was an overwhelmingly medieval-looking place, a fortress of gray stone, unlovely except for the one extravagance — a concession to the princess — of a single, pointed tower flying a lavender pennant. Inside there were tapestries on the walls, a suit of armor with French script over the visor, and, in black leotards, Clementine's slender mother. She was doing leg lifts.

"This is Callie," Clementine said. "She's coming over to play."

I beamed. I attempted a kind of curtsy. (This was my introduction to polite society, after all.) But Clementine's mother didn't so much as turn her head.

"We just moved in," I said. "We live in the house behind yours."

Now she frowned. I thought I'd said something wrong — my first etiquette mistake in Grosse Pointe. Mrs. Stark said, "Why don't you girls go upstairs?"

We did. In her bedroom Clementine mounted a rocking horse. For the next three minutes she rode it without saying another word. Then she abruptly got off. "I used to have a turtle but he escaped."

"He did?"

"My mom says he could survive if he made it outside."

"He's probably dead," I said.

Clementine accepted this bravely. She came over and held her arm next to mine. "Look, I've got freckles like the Big Dipper," she announced. We stood side to side before the full-length mirror, making faces. The rims of Clementine's eyes were inflamed. She yawned. She rubbed her nose with the heel of her hand. And then she asked, "Do you want to practice kissing?"

I didn't know what to answer. I already knew how to kiss, didn't I? Was there something more to learn? But while these questions were going through my head, Clementine was going ahead with the lesson. She came around to face me. With a grave expression she put her arms around my neck.

The necessary special effects are not in my possession, but what I'd like for you to imagine is Clementine's white face coming close to mine, her sleepy eyes closing, her medicine-sweet lips puckering up, and all the other sounds of the world going silent — the rustling of our dresses, her mother counting leg lifts downstairs, the airplane outside making an exclamation mark in the sky — all silent, as Clementine's highly educated, eight-year-old lips met mine.

And then, somewhere below this, my heart reacting.

Not a thump exactly. Not even a leap. But a kind of swish, like a frog kicking off from a muddy bank. My heart, that amphibian, moving that moment between two elements: one, excitement; the other, fear. I tried to pay attention. I tried to hold up my end of things. But Clementine was way ahead of me. She swiveled her head back and forth the way actresses did in the movies. I started doing the same, but out of the corner of her mouth she scolded, "You're the man." So I stopped. I stood stiffly with arms at my sides. Finally Clementine broke off the kiss. She looked at me blankly a moment, and then responded, "Not bad for your first time."

"Mo-om!" I shouted, coming home that evening. "I made a fri-end!" I told Tessie about Clementine, the old rugs on the walls, the pretty mother doing exercises, omitting only the kissing lessons. From the beginning I was aware that there was something improper about the way I felt about Clementine Stark, something I shouldn't tell my mother, but I wouldn't have been able to articulate it. I didn't connect this feeling to sex. I didn't know sex existed. "Can I invite her over?"

"Sure," said Tessie, relieved that my loneliness in the neighborhood was now over.

"I bet she's never seen a house like ours."

And now it is a cool, gray October day a week or so later. From the back of a yellow house, two girls emerge, playing geisha. We have coiled up our hair and crossed take-out chopsticks in it. We wear sandals and silk shawls. We carry umbrellas, pretending they're parasols. I know bits of *The Flower Drum Song*, which I sing as we traverse the courtyard and mount the steps to the bath-house. We come in the door, failing to notice a dark shape in the corner. Inside, the bath is a bright, bubbling turquoise. Silk robes fall to floor. Two giggling flamingos, one fair-skinned, the other light olive, test the water with one toe each. "It's too hot." "It's supposed to be that way." "You first." "No, you." "Okay." And then: in. Both of us. The smell of redwood and eucalyptus. The smell of sandalwood soap. Clementine's hair plastered to her skull. Her foot appearing now and then above the water like a shark fin. We laugh, float, waste my mother's bath beads. Steam rises from the surface so thick it obscures the walls, the ceiling, the dark shape in the corner. I'm examining the arches of my feet, trying to understand what it means that they have "fallen," when I see Clementine breasting through the water to me. Her face appears out of the steam. I think we're going to kiss again, but instead she wraps her legs around my waist. She's laughing hysterically, covering her mouth. Her eyes widen and she says into my ear, "Get some comfort." She hoots like a monkey and pulls me back onto a shelf in the tub. I fall between her legs, I fall on top of her, we sink . . . and then we're twirling, spinning in the water, me on top, then her, then me, and giggling, and making bird cries. Steam envelops us, cloaks us; light sparkles on the agitated water; and we keep spinning, so that at some point I'm not sure which hands are mine, which legs. We aren't kissing. This game is far less serious, more playful, free-style, but we're gripping each other, trying not to let the other's slippery body go, and our knees bump, our tummies slap, our hips slide back and forth. Various submerged softnesses on Clementine's body are delivering crucial information to mine, information I store away but won't understand until years later. How long do we spin? I have no idea. But at some point we get tired. Clementine beaches on the shelf, with me on top. I rise on my knees to get my bearings — and then freeze, hot water or not. For right there, sitting in the corner of the room — is my grandfather! I see him for a second, leaning over sideways — is he laughing? angry? — and then the steam rises again and blots him out.

I am too stunned to move or speak. How long has he been there? What did he see? "We were just doing water ballet," Clementine says lamely. The steam parts again. Lefty hasn't moved. He's sitting exactly as before, head tilted to one side. He looks as pale as Clementine. For one crazy second I think he's playing our driving game, pretending to sleep, but then I understand that he will never play anything ever again . . .

And next all the intercoms in the house are wailing. I shout to Tessie in the kitchen, who shouts to Milton in the den, who shouts to Desdemona in the guest house. "Come quick! Something's wrong with *papou!*" And then more screaming and an ambulance flashing its lights and my mother telling Clementine it's time for her to go home now.

Later that night: the spotlight rises on two rooms in our new house on Middlesex. In one pool of light, an old woman crosses herself and prays, while in the other a seven-year-old girl is also praying, praying for forgiveness, because it was clear to me that I was responsible. It was what I did . . . what Lefty saw . . . And I am promising never to do anything like that again and asking *Please don't let* papou *die* and swearing *It was Clementine's fault. She made me do it.*

(And now it's time for Mr. Stark's heart to have its moment. Its arteries coated with what looks like foie gras, it seizes up one day. Clementine's father crumples forward in the shower. Down on the first floor, sensing something, Mrs. Stark stops doing leg lifts; and three weeks later she sells the house and moves her daughter away. I never saw Clementine again . . .)

★ ★ ★

Lefty did recover and came home from the hospital. But this was only a pause in the slow but inevitable dissolution of his mind. Over the next three years, the hard disk of his memory slowly began to be erased, beginning with the most recent information and proceeding backward. At first Lefty forgot short-term things like where'd he put down his fountain pen or his glasses, and then he forgot what day it was, what month, and finally what year. Chunks of his life fell away, so that while we were moving ahead in time, he was moving back. In 1969 it became clear to us that he was living in 1968, because he kept shaking his head over the assassinations of Martin Luther King, Jr., and Robert Kennedy. By the time we crossed over into the valley of the seventies, Lefty was back in the fifties. Once again he was excited about the completion of the St. Lawrence Seaway, and he stopped referring to me altogether because I hadn't been born. He reexperienced his gambling mania and his feelings of uselessness after retiring, but this soon passed because it was the 1940s and he was running the bar and grill again. Every morning he got up as though he were going to work. Desdemona had to devise elaborate ruses to satisfy him, telling him that our kitchen was the Zebra Room, only redecorated, and lamenting at how bad business was. Sometimes she invited ladies from church over who played along, ordering coffee and leaving money on the kitchen counter.

In his mind Lefty Stephanides grew younger and younger while in actuality he continued to age, so that he often tried to lift things he couldn't or to tackle stairs his legs couldn't climb. Falls ensued. Things shattered. At these moments, bending to help him up, Desdemona would see a momentary clarity in her husband's eyes, as if he were playing along too, pretending to relive his life in the past so as not to face the present. Then he would begin to cry and Desdemona would lie down next to him, holding him until the fit ended.

But soon he was back in the thirties and was searching the radio, listening for speeches from FDR. He mistook our black milkman for Jimmy Zizmo and sometimes climbed up into his truck, thinking they were going rum-running. Using his chalkboard, he engaged the milkman in conversations about bootleg whiskey, and even if this had made sense, the milkman wouldn't have been able to understand, because right about this time Lefty's English began to deteriorate. He made spelling and grammatical mistakes he'd long mastered and soon he was writing broken English and then no English at all. He made written allusions to Bursa, and now Desdemona began to worry. She knew that the backward progression of her husband's mind could lead to only one place, back to the days when he wasn't her husband but her brother, and she lay in bed at night awaiting the moment with trepidation. In a sense she began to live in reverse, too, because she suffered the heart palpitations of her youth. *O God,* she prayed, *Let me die now. Before Lefty gets back to the boat.* And then one morning when she got up, Lefty was sitting at the breakfast table. His hair was pomaded à la Valentino with some Vaseline he'd found in the medicine chest. A dishrag was wrapped around his neck like a scarf. And on the table was the chalkboard, on which was written, in Greek, "Good morning, sis."

For three days he teased her as he used to do, and pulled her hair, and performed dirty Karaghiozis puppet shows. Desdemona hid his chalkboard, but it was no use. During Sunday dinner he took a fountain pen from Uncle Pete's shirt pocket and wrote on the tablecloth, "Tell my sister she's getting fat." Desdemona blanched. She put her hands to her face and waited for the blow she'd always feared to descend. But Peter Tatakis only took the pen from Lefty and said, "It appears that Lefty is now under the delusion that you are his sister." Everyone laughed. What else could they do? *Hey there, sis,* everyone kept saying to Desdemona all afternoon, and each time she jumped; each time she thought her heart would stop.

But this stage didn't last long. My grandfather's mind, locked in its graveyard spiral, accelerated as it hurtled toward its destruction, and three days later he started cooing like a baby and the next he started soiling himself. At that point, when there was almost nothing left of him, God allowed Lefty Stephanides to remain another three months, until the winter of 1970. In the end he became as fragmentary as the poems of Sappho he never succeeded in restoring, and finally one morning he looked up into the face of the woman who'd been the greatest love of his life and failed to recognize her. And then there was another kind of blow inside his head; blood pooled in his brain for the last time, washing even the last fragments of his self away.

From the beginning there existed a strange balance between my grandfather and me. As I cried my first cry, Lefty was silenced; and as he gradually lost the ability to see, to taste, to hear, to think or even remember, I began to see, taste, and remember everything, even stuff I hadn't

490

seen, eaten, or done. Already latent inside me, like the future 120 mph serve of a tennis prodigy, was the ability to communicate between the genders, to see not with the monovision of one sex but in the stereoscope of both. So that at the *makaria* after the funeral, I looked around the table at the Grecian Gardens and knew what everyone was feeling. Milton was beset by a storm of emotion he refused to acknowledge. He worried that if he spoke he might start to cry, and so said nothing throughout the meal, and plugged his mouth with bread. Tessie was seized with a desperate love for Chapter Eleven and me and kept hugging us and smoothing our hair, because children were the only balm against death. Sourmelina was remembering the day at Grand Trunk when she'd told Lefty that she would know his nose anywhere. Peter Tatakis was lamenting the fact that he would never have a widow to mourn his death. Father Mike was favorably reviewing the eulogy he'd given earlier that morning, while Aunt Zo was wishing she had married someone like her father.

The only one whose emotions I couldn't plumb was Desdemona. Silently, in the widow's position of honor at the head of the table, she picked at her whitefish and drank her glass of Mavrodaphne, but her thoughts were as obscured to me as her face behind her black veil.

Lacking any clairvoyance into my grandmother's state of mind that day, I'll just tell you what happened next. After the *makaria,* my parents, grandmother, brother, and I got into my father's Fleetwood. With a purple funeral pennant flying from the antenna, we left Greektown and headed down Jefferson. The Cadillac was three years old now, the oldest one Milton ever had. As we were passing the old Medusa Cement factory, I heard a long hiss and thought that my *yia yia,* sitting next to me, was sighing over her misfortunes. But then I noticed that the seat was tilting. Desdemona was sinking down. She who had always feared automobiles was being swallowed by the backseat.

It was the Air-Ride. You weren't supposed to turn it on unless you were going at least thirty miles per hour. Distracted by grief, Milton had been going only twenty-five. The hydraulic system ruptured. The passenger side of the car sloped down and stayed like that from then on. (And my father began trading his cars in every year.)

Limping, dragging, we returned home. My mother helped Desdemona out of the car and led her to the guest house out back. It took some time. Desdemona kept leaning on her cane to rest. Finally, outside her door, she announced, "Tessie, I am going to bed now."

"Okay, *yia yia*," my mother said. "You take a rest."

"I am going to bed," Desdemona said again. She turned and went inside. Beside the bed, her silkworm box was still open. That morning, she had taken out Lefty's wedding crown, cutting it away from her own so he could be buried with it. She looked into the box for a moment now before closing it. Then she undressed. She took off her black dress and hung it in the garment bag full of mothballs. She returned her shoes to the box from Penney's. After putting on her nightgown, she rinsed out her panty hose in the bathroom and hung them over the shower rod. And then, even though it was only three in the afternoon, she got into bed.

For the next ten years, except for a bath every Friday, she never got out again.

The Mediterranean Diet

She didn't like being left on earth. She didn't like being left in America. She was tired of living. She was having a harder and harder time climbing stairs. A woman's life was over once her husband died. Somebody had given her the evil eye.

Such were the answers Father Mike brought back to us the third day after Desdemona refused to get out of bed. My mother asked him to talk to her and he returned from the guest house with his Fra Angelico eyebrows lifted in tender exasperation. "Don't worry, it'll pass," he said. "I see this kind of thing with widows all the time."

We believed him. But as the weeks went by, Desdemona only became more depressed and withdrawn. A habitual early riser, she began to sleep late. When my mother brought in a breakfast tray, Desdemona opened one eye and gestured for her to leave it. Eggs got cold. Coffee filmed over. The only thing that roused her was her daily lineup of soap operas. She watched the cheating husbands and

494

scheming wives as faithfully as ever, but she didn't reprimand them anymore, as if she'd given up correcting the errors of the world. Propped up against the headboard, her hairnet cinched on her forehead like a diadem, Desdemona looked as ancient and indomitable as the elderly Queen Victoria. A queen of a sceptered isle that consisted only of a bird-filled bedroom. A queen in exile, with only two attendants remaining, Tessie and me.

"Pray for me to die," she instructed me. "Pray for *yia yia* to die and go be with *papou*."

. . . But before I go on with Desdemona's story, I want to update you on developments with Julie Kikuchi. With regard to the main point: there have been no developments. On our last day in Pomerania, we got very cozy, Julie and I. Pomerania belonged to East Germany. The seaside villas of Herringsdorf had been allowed to fall apart for fifty years. Now, after reunification, there is a real estate boom. Being Americans, Julie and I could not fail but be alert to this. As we strolled the wide boardwalk, holding hands, we speculated about buying this or that old, crumbling villa and fixing it up. "We could get used to the nudists," Julie said. "We could get a Pomeranian," I said. I don't know what came over us. That "we." We were prodigal in its usage, we were reckless with its implications. Artists have good instincts for real estate. And Herringsdorf energized Julie. We inquired about a few co-ops, a new thing here. We toured two or three mansions. It was all very marital. Under the influence of that old, aristocratic, nineteenth-century summer resort, Julie and I were acting old-fashioned, too. We discussed setting up house without even having slept together. But of course we never mentioned love or marriage. Only down payments.

But on the way back to Berlin a familiar fear descended on me. Humming over the road, I began to look ahead. I thought of the next step and what would be required of me. The preparations, the explanations, the very real possibility of shock, horror, withdrawal, rebuff. The usual reactions.

"What's the matter?" Julie asked me.

"Nothing."

"You seem quiet."

"Just tired."

In Berlin, I dropped her off. My hug was cold, peremptory. I haven't called her since. She left a message on my machine. I didn't respond. And now she has stopped calling, too. So it's all over with Julie. Over before it began. And instead of sharing a future with someone, I am back again with the past, with Desdemona who wanted no future at all . . .

I brought her dinner, sometimes lunch. I carried trays along the portico of brown metal posts. Above was the sun deck, underutilized, the redwood rotting. To my right was the bathhouse, smooth and poured. The guest house repeated the clean, rectilinear lines of the main house. The architecture of Middlesex was an attempt to rediscover pure origins. At the time, I didn't know about all that. But as I pushed through the door into the skylit guest house I was aware of the disparities. The boxlike room, stripped of all embellishment or parlor fussiness, a room that wished to be timeless or ahistorical, and there, in the middle of it, my deeply historical, timeworn grandmother. Everything about Middlesex spoke of forgetting and everything about Desdemona made plain the inescapability of remembering. Against her heap of pillows she lay, exuding woe vapors, but in a kindly way. That was the signature of my grandmother and the Greek ladies of her generation: the kindliness of their despair. How they moaned while offering you sweets! How they complained of physical ailments while patting your knee! My visits always cheered Desdemona up. "Hello, dolly *mou*," she

497

said, smiling. I sat on the bed as she stroked my hair, cooing endearments in Greek. With my brother Desdemona kept a happy face the entire time he was there. But with me, after ten minutes, her buoyant eyes subsided, and she told me the truth about how she felt. "I am too old now. Too old, honey."

Her lifelong hypochondria had never had a better field in which to flower. When she first sentenced herself to the mahogany limbo of her four-poster bed, Desdemona complained only of her usual heart palpitations. But a week later she began to suffer fatigue, dizziness, and circulation problems. "I am having in my legs pain. The blood it doesn't move."

"She's fine," Dr. Philobosian told my parents, after a half-hour examination. "Not young anymore, but I see nothing serious."

"I no can breathe!" Desdemona argued with him.

"Your lungs sound fine."

"My leg it is like needles."

"Try rubbing it. To stimulate the circulation."

"He's too old now too," Desdemona said after Dr. Phil had left. "Get me a new doctor who he isn't already dead himself."

My parents complied. Violating our family loyalty to Dr. Phil, they went behind his back and called in new physicians. A Dr. Tuttlesworth. A Dr. Katz. The unfortunately named Dr. Cold. Every single one gave Desdemona the same dire diagnosis that there was nothing wrong with her. They looked into the wrinkled prunes of her eyes; they peered into the dried apricots of her ears; they listened to the indestructible pump of her heart, and pronounced her well.

We tried to cajole her out of bed. We invited her to watch *Never on Sunday* on the big television. We called Aunt Lina in New Mexico and put the phone up to the intercom. "Listen, Des, why don't you visit me down here? It's so hot you'll think you're back in the *horeo*."

"I no can hear you, Lina!" Desdemona shouted, despite her lung problems. "It is working no good the machine!"

Finally, appealing to Desdemona's fear of God, Tessie told her that it was a sin to miss church when you were physically able to go. But Desdemona patted the mattress. "The next time I go to the church is in a coffin."

She began to make final preparations. From her bed she directed my mother to clean out the closets. "*Papou's* clothes you can give to the Goodwill. My nice dresses, too. Now I only need something for to bury me." The necessity of caring for her husband during his final years had made Desdemona a bundle of activity. Only a few months before, she'd been peeling and stewing the soft food he ate, changing his diapers, cleaning his bedding and pajamas, and harrying his body with moistened towels and Q-tips. But now, at seventy, the strain of having no one to care for but herself aged her overnight. Her salt-and-pepper hair turned completely gray and her robust figure sprang a slow leak, so that she seemed to be deflating day by day. She grew paler. Veins showed. Tiny red sunspots burst on her chest. She stopped checking her face in the mirror. Because of her poor dentures, Desdemona hadn't really had lips for years. But now she stopped putting lipstick even in the place where her lips used to be.

"Miltie," she asked my father one day, "you bought for me the place next to *papou?*"

"Don't worry, Ma. It's a double plot."

"Nobody they are going take it?"

"It's got your name on it, Ma."

"It *no* have my name, Miltie! That why I worry. It have *papou*'s name one side. Other side is grass only. I want you go put sign it says, this place is for *yia yia*. Some other lady maybe she die and try to get next to my husband."

But her funeral preparations didn't end

there. Not only did Desdemona pick out her burial plot. She also picked out her mortician. Georgie Pappas, Sophie Sassoon's brother who worked at the T. J. Thomas Funeral Home, arrived at Middlesex in April (when a bout of pneumonia was looking promising). He carried his sample cases of caskets, crematory urns, and flower arrangements out to the guest house and sat by Desdemona's bed while she looked the photographs over with the excitement of someone browsing travel brochures. She asked Milton what he could afford.

"I don't want to talk about it, Ma. You're not dying."

"I am no asking for the Imperial. Georgie says Imperial is top of line. But for *yia yia* Presidential is okay."

"When the time comes, you can have whatever you want. But —"

"And satin inside. Please. And a pillow. Like here. Page eight. Number five. Pay attention! And tell Georgie leave my glasses."

As far as Desdemona was concerned, death was only another kind of emigration. Instead of sailing from Turkey to America, this time she would be traveling from earth to heaven, where Lefty had already gotten his citizenship and had a place waiting.

Gradually we became accustomed to

Desdemona's retreat from the family sphere. By this time, the spring of 1971, Milton was busy with a new "business venture." After the disaster on Pingree Street, Milton vowed never to make the same mistake again. How do you escape the real estate rule of location, location, location? Simple: be everywhere at once.

"Hot dog stands," Milton announced at dinner one night. "Start with three or four and add on as you go."

With the remaining insurance money Milton rented space in three malls in the Detroit metropolitan area. On a pad of yellow paper, he came up with the design for the stands. "McDonald's has Golden Arches?" he said. "We've got the Pillars of Hercules."

If you ever drove along the blue highways anywhere from Michigan to Florida, anytime from 1971 to 1978, you may have seen the bright white neon pillars that flanked my father's chain of hot dog restaurants. The pillars combined his Greek heritage with the colonial architecture of his beloved native land. Milton's pillars were the Parthenon and the Supreme Court Building; they were the Herakles of myth as well as the Hercules of Hollywood movies. They also got people's attention.

Milton started out with three Hercules Hot Dogs™ but quickly added franchises as profits allowed. He began in Michigan but soon spilled over into Ohio, and from there went on down the Interstate to the deep South. The format was more like Dairy Queen than McDonald's. Seating was minimal or nonexistent (at most a couple of picnic tables). There were no play areas, no sweepstakes or "Happy Meals," no giveaways or promotions. What there was was hot dogs, Coney Island style, as that term was used in Detroit, meaning they were served with chili sauce and onions. Hercules Hot Dogs were side-of-the-road places, and usually not the nicest roads. By bowling alleys, by train stations, in small towns on the way to bigger ones, anywhere where real estate was cheap and a lot of cars or people passed through.

I didn't like the stands. To me they were a steep come-down from the romantic days of the Zebra Room. Where were the knickknacks, the jukebox, the glowing shelf of pies, the deep maroon booths? Where were the regulars? I couldn't understand how these hot dog stands could make so much more money than the diner ever had. But make money they did. After the first, touch-and-go year, my father's chain of hot dog restaurants began to make him a comfortably wealthy man. Aside from securing good locations, there was another element to my father's success. A gimmick or, in today's parlance, a "branding." Ball Park franks plumped when you cooked them, but Hercules Hot Dogs did something better. They came out of the package looking like normal, udder-pink wieners, but as they got hot, an amazing transformation took place. Sizzling on the grill, the hot dogs bulged in the middle, grew fatter, and, yes, *flexed*.

This was Chapter Eleven's contribution. One night, my then seventeen-year-old brother had gone down into the kitchen to make himself a late-night snack. He found some hot dogs in the refrigerator. Not wanting to wait for water to boil, he got out a frying pan. Next he decided to cut the hot dogs in half. "I wanted to increase the surface area," he explained to me later. Rather than slicing the hot dogs length-wise, Chapter Eleven tried various combinations to amuse himself. He made notches here and slits there and then he put all the hot dogs in a pan and watched what happened.

Not much, that first night. But a few of my brother's incisions resulted in the hot dogs assuming funny shapes. After that, it became a kind of game with him. He grew adept at manipulating the shapes of cooking hot dogs and, for fun, developed an entire line of gag frankfurters. There was the hot dog that stood on end when heated, resembling the Tower of Pisa. In honor of the moon landing, there was the Apollo 11, whose skin gradually stretched until, bursting, the wiener appeared to blast off into the air. Chapter Eleven made hot dogs that danced to Sammy Davis's rendition of "Bojangles" and others that formed letters, *L* and *S*, though he never accomplished a decent *Z*. (For his friends he had hot dogs do other things. Laughter emanated from the kitchen late at night. You heard Chapter Eleven: "I call this the Harry Reems," and then the other boys shouting: "No way, Stephanides!" And while we're on the subject, was I the only one who was shocked by those old Ball Park ads with their shots of red franks swelling and lengthening? Where were the censors? Did anyone notice the expressions on mothers' faces when those ads played, or the way, right afterward, they often discussed what kind of "buns" they preferred? I certainly noticed, because I was a girl at the time and those ads were designed to get my attention.)

Once you ate a Hercules hot dog you never forgot it. Very quickly they had wide name recognition. A large food processing company offered to buy the rights and sell the hot dogs in stores, but Milton, mistakenly thinking that popularity is eternal, rejected it.

Aside from inventing the Herculean frankfurters, my brother had little interest in the family business. "I'm an inventor," he said. "Not a hot dog man." In Grosse Pointe he fell into a group of boys whose main bond was their unpopularity. A hot Saturday night for them consisted of sitting in my brother's room, staring at Escher prints. For hours they followed figures up staircases that were also going down, or watched geese turn into fish and then into geese again. They ate peanut butter crackers, getting gunk all over their teeth while quizzing each other on the periodic table. Steve Munger, Chapter Eleven's best friend, used to infuriate my father with philosophical arguments. ("But how can you *prove* you exist, Mr. Stephanides?") Whenever we picked my brother up at school I saw him through a stranger's eyes. Chapter Eleven was geeky, nerdy. His body was a stalk supporting the tulip of his brain. As he walked to the car, his head was often tilted back, alert to phenomena in the trees. He didn't pick up on styles or trends. Tessie still bought his clothes for him. Because he was my older brother, I admired him; but because I was his sister, I felt superior. In doling out our respective gifts God had given me all the important ones. Mathematical aptitude: to Chapter Eleven. Verbal aptitude: to me. Fix-it handiness: to Chapter Eleven. Imagination: to me. Musical talent: to Chapter Eleven. Looks: to me.

The beauty I possessed as a baby only increased as I grew into a girl. It was no surprise why Clementine Stark had wanted to practice kissing with me. Everyone wanted to. Elderly waitresses bent close to take my order. Red-faced boys appeared at my desk, stammering, "Y-y-you dropped your eraser." Even Tessie, angry about something, would look down at me — at my Cleopatra eyes — and forget what she was mad about. Wasn't there the slightest rumble in the air whenever I brought in drinks to the Sunday debaters? Uncle Pete, Jimmy Fioretos, Gus Panos, men fifty, sixty, seventy years old looking up over expansive bellies and having thoughts they didn't admit? Back in Bithynios, where sustained respiration rendered a bachelor eligible, men of equivalent age had successfully asked for the hand of a girl like me. Were they remembering those days, lounging on our love seats? Were they thinking, "If this wasn't America, I just might . . ."? I can't say. Looking back now, I can only remember a time when the world seemed to have a million eyes, silently opening wherever I went. Most of the time they were camouflaged, like the closed eyes of green lizards in green trees.

But then they snapped open — on the bus, in the pharmacy — and I felt the intensity of all that looking, the desire and the desperation.

For hours at a time I would admire my looks myself, turning this way and that before the mirror, or assuming a relaxed pose to see what I looked like in real life. By holding a hand mirror I could see my profile, still harmonious at the time. I combed my long hair and sometimes stole my mother's mascara to do my eyes. But increasingly my narcissistic pleasure was tempered by the unlovely condition of the pool into which I gazed.

"He's popping his zits again!" I complained to my mother.

"Don't be so squeamish, Callie. It's just a little . . . here, I'll wipe it off."

"Gross!"

"Wait'll you get pimples!" Chapter Eleven shouted, ashamed and furious, from the hallway.

"I'm not going to."

"You will, too! Everybody's sebaceous glands overproduce when they go through puberty!"

"Quiet, both of you," said Tessie, but she didn't need to. I'd already gotten quiet on my own. It was that word: *puberty*. The source of a great amount of anxious speculation on my part at the time. A word that lay in wait for me, jumping out now and then, scaring me because I didn't know exactly what it meant. But now at least I knew one thing: Chapter Eleven was involved in it somehow. Maybe that explained not only the pimples but the other thing about my brother I'd been noticing lately.

Not long after Desdemona took to her bed, I'd begun to notice, in the vague creepy way of a sister with a brother, a new, solitary pastime of Chapter Eleven's. It was a matter of a perceptible activity behind the locked bathroom door. Of a certain strain to the reply, "Just a minute," when I knocked. Still, I was younger than he was and ignorant of the pressing needs of adolescent boys.

But let me backtrack a minute. Three years earlier, when Chapter Eleven was fourteen and I was eight, my brother had played a trick on me. It happened on a night when our parents had gone out to dinner. It was raining and thundering. I was watching television when Chapter Eleven suddenly appeared. He was holding out a lemon cake. "Look what I have!" he sang.

Magnanimously he cut me a slice. He watched me eat it. Then he said, "I'm telling! That cake was for Sunday."

"No fair!"

I ran at him. I tried to hit him, but he caught my arms. We wrestled standing up, until finally Chapter Eleven offered a deal.

As I said: in those days, the world was always growing eyes. Here were two more. They belonged to my brother, who, in the guest bathroom, amid the fancy hand towels, stood watching as I pulled down my underpants and lifted my skirt. (If I showed him, he wouldn't tell.) Fascinated as he was, he stayed at a distance. His Adam's apple rose and fell. He looked amazed and frightened. He didn't have much to compare me to, but what he saw didn't misinform him either: pink folds, a cleft. For ten seconds Chapter Eleven studied my documents, detecting no forgery, as the clouds burst overhead, and I made him get me one more piece of cake.

Apparently, Chapter Eleven's curiosity hadn't been satisfied by looking at his eight-year-old sister. Now, I suspected, he was looking at pictures of the real thing.

In 1971, all the men in our lives were gone, Lefty to death, Milton to Hercules Hot Dogs, and Chapter Eleven to bathroom solitaire. Leaving Tessie and me to deal with Desdemona.

We had to cut her toenails. We had to hunt down flies that found their way into her room. We had to move her birdcages around according to the light. We had to turn on the television for the day's soap operas and we had to turn it off before the murders on the evening news. Desdemona didn't want to lose her dignity, however. When nature called, she called us on the intercom, and we helped her out of bed and into the bathroom.

The simplest way to say it is: years passed. As the seasons changed outside the windows, as the weeping willows shed their million leaves, as snow fell on the flat roof and the angle of sunlight declined, Desdemona remained in bed. She was still there when the snow melted and the willows budded again. She was there when the sun, climbing higher, dropped a sunbeam straight through the skylight, like a ladder to heaven she was more than eager to climb.

What happened while Desdemona was in bed:

Aunt Lina's friend Mrs. Watson died, and with the poor judgment grief always brings, Sourmelina decided to sell their adobe house and move back north to be close to her family. She arrived in Detroit in February of 1972. The winter weather felt colder than she ever remembered. Worse, her time in the Southwest had changed her. Somehow in the course of her life Sourmelina had become an American. Almost nothing of the village remained in her. Her self-entombed cousin, on the other hand, had never left it. They were both in their seventies, but Desdemona was an old, gray-haired widow waiting to die while Lina, another kind of widow entirely, was a bottle redhead who drove a Firebird and wore belted denim skirts with turquoise belt buckles. After her life in the sexual counterculture, Lina found my parents' heterosexuality as quaint as a sampler. Chapter Eleven's acne alarmed her. She disliked sharing a shower with him. A strained atmosphere existed in our house while Sourmelina stayed with us. She was as garish and out of place in our living room as a retired Vegas showgirl, and because we watched her so closely out of the corners of our eyes, everything she did made too much noise, her cigarette smoke got into everything, she drank too much wine at dinner.

We got to know our new neighbors. There were the Picketts, Nelson, who'd played tackle for Georgia Tech and now worked for Parke-Davis, the pharmaceutical company, and his wife, Bonnie, who was always reading the miraculous tales in *Guideposts*. Across the street was Stew "Bright Eyes" Fiddler, an industrial parts salesman with a taste for bourbon and barmaids, and his wife, Mizzi, whose hair changed color like a mood ring. At the end of the block were Sam and Hettie Grossinger, the first Orthodox Jews we'd ever met, and their only child, Maxine, a shy violin prodigy. Sam, however, was funny, and Hettie was loud, and they talked about money without thinking it was impolite, and so we felt comfortable around them. Milt and Tessie often had the Grossingers over to dinner, though their dietary restrictions continually baffled us. My mother would drive all the way across town to buy kosher meat, for instance, only to serve it with a cream sauce. Or she would skip the meat and cream altogether and serve crab cakes. Though faithful to their religion, the Grossingers were midwestern Jews, low-key and assimilationist. They hid behind their wall of cypresses and at Christmas put up a Santa Claus along with lights.

In 1971: Judge Stephen J. Roth of the U.S. District Court ruled that *de jure* segregation existed in the Detroit school system. He immediately ordered the schools to be desegregated. There was only one problem. By 1971 the Detroit student population was 80 percent black. "That busing judge can bus all he wants," Milton crowed, reading about the decision in the paper. "Doesn't make any difference now. You see, Tessie? You understand why your dear old husband wanted to get the kids out of that school system? Because if I didn't, that goddamn Roth would be busing them to school in downtown Nairobi, that's why."

In 1972: Five-foot five-inch S. Miyamoto, rejected by the Detroit police force for failing to meet the five-foot seven-inch requirement (he had tried elevator heels, etc.), appeared on *The Tonight Show* to plead his case. I wrote a letter to the police commissioner myself in support of Miyamoto, but I never received a reply, and Miyamoto was rejected. A few months later, Police Commissioner Nichols was thrown from his horse during a parade. "That's what you get!" I said.

In 1972: H. D. Jackson and L. D. Moore, who had brought a police brutality case for four million dollars, hijacked a Southern Airways jet to Cuba, outraged at being awarded damages in the amount of twenty-five dollars.

In 1972: Mayor Roman Gribbs claimed that Detroit had turned around. The city had overcome the trauma of the '67 riots. Therefore, he wasn't planning on running for another term. A new candidate appeared, the man who would become the city's first African American mayor, Coleman A. Young.

And I turned twelve.

A few months earlier, on the first day of

sixth grade, Carol Horning came into class wearing a slight but unmistakably self-satisfied smile. Below this smile, as if displayed on a trophy shelf, were the new breasts she had gotten over the summer. She wasn't the only one. During the growing months, quite a few of my schoolmates had — as adults liked to say — "developed."

I wasn't entirely unprepared for this. I'd spent a month the previous summer at Camp Ponshewaing, near Port Huron. During the slow march of summer days I was aware, as one is aware of a drum steadily beating across a lake, of something unspooling itself in the bodies of my campmates. Girls were growing modest. They turned their backs to dress. Some had surnames stitched onto not only shorts and socks but training bras, too. Mostly, it was a personal matter that no one spoke about. But now and then there were dramatic manifestations. One afternoon during swimming hour, the tin door of the changing room clanged open and shut. The sound caromed off the trunks of pine trees, carrying past the meager beach out over the water, where I floated on an inner tube, reading *Love Story*. (Swimming hour was the only time I could get any reading done, and though the camp counselors tried to motivate me to practice my freestyle, I persevered every day in reading the new bestseller I'd found on my mother's night table.) Now I looked up. Along a dusty brown path in the pine needles, Jenny Simonson was advancing in a red, white, and blue swimsuit. All nature grew hushed at the sight. Birds fell silent. Lake swans unfurled tremendous necks to get a glimpse. Even a chainsaw in the distance cut its engine. I beheld the magnificence of Jenny S. The golden, late afternoon light intensified around her. Her patriotic swimsuit swelled in ways no one else's did. Muscles flexed in her long thighs. She ran to the end of the dock and plunged into the lake, where a throng of naiads (her friends from Cedar Rapids) swam over to meet her.

Lowering my book, I looked down at my own body. There it was, as usual: the flat chest, the nothing hips, the forked, mosquito-bitten legs. Lake water and sun were making my skin peel. My fingers had gotten all wrinkly.

Thanks to Dr. Phil's decrepitude and Tessie's prudishness, I arrived at puberty not knowing much about what to expect. Dr. Philobosian still had an office near Women's Hospital, though the hospital itself had been closed down by then. His practice had changed considerably. There were a few remaining elderly patients who, having survived so long under his care, were afraid to change doctors. The rest were welfare families. Nurse Rosalee ran the office. She and Dr. Phil had been married a year after they met delivering me. Now she did the scheduling and administered shots. Her Appalachian childhood had acquainted her with government assistance, and she was a whiz with the Medicaid forms.

In his eighties, Dr. Phil had taken up painting. His office walls were covered salon-style with thick, swirling oils. He didn't use a brush much, mainly a palette knife. And what did he paint? Smyrna? The quay at dawn? The terrible fire? No. Like many amateurs, Dr. Phil assumed that the only proper subject for art was a picturesque landscape that had nothing to do with his experience. He painted sea vistas he'd never seen and forest hamlets he'd never visited, complete with a pipe-smoking figure resting on a log. Dr. Philobosian never talked about Smyrna and left the room if anyone did. He never mentioned his first wife, or his murdered sons and daughters. Maybe this was the reason for his survival.

Nevertheless, Dr. Phil was becoming a fossil. For my annual physical in 1972 he used diagnostic methods popular back in medical school in 1910. There was a trick where he pretended to slap me in the face to check my reflexes. There was an auscultation accomplished with a wineglass. When he bent his head to listen to my heart I was treated to an aerial view of the Galápagos of scabs on his bald pate. (The archipelago changed position from year to year, continentally drifting across the globe of his skull but never healing.) Dr. Philobosian smelled like an old couch, of hair oil and spilled soup, of unscheduled naps. His medical diploma looked as if it were written on parchment. I wouldn't have been surprised if, to cure fever, Dr. Phil had written out a prescription for leeches. He was correct with me, never friendly, and directed most of his conversation to Tessie, who sat in a chair in the corner. What memories, I wonder, was Dr. Phil avoiding in not looking at me? Did the ghosts of Levantine girls haunt those cursory checkups, suggested by the fragility of my collarbone, or the birdcall of my small, congested lungs? Was he trying not to think of water palaces and loosened robes, or was he just tired, old, half-blind, and too proud to admit it?

Whatever the answer, year after year, Tessie faithfully took me to him, in repayment for an act of charity during a catastrophe he would no longer acknowledge. In his waiting room I encountered the same tattered *Highlights* magazine every visit.

"Can you find these?" the puzzle asked inside. And there in the spreading chestnut tree were the knife, the dog, the fish, the old woman, the candlestick — all circled by my own hand, shaky with earache, years and years before.

My mother avoided bodily matters, too. She never spoke openly about sex. She never undressed in front of me. She disliked dirty jokes or nudity in movies. For his own part, Milton was unable to discuss the birds and the bees with his young daughter, and so I was left, in those years, to figure things out for myself.

From hints Aunt Zo let slip in the kitchen I was aware that something happened to women every so often, something they didn't like, something men didn't have to put up with (like everything else). Whatever it was, it seemed safely far off, like getting married or giving birth. And then one day at Camp Ponshewaing, Rebecca Urbanus climbed up on a chair. Rebecca was from South Carolina. She had slave-owning ancestors and a trained voice. During dances with the boys from the neighboring camp, she waved a hand in front of her face as though holding a fan. Why was she up on a chair? We were having a talent show. Rebecca Urbanus was maybe singing or reciting the poetry of Walter de la Mare. The sun was still high and her shorts were white. And then suddenly, as she sang (or recited), the back of her white shorts darkened. At first it appeared to be only a shadow of the surrounding trees. Some kid's waving hand. But no: while our band of twelve-year-olds sat watching, each of us in camp T-shirt and Indian headband, we saw what Rebecca Urbanus didn't. While her upper half performed, her bottom half upstaged her. The stain grew, and it was red. Camp counselors were unsure how to react. Rebecca sang, arms outflung. She revolved on her chair before her theater-in-the-round: us, staring, perplexed and horrified. Certain "advanced" girls understood. Others, like me, thought: knife wound, bear attack. Right then Rebecca Urbanus saw us looking. She looked down herself. And screamed. And fled the stage.

I returned from camp browner and leaner, pinned with a single badge (ironically, for orienteering). But that other badge, which Carol Horning displayed so proudly the first day of school, I was still without. I felt ambivalent about this. On the one hand, if Rebecca Urbanus's mishap was any indication, it might be safer to stay the way I was. What if something similar happened to me? I went through my closet and threw out anything white. I stopped singing altogether. You couldn't control it.

You never knew. It could happen anytime.

Except, with me, it didn't. Gradually, as most of the other girls in my grade began to undergo their own transformations, I began to worry less about possible accidents and more about being left behind, left out.

I am in math class, sometime during the winter of sixth grade. Miss Grotowski, our youngish teacher, is writing an equation on the blackboard. Behind her, at wooden-topped desks, students follow her calculations, or doze, or kick each other from behind. A gray winter Michigan day. The grass outside resembles pewter. Overhead, fluorescent lights attempt to dispel the season's dimness. A picture of the great mathematician Ramanujan (whom we girls at first took to be Miss Grotowski's foreign boyfriend) hangs on the wall. The air is stuffy in the way only air at school can be stuffy.

And behind our teacher's back, in our desks, we are flying through time. Thirty kids, in six neat rows, being borne along at a speed we can't perceive. As Miss Grotowski sketches equations on the board, my classmates all around me begin to change. Jane Blunt's thighs, for instance, seem to get a little bit longer every week. Her sweater swells in front. Then one day Beverly Maas, who sits right next to me, raises her hand and I see darkness up her sleeve: a patch of light brown hair. When did it appear? Yesterday? The day before? The equations get longer and longer throughout the year, more complicated, and maybe it's all the numbers, or the multiplication tables; we are learning to quantify large sums as, by new math, bodies arrive at unexpected answers. Peter Quail's voice is two octaves lower than last month and he doesn't notice. Why not? He's flying too fast. Boys are getting peach fuzz on upper lips. Foreheads and noses are breaking out. Most spectacularly of all, girls are becoming women. Not mentally or emotionally even, but physically. Nature is making its preparations. Deadlines encoded in the species are met.

Only Calliope, in the second row, is motionless, her desk stalled somehow, so that she's the only one who takes in the true extent of the metamorphoses around her. While solving proofs she is aware of Tricia Lamb's purse on the floor next to her desk, of the tampon she glimpsed inside it that morning — which you use how, exactly? — and whom can she ask? Still pretty, Calliope soon finds herself the shortest girl in the room. She drops her eraser. No boy brings it back. In the Christmas pageant she is cast not as Mary as in past years but as an elf . . . But there's still hope, isn't there? . . .

because the desks are flying, day after day; arranged in their squadron, the students bank and roar through time, so that Callie looks up from her ink-stained paper one afternoon and sees it is spring, flowers budding, forsythia in bloom, elms greening; at recess girls and boys hold hands, kissing sometimes behind trees, and Calliope feels gypped, cheated. "Remember me?" she says, to nature. "I'm waiting. I'm still here."

As was Desdemona. By April of 1972, her application to join her husband in heaven was still working its way through a vast, celestial bureaucracy. Though Desdemona was perfectly healthy when she got into bed, the weeks, months, and finally years of inactivity, coupled with her own remarkable willpower to do away with herself, brought her the reward of a *Physician's Handbook* of ailments. During her bedridden years Desdemona had fluid in her lungs; lumbago; bursitis; a spell of eclampsia that manifested itself a half-century later than etiologically normal and then just as mysteriously vanished, to Desdemona's regret; a severe case of shingles that made her ribs and back the color and texture of ripe strawberries and stung like a cattle prod; nineteen colds; a week of purely figurative "walking" pneumonia; ulcers; psychosomatic cataracts which clouded her vision on the anniversaries of her husband's death and which she basically just cried away; and Dupuytren's contracture, where inflamed fascia in her hand curled her thumb and three fingers painfully into her palm, leaving her middle finger raised in an obscene gesture.

One doctor enrolled Desdemona in a longevity study. He was writing an article for a medical journal on "The Mediterranean Diet." To that end he plied Desdemona with questions about the cuisine of her homeland. How much yogurt had she consumed as a child? How much olive oil? Garlic? She answered every one of his queries because she thought his interest indicated that there was something, at last, organically the matter with her, and because she never missed a chance to stroll through the precincts of her childhood. The doctor's name was Müller. German by blood, he renounced his race when it came to its cooking. With postwar guilt, he decried bratwurst, sauerbraten, and Königsberger Klopse as dishes verging on poison. They were the Hitler of foods. Instead he looked to our own Greek diet — our eggplant aswim in tomato sauce, our cucumber dressings and fish-egg spreads, our *pilafi*, raisins, and figs — as potential curatives, as life-giving, artery-cleansing, skin-smoothing wonder drugs. And what

Dr. Müller said appeared to be true: though he was only forty-two, his face was wrinkled, burdened with jowls. Gray hair prickled up on the sides of his head; whereas my father, at forty-eight, despite the coffee stains beneath his eyes, was still the possessor of an unlined olive complexion and a rich, glossy, black head of hair. They didn't call it Grecian Formula for nothing. It was in our food! A veritable fountain of youth in our dolmades and taramasalata and even in our baklava, which didn't commit the sin of containing refined sugar but had only honey. Dr. Müller showed us graphs he'd made, listing the names and birth dates of Italians, Greeks, and a Bulgarian living in the Detroit metropolitan area, and we saw our own entrant — Desdemona Stephanides, age ninety-one — going strong in the midst of the rest. Plotted against Poles killed off by kielbasa, or Belgians done in by pommes frites, or Anglo-Saxons disappeared by puddings, or Spaniards stopped cold by chorizo, our Greek dotted line kept going where theirs tailed off in a tangle of downward trajectories. Who knew? As a people we hadn't had, for the past few millennia, that much to be proud of. So it was perhaps understandable that during Dr. Müller's house calls we failed to mention the troubling anomaly of Lefty's multiple strokes. We didn't want to skew the graph with new data, and so didn't mention that Desdemona was actually seventy-one, not ninety-one, and that she always confused sevens with nines. We didn't mention her aunts, Thalia and Victoria, who both died of breast cancer as young women; and we said nothing about the high blood pressure that taxed the veins within Milton's own smooth, youthful exterior. We couldn't. We didn't want to lose out to the Italians or even that one Bulgarian. And Dr. Müller, lost in his research, didn't notice the store display of mortuary services next to Desdemona's bed, the photograph of the dead husband next to the photograph of his grave, the abundant paraphernalia of a widow abandoned on earth. Not a member of a band of immortals from Mount Olympus. Just the only member left alive.

Meanwhile, tensions between my mother and me were rising.

"Don't *laugh!*"

"I'm sorry, honey. But it's just, you've got nothing to . . . to . . ."

"Mom!"

". . . to hold it up."

A tantrum-edged scream. Twelve-year-old feet running up the stairs, while Tessie called out, "Don't be so dramatic, Callie. We'll get you a bra if you want." Up into my bedroom, where, after locking the door, I pulled off my shirt before the mirror to see . . . that my mother was right. Nothing! Nothing at all to hold up anything. And I burst into tears of frustration and rage.

That evening, when I finally came back down to dinner, I retaliated in the only way I could.

"What's the matter? You're not hungry?"

"I want normal food."

"What do you mean normal food?"

"American food."

"I have to make what *yia yia* likes."

"What about what *I* like?"

"You like spanakopita. You've always liked spanakopita."

"Well, I don't anymore."

"Okay, then. Don't eat. Starve if you want. If you don't like what we give you, you can just sit at the table until we're finished."

Faced with the mirror's evidence, laughed at by my own mother, surrounded by developing classmates, I had come to a dire conclusion. I had begun to believe that the Mediterranean Diet that kept my grandmother alive against her will was also sinisterly retarding my maturity. It only served to reason that the olive oil Tessie drizzled over everything had some mysterious power to stop the body's clock, while the mind, impervious to cooking oils, kept going. That was why Desdemona had the despair and fatigue of a person of ninety along with the arteries of a fifty-year-old. Might it be, I wondered, that the omega-3 fatty acids and the three-vegetables-per-meal I consumed were responsible for retarding my sexual maturity? Was yogurt for breakfast stalling my breast development? It was possible.

"What's the matter, Cal?" asked Milton, eating while reading the evening newspaper. "Don't you want to live to be a hundred?"

"Not if I have to eat this stuff the whole time."

But now Tessie was the one tearing up. Tessie who for almost two years now had taken care of an old lady who wouldn't get out of bed. Tessie who had a husband more in love with hot dogs than her. Tessie who secretly monitored her children's bowel movements and so of course knew exactly how greasy American foods could disrupt their digestion. "You don't do the shopping," she said, tearfully. "You don't see what I see. When's the last time you've been to the drugstore, Little Miss Normal Food? You know what the shelves are full of? Laxatives! Every time I go to the drugstore the person in front of me is buying Ex-Lax. And not just one box.

They buy it by the bushel."

"That's just old people."

"It's not just old people. I see young mothers buying it. I see teenagers buying it. You want to know the truth? This entire country can't do number two!"

"Oh, now I really want to eat."

"Is this about the bra, Callie? Because if it is, I told you —"

"Mo-om!"

But it was too late. "What bra?" Chapter Eleven asked. And now, smiling: "Does the Great Salt Lake think she needs a bra?"

"Shut up."

"Here. My glasses must be dirty. Let me clean them. Ah, that's better. Now let's have a look —"

"Shut *up!*"

"No, I wouldn't say the Great Salt Lake has undergone any kind of geological —"

"Well, your face has, zithead!"

"Still as flat as ever. Perfect for time trials."

But then Milton shouted, "Goddamn it!" — drowning us both out.

We thought he was tired of our bickering.

"That goddamn judge!"

He wasn't looking at us. He was staring at the front page of *The Detroit News*. He was turning red and then — that high blood pressure we hadn't mentioned — almost purple.

That morning, at U.S. District Court, Judge Roth had devised a clever way to desegregate the schools. If there weren't enough white students left in Detroit to go around, he would get them from somewhere else. Judge Roth had claimed jurisdiction over the entire "metropolitan area." Jurisdiction over the city of Detroit and the surrounding fifty-three suburbs. Including Grosse Pointe.

"Just when we get you kids out of that hellhole," Milton was shouting, "that goddamn Roth wants to send you back!"

The Wolverette

"If you've just tuned in, we have one humdinger of a field hockey game on our hands! Final seconds of the last game of the season between those two archrivals, the BCDS Hornets and the B&I Wolverettes. Score tied 4 to 4. Face off at midfield and . . . the Hornets have it! Chamberlain stick-handling, passes to O'Rourke on the wing. O'Rourke faking left, going right . . . she's by one Wolverette, by another . . . and now she passes crossfield to Amigliato! Here comes Becky Amigliato down the sideline! Ten seconds left, nine seconds! In goal for the Wolverettes it's Stephanides and — oh my, my, she doesn't see Amigliato coming! What in the devil? . . . She's looking at a leaf, folks! Callie Stephanides is admiring a gorgeous, fire-red autumn leaf, but what a time to do it! Here comes Amigliato. Five seconds! Four seconds! This is it, folks, the championship of the Middle School Junior Varsity season is on the line — but hold on . . . Stephanides hears footsteps. Now she looks up . . . and Amigliato takes a slap shot! Ooowhee, it's a bullet! You can feel that one all the way up here in the booth. The ball's heading straight for Stephanides' head! She drops the leaf! She's watching it . . . watching it . . . gosh, you hate to see this, folks . . ."

Is it true that right before death (by field hockey ball or otherwise) your life flashes before your eyes? Maybe not your whole life, but parts of it. As Becky Amigliato's slap shot made for my face that fall day, the events of the last half year flickered in my possibly-soon-to-be-extinguished consciousness.

First of all, our Cadillac — by then the golden Fleetwood — wending its way the previous summer up the long driveway of the Baker & Inglis School for Girls. In the backseat, one very unhappy twelve-year-old, me, arriving under duress for an interview. "I don't want to go to a girls' school," I'm complaining. "I'd rather be bused."

And next another car picking me up, the following September, for my first day of seventh grade. Previously, I'd always walked to Trombley Elementary; but prep school has brought with it a host of changes: my new school uniform, for instance, crested and tartaned. Also: this carpool itself, a light green station wagon driven by a lady named Mrs. Drexel. Her hair is greasy, thinning. Above her upper lip, in an example of the foreshadowing I will learn to identify in the coming year's English class, is a mustache.

And now the station wagon is driving along a few weeks later. I'm looking out the window while Mrs. Drexel's cigarette uncoils a rope of smoke. We head into the heart of Grosse Pointe. We pass long, gated driveways, the kind that always fill my family with wonder and awe. But now Mrs. Drexel is turning up these drives. (It is my new classmates who live at the end of them.) We rumble past privet hedges and under topiary arches to arrive at secluded lakefront homes where girls wait with satchels, standing very straight. They wear the same uniform I do, but somehow it looks different on them, neater, more stylish. Occasionally there is also a well-coifed mother in the picture, clipping a rose from the garden.

And next it is two months later, near the end of the fall term, and the station wagon is climbing the hill to my no-longer-brand-new school. The car is full of girls. Mrs. Drexel is lighting another cigarette. She's pulling up to the curb and getting ready to lay a curse on us. Shaking her head at the view — of the hilly, green campus, the lake in the distance — she says, "Youse girls better enjoy it now. Best time of life is when you're young." (At twelve, I hated her for saying that. I couldn't imagine a worse thing to tell a kid. But maybe also, due to certain other changes that began that year, I suspected that the happy period of my childhood was coming to an end.)

What else came back to me, as the hockey ball zeroed in? Just about everything a field hockey ball could symbolize. Field hockey, that New England game, handed down from *old* England, just like everything else in our school. The building with its long echoing hallways and churchy smell, its leaded windows, its Gothic gloom. The Latin primers the color of gruel. The afternoon teas. The curtsying of our tennis team. The tweediness of our faculty, and the curriculum itself, which began, Hellenically, Byronically, with Homer, and then skipped straight to Chaucer, moving on to Shakespeare, Donne, Swift, Wordsworth, Dickens, Tennyson, and E. M. Forster. Only connect.

Miss Baker and Miss Inglis had founded the school back in 1911, in the words of the charter, "to educate girls in the humanities and sciences and to cultivate in them a love of learning, a modest comportment, an amiable grace, and an interest in civic duty above all." The two women had lived together on the far side of the campus in "The Cottage," a shingled bower that occupied a place in school mythology akin to Lincoln's log cabin in national legend. Fifth graders were given a tour every spring. They filed by the two single bedrooms (which fooled them maybe), the founders' writing desks still laid with fountain pens and licorice drops, and the gramophone on which they'd listened to Sousa marches. Miss Baker's and Miss Inglis's ghosts haunted the school, along with actual busts and portraits. A statue in the courtyard showed the bespectacled educators in a fanciful, springtime mood, Miss Baker gesturing, Pope-like, to bless the air, while Miss Inglis (forever the bottom) turned to see what her colleague was bringing to her attention. Miss Inglis's floppy hat obscured her plain features. In the work's only avant-garde touch, a thick wire extended from Miss Baker's head, at the top of which hovered the object of wonder: a hummingbird.

. . . All this was suggested by the spinning hockey ball. But there was something else, something more personal, that explained why I was its target. What was Calliope doing playing goalie? Why was she encumbered by mask and pads? Why was Coach Stork hollering at her to make the save?

To answer simply: I wasn't very good at sports. Softball, basketball, tennis: I was hopeless in every one. Field hockey was even worse. I couldn't get used to the funny little sticks or the nebulous, European strategies. Short on players, Coach Stork put me in goal and hoped for the best. It rarely happened. With a lack of team spirit, some Wolverettes maintained that I possessed no coordination whatsoever. Did this charge have merit? Is there any connection between my present desk job and a lack of physical grace? I'm not going to answer that. But in my defense I will say that none of my more athletic teammates ever inhabited such a problematic body. They didn't have, as I did, two testicles squatting illegally in their inguinal canals. Unknown to me, those anarchists had taken up residence in my abdomen, and were even hooked up to the utilities. If I crossed my leg the wrong way or moved too quickly, a spasm shot across my groin. On the hockey field I often doubled over, my eyes tearing up, while Coach Stork swatted me on the rump. "It's just a *cramp*, Stephanides. Run it off." (And now, as I moved to block the slap shot, just such a pain hit me. My insides twisted, erupting with a lava flow of pain. I bent forward, tripping on my goalie stick. And then I was tumbling, falling . . .)

But there's still time to record a few other physical changes. At the beginning of seventh grade I got braces, a full set. Rubber bands now hooked my upper and lower palates together. My jaw felt springy, like a ventriloquist dummy's. Every night before going to sleep I dutifully fit my medieval headgear on. But in the darkness, while my teeth were slowly coerced into straightness, the rest of my face had begun to give in to a stronger, genetic predisposition toward crookedness. To paraphrase Nietzsche, there are two types of Greek: the Apollonian and the Dionysian. I'd been born Apollonian, a sun-kissed girl with a face ringed with curls. But as I approached thirteen a Dionysian element stole over my features. My nose, at first delicately, then not so delicately, began to arch. My eyebrows, growing shaggier, arched, too. Something sinister, wily, literally "satyrical" entered my expression.

And so the last thing the hockey ball (coming closer now, unwilling to endure any more exposition) — the last thing the hockey ball symbolized was Time itself, the unstoppability of it, the way we're chained to our bodies, which are chained to Time.

The hockey ball rocketed forward. It hit the side of my mask, which deflected it into the center of the net. We lost. The Hornets celebrated.

In disgrace, as usual, I returned to the

gymnasium. Carrying my mask, I climbed out of the green bowl of the hockey field, which was like an outdoor theater. Taking small steps, I walked along the gravel path back to the school. In the distance, down the hill and across the road, lay Lake St. Clair, where my grandfather Jimmy Zizmo had faked his death. The lake still froze in winter, but bootleggers didn't drive over it anymore. Lake St. Clair had lost its sinister glamour and, like everything else, had become suburban. Freighters still plied the shipping channel, but now you mostly saw pleasure boats, Chris-Crafts, Santanas, Flying Dutchmen, 470s. On sunny days the lake still managed to look blue. Most of the time, however, it was the color of cold pea soup.

But I wasn't thinking about any of that. I was measuring my steps, trying to go as slowly as possible. I was looking at the gymnasium doors with an expression of wariness and anxiety.

It was now, when the game was over for everyone else, that it began for me. While my teammates were catching their breath, I was psyching myself up. I had to act with grace, with swift, athletic timing. I had to shout from the sidelines of my being, "Heads up, Stephanides!" I had to be coach, star player, and cheerleader all in one.

For despite the Dionysian revelry that had broken out in my body (in my throbbing teeth, in the wild abandon of my nose), not everything about me had changed. A year and a half after Carol Horning came to school with brand-new breasts, I was still without any. The brassiere I'd finally wheedled out of Tessie was still, like the higher physics, of only theoretical use. No breasts. No period, either. All through sixth grade I'd waited and then through the summer afterward. Now I was in seventh grade and still I was waiting. There were hopeful signs. From time to time my nipples became sore. Gingerly touching them, I felt a pebble beneath the pink, tender flesh. I always thought that this was the start of something. I thought I was budding. But time after time the swelling and soreness went away, and nothing came of it.

Of all the things I had to get used to at my new school, the most difficult, therefore, was the locker room. Even now with the season over, Coach Stork was standing by the door, barking. "Okay, ladies, hit the showers! Come on. Hustle up!" She saw me coming and managed to smile. "Good effort," she said, handing me a towel.

Hierarchies exist everywhere, but especially in locker rooms. The swampiness, the nudity bring back original conditions.

Let me perform a quick taxonomy of our locker room. Nearest the showers were the Charm Bracelets. As I passed by, I glanced down the steamy corridor to see them performing their serious, womanly movements. One Charm Bracelet was bending forward, wrapping a towel around her wet hair. She snapped upright, twisting it into a turban. Next to her another Bracelet was staring into space with empty blue eyes as she anointed herself with moisturizer. Still another Bracelet lifted a water bottle to her lips, exposing the long column of her neck. Not wanting to stare, I looked away, but I could still hear the sound they made getting dressed. Above the hiss of shower heads and the slap of feet on tiles, a high, thin tinkling reached my ears, a sound almost like the tapping of champagne flutes before a toast. What was it? Can't you guess? From the slender wrists of these girls, tiny silver charms were chiming together. It was the ringing of tiny tennis rackets against tiny snow skis, of miniature Eiffel Towers against half-inch ballerinas on point. It was the sound of Tiffany frogs and whales chiming together; of puppies tinkling against cats, of seals with balls on their noses hitting monkeys with hand organs, of wedges of cheese ringing against clowns' faces, of strawberries singing with inkwells, of valentine hearts striking the bells around the necks of Swiss cows. In the midst of all this soft chiming, one girl held out her wrist to her friends, like a lady recommending a perfume. Her father had just returned from a business trip, bringing her back this latest present.

The Charm Bracelets: they were the rulers of my new school. They'd been going to Baker & Inglis since kindergarten. Since pre-kindergarten! They lived near the water and had grown up, like all Grosse Pointers, pretending that our shallow lake was no lake at all but actually the ocean. The Atlantic Ocean. Yes, that was the secret wish of the Charm Bracelets and their parents, to be not Midwesterners but Easterners, to affect their dress and lockjaw speech, to summer in Martha's Vineyard, to say "back East" instead of "out East," as though their time in Michigan represented only a brief sojourn away from home.

What can I say about my well-bred, small-nosed, trust-funded schoolmates? Descended from hardworking, thrifty industrialists (there were two girls in my class who had the same last names as American car makers), did they show aptitudes for math or science? Did they display mechanical ingenuity? Or a commitment to the Protestant work ethic? In a word: no. There is no evidence against genetic determinism more persuasive than the children of the rich. The Charm Bracelets didn't study. They never raised their hands in class. They sat in the back, slumping, and went home each day carrying the prop of a notebook. (But maybe the Charm Bracelets understood more about life than I did. From an early age they knew what little value the world placed in books, and so didn't waste their time with them. Whereas I, even now, persist in believing that these black marks on white paper bear the greatest significance, that if I keep writing I might be able to catch the rainbow of consciousness in a jar. The only trust fund I have is this story, and unlike a prudent Wasp, I'm dipping into principal, spending it all . . .)

Passing by their lockers in seventh grade, I wasn't aware of all this yet. I look back now (as Dr. Luce urged me to do) to see exactly what twelve-year-old Calliope was feeling, watching the Charm Bracelets undress in steamy light. Was there a shiver of arousal in her? Did flesh respond beneath goalie pads? I try to remember, but what comes back is only a bundle of emotions: envy, certainly, but also disdain. Inferiority and superiority at once. Above all, there was panic.

In front of me girls were entering and exiting the showers. The flashes of nakedness were like shouts going off. A year or so earlier these same girls had been porcelain figurines, gingerly dipping their toes into the disinfectant basin at the public pool. Now they were magnificent creatures. Moving through the humid air, I felt like a snorkeler. On I came, kicking my heavy, padded legs and gaping through the goalie mask at the fantastic underwater life all around me. Sea anemones sprouted from between my classmates' legs. They came in all colors, black, brown, electric yellow, vivid red. Higher up, their breasts bobbed like jellyfish, softly pulsing, tipped with stinging pink. Everything was waving in the current, feeding on microscopic plankton, growing bigger by the minute. The shy, plump girls were like sea lions, lurking in the depths.

The surface of the sea is a mirror, reflecting divergent evolutionary paths. Up above, the creatures of air; down below, those of water. One planet, containing two worlds. My classmates were as unastonished by their extravagant traits as a blowfish is by its quills. They seemed to be a different species. It was as if they had scent glands or marsupial pouches, adaptations for fecundity, for procreating in the wild, which had nothing to do with skinny, hairless, domesticated me. I hurried by, desolate, my ears ringing with the noise of the place.

Beyond the Charm Bracelets I passed next into the area of the Kilt Pins. The most populous phylum in our locker room, the Kilt Pins took up three rows of lockers. There they were, fat and skinny, pale and freckled, clumsily putting on socks or pulling up unbecoming underwear. They were like the devices that held our tartans together, unremarkable, dull, but necessary in their way. I don't remember any of their names.

Past the Charm Bracelets, through the Kilt Pins, deeper into the locker room, Calliope limped. Back to where the tiles were cracked and the plaster yellowing, under the flickering light fixtures, by the drinking fountain with the prehistoric piece of gum in the drain, I hurried to where I belonged, to my niche of the local habitat.

I wasn't alone that year in having my circumstances altered. The specter of busing had started other parents looking into private schools. Baker & Inglis, with an impressive physical plant but a small endowment, wasn't averse to increasing enrollment. And so, in the autumn of 1972, we had arrived (the steam thins out this far from the showers and I can see my old friends clearly): Reetika Churaswami, with her enormous yellow eyes and sparrow's waist; and Joanne Maria Barbara Peracchio, with her corrected clubfoot and (it must be admitted) John Birch Society affiliation; Norma Abdow, whose father had gone away on the Haj and never come back; Tina Kubek, who was Czech by blood; and Linda Ramirez, half Spanish, half Filipina, who was standing still, waiting for her glasses to unfog. "Ethnic" girls we were called, but then who wasn't, when you got right down to it? Weren't the Charm Bracelets every bit as ethnic? Weren't they as full of strange rituals and food? Of tribal speech? They said "bogue" for repulsive and "queer" for weird. They ate tiny, crustless sandwiches on white bread — cucumber sandwiches, mayonnaise, and something called "watercress." Until we came to Baker & Inglis my friends and I had always felt completely American. But now the Bracelets' upturned noses suggested that there was another America to which we could never gain admittance. All of a sudden America wasn't about hamburgers and hot rods anymore. It was about the *Mayflower* and Plymouth Rock. It was about something that had happened for two minutes four hundred years ago, instead of everything that had happened since. Instead of everything that was happening now!

Suffice it to say that, in seventh grade, Calliope found herself aligned with, taken in by, nurtured and befriended by the year's newcomers. As I opened my locker, my friends said nothing about my porous goaltending. Instead Reetika kindly turned the subject to an upcoming math test. Joanne Maria Barbara Peracchio slowly peeled off a knee sock. Correctional surgery had left her right ankle as thin as a broomstick. The sight of it always made me feel better about myself. Norma Abdow opened her locker, looked in, and shouted, "Gross!" I stalled, unlacing my pads. On either side, my friends, with quick, shivery movements, stripped off their clothes. They wrapped themselves in towels. "You guys?" Linda Ramirez asked. "Can I borrow some shampoo?" "Only if you're my lunch peon tomorrow." "No way!" "Then no shampoo." "Okay, okay." "Okay, what?" "Okay, Your Highness."

I waited until they left before I undressed. First I took off my knee socks. I reached under my athletic tunic and pulled down my shorts. After tying a bath towel around my waist, I unbuttoned the shoulder straps of my tunic and pulled it over my head. This left me with the towel and my jersey on. Now came the tricky part. The brassiere I had was size 30 AA. It had a tiny rosette between the cups and a label that read "Young Miss by Olga." (Tessie had urged me to get an old-fashioned training bra, but I wanted something that looked like what my friends had, and preferably padded.) I now fastened this item around my waist, clasps in front, and then rotated it into position. At that point, one sleeve at a time, I pulled my arms inside my jersey so that it sat on my shoulders like a cloak. Working inside it, I slid the bra up my torso until I could slip my arms through the armholes. When that was accomplished, I put my kilt on under my towel, removed my jersey, put on my blouse, and tossed the towel away. I wasn't naked for a second.

The only witness to my cunning was our school mascot. On the wall behind me a faded felt banner proclaimed: "1955 State Field Hockey Champions." Below this, striking her customary insouciant pose, was the B&I Wolverette. With her beady eyes, sharp teeth, and tapering snout, she stood leaning on her hockey stick, right foot crossed over left ankle. She wore a blue tunic with a red sash. A red ribbon sat between her furry ears. It was difficult to tell if she was smiling or snarling. There was something of the Yale bulldog's tenacity in our Wolverette, but there was elegance, too. The Wolverette didn't just play to win. She played to keep her figure.

At the nearby drinking fountain, I pressed one finger over the hole, making the water squirt high in the air. I put my head into this stream. Coach Stork always touched our hair before letting us leave, making sure it was wet.

The year I was packed off to private school, Chapter Eleven went off to college. Although he was safe from the long arm of Judge Roth, other arms had been reaching for him. One hot day the previous July, as I was passing down our upstairs hall, I heard a strange voice emanating from Chapter Eleven's bedroom. The voice was a man's and he was reading numbers and dates. "February fourth," the voice said, "thirty-two. February fifth — three hundred and twenty-one. February sixth . . ." The accordion door wasn't latched, so I peeked in.

My brother was lying on his bed, wrapped in an old afghan Tessie had crocheted for him. His head extended from one end — eyes glazed — and his white legs from the other. Across the room his stereo amplifier was on, the radio needle jumping.

That spring, Chapter Eleven had received two letters, one from the University of Michigan informing him of his acceptance and the other from the U.S. government informing him of his eligibility for the draft. Since then my apolitical brother had been taking an unusual interest in current events. Every night, he watched the news with Milton, tracking military developments and paying close attention to the guarded statements of Henry Kissinger at the Paris peace talks. "Power is the greatest aphrodisiac," Kissinger famously said, and it must have been true: because Chapter Eleven was glued to the set night after night, following the machinations of diplomacy. At the same time, Milton was pricked by the strange desire of parents, and especially of fathers, to see their children repeat their own sufferings. "Might do you some good being in the service," he said. To which Chapter Eleven replied, "I'll go to Canada." "You will not. If they call you up, you'll serve your country just like I did." And then Tessie: "Don't worry. The whole thing'll be over before they can get you."

In the summer of '72, however, as I watched my number-stunned brother, the war was still officially on. Nixon's Christmas bombings were still awaiting their holiday season. Kissinger was still shuttling between Paris and Washington to maintain his sex appeal. In actuality, the Paris Peace Accords would be signed the following January and the last American troops would pull out of Vietnam in March. But as I peeked in at my brother's inert body, no one knew that yet. I was aware only of what a strange thing it was to be male. Society discriminated against women, no question. But what about the discrimination of being sent to war? Which sex was really thought to be expendable? I felt a sympathy and protectiveness for my brother I'd never felt before. I thought of Chapter Eleven in an army uniform, squatting in the jungle. I imagined him wounded on a stretcher, and I started to cry. The voice on the radio droned on: "February twenty-first — one hundred and forty-one. February twenty-second — seventy-four. February twenty-third — two hundred and six."

I waited until March 20, Chapter Eleven's birthday. When the voice announced his draft number — it was two hundred and ninety, he would never go to war — I burst into his room. Chapter Eleven leapt out of bed. We looked at each other and — almost unheard of between us — we hugged.

The next fall, my brother left not for Canada but for Ann Arbor. Once again, as when Chapter Eleven's egg had dropped, I was left alone. Alone at home to note my father's growing anger at the nightly news, his frustration at the "half-assed" way the Americans were waging the war (napalm notwithstanding) and his increasing sympathy for President Nixon. Alone, also, to detect a feeling of uselessness that began to plague my mother. With Chapter Eleven out of the house and me growing up, Tessie found herself with too much time on her hands. She began to fill her days with classes at the War Memorial Community Center. She learned decoupage. She wove plant hangers. Our house began to fill up with her craft projects. There were painted baskets and beaded curtains, paperweights with various objects suspended in them, dried flowers, colored grains and beans. She went antiquing and hung an old washboard on the wall. She took yoga, too.

It was the combination of Milton's disgust at the antiwar movement and Tessie's sense of uselessness that led them to begin reading the entire one-hundred-and-fifteen-volume set of the Great Books series. Uncle Pete had been touting these books for a long time, not to mention quoting from them liberally to score points in Sunday debates. And now, with so much learning in the air — Chapter Eleven majoring in engineering, I myself taking first-year Latin with Miss Silber, who wore sunglasses in class — Milton and Tessie decided it was time to round out their education. The Great Books arrived in ten boxes stamped with their contents. Aristotle, Plato, and Socrates in one; Cicero, Marcus Aurelius, and Virgil in another. As we shelved the books in the built-in stacks on Middlesex, we read the names, many familiar (Shakespeare), others not (Boethius). Canon-bashing wasn't in vogue yet, and besides, the Great Books began with names not unlike our own (Thucydides), so we felt included. "Here's a good one," said Milton, holding up Milton. The only thing that disappointed him was that the series didn't contain a book by Ayn Rand. Nevertheless, that evening after dinner, Milton began reading aloud to Tessie.

They went chronologically, starting with volume one and working their way toward one hundred and fifteen. While I did my homework in the kitchen I heard Milton's resonant, drill-like voice saying, "Socrates: 'There seem to be two causes of the deterioration of the arts.' Adeimantus: 'What are they?' Socrates: 'Wealth, I said, and poverty.' " When the Plato got to be hard going, Milton suggested skipping ahead to Machiavelli. After a few days of that, Tessie asked for Thomas Hardy, but an hour later Milton put the book down, unimpressed. "Too many heaths," he complained. "Heath this and heath that." Then they read *The Old Man and the Sea* by Ernest Hemingway, which they enjoyed, and then they gave the project up.

I bring up my parents' failed assault on the Great Books for a reason. Throughout my formative years, the set remained on our library shelves, weighty and regal-looking with its gold spines. Even back then the Great Books were working on me, silently urging me to pursue the most futile human dream of all, the dream of writing a book worthy of joining their number, a one hundred and sixteenth Great Book with another long Greek name on the cover: Stephanides. That was when I was young and full of grand dreams. Now I've given up any hope of lasting fame or literary perfection. I don't care if I write a great book anymore, but just one which, whatever its flaws, will leave a record of my impossible life.

The life which, as I shelved books, was finally revealing itself. Because here is Calliope, opening another carton. Here she is taking out number forty-five (Locke, Rousseau). Here she is reaching up, without resorting to tiptoes, to put it on the top shelf. And here is Tessie, looking up and saying, "I think you're growing, Cal."

It turned out to be an understatement. Beginning in January of seventh grade and continuing into the following August, my previously frozen body underwent a growth spurt of uncommon proportions and unforeseeable consequences. Though at home I was still kept on the Mediterranean Diet, the food at my new school — chicken pot pies, Tater Tots, cubed Jell-O — canceled out its fountain-of-youth effects and, in all ways but one, I began to grow up. I sprouted with the velocity of the mung beans we studied in Earth Science. Learning about photosynthesis, we kept one tray in the dark and one in the light, and measured them every day with metric rulers. Like a mung bean my body stretched up toward the great grow lamp in the sky, and my case was even more significant because I continued to grow in the dark. At night, my joints ached. I had trouble sleeping. I wrapped my legs in heating pads, smiling through the pain. Because along with my new height, something else was finally happening. Hair was beginning to appear in the required places. Every night, after locking my bedroom door, I angled my desk lamp just so and began to count the hairs. One week there were three; the next, six; two weeks later, seventeen. In a grand mood one day I ran a comb through them. "About time," I said, and even that was different: my voice was beginning to change.

It didn't do so overnight. I don't remember any cracking. Instead my voice began a slow descent that continued for the next couple of years. The earsplitting quality it had had — which I used as a weapon against my brother — disappeared.

Hitting the "free" in the national anthem was a thing of the past. My mother kept thinking that I had a cold. Sales ladies looked past me for the woman who had asked for help. It was a not unbewitching sound, a mix of flute and bassoon, my consonants slightly slurred, a rush and breathiness to most of my pronouncements. And there were the signs only a linguist could pick up, middle-class elisions, grace notes passed down from Greek into midwestern twang, the heritage from my grandparents and parents that lived on in me like everything else.

I grew tall. My voice matured. But nothing seemed unnatural. My slight build, my thin waist, the smallness of my head, hands, and feet raised no questions in anybody's mind. Many genetic males raised as girls don't blend in so easily. From an early age they look different, move differently, they can't find shoes or gloves that fit. Other kids call them tomboys or worse: ape-women, gorillas. My skinniness disguised me. The early seventies were a good time to be flat-chested. Androgyny was in. My rickety height and foal's legs gave me the posture of a fashion model. My clothes weren't right, my face wasn't right, but my angularity was. I had that saluki look. Plus, for whatever reason — my dreamy temperament, my bookishness — I fit right in.

Still, it wasn't uncommon for certain innocent, excitable girls to respond to my presence in ways they weren't aware of. I'm thinking of Lily Parker, who used to lie down on the lobby couches and rest her head in my lap, looking up and saying, "You have the most perfect chin." Or of June James, who used to pull my hair over her own head, so that we could share it like a tent. My body might have released pheromones that affected my schoolmates. How else to explain the way my friends tugged on me, leaned on me? At this early stage, before my male secondary characteristics had manifested themselves, before there were whispers about me in the halls and girls thought twice about laying their heads in my lap — in seventh grade, when my hair was glossy instead of frizzy, my cheeks still smooth, my muscles undeveloped, and yet, invisibly but unmistakably, I began to exude some kind of masculinity, in the way I tossed up and caught my eraser, for instance, or in the way I dive-bombed people's desserts with my spoon, in the intensity of my knit brow or my eagerness to debate anyone on anything in class; when I was a changeling, before I changed, I was quite popular at my new school.

But this stage was brief. Soon my headgear lost its nighttime war against the forces of crookedness. Apollo gave in to Dionysius. Beauty may always be a little bit freakish, but the year I turned thirteen I was becoming freakier than ever.

Consider the yearbook. In the field hockey team photo, taken in the fall, I am on one knee in the front row. With my homeroom in the spring, I am stooping in the back. My face is shadowed with self-consciousness. (Over the years my perpetually perplexed expression would drive photographers to distraction. It ruined class photos and Christmas cards until, in the most widely published pictures of me, the problem was finally solved by blocking out my face altogether.)

If Milton missed having a beautiful daughter, I never knew it. At weddings he still asked me to dance, regardless of how ridiculous we looked together. "Come on, *kukla*," he'd say, "let's cut the rug," and we'd be off, the squat, plump father leading with confident, old-fashioned, fox-trot steps, and the awkward praying mantis of a daughter trying to follow along. My parents' love for me didn't diminish with my looks. I think it's fair to say, however, that as my appearance changed in those years a species of sadness infiltrated my parents' love. They worried that I wouldn't attract boys, that I would be a wallflower, like Aunt Zo. Sometimes when we were dancing, Milton squared his shoulders and looked around the floor, as if daring anyone to make a crack.

My response to all this growing was to grow my hair. Unlike the rest of me, which seemed bent on doing whatever it wanted, my hair remained under my control. And so like Desdemona after her disastrous YWCA makeover, I refused to let anyone cut it. All through seventh grade and into eighth I pursued my goal. While college students marched against the war, Calliope protested against hair clippers. While bombs were secretly dropped on Cambodia, Callie did what she could to keep her own secrets. By the spring of 1973, the war was officially over. President Nixon would be out of office in August of the next year. Rock music was giving way to disco. Across the nation, hairstyles were changing. But Calliope's head, like a midwesterner who always got the fashions late, still thought it was the sixties.

My hair! My unbelievably abundant, thirteen-year-old hair! Has there ever existed a head of hair like mine at thirteen? Did any girl ever summon as many Roto-Rooter men out of their trucks? Monthly, weekly, semiweekly, the drains in our house clogged. "Jesus Christ," Milton complained, writing out yet another check, "you're worse than those goddamn tree roots." Hair like a ball of tumbleweed, blowing through the rooms of Middlesex. Hair like a black tornado wheeling across an amateur newsreel. Hair so vast it seemed to possess its own weather systems, because my dry split ends crackled with static electricity whereas closer in, near my scalp, the atmosphere grew warm and moist like a rain forest. Desdemona's hair was long and silky, but I'd gotten Jimmy Zizmo's spikier variety. Pomade would never subdue it. First ladies would never buy it. It was hair that could turn the Medusa to stone, hair snakier than all the snake pits in a minotaur movie.

My family suffered. My hair turned up in every corner, every drawer, every *meal*. Even in the rice puddings Tessie made, covering each little bowl with wax paper before putting it away in the fridge — even into these prophylactically secure desserts my hair found its way! Jet black hairs wound themselves around bars of soap. They lay pressed like flower stems between the pages of books. They turned up in eye-glass cases, birthday cards, once — I swear — inside an egg Tessie had just cracked. The next-door neighbor's cat coughed up a hairball one day and the hair was not the cat's. "That's so gross!" Becky Turnbull shouted. "I'm calling the SPCA!" In vain Milton tried to get me to wear one of the paper hats his employees had to wear by law. Tessie, as though I were still six, took a hairbrush to me.

"I — don't — see — why — you — won't — let — Sophie — do — something — with — your — hair."

"Because I see what she does to her hair."

"Sophie has a perfectly nice hairstyle."

"Ow!"

"Well, what do you expect? It's a rat's nest."

"Just leave it."

"Be still." More brushing, tugging. My head jerking with every stroke. "Short hair's the style now anyway, Callie."

"Are you finished?"

A few final, frustrated strokes. Then, plaintively: "At least tie it back. Keep it out of your face."

What could I tell her? That that was the whole point of having long hair? To keep it *in* my face? Maybe I didn't look like Dorothy Hamill. Maybe I was even starting to bear a strong resemblance to our weeping willow trees. But there were virtues to my hair. It covered tinsel teeth. It covered satyrical nose. It hid blemishes and, best of all, it hid me. Cut my hair? Never! I was still growing it out. My dream was to someday live inside it.

Imagine me then at unlucky thirteen as I

entered the eighth grade. Five feet ten inches tall, weighing one hundred and thirty-one pounds. Black hair hanging like drapes on either side of my nose. People knocking on the air in front of my face and calling out, "Anybody in there?"

I was in there all right. Where else could I go?

Waxing Lyrical

❧❧❧

I am back to my old ways. To my solitary walks through Victoriapark. To my Romeo y Julietas, my Davidoff Grand Crus. To my embassy receptions, my Philharmonie concerts, my nightly rounds at the Felsenkeller. It's my favorite time of year, fall. The slight chill to the air, quickening the brain, and all the schoolkid, school-year memories attached to autumn. You don't get the bright leaves here in Europe the way you do in New England. The leaves smolder but never catch flame. It's still warm enough to bicycle. Last night I rode from Schöneberg to Orianenburgstrasse in Mitte. I met a friend for a drink. Leaving, riding through the streets, I was hailed by the intergalactic streetwalkers. In their Manga suits, their moon boots, they tossed their teased doll's hair and called, Hallohallo. Maybe they would be just the thing for me. Remunerated to tolerate most anything. Shocked by nothing. And yet, as I pedaled past their lineup, their *Strich*, my feelings toward them were not a man's. I was aware of a good girl's reproachfulness and disdain, along with a perceptible, physical empathy. As they shifted their hips, hooking me with their darkly painted eyes, my mind filled not with images of what I might do with them, but with what it must be like for them, night after night, hour after hour, to have to do it. The *Huren* themselves didn't look too closely at me. They saw my silk scarf, my Zegna pants, my gleaming shoes. They saw the money in my wallet. Hallo, they called. Hallo. Hallo.

⚜

It was fall then, too, the fall of 1973. I was only a few months from turning fourteen. And one Sunday after church Sophie Sassoon whispered in my ear, "Hon? You're getting just the tiniest bit of a mustache. Have your mother bring you by the shop. I'll take care of it for you."

A mustache? Was it true? Like Mrs. Drexel? I hurried to the bathroom to see. Mrs. Tsilouras was reapplying lipstick, but as soon as she left I put my face up to the mirror. Not a full-fledged mustache: only a few darkish hairs above my upper lip. This wasn't as surprising as it may seem. In fact, I'd been expecting it.

Like the Sun Belt or the Bible Belt, there exists, on this multifarious earth of ours, a Hair Belt. It begins in southern Spain, congruent with Moorish influence. It extends

563

over the dark-eyed regions of Italy, almost all of Greece, and absolutely all of Turkey. It dips south to include Morocco, Tunisia, Algeria, and Egypt. Continuing on (and darkening in color as maps do to indicate ocean depth) it blankets Syria, Iran, and Afghanistan, before lightening gradually in India. After that, except for a single dot representing the Ainu in Japan, the Hair Belt ends.

Sing, Muse, of Greek ladies and their battle against unsightly hair! Sing of depilatory creams and tweezers! Of bleach and beeswax! Sing how the unsightly black fuzz, like the Persian legions of Darius, sweeps over the Achaean mainland of girls barely into their teens! No, Calliope was not surprised by the appearance of a shadow above her upper lip. My Aunt Zo, my mother, Sourmelina, and even my cousin Cleo all suffered from hair growing where they didn't want it to. When I close my eyes and summon the fond smells of childhood, do I smell gingerbread baking or the pine-fresh scent of Christmas trees? Not primarily. The aroma that fills, as it were, the nostrils of my memory is the sulfurous, protein-dissolving fetor of Nair.

I see my mother, with her feet in the tub, waiting for the bubbling, stinging foam to work. I see Sourmelina, heating up a tin of wax on the stove. The pains they took to make themselves smooth! The rashes the creams left! The futility of it all! The enemy, hair, was invincible. It was life itself.

I told my mother to make an appointment for me at Sophie Sassoon's beauty parlor at the Eastland Mall.

Wedged between a movie theater and a submarine sandwich shop, the Golden Fleece did what it could to distance itself socially from its neighbors. A tasteful awning hung over the entrance, bearing the silhouette of a Parisian *grande dame*. Inside, flowers sat on the front desk. Just as colorful as the flowers was Sophie Sassoon herself. In a purple muumuu, braceleted and begemmed, she glided from chair to chair. "How we doing here? Oh, you look gorgeous. That color takes ten years off." Then to the next customer: "Don't look so worried. Trust me. This is how they're wearing their hair now. Reinaldo, tell her." And Reinaldo in his hip-huggers: "Like Mia Farrow in *Rosemary's Baby*. Sick flick, but she looked great." By then Sophie had moved on to the next person. "Hon, let me give you some advice. Don't blow-dry your hair. Let it dry wet. Also I've got a conditioner for you you won't believe. I'm an authorized dealer." It was Sophie Sassoon's personal attention the women came for, the feeling of safety the salon gave them, the assurance that in here they could expose their flaws without embarrassment and Sophie would take care of them. It must have been the love they came for. Otherwise the customers would have noticed that Sophie Sassoon was herself in need of beauty advice. They would have seen that her eyebrows were drawn on as though by Magic Marker, and that her face, owing to the Princess Borghese makeup she sold on commission, was the color of a brick. But did I see it that day myself, or in the weeks that followed? Like everyone else, instead of judging the final effect of Sophie Sassoon's makeup job, I was impressed by the complexity of it. I knew, as did my mother and the other ladies, that to "put on her face" every morning it took Sophie Sassoon no less than one hour and forty-five minutes. She had to apply eye creams and under-eye creams. She had to lay down various layers, like shellacking a Stradivarius. In addition to the brick-colored final coat there were others: dabs of green to control redness, pinks to add blush, blues above the eyes. She used dry eyeliner, liquid eyeliner, lip liner, lip conditioner, a frosted highlighter, and a pore minimizer. Sophie Sassoon's face: it was created with the rigor of a sand painting blown grain by grain by Tibetan monks. It lasted only a day and then it was gone.

This face now said to us, "Right this way, ladies." Sophie was warm, as always, loving as always. Her hands, treated every night with vanishing cream, fluttered around us, stroking, rubbing. Her earrings looked like something Schliemann had dug up at Troy. She led us past a line of women having their hair set, across a stifling ghetto of hair dryers, and through a blue curtain. In the front of the Golden Fleece, Sophie fixed people's hair; in the back she removed it. Behind the blue curtain half-naked women presented portions of themselves to wax. One large woman was on her back, her blouse pulled up to expose her navel. Another was lying on her stomach, reading a magazine while wax dried on the back of her thighs. There was a woman sitting in a chair, her sideburns and chin smeared with dark golden wax, and there were two beautiful young women lying naked from the waist down, having their bikini lines done. The smell of the beeswax was strong, pleasant. The atmosphere was like a Turkish bath without the heat, a lazy, draped feeling to everything, steam curling off pots of wax.

"I'm only having my face done," I told Sophie.

"She sounds like she's paying," Sophie joked to my mother.

My mother laughed, and the other women joined in. Everyone was looking our way, smiling. I'd come from school and was still in my uniform.

"Be glad it's just your face," said one of the bikini-liners.

"Few years from now," said the other, "you might be heading south."

Laughter. Winks. Even, to my astonishment, a sly smile spreading over my mother's face. As if behind the blue curtain Tessie was another person. As if, now that we were getting waxed together, she could treat me like an adult.

"Sophie, maybe you can convince Callie to get her hair cut," Tessie said.

"It's a little bushy, hon," Sophie leveled with me. "For your face shape."

"Just a wax, please," I said.

"She won't listen," said Tessie.

A Hungarian woman (from the outskirts of the Hair Belt) did the honors. With the short-order efficiency of Jimmy Papanikolas, she positioned us around the room like food on a grill: in one corner the large woman as pink as a slab of Canadian bacon; down at the bottom Tessie and me, lumped together like home fries; over on the left the bikini-liners, lying sunny side up. Helga kept us all sizzling. Holding her aluminum tray, she moved from body to body, spreading maple-syrup-colored wax

568

where it was needed with a flat wooden spoon, and pressing in strips of gauze before it hardened. When the large woman was done on one side, Helga flipped her over. Tessie and I lay in our chairs, listening to wax being violently removed. "Oh my!" cried the large lady. "Is nothing," belittled Helga. "I do it perfect." "Oweee!" yelped a bikini-liner. And Helga, taking an oddly feminist stance: "See what you do for the mens? You suffer. Is not worth it."

Now Helga came over to me. She took hold of my chin and moved my head from side to side, examining. She spread wax above my upper lip. She moved to my mother and did the same. Thirty seconds later the wax had hardened.

"I have a surprise for you," Tessie said.

"What?" I asked, as Helga ripped. I was certain my fledgling mustache was gone. Also, my upper lip.

"Your brother's coming home for Christmas."

My eyes were tearing. I blinked and said nothing, momentarily dumbfounded. Helga turned to my mother.

"Some surprise," I said.

"He's bringing a girlfriend."

"He's got a girlfriend? Who would go out with him?"

"Her name is . . ." Helga ripped. After a

moment my mother resumed, "Meg."

From then on, Sophie Sassoon took care of my facial hair. I went in about twice a month, adding depilation to an ever-growing list of upkeep requirements. I started shaving my legs and underarms. I plucked my eyebrows. The dress code at my school forbade cosmetics. But on weekends I got to experiment, within limits. Reetika and I painted our faces in her bedroom, passing a hand mirror back and forth. I was particularly given to dramatic eyeliner. My model here was Maria Callas, or possibly Barbra Streisand in *Funny Girl*. The triumphant, long-nosed divas. At home I snooped in Tessie's bathroom. I loved the amulet-like vials, the sweet-smelling, seemingly edible creams. I tried out her facial steamer, too. You put your face to the plastic cone and were blasted by heat. I stayed away from greasy moisturizers, worried they would make me break out.

With Chapter Eleven off at college — he was a sophomore now — I had the bathroom to myself. This was evident from the medicine cabinet. Two pink Daisy razors stood upright in a small drinking cup, next to a spray can of Pssssssst instant shampoo. A tube of Dr Pepper Lip Smacker, which tasted like the soft drink, kissed a bottle of "Gee, Your Hair Smells Terrific." My Breck Creme Rinse with Body promised to make me "the girl with the hair" (but wasn't I already?). From there we move on to the facial products: my Epi*Clear Acne Kit; my Crazy Curl hair iron; a bottle of FemIron pills which I was hoping to someday need; and a shaker of Love's Baby Soft body powder. Then there was my aerosol can of Soft & Dri non-sting antiperspirant and my two bottles of perfume: Woodhue, a mildly disturbing Christmas present from my brother, which I consequently never wore; and L'Air du Temps by Nina Ricci ("Only the romantic need apply"). I also had a tub of Jolén Creme Bleach, for between appointments at the Golden Fleece. Interspersed amid these totemic items were stray Q-tips and cotton balls, lip liners, Max Factor eye makeup, mascara, blush, and everything else I used in a losing battle to make myself beautiful. Finally, hidden in the back of the cabinet, was the box of Kotex pads, which my mother had given me one day. "We better just keep these on hand," she'd said, astonishing me completely. No further explanation than that.

The hug I had given Chapter Eleven in the summer of '72 turned out to be a kind of farewell, because when he returned home from college after his freshman year my brother had become another person.

He'd grown his hair out (not as long as mine, but still). He'd started learning the guitar. Perched on his nose was a pair of granny glasses and instead of straight-legs he now wore faded bell-bottom jeans. The members of my family have always had a knack for self-transformation. While I finished my first year at Baker & Inglis and began my second, while I went from being a short seventh grader to an alarmingly tall eighth grader, Chapter Eleven, up at college, went from science geek to John Lennon look-alike.

He bought a motorcycle. He started meditating. He claimed to understand *2001: A Space Odyssey*, even the ending. But it wasn't until Chapter Eleven descended into the basement to play Ping-Pong with Milton that I understood what was behind all this. We'd had a Ping-Pong table for years, but so far, no matter how much my brother or I practiced, we had never come close to beating Milton. Neither my new long reach nor Chapter Eleven's beetle-browed concentration was sufficient to counter Milton's wicked spin or his "killer shot" which left red marks on our chests, *through our clothes*. But that summer, something was different. When Milton used his extra-fast serve, Chapter Eleven returned it with a minimum of effort. When Milton employed the "English" he'd learned in the Navy, Chapter Eleven counter-spun. Even when Milton smashed a winner across the table, Chapter Eleven, with stupendous reflexes, sent it back where it came from. Milton began to sweat. His face turned red. Chapter Eleven remained cool. He had a strange, distracted look on his face. His pupils were dilated. "Go!" I cheered him on. "Beat Dad!" 12–12. 12–14. 14–15. 17–18. 18–21! Chapter Eleven had done it! He'd beaten Milton!

"I'm on acid," he explained later.

"What?"

"Windowpane. Three hits."

The drug had made everything seem as if it were happening in slow motion. Milton's fastest serves, his most arching spin shots and smashes, seemed to float in the air.

LSD? Three hits? Chapter Eleven had been tripping the whole time! He had been tripping during dinner! "That was the hardest part," he said. "I was watching dad carve the chicken and then it flapped its wings and flew away!"

"What's the matter with that kid?" I heard my father ask my mother through the wall separating our rooms. "Now he's talking about dropping out of engineering. Says it's too boring."

"It's just a stage. It'll pass."

"It better."

Shortly thereafter, Chapter Eleven had returned to college. He hadn't come back for Thanksgiving. And so, as Christmas of '73 approached, we all wondered what he would be like when we saw him again.

We quickly found out. As my father had feared, Chapter Eleven had scuttled his plans to become an engineer. Now, he informed us, he was majoring in anthropology.

As part of an assignment for one of his courses, Chapter Eleven conducted what he called "fieldwork" during most of that vacation. He carried a tape recorder around with him, recording everything we said. He took notes on our "ideation systems" and "rituals of kin bonding." He said almost nothing himself, claiming that he didn't want to influence the findings. Every now and then, however, while observing our extended family eat and joke and argue, Chapter Eleven would let out a laugh, a private Eureka that made him fall back in his chair and lift his Earth shoes off the floor. Then he would lean forward and begin writing madly in his notebook.

As I've mentioned, my brother didn't pay much attention to me while we were growing up. That weekend, however, spurred on by his new mania for observation, Chapter Eleven took a new interest in me. On Friday afternoon while I was diligently doing some advance homework at the kitchen table, he came and sat down. He stared at me thoughtfully for a long time.

"Latin, huh? That what they're teaching you in that school?"

"I like it."

"You a necrophiliac?"

"A what?"

"That's someone who gets off on dead people. Latin's dead, isn't it?"

"I don't know."

"I know some Latin."

"You do?"

"Cunnilingus."

"Don't be gross."

"Fellatio."

"Ha ha."

"Mons veneris."

"I'm dying of laughter. You're killing me. Look, I'm dead."

Chapter Eleven was quiet for a while. I tried to go on studying but felt him staring at me. Finally, exasperated, I closed my book. "What are you looking at?" I said.

There was a pause characteristic of my brother. Behind his granny glasses his eyes looked bland, but the mind behind them was working things out.

"I'm looking at my little sister," he said.

"Okay. You saw her. Now go."

"I'm looking at my little sister and

thinking she doesn't look like my little sister anymore."

"What's that supposed to mean?" I asked.

Again the pause. "I don't know," said my brother. "I'm trying to figure it out."

"Well, when you figure it out, let me know. Right now I've got stuff to do."

On Saturday morning, Chapter Eleven's girlfriend arrived. Meg Zemka was as small as my mother and as flat-chested as me. Her hair was a mousy brown, her teeth, owing to an impoverished childhood, not well cared for. She was a waif, an orphan, a runt, and six times as powerful as my brother.

"What are you studying up at college, Meg?" my father asked at dinner.

"Poli. sci."

"That sounds interesting."

"I doubt you'd like my emphasis. I'm a Marxist."

"Oh, you are, are you?"

"You run a bunch of restaurants, right?"

"That's right. Hercules Hot Dogs. Haven't you ever had one? We'll have to take you down to one of our stands."

"Meg doesn't eat meat," my mother reminded.

"Oh yeah, I forgot," said Milton. "Well, you can have some french fries. We've got french fries."

"What do you pay your workers?" Meg asked.

"The ones behind the counter? They get minimum wage."

"And you live out here in this big house in Grosse Pointe."

"That's because I handle the entire business and accept the risk."

"Sounds like exploitation to me."

"It does, does it?" Milton smiled. "Well, if giving somebody a job is exploiting them, then I guess I'm an exploiter. Those jobs didn't exist before I started the business."

"That's like saying that the slaves didn't have jobs until they built the plantations."

"You got a real live wire here," Milton said, turning to my brother. "Where did you find her?"

"I found him," said Meg. "On top of an elevator."

That was when we learned how Chapter Eleven was spending his time at college. His favorite pastime was to unscrew the ceiling panel on the dorm elevator and climb up on top. He sat there for hours, riding up and down in the darkness.

"The first time I did it," Chapter Eleven now confessed, "the car started going up to the top. I thought I might get crushed. But they leave some air space."

"This is what we're paying your tuition

for?" Milton asked.

"That's what you're exploiting your workers for," said Meg.

Tessie made Chapter Eleven and Meg sleep in separate bedrooms, but in the middle of the night there was a lot of tip-toeing and giggling in the dark. Trying to be the big sister I never had, Meg gave me a copy of *Our Bodies, Ourselves*.

Chapter Eleven, swept up in the sexual revolution, tried to educate me, too.

"You ever masturbate, Cal?"

"What!"

"You don't have to be embarrassed. It's natural. This friend of mine told me you could do it with your hand. So I went into the bathroom —"

"I don't want to hear about —"

"— and tried it out. All of a sudden, all the muscles in my penis started contracting —"

"In our bathroom?"

"— And then I ejaculated. It felt really amazing. You should try it, Cal, if you haven't already. Girls are a little different, but physiologically it's pretty much the same. I mean, the penis and the clitoris are analogous structures. You gotta experiment to see what works."

I put my fingers in my ears and started humming.

"You don't have to have any hang-ups

with me," Chapter Eleven said loudly. "I'm your brother."

The rock music, the reverence for Maharishi Mahesh Yogi, the avocado pits sprouting on the windowsill, the rainbow-colored rolling papers. What else? Oh yeah: my brother had stopped using deodorant.

"You stink!" I objected one day, sitting next to him in the TV room.

Chapter Eleven gave the tiniest of shrugs. "I'm a human," he said. "This is what humans smell like."

"Then humans stink."

"Do you think I stink, Meg?"

"No way," nuzzling up to his armpit. "It turns me *on*."

"Will you guys get out of here! I'm trying to watch this show."

"Hey, baby, my little sister wants us to split. What do you say to a little nookie?"

"Groovy."

"See you, sis. We'll be upstairs *in flagrante delicto*."

Where could all this lead? Only to family dissension, shouting matches, and heartbreak. On New Year's Eve, as Milton and Tessie toasted the new year with glasses of Cold Duck, Chapter Eleven and Meg swigged on bottles of Elephant Malt Liquor, going outside every so often to secretly smoke a joint. Milton said, "You know, I've been thinking about finally making that trip to the old country. We could go back and see *papou* and *yia yia*'s village."

"And fix that church, like you promised," said Tessie.

"What do you think?" Milton asked Chapter Eleven. "Maybe we could take a family vacation this summer."

"Not me," said Chapter Eleven.

"Why not?"

"Tourism is just another form of colonialism."

And so on and so forth. Before long, Chapter Eleven declared that he didn't share Milton and Tessie's values. Milton asked what was wrong with their values. Chapter Eleven said he was against materialism. "All you care about is money," he told Milton. "I don't want to live like this." He gestured toward the room. Chapter Eleven was against our living room, everything we had, everything Milton had worked for. He was against Middlesex! Then shouting; and Chapter Eleven uttering two words to Milton, one beginning with *f,* the other with *y;* and more shouting, and Chapter Eleven's motorcycle roaring away, with Meg on the back.

What had happened to Chapter Eleven? Why had he changed so much? It was being away from home, Tessie said. It was the times. It was all this trouble with the war. I, however, have a different answer. I suspect that Chapter Eleven's transformation was caused in no small part by that day on his bed when his life was decided by lottery. Am I projecting? Saddling my brother with my own obsessions with chance and fate? Maybe. But as we planned a trip — a trip that had been promised when Milton was saved from another war — it appeared that Chapter Eleven, taking chemical trips of his own, was trying to escape what he had dimly perceived while wrapped in an afghan: the possibility that not only his draft number was decided by lottery, but that everything was. Chapter Eleven was hiding from this discovery, hiding behind windowpane, hiding on the top of elevators, hiding in the bed of Meg Zemka with her multiple O's and bad teeth, Meg Zemka who hissed in his ear while they made love, *"Forget your family, man! They're bourgeois pigs! Your dad's an exploiter, man! Forget 'em. They're dead, man. Dead. This is what's real. Right here. Come and get it, baby!"*

The Obscure Object

❦

It occurred to me today that I'm not as far along as I thought. Writing my story isn't the courageous act of liberation I had hoped it would be. Writing is solitary, furtive, and I know all about those things. I'm an expert in the underground life. Is it really my apolitical temperament that makes me keep my distance from the intersexual rights movement? Couldn't it also be fear? Of standing up. Of becoming one of *them*.

Still, you can only do what you're able. If this story is written only for myself, then so be it. But it doesn't feel that way. I feel you out there, reader. This is the only kind of intimacy I'm comfortable with. Just the two of us, here in the dark.

Things weren't always like this. In college, I had a girlfriend. Her name was Olivia. We were drawn together by our common woundedness. Olivia had been savagely attacked when she was only thirteen, nearly raped. The police had caught the guy who did it and Olivia had testified in court numerous times. The ordeal had arrested her development. Instead of doing the normal things a high school girl did, she had had to remain that thirteen-year-old girl on the witness stand. While Olivia and I were both intellectually capable of handling the college curriculum, of excelling in it even, we remained in key ways emotionally adolescent. We cried a lot in bed. I remember the first time we took off our clothes in front of each other. It was like unwinding bandages. I was as much of a man as Olivia could bear at that point. I was her starter kit.

After college, I took a trip around the world. I tried to forget my body by keeping it in motion. Nine months later, back home, I took the Foreign Service exam and, a year after that, started working for the State Department. A perfect job for me. Three years in one place, two in another. Never long enough to form a solid attachment to anyone. In Brussels, I fell in love with a bartender who claimed not to care about the uncommon way I was made. I was so grateful that I asked her to marry me, though I found her dull company, ambitionless, too much of a shouter, a hitter. Fortunately, she refused my proposal and ran off with someone else. Who has there been since? A few here and there, never long-lasting. And so, without permanence, I have fallen into the routine of my incomplete seductions. The chatting up I'm good at. The dinners and drinks. The clinches in doorways. But then I'm off. "I've got a meeting with the ambassador in the morning," I say. And they believe me. They believe the ambassador wants to be briefed on the upcoming Aaron Copland tribute.

It's getting harder all the time. With Olivia and every woman who came after her there has been this knowledge to deal with: the great fact of my condition. The Obscure Object and I met unawares, however, in blissful ignorance.

After all the screaming in our house, there reigned, that winter on Middlesex, only silence. A silence so profound that, like the left foot of the President's secretary, it erased portions of the official record. A soggy, evasive season during which Milton, unable to admit that Chapter Eleven's attack had broken his heart, began visibly to swell with rage, so that almost anything set him off, a long red light, ice milk for dessert instead of ice cream. (His was a loud silence but a silence nonetheless.) A winter during which Tessie's worries about her children immobilized her, so that she failed to return Christmas presents that didn't fit, and merely put them in the closet, without getting a refund. At the end of this wounded, dishonest season, as the first crocuses appeared, returning from their winter in the underworld, Calliope Stephanides, who also felt something stirring in the soil of her being, found herself reading the classics.

Spring semester of eighth grade brought me into Mr. da Silva's English class. A group of only five students, we met in the greenhouse on the second floor. Spider plants let down vines from the glass roof. Closer to our heads geraniums crowded in, giving off a smell somewhere between licorice and aluminum. In addition to me, there was Reetika, Tina, Joanne, and Maxine Grossinger. Though our parents were friends, I hardly knew Maxine. She didn't mix with the other kids on Middlesex. She was always practicing her violin. She was the only Jewish kid at school. She ate lunch alone, spooning kosher food from Tupperware. I assumed her pallor was the result of being indoors all the time and that the blue vein that beat wildly at her temple was a kind of inner metronome.

Mr. da Silva had been born in Brazil. This was hard to notice. He wasn't exactly the Carnival type. The Latin details of his childhood (the hammock, the outdoor tub) had been erased by a North American education and a love of the European novel.

Now he was a liberal Democrat and wore black armbands in support of radical causes. He taught Sunday school at a local Episcopal church. He had a pink, cultivated face and dark blond hair that fell into his eyes when he recited poetry. Sometimes he picked thistles or wildflowers from the green and wore them in the lapel of his jacket. He had a short, compact body, and often did isometric exercises between class periods. He played the recorder, too. A music stand in his classroom held sheet music, early Baroque pieces, mostly.

He was a great teacher, Mr. da Silva. He treated us with complete seriousness, as if we eighth graders, during fifth period, might settle something scholars had been arguing about for centuries. He listened to our chirping, his hairline pressing down on his eyes. When he spoke himself, it was in complete paragraphs. If you listened closely it was possible to hear the dashes and commas in his speech, even the colons and semicolons. Mr. da Silva had a relevant quotation for everything that happened to him and in this way evaded real life. Instead of eating his lunch, he told you what Oblonsky and Levin had for lunch in *Anna Karenina*. Or, describing a sunset from *Daniel Deronda*, he failed to notice the one that was presently falling over Michigan.

Mr. da Silva had spent a summer in Greece six years before. He was still keyed up about it. When he described visiting the Mani, his voice became even mellower than usual, and his eyes glistened. Unable to find a hotel one night, he had slept on the ground, awaking the next morning to find himself beneath an olive tree. Mr. da Silva had never forgotten that tree. They had had a meaningful exchange, the two of them. Olive trees are intimate creatures, eloquent in their twistedness. It's easy to understand why the ancients believed human spirits could be trapped inside them. Mr. da Silva had felt this, waking up in his sleeping bag.

I was curious about Greece myself, of course. I was eager to visit. Mr. da Silva encouraged me in feeling Greek.

"Miss Stephanides," he called on me one day. "Since you hail from Homer's own land, would you be so kind as to read aloud?" He cleared his throat. "Page eighty-nine."

That semester, our less academically inclined sisters were reading *The Light in the Forest*. But in the greenhouse we were making our way through *The Iliad*. It was a paperback prose translation, abridged, set loose from its numbers, robbed of the music of the ancient Greek but — as far as I was concerned — still a terrific read.

God, I loved that book! From the pouting of Achilles in his tent (which reminded me of the President's refusal to hand over the tapes) to Hector's being dragged around the city by his feet (which made me cry), I was riveted. Forget *Love Story*. Harvard couldn't match Troy as a setting, and in Segal's whole novel only one person died. (Maybe this was another sign of the hormones manifesting themselves silently inside me. For while my classmates found *The Iliad* too bloody for their taste, an endless catalogue of men butchering one another after formally introducing themselves, I thrilled to the stabbings and beheadings, the gouging out of eyes, the juicy eviscerations.)

I opened my paperback and lowered my head. My hair fell forward, cutting off everything — Maxine, Mr. da Silva, the greenhouse's geraniums — except the book. From behind the velvet curtain, my lounge singer's voice began to purr. "Aphrodite put off her famous belt, in which all the charms of love are woven, potency, desire, lovely whispers, and the force of seduction, which takes away foresight and judgment even from the most reasonable people."

It was one o'clock. An after-lunch lethargy lay over the room. Outside, rain threatened. There was a knock at the door.

"Excuse me, Callie. Could you stop for a moment, please?" Mr. da Silva turned toward the door. "Come in."

Along with everyone else, I looked up. Standing in the doorway was a redheaded girl. Two clouds bumped up above, skidding past each other, and let down a beam of light. This beam struck the glass roof of the greenhouse. Passing through the hanging geraniums, it picked up the rosy light which now, in a kind of membrane, enveloped the girl. It was also possible that the sun wasn't doing this at all, but a certain intensity, a soul ray, from my eyes.

"We're in the middle of class, dear."

"I'm supposed to be in this class," said the girl, unhappily. She held out a slip of paper.

Mr. da Silva examined it. "Are you sure Miss Durrell wants you transferred into *this* class?" he said.

"Mrs. Lampe doesn't want me in her class anymore," replied the girl.

"Take a seat. You'll have to share with someone. Miss Stephanides has been reading from Book Three of *The Iliad* for us."

I started reading again. That is, my eyes kept tracing over the sentences and my mouth kept forming the words. But my mind had stopped paying attention to their meaning. When I finished I didn't toss my hair back. I let it stay hanging over my face. Through a keyhole in it I peeked out.

The girl had taken a seat across from me. She was leaning toward Reetika as though to look on with her, but her eyes were taking in the plants. Her nose wrinkled up at the mulchy smell.

Part of my interest was scientific, zoological. I'd never seen a creature with so many freckles before. A Big Bang had occurred, originating at the bridge of her nose, and the force of this explosion had sent galaxies of freckles hurtling and drifting to every end of her curved, warm-blooded universe. There were clusters of freckles on her forearms and wrists, an entire Milky Way spreading across her forehead, even a few sputtering quasars flung into the wormholes of her ears.

Since we're in English class, let me quote a poem. Gerard Manley Hopkins's "Pied Beauty," which begins, "Glory be to God for dappled things." When I think back about my immediate reaction to that redheaded girl, it seems to spring from an appreciation of natural beauty. I mean the heart pleasure you get from looking at speckled leaves or the palimpsested bark of plane trees in Provence. There was something richly appealing in her color combination, the ginger snaps floating in the milk-white skin, the gold highlights in the strawberry hair. It was like autumn, looking at her. It was like driving up north to see the colors.

Meanwhile she remained slumped sideways in her desk, her legs with the blue knee socks shoved out, revealing the worn heels of her shoes. Because she hadn't done the reading she was exempt from being called on, but Mr. da Silva sent concerned looks her way. The new girl didn't notice. She sprawled in her orange light and sleepily opened and closed her eyes. At one point she yawned and, halfway through, cut the yawn off, as though it hadn't gone right. She swallowed something back and pounded a fist against her breastbone. She burped quietly and whispered to herself, *"Ay, caramba."* As soon as class was over she was gone.

Who was she? Where had she come from? Why had I never noticed her in school before? She was obviously not new at Baker & Inglis. Her oxfords were stamped down at the heels so that she could slip into them like clogs. This was something the Charm Bracelets did. Also, she had an antique ring on her finger, with real rubies in it. Her lips were thin, austere, Protestant. Her nose was not really a nose at all. It was only a beginning.

She came to class every day wearing the

same distant, bored expression. She shuffled in her oxford-clogs, with a gliding or skating motion, her knees bent and her weight thrust forward. It added to the overall desultory impression. I would be watering Mr. da Silva's plants when she entered. He asked me to do this before class. So every day began like that, me at one end of the crystal room, engulfed by geranium blooms, and this answering burst of red coming through the door.

The way she dragged her feet made it clear how she felt about the weird, old, dead poem we were reading. She wasn't interested. She never did the homework. She tried to bluff her way through class. She hacked up the quizzes and tests. If she'd had a fellow Charm Bracelet with her, they could have formed a faction of uninterested note-passers. Alone, she could only mope. Mr. da Silva gave up trying to teach her anything and called on her as little as possible.

I watched her in class and I watched her outside it, too. As soon as I arrived at school I was on the lookout. I sat in one of the lobby's yellow wing chairs, pretending to do homework, and waited for her to pass. Her brief appearances always knocked me out. I was like somebody in a cartoon, with stars vibrating around the head. She would come around the corner, chewing on a Flair pen and shuffling, as if wearing slippers. There was always a rush to her walk. If she didn't keep her feet digging forward her crushed-down shoes would fly off. This brought out the muscles in her calves. She was freckled down there, too. It was almost a kind of suntan. Sliding, she charged by, talking to some other Charm Bracelet, both of them moving with that lazy, confident hauteur they all had. Sometimes she looked at me but showed no recognition. A nictitating membrane lowered itself over her eyes.

Allow me an anachronism. Luis Buñuel's *That Obscure Object of Desire* didn't come out until 1977. By that time the redheaded girl and I were no longer in touch. I doubt she ever saw the movie. Nevertheless, *That Obscure Object of Desire* is what I think about when I think about her. I saw it on television, in a Spanish bar, when I was stationed in Madrid. I didn't catch most of the dialogue. The plot was clear enough, though. An older gentleman played by Fernando Rey is smitten with a young and beautiful girl played by Carole Bouquet and Angela Molina. I didn't care about any of that. It was the surrealist touch that got me. In many scenes Fernando Rey is shown holding a heavy sack over his shoulder. The reason for this sack is never mentioned. (Or if it is, I missed that, too.)

He just goes around lugging this sack, into restaurants and through city parks. That was exactly how I felt, following my own Obscure Object. As though I were carrying around a mysterious, unexplained burden or weight. I'm going to call her that, if you don't mind. I'm going to call her the Obscure Object. For sentimental reasons. (I also have to protect her identity.)

There she was in gym class, malingering. There she was at lunch, having a laugh attack. Doubled over the table, she tried to hit the joker responsible. Her mouth bubbled milk. Her nose leaked a few drops, which started everyone laughing harder. Next I saw her after school, riding double with an unknown boy. She climbed up on the bicycle seat while he stood on the pedals. She didn't put her arms around his waist. She managed the thing by balance alone. This gave me hope.

One day in class Mr. da Silva asked the Object to read aloud.

She was lounging in her desk as usual. At a girls' school you didn't have to be so vigilant about keeping your knees together or your skirt tugged down. The Object's knees were spread apart and her legs, which were somewhat heavy in the thigh, were bare high up. Without moving, she said, "I forgot my book."

Mr. da Silva compressed his lips.

"You can look on with Callie."

The only sign of agreement she gave was to sweep her hair off her face. She placed a hand to her forehead and ran it back like a plow through her hair, her fingers leaving furrows. At the end of the stroke came a little flick of the head, a flourish. There was her cheek, permitting approach. I scooted over. I slid my book onto the crack between our desks. The Object leaned over it.

"From where?"

"Top of page one hundred and twelve. The description of the shield of Achilles."

I'd never been this close to the Obscure Object before. It was hard on my organism. My nervous system launched into "Flight of the Bumblebee." The violins were sawing away in my spine. The timpani were banging in my chest. At the same time, trying to conceal all this, I didn't move a muscle. I hardly breathed. That was the deal basically: catatonia without; frenzy within.

I could smell her cinnamon gum. It was still in the back of her mouth somewhere. I didn't look directly at her. I kept my eyes on the book. A strand of her red-gold hair fell onto the desk between us. Where the sun hit the hair, there was a prismatic effect. But while I was witnessing the half-inch rainbow she began to read.

I expected a nasal monotone, riddled with mispronunciations. I expected bumps, swerves, screeching brakes, head-on collisions. But the Obscure Object had a good reading voice. It was clear, strong, supple in its rhythms. It was a voice she'd picked up at home, from poetry-reciting uncles who drank too much. Her expression changed, too. A concentrated dignity, previously absent, marked her features. Her head rose on a proud neck. Her chin was lifted. She sounded twenty-four instead of fourteen. I wonder which was stranger, the Eartha Kitt voice that came out of my mouth or the Katharine Hepburn that came out of hers.

When she was finished there was silence. "Thank you," said Mr. da Silva, as surprised as the rest of us. "That was very nicely done."

The bell rang. Immediately the Object leaned away from me. She ran a hand through her hair again, as though rinsing it in the shower. She slipped out of the desk and left the room.

On certain days, when the greenhouse was lit just so and the Obscure Object's blouse unbuttoned two buttons, when the light illuminated the scapulars dangling between the cups of her brassiere, did Calliope feel any inkling of her true biological nature? Did she ever, while the Obscure Object passed in the hall, think that what she was feeling was wrong? Yes and no. Let me remind you where all this was happening.

It was perfectly acceptable at Baker & Inglis to get a crush on a fellow classmate. At a girls' school a certain amount of emotional energy, normally expended on boys, gets redirected into friendships. Girls walked arm in arm at B&I, the way French schoolgirls do. They competed for affection. Jealousies arose. Betrayals occurred. It was common to come into the bathroom and hear somebody sobbing in one of the stalls. Girls cried because so-and-so wouldn't sit by them at lunch, or because their best friend had a new boyfriend who monopolized her time. On top of this, school rituals reinforced an intimate atmosphere. There was Ring Day, where Big Sisters initiated Little Sisters into maturity by giving them flowers and gold bands. There was the Distaff Dance, a maypole without men, held in the spring. There were the bimonthly "Heart-to-Hearts," confessional meetings run by the school chaplain, which invariably ended in paroxysms of hugging and weeping. Nevertheless, the ethos of the school remained militantly heterosexual. My classmates might act cozy during the day, but boys were the number one after-school activity. Any girl suspected of being attracted to girls was gossiped about, victimized, and shunned. I was aware of all this. It scared me.

I didn't know if the way I felt about the Obscure Object was normal or not. My friends tended to get envious crushes on other girls. Reetika swooned over the way Alwyn Brier played *Finlandia* on the piano. Linda Ramirez was smitten with Sofia Cracchiolo because she was taking three languages at once. Was that it? Was the crush I had on the Object a result of her elocutionary talent? I doubted it. It felt physical, my crush. It wasn't a judgment but a tumult in my veins. For that reason I kept quiet about it. I hid out in the basement bathroom to think the matter through. Every day, whenever I could, I took the back stairs down to the deserted washroom and shut myself up for at least half an hour.

Is there anyplace as comforting as an old, institutional, prewar bathroom? The kind of bathroom they used to build in America when the country was on the rise. The basement bathroom at Baker & Inglis was done up like a box at the opera. Edwardian lighting fixtures gleamed overhead. The sinks were deep white bowls set in blue slate. When you bent to wash your face you saw tiny cracks in the porcelain, as in a Ming vase. Gold chains held the drain-stoppers in place. Beneath the taps, dripping had worn the porcelain thin in green stripes.

Above each sink hung an oval mirror. I wanted nothing to do with any of them. ("The hatred of mirrors that begins in middle age" started early for me.) Avoiding my reflection, I headed straight for the toilet stalls. There were three, and I chose the middle. Like the others, it was marble. Gray New England marble, two inches thick, quarried in the nineteenth century and studded with fossils millions of years old. I closed the door and latched it. I took a Safe-T-Guard from the dispenser and laid it over the toilet seat. Germ-protected, I lowered my underpants, lifted my kilt, and sat. Right away I could feel my body relaxing, my stoop unkinking itself. I brushed my hair out of my face so that I could see. There were little fern-shaped fossils, and fossils that looked like scorpions stinging themselves to death. Down beneath my legs the toilet bowl had a rust stain, ancient, too.

The basement bathroom was the opposite of our locker room. The stalls were seven feet high and extended all the way to the floor. Fossilized marble concealed me even better than my hair. In the basement bathroom was a time frame I felt much more comfortable with, not the rat race of the school upstairs but the slow, evolutionary progress of the earth, of its plant and animal life forming out of the generative, primeval mud. The faucets dripped with the slow, inexorable movement of time and I was alone down there, and safe. Safe from my confused feelings about the Obscure Object; and safe, too, from the bits of conversation I'd been overhearing from my parents' bedroom. Just the night before, Milton's exasperated voice had reached my ears: "You still got a headache? Christ, take some aspirin." "I took some already," my mother replied. "Nothing helps." Then my brother's name, and my father grumbling something I couldn't make out. Then Tessie: "I'm worried about Callie, too. She still hasn't gotten her period." "Hell, she's only thirteen." "She's *fourteen*. And look how tall she is. I think something's wrong." Silence a moment, after which my father asked, "What does Dr. Phil say?" "Dr. Phil! He doesn't say anything. I want to take her to someone else."

The humming of my parents' voices from behind my bedroom wall, which throughout my childhood had filled me with a sense of security, had now become a source of anxiety and panic. So I exchanged it for walls of marble, which echoed only with the sound of dripping water, of the flushing of my toilet, or of my voice softly reading *The Iliad* aloud.

And when I got tired of Homer, I started reading the walls.

That was another selling point of the basement bathroom. It was covered with graffiti. Upstairs, class photos showed rows and rows of student faces. Down here it was mostly bodies. Sketched in blue ink were little men with gigantic sexual parts. And women with enormous breasts. Also various permutations: men with dinky penises; and women with penises, too. It was an education both in what was and what might be. Over the gray marble this new, jagged etching of bodies doing things, growing parts, fitting together, changing shape. Plus also jokes, words to the wise, confessions. In one spot: "I love sex." In another, "Patty C. is a slut." Where else would a girl like me, hiding from the world a knowledge she didn't quite understand herself — where else would she feel more comfortable than in this subterranean realm where people wrote down what they couldn't say, where they gave voice to their most shameful longings and knowledge?

For that spring, while the crocuses bloomed, while the headmistress checked on the daffodil bulbs in the flower beds,

Calliope, too, felt something budding. An obscure object all her own, which in addition to the need for privacy was responsible for bringing her down to the basement bathroom. A kind of crocus itself, just before flowering. A pink stem pushing up through dark new moss. But a strange kind of flower indeed, because it seemed to go through a number of seasons in a single day. It had its dormant winter when it slept underground. Five minutes later, it stirred in a private springtime. Sitting in class with a book in my lap, or riding home in car pool, I'd feel a thaw between my legs, the soil growing moist, a rich, peaty aroma rising, and then — while I pretended to memorize Latin verbs — the sudden, squirming life in the warm earth beneath my skirt. To the touch, the crocus sometimes felt soft and slippery, like the flesh of a worm. At other times it was as hard as a root.

How did Calliope feel about her crocus? This is at once the easiest and the hardest thing to explain. On the one hand she liked it. If she pressed the corner of a textbook against it, the sensation was pleasurable. This wasn't new. It had always felt nice to apply pressure there. The crocus was part of her body, after all. There was no reason to ask questions.

But there were times when I felt that

something was different about the way I was made. At Camp Ponshewaing I'd learned, on certain humid bunkhouse nights, of the bicycle seats and fence posts that had seduced my campmates at tender ages. Lizzie Barton, roasting a marshmallow on a stick, told us how she had become fond of the post of a leather saddle. Margaret Thompson was the first girl in town whose parents owned a massaging shower head. I added my own sense data to these clinical histories (that was the year I fell in love with gym ropes), but there remained a vague, indefinable gap between the stirrings my friends reported and the clutching ecstasy of my own dry spasms. Sometimes, hanging down from my top bunk into the beam of someone's flashlight, I would finish my little self-revelation with "You know?" And in the dimness three or four stringy-haired girls would nod, once, and bite the corner of their lips, and shift their eyes away. They didn't know.

I worried at times that my crocus was too elaborate a bloom, not a common perennial but a hothouse flower, a hybrid named by its originator like a rose. Iridescent Hellene. Pale Olympus. Greek Fire. But no — that wasn't right. My crocus wasn't for show. It was in a state of becoming and might turn out fine if I waited patiently. Maybe it happened like this to everybody. In the meantime, it was best to keep everything under wraps. Which was what I was doing down in the basement.

Another tradition at Baker & Inglis: every year the eighth graders put on a classical Greek play. Originally, these plays had been performed in the Middle School auditorium. But after Mr. da Silva took his trip to Greece, he got the idea of converting the hockey field into a theater. With its bleachers set into the slope and its natural acoustics, it was a perfect mini-Epidaurus. The custodial staff brought risers out and set up a stage on the grass.

The year of my infatuation with the Obscure Object, the play Mr. da Silva selected was *Antigone*. There were no auditions. Mr. da Silva filled the major roles with his pets from Advanced English. Everyone else he stuck in the chorus. So the cast list read like this: Joanne Maria Barbara Peracchio as Creon; Tina Kubek as Eurydice; Maxine Grossinger as Ismene. In the role of Antigone herself — the only real possibility from even a physical standpoint — was the Obscure Object. Her midterm grade had been only a C minus. Still, Mr. da Silva knew a star when he saw one.

"We have to learn all these lines?" asked Joanne Maria Barbara Peracchio at our first rehearsal. "In two weeks?"

"Learn what you can," said Mr. da Silva. "Everyone's going to be wearing a robe. You can keep your script underneath. Miss Fagles will also be our prompter. She'll be in the orchestra pit."

"We're going to have an orchestra?" Maxine Grossinger wanted to know.

"The orchestra," Mr. da Silva said, pointing to his recorder, "is I."

"I hope it doesn't rain," said the Object.

"Will it rain the Friday after next?" said Mr. da Silva. "Why don't we ask our Tiresias?" And then he turned to me.

You expected someone else? No, if the Obscure Object was perfect to play the avenging sister, I was a shoo-in to play the old, blind prophet. My wild hair suggested clairvoyance. My stoop made me appear brittle with age. My half-changed voice had a disembodied, inspired quality. Tiresias had also been a woman, of course. But I didn't know that then. And it wasn't mentioned in the script.

I didn't care what part I played. All that mattered, all I could think about, was that now I would be near the Obscure Object. Not near her as I was during class, when it was impossible to speak. Not near her as I was in the lunchroom, when she was spitting milk at another table. But near her in rehearsals for a school play, with all the waiting around that implied, all the backstage intimacy, all the intense, fraught, giddy, emotional abandon brought on by assuming identities not your own.

"I don't think we should use scripts," the Obscure Object now declared. She had arrived for rehearsal looking professional, all her lines highlighted in yellow. Her sweater was tied around her shoulders like a cloak. "I think we should all memorize our lines." She looked from face to face. "Otherwise it'll be too fakey."

Mr. da Silva was smiling. Learning lines would require effort on the Object's part. A novel undertaking. "Antigone has far and away the most lines," he said. "So if Antigone wants to be off book, then I think the rest of you should be off book, too."

The other girls groaned. But Tiresias, already having a vision of the future, turned toward the Object. "I'll go over your lines with you. If you want."

The future. It was already happening. The Object was looking at me. The nictitating membranes were lifting. "Okay," she said, distantly.

We agreed to meet the next day, a Tuesday evening. The Obscure Object wrote out her address and Tessie dropped me at the house. She was sitting on a green velvet sofa when I was shown into the library. Her oxfords were off but she still had her uniform on. Her long red hair was tied back, the better to do what she was doing, which was to light her cigarette. Sitting Indian style, the Object leaned forward, holding the cigarette in her mouth over a green ceramic lighter shaped like an artichoke. The lighter was low on fluid. She shook it and flicked the button with her thumb until at last a small flame shot out.

"Your parents let you smoke?" I said.

She looked up, surprised, then returned to the work at hand. She got the cigarette going, inhaled deeply, and let it out, slowly, satisfyingly. "*They* smoke," she said. "They'd be pretty big hypocrites if they didn't let me smoke."

"But they're adults."

"Mummy and Daddy know I'm going to smoke if I want to. If they don't let me do it, I'll just sneak it."

By the looks of it, this dispensation had been in effect for some time. The Object was not new to smoking. She was already a professional. As she sized me up, her eyes narrowing, the cigarette hung aslant from her mouth. Smoke drifted close to her face. It was a strange opposition: the hard-bitten private-eye expression on the face of a girl wearing a uniform for private school. Finally she reached up and took the cigarette out of her mouth. Without looking for the ashtray, she flicked her ash. It fell in.

"I doubt a kid like you smokes," she said.

"That would be a good guess."

"You interested in starting?" She held out her pack of Tareytons.

"I don't want to get cancer."

She tossed the pack down, shrugging. "I figure they'll be able to cure it by the time I get it."

"I hope so. For your sake."

She inhaled again, even more deeply. She held the smoke in and then turned in cinematic profile and let it out.

"You don't have any bad habits, I bet," she said.

"I've got tons of bad habits."

"Like what?"

"Like I chew my hair."

"I bite my nails," she said competitively. She lifted one hand to show me. "Mummy got me this stuff to put on them. It tastes like shit. It's supposed to help you quit."

"Does it work?"

"At first it did. But now I sort of like the taste." She smiled. I smiled. Then, briefly, trying it out, we laughed together.

"That's not as bad as chewing your hair," I resumed.

"Why not?"

"Because when you chew your hair it starts smelling like what you had for lunch."

She made a face and said, "Bogue."

At school we would have felt funny talking together, but here no one could see us. In the bigger scheme of things, out in the world, we were more alike than different. We were both teenagers. We were both from the suburbs. I set down my bag and came over to the sofa. The Object put her Tareyton in her mouth. Planting her palms on either side of her crossed legs, she lifted herself up, like a yogi levitating, and scooted over to make room for me.

"I've got a history test tomorrow," she said.

"Who do you have for history?"

"Miss Schuyler."

"Miss Schuyler has a vibrator in her desk."

"A what!"

"A vibrator. Liz Clark saw it. It's in her bottom drawer."

"I can't believe it!" The Object was shocked, amused. But then she squinted, thinking. In a confidential voice she asked, "What are those for, anyway?"

"Vibrators?"

"Yeah." She knew she was supposed to know. But she trusted I wouldn't make fun of her. This was the form of the pact we made that day: I would handle the deep intellectual matters, like vibrators; she would handle the social sphere.

"Most women can't have orgasms by

regular intercourse," I said, quoting from the copy of *Our Bodies, Ourselves* Meg Zemka had given me. "They need clitoral stimulation."

Behind her freckles, a blush rose to the Object's face. She was, of course, transfixed by such information. I was speaking into her left ear. The blush spread across her face from that side, as if my words left a visible trace.

"I can't believe you know all this stuff."

"I'll tell you who knows about it. Miss Schuyler, that's who."

The laugh, the hoot, shot out of her mouth like a geyser, and then the Object was falling back on the couch. She screamed, with delight, with revulsion. She kicked her legs, knocking her cigarettes off the table. She was fourteen again, instead of twenty-four, and against all odds we were becoming friends.

" 'Unwept, unfriended, without marriage song, I am led forth in my horror —' "

" '— sorrow —' "

" '— in my sorrow on this journey that can be delayed no more. No longer . . .' "

" '. . . hapless one . . .' "

" 'Hapless one!' I hate that! 'No longer, hapless one, may I behold yon day-star's sacred eye; but for my fate no tear is shed, no . . . no . . .' "

" 'No friend makes moan.' "
" 'No friend makes moan.' "

We were at the Object's house again, going over our lines. We were in the sun room, sprawled on the Caribbean sofas. Parrots flocked behind the Object's head as she squeezed her eyes shut, reciting. We'd been at it for two hours. The Object had gone through almost a full pack. Beulah, the maid, brought us sandwiches on a tray along with two sixty-four-ounce bottles of Tab. The sandwiches were white, crustless, but not cucumber or watercress. A salmon-colored spread caked the spongy bread.

We took frequent breaks. The Object required constant refreshment. I still wasn't comfortable in the house. I couldn't get used to being waited on. I kept jumping up to serve myself. Beulah was black, too, which didn't make it any easier.

"I'm really glad we're in this play together," the Object said, munching. "I would've never talked to a kid like you." She paused, realizing how this sounded. "I mean, I never knew you were such a cool kid."

Cool? Calliope cool? I had never dreamed of such a thing. But I was ready to accept the Object's judgment.

"Can I tell you something, though?" she asked. "About your part?"

"Sure."

"You know how you're supposed to be blind and everything? Well, where we go in Bermuda there's this man who runs a hotel. And he's blind. And the thing about him is, it's like his ears are his eyes. Like if someone comes into the room, he turns one ear that way. The way *you* do it —" She stopped suddenly and seized my hand. "You're not getting mad at me, are you?"

"No."

"You've got the worst expression on your face, Callie!"

"I do?"

She had my hand. She wasn't letting go. "You sure you're not mad?"

"I'm not mad."

"Well, the way you pretend to be blind is you just, sort of, stumble around a lot. But the thing is, this blind man down in Bermuda, he never stumbles. He stands up really straight and he knows where everything is. And his ears are always focusing in on stuff."

I turned my face away.

"See, you're mad!"

"I'm not."

"You *are*."

"I'm being blind," I said. "I'm looking at you with my ear."

"Oh. That's good. Yeah, like that. That's really good."

Without letting go of my hand, she

leaned closer and I heard, felt, very softly, her hot breath in my ear. "Hi, Tiresias," she said, giggling. "It's me. Antigone."

The day of the play arrived ("opening night" we called it, though there would be no others). In an improvised "dressing room" behind the stage we lead actors sat on folding chairs. The rest of the eighth graders were already onstage, standing in a big semicircle. The play was set to begin at seven o'clock and finish before sunset. It was 6:55. Beyond the flats we could hear the hockey field filling up. The low rumble got steadily louder — voices, footsteps, the creaking of bleachers, and the slamming of car doors up in the parking lot. We were each dressed in a floor-length robe, tie-dyed black, gray, and white. The Obscure Object, however, was wearing a white robe. Mr. da Silva's concept was minimal: no makeup, no masks.

"How many people are out there?" Tina Kubek asked.

Maxine Grossinger peeked out. "Tons."

"You must be used to this, Maxine," I said. "From all your recitals."

"I don't get nervous when I'm playing the violin. This is way worse."

"I am sooo nervous," the Object said.

In her lap she had a jar of Rolaids, which she was eating like candy. I understood now why she had pounded her chest the first day of class. The Obscure Object suffered from a more or less constant case of heartburn. It was worse during times of stress. A few minutes earlier, she had wandered off to smoke her last cigarette before showtime. Now she was chewing on the antacid tablets. Part of coming from old money, apparently, was having old-person habits, those gross, adult needs and desperate palliatives. The Object was still too young for the effects to tell on her. She didn't have eye bags yet or stained fingernails. But the appetite for sophisticated ruin was already there. She smelled like smoke, if you got close. Her stomach was a mess. But her face continued to give off its autumnal display. The cat eyes above the snub nose were alert, blinking and resetting their attention to the growing noise beyond the flats.

"There's my mom and dad!" Maxine Grossinger shouted. She turned back to us and broke into a big smile. I'd never seen Maxine smile before. Her teeth were jagged and gappy, like those of a Sendak creature. She had braces, too. Her unconcealed joy made me understand her. She had a whole other life apart from school. Maxine was happy in her house behind the cypresses. Meanwhile, curly hair gushed from her fragile, musical head.

614

"Oh, Jesus." Maxine was peeking out again. "They're sitting right in the front row. They're going to be staring right at me."

We all peeked out, each in our turn. Only the Obscure Object remained seated. I saw my parents arrive. Milton stopped at the crest of the slope to look down at the hockey field. His expression suggested that the spectacle before him, the emerald grass, the white wooden bleachers, the school in the distance with its blue slate roof and ivy, pleased him. In America, England is where you go to wash yourself of ethnicity. Milton had on a blue blazer and cream-colored trousers. He looked like the captain of a cruise ship. With one arm on her back, he was gently leading Tessie down the steps to get a good seat.

We heard the audience grow quiet. Then a pan flute was heard — Mr. da Silva playing his recorder.

I went over to the Object and said, "Don't worry. You'll be fine."

She had been repeating her lines silently to herself but now stopped.

"You're a really good actress," I continued.

She turned away and lowered her head, moving her lips again.

"You won't forget your lines. We went over them a billion times. You had them down perfect yester—"

"Will you stop bugging me for a minute?" the Object snapped. "I'm trying to get psyched up." She glared at me. Then she turned and walked off.

I stood watching her, crestfallen, hating myself. Cool? I was anything but. I'd already made the Obscure Object sick of me. Feeling as if I might cry, I grabbed one of the black curtains and wrapped myself up in it. I stood in the darkness, wishing I were dead.

I hadn't just been flattering her. She *was* good. Onstage, the Object's fidgetiness stilled itself. Her posture improved. And of course there was the sheer physical fact of her, the blood-tinged blade that she was, the riot of color that caught everyone's attention. The pan flute stopped and the hockey field got silent again. People coughed, getting it out of their systems. I peeked out from the curtains and saw the Object waiting to go on. She was standing just inside the middle arch, no more than ten feet from me. I had never seen her so serious before, so concentrated. Talent is a kind of intelligence. As she waited to go on, the Obscure Object was coming into hers. Her lips moved as if she were speaking Sophocles' lines to Sophocles himself, as if, contrary to all intellectual evidence, she understood the literary reasons for their endurance. So the Object stood, waiting to go on. Far away from her cigarettes and her snobbishness, her cliquish friends, her atrocious spelling. This was what she was good at: appearing before people. Stepping out and standing there and speaking. She was just beginning to realize it then. What I was witnessing was a self discovering the self it could be.

On cue, our Antigone took a deep breath and walked onstage. Her white robe was cinched around her torso with silver braid. The robe fluttered as she stepped out in the warm breeze.

"Wilt thou aid this hand to lift the dead?"

Maxine-Ismene replied, "Thou wouldst bury him, when 'tis forbidden to Thebes?"

"I will do my part, and thou wilt not, to a brother. False to him will I never be found."

I wasn't on for a while. Tiresias wasn't that big a part. So I closed the curtain around me again and waited. I had a staff in my hand. It was my only prop, a plastic stick painted to look like wood.

It was then I heard a small, choking sound. Again the Object said, "False to him will I never be found." Followed by silence. I peeked out the curtain. Through the central arch I could see them. The Object had her back to me. Farther downstage

Maxine Grossinger stood with a blank look on her face. Her mouth was open, though no words were coming out. Beyond, just above the lip of the stage, was Miss Fagles's florid face, whispering Maxine's next line.

It wasn't stage fright. An aneurysm had burst in Maxine Grossinger's brain. At first, the audience took her quick stagger and shocked expression to be part of the play. Titters had begun at the way the girl playing Ismene was hamming it up. But Maxine's mother, knowing exactly what pain looked like on her child's face, shot up out of her seat. "No," she cried. "No!" Twenty feet away, elevated under a setting sun, Maxine Grossinger was still mute. A gurgle escaped from her throat. With the suddenness of a lighting cue her face went blue. Even in the back rows people could see the oxygen leave her blood. Pinkness drained away, down her forehead, her cheeks, her neck. Later, the Obscure Object would swear that Maxine had been looking at her with a kind of appeal, that she had seen the light go out of Maxine's eyes. According to the doctors, however, this was probably not true. Wrapped in her dark robe, still on her feet, Maxine Grossinger was already dead. She toppled forward seconds later.

Mrs. Grossinger scrambled up onstage.

She made no sound now. No one did. In silence she reached Maxine and tore open her robe. In silence the mother began to give the daughter mouth-to-mouth. I froze. I let the curtains untwist and I stepped out and gawked. Suddenly a white blur filled the arch. The Obscure Object was fleeing the stage. For a second I had a crazy idea. I thought Mr. da Silva had been holding out on us. He was doing things the traditional way after all. Because the Obscure Object was wearing a mask. The mask for tragedy, her eyes like knife slashes, her mouth a boomerang of woe. With this hideous face she threw herself on me. "Oh my God!" she sobbed. "Oh my God, Callie," and she was shaking and needing me.

Which leads me to a terrible confession. It is this. While Mrs. Grossinger tried to breathe life back into Maxine's body, while the sun set melodramatically over a death that wasn't in the script, I felt a wave of pure happiness surge through my body. Every nerve, every corpuscle, lit up. I had the Obscure Object in my arms.

Tiresias In Love

❧

"I made a doctor's appointment for you."

"I just went to the doctor."

"Not with Dr. Phil. With Dr. Bauer."

"Who's Dr. Bauer?"

"He's . . . a ladies' doctor."

There was a hot bubbling in my chest. As if my heart were eating Pop Rocks. But I played it cool, looking out at the lake.

"Who says I'm a lady?"

"Very funny."

"I just *went* to the doctor, Mom."

"That was for your physical."

"What's this for?"

"When girls get to be a certain age, Callie, they have to go get checked."

"Why?"

"To make sure everything's okay."

"What do you mean, everything?"

"Just — everything."

We were in the car. The second-best Cadillac. When Milton got a new car he gave Tessie his old one. The Obscure Object had invited me to spend the day at her club and my mother was taking me to her house.

It was summer now, two weeks since Maxine Grossinger had collapsed onstage. School was out. On Middlesex preparations were under way for our trip to Turkey. Determined not to let Chapter Eleven's condemnation of tourism ruin our travel plans, Milton was making airplane reservations and haggling with car rental agencies. Every morning he scanned the newspaper, reporting the weather conditions in Istanbul. "Eighty-one degrees and sunny. How does that sound, Cal?" In response to which I generally twirled an index finger. I wasn't keen on visiting the homeland anymore. I didn't want to waste my summer painting a church. Greece, Asia Minor, Mount Olympus, what did they have to do with me? I'd just discovered a whole new continent only a few miles away.

In the summer of 1974 Turkey and Greece were about to be in the news again. But I didn't pay any mind to the rising tensions. I had troubles of my own. More than that, I was in love. Secretly, shamefully, not entirely consciously, but for all that quite head-over-heels in love.

Our pretty lake was trimmed in filth. The usual June scum of fish flies. There was also a new guardrail, which gave me a somber feeling as we drove past. Maxine Grossinger wasn't the only girl at school who had died that year. Carol Henkel, a junior, had died in a car accident. One Saturday night her drunken boyfriend, a guy named Rex Reese, had plunged his parents' car into the lake. Rex had survived, swimming back to shore. But Carol had been trapped inside the car.

We passed Baker & Inglis, closed for vacation and succumbing to the unreality of schools during summertime. We turned up Kerby Road. The Object lived on Tonnacour, in a gray stone and clapboard house with a weather vane. Parked on the gravel was an unprepossessing Ford sedan. I felt self-conscious in the second-best Cadillac and got out quickly, wishing my mother gone.

When I rang the bell, Beulah answered. She led me to the staircase and pointed up. That was all. I climbed to the second floor. I'd never been upstairs at the Object's house before. It was messier than ours, the carpeting not new. The ceiling hadn't been painted in years. But the furniture was impressively old, heavy, and sent out signals of permanence and settled judgment.

I tried three rooms before I found the Object's. Her shades were drawn. Clothes were scattered all over the shag carpeting and I had to wade through them to reach the bed. But there she was, sleeping, in a Lester Lanin T-shirt. I called her name. I jiggled her. Finally she sat up against her pillows and blinked.

"I must look like shit," she said after a moment.

I didn't say whether she did or not. It strengthened my position to keep her in doubt.

We had breakfast in the breakfast nook. Beulah served us without elaboration, bringing and taking plates. She wore an actual maid's uniform, black, with white apron. Her eyeglasses hailed from her other, more stylish life. In gold script her name curled across the left lens.

Mrs. Object arrived, clacking in sensible heels: "Good morning, Beulah. I'm off to the vet's. Sheba's getting a tooth pulled. I'll drop her back here, but then I'm off to lunch. They say she'll be woozy. Oh — and the men are coming for the drapes today. Let them in and give them the check that's on the counter. Hello, girls! I didn't see you. You must be a good influence, Callie. Nine-thirty and this one's up already?" She mussed the Object's hair. "Are you spending the day at the Little Club, dear? Good. Your father and I are going out with the Peterses tonight. Beulah will leave something for you in the fridge. Bye, all!"

All this while, Beulah rinsed glasses. Keeping to her strategy. Giving Grosse

Pointe the silent treatment.

The Object spun the lazy Susan. French jams, English marmalades, an unclean butter dish, bottles of ketchup and Lea & Perrins circled past, before what the Object wanted: an economy-size jar of Rolaids. She shook out three tablets.

"What is heartburn, anyway?" I said.

"You've never had heartburn?" asked the Object, amazed.

The Little Club was only a nickname. Officially the club was known as the Grosse Pointe Club. Though the property was on the lake, there were no docks or boats in sight, only a mansion-like club-house, two paddle tennis courts, and a swimming pool. It was beside this pool that we lay every day that June and July.

As far as swimwear went, the Obscure Object favored bikinis. She looked good in them but by no means perfect. Like her thighs, her hips were on the large side. She claimed to envy my thin, long legs, but she was only being nice. Calliope appeared poolside, that first day and every day thereafter, in an old-fashioned one-piece with a skirt. It had belonged to Sourmelina during the 1950s. I found it in an old trunk. The stated intent was to look funky, but I was grateful for the full coverage. I also hung a beach towel around my neck or wore an alligator shirt over my suit. The bodice of the bathing suit was a plus, too. The cups were rubberized, pointy, and beneath a towel or a shirt gave me the suggestion of a bust I didn't have.

Beyond us, pelican-bellied ladies in swim caps followed kickboards back and forth across the pool. Their bathing suits were a lot like mine. Little kids waded and splashed in the shallow end. There is a small window of opportunity for freckled girls to tan. The Object was in it. As we revolved on our towels that summer, self-basting, the Object's freckles darkened, going from butterscotch to brown. The skin between them darkened, too, knitting her freckles together into a speckled harlequin mask. Only the tip of her nose remained pink. The part in her hair flamed with sunburn.

Club sandwiches, on wave-rimmed plates, sailed out to us. If we were feeling sophisticated, we ordered the French dip. We had milk shakes, too, ice cream, french fries. For everything the Object signed her father's name. She talked about Petoskey, where her family had a summer house. "We're going up in August. Maybe you could come up."

"We're going to Turkey," I said unhappily.

"Oh, right. I forgot." And then: "Why

do you have to paint a church?"

"My dad made this promise."

"How come?"

Behind us married couples were playing paddle tennis. Pennants flew from the clubhouse roof. Was this the place to mention St. Christopher? My father's war stories? My grandmother's superstitions?

"You know what I keep thinking?" I said.

"What?"

"I keep thinking about Maxine. I can't believe she's dead."

"I know. It doesn't seem like she's really dead. It's like I dreamed it."

"The only way we know it's true is that we both dreamed it. That's what reality is. It's a dream everyone has together."

"That's deep," said the Object.

I smacked her.

"Ow!"

"That's what you get."

Bugs were attracted by our coconut oil. We killed them without mercy. The Object was making a slow, scandalized progress through *The Lonely Lady* by Harold Robbins. Every few pages she shook her head and announced, "This book is sooo dirty." I was reading *Oliver Twist*, one of the assigned volumes for our summer reading list.

Suddenly the sun went in. A drop of

water hit my page. But this was nothing compared to the cascade that was being shaken onto the Obscure Object. An older boy was leaning over sideways, shaking his wet mop of hair.

"Goddamn you," she said, "cut it out!"

"What's the matter? I'm cooling you off."

"Quit it!"

Finally, he did. He straightened up. His bathing suit had fallen down over his skinny hipbones. This exposed an ant trail of hair running down from his navel. The ant trail was red. But on his head the hair was jet black.

"Who's the latest victim of your hospitality?" the boy asked.

"This is Callie," said the Object. Then to me: "This is my brother. Jerome."

The resemblance was clear. The same palette had gone into Jerome's face (oranges and pale blues, primarily) but there was a crudeness to the overall sketch, something bulbous about the nose, the eyes on the squinty side, pinpricks of light. What threw me at first was the dark, sheenless hair, which I soon realized was dyed.

"You were the one in the play, right?"

"Yes."

Jerome nodded. With slitty eyes glinting he said, "A thespian, eh? Just like you. Right, sis?"

"My brother has a lot of problems," the Object said.

"Hey, since you gals are into the thee-a-tah, maybe you want to be in my next film." He looked at me. "I'm making a vampire movie. You'd make a great vampire."

"I would?"

"Let me see your teeth."

I didn't oblige, taking my cue from the Object not to be too friendly.

"Jerome is into monster movies," she said.

"Horror films," he corrected, still directing his words to me. "Not monster movies. My sister, as usual, belittles my chosen medium. Want to know the title?"

"No," said the Object.

"*Vampires in Prep School*. It's about this vampire, played by *moi*, who gets sent off to prep school because his affluent but terribly unhappy parents are going through a divorce. Anyway, he doesn't get along too well out there at boarding school. He doesn't wear the right clothes. He doesn't have the right haircut. But then one day after this kegger he takes a walk across campus and gets attacked by a vampire. And — here's the kicker — the vampire is smoking a pipe. He's wearing a Harris tweed. It's the fucking headmaster, man! So the next morning, our hero wakes up and goes right out and buys a blue blazer and some Top-Siders and — presto — he's a total prep!"

"Will you move, you're blocking my sun."

"It's a metaphor for the whole boarding school experience," Jerome said. "Each generation puts the bite on the next, turning them into the living dead."

"Jerome has been kicked out of two boarding schools."

"And I shall have my revenge upon them!" Jerome proclaimed in a hoary voice, shaking his fist in the air. Then without another word he ran to the pool and jumped. As he did, he spun around so he was facing us. There Jerome hung, skinny, sunken-chested, as white as a saltine, his face scrunched up and one hand clutching his nuts. He held that pose all the way down.

I was too young to ask myself what was behind our sudden intimacy. In the days and weeks that followed, I didn't consider the Object's own motivations, her love vacuum. Her mother had engagements all day long. Her father left for the office at six forty-five. Jerome was a brother and therefore useless. The Object didn't like being alone. She had never learned to amuse herself. And so one evening at her house, as I was about to get on my bike and ride home, she suggested that I sleep over.

"I don't have my toothbrush."

"You can use mine."

"That's gross."

"I'll get you a new toothbrush. We've got a box of them. God, you're such a priss."

I was only feigning squeamishness. In actuality I wouldn't have minded sharing the Object's toothbrush. I wouldn't have minded *being* the Object's toothbrush. I was already well acquainted with the splendors of her mouth. Smoking is good for that. You get a full display of the puckering and the sucking. The tongue often makes an appearance, licking from the lips any stickiness imparted by the filter. Sometimes bits of paper adhere to the bottom lip and the smoker, pulling them away, reveals the candied lower teeth against the pulpy gums. And if the smoker is a blower of smoke rings, you get to see all the way in to the dark velvet of the inner cheeks.

That was how it went with the Obscure Object. A cigarette in bed was the tombstone marking each day's end and the reed through which she breathed herself back to life each morning. You've heard of installation artists? Well, the Object was an *exhalation* artist. She had a whole repertoire. There was the Sidewinder, where she politely funneled smoke away from the person she was talking to out the corner of her mouth. There was the Geyser when she was angry. There was the Dragon Lady, featuring a plume from each nostril. There was the French Recycle, where she let smoke out her mouth only to inhale it back through her nose. And there was the Swallow. The Swallow was reserved for crisis situations. Once, in the Science Wing bathroom, the Object had just finished taking a long drag when a teacher charged in. My friend had time to flick her cigarette into the toilet bowl and flush. But what about the smoke? Where could it go?

"Who's been smoking in here?" the teacher asked.

The Object shrugged, keeping her mouth closed. The teacher leaned toward her, sniffing. And the Object swallowed. No smoke came out. Not a wisp. Not a puff. A little moistness in her eyes the only sign of the Chernobyl in her lungs.

I accepted the Object's invitation to sleep over. Mrs. Object called Tessie to see if it was all right and, by eleven o'clock, my friend and I went up to bed together. She gave me a T-shirt to wear. It said "Fessenden" on the front. I put it on and the Object snickered.

"What?"

"That's Jerome's T-shirt. Does it reek?"

"Why'd you give me his shirt?" I said, going stiff, shrinking from the cotton's touch while still wearing it.

"Mine are too small. You want one of Daddy's? They smell like cologne."

"Your dad wears cologne?"

"He lived in Paris after the war. He's got all kinds of fruity habits." She was climbing up onto the big bed now. "Plus he slept with about a million French prostitutes."

"He told you that?"

"Not exactly. But whenever Daddy talks about France he acts all horny. He was in the Army there. He was like in charge of running Paris after the war. And Mummy gets really pissed when he talks about it." She imitated her mother now. " 'That's enough Francophilia for one evening, dear.' " As usual, when she did something dramatic, her IQ suddenly soared. Then she flopped onto her stomach. "He killed people, too."

"He did?"

"Yeah," said the Object, adding by way of explanation, "Nazis."

I climbed into the big bed. At home I had one pillow. Here there were six.

"Back rub," the Object called out cheerily.

"I'll do you if you do me."

"Deal."

I sat astride her, on the saddle of her

hips, and started with her shoulders. Her hair was in the way, so I moved it. We were quiet for a while, me rubbing, and then I asked, "Have you ever been to a gynecologist?"

The Object nodded into her pillow.

"What's it like?"

"It's torture. I hate it."

"What do they do?"

"First they make you strip and put this little gown on. It's made of paper and all this cold air gets in. You freeze. Then they make you lie on this table, spread-eagled."

"Spread-eagled?"

"Yep. You have to put your legs in these metal things. Then the gyno gives you a pelvic exam, *which kills*."

"What do you mean, pelvic exam?"

"I thought you were supposed to be the sex expert."

"Come on."

"A pelvic exam is, you know, *inside*. They shove this little doohickey in you to spread you all open and everything."

"I can't believe this."

"It kills. And it's freezing. Plus you've got the gyno making lame jokes while he's nosing around in there. But the worst is what he does with his hands."

"What?"

"Basically he reaches in until he can tickle your tonsils."

Now I was mute. Absolutely paralyzed with shock and fear.

"Who are you going to?" the Object asked.

"Someone named Dr. Bauer."

"Dr. Bauer! That's Renee's dad. He's a total perv!"

"What do you mean?"

"I went swimming over at Renee's one time. They have a pool. Dr. Bauer came out and stood there, watching. Then he goes, 'Your legs have perfect proportions. Absolutely perfect proportions.' God, what a perv! Dr. Bauer. I pity you."

She raised her stomach in order to free her shirt. I massaged her lower back, reaching under the shirt to knead her shoulder blades.

The Object got quiet after that. So did I. I kept my mind off gynecology by losing myself in the back rub. It wasn't hard. Her honey- or apricot-colored back tapered at the waist in a way mine didn't. There were white spots here and there, anti-freckles. Wherever I rubbed, her skin flushed. I was aware of the blood underneath, coursing and draining. Her underarms were rough like a cat's tongue. Below them the sides of her breasts swelled out, flattened against the mattress.

"Okay," I said, after a long while, "my turn."

But that night was like all the others. She was asleep.

It was never my turn with the Object.

They come back to me, the scattered days of that summer with the Object, each encased in a souvenir snow globe. Let me shake them up again. Watch the flakes float down:

We are lying in bed together on a Saturday morning. The Object is on her back. I'm fulcrumed on one elbow, leaning over to inspect her face.

"You know what sleep is?" I say.

"What?"

"Snot."

"It is not."

"It *is*. It's mucus. It's snot that comes out your eyes."

"That's so gross!"

"You've got a little sleep in your eyes, my dear," I say in a fake deep voice. With my finger I flick the crust from the Object's eyelashes.

"I can't believe I'm letting you do this," she says. "You're touching my snot."

We look at each other a moment.

"I'm touching your snot!" I scream. And we writhe around, throwing pillows and screaming some more.

On another day, the Object is taking a

bath. She has her own bathroom. I'm on the bed, reading a gossip magazine.

"You can tell Jane Fonda isn't really naked in that movie," I say.

"How?"

"She's got a body stocking on. You can see it."

I go into the bathroom to show her. In the claw-footed tub, under a layer of whipped cream, the Object lolls, pumicing one heel.

She looks at the photograph and says, "You're never naked, either."

I am frozen, speechless.

"Do you have some kind of complex?"

"No, I don't have a complex."

"What are you afraid of, then?"

"I'm not afraid."

The Object knows this isn't true. But her intentions aren't malicious. She isn't trying to catch me out, only to put me at ease. My modesty baffles her.

"I don't know what you're so worried about," she says. "You're my best friend."

I pretend to be engrossed in the magazine. I can't get myself to look away. Inside, however, I'm bursting with happiness. I'm erupting with joy, but I keep staring at the magazine as though I'm mad at it.

It's late. We've stayed up watching TV. The Object is brushing her teeth when I come into the bathroom. I pull down my underpants and sit on the toilet. I do this sometimes as a compensatory tactic. The T-shirt is long enough to cover my lap. I pee while the Object brushes.

It's then I smell smoke. Looking up, I see, besides a toothbrush in the Object's mouth, a cigarette.

"You even smoke while you brush your teeth?"

She looks at me sideways. "Menthol," she says.

The thing about those souvenirs, though: the glitter falls fast.

A reminder taped to our refrigerator brought me back to reality: "Dr. Bauer, July 22, 2 p.m."

I was filled with dread. Dread of the perverted gynecologist and his inquisitorial instruments. Dread of the metal things that would spread my legs and of the doohickey that would spread something else. And dread of what all this spreading might reveal.

It was in this state, this emotional foxhole, that I started going to church again. One Sunday in early July my mother and I dressed up (Tessie in heels, me not) and drove down to Assumption. Tessie was suffering, too. It had been six months since Chapter Eleven had sped away from

Middlesex on his motorcycle, and since that time he hadn't been back. Worse, in April he had broken the news that he was dropping out of college. He was planning to move to the Upper Peninsula with some friends and, as he put it, live off the land. "You don't think he'd do something crazy like run off and marry that Meg, do you?" Tessie asked Milton. "Let's hope not," he answered. Tessie worried that Chapter Eleven wasn't taking care of himself, either. He wasn't going to the dentist regularly. His vegetarianism made him pale. And he was losing his hair. At the age of twenty. This made Tessie feel suddenly old.

United in anxiety, seeking solace for differing complaints (Tessie wanting to get rid of her pains while I wanted mine to begin), we entered the church. As far as I could tell, what happened every Sunday at Assumption Greek Orthodox Church was that the priests got together and read the Bible out loud. They started with Genesis and kept going straight through Numbers and Deuteronomy. Then on through Psalms and Proverbs, Ecclesiastes, Isaiah, Jeremiah, and Ezekiel, all the way up to the New Testament. Then they read that. Given the length of our services, I saw no other possibility.

They chanted as the church slowly filled

up. Finally the central chandelier flicked on and Father Mike, like a life-size puppet, sprang through the icon screen. The transformation my uncle went through every Sunday always amazed me. At church Father Mike appeared and disappeared with the capriciousness of a divinity. One minute he was up on the balcony, singing in his tender, tone-deaf voice. The next minute he was back on ground level, swinging his censer. Glittering, bejeweled, as overdone in his vestments as a Fabergé egg, he promenaded around the church, giving us God's blessing. Sometimes his censer produced so much smoke it seemed that Father Mike had the ability to cloak himself in a mist. When the mist dispersed, however, later that afternoon in our living room, he was once again a short, shy man, in black, polyester-blend clothes and a plastic collar.

Aunt Zoë's authority went in the opposite direction. At church she was meek. The round gray hat she wore looked like the head of a screw fastening her to her pew. She was constantly pinching her sons to keep them awake. I could barely connect the anxious person hunched down every week in front of us to the funny woman who, under the inspiration of wine, launched into comedy routines in our kitchen. "You men stay out!" she'd shout, dancing with my mother. "We've got knives in here."

So startling was the contrast between churchgoing Zoë and wine-drinking Zoë that I always made a point of watching her closely during the liturgy. On most Sundays, when my mother tapped her on the shoulder in greeting, Aunt Zo responded only with a weak smile. Her large nose looked swollen with grief. Then she turned back, crossed herself, and settled in for the duration.

And so: Assumption Church that July morning. Incense rising with the pungency of irrational hope. Closer in (it had been drizzling out), the smell of wet wool. The dripping of umbrellas stashed under pews. The rivulets from these umbrellas flowing down the uneven floor of our poorly built church, pooling in spots. The smell of hairspray and perfume, of cheap cigars, and the slow ticking of watches. The grumbling of more and more stomachs. And the yawning. The nodding off and the snoring and the being elbowed awake.

Our liturgy, endless; my own body immune to the laws of time. And right in front of me, Zoë Antoniou, on whom time had also been doing a number.

The life of a priest's wife had been even worse than Aunt Zo had expected. She had hated her years in the Peloponnese. They had lived in a small, unheated stone house. Outside, the village women spread blankets under olive trees, beating the branches until the olives fell. "Can't they stop that damn racket!" Zoë had complained. In five years, to the incessant sound of trees being clubbed to death, she bore four children. She sent letters to my mother detailing her hardships: no washing machine, no car, no television, a backyard full of boulders and goats. She signed her letters, "St. Zoë, Church martyr."

Father Mike had liked Greece better. His years there represented the best period of his priesthood. In that tiny Peloponnesian village the old superstitions survived. People still believed in the evil eye. Nobody pitied him for being a priest, whereas later on in America his parishioners always treated him with a slight but unmistakable condescension, like a crazy person whose delusions had to be humored. The humiliation of being a priest in a market economy didn't plague Father Mike while he was in Greece. In Greece he could forget about my mother, who had jilted him, and he could escape comparison with my father, who made so much more money. His wife's nagging complaints hadn't begun to make Father Mike think about leaving the priesthood yet, and hadn't led him to his desperate act . . .

In 1956 Father Mike was reappointed

stateside to a church in Cleveland. In 1958 he became a priest at Assumption. Zoë was happy to be back home, but she never got used to her position as *presvytera*. She didn't like being a role model. She found it difficult to keep her children looking neat and well dressed. "On what money?" she shouted at her husband. "Maybe if they paid you halfway decent the kids would look better." My cousins — Aristotle, Socrates, Cleopatra, and Plato — had the thwarted, overbrushed look of ministers' children. The boys wore cheap, garishly colored double-breasted suits. They had Afros. Cleo, who was as beautiful and almond-eyed as her namesake, made do with dresses from Montgomery Ward. She rarely spoke, and played cat's cradle with Plato during the service.

I always liked Aunt Zo. I liked her big, grandstanding voice. I liked her sense of humor. She was louder than most men; she could make my mother laugh like nobody else.

That Sunday, for instance, during one of the many lulls, Aunt Zo turned around and dared to joke. "I *have* to be here, Tessie. What's your excuse?"

"Callie and I just felt like coming to church," my mother answered.

Plato, who was small like his father, sang out with mock censure, "Shame on you,

Callie. What did you do?" He rubbed his right index finger repeatedly over his left.

"Nothing," I said.

"Hey, Soc," Plato whispered to his brother. "Is cousin Callie blushing?"

"She must have done something she doesn't want to tell us."

"Shush up now, you," said Aunt Zo. For Father Mike was approaching with the censer. My cousins turned around. My mother bowed her head to pray. I did, too. Tessie prayed for Chapter Eleven to come to his senses. And me? That's easy. I prayed for my period to come. I prayed to receive the womanly stigmata.

Summer sped on. Milton brought our suitcases up from the basement and told my mother and me to start packing. I tanned with the Object at the Little Club. Dr. Bauer haunted my mind, judging the proportions of my legs. The appointment was a week away, then half a week, then two days . . .

And so we come to the preceding Saturday night, July 20, 1974. A night full of departures and secret plans. In the early hours of Sunday morning (which was still Saturday night back in Michigan), Turkish jets took off from bases on the mainland. They headed southeast over the Mediterranean Sea toward the island of Cyprus. In the ancient myths, gods favoring mortals often hid them away. Aphrodite blotted out Paris once, saving him from certain death at the hands of Menelaus. She wrapped Aeneas in a coat to sneak him off the battlefield. Likewise, as the Turkish jets roared over the sea, they were also hidden. That night, Cypriot military personnel reported a mysterious malfunctioning of their radar screens. The screens filled with thousands of white blips: an electromagnetic cloud. Invisible inside this, the Turkish jets reached the island and began dropping their bombs.

Meanwhile, back in Grosse Pointe, Fred and Phyllis Mooney were also leaving home base, heading to Chicago. On the front porch, waving goodbye, stood their children, Woody and Jane, who had secret plans of their own. Flying toward the Mooneys' house at that moment were the silver bombers of beer kegs and the tight formations of six-packs. Cars full of teenagers were on their way. And so were the Object and I. Powdered and glossed, our hair hot-combed into wings, we had set off for the party ourselves. In thin corduroy skirts and clogs we came up the front lawn. But the Object stopped me on the porch before we went in. She was biting her lip.

"You're my best friend, right?"

"Right."

"Okay. Sometimes I think I have bad breath." She stopped. "The thing is, you can never tell if you *have* bad breath or not. So the thing is" — she paused — "I want you to check it for me."

I didn't know what to say and so said nothing.

"Is that too disgusting?"

"No," I said, finally.

"Okay, here goes." She leaned toward me and huffed a single breath into my face.

"It's okay," I said.

"Good. Now you."

I leaned down and exhaled in her face.

"It's fine," she said, decisively. "Okay. Now we can go to the party."

I'd never been to a party before. I felt for the parents. As we squeezed by the throngs in the throbbing house, I cringed at the destruction under way. Cigarette ashes were dropping on Pierre Deux upholstery. Beer cans were spilling onto heirloom carpets. In the den I saw two laughing boys urinating into a tennis trophy. It was mostly older kids. A few couples climbed the stairs, disappearing into bedrooms.

The Object was trying to act older herself. She was copying the superior, bored expressions of the high school girls. She crossed to the back porch ahead of me and got in the line for the keg.

"What are you doing?" I asked.

"I'm getting a beer. What do you think?"

It was fairly dark outside. As in most social situations, I let my hair fall into my face. I was standing behind the Object, looking like Cousin It, when someone put his hands over my eyes.

"Guess who?"

"Jerome."

I pulled his hands off my face and turned around.

"How did you know it was me?"

"The curious smell."

"Ouch," said a voice behind Jerome. I looked over and received a shock. Standing with Jerome was Rex Reese, the guy who had driven Carol Henkel to her watery death. Rex Reese, our local Teddy Kennedy. He didn't look particularly sober now, either. His dark hair covered his ears and he wore a piece of blue coral on a leather thong around his throat. I searched his face for signs of remorse or repentance. Rex wasn't searching my face, however. He was eyeing the Object, his hair falling into his eyes above the curl of a smile.

Deftly, the two boys moved in between us, turning their backs to each other. I had a final glimpse of the Obscure Object. She had her hands in the back pockets of her corduroy skirt. This looked casual but had the effect of pushing out her chest. She was looking up at Rex and smiling.

"I start filming tomorrow," Jerome said.

I looked blank.

"My movie. My vampire movie. You sure you don't want to be in it?"

"We're going on vacation this week."

"That sucks," said Jerome. "It's going to be genius."

We stood silent. After a moment I said, "Real geniuses never think they're geniuses."

"Who says?"

"Me."

"Because why?"

"Because genius is nine-tenths perspiration. Haven't you ever heard that? As soon as you *think* you're a genius, you slack off. You think everything you do is so great and everything."

"I just want to make scary movies," Jerome replied. "With occasional nudity."

"Just don't try to be a genius and maybe you'll end up being one by accident," I said.

He was looking at me in a funny way, intense, but also grinning.

"What?"

"Nothing."

"Why are you looking at me like that?"

"Looking at you like what?"

In the dark, Jerome's resemblance to the Obscure Object was even more pronounced. The tawny eyebrows, the butterscotch complexion — here they were again, in permissible form.

"You're a lot smarter than most of my sister's friends."

"You're a lot smarter than most of my friends' brothers."

He leaned toward me. He was taller than I was. That was the big difference between him and his sister. It was enough to wake me from my trance. I turned away. I circled around him back to the Object. She was still staring up bright-faced at Rex.

"Come on," I said. "We've got to go to that thing."

"What thing?"

"You know. That thing."

Finally I managed to pull her away. She left trailing smiles and significant looks. As soon as we got off the porch she was frowning at me.

"Where are you taking me?" she said angrily.

"Away from that creep."

"Can't you leave me alone for a minute?"

"You want me to leave you alone?" I said. "Okay, I'll leave you alone." I didn't move.

"Can't I even talk to a boy at a party?" the Object asked.

"I was taking you away before it was too late."

"What do you mean?"

"You've got bad breath."

This checked the Object. This struck her to her core. She wilted. "I do?" she asked.

"It's just a little oniony," I said.

We were on the back lawn now. Kids were sitting on the stone porch rail, their cigarette tips glowing in the darkness.

"What do you think of Rex?" the Object whispered.

"What? Don't tell me you like him."

"I didn't say I like him."

I scoped her face, seeking the answer. She noticed this and walked farther away over the lawn. I followed. I said earlier that most of my emotions are hybrids. But not all. Some are pure and unadulterated. Jealousy, for instance.

"Rex is okay," I said when I had caught up to her. "If you like manslaughterers."

"That was an accident," said the Object.

The moon was three-quarters full. It silvered the fat leaves of the trees. The grass was wet. We both kicked off our clogs to stand in it. After a moment, sighing, the Object laid her head on my shoulder.

"It's good you're going away," she said.

"Why?"

"Because this is too weird." I looked back to see if anyone could see us. No one could. So I put my arm around her.

For the next few minutes we stood under

649

the moon-blanched trees, listening to the music blaring from the house. The cops would come soon. The cops always came. That was something you could depend on in Grosse Pointe.

The next morning, I went to church with Tessie. As usual, Aunt Zo was down in front, setting an example. Aristotle, Socrates, and Plato were wearing their gangster suits. Cleo was sunk into her black mane, about to doze off.

The rear and sides of the church were dark. Icons gloomed from the porticoes or raised stiff fingers in the glinting chapels. Beneath the dome, light fell in a chalky beam. The air was already thick with incense. Moving back and forth, the priests looked like men at a hammam.

Then it was showtime. One priest flicked a switch. The bottom tier of the enormous chandelier blazed on. From behind the iconostasis Father Mike entered. He was wearing a bright turquoise robe with a red heart embroidered on his back. He crossed the solea and came down among the parishioners. The smoke from his censer rose and curled, fragrant with antiquity. *"Kyrie eleison,"* Father Mike sang. *"Kyrie eleison."* And though the words meant nothing to me, or almost nothing, I felt their weight, the deep groove they made in the air of time. Tessie crossed herself, thinking about Chapter Eleven.

First Father Mike did the left side of the church. In blue waves, incense rolled over the gathered heads. It dimmed the circular lights of the chandelier. It aggravated the widows' lung conditions. It subdued the brightness of my cousins' suits. As it wrapped me in its dry-ice blanket, I breathed it in and began to pray myself. *Please God let Dr. Bauer not find anything wrong with me. And let me be just friends with the Object. And don't let her forget about me while we're in Turkey. And help my mother not to be so worried about my brother. And make Chapter Eleven go back to college.*

Incense serves a variety of purposes in the Orthodox church. Symbolically, it's an offering to God. Like the burnt sacrifices in pagan times, the fragrance drifts upward to heaven. Before the days of modern embalming, incense had a practical application. It covered the smell of corpses during funerals. It can also, when inhaled in sufficient amounts, create a lightheadedness that feels like religious reverie. And if you breathe in enough of it, it can make you sick.

"What's the matter?" Tessie's voice in my ear. "You look pale."

I stopped praying and opened my eyes. "I do?"

"Do you feel okay?"

I began to answer in the affirmative. But then I stopped myself.

"You look really pale, Callie," Tessie said again. She touched her hand to my forehead.

Sickness, reverie, devotion, deceit — they all came together. If God doesn't help you, you have to help yourself.

"It's my stomach," I said.

"What have you been eating?"

"Or not exactly my stomach. It's lower down."

"Do you feel faint?"

Father Mike passed by again. He swung the censer so high it nearly touched the tip of my nose. And I widened my nostrils and breathed in as much smoke as possible to make myself even paler than I already was.

"It's like somebody's twisting something inside me," I hazarded.

Which must have been more or less right. Because Tessie was now smiling. "Oh, honey," she said. "Oh, thank God."

"You're happy I'm sick? Thanks a lot."

"You're not sick, honey."

"Then what am I? I don't feel good. It *hurts*."

My mother took my hand, still beaming. "Hurry, hurry," she said. "We don't want an accident."

★ ★ ★

By the time I closed myself into a church bathroom stall, news of the Turkish invasion of Cyprus had reached the United States. When Tessie and I arrived back home, the living room was filled with shouting men.

"Our battleships are sitting off the coast to intimidate the Greeks," Jimmy Fioretos was yelling.

"Sure they're sitting off the coast," Milton now, "what do you expect? The Junta comes in and throws Makarios out. So the Turks are getting anxious. It's a volatile situation."

"Yeah, but to help the Turks —"

"The U.S. isn't helping the Turks," Milton went on. "They just don't want the Junta to get out of hand."

In 1922, while Smyrna burned, American warships sat idly by. Fifty-two years later, off the coast of Cyprus, they also did nothing. At least ostensibly.

"Don't be so naïve, Milt," Jimmy Fioretos again. "Who do you think's jamming the radar? It's the Americans, Milt. It's us."

"How do you know?" my father challenged.

And now Gus Panos through the hole in his throat: "It's that goddamned — sssss — Kissinger. He must have — sssss — made

653

a deal with the Turks."

"Of course he did." Peter Tatakis nodded, sipping his Pepsi. "Now that the Vietnam crisis is over, Herr Doktor Kissinger can get back to playing Bismarck. He would like to see NATO bases in Turkey? This is his way to get them."

Were these accusations true? I can't say for sure. All I know is this: on that morning, somebody jammed the Cypriot radar, guaranteeing the success of the Turkish invasion. Did the Turks possess such technology? No. Did the U.S. war- ships? Yes. But this isn't something you can prove . . .

Plus, it didn't matter to me, anyway. The men cursed, and shook their fingers at the television and pounded the radio, until Aunt Zo unplugged them. Unfortunately, she couldn't unplug the men. All through dinner the men shouted at each other. Knives and forks waved in the air. The ar- gument over Cyprus lasted for weeks and would finally put an end to those Sunday dinners once and for all. But as for myself, the invasion had only one meaning.

As soon as I could, I excused myself and ran off to call the Object. "Guess what?" I cried out with excitement. "We're not going on vacation. There's a war!"

Then I told her I had cramps and that I'd be right over.

Flesh and Blood

❧

I'm quickly approaching the moment of discovery: of myself by myself, which was something I knew all along and yet didn't know; and the discovery by poor, half-blind Dr. Philobosian of what he'd failed to notice at my birth and continued to miss during every annual physical thereafter; and the discovery by my parents of what kind of child they'd given birth to (answer: the same child, only different); and finally, the discovery of the mutated gene that had lain buried in our bloodline for two hundred and fifty years, biding its time, waiting for Atatürk to attack, for Hajienestis to turn into glass, for a clarinet to play seductively out a back window, until, coming together with its recessive twin, it started the chain of events that led up to me, here, writing in Berlin.

That summer — while the President's lies were also getting more elaborate — I started faking my period. With Nixonian cunning, Calliope unwrapped and flushed away a flotilla of unused Tampax. I feigned symptoms from headache to fatigue. I did cramps the way Meryl Streep did accents. There was the twinge, the dull ache, the sucker punch that made me curl up on my bed. My cycle, though imaginary, was rigorously charted on my desk calendar. I used the catacomb fish symbol ⟩○ to mark the days. I scheduled my periods right through December, by which time I was certain my real menarche would have finally arrived.

My deception worked. It calmed my mother's anxieties and somehow even my own. I felt I'd taken charge of things. I wasn't at the mercy of nature anymore. Even better, with our trip to Bursa canceled — as well as my appointment with Dr. Bauer — I was free to accept the Object's invitation to visit her family's summer house. In preparation I bought a sun hat, sandals, and a pair of rustic overalls.

I wasn't particularly tuned in to the political events unfolding in the nation that summer. But it was impossible to miss what was going on. My father's identification with Nixon only grew stronger as the President's troubles mounted. In the long-haired war protesters Milton saw his own shaggy, condemnatory son. Now, in the Watergate scandal, my father recognized his own dubious behavior during the riots. He thought the break-in was a mistake, but also believed that it was no big deal. "You don't think the Democrats aren't doing the same thing?" Milton asked the Sunday debaters. "The liberals just want to stick it to him. So they're playing pious." Watching the evening news, Milton delivered a running commentary to the screen. "Oh yeah?" he'd say. "Bullshit." Or: "This guy Proxmire's a total zero." Or: "What these pointy-headed intellectuals should be worrying about is foreign policy. What to do about the goddamn Russians and the Red Chinese. Not pissing and moaning about a robbery at a lousy campaign office." Hunkered down behind his TV tray, Milton scowled at the left-wing press, and his growing resemblance to the President couldn't be ignored.

On weeknights he argued with the television, but on Sundays he faced a live audience. Uncle Pete, who was usually as dormant as a snake while digesting, was now animated and jovial. "Even from a chiropractic standpoint, Nixon is a questionable character. He has the skeleton of a chimpanzee."

Father Mike joined the needling. "So what do you think about your friend Tricky Dicky now, Milt?"

"I think it's a lot of hoo-ha."

Things got worse when the conversation turned to Cyprus. In domestic affairs

Milton had Jimmy Fioretos on his side. But when it came to the Cyprus situation they parted company. A month after the invasion, just as the UN was about to conclude a peace negotiation, the Turkish Army had launched another attack. This time the Turks claimed a large portion of the island. Now barbed wire was going up. Guard towers were being erected. Cyprus was being cut in half like Berlin, like Korea, like all the other places in the world that were no longer one thing or the other.

"Now they're showing their true stripes," Jimmy Fioretos said. "The Turks wanted to invade all along. That malarkey about 'protecting the Constitution' was just a pretext."

"They hit us . . . sssss . . . while our backs were turned," croaked Gus Panos.

Milton snorted. "What do you mean 'us'? Where were you born, Gus, Cyprus?"

"You know . . . sssss . . . what I mean."

"America betrayed the Greeks!" Jimmy Fioretos jabbed a finger in the air. "It's that two-faced son of a bitch Kissinger. Shakes your hand while he pisses in your pocket!"

Milton shook his head. He lowered his chin aggressively and made a little sound, a bark of disapproval, deep in his throat. "We have to do whatever's in our national interest."

And then Milton lifted his chin and said it: "To hell with the Greeks."

In 1974, instead of reclaiming his roots by visiting Bursa, my father renounced them. Forced to choose between his native land and his ancestral one, he didn't hesitate. Meanwhile, we could hear it all the way from the kitchen: shouting; and a coffee cup breaking; swear words in both English and Greek; feet stomping out of the house.

"Get your coat, Phyllis, we're leaving," Jimmy Fioretos said.

"It's summer," said Phyllis. "I don't have a coat."

"Then get whatever the hell it is you have to get."

"We're going, too . . . sssss . . . I've lost my . . . sssss . . . appetite."

Even Uncle Pete, the self-educated opera buff, drew the line. "Maybe Gus didn't grow up in Greece," he said, "but I'm sure you remember that I did. You are talking about my native land, Milton. And your parents' own true home."

The guests left. They didn't come back. Jimmy and Phyllis Fioretos. Gus and Helen Panos. Peter Tatakis. The Buicks pulled away from Middlesex, leaving behind a negative space in our living room. After that, there were no more Sunday dinners. No more large-nosed men blowing their noses like muted trumpets. No more cheek-pinching women who resembled Melina Mercouri in her later years. Most of all, no more living room debates. No more arguing and citing examples and quoting the famous dead and castigating the infamous living. No more running the government from our love seats. No more revamping of the tax code or philosophical fights about the role of government, the welfare state, the Swedish health system (designed by a Dr. Fioretos, no relation). The end of an era. Never again. Never on Sunday.

The only people who stayed were Aunt Zo, Father Mike, and our cousins, because they were related to us. Tessie was angry with Milton for causing a fight. She told him so, he exploded at her, and she gave him the silent treatment for the rest of the day. Father Mike took advantage of this to lead Tessie up to the sun deck. Milton got in his car and drove off. I was with Aunt Zo when we later brought refreshments up to the deck. I had just stepped out onto the gravel between the thick redwood railings when I saw Tessie and Father Mike sitting on the black iron patio furniture. Father Mike was holding my mother's hand, leaning his bearded face close to her and looking into her eyes as he spoke softly. My mother had been crying, apparently. She had a tissue balled in one hand. "Callie's got iced tea," Aunt Zo announced as she came out, "and I've got the booze." But then she saw how Father Mike was looking at my mother and she went silent. My mother stood up, blushing. "I'll take the booze, Zo." Everyone laughed nervously. Aunt Zo poured the glasses. "Don't look, Mike," she said. "The *presvytera*'s getting drunk on Sunday."

The following Friday I drove up with the Object's father to their summer house near Petoskey. It was a grand Victorian, covered with gingerbread, and painted the color of pistachio saltwater taffy. I was dazzled by the sight of the house as we drove up. It sat on a rise above Little Traverse Bay, guarded by tall pines, all its windows blazing.

I was good with parents. Parents were my specialty. In the car on the way up I had carried on a lively and wide-ranging conversation with the Object's father. It was from him that she had gotten her coloring. Mr. Object had the Celtic tints. He was in his late fifties, however, and his reddish hair had been bleached almost colorless now, like a dandelion gone to seed. His freckled skin looked blown out, too. He wore a khaki poplin suit and bow tie. After he picked me up, we stopped at a party store near the highway, where Mr. Object bought a six-pack of Smirnoff cocktails.

"Martinis in a can, Callie. We live in an age of wonders."

Five hours later, not at all sober, he turned up the unpaved road that led to the summer house. It was ten o'clock by this time. In moonlight we carried our bags up to the back porch. Mushrooms dotted the pine-needled path between the thin gray pines. Next to the house an artesian well chimed among mossy rocks.

When we came in the kitchen door, we found Jerome. He was sitting at the table, reading the *Weekly World News*. The pallor of his face suggested that he had been there pretty much all month. His lusterless black hair looked particularly inert. He had on a Frankenstein T-shirt, seersucker shorts, white canvas Top-Siders without socks.

"I present to you Miss Stephanides," Mr. Object said.

"Welcome to the hinterland." Jerome stood up and shook his father's hand. They attempted a hug.

"Where's your mother?"

"She's upstairs getting dressed for the party you're incredibly late for. Her mood reflects that."

"Why don't you take Callie up to her room? Show her around."

"Check," said Jerome.

We went up the back stairs off the kitchen. "The guest room's being painted," Jerome told me. "So you're staying in my sister's room."

"Where is she?"

"She's out on the back porch with Rex."

My blood stopped. "Rex *Reese?*"

"His 'rents have a place up here, too."

Jerome then showed me the essentials, guest towels, bathroom location, how to work the lights. But his manners were lost on me. I was wondering why the Object hadn't mentioned anything about Rex on the phone. She had been up here three weeks and said nothing.

We came back into her bedroom. Her rumpled clothes lay on the unmade bed. There was a dirty ashtray on one pillow.

"My little sister is a creature of slovenly habits," Jerome said, looking around. "Are you neat?"

I nodded.

"Me too. Only way to be. Hey." He came around to face me now. "What happened to your trip to Turkey?"

"It got canceled."

"Excellent. Now you can be in my film. I'm shooting it up here. Are you up for that?"

"I thought it took place in a boarding school."

"I decided to make it a boarding school in the boonies." Jerome was standing somewhat close to me. His hands flopped around in his pockets as he squinted at me and rocked on his heels.

"Should we go downstairs?" I finally asked.

"What? Oh, right. Yeah. Let's go." Jerome turned and bolted. I followed him back down and through the kitchen. As we were crossing the living room I heard voices out on the porch.

"So Selfridge, that lightweight, *pukes*," Rex Reese was saying. "Doesn't even make it to the bathroom. Pukes right on the bar."

"I can't believe it! Selfridge!" It was the Object now, crying out with amusement.

"He blew chunks. Right into his stinger. I couldn't believe it. It was like the Niagara Falls of puke. Selfridge woofs on the bar and everybody jumps off their stools, right? Selfridge is facedown in his own puke. For a minute there's total silence. Then this one girl starts gagging . . . and it's like a chain reaction. The whole place starts gagging, puke's dripping everywhere, and the bartender is — *pissed*. He's huge, too. He's fucking *huge*. He comes over and looks down at Selfridge. I'm going like I don't know this guy. Never saw him before. And then guess what?"

"What?"

"The bartender reaches out and grabs hold of Selfridge. He's got him by the collar and the belt, right? And he lifts Selfridge like a foot up in the air — and Zambonis the bar with him!"

"No way!"

"I'm not kidding. Zambonied the Fridge right in his own barf!"

At that point we stepped out onto the porch. The Object and Rex Reese were sitting together on a white wicker couch. It was dark out, coolish, but the Object was still in her swimsuit, a shamrock bikini. She had a beach towel wrapped around her legs.

"Hi," I called out.

The Object turned. She looked at me blankly. "Hey," she said.

"She's here," said Jerome. "Safe and sound. Dad didn't run off the road."

"Daddy's not that bad a driver," said the Object.

"When he's not drinking he's not. But tonight I'd wager he had the old martini thermos on the front seat."

"Your old man likes to party!" Rex called out hoarsely.

"Did my dad have occasion to quench his thirst on the drive up?" Jerome asked.

"More than one occasion," I said.

Now Jerome laughed, going loose in the body and slapping his hands together.

Meanwhile Rex was saying to the Object, "Okay. She's here. So let's party."

"Where should we go?" the Object said.

"Hey, Je-roman, didn't you say there was some old hunting lodge out in the woods?"

"Yeah. It's about half a mile in."

"Think you could find it in the dark?"

"With a flashlight maybe."

"Let's go." Rex stood up. "Let's take some beers and hike on in there."

The Object got up, too. "Let me put on some pants." She crossed the porch in her swimsuit. Rex watched. "Come on, Callie," she said. "You're staying in my room."

I followed the Object inside. She went quickly, almost running, and didn't look back at me. As she climbed the stairs ahead of me, I whacked her from behind.

"I hate you," I said.

"What?"

"You're so tan!"

She flashed a smile over her shoulder.

As the Object dressed, I snooped around the bedroom. The furniture was white wicker up here, too. There were amateur sailing prints on the walls and on the shelves Petoskey stones, pinecones, musty paperbacks.

"What are we going to do in the woods?" I said, with a note of complaint.

The Object didn't answer.

"What are we going to do in the woods?" I repeated.

"We're going for a walk," she said.

"You just want Rex to molest you."

"You have such a dirty mind, Callie."

"Don't deny it."

She turned around and smiled. "I know who wants to molest *you*," she said.

For a second, an irrepressible happiness flooded me.

"Jerome," she finished.

"I don't want to go out in the woods," I said. "There's bugs and stuff."

"Don't be a such a wuss," she said. I had never heard her say "wuss" before. It was a word boys used; boys like Rex. Finished dressing, the Object stood before the mirror, picking at some dry skin on her cheek. She ran a brush through her hair and put on lip gloss. Then she came over to me. She came up very close. She opened her mouth and blew her breath into my face.

"It's fine," I said, and moved away.

"Don't you want me to check yours?"

"No biggie," I said.

I decided that if the Object was going to ignore me and flirt with Rex, I would ignore her and flirt with Jerome. After she left, I combed my hair. From the collection of atomizers on the dresser, I chose one and squeezed the bulb, but no perfume came out. I went into the bathroom and undid the straps of my overalls. Lifting my shirt, I stuffed a few tissues in my brassiere. Then I shook my hair back, hitched up my overalls, and hurried outside for our walk in the woods.

They were waiting for me under a yellow bug light on the porch. Jerome held a silver flashlight. Slung over Rex's shoulder was an army surplus backpack, filled with Stroh's. We came down the steps onto the lawn. The ground was uneven, treacherous with roots, but the pine needles were soft underfoot. For a moment, despite my foul mood, I felt it: the crisp northern Michigan delight. A slight chill to the air, even in August, something almost Russian. The indigo sky above the black bay. The smell of cedar and pine.

At the edge of the woods the Object stopped. "Is it going to be wet?" she said. "I only have my Tretorns on."

"Come on," said Rex Reese, pulling her by the hand. "Get wet."

She screamed, theatrically. Leaning back like someone on a rope tow, she was pulled unsteadily into the trees. I paused, too, peering in, waiting for Jerome to do the same. He didn't, though. Instead he stepped straight into the swamp and then slowly melted below the knees. "Quicksand!" he cried. "Help me! I'm sinking! Please somebody help . . . glub glub glub glub glub." Up ahead, already invisible, Rex and the Object were laughing.

The cedar swamp was an ancient place. No logging had ever been done here. The ground wasn't suitable for houses. The trees had been alive for hundreds of years and when they fell over they fell over for good. Here in the cedar swamp verticality wasn't an essential property of trees. Many cedars were standing straight up but many were leaning over. Still others had fallen against nearby trees, or crashed to the ground, popping up root systems. There was a graveyard feeling: everywhere the gray skeletons of trees. The moonlight filtering in lit up silver puddles and sprays of cobweb. It glanced off the Object's red hair as she moved and darted ahead of me.

We made a clumsy, yahoo progress through the swamp. Rex imitated animal sounds that sounded like no animal. Beer cans dinged in his backpack. Our deracinated feet stomped along in the mud.

After twenty minutes we found it: a one-room shack made of unpainted boards. The roof wasn't much taller than I was. The circular flashlight beam showed tar paper covering the narrow door.

"It's locked. Fuck," said Rex.

"Let's try the window," Jerome suggested. They disappeared, leaving the Object and me alone. I looked at her. For the first time since I'd arrived she really looked at me. There was just enough moonlight to accomplish this silent exchange between our eyes.

"It's dark out here," I said.

"I know it," said the Object.

There was a crash behind the shack, followed by laughter. The Object took a step closer to me. "What are they doing in there?"

"I don't know."

Suddenly the small window of the shack lit up. The boys had lit a Coleman lantern inside. Next the front door opened and Rex stepped out. He was smiling like a salesman. "Got a guy here wants to meet you." At which point he held up a mousetrap dangling the jellied mouse.

The Object screamed. "Rex!" She jumped back and held on to me. "Take it away!"

Rex dangled it some more, laughing, and then tossed it into the woods. "Okay, okay. Don't have a shit fit." He went back inside.

The Object was still clinging to me.

"Maybe we should go back," I ventured.

"Do you think you know the way? I'm totally lost."

"I can find it."

She turned and looked into the black woods. She was thinking about it. But then Rex reappeared in the doorway. "Come on in," he said. "Check it out."

And now it was too late. The Object let go of me. Throwing the red scarf of her hair over her shoulder, she ducked through the low threshold into the hunting shack.

Inside were two cots with Hudson's Bay blankets. They stood at either end of the small space separated by a crude kitchen with a camp stove. Empty bourbon bottles lined the windowsill. The walls were covered with yellowed clippings from the local paper, angling competitions, soap box derbies. There was also a taxidermied pike, jaws agape. Low on kerosene, the lantern sputtered. The light was butter-colored, the ripple of smoke greasing the air. It was opium den light, which was appropriate, because already Rex had plucked a joint from his pocket and was lighting it with a safety match.

Rex was on one cot, Jerome on the other. Casually the Object sat down next to Rex. I stood in the middle of the floor, hunching. I could feel Jerome watching me. I pretended to examine the shack but then turned, expecting to meet his gaze. This didn't happen, however. Jerome's eyes were focused on my chest. On my falsies. He liked me already. Now here was an added attraction, like a bonus for good intentions.

Maybe I should have been pleased by the trance he was in. But my revenge fantasy had already gone bust. My heart wasn't in it. Still, having no alternative, I went ahead and sat beside Jerome. Across the shack Rex Reese had the joint in his mouth.

Rex was wearing shorts and a monogrammed shirt, ripped at the shoulder, showing tanned skin. There was a red mark on his flamenco dancer's neck: a bug bite, a fading hickey. He closed his eyes to inhale deeply, his long eyelashes coming together. The hair on his head was as thick and oiled as an otter's pelt. Finally he opened his eyes and passed the joint to the Object.

To my surprise she took it. As though it were one of her beloved Tareytons, she put it between her lips and inhaled.

"Won't that make you paranoid?" I said.

"No."

"I thought you told me pot always makes you paranoid."

"Not when I'm out in nature," said the Object. She gave me a hard look. Then she took another toke.

"Don't bogart it," said Jerome. He got up to take the joint from her. He smoked half-standing, and then turned and held it out to me. I looked at the joint. One end burned; the other was mashed and wet. I had an idea that this was all part of the boys' plan, the woods, the shack, the cots, the drugs, the sharing of saliva. Here's a question I still can't answer: Did I see through the male tricks because I was destined to scheme that way myself? Or do girls see through the tricks, too, and just pretend not to notice?

For one second I thought of Chapter Eleven. He was living in a shack in the woods like this. I asked myself if I missed my brother. I couldn't tell if I did or not. I never know what I feel until it's too late. Chapter Eleven had smoked his first joint at college. I was four years ahead of him.

"Hold it in," Rex coached me.

"You have to let the THC build up in your bloodstream," said Jerome.

There was a sound out in the woods, twigs snapping. The Object grabbed Rex's arm. "What was that?"

"Maybe a bear," Jerome said.

"Neither of you girls are on the rag, I hope," said Rex.

"Rex!" the Object protested.

"Hey, I'm serious. Bears can smell it. I was out camping in Yellowstone one time and there was this woman out there who got killed. Grizzly could smell the blood."

"That is not true!"

"I swear. This guy I know told me. He

was an Outward Bound guide."

"Well, I don't know about Callie, but I'm not," said the Object.

They all looked at me. "I'm not either," I said.

"I guess we're safe, then, Roman," said Rex, and laughed.

The Object was still holding on to him for protection. "You want to do a shotgun?" he asked her.

"What's that?"

"Here." He turned to face her. "What you do is one person opens their mouth and the other person blows the smoke into it. You get totally fucked up. It's excellent."

Rex put the lit end of the joint in his mouth. He leaned toward the Object. She leaned forward too. She opened her mouth. And Rex began to blow. The Obscure Object's lips were a perfect ripe oval and into that target, that bull's-eye, Rex Reese directed the stream of musky smoke. I could see the column rush into the Object's mouth. It disappeared down her throat like whitewater over falls. Finally she coughed and he stopped.

"Good hit. Now do me."

The Object's green eyes were watering. But she took the joint and inserted it between her lips. She leaned toward Rex Reese, who opened his own mouth wide.

When they were finished, Jerome took the joint from his sister. "Let me see if I can master the technical difficulties here," he said. The next thing I knew, his face was close to mine. So finally I did it, too. Leaned forward, closed my eyes, parted my lips, and let Jerome shotgun into my mouth a long, dirty plume of smoke.

Smoke filled my lungs, which began to burn. I coughed and let it out. When I opened my eyes again, Rex had his arm around the Object's shoulder. She was trying to act casual about it. Rex finished his beer. He opened two more, one for him and one for her. He turned toward the Object. He smiled. He said something I couldn't hear. And then while I was still blinking he covered the Object's lips with his sour, handsome, pot-smoking mouth.

Across the flickering shack Jerome and I were left pretending not to notice. The joint was ours now to bogart as we wished. We passed it back and forth in silence and sipped our beers.

"I'm having this weird thing where my feet look extremely far away," Jerome said after a while. "Do your feet look extremely far away to you?"

"I can't see my feet," I said. "It's dark in here."

He passed me the joint again and I took it. I inhaled and held the smoke in. I let it keep burning my lungs because I wanted to distract myself from the pain in my heart. Rex and the Object were still kissing. I looked away, out the dark, grimy window.

"Everything looks really blue," I said. "Did you notice that?"

"Oh yeah," said Jerome. "All kinds of strange epiphenomena."

The Oracle of Delphi had been a girl about my same age. All day long she sat over a hole in the ground, the *omphalos*, the navel of the earth, breathing petrochemical fumes escaping from underneath. A teenage virgin, the Oracle told the future, speaking the first metered verse in history. Why do I bring this up? Because Calliope was also a virgin that night (for a little while longer at least). And she, too, had been inhaling hallucinogens. Ethylene was escaping from the cedar swamp outside the shack. Dressed not in a diaphanous robe but a pair of overalls, Calliope began to feel very funny indeed.

"Want another beer?" Jerome asked.

"Okay."

He handed me a golden can of Stroh's. I put the sweating can to my lips and drank. Then I drank some more. Jerome and I both felt the weight of the obligation. We smiled at each other nervously. I looked down and rubbed my knee through my overalls. And when I looked up again

Jerome's face was close. His eyes were shut, like the eyes of a boy jumping feet first off the high dive. Before I knew what was happening he was kissing me. Kissing the girl who had never been kissed. (Not since Clementine Stark, anyway.) I didn't stop him. I remained completely still while he did his thing. Despite my light-headedness, I could feel everything. The shocking wetness of his mouth. The whiskery feel of his lips. His barging tongue. Certain flavors, too, the beer, the dope, a lingering breath mint, and beneath all that the actual, animal taste of a boy's mouth. I could taste the gamy tang of Jerome's hormones and the metal of his fillings. I opened one eye. Here was the fine hair I'd spent so much time admiring on another head. Here were the freckles on the forehead, on the bridge of the nose, along the ears. But it wasn't the right face; they weren't the right freckles, and the hair was dyed black. Behind my impassive face my soul curled up into a ball, waiting until the unpleasantness was over.

Jerome and I were still sitting up. He was pressing his face against mine. By maneuvering a little, I could see across the room to where Rex and the Object were. They were lying down now. The tails of Rex's blue shirt seemed to flap in the wavering light. Beneath him one of the Object's legs dangled off the bed, the cuff of her pants muddy. I heard them whispering and laughing, then silence again. I watched the Object's mud-stained leg dancing. I concentrated on that leg, so that I hardly noticed when Jerome began to pull me down on our cot. I let him; I gave in to our slow collapse, all the while watching Rex Reese and the Object out of one eye. Rex's hands were moving over the Object's body now. They were pulling up her shirt, moving under it. Then their bodies shifted so that I saw their faces in profile. The Object's face, as still as a death mask, waited with eyes closed. Rex's profile was rampant, flushed. Meanwhile Jerome's hands were moving over me. He was rubbing my overalls, but I was no longer in them exactly. My focus on the Object was too intense.

Ecstasy. From the Greek *Ekstasis*. Meaning not what you think. Meaning not euphoria or sexual climax or even happiness. Meaning, literally: a state of displacement, of being driven out of one's senses. Three thousand years ago in Delphi the Oracle became ecstatic every single working hour. That night in a hunting cabin in northern Michigan, so did Calliope. High for my first time, drunk for my first time, I felt myself dissolving, turning to vapor. Like the incense at church my soul rose toward the dome of my skull — and then broke through. I drifted over the plank floor. I floated above the little camp stove. Passing by the bourbon bottles, I hovered over the other cot, looking down at the Object. And then, because I suddenly knew that I could, I slipped into the body of Rex Reese. I entered him like a god so that it was me, and not Rex, who kissed her.

An owl hooted in a tree somewhere. Bugs assailed the windows, attracted by the light. In my Delphic state I was simultaneously aware of both make-out sessions. By way of Rex's body I was hugging the Obscure Object, nuzzling her ear . . . while at the same time I was also aware of Jerome's hands ranging over my body, the one I'd left on the other cot. He was on top of me, crushing one of my legs, so I moved it, spread my legs apart, and he fell between them. He made little sounds. I put my arms around him, appalled and moved by his thinness. He was even skinnier than I was. Now Jerome was kissing my neck. Now, advised by some magazine column, he was paying attention to my earlobe. His hands moved up. They were heading for my chest. "Don't," I said, scared he'd find my tissues. And Jerome obeyed . . .

. . . while on the other cot Rex was meeting with no such resistance. With consummate skill he had undone the Object's brassiere with one hand. Because he was more experienced than me I let him deal with the shirt buttons, but it was my hands that took hold of her bra and, as if snapping up a windowshade, let into the room the pale light of the Object's breasts. I saw them; I touched them; and since it wasn't me who did this but Rex Reese I didn't have to feel guilty, didn't have to ask myself if I was having unnatural desires. How could I be when I was on the other cot fooling around with Jerome? . . . and so, just to be safe, I returned my attention to him. He was now in some kind of agony. He was rubbing against me and then he stopped and reached down to adjust himself. There was the sound of a zipper. I peeked at him through the corner of my eyes. I saw him thinking, concentrating on the puzzle of the overalls.

He didn't seem to be getting anywhere, so once again I floated back across the room and entered the body of Rex Reese. For a minute I could feel the Object responding to my touch, the startled, eager wakefulness in her skin and muscles. And now I felt something else, Rex, or me, lengthening, expanding. I felt that for only a second and then something was pulling me back . . .

Jerome had his hand on my bare

stomach. While I'd been off inhabiting Rex's body Jerome had taken the opportunity to undo my shoulder straps. He had flicked open the silver buttons at my waist. Now he was pulling down my overalls and I was trying to wake up. Now he was tugging on my underpants and I was realizing how drunk I was. Now he was inside my underpants and now he was . . . *inside me!*

And then: pain. Pain like a knife, pain like fire. It ripped into me. It spread up my belly all the way to my nipples. I gasped; I opened my eyes; I looked up and saw Jerome looking down at me. We gaped at each other and I knew he knew. Jerome knew what I was, as suddenly I did, too, for the first time clearly understood that I wasn't a girl but something in between. I knew this from how natural it had felt to enter Rex Reese's body, *how right it felt,* and I knew this from the shocked expression on Jerome's face. All this was conveyed in an instant. Then I pushed Jerome away. He pulled back, pulled out, and slid off the bed onto the floor.

Silence. Only the two of us, catching our breath. I lay on my back on the camp bed. Beneath the newspaper clippings. With only a mounted pike as witness. I pulled up my overalls and felt very sober indeed.

It was all over now. There was nothing I could do. Jerome would tell Rex. Rex would tell the Object. She would stop being my friend. By the time school started, everyone at Baker & Inglis would know that Calliope Stephanides was a freak. I was waiting for Jerome to jump up and run. I felt panicked and, at the same time, strangely calm. I was putting things together in my head. Clementine Stark and kissing lessons; and spinning together in a hot tub; an amphibian heart and a crocus blooming; blood and breasts that didn't come; and a crush on the Object that did, that *had*, that looked as if it was here to stay.

A few moments of clarity and then panic again whined in my ears. I wanted to run myself. Before Jerome had a chance to say anything. Before anyone found out. I could leave tonight. I could find my way back through the cedar swamp to the house. I could steal the Object's parents' car. I could drive north, through the Upper Peninsula to Canada, where Chapter Eleven had once thought of going to escape the draft. As I contemplated my life on the run I peeked over the edge of the cot to see what Jerome was doing.

He was flat on his back, eyes closed. And he was smiling to himself.

Smiling? Smiling how? In ridicule? No. In shock? Wrong again. How then? *In contentment.* Jerome had the smile of a boy who, on a summer night, had gone all the way. He had the smile of a guy who couldn't wait to tell his friends.

Reader, believe this if you can: he hadn't noticed a thing.

The Gun on the Wall

❦

I woke up back at the house. I had a vague memory of how I got there, of trudging back through the bog. My overalls were still on. My crotch felt hot and spongy. The Object was already out of bed or had slept somewhere else. I reached down and unstuck my underpants from my skin. Something about this act, the little puff of air, the rising aroma, reiterated the brand-new fact about myself. But it wasn't a fact exactly. It was nothing as solid as a fact right then. It was just an intuition I'd had about myself, to which the coming of morning brought no clarity. It was just an idea that was already beginning to fade, to become part of the drunkenness in the woods of the night before.

When the Oracle awoke after one of her wild, prophesying nights, she probably had no memory of the things she'd said. Whatever truths she'd hit on were secondary to the immediate sensations: the headache, the singed throat. It was the same for Calliope. I had a sense of having been dirtied and initiated. I felt all grown up. But mostly I felt sick and didn't want to think about what had happened at all.

In the shower I tried to rinse the experience away, scrubbing methodically, lifting my face to the slanting water. Steam filled the air. The mirrors and the windows dripped. The towels grew damp. I used every kind of soap within reach, Lifebuoy, Ivory, plus a local, rustic brand that felt like sandpaper. I got dressed and came down the stairs quietly. As I crossed the living room I noticed an old hunting rifle over the mantel. Another gun on the wall. I tiptoed by it. In the kitchen, the Object was eating cereal and reading a magazine. She didn't look up when I entered. I got a bowl myself and sat down across from her. Maybe I grimaced in doing so.

"What's the matter?" sneered the Object. "Sore?" Her sarcastic face rested on one palm. She didn't look so hot herself. She was puffy under the eyes. There were times when her freckles were not sunny but like corrosion or rust.

"You're the one that should be sore," I replied.

"I'm not sore at all," said the Object, "if you want to know."

"I forgot," I said; "you're used to it."

Suddenly her face was full of anger, shaking. Cords stretched and pulled beneath her skin, making lines. "You were a total slut last night," she charged.

"Me? What about you? You were throwing yourself at Rex the whole time."

"I was not. We didn't even do that much."

"You could have fooled me."

"At least he's not your *brother*." She got to her feet, glaring. She looked like she might cry. She hadn't wiped her mouth. There was jam on it, crumbs. I was struck dumb by the sight of this beloved face working itself up into what looked like hatred. My own face must have been reacting, too. I could feel my eyes going wide and scared. The Object was waiting for me to say something but nothing came to mind. So finally she shoved her chair away and said, "Jerome's upstairs. Why don't you go climb in bed with him." And she stormed off.

A low moment followed. Regret, already sogging me down, burst its dam. It seeped into my legs, it pooled in my heart. On top of panic that I'd lost my friend, I was suddenly beset by worries about my reputation. Was I really a slut? I hadn't even liked it. But I had done it, hadn't I? I had let him do it. Fear of retribution came next. What if I got pregnant? What then? My face at the breakfast table was the face of all mathematical girls, counting days, measuring liquids. It was at least a minute before I remembered that I couldn't be pregnant. That was one good thing about being a late bloomer. Still, I was upset. I was certain that the Object would never talk to me again.

I climbed the stairs and got back into bed, pulling a pillow over my face to block out the summer light. But there was no hiding from reality that morning. No more than five minutes later the bedsprings sagged under new weight. Peeking out, I saw that Jerome had come to visit.

He was lying on his back, looking cozy, already installed. Instead of a robe he had on a duck hunting coat. The ends of his frayed boxer shorts were visible below. He had a mug of coffee in one hand and I noticed that his fingernails were painted black. The morning light coming from the side window showed stubble on his chin and above his upper lip. Against the flat, wasted, dyed hair these orange shoots were like life returning to a scorched landscape.

"Good morning, dahling," he said.

"Hi."

"Feeling a little under the weather, are we?"

"Yeah," I said. "I was pretty drunk last night."

"You didn't seem that drunk to me, dahling."

"Well, I was."

Jerome now dropped the bit. He flopped back into the pillows and sipped his coffee and sighed. With one finger he tapped his forehead for a while. Then he spoke. "Just in case you were having any of the hackneyed worries, you should know that I still respect you and all that shit."

I didn't respond. Responding would only confirm the facts of what had happened, whereas I wanted to cast them in doubt. After a while Jerome set the coffee mug down and turned onto his side. He wriggled over toward me and rested his head against my shoulder. He lay there breathing. Then, with closed eyes, he moved his head and tunneled under the pillow with me. He started to nuzzle me. He brought his hair across the skin of my neck and after that came the sensitive organs. His eyelashes made butterfly kisses on my chin. His nose snuffled in the hollow of my throat. And then his lips arrived, avid, clumsy. I wanted him off me. At the same time I asked myself if I had brushed my teeth. Jerome was sliding and climbing on top of me and it felt like it had the night before, like a crushing weight. So do boys and men announce their intentions. They cover you like a sarcophagus lid. And call it love.

For a minute it was tolerable. But soon the duck coat rode up and Jerome's urgency was pressing itself upon me. He was trying to reach up under my shirt again. I didn't have a bra on. After my shower I had gone without it, flushing away the Kleenex. I was done with them. Jerome's hands moved higher. I didn't care. I let him feel me up. For what it was worth. But if I was hoping to disappoint him, it didn't work. He stroked and squeezed while his lower half swished like a crocodile's tail. And then he said an unironic thing. Fervently he whispered, "I'm really into you."

His lips closed, seeking mine. His tongue entered. The first penetration that augured the next. But not now, not this time.

"Stop," I said.

"What?"

"Stop."

"Why stop?"

"Because."

"Because why?"

"Because I don't like you like that."

He sat up. Like the guy in the old vaudeville skit, the guy in the folding cot that won't stay folded, Jerome flipped straight up, wide awake. Then he jumped off the bed.

"Don't be mad at me," I said.

"Who says I'm mad?" said Jerome, and left.

The rest of the day went slowly. I stayed

in my room until I saw Jerome leave the house, carrying his movie camera. I guessed that I was no longer in the cast. The Object's parents returned from their morning tennis foursome. Mrs. Object came up the stairs to the master bathroom. From my window I saw Mr. Object climb into the backyard hammock with a book. I waited for the shower to turn on and then came down the back stairs and out the kitchen door. I walked down to the bay, feeling melancholy.

The cedar swamp lay on one side of the house. On the other was a dirt and gravel road that led through an open field, treeless, with high yellow grass. The absence of trees was noticeable, and poking around out there I came upon a historical marker, nearly overgrown. It marked the site of a fort or a massacre, I don't remember which. Moss encroached upon the raised letters and I didn't read the whole plaque. I stood there for a while thinking about the first settlers and how they had killed one another over beaver and fox pelts. I put my foot on the plaque, kicking off the moss with my sneaker, until I got tired of that. It was almost noon by now. The bay was bright blue. Over the rise I could sense the city of Petoskey, the smoke of stoves and chimneys down there. The grass got marshy near the water. I climbed up on the breakwall and walked back and forth, keeping my balance. I held my arms out and pranced, Olga Korbut style. But my heart wasn't in it. And I was way too tall to be Olga Korbut. Sometime later the whir of an outboard engine reached me. I shaded my eyes with my hand to look out over the shimmering water. A speedboat was shooting past. At the wheel was Rex Reese. Bare-chested, drinking a beer and wearing sunglasses, he gunned the throttle, towing a water-skier. It was the Object, of course, in her shamrock bikini. She looked almost naked against the expanse of water, only those two little strips, one above, one below, separating her from Eden. Her red hair flapped like a gale warning. She wasn't a beautiful skier. She leaned too far forward, bowlegged on the pontoons. But she didn't fall. Rex kept turning around to check on her while he sipped his beer. Finally the boat made a sharp turn and the Object crossed her wake, whipping along past the shore.

A terrible thing happens when you water-ski. After you release the rope, you keep skimming over the water for a while, free. But there comes an inevitable moment when your speed fails to sustain your forward progress. The surface of the water breaks like glass. The depths open up to claim you. That was how I felt on land, watching the Object ski past. That same plunging, hopeless feeling, that emotional physics.

When I got back at dinnertime the Object was still not there. Her mother was angry, thinking it rude of the Object to leave me alone. Jerome, too, was out with friends. So I ate dinner with the Object's parents. I felt too desolate to charm the grownups that night. I ate in silence and afterward sat in the living room pretending to read. The clock ticked on. The night labored and creaked. When I felt I might fall apart I went into the bathroom and threw water on my face. I held a warm washcloth over my eyes and pressed my hands against my temples. I wondered what the Object and Rex were doing. I pictured her socks in the air, her little tennis socks with the balls at the heels, those ensanguined balls, bouncing.

It was obvious that Mr. and Mrs. Object were staying up just to keep me company. So finally I said good night and went up to bed myself. I got in and immediately started crying. I cried for a long time, trying not to make any noise. While I sobbed I said things in an aggrieved whisper. I cried, "Why don't you like me?" and "I'm sorry, I'm sorry!" I didn't care what I sounded like. There was a poison in my system and I needed to purge it. While

I was carrying on like that, I heard the screen door bang shut downstairs. I wiped my nose on the sheets and tried to settle down and listen. Footsteps climbed the stairs, and in another moment the door of the bedroom opened and closed. The Object entered and stood there in darkness. She might have been waiting for her eyes to adjust. I lay on my side, pretending to be asleep. The floorboards creaked as she came over to my side of the bed. I felt her standing over me, looking down. Then she went to the other side of the bed, took off her shoes and shorts, put on a T-shirt, and got in.

The Object slept on her back. She told me once that back-sleepers were the leaders in life, born performers or exhibitionists. Stomach-sleepers like me were in retreat from reality, given to dark perception and the meditative arts. This theory applied in our case. I lay prone, my nose and eyes sore from crying. The Object, supine, yawned and (like a born performer, perhaps) soon fell asleep.

I waited ten or so minutes, just to be safe. Then, as though tossing in my sleep, I rolled over so that I was looking at the Object. The moon was gibbous and filled the room with blue light. There upon the wicker bed the Obscure Object slept. The top of her Groton T-shirt was visible. It was an old one of her father's, with a few holes. She had one arm crossed over her face, like a slash on a sign that meant "No Touching." So I looked instead. Over the pillow her hair was spread out. Her lips were parted. Something glinted inside her ear, grains of sand from the beach maybe. Beyond, the atomizers glowed on the dresser. The ceiling was up above somewhere. I could feel the spiders working in the corners. The sheets were cool. The fat duvet rolled up at our feet was leaking feathers. I'd grown up around the smell of new carpeting, of polyester shirts hot from the dryer. Here the Egyptian sheets smelled like hedges, the pillows like water fowl. Thirteen inches away, the Object was part of all this. Her colors seemed to agree with the American landscape, her pumpkin hair, her apple cider skin. She made a sound and went still again.

Gently, I pulled the covers off her. In the dimness her outline appeared, the rise of her breasts beneath the T-shirt, the soft hill of her belly, and then the brightness of her underpants, converging in their V shape. She didn't stir at all. Her chest rose and fell with her breath. Slowly, trying not to make a sound, I moved closer to her. Tiny muscles in my flank, muscles I hadn't known I possessed, suddenly made themselves available. They propelled me millimeter by millimeter across the sheets. The old bedsprings gave me trouble. As I tried nonchalantly to advance, they called out ribald encouragement. They cheered, they sang. I kept stopping and starting. It was hard work. I breathed through my mouth, quieter that way.

Over the course of ten minutes I slid nearer and nearer to her. Finally I felt the heat of her body along my entire length. We were still not touching, only radiating against each other. She was breathing deeply. So was I. We breathed together. Finally, gathering courage, I flung my arm across her waist.

Then nothing more for a long while. Having achieved this much, I was scared to go further. So I remained frozen, half hugging her. My arm grew stiff. It began to throb and finally went numb. The Object might have been drugged or comatose. Still, I sensed an alertness in her skin, in her muscles. After another long while I plunged ahead. I took hold of her T-shirt and lifted it up. I gazed at her naked belly for a long while and, finally, with a kind of woefulness, bowed my head. I bowed my head to the god of desperate longing. I kissed the Object's belly and then slowly, gathering confidence, worked my way up.

Do you remember my frog heart? In Clementine Stark's bedroom it had kicked off from a muddy bank, moving between two elements. Now it did something even more amazing — it crept up onto land. Squeezing millennia into thirty seconds, it developed consciousness. While kissing the Object's belly, I wasn't just reacting to pleasurable stimuli, as I had been with Clementine. I didn't vacate my body, as I had with Jerome. Now I was aware of what was happening. I was thinking about it.

I was thinking that this was what I'd always wanted. I was realizing that I wasn't the only faker around. I was wondering what would happen if someone discovered what we were doing. I was thinking that it was all very complicated and would only get more so.

I reached down and touched her hips. I hooked my fingers in the waistband of her underpants. I began to slip them off. Just then, the Object lifted her hips, very slightly, to make it easier for me. This was her only contribution.

The next day we didn't mention it. When I got up, the Object was already out of bed. She was in the kitchen, observing her father's preparation of scrapple. Making scrapple was Mr. Object's Sunday morning ritual. He presided over the bubbling fat and grease while the Object periodically looked into the frying pan and said, "That is so disgusting." Soon she was working on a plate of it, and made me have one, too. "I'm going to have the worst heartburn," she said.

I understood the unspoken message immediately. The Object wanted no dramatics, no guilt. No show of romance, either. She was going on about the scrapple to separate night from day, to make it clear that what happened at night, what we did at night, had nothing to do with daylight hours. She was a good actress, too, and at times I wondered if maybe she really had been sleeping through the whole thing. Or maybe I had only been dreaming it.

She gave only two signs during the day that anything had changed between us. In the afternoon Jerome's film crew arrived. This consisted of two friends of his, carrying boxes and cables and a long, fuzzy microphone like a dirty, rolled-up bathmat. Jerome was by this time pointedly not speaking to me. They set up in a small equipment shed on the property. The Object and I decided to see what they were doing. Jerome had told us to stay away, so we couldn't resist. We crept up, moving from tree to tree. We had to stop often to fight off laugh attacks, slapping at each other, avoiding each other's eyes until we could control ourselves. At the back window of the equipment shed we peeked in. Not much was happening. One of Jerome's friends was taping a light to the wall. It was hard for us both to see through the small window at once, so the Object got in front of me. She placed my hands on her belly and held my wrists. Still, her attention was officially given over to what was going on inside the shed.

Jerome appeared, dressed as the preppy vampire. Inside the traditional Dracula waistcoat, he wore a pink Lacoste shirt. Instead of a bow tie he had an ascot. His black hair was slicked back, his face whitened with a cosmetic, and he carried a cocktail shaker. One of his friends held a broomstick dangling a rubber bat. Another operated the camera. "Action," said Jerome. He lifted the cocktail shaker. He shook it with both hands. Meanwhile the bat swooped and fluttered above his head. Jerome removed the lid and poured the blood into the martini glasses. He held one up for his friend the bat, who promptly plopped into it. Jerome sipped his blood cocktail. "Just how you like it, Muffie," he said to the bat. "*Very* dry."

Under my hands the Object's stomach jiggled as she laughed. She leaned back into me and her flesh captured in my arms shook and yielded. I pressed my pelvis against her. All this went on secretly behind the shed, like a game of footsie. But then the cameraman lowered his camera. He pointed at us and Jerome turned around. His eyes fixed on my hands and then rose to my eyes. He bared his fangs, burning me with a look. And then shouted in his regular voice, "Get the hell out of here, you fuckers! We're shooting." He came up to the window and struck it, but we were already running away.

Later, around evening, the phone rang. The Object's mother answered it. "It's Rex," she said. The Object got up from the sofa where we were playing backgammon. I restacked my chips to have something to do. I tidied them up, over and over, while the Object talked to Rex. She had her back to me. She moved around as she talked, playing with the cord. I kept looking down at the chips, moving them. Meanwhile I paid close attention to the conversation. "Nothing much, just playing back-gammon . . . with Callie . . . He's making his stupid film . . . I can't, we're supposed to have dinner soon . . . I don't know, maybe later . . . I'm sort of tired, actually." Suddenly she wheeled around to face me. With effort I looked up. The Object pointed at the phone and then, opening her mouth wide, stuck her finger down her throat. My heart brimmed.

Night came again. In bed we went

through the preliminaries, plumping our pillows, yawning. We tossed around to get comfortable. And then after an appropriate time of silence the Object made a noise. It was a murmur, a cry caught in the throat, as if she were talking in her sleep. After this, her breathing became deeper. And taking this as the okay, Calliope began the long trek across the bed.

So that was our love affair. Wordless, blinkered, a nighttime thing, a dream thing. There were reasons on my side for this as well. Whatever it was that I was was best revealed slowly, in flattering light. Which meant not much light at all. Besides, that's the way it goes in adolescence. You try things out in the dark. You get drunk or stoned and extemporize. Think back to your backseats, your pup tents, your beach bonfire parties. Did you ever find yourself, without admitting it, tangled up with your best friend? Or in a dorm room bed with two people instead of one, while Bach played on the chintzy stereo, orchestrating the fugue? It's a kind of fugue state, anyway, early sex. Before the routine sets in, or the love. Back when the groping is largely anonymous. Sandbox sex. It starts in the teens and lasts until twenty or twenty-one. It's all about learning to share. It's about sharing your toys.

Sometimes when I climbed on top of the Object she would almost wake up. She would move to accommodate me, spreading her legs or throwing an arm around my back. She swam up to the surface of consciousness before diving again. Her eyelids fluttered. A responsiveness entered her body, a flex of abdomen in rhythm with mine, her head thrown back to offer up her throat. I waited for more. I wanted her to acknowledge what we were doing, but I was scared, too. So the sleek dolphin rose, leapt through the ring of my legs, and disappeared again, leaving me bobbing, trying to keep my balance. Everything was wet down there. From me or her I didn't know. I laid my head on her chest beneath the bunched-up T-shirt. Her underarms smelled like overripe fruit. The hair there was very sparse. "You luck," I would have said, back in our daytime life. "You don't even have to shave." But the nighttime Calliope only stroked the hair, or tasted it. One night, as I was doing this and other things, I noticed a shadow on the wall. I thought it was a moth. But, looking closer, I saw that it was the Object's hand, raised behind my head. Her hand was completely awake. It clenched and unclenched, siphoning all the ecstasy from her body into its secret flowerings.

What the Object and I did together was

played out under these loose rules. We weren't too scrupulous about the details. What pressed on our attention was that it was happening, sex was happening. That was the great fact. How it happened exactly, what went where, was secondary. Plus, we didn't have much to compare it to. Nothing but our night in the shack with Rex and Jerome.

As far as the crocus was concerned, it wasn't so much a piece of me as something we discovered and enjoyed together. Dr. Luce will tell you that female monkeys exhibit mounting behavior when administered male hormones. They seize, they thrust. Not me. Or at least not at first. The blooming of the crocus was an impersonal phenomenon. It was a kind of hook that fastened us together, more a stimulant to the Object's outer parts than a penetration of her inner. But, apparently, effective enough. Because after the first few nights, she was eager for it. Eager, that is, while ostensibly remaining unconscious. As I hugged her, as we languorously shifted and knotted, the Object's attitudes of insensibility included favorable positioning. Nothing was made ready or caressed. Nothing was aimed. But practice brought about a fluid gymnastics to our sleep couplings. The Object's eyes remained closed throughout; her head was often turned

702

slightly away. She moved under me as a sleeping girl might while being ravished by an incubus. She was like somebody having a dirty dream, confusing her pillow for a lover.

Sometimes, before or afterward, I switched on the bedside lamp. I pulled her T-shirt up as far as it would go and slid her underpants down below her knees. And then I lay there, letting my eyes have their fill. What else compares? Gold filings shifted around the magnet of her navel. Her ribs were as thin as candy canes. The spread of her hips, so different from mine, looked like a bowl offering up red fruit. And then there was my favorite spot, the place where her ribcage softened into breast, the smooth, white dune there.

I turned the light off. I pressed against the Object. I took the backs of her thighs in my hands, adjusting her legs around my waist. I reached under her. I brought her up to me. And then my body, like a cathedral, broke out into ringing. The hunchback in the belfry had jumped and was swinging madly on the rope.

Through all this I made no lasting conclusions about myself. I know it's hard to believe, but that's the way it works. The mind self-edits. The mind airbrushes. It's a different thing to be inside a body than outside. From outside, you can look, inspect, compare. From inside there is no comparison. In the past year the crocus had lengthened considerably. At its most demonstrative it was now about two inches long. Most of this length, however, was concealed by the flaps of skin from which it issued. Then there was the hair. In its quiet state, the crocus was barely noticeable. What I saw looking down at myself was only the dark triangular badge of puberty. When I touched the crocus it expanded, swelling until with a kind of pop it slid free of the pouch it was in. It poked its head up into the air. Not too far, though. No more than an inch past the tree line. What did this mean? I knew from personal experience that the Object had a crocus of her own. It swelled, too, when touched. Mine was just bigger, more effusive in its feelings. My crocus wore its heart on its sleeve.

The crucial feature was this: the crocus didn't have a hole at the tip. This was certainly not what a boy had. Put yourself in my shoes, reader, and ask yourself what conclusion you would have come to about your sex, if you had what I had, if you looked the way I looked. To pee I had to sit. The stream issued from underneath. I had an interior like a girl. It was tender inside, almost painful if I inserted my finger.

True, my chest was completely flat. But there were other ironing boards at my school. And Tessie insisted I took after her in that department. Muscles? Not much to speak of. No hips either, no waist. A dinner plate of a girl. The low-Cal special.

Why should I have thought I was anything other than a girl? Because I was *attracted* to a girl? That happened all the time. It was happening more than ever in 1974. It was becoming a national pastime. My ecstatic intuition about myself was now deeply suppressed. How long I would have managed to keep it down is anybody's guess. But in the end it wasn't up to me. The big things never are. Birth, I mean, and death. And love. And what love bequeaths to us before we're born.

The following Thursday morning was hot. It was one of those humid days when the atmosphere gets confused. Sitting on the porch, you could feel it: the air wishing it was water. The Object was draggy in any kind of heat. She claimed her ankles swelled. All morning she'd been a trying companion, demanding, sullen. While I was dressing she'd come back from the bathroom to accuse me from the doorway, "What did you do with the shampoo?"

"I didn't do anything with it."

"I left it right on the windowsill. You're

the only other person who uses it."

I squeezed past her and went down the hall. "It's right here in the tub," I said.

The Object took it from me. "I feel totally gross and sticky!" she said, by way of apology. Then she got into the shower while I brushed my teeth. After a minute her oval face appeared, the shower curtain snug around it. She looked bald and big-eyed like an alien. "Sorry I'm such a bitch today," she said.

I kept brushing, wanting her to suffer a little.

The Object's forehead wrinkled and her eyes grew soft in appeal. "Do you hate me?"

"I'm still deciding."

"You're so mean!" she said, comically frowning, and snapped the curtain shut.

After breakfast, we were on the porch swing, drinking lemonade and gliding back and forth to create a breeze. I had my feet up on the railing, pushing off from it. The Object was lying sideways, her legs spread over my lap, her head resting against the arm of the swing. She had on cutoffs, short enough to reveal the white lining of the pockets, and her bikini top. I was wearing khaki shorts and a white alligator shirt.

Out in front of us, the bay flashed silver. The bay had scales, like the fish beneath.

"Sometimes I get really sick of having a body," the Object said.

"Me too."

"You too?"

"Especially when it's hot like this. It's like torture just moving around."

"Plus I hate sweating."

"I can't stand to sweat," I said. "I'd rather pant like a dog."

The Object laughed. She was smiling at me, marveling. "You understand everything I say," she said. She shook her head. "Why can't you be a guy?"

I shrugged, indicating that I had no answer. I was aware of no irony in this. Neither was the Object.

She was looking at me, low-lidded. Her eyes in the brightness of day with heat currents rising over the baking grass looked very green, even if they were only slits, crescents. Her head was bent forward against the arm of the swing; she had to look up to see me. This gave her a vixenish attitude. Without taking her eyes off mine, she adjusted her legs, spreading them slightly.

"You have the most amazing eyes," she said.

"Your eyes are really green. They almost look fake."

"They are fake."

"You've got glass eyes?"

"Yeah, I'm blind. *I'm* Tiresias."

This was a new way to do it. We'd just discovered it. Staring into each other's eyes was another way of keeping them closed, or off the details at hand, anyway. We locked onto each other. Meanwhile the Object was very subtly flexing her legs. I was aware of the mound beneath her cutoffs rising toward me, just a little, rising and suggesting itself. I put my hand on the Object's thigh, palm down. And as we continued to swing, looking at each other while crickets played their fiddles in the grass, I slid my hand sideways up toward the place where the Object's legs joined. My thumb went under her cutoffs. Her face showed no reaction. Her green eyes under the heavy lids remained fastened on mine. I felt the fluffiness of her underpants and pressed down, sliding under the elastic. And then with our eyes wide open but confined in that way my thumb slipped inside her. She blinked, her eyes closed, her hips rose higher, and I did it again. And again after that. The boats in the bay were part of it, and the string section of crickets in the baking grass, and the ice melting in our lemonade glasses. The swing moved back and forth, creaking on its rusted chain, and it was like that old nursery rhyme, Little Jack Horner sat in the corner eating his Christmas pie. He stuck in his thumb and pulled out a plum . . . After the first roll of her eyes the Object resettled her gaze on mine, and then what she was feeling showed only there, in the green depths her eyes revealed. Otherwise she was motionless. Only my hand moved, and my feet on the rail, pushing the swing. This went on for three minutes, or five, or fifteen. I have no idea. Time disappeared. Somehow we were still not quite conscious of what we were doing. Sensation dissolved straight into forgetting.

When the floor of the porch creaked behind us, I jumped. I withdrew my thumb from the Object's pants and sat up straight. I saw something in the corner of my eyes and turned. Perched on the railing to our right was Jerome. He was in his vampire costume, despite the heat. The powder on his face was burning off in spots but he still looked very pale. He was gazing down on us with his best haunted expression. His *Turn of the Screw* expression. The young master led astray by the gardener. The boy in the frock coat who'd drowned in the well. Everything was dead except the eyes. His eyes fixed on us — on the Object's bare legs lying in my lap — while his face remained embalmed.

Then the apparition spoke:

"Carpet munchers."

"Just ignore him," the Object said.

"Carrrrpet muncherrrrs," Jerome repeated. It came out in a croak.

"Shut *up!*"

Jerome remained still and ghoul-like on the rail. His hair wasn't slicked back but fell limp on either side of his face. He was very controlled and intent about what he was doing, as if following a time-honored procedure. "Carpet muncher," he said again. "Carpet muncher, carpet muncher." Singular now. This was between him and his sister.

"I said quit it, Jerome." The Object now tried to rise. She swung her legs off my lap and started to roll out of the swing. But Jerome moved first. He spread his jacket like wings and jumped off the railing. He swooped down on the Object. Still his face was completely impassive. No muscles moved except those of his mouth. Into the Object's face, into her ears he kept hissing and croaking. "Carpet muncher, carpet muncher, carpet muncher, carpet muncher."

"Stop it!"

She tried to hit him but he caught her arms. He held both of her wrists in one hand. With his other hand Jerome made a V with his fingers. He pressed this V to his mouth and between this suggestive triangle flicked his tongue back and forth. At the crudity of this gesture the Object's calm began to crack. A sob rose in her. Jerome sensed its arrival. He had reduced his sister to tears for over a decade; he knew how to do it; he was like a kid burning an ant with a magnifying glass, focusing the beam in hotter and hotter.

"Carpet muncher, carpet muncher, carpet muncher . . ."

And then it happened. The Object broke down. She began to bawl like a little girl. Her face turned red and she swung her fists wildly before finally running away into the house.

At that point Jerome's fierce activity ceased. He adjusted his jacket. He smoothed his hair and, leaning against the porch rail, stared peacefully out at the water.

"Don't worry," he said to me. "I won't tell anyone."

"Tell anyone what?"

"You're lucky I'm such a liberal and freethinking type of guy," he continued. "Most guys wouldn't be so happy to find out that they'd been two-timed by a lesbian with their own sister. It's sort of embarrassing, don't you think? But I'm such a freethinker that I'm willing to overlook your proclivities."

"Why don't you shut up, Jerome?"

"I'll shut up when I want to," he said. Then he turned his head and looked at me. "You know where you are now? Splitsville,

Stephanides. Get out of here and don't come back. And keep your hands off my sister."

I was already jumping up. My blood rocketed. It shot up my spine and rang a bell in my head, and I charged Jerome in a blaze of fury. He was bigger than me but unprepared. I hit him in the face. He tried to move away but I crashed into him, my momentum knocking him to the floor. I climbed on his chest, pinning his arms with my legs. Finally Jerome stopped resisting. He lay on his back and tried to look amused.

"Any time you're finished," he said.

It was an exhilarating feeling to be on top of him. Chapter Eleven had pinned me all my life. This was the first time I'd done it to somebody else, especially a boy older than me. My long hair was falling into Jerome's face. I swept it back and forth, tormenting him. Then I remembered something else my brother used to do.

"No," Jerome cried. "Come on. *Don't!*"

I let it fall. Like a raindrop. Like a tear. But neither of those things. The spit plopped right between Jerome's eyes. And then the earth opened up beneath us. With a roar Jerome rose up, sending me backward. My supremacy had been brief. Now it was time to run.

I took off across the porch. I jumped

down the steps and tore across the back lawn, barefoot. Jerome came after me in his Dracula getup. He stopped to fling off the coat and I increased the distance between us. Through the backyards of the neighboring houses I ran, ducking under pine branches. I dodged bushes and barbecues. The pine needles gave good traction under my feet. Finally I reached the open field beyond and fled into it. When I looked back Jerome was gaining on me.

Through the high, yellow grass along the bayshore we flew. I jumped over the historical marker, grazing my foot, then hopped in pain and continued on. Jerome cleared it without a hitch. On the other side of the field was the road that led back to the house. If I could get over the rise, I could double back without Jerome seeing me. The Object and I could barricade ourselves in our room. I reached the hill and started up. Jerome came after me, scowling, still gaining.

We were like runners in a frieze. In profile, with pumping thighs and knifing arms, we cut through the shin-whipping grass. By the time I reached the bottom of the hill Jerome seemed to be slowing down. He was waving his hand in defeat. He was waving it and shouting something I couldn't hear . . .

The tractor had just made a turn onto

the road. High in his seat, the farmer didn't see me. I was looking back to check on Jerome. When I finally turned forward it was too late. Right in front of me was the tractor tire. I hit it dead on. In the terra-cotta dust I was spun upward into the air. At the apex of my arc I saw the raised plow blades behind, the corkscrewing metal covered with mud, and then the race was over.

I awoke later, in the backseat of a strange automobile. A rattletrap, with blankets covering the seats. A decal of a hooked, flapping trout was pasted to the rear window. The driver wore a red cap. The little space above the cap's adjustable headband showed the buzzed hairline of his seamed neck.

My head felt soft, as if covered in gauze. I was wrapped in an old blanket, stiff and spoked with hay. I turned my head and looked up and saw a beautiful sight. I saw the Object's face from below. My head was in her lap. My right cheek was flush against the warm upholstery of her tummy. She was still in her bikini top and cutoffs. Her knees were spread and her red hair fell over me, darkening things. I gazed up through this maroon or oxblood space and saw what I could of her, the dark band of her swimsuit top, her clavicles set forward. She was chewing one cuticle. It was going to bleed if she kept it up. "Hurry," she was saying, from the other side of the falling hair. "Hurry up, Mr. Burt."

It was the farmer who was driving. The farmer whose tractor I'd run into. I hoped he wasn't listening. I didn't want him to hurry. I wanted this ride to go on for as long as possible. The Object was stroking my head. She'd never done this in daylight before.

"I beat up your brother," I said out of the blue.

With one hand the Object swept her hair away. The light knifed in.

"Callie! Are you okay?"

I smiled up at her. "I got him good."

"Oh God," she said. "I was so scared. I thought you were dead. You were just ly— ly" — her voice broke — "*lying* there in the road!"

The tears came on, tears of gratitude now, not anger like before. The Object sobbed. With awe I beheld the storm of emotion racking her. She dipped her head. She pressed her snuffling, wet face against mine and, for the first and last time, we kissed. We were hidden by the backrest, by the wall of hair, and who was the farmer to tell anyway? The Object's anguished lips met mine, and there was a sweet taste and a taste of salt.

"I'm all snotty," she said, lifting her face

up again. She managed to laugh.

But already the car was stopping. The farmer was jumping out, shouting things. He swung open the back door. Two orderlies appeared and lifted me onto a stretcher. They wheeled me across the sidewalk into the hospital doors. The Object remained at my side. She took my hand. For a moment she seemed to register her near nakedness. She looked down at herself when her bare feet hit the cold linoleum. But she shrugged this off. All the way down the hall, until the orderlies told her to stop, she held on to my hand. As though it were a string of Piraeus yarn. "You can't come in, miss," the orderlies said. "You have to wait here." And so she did. But still she didn't let go of my hand. Not for a while longer yet. The stretcher was wheeled down the corridor and my arm stretched out toward the Object. I had already left on my voyage. I was sailing across the sea to another country. Now my arm was twenty feet long, thirty, forty, fifty. I lifted my head from the stretcher to gaze at the Object. To gaze at the Obscure Object. For once more she was becoming a mystery to me. What ever happened to her? Where is she now? She stood at the end of the hall, holding my unraveling arm. She looked cold, skinny, out of place, lost. It was almost as if she knew we would never see each other again. The stretcher was picking up speed. My arm was only a thin ribbon now, curling through the air. Finally the inevitable moment came. The Object let go. My hand flew up, free, empty.

Lights overhead, bright and round, as at my birth. The same squeaking of white shoes. But Dr. Philobosian was nowhere to be found. The doctor who smiled down at me was young and sandy-haired. He had a country accent. "I'm gonna ask you a few questions, okay?"

"Okay."

"Start off with your name."

"Callie."

"How old are you, Callie?"

"Fourteen."

"How many fingers am I holding out?"

"Two."

"I want you to count backward for me. Start from ten."

"Ten, nine, eight . . ."

And all the while, he was pressing me, feeling for breaks. "Does this hurt?"

"No."

"This?"

"Uh-uh."

"How about here?"

Suddenly it did hurt. A bolt, a cobra bite, beneath my navel. The cry I let out was answer enough.

"Okay, okay, we're gonna go easy here. I just need to take a look. Lie still now."

The doctor signaled the intern with his eyes. From either side they began to undress me. The intern pulled my shirt over my head. There was my chest, green and bleak. They paid no notice. Neither did I. Meanwhile the doctor had unfastened my belt. He was undoing the clasp of my khakis: I let him. Down came the pants. I watched as if from far away. I was thinking about something else. I was remembering how the Object would lift her hips to help me get her underpants off. That little signal of compliance, of desire. I was thinking how much I loved it when she did that. Now the intern was reaching under me. And so I lifted my hips.

They took hold of my underpants. They tugged them down. The elastic caught on my skin, then gave.

The doctor bent closer, mumbling to himself. The intern, rather unprofessionally, raised one hand to her throat and then pretended to fix her collar.

Chekhov was right. If there's a gun on the wall, it's got to go off. In real life, however, you never know where the gun is hanging. The gun my father kept under his pillow never fired a shot. The rifle over the Object's mantel never did either. But in the emergency room things were different.

There was no smoke, no gunpowder smell, absolutely no sound at all. Only the way the doctor and nurse reacted made it clear that my body had lived up to the narrative requirements.

One scene remains to be described in this portion of my life. It took place a week later, back on Middlesex, and featured me, a suitcase, and a tree. I was in my bedroom, sitting on the window seat. It was just before noon. I was dressed in traveling clothes, a gray pantsuit with a white blouse. I was reaching out my window, picking berries off the mulberry tree that grew outside. For the last hour I'd been eating the berries to distract myself from the sound coming from my parents' bedroom.

The mulberries had ripened in the last week. They were fat and juicy. The berries stained my hands. Outside, the sidewalk was splotched purple, as was the grass itself, and the rocks in the flower beds. The sound in my parents' bedroom was my mother weeping.

I got up. I went over to the open suitcase and checked again to see if I'd packed everything. My parents and I were leaving in an hour. We were going to New York City to see a famous doctor. I didn't know how long we'd be gone or what was wrong with me. I didn't pay much attention to the details. I only knew I was no longer a girl like other girls.

Orthodox monks smuggled silk out of China in the sixth century. They brought it to Asia Minor. From there it spread to Europe, and finally traveled across the sea to North America. Benjamin Franklin fostered the silk industry in Pennsylvania before the American Revolution. Mulberry trees were planted all over the United States. As I picked those berries out my bedroom window, however, I had no idea that our mulberry tree had anything to do with the silk trade, or that my grandmother had had trees just like it behind her house in Turkey. That mulberry tree had stood outside my bedroom on Middlesex, never divulging its significance to me. But now things are different. Now all the mute objects of my life seem to tell my story, to stretch back in time, if I look closely enough. So I can't possibly finish up this section of my life without mentioning the following fact:

The most widely raised type of silkworm, the larva of the *Bombyx mori,* no longer exists anywhere in a natural state. As my encyclopedia poignantly puts it: "The legs of the larvae have degenerated, and the adults do not fly."

Book four

Book Four

The Oracular Vulva

꧁❦꧂

From my birth when they went undetected, to my baptism where they upstaged the priest, to my troubled adolescence when they didn't do much of anything and then did everything at once, my genitals have been the most significant thing that ever happened to me. Some people inherit houses; others paintings or highly insured violin bows. Still others get a Japanese tansu or a famous name. I got a recessive gene on my fifth chromosome and some very rare family jewels indeed.

My parents had at first refused to believe the emergency room doctor's wild claim about my anatomy. The diagnosis, delivered over the phone to a largely uncomprehending Milton and then bowdlerized by him for Tessie's benefit, amounted to a vague concern about the formation of my urinary tract along with a possible hormonal deficiency. The doctor in Petoskey hadn't performed a karyotype. His job was to treat my concussion and contusions, and when he was done with that, he let me go.

My parents wanted a second opinion. At Milton's insistence I had been taken one last time to see Dr. Phil.

In 1974, Dr. Nishan Philobosian was eighty-eight years old. He still wore a bow tie, but his neck no longer filled out the collar of his shirt. He was reduced in all his parts, freeze-dried. Nevertheless, green golf slacks extended from the hem of his white coat and a pair of tinted aviator-style glasses gripped his hairless head.

"Hello, Callie, how are you?"

"Fine, Dr. Phil."

"Starting school again? What grade are you in now?"

"I'll be in ninth this year. High school."

"High school? Already? I must be getting old."

His courtly manner was no different than it had ever been. The foreign sounds he still made, the evidence of the Old World in his teeth, put me somewhat at ease. All my life dignified foreigners had petted and pampered me. I was a sucker for the soft-handed Levantine affections. As a little girl I had sat on Dr. Philobosian's knee while his fingers climbed my spinal column, counting off the vertebrae. Now I was taller than he was, gangly, freak-haired, a Tiny Tim of a girl, sitting in gown, bra, and underpants on the edge of an old-fashioned medical table with step-drawers of vulcanized rubber. He listened to my heart and lungs, his bald head dipping on the long neck like that of a brontosaurus, sampling leaves.

"How's your father, Callie?"

"Fine."

"How's the hot dog business?"

"Good."

"How many hot dog places your dad has now?"

"Like fifty or something."

"There's one not too far from where Nurse Rosalee and I go in the winter. Pompano Beach."

He examined my eyes and ears and then politely asked me to stand and lower my underpants. Fifty years earlier, Dr. Philobosian had made his living treating Ottoman ladies in Smyrna. Propriety was an old habit with him.

My mind was not fuzzy, as it had been up in Petoskey. I was fully aware of what was happening and where the focus of medical scrutiny lay. After I had pulled my panties down to my knees, a hot wave of embarrassment swept through me and by reflex I covered myself with my hand. Dr. Philobosian, not entirely gently, moved this aside. There was something of the impatience of the old in this. He forgot himself momentarily, and behind his aviator lenses his eyes glared. Still, he didn't look down at me. He gazed gallantly off at the far wall while feeling for information with his hands. We were as close as dancing. Dr. Phil's breathing was noisy; his hands shook. I glanced down myself only once. My embarrassment had retracted me. From my angle I was a girl again, white belly, dark triangle, foreshortened legs shaved smooth. My brassiere was bandoliered across my chest.

It took only a minute. The old Armenian, crouching, lizard-backed, ran his yellowed fingers over my parts. It was no surprise that Dr. Philobosian had never noticed anything. Even now, alerted to the possibility, he didn't seem to want to know.

"You can get dressed now," was all he said. He turned and walked very carefully to the sink. He turned on the water and thrust his hands into the stream. They seemed to be trembling more than ever. Liberally he squirted out the antibacterial soap. "Say hello to your dad," he said before I left the room.

Dr. Phil referred me to an endocrinologist at Henry Ford Hospital. The endocrinologist tapped a vein in my arm, filling an alarming number of vials with my blood. Why all this blood was needed he didn't say. I was too frightened to ask. That night, however, I put my ear to my bedroom wall in hopes of finding out what was going on. "So what did the doctor say?" Milton was asking. "He said Dr. Phil should have noticed when Callie was born," Tessie answered. "This whole thing could have been fixed back then." And then Milton again: "I can't believe he'd miss something like that." ("Like what?" I silently asked the wall, but it didn't specify.)

Three days later we arrived in New York.

Milton had booked us into a hotel called the Lochmoor in the East Thirties. He had stayed there twenty-three years earlier as a navy ensign. Always a thrifty traveler, Milton was also encouraged by the room rates. Our stay in New York was open-ended. The doctor Milton had spoken to — the specialist — refused to discuss details before he'd had a chance to examine me. "You'll like it," Milton assured us. "It's pretty swank, as I remember."

It was not. We arrived from La Guardia in a taxi to find the Lochmoor fallen from its former glory. The desk clerk and cashier worked behind bulletproof glass. The Viennese carpeting was wet beneath the dripping radiators and the mirrors had been removed, leaving ghostly rectangles of plaster and ornamental screws. The elevator was prewar, with gilded, curving bars like a birdcage. Once upon a time, there had been an operator; no longer. We crammed our suitcases into the small space and I slid the gate closed. It kept coming off its track. I had to do it three times before the electrical current would flow. Finally the contraption rose and through the spray-painted bars we watched the floors pass by, each dim and identical except for the variation of a maid in uniform, or a room service tray outside a door, or a pair of shoes. Still, there was a feeling of ascension in that old box, of rising up out of a pit, and it was a letdown to get to our floor, number eight, and find it just as drab as the lobby.

Our room had been carved out of a once-bigger suite. Now the angles of the walls were skewed. Even Tessie, pint-sized, felt constricted. For some reason the bathroom was nearly as large as the bedroom. The toilet stood stranded on loose tiles and ran continuously. The tub had a skid mark where the water drained out.

There was a queen-size bed for my parents and, in the corner, a cot set up for me. I hauled my suitcase up onto it. My suitcase was a bone of contention between Tessie and me. She had picked it out for me before our trip to Turkey. It had a floral pattern of turquoise and green blossoms which I found hideous. Since going off to private school — and hanging around the Object — my tastes had been changing, becoming refined, I thought. Poor Tessie no longer knew what to buy me. Anything she chose was greeted by wails of horror. I was adamantly opposed to anything synthetic or with visible stitching. My parents found my new urge for purity amusing. Often my father would rub my shirt between his thumb and fingers and ask, "Is this preppy?"

With the suitcase Tessie had had no time to consult me, and so there it was, bearing a design like a place mat's. Unzipping the suitcase and flipping it open, I felt better. Inside were all the clothes I'd chosen myself: the crew neck sweaters in primary colors, the Lacoste shirts, the wide-wale corduroys. My coat was from Papagallo, lime green with horn-shaped buttons made from bone.

"Do we have to unpack or can we leave everything in our suitcases?" I asked.

"We better unpack and put our suitcases in the closet," Milton answered. "Give us a little more room in here."

I put my sweaters neatly in the dresser drawers, my socks and underpants, too, and hung my pants up. I took my toiletry case into the bathroom and put it on the shelf. I had brought lip gloss and perfume with me. I wasn't certain that they were obsolete.

I closed the bathroom door, locked it, and bent close to the mirror to examine my face. Two dark hairs, still short, were visible above my upper lip. I got tweezers out of my case and plucked them. This made my eyes water. My clothes felt tight. The sleeves of my sweater were too short. I combed my hair and, optimistically, desperately, smiled at myself.

I knew that my situation, whatever it was, was a crisis of some kind. I could tell that from my parents' false, cheery behavior and from our speedy exit from home. Still, no one had said a word to me yet. Milton and Tessie were treating me exactly as they always had — as their daughter, in other words. They acted as though my problem was medical and therefore fixable. So I began to hope so, too. Like a person with a terminal illness, I was eager to ignore the immediate symptoms, hoping for a last-minute cure. I veered back and forth between hope and its opposite, a growing certainty that something terrible was wrong with me. But nothing made me more desperate than looking in the mirror.

I opened the door and stepped back into the room. "I hate this hotel," I said. "It's gross."

"It's not too nice," Tessie agreed.

"It used to be nicer," said Milton. "I

don't understand what happened."

"The carpet smells."

"Let's open a window."

"Maybe we won't have to be here that long," Tessie said, hopefully, wearily.

In the evening we ventured outside, looking for something to eat, and then returned to the room to watch TV. Later, after we switched off the lights, I asked from my cot, "What are we doing tomorrow?"

"We have to go to the doctor's in the morning," said Tessie.

"After that we have to see about some Broadway tickets," said Milton. "What do you want to see, Cal?"

"I don't care," I said gloomily.

"I think we should see a musical," said Tessie.

"I saw Ethel Merman in *Hello, Dolly!*" Milton recalled. "She came down this big, long staircase, singing. When she finished, the place went wild. She stopped the show. So she just went right back up the staircase and sang the song over again."

"Would you like to see a musical, Callie?"

"Whatever."

"Damnedest thing I ever saw," said Milton. "That Ethel Merman can really belt it out."

No one spoke after that. We lay in the

dark, in our strange beds, until we fell asleep.

The next morning after breakfast we set off to see the specialist. My parents tried to seem excited as we left the hotel, pointing out sights from the taxi window. Milton exuded the boisterousness he reserved for all difficult situations. "This is some place," he said as we drove up to New York Hospital. "River view! I might just check myself in."

Like any teenager, I was largely oblivious to the clumsy figure I cut. My stork movements, my flapping arms, my long legs kicking out my undersized feet in their fawn-colored Wallabees — all that machinery clanked beneath the observation tower of my head, and I was too close to see it. My parents did. It pained them to watch me advance across the sidewalk toward the hospital entrance. It was terrifying to see your child in the grip of unknown forces. For a year now they had been denying how I was changing, putting it down to the awkward age. "She'll grow out of it," Milton was always telling my mother. But now they were seized with a fear that I was growing out of control.

We found the elevator and rode up to the fourth floor, then followed the arrows to something called the Psychohormonal

Unit. Milton had the office number written out on a card. Finally we found the right room. The gray door was unmarked except for an extremely small, unobtrusive sign halfway down that read:

Sexual Disorders and Gender Identity Clinic

If my parents saw the sign, they pretended not to. Milton lowered his head, bull-like, and pushed the door open.

The receptionist welcomed us and told us to have a seat. The waiting room was unexceptional. Chairs lined the walls, divided evenly by magazine tables, and there was the usual rubber tree expiring in the corner. The carpeting was institutional, with a hectic, stain-camouflaging pattern. There was even a reassuringly medicinal smell in the air. After my mother filled out the insurance forms, we were shown into the doctor's office. This, too, inspired confidence. An Eames chair stood behind the desk. By the window was a Le Corbusier chaise, made of chrome and cowhide. The bookshelves were filled with medical books and journals and the walls tastefully hung with art. Big-city sophistication attuned to a European sensibility. The surround of a triumphant psychoanalytic world-view. Not to mention the East River view out the windows. We were a long way from Dr. Phil's office with its amateur oils and Medicaid cases.

It was two or three minutes before we noticed anything out of the ordinary. At first the curios and etchings had blended in with the scholarly clutter of the office. But as we sat waiting for the doctor, we became aware of a silent commotion all around us. It was like staring at the ground and realizing, suddenly, that it is swarming with ants. The restful doctor's office was churning with activity. The paperweight on his desk, for instance, was not a simple, inert rock but a tiny priapus carved from stone. The miniatures on the walls revealed their subject matter under closer observation. Beneath yellow silk tents, on paisley pillows, Mughal princes acrobatically copulated with multiple partners, keeping their turbans in place. Tessie blushed, looking; while Milton squinted; and I hid inside my hair as usual. We tried to look someplace else and so looked at the bookshelves. But here it wasn't safe either. Amid a dulling surround of issues of *JAMA* and *The New England Journal of Medicine* were some eye-popping titles. One, with entwining snakes on the spine, was called *Erotosexual Pair Bonding*. There was a purple, pamphlety thing entitled *Ritualized Homosexuality: Three Field Studies*. On the desk itself, with a bookmark in it, was a manual called *Hap-Penis: Surgical Techniques in Female-to-Male Sex Reassignment*. If the sign on the front door hadn't already, Luce's office made it clear just what kind of specialist my parents had brought me to see. (And, worse, to see me.) There were sculptures, too. Reproductions from the temple at Kujaraho occupied corners of the room along with huge jade plants. Against the waxy green foliage, melon-breasted Hindu women bent over double, offering up orifices like prayers to the well-endowed men who answered them. An overloaded switchboard, a dirty game of Twister everywhere you turned.

"Will you look at this place?" Tessie whispered.

"Sort of unusual decor," said Milton.

And I: "What are we doing here?"

It was right then that the door opened and Dr. Luce presented himself.

At that stage, I didn't know about his glamour status in the field. I had no idea of the frequency with which Luce's name appeared in the relevant journals and papers. But I saw right away that Luce wasn't your normal-looking doctor. Instead of a medical coat he wore a suede vest with fringe. Silver hair touched the collar of his beige turtleneck. His pants were flared and on his feet were a pair of ankle boots with zippers on the sides. He had eyeglasses, too, silver wire-rims, and a gray mustache.

"Welcome to New York," he said. "I'm Dr. Luce." He shook my father's hand, then my mother's, and finally came to me. "You must be Calliope." He was smiling, relaxed. "Let's see if I can remember my mythology. Calliope was one of the Muses, right?"

"Right."

"In charge of what?"

"Epic poetry."

"You can't beat that," said Luce. He was trying to act casual, but I could see he was excited. I was an extraordinary case, after all. He was taking his time, savoring me. To a scientist like Luce I was nothing less than a sexual or genetic Kaspar Hauser. There he was, a famous sexologist, a guest on *Dick Cavett*, a regular contributor to *Playboy*, and suddenly on his doorstep, arriving out of the woods of Detroit like the Wild Boy of Aveyron, was me, Calliope Stephanides, age fourteen. I was a living experiment dressed in white corduroys and a Fair Isle sweater. This sweater, pale yellow, with a floral wreath at the neck, told Luce that I refuted nature in just the way his theory predicted. He must have hardly been able to contain himself, meeting me. He was a brilliant, charming, work-obsessed man, and watched me from behind his desk with keen eyes. While he chatted, speaking primarily to my parents, gaining their confidence, Luce was nevertheless making mental notes. He registered my tenor voice. He noted that I sat with one leg tucked under me. He watched how I examined my nails, curling my fingers into my palm. He paid attention to the way I coughed, laughed, scratched my head, spoke; in sum, all the external manifestations of what he called my gender identity.

He kept up the calm manner, as if I had come to the Clinic with nothing more than a sprained ankle. "The first thing I'd like to do is give Calliope a short examination. If you'd care to wait here in my office, Mr. and Mrs. Stephanides." He stood up. "Would you come with me please, Calliope?"

I got up from my chair. Luce watched as the various segments, like those of a collapsible ruler, unfolded themselves, and I attained my full height, an inch taller than he was himself.

"We'll be right here, honey," Tessie said.

"We're not going anywhere," said Milton.

Peter Luce was considered the world's leading authority on human hermaphroditism. The Sexual Disorders and Gender Identity Clinic, which he founded in 1968, had become the foremost facility in the world for the study and treatment of conditions of ambiguous gender. He was the author of a major sexological work, *The Oracular Vulva*, which was standard in a variety of disciplines ranging from genetics and pediatrics to psychology. He had written a column by the same name for *Playboy* from August 1972 to December 1973 in which the conceit was that a personified and all-knowing female pudendum answered the queries of male readers with witty and sometimes sibylline responses. Hugh Hefner had come across Peter Luce's name in the papers in connection with a demonstration for sexual freedom. Six Columbia students had staged an orgy in a tent on the main green, which the cops broke up, and when asked what he thought about such activity on campus, Prof. Peter Luce, 46, had been quoted as saying, "I'm in favor of orgies wherever they happen." That caught Hef's eye. Not wanting to replicate Xaviera Hollander's "Call Me Madam" column in *Penthouse*, Hefner saw Luce's contribution as being devoted to the scientific and historical side of sex. Thus, in her first three issues, the Oracular Vulva delivered disquisitions on the erotic art of the Japanese painter Hiroshi Yamamoto, the epidemiology of syphilis, and the sex life of St. Augustine.

The column proved popular, though intelligent queries were always hard to come by, the readership being more interested in the "Playboy Advisor" 's cunnilingus tips or remedies for premature ejaculation. Finally, Hefner told Luce to write his own questions, which he was only too glad to do.

Peter Luce had appeared on *Phil Donahue* along with two hermaphrodites and a transsexual to discuss both the medical and psychological aspects of these conditions. On that program, Phil Donahue said, "Lynn Harris was born and raised a girl. You won the Miss Newport Beach Contest in 1964 in good old Orange County, California? Boy, wait till they hear this. You lived as a woman to the age of twenty-nine and then you switched to living as a man. He has the anatomical characteristics of both a man and a woman. If I'm lyin', I'm dyin'."

He also said, "Here's what's not so funny. These live, irreplaceable sons and daughters of God, human beings all, want you to know, among other things, that that's exactly what they are, human beings."

Because of certain genetic and hormonal conditions, it was sometimes very difficult to determine the sex of a newborn baby. Confronted with such a child, the Spartans had left the infant on a rocky hillside to die. Luce's own forebears, the English, didn't even like to mention the subject, and might never have done so had the nuisance of mysterious genitalia not thrown a wrench into the smooth workings of inheritance law. Lord Coke, the great British jurist of the seventeenth century, tried to clear up the matter of who would get the landed estates by declaring that a person should "be either male or female, and it shall succeed according to the kind of sex which doth prevail." Of course, he didn't specify any precise method for determining which sex *did* prevail. For most of the twentieth century, medicine had been using the same primitive diagnostic criterion of sex formulated by Klebs way back in 1876. Klebs had maintained that a person's gonads determined sex. In cases of ambiguous gender, you looked at the gonadal tissue under the microscope. If it was testicular, the person was male; if ovarian, female. The hunch here was that a person's gonads would orchestrate sexual development, especially at puberty. But it turned out to be more complicated than that. Klebs had begun the task, but the world had to wait another hundred years for Peter Luce to come along and finish it.

In 1955, Luce published an article called "Many Roads Lead to Rome: Sexual Concepts of Human Hermaphroditism." In twenty-five pages of forthright, high-toned prose, Luce argued that gender is determined by a variety of influences: chromosomal sex; gonadal sex; hormones; internal genital structures; external genitals; and, most important, the sex of rearing. Drawing on studies of patients at the pediatric endocrine clinic at New York Hospital, Luce was able to compile charts demonstrating how these various factors came into play, and showing that a patient's gonadal sex often didn't determine his or her gender identity. The article made a big splash. Within months, pretty much everyone had given up Klebs's criterion for Luce's criteria.

On the strength of this success, Luce was given the opportunity to open the Psychohormonal Unit at New York Hospital. In those days he saw mostly kids with adrenogenital syndrome, the most common form of female hermaphroditism. The hormone cortisol, recently synthesized in the lab, had been found to arrest the virilization these girls normally underwent, allowing them to develop as normal females. The endocrinologists administered the cortisol and Luce oversaw the girls' psychosexual development. He learned a lot. In a decade of solid, original research, Luce made his second great discovery: that gender identity is established very early on in life, about the age of two. Gender was like a native tongue; it didn't exist before birth but was imprinted in the brain during childhood, never disappearing. Children learn to speak Male or Female the way they learn to speak English or French.

He published this theory in 1967, in an article in *The New England Journal of Medicine* entitled "Early Establishment of Gender Identity: The Terminal Twos." After that, his reputation reached the stratosphere. The funding flowed in, from the Rockefeller Foundation, the Ford Foundation, and the N.I.S. It was a great time to be a sexologist. The Sexual Revolution provided new opportunities for the enterprising sex researcher. It was a matter of national interest, for a few years there, to examine the mechanics of the female orgasm. Or to plumb the psychological reasons why certain men exhibited themselves on the street. In 1968, Dr. Luce opened the Sexual Disorders and Gender Identity Clinic. Luce treated everybody: the webbed-necked girl teens with Turner's syndrome, who had only one sex chromosome, a lonely X; the leggy beauties with Androgen Insensitivity; or the XYY boys, who tended to be dreamers and loners. When babies with ambiguous genitalia were born at the hospital, Dr. Luce was called in to discuss the matter with the bewildered parents. Luce got the transsexuals, too. Everyone came to the Clinic, with the result that Luce had at his disposal a body of research material — of living, breathing specimens — no scientist had ever had before.

And now Luce had me. In the examination room, he told me to get undressed and put on a paper gown. After taking some blood (only one vial, thankfully), he had me lie down on a table with my legs up in stirrups. There was a pale green curtain, the same color as my gown, that could be pulled across the table, dividing my upper and lower halves. Luce didn't close it that first day. Only later, when there was an audience.

"This shouldn't hurt but it might feel a little funny."

I stared up at the ring light on the ceiling. Luce had another light on a stand, which he angled to suit his purposes. I could feel its heat between my legs as he pressed and prodded me.

For the first few minutes I concentrated on the circular light, but finally, drawing in my chin, I looked down to see that Luce was holding the crocus between his thumb and forefinger. He was stretching it out with one hand while measuring it with the other. Then he let go of the ruler and made notes. He didn't look shocked or appalled. In fact he examined me with great curiosity, almost connoisseurship. There was an element of awe or appreciation in his face. He took notes as he proceeded but made no small talk. His concentration was intense.

After a while, still crouching between my legs, Luce turned his head to search for another instrument. Between the sight lines of my raised knees his ear appeared, an amazing organ all its own, whorled and flanged, translucent in the bright lights. His ear was very close to me. It seemed for a moment as though Luce were listening at my source. As though some riddle were being imparted to him from between my legs. But then he found what he had been looking for and turned back.

He began to probe inside.

"Relax," he said.

He applied a lubricant, huddled in closer.

"Re*lax*."

There was a hint of annoyance, of command in his voice. I took a deep breath and did the best I could. Luce poked inside. For a moment it felt merely strange, as he'd suggested. But then a sharp pain shot through me. I jerked back, crying out.

"Sorry."

Nevertheless, he kept on. He placed one hand on my pelvis to steady me. He probed in farther, though he avoided the painful area. My eyes were welling with tears.

"Almost finished," he said.

But he was only getting started.

The chief imperative in cases like mine was to show no doubt as to the gender of the child in question. You did not tell the parents of a newborn, "Your baby is a hermaphrodite." Instead, you said, "Your daughter was born with a clitoris that is a little larger than a normal girl's. We'll need to do surgery to make it the right size." Luce felt that parents weren't able to cope with an ambiguous gender assignment. You had to tell them if they had a boy or a girl. Which meant that, before you said anything, you had to be sure what the prevailing gender was.

Luce could not do this with me yet. He had received the results of the endocrinological tests performed at Henry Ford Hospital, and so knew of my XY karyotype, my high plasma testosterone levels, and the absence in my blood of dihydrotestosterone. In other words, before even seeing me, Luce was able to make an educated guess that I was a male pseudohermaphrodite — genetically male but appearing otherwise, with 5-alpha-reductase deficiency syndrome. But that, according to Luce's thinking, did not mean that I had a male gender identity.

My being a teenager complicated things. In addition to chromosomal and hormonal factors, Luce had to consider my sex of rearing, which had been *female*. He suspected that the tissue mass he had palpated inside me was testicular. Still, he couldn't be sure until he had looked at a sample under a microscope.

All this must have been going through Luce's mind as he brought me back to the waiting room. He told me he wanted to speak to my parents and that he would send them out when he was finished. His intensity had lessened and he was friendly again, smiling and patting me on the back.

In his office Luce sat down in his Eames chair, looked up at Milton and Tessie, and adjusted his glasses.

"Mr. Stephanides, Mrs. Stephanides, I'll be frank. This a complicated case. By complicated I don't mean irremediable. We have a range of effective treatments for cases of this kind. But before I'm ready to begin treatment there are a number of questions I have to answer."

My mother and father were sitting only a foot apart during this speech, but each heard something different. Milton heard the words that were there. He heard "treatment" and "effective." Tessie, on the other hand, heard the words that weren't there. The doctor hadn't said my name, for instance. He hadn't said "Calliope" or "Callie." He hadn't said "daughter," either. He didn't use any pronouns at all.

"I'll need to run further tests," Luce was continuing. "I'll need to perform a complete psychological assessment. Once I have the necessary information, then we can discuss in detail the proper course of treatment."

Milton was already nodding. "What kind of time line are we talking about, Doctor?"

Luce jutted out a thoughtful lower lip. "I want to redo the lab tests, just to be sure. Those results will be back tomorrow. The psychological evaluation will take longer. I'll need to see your child every day for at least a week, maybe two. Also it would be helpful if you could give me any childhood photographs or family movies you might have."

Milton turned to Tessie. "When does Callie start school?"

Tessie didn't hear him. She was distracted by Luce's phrase: "your child."

"What kind of information are you trying to get, Doctor?" Tessie asked.

"The blood tests will tell us hormone levels. The psychological assessment is routine in cases like this."

"You think it's some kind of hormone thing?" Milton asked. "A hormone imbalance?"

"We'll know after I've had time to do what I need to do," said Luce.

Milton stood up and shook hands with the doctor. The consultation was over.

Keep in mind: neither Milton nor Tessie had seen me undressed for years. How were they to know? And not knowing, how could they imagine? The information available to them was all secondary stuff — my husky voice, my flat chest — but these things were far from persuasive. A hormonal thing. It could have been no more serious than that. So my father believed, or wanted to believe, and so he tried to convince Tessie.

I had my own resistance. "Why does he have to do a psychological evaluation?" I asked. "It's not like I'm crazy."

"The doctor said it was routine."

"But why?"

With this question I had hit upon the crux of the matter. My mother has since told me that she intuited the real reason for the psychological assessment, but chose not to dwell on it. Or, rather, didn't choose. Let Milton choose for her. Milton preferred to treat the problem pragmatically. There was no sense in worrying about a psychological assessment that could only confirm what was obvious: that I was a normal, well-adjusted girl. "He probably bills the insurance extra for the psychological stuff," Milton said. "Sorry, Cal, but you'll have to put up with it. Maybe he can cure your neuroses. Got any neuroses? Now's your time to let 'em out." He put his arms around me, squeezed hard, and roughly kissed the side of my head.

Milton was so convinced that everything was going to be okay that on Tuesday morning he flew down to Florida on business. "No sense cooling my heels in this hotel," he told us.

"You just want to get out of this pit," I said.

"I'll make it up to you. Why don't you and your mother go out for a fancy dinner tonight. Anyplace you want. We're saving a couple bucks on this room, so you gals can splurge. Why don't you take Callie to Delmonico's, Tess."

"What's Delmonico's?" I asked.

"It's a steak joint."

"I want lobster. And baked Alaska," I said.

"Baked Alaska! Maybe they have that, too."

Milton left, and my mother and I tried

to spend his money. We went shopping at Bloomingdale's. We had high tea at the Plaza. We never made it to Delmonico's, preferring a moderately priced Italian restaurant near the Lochmoor, where we felt more comfortable. We ate there every night, doing our best to pretend we were on a real trip, a vacation. Tessie drank more wine than usual and got tipsy, and when she went to the bathroom I drank her wine myself.

Normally the most expressive thing about my mother's face was the gap between her front teeth. When she was listening to me, Tessie's tongue often pressed against that divot, that gate. This was the signal of her attention. My mother always paid great attention to whatever I said. And if I told her something funny, then her tongue dropped away, her head fell back, her mouth opened wide, and there were her front teeth, riven and ascendant.

Every night at the Italian restaurant I tried to make this happen.

In the mornings, Tessie took me to the Clinic for my appointments.

"What are your hobbies, Callie?"
"Hobbies?"
"Is there anything you especially like to do?"
"I'm not really a hobby-type person."

750

"What about sports? Do you like any sports?"

"Does Ping-Pong count?"

"I'll put it down." Luce smiled from behind his desk. I was on the Le Corbusier daybed across the room, lounging on the cowhide.

"What about boys?"

"What about them?"

"Is there a boy at school you like?"

"I guess you've never been to my school, Doctor."

He checked his file. "Oh, it's a girls' school, isn't it?"

"Yup."

"Are you sexually attracted to girls?" Luce said this quickly. It was like a tap from a rubber hammer. But I stifled my reflex.

He put down his pen and knit his fingers together. He leaned forward and spoke softly. "I want you to know that this is all between us, Callie. I'm not going to tell your parents anything that you tell me here."

I was torn. Luce in his leather chair, with his longish hair and ankle boots, was the kind of adult a kid might open up to. He was as old as my father but in league with the younger generation. I longed to tell him about the Object. I longed to tell somebody, anybody. My feelings for her were still so strong they rushed up my throat. But I held them back, wary. I didn't believe this was all private.

"Your mother says you have a close relationship with a friend of yours," Luce began again. He said the Object's name. "Do you feel sexually attracted to her? Or have you had sexual relations with her?"

"We're just friends," I insisted, a little too loudly. I tried again in a quieter voice. "She's my best friend." In response Luce's right eyebrow rose from behind his glasses. It came out of hiding as though it, too, wanted to get a good look at me. And then I found a way out:

"I had sex with her brother," I confessed. "He's a junior."

Again Luce showed neither surprise, disapproval, or interest. He made a note on his pad, nodding once. "And did you enjoy it?"

Here I could tell the truth. "It hurt," I said. "Plus I was scared about getting pregnant."

Luce smiled to himself, jotting in his notebook. "Not to worry," he said.

That was how it went. Every day for an hour I sat in Luce's office and talked about my life, my feelings, my likes and dislikes. Luce asked all kinds of questions. The answers I gave were sometimes not as important as the way I answered them. He watched my facial expressions; he noted my style of argument. Females tend to smile at their interlocutors more than males do. Females pause and look for signs of agreement before continuing. Males just look into the middle distance and hold forth. Women prefer the anecdotal, men the deductive. It was impossible to be in Luce's line of work without falling back on such stereotypes. He knew their limitations. But they were clinically useful.

When I wasn't being questioned about my life and feelings, I was writing about them. Most days I sat typing up what Luce called my "Psychological Narrative." That early autobiography didn't begin: "I was born twice." Flashy, rhetorical openings were something I had to get the hang of. It started simply, with the words "My name is Calliope Stephanides. I am fourteen years old. Going on fifteen." I began with the facts and followed them as long as I could.

Sing, Muse, how cunning Calliope wrote on that battered Smith Corona! Sing how the typewriter hummed and trembled at her psychiatric revelations! Sing of its two cartridges, one for typing and one for correcting, that so eloquently represented her predicament, poised between the print of genetics and the Wite-Out of surgery. Sing of the weird smell the typewriter gave off,

753

like WD-40 and salami, and of the Day-Glo flower decal the last person who'd used it had applied, and of the broken F key, which stuck. On that newfangled but soon-to-be obsolete machine I wrote not so much like a kid from the Midwest as a minister's daughter from Shropshire. I still have a copy of my psychological narrative somewhere. Luce published it in his collected works, omitting my name. "I would like to tell of my life," it runs at one point, "and of the experiences that make myriad my joys and sorrows upon this planet we call Earth." In describing my mother, I say, "Her beauty is the kind which seems to be thrown into relief by grief." A few pages on there comes the subheading "Calumnies Caustic and Catty by Callie." Half the time I wrote like bad George Eliot, the other half like bad Salinger. "If there's one thing I hate it's television." Not true: I loved television! But on that Smith Corona I quickly discovered that telling the truth wasn't nearly as much fun as making things up. I also knew that I was writing for an audience — Dr. Luce — and that if I seemed normal enough, he might send me back home. This explains the passages about my love of cats ("feline affection"), the pie recipes, and my deep feelings for nature.

Luce ate it all up. It's true; I have to give

credit where credit's due. Luce was the first person to encourage my writing. Every night he read through what I had typed up during the day. He didn't know, of course, that I was making up most of what I wrote, pretending to be the all-American daughter my parents wanted me to be. I fictionalized early "sex play" and later crushes on boys; I transferred my feeling for the Object onto Jerome and it was amazing how it worked: the tiniest bit of truth made credible the greatest lies.

Luce was interested in the gender giveaways of my prose, of course. He measured my *jouissance* against my linearity. He picked up on my Victorian flourishes, my antique diction, my girls' school propriety. These all weighed heavily in his final assessment.

There was also the diagnostic tool of pornography. One afternoon when I arrived for my session with Dr. Luce, there was a movie projector in his office. A screen had been set up before the bookcase, and the blinds drawn. In syrupy light Luce was feeding the celluloid through the sprocket wheel.

"Are you going to show me my dad's movie again? From when I was little?"

"Today I've got something a little different," said Luce.

I took up my customary position on the

chaise, my arms folded behind me on the cowhide. Dr. Luce switched off the lights and soon the movie began.

It was about a pizza delivery girl. The title was, in fact, *Annie Delivers to Your Door.* In the first scene, Annie, wearing cutoffs and a midriff-revealing, Ellie-May blouse, gets out of her car before an ocean-side house. She rings the bell. No one is at home. Not wanting the pizza to go to waste, she sits down next to the pool and begins to eat.

The production values were low. The pool boy, when he arrived, was badly lit. It was hard to hear what he was saying. But soon enough he was no longer saying anything. Annie had begun to remove her clothes. She was down on her knees. The pool boy was naked, too, and then they were on the steps, in the pool, on the diving board, pumping, writhing. I closed my eyes. I didn't like the raw meat colors of the film. It wasn't at all beautiful like the tiny paintings in Luce's office.

In a straightforward voice Luce asked from the darkness, "Which one turns you on?"

"Excuse me?"

"Which one turns you on? The woman or the man?"

The true answer was neither. But truth would not do.

Sticking to my cover story, I managed to get out, very quietly, "The boy."

"The pool boy? That's good. I dig the pizza girl myself. She's got a great bod." A sheltered child once, from a reserved Presbyterian home, Luce was now liberated, free of antisexualism. "She's got incredible tits," he said. "You like her tits? Do they turn you on?"

"No."

"The guy's cock turns you on?"

I nodded, barely, wishing it would be over. But it was not over for a while yet. Annie had other pizzas to deliver. Luce wanted to watch each one.

Sometimes he brought other doctors to see me. A typical unveiling went as follows. I was summoned from my writing studio in the back of the Clinic. In Luce's office two men in business suits were waiting. They stood when I came in. Luce made introductions. "Callie, I want to you meet Dr. Craig and Dr. Winters."

The doctors shook my hand. It was their first bit of data: my handshake. Dr. Craig squeezed hard, Winters less so. They were careful about not seeming too eager. Like men meeting a fashion model, they trained their eyes away from my body and pretended to be interested in me as a person. Luce said, "Callie's been here at the Clinic for just about a week now."

"How do you like New York?" asked Dr. Craig.

"I've hardly seen it."

The doctors gave me sightseeing suggestions. The atmosphere was light, friendly. Luce put his hand on the small of my back. Men have an annoying way of doing that. They touch your back as though there's a handle there, and direct you where they want you to go. Or they place their hand on top of your head, paternally. Men and their hands. You've got to watch them every minute. Luce's hand was now proclaiming: Here she is. My star attraction. The terrible thing was that I responded to it; I liked the feel of Luce's hand on my back. I liked the attention. Here were all these people who wanted to meet me.

Pretty soon Luce's hand was escorting me down the hall into the examination room. I knew the drill. Behind the screen I undressed while the doctors waited. The green paper gown was folded on the chair.

"The family comes from where, Peter?"

"Turkey. Originally."

"I'm only acquainted with the Papua New Guinea study," said Craig.

"Among the Sambia, right?" asked Winters.

"Yes, that's right," Luce answered. "There's a high incidence of the mutation there as well. The Sambia are interesting from a sexological point of view, too. They practice ritualized homosexuality. Sambia males consider contact with females highly polluting. So they've organized social structures to limit exposure as much as possible. The men and boys sleep on one side of the village, the women and girls on the other side. The men go into the women's longhouse only to procreate. In and out. In fact, the Sambia word for 'vagina' translates literally as 'that thing which is truly no good.' "

Soft chuckling came from the other side of the screen.

I came out, feeling awkward. I was taller than everyone else in the room, though I weighed much less. The floor felt cold against my bare feet as I crossed to the exam table and jumped up.

I lay back. Without having to be told, I lifted my legs and fit my heels in the gynecological stirrups. The room had gone ominously silent. The three doctors came forward, staring down. Their heads formed a trinity above me. Luce pulled the curtain across the table.

They bent over me, studying my parts, while Luce led a guided tour. I didn't know what most of the words meant but after the third or fourth time I could recite the list by heart. "Muscular habitus . . . no gynecomastia . . . hypospadias . . . urogenital sinus . . . blind vaginal pouch . . ." These were my claim to fame. I didn't feel famous, however. In fact, behind the curtain, I no longer felt as if I were in the room.

"How old is she?" Dr. Winters asked.

"Fourteen," Luce answered. "She'll be fifteen in January."

"So your position is that chromosomal status has been completely overridden by rearing?"

"I think that's pretty clear."

As I lay there, letting Luce, in rubber gloves, do what he had to do, I got a sense of things. Luce wanted to impress the men with the importance of his work. He needed funding to keep the clinic running. The surgery he performed on transsexuals wasn't a selling point over at the March of Dimes. To get them interested you had to pull at the heartstrings. You had to put a face on suffering. Luce was trying to do that with me. I was perfect, so polite, so midwestern. No unseemliness attached itself to me, no hint of cross-dresser bars or ads in the back of louche magazines.

Dr. Craig wasn't convinced. "Fascinating case, Peter. No question. But my people will want to know the applications."

"It's a very rare condition," Luce admitted. "Exceedingly rare. But in terms of research, its importance can't be overstated. For the reasons I outlined in my office." Luce remained vague for my benefit, but still persuasive enough for theirs. He hadn't gotten where he was without certain lobbyist gifts. Meanwhile I was there and not there, cringing at Luce's touch, sprouting goose bumps, and worrying that I hadn't washed properly.

I remember this, too. A long narrow room on a different floor of the hospital. A riser set up at one end before a butterfly light. The photographer putting film in his camera.

"Okay, I'm ready," he said.

I dropped my robe. Almost used to it now, I climbed up on the riser before the measuring chart.

"Hold your arms out a little."

"Like this?"

"That's good. I don't want a shadow."

He didn't tell me to smile. The textbook publishers would make sure to cover my face. The black box: a fig leaf in reverse, concealing identity while leaving shame exposed.

Every night Milton called us in our room. Tessie put on a bright voice for him. Milton tried to sound happy when I got on the line. But I took the opportunity to whine and complain.

"I'm sick of this hotel. When can we go home?"

"Soon as you're better," Milton said.

When it was time for sleep, we drew the window curtains and turned off the lights.

"Good night, honey. See you in the morning."

"Night."

But I couldn't sleep. I kept thinking about that word: "better." What did my father mean? What were they going to do to me? Street sounds made it up to the room, curiously distinct, echoing off the stone building opposite. I listened to the police sirens, the angry horns. My pillow was thin. It smelled like a smoker. Across the strip of carpet my mother was already asleep. Before my conception, she had agreed to my father's outlandish plan to determine my sex. She had done this so that she wouldn't be alone, so that she would have a girlfriend in the house. And I had been that friend. I had always been close to my mother. Our temperaments were alike. We liked nothing better than to sit on park benches and watch the faces go by. Now the face I was watching was Tessie's in the other bed. It looked white, blank, as if her cold cream had removed not only her makeup but her personality. Tessie's eyes were moving, though; under the lids they skated back and forth. Callie couldn't imagine the things Tessie was seeing in her dreams back then. But I can. Tessie was dreaming a family dream. A version of the nightmares Desdemona had after listening to Fard's sermons. *Dreams of the germs of infants bubbling, dividing. Of hideous creatures growing up from pale foam.* Tessie didn't allow herself to think about such things during the day, so they came to her at night. Was it her fault? Should she have resisted Milton when he tried to bend nature to his will? Was there really a God after all, and did He punish people on Earth? These Old World superstitions had been banished from my mother's conscious mind, but they still operated in her dreams. From the other bed I watched the play of these dark forces on my mother's sleeping face.

Looking Myself Up
in Webster's

❧

I tossed and turned every night, unable to sleep straight through. I was like the princess and the pea. A pellet of disquiet kept unsettling me. Sometimes I awoke with the feeling that a spotlight had been trained on me while I slept. It was as if my ether body had been conversing with angels, somewhere up near the ceiling. When I opened my eyes they fled. But I could hear the traces of the communication, the fading echoes of the crystal bell. Some essential information was rising from the depths of my being. This information was on the tip of my tongue and yet never surfaced. One thing was certain: it was all connected with the Object somehow. I lay awake thinking about her, wondering how she was, and pining, grieving.

I thought of Detroit, too, of its vacant lots of pale Osiris grass springing up between the condemned houses and those not yet condemned, and of the river with its iron runoff, the dead carp floating on the surface, white bellies flaking. I thought of fishermen standing on the concrete freighter docks with their bait buckets and tallboys, the baseball game on the radio. It's often said that a traumatic experience early in life marks a person forever, pulls her out of line, saying, "Stay there. Don't move." My time at the Clinic did that to me. I feel a direct line extending from that girl with her knees steepled beneath the hotel blankets to this person writing now in an Aeron chair. Hers was the duty to live out a mythical life in the actual world, mine to tell about it now. I didn't have the resources at fourteen, didn't know enough, hadn't been to the Anatolian mountain the Greeks call Olympus and the Turks Uludag, just like the soft drink. I hadn't gotten old enough yet to realize that living sends a person not into the future but back into the past, to childhood and before birth, finally, to commune with the dead. You get older, you puff on the stairs, you enter the body of your father. From there it's only a quick jump to your grandparents, and then before you know it you're time-traveling. In this life we grow backwards. It's always the gray-haired tourists on Italian buses who can tell you something about the Etruscans.

In the end, it took Luce two weeks to make his determination about me. He scheduled an appointment with my parents for the following Monday.

Milton had been jetting around during the two weeks, checking on his Hercules franchises, but on the Friday preceding the appointment he flew back to New York. We spent the weekend spiritlessly sightseeing, assailed by unspoken anxieties. On Monday morning my parents dropped me off at the New York Public Library while they went to see Dr. Luce.

My father had dressed that morning with special care. Despite an outward show of tranquillity, Milton was beset by an unaccustomed feeling of dread, and so armored himself in his most commanding clothes: over his plump body, a charcoal pinstripe suit; around his bullfrog neck, a Countess Mara necktie; and in the buttonholes of his shirtsleeves, his "lucky" Greek Drama cuff links. Like our Acropolis night-light, the cuff links had come from Jackie Halas's souvenir shop in Greektown. Milton wore them whenever he met with bank loan officers or auditors from the IRS. That Monday morning, however, he had trouble putting the cuff links in; his hands were not steady enough. In exasperation he asked Tessie to do it. "What's the matter?" she asked tenderly. But Milton snapped, "Just put the cuff links in, will you?" He held out his arms, looking away, embarrassed by his body's weakness.

Silently Tessie inserted the links, tragedy in one sleeve, comedy in the other. As we came out of the hotel that morning they glittered in the early morning sun, and under the influence of those two-sided accessories, what happened next took on contrasting tones. There was tragedy, certainly, in Milton's expression as they left me off at the library. During Milton's time away, his image of me had reverted to the girl I'd been a year earlier. Now he faced the real me again. He saw my ungainly movements as I climbed the library steps, the broadness of my shoulders inside my Papagallo coat. Watching from the cab, Milton came face-to-face with the essence of tragedy, which is something determined before you're born, something you can't escape or do anything about, no matter how hard you try. And Tessie, so used to feeling the world through her husband, saw that my problem was getting worse, was accelerating. Their hearts were wrung with anguish, the anguish of having children, a vulnerability as astonishing as the capacity for love that parenthood brings, in a cuff link set all its own . . .

. . . But now the cab was driving away, Milton was wiping his brow with his handkerchief; and the grinning face in his right sleeve came into view, for there was a comic aspect to events that day, too. There was comedy in the way Milton, while still worrying about me, kept one eye on the rocketing taxi meter. At the Clinic, there was comedy in the way Tessie, idly picking up a waiting-room magazine, found herself reading about the juvenile sexual rehearsal play of rhesus monkeys. There was even a brand of harsh satire in my parents' quest itself, because it typified the American belief that everything can be solved by doctors. All this comedy, however, is retrospective. As Milton and Tessie prepared to see Dr. Luce, a hot foam was rising in their stomachs. Milton was thinking back to his early navy days, to his time in the landing craft. This was just like that. Any minute the door was going to drop away and they would have to plunge into the churning night surf . . .

In his office Luce got straight to the point. "Let me review the facts of your daughter's case," he said. Tessie noted the change at once. Daughter. He had said "daughter."

The sexologist was looking reassuringly medical that morning. Over his cashmere turtleneck he wore an actual white coat. In his hand he held a sketchpad. His ballpoint pen bore the name of a pharmaceutical company. The blinds were drawn, the light low. The couples in the Mughal miniatures had modestly covered themselves in shadow. Sitting in his designer chair, with tomes and journals rising behind him, Dr. Luce appeared serious, full of expertise, as was his speech. "What I'm drawing here," he began, "are the fetal genital structures. In other words, this is what a baby's genitals look like in the womb, in the first few weeks after conception. Male or female, it's all the same. These two circles here are what we call the all-purpose gonads. This little squiggle here is a Wolffian duct. And this other squiggle is a Müllerian duct. Okay? The thing to keep in mind is that everybody starts out like this. We're all born with potential boy parts and girl parts. You, Mr. Stephanides, Mrs. Stephanides, me — everybody. Now" — he started drawing again — "as the fetus develops in the womb, what happens is that hormones and enzymes are released — let's make them arrows. What do these hormones and enzymes do? Well, they turn these circles and squiggles into either boy parts or girl parts. See this circle, the all-purpose gonad? It can become either an ovary or a testis. And this squiggly Müllerian duct can either wither up" — he scratched it out — "or grow into a uterus, fallopian tubes, and the inside of the vagina. This Wolffian duct can either wither away or grow into a seminal vesicle, epididymis, and vas deferens.

Depending on the hormonal and enzymatic influences." Luce looked up and smiled. "You don't have to worry about the terminology. The main thing to remember is this: every baby has Müllerian structures, which are potential girl parts, and Wolffian structures, which are potential boy parts. Those are the internal genitalia. But the same thing goes for the *external* genitalia. A penis is just a very large clitoris. They grow from the same root."

Dr. Luce stopped once more. He folded his hands. My parents, leaning forward in the chairs, waited.

"As I explained, any determination of gender identity must take into account a host of factors. The most important, in your daughter's case" — there it was again, confidently proclaimed — "is that she has been raised for fourteen years as a girl and indeed thinks of herself as female. Her interests, gestures, psychosexual makeup — all these are female. Are you with me so far?"

Milton and Tessie nodded.

"Due to her 5-alpha-reductase deficiency, Callie's body does not produce dihydrotestosterone. What this means is that, in utero, she followed a primarily female line of development. Especially in terms of the external genitalia. That, coupled with her being brought up as a girl, resulted in her thinking, acting, and looking like a girl. The problem came when she started to go through puberty. At puberty, the other androgen — testosterone — started to exert a strong effect. The simplest way to put it is like this: Callie is a girl who has a little too much male hormone. We want to correct that."

Neither Milton nor Tessie said a word. They weren't following everything the doctor was saying but, as people do with doctors, they were attentive to his manner, trying to see how serious things were. Luce seemed optimistic, confident, and Tessie and Milton began to be filled with hope.

"That's the biology. It's a very rare genetic condition, by the way. The only other populations where we know of this mutation expressing itself are in the Dominican Republic, Papua New Guinea, and southeastern Turkey. Not that far from the village your parents came from. About three hundred miles, in fact." Luce removed his silver glasses. "Do you know of any family member who may have had a similar genital appearance to your daughter's?"

"Not that we know of," said Milton.

"When did your parents immigrate?"

"Nineteen twenty-two."

"Do you have any relatives still living in Turkey?"

"Not anymore."

Luce looked disappointed. He had one arm of his glasses in his mouth, and was chewing on it. Possibly he was imagining what it would be like to discover a whole new population of carriers of the 5-alpha-reductase mutation. He had to content himself with discovering me.

He put his glasses back on. "The treatment I'd recommend for your daughter is twofold. First, hormone injections. Second, cosmetic surgery. The hormone treatments will initiate breast development and enhance her female secondary sex characteristics. The surgery will make Callie look exactly like the girl she feels herself to be. In fact, she will be that girl. Her outside and inside will conform. She will look like a normal girl. Nobody will be able to tell a thing. And then Callie can go on and enjoy her life."

Milton's brow was still furrowed with concentration but from his eyes there was light appearing, rays of relief. He turned toward Tessie and patted her leg.

But in a timid, breaking voice Tessie asked, "Will she be able to have children?"

Luce paused only a second. "I'm afraid not, Mrs. Stephanides. Callie will never menstruate."

"But she's been menstruating for a few months now," Tessie objected.

"I'm afraid that's impossible. Possibly

there was some bleeding from another source."

Tessie's eyes filled with tears. She looked away.

"I just got a postcard from a former patient," Luce said consolingly. "She had a condition similar to your daughter's. She's married now. She and her husband adopted two kids and they're as happy as can be. She plays in the Cleveland Orchestra. Bassoon."

There was a silence, until Milton asked, "Is that it, Doctor? You do this one surgery and we can take her home?"

"We may have to do additional surgery at a later date. But the immediate answer to your question is yes. After the procedure, she can go home."

"How long will she be in the hospital?"

"Only overnight."

It was not a difficult decision, especially as Luce had framed it. A single surgery and some injections would end the nightmare and give my parents back their daughter, their Calliope, intact. The same enticement that had led my grandparents to do the unthinkable now offered itself to Milton and Tessie. No one would know. No one would ever know.

While my parents were being given a crash course in gonadogenesis, I — still of-

ficially Calliope — was doing some homework myself. In the Reading Room of the
New York Public Library I was looking up
something in the dictionary. Dr. Luce was
correct in thinking that his conversations
with colleagues and medical students were
over my head. I didn't know what "5-
alpha-reductase" meant, or "gynecomastia,"
or "inguinal canal." But Luce had under-
estimated my abilities, too. He didn't take
into consideration the rigorous curriculum
at my prep school. He didn't allow for my
excellent research and study skills. Most of
all, he didn't factor in the power of my
Latin teachers, Miss Barrie and Miss Silber.
So now, as my Wallabees made squishing
sounds between the reading tables, as a few
men looked up from their books to see
what was coming and then looked down
(the world was no longer full of eyes), I
heard Miss Barrie's voice in my ear. "Infants, define this word for me: *hypospadias.*
Use your Greek or Latin roots."

The little schoolgirl in my head wriggled
in her desk, hand raised high. "Yes, Calliope?" Miss Barrie called on me.

"*Hypo*. Below or beneath. Like 'hypo-
dermic.' "

"Brilliant. And *spadias?*"

"Um um . . ."

"Can anyone come to our poor muse's
aid?"

But, in the classroom of my brain, no one could. So that was why I was here. Because I knew that I had something below or beneath but I didn't know what that something was.

I had never seen such a big dictionary before. The Webster's at the New York Public Library stood in the same relation to other dictionaries of my acquaintance as the Empire State Building did to other buildings. It was an ancient, medieval-looking thing, bound in brown leather that brought to mind a falconer's gauntlet. The pages were gilded like the Bible's.

Flipping pages through the alphabet, past *cantabile* to *eryngo*, past *fandango* to *formicate* (that's with an *m*), past *hypertonia* to *hyposensitivity*, and there it was:

hypospadias New Latin, from Greek, man with hypospadias fr. *hypo-* + prob from *spadon*, eunuch, fr. *span*, to tear, pluck, pull, draw. — An abnormality of the penis in which the urethra opens on its under surface. *See* synonyms at EUNUCH.

I did as instructed and got

eunuch — 1. A castrated man; especially, one of those who were employed as harem attendants or functionaries in certain Oriental courts. **2.** A man whose testes have not developed. *See* synonyms at HERMAPHRODITE.

Following where the trail led, I finally reached

hermaphrodite — 1. One having the sex organs and many of the secondary sex characteristics of both male and female. **2.** Anything comprised of a combination of diverse or contradictory elements. *See* synonyms at MONSTER.

And that is where I stopped. And looked up, to see if anyone was watching. The vast Reading Room thrummed with silent energy: people thinking, writing. The painted ceiling bellied overhead like a sail, and down below the green desk lamps glowed, illuminating faces bent over books. I was stooping over mine, my hair falling onto the pages, covering up the definition of myself. My lime green coat was hanging open. I had an appointment with Luce later in the day and my hair was washed, my underpants fresh. My bladder was full and I crossed my legs, putting off a trip to the bathroom. Fear was stabbing me. I longed to be held, caressed, and that was impossible. I laid my hand on the dictionary and looked at it. Slender, leaf-shaped, it had a braided rope ring on one finger, a gift from the Object. The rope was getting dirty. I looked at my pretty hand and then pulled it away and faced the word again.

There it was, *monster*, in black and white, in a battered dictionary in a great city library. A venerable, old book, the shape and size of a headstone, with yellowing pages that bore marks of the multitudes who had consulted them before me. There were pencil scrawls and ink stains, dried blood, snack crumbs; and the leather binding itself was secured to the lectern by a chain. Here was a book that contained the collected knowledge of the past while giving evidence of present social conditions. The chain suggested that some library visitors might take it upon themselves to see that the dictionary circulated. The dictionary contained every word in the English language but the chain knew only a few. It knew *thief* and *steal* and, maybe, *purloined*. The chain spoke of *poverty* and *mistrust* and *inequality* and *decadence*. Callie herself was holding on to this chain now. She was tugging on it, winding it around her hand so that her fingers went white, as she stared down at that word. *Monster*. Still there. It had not moved. And she wasn't reading this word on the wall of her old bathroom stall. There was graffiti in Webster's but the synonym wasn't part of it.

The synonym was official, authoritative; it was the verdict that the culture gave on a person like her. *Monster.* That was what she was. That was what Dr. Luce and his colleagues had been saying. It explained so much, really. It explained her mother crying in the next room. It explained the false cheer in Milton's voice. It explained why her parents had brought her to New York, so that the doctors could work in secret. It explained the photographs, too. What did people do when they came upon Bigfoot or the Loch Ness Monster? They tried to get a picture. For a second Callie saw herself that way. As a lumbering, shaggy creature pausing at the edge of woods. As a humped convolvulus rearing its dragon's head from an icy lake. Her eyes were filling now, making the print swim, and she turned away and hurried out of the library.

But the synonym pursued her. All the way out the door and down the steps between the stone lions, Webster's Dictionary kept calling after her, *Monster, Monster!* The bright banners hanging from the tympanum proclaimed the word. The definition inserted itself into billboards and the ads on passing buses. On Fifth Avenue a cab was pulling up. Her father jumped out, smiling and waving. When Callie saw him, her heart lifted. The voice of Webster's stopped speaking in her head. Her father wouldn't be smiling like that unless the news from the doctor had been good. Callie laughed and sprinted down the library steps, almost tripping. Her emotions soared for the time it took to reach the street, maybe five or eight seconds. But coming closer to Milton, she learned something about medical reports. The more people smile, the worse the news. Milton grinned at her, perspiring in pinstripes, and once again the tragedy cuff link glinted in the sun.

They knew. Her parents knew she was a monster. And yet here was Milton, opening the car door for her; here was Tessie, inside, smiling as Callie climbed in. The cab took them to a restaurant and soon the three of them were looking over menus and ordering food.

Milton waited until the drinks were served. Then, somewhat formally, he began. "Your mother and I had a little chat with the doctor this morning, as you are aware. The good news is that you'll be back at home this week. You won't miss much school. Now for the bad news. Are you ready for the bad news, Cal?"

Milton's eyes were saying that the bad news was not all that bad.

"The bad news is you have to have a little operation. Very minor. 'Operation' isn't really the right word. I think the doctor called it a 'procedure.' They have to knock you out and you have to stay overnight in the hospital. That's it. There'll be some pain but they can give you painkillers for it."

With that, Milton rested. Tessie reached out and patted Callie's hand. "It'll be okay, honey," she said in a thickened voice. Her eyes were watery, red.

"What kind of operation?" Callie asked her father.

"Just a little cosmetic procedure. Like getting a mole removed." He reached out and playfully caught Callie's nose between his knuckles. "Or getting your nose fixed."

Callie pulled her head away, angry. "Don't do that!"

"Sorry," said Milton. He cleared his throat, blinking.

"What's wrong with me?" Calliope asked, and now her voice broke. Tears were running down her cheeks. "What's wrong with me, Daddy?"

Milton's face darkened. He swallowed hard. Callie waited for him to say the word, to quote Webster's, but he didn't. He only looked at her across the table, his head low, his eyes dark, warm, sad, and full of love. There was so much love in Milton's eyes that it was impossible to look for truth.

"It's a hormonal thing, what you've got," he said. "I was always under the impression that men had male hormones and women had female hormones. But everybody has both, apparently."

Still Callie waited.

"What you've got, see, is you've got a little too much of the male hormones and not quite enough of the female hormones. So what the doctor wants to do is give you a shot every now and then to get everything working right."

He didn't say the word. I didn't make him.

"It's a hormonal thing," Milton repeated. "In the grand scheme of things, no big deal."

Luce believed that a patient of my age was capable of understanding the essentials. And so, that afternoon, he did not mince words. In his mellow, pleasing, educated voice, looking directly into my eyes, Luce declared that I was a girl whose clitoris was merely larger than those of other girls. He drew the same charts for me as he had for my parents. When I pressed him on the details of my surgery, he said only this: "We're going to do an operation to finish your genitalia. They're not quite finished yet and we want to finish them."

He never mentioned anything about

hypospadias, and I began to hope that the word didn't apply to me. Maybe I had taken it out of context. Dr. Luce may have been referring to another patient. Webster's had said that hypospadias was an abnormality of the penis. But Dr. Luce was telling me that I had a clitoris. I understood that both these things grew out of the same fetal gonad, but that didn't matter. If I had a clitoris — and a specialist was telling me that I did — what could I be but a girl?

The adolescent ego is a hazy thing, amorphous, cloudlike. It wasn't difficult to pour my identity into different vessels. In a sense, I was able to take whatever form was demanded of me. I only wanted to know the dimensions. Luce was providing them. My parents supported him. The prospect of having everything solved was wildly attractive to me, too, and while I lay on the chaise I didn't ask myself where my feelings for the Object fit in. I only wanted it all to be over. I wanted to go home and forget it had ever happened. So I listened to Luce quietly and made no objections.

He explained the estrogen injections would induce my breasts to grow. "You won't be Raquel Welch, but you won't be Twiggy either." My facial hair would diminish. My voice would rise from tenor to alto. But when I asked if I would finally get my period, Dr. Luce was frank. "No. You won't. Ever. You won't be able to have a baby yourself, Callie. If you want to have a family, you'll have to adopt."

I received this news calmly. Having children wasn't something I thought much about at fourteen.

There was a knock on the door, and the receptionist stuck her head in. "Sorry, Dr. Luce. But could I bother you a minute?"

"That depends on Callie." He smiled at me. "You mind taking a little break? I'll be right back."

"I don't mind."

"Sit there a few minutes and see if any other questions occur to you." He left the room.

While he was gone, I didn't think of any other questions. I sat in my chair, not thinking anything at all. My mind was curiously blank. It was the blankness of obedience. With the unerring instinct of children, I had surmised what my parents wanted from me. They wanted me to stay the way I was. And this was what Dr. Luce now promised.

I was brought out of my abstracted state by a salmon-colored cloud passing low in the sky. I got up and went to the window to look out at the river. I pressed my cheek against the glass to see as far south as possible, where the skyscrapers rose. I told myself that I would live in New York when I grew up. "This is the city for me," I said. I had begun to cry again. I tried to stop. Dabbing at my eyes, I wandered around the office and finally found myself in front of one of the Mughal miniatures. In the small, ebony frame, two tiny figures were making love. Despite the exertion implied by their activity, their faces looked peaceful. Their expressions showed neither strain nor ecstasy. But of course the faces weren't the focal point. The geometry of the lovers' bodies, the graceful calligraphy of their limbs led the eye straight to the fact of their genitalia. The woman's pubic hair was like a patch of evergreen against white snow, the man's member like a redwood sprouting from it. I looked. I looked once again to see how other people were made. As I looked, I didn't take sides. I understood both the urgency of the man and the pleasure of the woman. My mind was no longer blank. It was filling with a dark knowledge.

I swung around. I wheeled and looked at Dr. Luce's desk. A file sat open there. He had left it when he hurried off.

PRELIMINARY STUDY:
GENETIC XY (MALE) RAISED AS FEMALE

The following illustrative case indicates

that there is no preordained correspondence between genetic and genital structure, or between masculine or feminine
behavior and chromosomal status.

SUBJECT: Calliope Stephanides
INTERVIEWER: Peter Luce, M.D.

INTRODUCTORY DATA: The patient is
fourteen years old. She has lived as a
female all her life. At birth, somatic appearance was of a penis so small as to
appear to be a clitoris. The subject's XY
karyotype was not discovered until puberty, when she began to virilize. The
girl's parents at first refused to believe
the doctor who delivered the news
and subsequently asked for two other
opinions before coming to the Gender
Identity Clinic and New York Hospital
Clinic.
    During examination, undescended
testes could be palpated. The "penis"
was slightly hypospadiac, with the urethra opening on the underside. The girl
has always sat to urinate like other girls.
Blood tests confirmed an XY chromosomal status. In addition, blood tests revealed that the subject was suffering
from 5-alpha-reductase deficiency syndrome. An exploratory laparotomy was
not performed.

A family photograph (see case file) shows her at age twelve. She appears to be a happy, healthy girl with no visible signs of tomboyishness, despite her XY karyotype.

FIRST IMPRESSION: The subject's facial expression, though somewhat stern at times, is overall pleasant and receptive, with frequent smiling. The subject often casts her eyes downward in a modest or coy manner. She is feminine in her movements and gestures, and the slight gracelessness of her walk is in keeping with females of her generation. Though due to her height some people may find the subject's gender at first glance somewhat indeterminate, any prolonged observation would result in a decision that she was indeed a girl. Her voice, in fact, has a soft, breathy quality. She inclines her head to listen when another person speaks and does not hold forth or assert her opinions in a bullying manner characteristic of males. She often makes humorous remarks.

FAMILY: The girl's parents are fairly typical Midwesterners of the World War II generation. The father identifies himself as a Republican. The mother is a friendly, intelligent, and caring person, perhaps slightly prone to depression or neurosis. She accedes to the subservient wifely role typical of women of her generation. The father only came to the Clinic twice, citing business obligations, but from those two meetings it is apparent that he is a dominating presence, a "self-made" man and former naval officer. In addition, the subject has been raised in the Greek Orthodox tradition, with its strongly sex-defined roles. In general the parents seem assimilationist and very "all-American" in their outlook, but the presence of this deeper ethnic identity should not be overlooked.

SEXUAL FUNCTION: The subject reports engaging in childhood sexual play with other children, in every case of which she acted as the feminine partner, usually pulling up her dress and letting a boy simulate coition atop her. She experienced pleasurable erotosexual sensations by positioning herself by the water jets of a neighbor's swimming pool. She masturbated frequently from a young age.

The subject has had no serious boyfriends, but this may be due to her attending an all-girls school or from a feeling of shame about her body. The subject is aware of the abnormal appearance of her genitalia and has gone to great lengths in the locker room and

other communal dressing areas to avoid being seen naked. Nevertheless, she reports having had sexual intercourse, one time only, with the brother of her best friend, an experience she found painful but which was successful from the point of view of teenage romantic exploration. INTERVIEW: The subject spoke in rapid bursts, clearly and articulately but with the occasional breathlessness associated with anxiety. Speech patterning and characteristics appeared to be feminine in terms of oscillation of pitch and direct eye contact. She expresses sexual interest in males exclusively.
CONCLUSION: In speech, mannerisms, and dress, the subject manifests a feminine gender identity and role, despite a contrary chromosomal status.

It is clear by this that sex of rearing, rather than genetic determinants, plays a greater role in the establishment of gender identity.

As the girl's gender identity was firmly established as female at the time her condition was discovered, a decision to implement feminizing surgery along with corresponding hormonal treatments seems correct. To leave the genitals as they are today would expose her to all manner of humiliation. Though it is possible that the surgery may result in partial or total loss of erotosexual sensation, sexual pleasure is only one factor in a happy life. The ability to marry and pass as a normal woman in society are also important goals, both of which will not be possible without feminizing surgery and hormone treatment. Also, it is hoped that new methods of surgery will minimize the effects of erotosexual dysfunction brought about by surgeries in the past, when feminizing surgery was in its infancy.

That evening, when my mother and I got back to the hotel, Milton had a surprise. Tickets to a Broadway musical. I acted excited but later, after dinner, crawled into my parents' bed, claiming I was too tired to go.

"Too tired?" Milton said. "What do you mean you're too tired?"

"That's okay, honey," said Tessie. "You don't have to go."

"Supposed to be a good show, Cal."

"Is Ethel Merman in it?" I asked.

"No, smart-ass," Milton said, smiling. "Ethel Merman is not in it. She's not on Broadway right now. So we're seeing something with Carol Channing. She's pretty good, too. Why don't you come along?"

"No thanks," I said.

"Okay, then. You're missing out."

They started to go. "Bye, honey," my mother said.

Suddenly I jumped out of bed and ran to Tessie, hugging her.

"What's this for?" she asked.

My eyes brimmed with tears. Tessie took them to be tears of relief at everything we'd been through. In the narrow entryway carved from a former suite, cockeyed, dim, the two of us stood hugging and crying.

When they were gone, I got my suitcase from the closet. Then, looking at the turquoise flowers, I exchanged it for my father's suitcase, a gray Samsonite. I left my skirts and my Fair Isle sweater in the dresser drawers. I packed only the darker garments, a blue crew neck, the alligator shirts, and my corduroys. The brassiere I abandoned, too. For the time being, I held on to my socks and panties, and I tossed in my toiletry case entire. When I was finished, I searched in Milton's garment bag for the cash he'd hidden there. The wad was fairly large and came to nearly three hundred dollars.

It wasn't all Dr. Luce's fault. I had lied to him about many things. His decision was based on false data. But he had been false in turn.

On a piece of stationery, I left a note for my parents.

Dear Mom and Dad,

I know you're only trying to do what's best for me, but I don't think anyone knows for sure what's best. I love you and don't want to be a problem, so I've decided to go away. I know you'll say I'm not a problem, but I know I am. If you want to know why I'm doing this, you should ask Dr. Luce, <u>who is a big liar</u>! I am <u>not</u> a girl. I'm a <u>boy</u>. That's what I found out today. So I'm going where no one knows me. Everyone in Grosse Pointe will talk when they find out.

Sorry I took your money, Dad, but I promise to pay you back someday, with interest.

Please don't worry about me. I will be <u>ALL RIGHT</u>!

Despite its content, I signed this declaration to my parents: "Callie."

It was the last time I was ever their daughter.

Go West, Young Man

❧

Once again, in Berlin, a Stephanides lives among the Turks. I feel comfortable here in Schöneberg. The Turkish shops along Hauptstrasse are like those my father used to take me to. The food is the same, the dried figs, the halvah, the stuffed grape leaves. The faces are the same, too, seamed, dark-eyed, significantly boned. Despite family history, I feel drawn to Turkey. I'd like to work in the embassy in Istanbul. I've put in a request to be transferred there. It would bring me full circle.

Until that happens, I do my part this way. I watch the bread baker in the döner restaurant downstairs. He bakes bread in a stone oven like those they used to have in Smyrna. He uses a long-handled spatula to shift and retrieve the bread. All day long he works, fourteen, sixteen hours, with unflagging concentration, his sandals leaving prints in the flour dust on the floor. An artist of bread baking. Stephanides, an American, grandchild of Greeks, admires this Turkish immigrant to Germany, this

Gastarbeiter, as he bakes bread on Haupt-strasse here in the year 2001. We're all made up of many parts, other halves. Not just me.

⚜

The bell on the door of Ed's Barbershop in the Scranton bus station merrily rang. Ed, who had been reading the newspaper, lowered it to greet his next customer.

There was a pause. And then Ed said, "What happened? You lose a bet?"

Standing inside the door but looking as though he might flee back out of it was a teenage kid, tall, stringy, and an odd mix if ever Ed saw one. His hair was a hippie's and came down past his shoulders. But he was wearing a dark suit. The jacket was baggy and the trousers were too short, riding high above his chunky tan, square-toed shoes. Even from across the shop Ed detected a musty, thrift-store smell. Yet the kid's suitcase was big and gray, a business-man's.

"I'm just tired of the style," the kid answered.

"You and me both," said Ed the barber.

He directed me to a chair. I — the easily rechristened Cal Stephanides, teen run-away — set my suitcase down and hung my jacket on the rack. I walked across the room, concentrating as I did on walking like a boy. Like a stroke victim, I was having to relearn all the simple motor skills. As far as walking went, this wasn't too difficult. The time when Baker & Inglis girls had balanced books on their heads was long gone. The slight gracelessness of my walk, which Dr. Luce had commented on, predisposed me to join the graceless sex. My skeleton was a male's, with its higher center of gravity. It promoted a tidy, forward thrust. It was my knees that gave me trouble. I had a tendency to walk knock-kneed, which made my hips sway and my back end twitch. I tried to keep my pelvis steady now. To walk like a boy you let your shoulders sway, not your hips. And you kept your feet farther apart. All this I had learned in a day and a half on the road.

I climbed into the chair, glad to stop moving. Ed the barber tied a paper bib around my neck. Next he draped an apron over me. All the while he was taking my measure and shaking his head. "I never understood what it was with you young people and the long hair. Nearly ruined my business. I get mostly retired fellas in here. Guys who come in my shop for a haircut, they don't *have* any hair." He chuckled, but only briefly. "Okay, so nowadays the hairstyles are a little bit shorter. I think, good, maybe I can make a living. But no. Now everyone wants to go unisex. They want to be *shampooed*." He leaned toward me, suspicious. "You don't want a shampoo, do you?"

"Just a haircut."

He nodded, satisfied. "How do you want it?"

"Short," I ventured.

"Short short?" he asked.

"Short," I said, "but not too short."

"Okay. Short but not too short. Good idea. See how the other half lives."

I froze, thinking he meant something by this. But he was only joking.

As for himself, Ed kept a neat head. What hair he had was slicked back. He had a brutal, pugnacious face. His nostrils were dark and fiery as he labored around me, pumping up the chair and stropping his razor.

"Your father let you keep your hair like this?"

"Up until now."

"So the old man is finally straightening you out. Listen, you won't regret it. Women don't want a guy looks like a girl. Don't believe what they tell you, they want a sensitive male. Bullshit!"

The swearing, the straight razors, the shaving brushes, all these were my welcome to the masculine world. The barber had the football game on the TV. The calendar showed a vodka bottle and a pretty girl in a white fur bikini. I planted my feet on the waffle iron of the footrest while he swiveled me back and forth before the flashing mirrors.

"Holy mackerel, when's the last time you had a haircut anyway?"

"Remember the moon landing?"

"Yeah. That's about right."

He turned me to face the mirror. And there she was, for the last time, in the silvered glass: Calliope. She still wasn't gone yet. She was like a captive spirit, peeking out.

Ed the barber put a comb in my long hair. He lifted it experimentally, making snipping sounds with his scissors. The blades weren't touching my hair. The snipping was only a kind of mental barbering, a limbering up. This gave me time for second thoughts. What was I doing? What if Dr. Luce was right? What if that girl in the mirror really *was* me? How did I think I could defect to the other side so easily? What did I know about boys, about men? I didn't even like them that much.

"This is like taking down a tree," opined Ed. "First you gotta go in and lop off the branches. Then you chop down the trunk."

I closed my eyes. I refused to return Calliope's gaze any longer. I gripped the armrests and waited for the barber to do his work. But in the next second the scissors clinked onto the shelf. With a buzz, the electric clippers switched on. They circled my head like bees. Again Ed the barber lifted my hair with his comb and I heard the buzzer dive in toward my head. "Here we go," he said.

My eyes were still closed. But I knew there was no going back now. The clippers raked across my scalp. I held firm. Hair fell away in strips.

"I should charge you extra," said Ed.

Now I did open my eyes, alarmed about the cost. "How much is it?"

"Don't worry. Same price. This is my patriotic deed today. I'm making the world safe for democracy."

My grandparents had fled their home because of a war. Now, some fifty-two years later, I was fleeing myself. I felt that I was saving myself just as definitively. I was fleeing without much money in my pocket and under the alias of my new gender. A ship didn't carry me across the ocean; instead, a series of cars conveyed me across a continent. I was becoming a new person, too, just like Lefty and Desdemona, and I didn't know what would happen to me in this new world to which I'd come.

I was also scared. I had never been out on my own before. I didn't know how the world operated or how much things cost. From the Lochmoor Hotel I had taken a cab to the bus terminal, not knowing the way. At Port Authority I wandered past the tie shops and fast-food stalls, looking for the ticket booths. When I found them I bought a ticket for a night bus to Chicago, paying the fare as far as Scranton, Pennsylvania, which was as much as I thought I could afford. The bums and druggies occupying the scoop benches looked me over, sometimes hissing or smacking their lips. They scared me, too. I nearly gave up the idea of running away. If I hurried, I could make it back to the hotel before Milton and Tessie returned from seeing Carol Channing. I sat in the waiting area, considering this, the edge of the Samsonite clamped between my knees as though any minute someone might try to snatch it away. I played out scenes in my head where I declared my intention of living as a boy and my parents, at first protesting but then breaking down, accepted me. A policeman passed by. When he was gone I went to sit next to a middle-aged woman, hoping to be taken for her daughter. Over the loudspeaker a voice announced that my bus was boarding. I looked up at the other passengers, the poor traveling by night. There was an aging cowboy carrying a duffel bag and a souvenir Louis Armstrong statuette; there were two Sri Lankan Catholic priests; there were no less than three overweight mothers loaded down with children and bedding, and a little man who turned out to be a horse jockey, with cigarette wrinkles and brown teeth. They lined up to board the bus while the scene in my head began to go off on its own, to stop taking my directorial notes. Now Milton was shaking his head no, and Dr. Luce was putting on a surgical mask, and my schoolmates back in Grosse Pointe were pointing at me and laughing, their faces lit with malicious joy.

In a trance of fear, dazed yet trembling, I proceeded onto the dark bus. For protection I took a seat next to the middle-aged lady. The other passengers, accustomed to these night journeys, were already taking out thermoses and unwrapping sandwiches. The smell of fried chicken began to waft from the back seats. I was suddenly very hungry. I wished that I were back at the hotel, ordering room service. I would have to get new clothes soon. I needed to look older and less like prey. I had to start dressing like a boy. The bus pulled out of Port Authority and I watched, terrified at what I was doing but unable to stop myself, as we made our way out of the city and through the long yellow-lit dizzy tunnel that led to New Jersey. Going underground, through the rock, with the filthy river bottom above us, and fish swimming in the black water on the other side of the curving tiles.

At a Salvation Army outlet in Scranton, not far from the bus station, I went looking for a suit. I pretended I was shopping for my brother, though no one asked any questions. Male sizes baffled me. I held the jackets discreetly against me to see what might fit. Finally I found a suit roughly my size. It was sturdy-looking and all-weather. The label inside said "Durenmatt's Men's Clothiers, Pittsburgh." I took off my Papagallo. Checking to see if anyone was watching, I tried the jacket on. I didn't feel what a boy would feel. It wasn't like putting on your father's jacket and becoming a man. It was like being cold and having your date give you his jacket to wear. As it settled on my shoulders, the jacket felt big, warm, comforting, alien. (And who was my date in this case? The football captain? No. My steady was the World War II vet, dead of heart disease. My guy was the Elks Lodge member who had moved to Texas.)

The suit was only part of my new identity. It was the haircut that mattered most. Now, in the barbershop, Ed was going at me with a whisk brush. The bristles cast a powder in the air and I closed my eyes. I felt myself being wheeled around again and the barber said, "Okay, that's it."

I opened my eyes. And in the mirror I didn't see myself. Not the Mona Lisa with the enigmatic smile any longer. Not the shy girl with the tangled black hair in her face, but instead her fraternal twin brother. With the screen of my hair removed, the recent changes in my face were far more evident. My jaw looked squarer, broader, my neck thicker, with a bulge of Adam's apple in the center. It was unquestionably a male face, but the feelings inside that boy were still a girl's. To cut off your hair after a breakup was a feminine reaction. It was a way to start over, to renounce vanity, to spite love. I knew that I would never see the Object again. Despite bigger problems, greater worries, it was heartbreak that seized me when I first saw my male face in the mirror. I thought: it's over. By cutting off my hair I was punishing myself for loving someone so much. I was trying to be stronger.

By the time I came out of Ed's Barber-shop, I was a new creation. The other people passing through the bus station, to the extent they noticed me at all, took me for a student at a nearby boarding school. A prep school kid, a touch arty, wearing an old man's suit and no doubt reading Camus or Kerouac. There was a kind of beatnik quality to the Durenmatt's suit. The trousers had a sharkskin sheen. Because of my height I could pass for older than I was, seventeen, maybe eighteen. Under the suit was a crew neck sweater, under the sweater was an alligator shirt, two protective layers of parental money next to my skin, plus the golden Wallabees on my feet. If anyone noticed me, they thought I was playing dress-up, as teenagers do.

Inside these clothes my heart was still beating like mad. I didn't know what to do next. Suddenly I had to pay attention to things I'd never paid any attention to. To bus schedules and bus fares, to budgeting money, to *worrying* about money, to scanning a menu for the absolutely cheapest thing that would fill me up, which that day in Scranton turned out to be chili. I ate a bowl of it, stirring in multiple packets of crackers, and looked over the bus routes. The best thing to do, it being fall, was to head south or west for the winter, and because I didn't want to go south I decided to go west. To California. Why not? I checked to see what the fare would be. As I feared, it was too much.

Throughout the morning it had drizzled on and off, but now the clouds were breaking up. Across the desperate eatery, through the rain-greased windows and beyond the access road that bounded a strip of sloping littered grass, ran the Interstate.

I watched the traffic whizzing along, feeling less hungry now but still lonely and scared. The waitress came over and asked if I wanted coffee. Though I had never had a cup of coffee before, I said yes. After she served it to me, I doctored it with two packets of creamer and four of sugar. When it tasted roughly like coffee ice cream, I drank it.

From the terminal buses were steadily pulling out, leaving gassy trails. Down on the highway cars sped along. I wanted to take a shower. I wanted to lie down in clean sheets and go to sleep. I could get a motel room for $9.95, but I wanted to be farther away before I did that. I sat in the booth for a long time. I couldn't see my way to the next step. Finally, an idea occurred to me. Paying my bill, I left the bus terminal. I crossed the access road and shuffled down the slope. I set down my suitcase on the shoulder and, stepping out to face the oncoming traffic, tentatively stuck out my thumb.

My parents had always cautioned me against hitchhiking. Sometimes Milton pointed out stories in the newspaper detailing the gruesome ends of coeds who had made that mistake. My thumb was not very high in the air. Half of me was against the idea. Cars sped past. No one stopped. My reluctant thumb was shaking.

I had miscalculated with Luce. I thought that after talking to me he would decide that I was normal and leave me alone. But I was beginning to understand something about normality. Normality wasn't normal. It couldn't be. If normality were normal, everybody could leave it alone. They could sit back and let normality manifest itself. But people — and especially doctors — had doubts about normality. They weren't sure normality was up to the job. And so they felt inclined to give it a boost.

As for my parents, I held them blameless. They were only trying to save me from humiliation, lovelessness, even death. I learned later that Dr. Luce had emphasized the medical risk in letting my condition go untreated. The "gonadal tissue," as he referred to my undescended testes, often became cancerous in later years. (I'm forty-one now, however, and so far nothing has happened.)

A semi appeared around the bend, blowing black smoke from an upright exhaust pipe. In the window of the red cab the driver's head was bouncing like the head of a doll on a spring. His face turned in my direction, and as the huge truck roared past, he engaged the brakes. The rear wheels of the cab smoked a little, squealed, and then twenty yards ahead of me the truck was waiting.

Lifting my suitcase, with a wild excitement, I ran up to the truck. But when I reached it I stopped. The door looked so high up. The huge vehicle sat rumbling, shuddering. I couldn't see the driver from my vantage point and stood paralyzed with indecision. Then suddenly the trucker's face appeared in the window, startling me. He opened the door.

"You coming up or what?"

"Coming," I said.

The cab was not clean. He had been traveling for some time and there were food containers and bottles strewn around.

"Your job is to keep me awake," the trucker said.

When I didn't respond right away he looked over at me. His eyes were red. Red, too, were the Fu Manchu mustache and the long sideburns. "Just keep talking," he said.

"What do you want to talk about?"

"Fuck-all if I know!" he shouted angrily. But just as suddenly: "Indians! You know anything about Indians?"

"American Indians?"

"Yeah. I pick up a lot of Injuns when I drive out west. Those are some of the craziest motherfuckers I ever heard. They got all kinds of theories and shit."

"Like what?"

"Like some of 'em say they didn't come

over the Bering land bridge. Are you familiar with the Bering land bridge? That's up there in Alaska. Called the Bering Strait now. It's water. Little sliver of water between Alaska and Russia. Long time ago, though, it was land, and that's where the Indians came over from. From like China or Mongolia. Indians are really Orientals."

"I didn't know that," I said. I was feeling less scared now than before. The trucker was apparently taking me at face value.

"But some of these Indians I pick up, they say their people didn't come over the land bridge. They say they come from a lost island, like Atlantis."

"Join the club."

"You know what else they say?"

"What?"

"They say it was Indians wrote the *Constitution*. The U.S. *Constitution!*"

As it turned out, he did most of the talking. I said very little. But my presence was enough to keep him awake. Talking about Indians reminded him about meteors; there was a meteor in Montana that the Indians considered sacred, and soon he was telling me about the celestial sights a trucker's life acquainted a person with, the shooting stars and comets and green rays. "You ever seen a green ray?" he asked me.

"No."

"They say you can't take a picture of a

green ray, but I got one. I always keep a camera in the cab in case I come across some mind-blowing shit like that. And one time I saw this green ray and I grabbed my camera and I got it. I've got the picture at home."

"What is a green ray?"

"It's the color the sun makes when it rises and sets. For two seconds. You can see it best in the mountains."

He took me as far as Ohio and let me off in front of a motel. I thanked him for the ride and carried my suitcase up to the office. Here the suit also came in useful. Plus the expensive luggage. I didn't look like a runaway. The motel clerk may have had doubts about my age, but I laid money on the counter right away, and the key was forthcoming.

After Ohio came Indiana, Illinois, Iowa, and Nebraska. I rode in station wagons, sport cars, rented vans. Single women never picked me up, only men, or men with women. A pair of Dutch tourists stopped for me, complaining about the frigidity of American beer, and sometimes I got rides from couples who were fighting and tired of each other. In every case, people took me for the teenage boy I was every minute more conclusively becoming. Sophie Sassoon wasn't around to wax my mustache, so it began to fill in, a smudge above my upper lip. My voice continued to deepen. Every jolt in the road dropped my Adam's apple another notch in my neck.

If people asked, I told them I was on my way to California for my freshman year at college. I didn't know much about the world, but I knew something about colleges, or at least about homework, and so claimed that I was going to Stanford to live in a dorm. To be honest, my drivers weren't too suspicious. They didn't care one way or another. They had their own agendas. They were bored, or lonely, and wanted someone to talk to.

Like a convert to a new religion, I overdid it at first. Somewhere near Gary, Indiana, I adopted a swagger. I rarely smiled. My expression throughout Illinois was the Clint Eastwood squint. It was all a bluff, but so was it on most men. We were all walking around squinting at each other. My swagger wasn't that different from what lots of adolescent boys put on, trying to be manly. For that reason it was convincing. Its very falseness made it credible. Now and then I fell out of character. Feeling something stuck to the bottom of my shoe, I kicked up my heel and looked back over my shoulder to see what it was, rather than crossing my leg in front of me and twisting up my shoe. I picked correct change from my open palm instead of my trouser pocket. Such slips made me panic, but needlessly. No one noticed. I was aided by that: as a rule people don't notice much.

It would be a lie to tell you I understood everything I was feeling. You don't, at fourteen. An instinct for self-preservation told me to run, and I was running. Dread pursued me. I missed my parents. I felt guilty for making them worry. Dr. Luce's report haunted me. At night, in various motels, I cried myself to sleep. Running away didn't make me feel any less of a monster. I saw ahead of me only humiliation and rejection, and I wept for my life.

But in the mornings I woke up feeling better. I left my motel room and went out to stand in the air of the world. I was young, and, despite dread, full of animal spirits; it was impossible for me to take a dark view too long. Somehow I was able to forget about myself for long stretches. I ate doughnuts for breakfast. I kept drinking very sweet, milky coffee. To lift my mood, I did things my parents wouldn't have let me do, ordering two and sometimes three desserts and never eating salads. I was free now to let my teeth rot or to put my feet up on the backs of seats. Sometimes while I was hitching I saw other runaways. Under overpasses or in runoff drains they congregated, smoking cigarettes, the hoods of their sweatshirts pulled up. They were tougher than I was, scroungier. I steered clear of their packs. They were from broken homes, had been physically abused and now abused others. I wasn't anything like them. I had brought my family's upward mobility out onto the road. I joined no packs but went my way alone.

And now, amid the prairie, appears the recreation vehicle belonging to Myron and Sylvia Bresnick, of Pelham, New York. Like a modern-day covered wagon, it rolls out of the waving grasslands and stops. A door opens, like the door of a house, and standing inside is a perky woman in her late sixties.

"I think we've got room for you," she says.

A moment before, I had been on Route 80 in western Iowa. But now as I carry my suitcase onto this ship of the prairie, I am suddenly in the Bresnicks' living room. Framed photographs of their children hang on the walls, along with Chagall prints. The history of Winston Churchill that Myron is working his way through at night at the hookups sits on the coffee table.

Myron is a retired parts salesman, Sylvia a former social worker. In profile she resembles a cute Punchinello, her cheeks expressive, painted, and the nose carved for comic effect. Myron works his lips around his cigar, foul and intimate with his own juices.

While Myron drives, Sylvia gives me a tour of the beds, the shower, the living area. What school do I go to? What do I want to be? She peppers me with questions.

Myron turns from the wheel and booms, "Stanford! Good school!"

And it is right then that it happens. At some moment on Route 80 something clicks in my head and suddenly I feel I am getting the hang of it. Myron and Sylvia are treating me like a son. Under this collective delusion I become that, for a little while at least. I become male-identified.

But something daughterly must cling to me, too. For soon Sylvia has taken me aside to complain about her husband. "I know it's tacky. This whole RV thing. You should see the people we meet in these camps. They call it the 'RV lifestyle.' Oh, they're nice enough — but boring. I miss going to cultural events. Myron says he spent his life traveling around the country too busy to see it. So he's doing it over again — slowly. And guess who gets dragged along?"

"My heart?" Myron is calling to her. "Could you bring your husband an iced tea, please? He's parched."

They let me off in Nebraska. I counted my money and found I had two hundred and thirty dollars left. I found a cheap room in a kind of boardinghouse and stayed the night. I was still too scared to hitchhike in the dark.

On the road there was time for minor adjustments. Many of the socks I'd brought were the wrong color — pink, white, or covered with whales. Also my underpants weren't the right kind. At a Woolworth's in Nebraska City I bought a three-pack of boxer shorts. As a girl, I had worn size large. As a boy, medium. I trolled through the toiletries section, too. Instead of row upon row of beauty products there was only a single rack of hygienic essentials. The explosion in men's cosmetics hadn't happened yet. There were no pampering unguents disguised by rugged names. No Heavy-Duty Skin Repair. No Anti-Burn Shave Gel. I selected deodorant, disposable razors, and shaving cream. The colorful cologne bottles attracted me, but my experience with after-shaves was not favorable. Cologne made me think of voice coaches, of maître d's, of old men and their unwanted embraces. I picked out a man's wallet, too. At the register, I couldn't look the cashier in the face, as embarrassed as if I were buying condoms. The cashier wasn't much older than I was, with blond, feathered hair. That heartland look.

At restaurants I began to use the men's rooms. This was perhaps the hardest adjustment. I was scandalized by the filth of men's rooms, the rank smells and pig sounds, the grunting and huffing from the stalls. Urine was forever puddled on the floors. Scraps of soiled toilet paper adhered to the commodes. When you entered a stall, more often than not a plumbing emergency greeted you, a brown tide, a soup of dead frogs. To think that a toilet stall had once been a haven for me! That was all over now. I could see at once that men's rooms, unlike the ladies', provided no comfort. Often there wasn't even a mirror, or any hand soap. And while the closeted, flatulent men showed no shame, at the urinals men acted nervous. They looked straight ahead like horses with blinders.

I understood at those times what I was leaving behind: the solidarity of a shared biology. Women know what it means to have a body. They understand its difficulties and frailties, its glories and pleasures. Men think their bodies are theirs alone. They tend them in private, even in public.

A word on penises. What was Cal's official position on penises? Among them, surrounded by them, his feelings were the same as they had been as a girl: by equal measures fascinated and horrified. Penises had never really done that much for me. My girlfriends and I had a comical opinion of them. We hid our guilty interest by giggling or pretending disgust. Like every schoolgirl on a field trip, I'd had my blushing moments among the Roman antiquities. I'd stolen peeks when the teacher's back was turned. It's our first art lesson as kids, isn't it? The nudes are dressed. They're dressed in high-mindedness. Being six years older, my brother had never shared a bathtub with me. The glimpses of his genitals I'd had over the years were fleeting. I'd studiously looked away. Even Jerome had penetrated me without my seeing what went on. Anything so long concealed couldn't fail to intrigue me. But the glimpses those men's rooms afforded were on the whole disappointing. The proud phallus was nowhere in evidence, only the feed bag, the dry tuber, the snail that had lost its shell.

And I was scared to death of being caught looking. Despite my suit, my haircut, and my height, every time I went into a men's room a shout rang out in my head: "You're in the men's!" But the men's was where I was supposed to be. Nobody said a word. Nobody objected to my presence. And so I searched for a stall that looked halfway clean. I had to sit to urinate. Still do.

At night, on the fungal carpets of motel rooms, I did exercises, push-ups and sit-ups. Wearing nothing but my new boxers, I examined my physique in the mirror. Not long ago I'd fretted over my failure to develop. That worry was gone now. I didn't have to live up to that standard anymore. The impossible demands had been removed and I felt a vast relief. But there were also moments of dislocation, staring at my changing body. Sometimes it didn't feel like my own. It was hard, white, bony. Beautiful in its own way, I supposed, but Spartan. Not receptive or pliant at all. Contents under pressure, rather.

It was in those motel rooms that I learned about my new body, its specific instructions and contraindications. The Object and I had worked in the dark. She had never really explored my apparatus much. The Clinic had medicalized my genitals. During my time there they were numb or slightly tender from the constant examinations. My body had shut down in order to get through the ordeal. But traveling woke it up. Alone, with the door locked and the chain on, I experimented with myself. I put pillows between my legs. I lay on top of them. Half paying attention, while I watched Johnny Carson, my hand prospected. The anxiety I'd always felt about how I was made had kept me from exploring the way most kids did. So it was only now, lost to the world and everyone I knew, that I had the courage to try it out. I can't discount the importance of this. If I had doubts about my decision, if I sometimes thought about turning back, running back to my parents and the Clinic and giving in, what stopped me was this private ecstasy between my legs. I knew it would be taken from me. I don't want to overestimate the sexual. But it was a powerful force for me, especially at fourteen, with my nerves bright and jangling, ready to launch into a symphony at the slightest provocation. That was how Cal discovered himself, in voluptuous, liquid, sterile culmination, couchant upon two or three deformed pillows, with the shades drawn and the drained swimming pool outside and the cars passing, endlessly, all night.

Outside Nebraska City, a silver Nova hatchback pulled over. I ran up with my suitcase and opened the passenger door. At the wheel was a good-looking man in his early thirties. He wore a tweed coat and yellow V-neck sweater. His plaid shirt was open at the collar, but the wings were crisp with starch. The formality of his clothes contrasted with his relaxed manner. "Hello deh," he said, doing a Brooklyn accent.

"Thanks for stopping."

He lit a cigarette and introduced himself, extending his hand. "Ben Scheer."

"My name's Cal."

He didn't ask the usual questions about my origin and destination. Instead, as we drove off, he asked, "Where did you get that suit?"

"Salvation Army."

"Real nice."

"Really?" I said. And then reconsidered. "You're teasing."

"No, I'm not," said Scheer. "I like a suit somebody died in. It's very existential."

"What's that?"

"What's what?"

"Existential?"

He gave me a direct look. "An existentialist is someone who lives for the moment."

No one had ever talked to me like this before. I liked it. As we drove on through the yellow country, Scheer told me other interesting things. I learned about Ionesco and the Theater of the Absurd. Also about Andy Warhol and the Velvet Underground. It's hard to express the excitement such phrases instilled in a kid like me from the cultural sticks. The Charm Bracelets wanted to pretend they were from the East, and I guess I had picked up that urge, too.

"Did you ever live in New York?" I asked.

"Used to."

"I was just there. I want to live there someday."

"I lived there ten years."

"Why did you leave?"

Again the direct look. "I woke up one morning and realized, if I didn't, I'd be dead in a year."

This, too, seemed marvelous.

Scheer's face was handsome, pale, with an Asiatic cast to his gray eyes. His light brown frizzy hair was scrupulously brushed, and parted by fiat. After a while I noticed other niceties of his dress, the monogrammed cuff links, the Italian loafers. I liked him immediately. Scheer was the kind of man I thought I would like to be myself.

Suddenly, from the rear of the car there erupted a magnificent, weary, soul-emptying sigh.

"How ya doin', Franklin?" Scheer called.

On hearing his name, Franklin lifted his troubled, regal head from the recesses of the hatchback, and I saw the black-and-white markings of an English setter. Ancient, rheumy-eyed, he gave me the once-over and dropped back out of sight.

Scheer was meanwhile pulling off the highway. He had a breezy highway driving style, but when making any kind of maneuver he snapped into military action, pummeling the wheel with strong hands. He pulled into the parking lot of a convenience store. "Back in a minute."

Holding a cigarette at his hip like a riding crop, he walked with clipped steps into the store. While he was gone I looked around the car. It was immaculately clean, the floor mats freshly vacuumed. The glove box contained orderly maps and tapes of Mabel Mercer. Scheer reappeared with two full shopping bags.

"I think road drinks are in order," he said.

He had a twelve-pack carton of beer, two bottles of Blue Nun, and a bottle of Lancers rosé, in a faux clay bottle. He set all of these on the backseat.

This was part of being sophisticated, too. You drank cheap Liebfraumilch in plastic cups, calling it cocktails, and carved off hunks of Cheddar cheese with a Swiss Army knife. Scheer had assembled a nice hors d'oeuvre platter from meager sources. There were also olives. We headed back out across the no-man's-land, while Scheer directed me to open the wine and serve him snacks. I was now his page. He had me put in the Mabel Mercer tape and then enlightened me about her meticulous phrasing.

Suddenly he raised his voice. "Cops. Keep your glass down."

I quickly lowered my Blue Nun and we drove on, acting cool as the state trooper passed on our left.

By now Scheer was doing the cop's voice. "I know city slickers when I see 'em and them thar's two of the slickest of 'em all. I'd wager they're up to no good."

To all this I responded with laughter, happy to be in league against the world of hypocrites and rulemongers.

When it began to grow dark, Scheer chose a steak house. I was worried it might be too expensive, but he told me, "Dinner's on me tonight."

Inside, it was busy, a popular place, the only table open a small one near the bar.

To the waitress Scheer said, "I'll have a vodka martini, very dry, *two* olives, and my son here will have a beer."

The waitress looked at me.

"He got any ID?"

"Not on me," I said.

"Can't serve you, then."

"I was there at his birth. I can vouch for him," said Scheer.

"Sorry, no ID, no alcohol."

"Okay, then," said Scheer. "Changed my mind. I'll have a vodka martini, very dry, two olives, and a beer chaser."

Through her tight lips the waitress said,

"You gonna let your friend drink that beer I can't serve it to you."

"They're both for me," Scheer assured her. He deepened his voice a little, opened the tone a little, injecting it with an Eastern or Ivy League authority whose influence did not entirely dissipate even all the way out here in the steak house on the plains. The waitress, resentful, complied.

She walked off and Scheer leaned toward me. He did his hick voice again. "Nothing wrong with that gal that a good poke in the hay barn wouldn't fix. And you're just the stud for the job." He didn't seem drunk, but this crudeness was new; he was a little less precise in his movements now, his voice louder. "Yeah," said Scheer, "I think she's sweet on you. You and Mayella could be happy together." I was feeling the wine strongly, too, my head like a mirrored ball, flashing lights.

The waitress brought the drinks, setting them demonstratively on Scheer's side of the table. As soon as she disappeared, he pushed the beer toward me and said, "There you go."

"Thanks." I drank the beer in gulps, pushing it back across the table whenever the waitress passed by. It was fun to be sneaking it like this.

But I was not unobserved. A man at the bar was watching me. Wearing a Hawaiian shirt and sunglasses, he looked as though he disapproved. But then his face broke into a big, knowing smile. The smile made me uncomfortable and I looked away.

When we came out again, the sky was completely dark. Before leaving, Scheer opened the hatch of the Nova to get Franklin out. The old dog could no longer walk, and Scheer had to lift him bodily out of the car. "Let's go, Franks," Scheer said, gruffly affectionate, and with a lit cigarette between his teeth, angled up in a patrician manner not unlike that of Franklin Roosevelt himself, in Gucci loafers and side-vented, gold-hued tweed jacket, his strong polo player's legs braced under the weight, he carried the aged beast into the weeds.

Before going back to the highway, he stopped at a convenience store to get more beer.

We drove for another hour or so. Scheer consumed many beers; I worked my way through one or two. I was not at all sober and feeling sleepy. I leaned against my door, blearily looking out. A long white car came alongside us. The driver looked at me, smiling, but I was already falling asleep.

Sometime later, Scheer shook me awake. "I'm too wrecked to drive. I'm pulling over."

I said nothing to this.

"I'm going to find a motel. I'll get you a room, too. On me."

I didn't object. Soon I saw hazy motel lights. Scheer left the car and returned with my room key. He led me to my room, carrying my suitcase, and opened the door for me. I went to the bed and collapsed.

My head was spinning. I managed to pull down the bedspread and get at the pillows.

"You gonna sleep in your clothes?" Scheer asked as if amused.

I felt his hand on my back, rubbing it. "You shouldn't sleep in your clothes," he said. He started to undress me, but I roused myself. "Just let me sleep," I said.

Scheer bent closer. In a thick voice he said, "Your parents kick you out, Cal? Is that it?" He sounded suddenly very drunk, as if all the day's and night's drinking had finally hit him.

"I'm going to sleep," I said.

"Come on," whispered Scheer. "Let me take care of you."

I curled up protectively, keeping my eyes closed. Scheer nuzzled me, but when I didn't respond, he stopped. I heard him open the door and then close it behind him.

When I awoke again, it was early in the morning. Light was coming in the windows. And Scheer was right next to me.

He was hugging me clumsily, his eyes squeezed shut. "Just wanna sleep here," he said, slurring. "Just wanna sleep." My shirt had been unbuttoned. Scheer was wearing only his underwear. The television was on, and there were empty beers on it.

Scheer clutched me, pressing his face into mine, making sounds. I tolerated this, feeling obliged for some reason. But when his drunken attentions became more avid, more targeted, I pushed him off me. He didn't protest. He crumpled into a ball and quickly passed out.

I got up and went into the bathroom. For a long while I sat on the toilet lid, hugging my knees. When I peeked out again, Scheer was still sound asleep. There was no lock on the door, but I was desperate for a shower. I took a quick one, keeping the curtain open and my eyes on the door. Then I changed into a new shirt, put my suit back on, and let myself out of the room.

It was very early. No traffic was passing along the road. I walked away from the motel and sat on my Samsonite, waiting. Big open sky. A few birds in it. I was hungry again. My head hurt. I got out my wallet and counted my dwindling money. I contemplated calling home for the hundredth time. I started to cry but stopped myself. Then I heard a car coming. From the motel parking lot a white Lincoln Continental emerged. I put out my thumb. The car stopped alongside me and the power window slowly went down. At the wheel was the man from the restaurant the day before.

"Where you headed?"

"California."

That smile again. Like something bursting. "Well then, this is your lucky day. That's where I'm headed, too."

I hesitated only a moment. Then I opened the back door of the big car and slid my suitcase in. I didn't have, at that point, much choice in the matter.

Gender Dysphoria
in San Francisco

❧❧❧

His name was Bob Presto. He had soft, white, fat hands and a plump face and wore a white guayabera shot with gold threads. He was vain of his voice, had been a radio announcer for many years before getting into his present line of business. What that was he didn't specify. But its lucrative nature was evident in the white Continental with red leather seats and in Presto's gold watch and jeweled rings, his newscaster's hair. Despite these grown-man touches, there was much of the mama's boy to Presto. He had the body of a little fatty, though he was big, close to two hundred pounds. He reminded me of the Big Boy at the Elias Brothers' chain of restaurants, only older, coarsened and bloated by adult vices.

Our conversation began the usual way, Presto asking me about myself and I giving the standard lies.

"Where you off to in California?"

"College."

"What school?"

"Stanford."

"I'm impressed. I've got a brother-in-law went to Stanford. Big muckety-muck. Where is that again?"

"Stanford?"

"Yeah, what city?"

"I forget."

"You forget? I thought Stanford students were supposed to be smart. How are you going to get there if you don't know where it is?"

"I'm meeting my friend. He's got all the details and stuff."

"It's nice to have friends," Presto said. He turned and winked at me. I didn't know how to interpret this wink. I kept quiet, staring forward at the road ahead.

On the buffet-like front seat between us were many supplies, soft drink bottles and bags of chips and cookies. Presto offered me whatever I wanted. I was too hungry to refuse, and took a few cookies, trying not to wolf them down.

"I'll tell you," Presto said, "the older I get, the younger college kids look. If you asked me, I'd say you were still in high school. What year you in?"

"Freshman."

Again Presto's face broke into the candy-apple grin. "I wish I were in your shoes. College is the best time of life. I hope you're ready for all the girls."

A chuckle accompanied this, to which I was obliged to add one of my own. "I had a lot of girlfriends in college, Cal," Presto said. "I worked for the college radio station. I used to get all kinds of free records. And if I liked a girl, I used to dedicate songs to her." He gave me a sample of his style, crooning low: "This one goes out to Jennifer, queen of Anthro 101. I'd love to study your culture, baby."

Presto's jowly head bowed and his eyebrows rose in modest recognition of his vocal gifts. "Let me give you a little advice about women, Cal. Voice. Voice is a big turn-on for women. Never discount voice." Presto's was indeed deep, dimorphically masculine. The fat of his throat increased its resonance as he explained, "Take my ex-wife, for example. When we first met, I could say anything to her and she'd go bananas. We'd be fucking and I'd say 'English muffin' — and she'd come."

When I didn't reply, Presto said, "I'm not offending you, am I? You're not one of those Mormon kids on your mission, are you? In that suit of yours?"

"No."

"Good. You had me worried for a minute. Let's hear your voice again," Presto said. "Come on, give me your best shot."

"What do you want me to say?"

"Say 'English muffin.' "

"English muffin."

"I don't work in radio anymore, Cal. I am not a professional broadcaster. But my humble opinion is that you are not DJ material. What you've got is a thin tenor. If you want to get laid, you'd better learn to sing." He laughed, grinning at me. His eyes showed no merriment, however, but were hard, examining me closely. He drove one-handed, eating potato chips with the other.

"Your voice has an unusual quality, actually. It's hard to place."

It seemed best to keep quiet.

"How old are you, Cal?"

"I just told you."

"No, you didn't."

"I just turned eighteen."

"How old do you think I am?"

"I don't know. Sixty?"

"Okay, you can get out now. Sixty! I'm fifty-two, for Christ's sake."

"I was going to say fifty."

"It's all this weight." He was shaking his head. "I didn't look old until I gained all this weight. Skinny kid like you wouldn't know about that, would you? I thought you were a chick at first, when I saw you standing by the road. I didn't register the suit. I just saw your outline. And I thought, Jesus, what's a young chick like that doing hitchhiking?"

I was unable to meet Presto's gaze now. I was beginning to feel scared again and very uncomfortable.

"That's when I recognized you. I saw you before. At that steak house. You were with that queer." There was a pause. "I had him for a chicken hawk. Are you gay, Cal?"

"What?"

"You can tell me if you want. I'm not gay but I've got nothing against it."

"I'd like to get out now. Could you let me out?"

Presto let go of the wheel and held his palms up in the air. "I'm sorry. I apologize. No more third degree. I won't say another word."

"Just let me out."

"If that's what you want, okay. But it doesn't make sense. We're going the same way, Cal. I'll take you to San Francisco." He didn't slow down and I didn't ask him to. He was true to his word and from then on remained mostly quiet, humming along to the radio. Every hour he made a pit stop to relieve himself and to buy more economy-sized bottles of Pepsi, more chocolate chip cookies, more red licorice and corn chips. Back on the road, he tanked up. He tilted his head back while he chewed, wary about getting crumbs on his shirtfront. Soft drinks glugged down his throat. Our conversation remained general. We drove up through the Sierra, out of Nevada and into California. We got lunch at a drive-thru. Presto paid for the hamburgers and milk shakes and I decided he was all right, friendly enough, and not after anything physical from me.

"Time for my pills," he said after we had eaten. "Cal, can you hand me my pill bottles? They're in the glove compartment."

There were five or six different bottles. I handed them to Presto and he tried to read their labels, slanting his eyes. "Here," he said, "steer for a minute." I leaned over to take hold of the wheel, closer to Bob Presto than I wanted to be, while he struggled with the caps and shook out pills. "My liver's all fucked up. Because of this hepatitis I picked up in Thailand. Fucking country almost killed me." He held up a blue pill. "This is the one for the liver. I've got a blood thinner, too. And one for blood pressure. My blood's all fucked up. I'm not supposed to eat so much."

In this way we drove all day, reaching San Francisco in the evening. When I saw the city, pink and white, a wedding cake arrayed on hills, a new anxiety took hold of me. All the way across the country I had absorbed myself in reaching my destination. Now I was there and I didn't know what I would do or how I would survive.

"I'll drop you wherever you want," Presto said. "You got an address where you're staying, Cal? Your friend's place?"

"Anywhere's fine."

"I'll take you up to the Haight. That'll be a good place for you to get your bearings." We drove into the city and finally Bob Presto pulled his car over and I opened my door.

"Thanks for the ride," I said.

"Sure, sure," said Presto. He held out his hand. "And by the way, it's Palo Alto."

"What?"

"Stanford's in Palo Alto. You should get that straight if you want anyone to believe you're in college." He waited for me to speak. Then in a surprisingly tender voice, a professional trick, too, no doubt, but not without effect, Presto asked, "Listen, guy, you got any place to stay?"

"Don't worry about me."

"Can I ask you something, Cal? What are you, anyway?"

Without answering I got out of the car and opened the back door to get my suitcase. Presto turned around in his seat, a difficult maneuver for him. His voice remained soft, deep, fatherly. "Come on. I'm in the business. I might be able to help you out. You a tranny?"

"I'm going now."

"Don't get offended. I know all about pre-op and post-op and all that stuff."

"I don't know what you're talking about." I pulled my suitcase off the seat.

"Hey, not so fast. Here. At least take my number. I could use a kid like you. Whatever you are. You need some money, don't you? You need an easy way to make some good money, you give your old friend Bob Presto a call."

I took the number to get rid of him. Then I turned and walked off as though I knew where I was going.

"Watch out in the park at night," Presto called after me in his booming voice. "Lot of lowlifes in there."

My mother used to say that the umbilical cord attaching her to her children had never been completely cut. As soon as Dr. Philobosian had severed the cord of flesh, another, spiritual connection had grown up in its place. After I went missing, Tessie felt that this fanciful idea was truer than ever. In the nights, while she lay in bed waiting for the tranquilizers to take effect, she often put her hand to her navel, like a fisherman checking his line. It seemed to Tessie that she felt something. Faint vibrations reached her. From these she could tell that I was still alive, though far away, hungry, and possibly unwell. All this came in a kind of singing along the invisible cord, a singing such as whales do, crying out to one another in the deep.

For almost a week after I disappeared, my parents had remained at the Lochmoor Hotel, hoping I might return. Finally, the NYPD detective assigned to the case told them that the best thing to do was return home. "Your daughter might call. Or turn up there. Kids usually do. If we find her, we'll let you know. Believe me. The best thing to do is go home and stay by the phone." Reluctantly, my parents took this advice.

Before leaving, however, they had made an appointment with Dr. Luce. "A little knowledge is a dangerous thing," Dr. Luce told them, offering an explanation for my disappearance. "Callie may have stolen a look at her file while I was out of my office. But she didn't understand what she was reading."

"But what would make her run away?" Tessie asked. Her eyes were wide, imploring.

"She misconstrued the facts," Luce answered. "She oversimplified them."

"I'll be honest with you, Dr. Luce," said Milton. "Our daughter called you a liar in that note she left. I'd like an explanation why she might say something like that."

Luce smiled tolerantly. "She's fourteen. Distrustful of adults."

"Can we take a look at that file?"

"It won't help you to see the file. Gender identity is very complex. It's not a matter of sheer genetics. Neither is it a matter of purely environmental factors. Genes and environment come together at a critical moment. It's not di-factorial. It's tri-factorial."

"Let me get one thing straight," Milton interrupted. "Is it, or is it not, still your medical opinion that Callie should stay the way she is?"

"From the psychological assessment I was able to make during the brief time I treated Callie, I would say yes, my opinion is that she has a female gender identity."

Tessie's composure broke and she sounded frantic. "Why does she say she's a boy, then?"

"She never said that to me," said Luce. "That's a new piece of the puzzle."

"I want to see that file," demanded Milton.

"I'm afraid that's not possible. The file is for my own private research purposes. You're free to see Callie's blood work and the other test results."

Milton exploded then. Shouting, swearing at Dr. Luce. "I hold you responsible. You hear me? Our daughter isn't the kind to just run off like that. You must have done something to her. Scared her."

"Her situation scared her, Mr. Stephanides," said Luce. "And let me emphasize something to you." He rapped his knuckles against his desk. "It is of tantamount importance that you find her as soon as possible. The repercussions could be severe."

"What are you saying?"

"Depression. Dysphoria. She's in a very delicate psychological state."

"Tessie," Milton looked at his wife, "you want to see the file or should we get out of here and let this bastard go screw himself."

"I want to see the file." She was sniffling now. "And watch your language, please. Let's try to be cordial."

Finally, Luce had given in and let them see it. After they had read the file, he offered to reevaluate my case at a future time, and expressed hope that I would soon be found.

"I'd never take Callie back to him in a million years," my mother said as they left.

"I don't know what he did to upset Callie," said my father, "but he did something."

They returned to Middlesex in late September. The leaves were falling from the elms, robbing the street of shelter. The weather began to turn colder, and from her bed at night Tessie listened to the wind and the rustling leaves, wondering where I was sleeping and if I was safe. The tranquilizers didn't subdue her panic so much as displace it. Under their sedation Tessie withdrew into an inner core of herself, a kind of viewing platform from which she could observe her anxiety. The fear was a little less with her at those times. The pills made her mouth dry. They made her head feel as though it were wrapped in cotton, and turned the periphery of her vision starry. She was supposed to take only one pill at a time, but she often took two.

There was a place halfway between consciousness and unconsciousness where Tessie did her best thinking. During the day she busied herself with company — people were constantly stopping by the house with food, and she had to set out trays and clean up after them — but in the nights, approaching stupefaction, she had the courage to try to come to terms with the note I'd left behind.

It was impossible for my mother to think of me as anything but her daughter. Her thoughts went in the same circle again and again. With her eyes half-open, Tessie gazed out across the dark bedroom glinting and sparking in the corners, and saw before her all the items I had ever worn or possessed. They all seemed to be heaped at the foot of her bed — the beribboned socks, the dolls, the hair clips, the full set of Madeline books, the party dresses, the red Mary Janes, the jumpers, the Easy-Bake Oven, the hula hoop. These objects were the trail that led back to me. How could such a trail lead to a boy?

And yet now, apparently, it did. Tessie went back over the events of the last year and a half, looking for signs she might have missed. It wasn't so different from what any mother would do, confronted with a shocking revelation about her teenage daughter. If I had died of a drug overdose or joined a cult, my mother's thinking would have taken essentially the same form. The reappraisal was the same but the questions were different. Was that why I was so tall? Did it explain why I hadn't gotten my period? She thought about our waxing appointments at the Golden Fleece and my husky alto — everything, really: the way I never filled out dresses right, the way women's gloves no longer fit me. All the things Tessie had accepted as part of the awkward age suddenly seemed ominous to her. How could she not have known! She was my mother, she had given birth to me, she was closer to me than I was to myself. My pain was her pain, my joy her joy. But didn't Callie's face have a strange look sometimes? So intense, so . . . masculine. And no fat on her, nowhere at all, all bones, no hips. But it wasn't possible . . . and Dr. Luce had said that Callie was a . . . and why hadn't he mentioned anything about chromosomes . . . and how could it be true? So ran my mother's thoughts, as her mind darkened and the glinting stopped. And after she had thought all these things, Tessie thought about the Object, about my close friendship with the Object. She remembered that day when the girl had died during the play, recalled rushing backstage to find me hugging the Object, comforting her, stroking her hair, and the wild look on my face, not really sadness at all . . .

From this last thought Tessie turned back.

Milton, on the other hand, didn't waste time reevaluating the evidence. On hotel stationery Callie had proclaimed, "I am *not* a girl." But Callie was just a kid. What did she know? Kids said all kinds of crazy things. My father didn't understand what had made me flee my surgery. He couldn't fathom why I wouldn't want to be fixed, cured. And he was certain that speculating about my reasons for running away was beside the point. First they had to find me. They had to get me back safe and sound. They could deal with the medical situation later.

Milton now dedicated himself to that

end. He spent much of every day on the phone, calling police departments across the country. He pestered the detective in New York, asking if there was any progress in my case. At the public library he consulted telephone books, writing down the numbers and addresses of police departments and runaway shelters, and then he methodically went down this list, calling every number and asking if anyone had seen someone who fit my description. He sent my photograph to these police stations and he sent a memo to his franchise operators, asking them to post my picture at every Hercules restaurant. Long before my naked body appeared in medical textbooks, my face appeared on bulletin boards and in windows across the nation. The police station in San Francisco received one of the photographs, but there was little chance of my being recognized by it now. Like a real outlaw, I had already changed my appearance. And biology was perfecting my disguise day by day.

Middlesex began to fill up with friends and relatives again. Aunt Zo and our cousins came over to give my parents moral support. Peter Tatakis closed his chiropractic office early one day and drove in from Birmingham to have dinner with Milt and Tessie. Jimmy and Phyllis Fioretos brought *koulouria* and ice cream.

It was as if the Cyprus invasion had never happened. The women congregated in the kitchen, preparing food, while the men sat in the living room, conversing in low tones. Milton got the dusty bottles from the liquor cabinet. He removed the bottle of Crown Royal from its purple velvet sack and set it out for the guests. Our old backgammon set came out from under a stack of board games, and a few of the older women began to count their worry beads. Everyone knew that I had run away but no one knew why. Privately, they said to each other, "Do you think she's pregnant?" And, "Did Callie have a boyfriend?" And, "She always seemed like a good kid. Never would have thought she'd pull something like this." And, "Always crowing about their kid with the straight A's at that hoity-toity school. Well, they're not crowing now."

Father Mike held Tessie's hand as she lay suffering on the bed upstairs. Removing his jacket, wearing only his black short-sleeved shirt and collar, he told her that he would pray for my return. He advised Tessie to go to church and light a candle for me. I ask myself now what Father Mike's face looked like as he held my mother's hand in the master bedroom. Was there any hint of *Schadenfreude?* Of taking pleasure in the unhappiness of his former fiancée? Of enjoyment at the fact that his brother-in-law's money couldn't protect him from this misfortune? Or of relief that for once, on the ride home, his wife, Zoë, wouldn't be able to compare him unfavorably with Milton? I can't answer these questions. As for my mother, she was tranquilized, and remembers only that the pressure in her eyes made Father Mike's face appear oddly elongated, like a priest in a painting by El Greco.

At night Tessie slept fitfully. Panic kept waking her up. In the morning she made the bed but, after breakfast, sometimes went to lie on it again, leaving her tiny white Keds neatly on the carpet and closing the shades. The sockets of her eyes darkened and the blue veins at her temples visibly throbbed. When the telephone rang, her head felt as if it would explode.

"Hello?"

"Any word?" It was Aunt Zo. Tessie's heart sank.

"No."

"Don't worry. She'll turn up."

They spoke for a minute before Tessie said she had to go. "I shouldn't tie up the line."

Every morning a great wall of fog descends upon the city of San Francisco. It begins far out at sea. It forms over the

Farallons, covering the sea lions on their rocks, and then it sweeps onto Ocean Beach, filling the long green bowl of Golden Gate Park. The fog obscures the early morning joggers and the lone practitioners of tai chi. It mists up the windows of the Glass Pavilion. It creeps over the entire city, over the monuments and movie theaters, over the Panhandle dope dens and the flophouses in the Tenderloin. The fog covers the pastel Victorian mansions in Pacific Heights and shrouds the rainbow-colored houses in the Haight. It walks up and down the twisting streets of Chinatown; it boards the cable cars, making their clanging bells sound like buoys; it climbs to the top of Coit Tower until you can't see it anymore; it moves in on the Mission, where the mariachi players are still asleep; and it bothers the tourists. The fog of San Francisco, that cold, identity-cleansing mist that rolls over the city every day, explains better than anything else why that city is what it is. After the Second World War, San Francisco was the main point of reentry for sailors returning from the Pacific. Out at sea, many of these sailors had picked up amatory habits that were frowned upon back on dry land. So these sailors stayed in San Francisco, growing in number and attracting others, until the city became the gay capital, the homosexual

Hauptstadt. (Further evidence of life's unpredictability: the Castro is a direct outcome of the military-industrial complex.) It was the fog that appealed to those sailors because it lent the city the shifting, anonymous feeling of the sea, and in such anonymity personal change was that much easier. Sometimes it was hard to tell whether the fog was rolling in over the city or whether the city was drifting out to meet it. Back in the 1940s, the fog hid what those sailors did from their fellow citizens. And the fog wasn't done. In the fifties it filled the heads of the Beats like the foam in their cappuccinos. In the sixties it clouded the minds of the hippies like the pot smoke rising in their bongs. And in the seventies, when Cal Stephanides arrived, the fog was hiding my new friends and me in the park.

On my third day in the Haight, I was in a café, eating a banana split. It was my second. The kick of my new freedom was wearing off. Gorging on sweets didn't chase away the blues as it had a week earlier.

"Spare some change?"

I looked up. Slouching beside my small marble-topped table was a type I knew well. It was one of the underpass kids, the scroungy runaways I kept my distance from. The hood of his sweatshirt was up, framing a flushed face, ripe with pimples.

"Sorry," I said.

The boy bent over, his face getting closer to mine. "Spare some change?" he said again.

His persistence annoyed me. So I glowered at him and said, "I should ask you the same question."

"I'm not the one pigging out on a sundae."

"I told you I don't have any spare change."

He glanced behind me and asked more affably, "How come you're carrying that humongous suitcase around?"

"That's my business."

"I saw you yesterday with that thing."

"I have enough money for this ice cream but that's it."

"Don't you have any place to stay?"

"I've got tons of places."

"You buy me a burger I'll show you a good place."

"I said I've got tons."

"I know a good place in the park."

"I can go into the park myself. *Anyone* can go into the park."

"Not if they don't want to get rolled they can't. You don't know what's up, man. There's places in the Gate that are safe and places that aren't. Me and my friends got a nice place. Real secluded. The cops don't even know about it, so we can just party all the time. Might let you stay there but first I need that double cheese."

"It was a hamburger a minute ago."

"You snooze, you lose. Price is going up all the time. How old are you, anyway?"

"Eighteen."

"Yeah, right, like I'll believe that. You ain't no eighteen. I'm sixteen and you're not any older than me. You from Marin?"

I shook my head. It had been a while since I had spoken to anyone my age. It felt good. It made me less lonely. But I still had my guard up.

"You're a rich kid, though, right? Mr. Alligator?"

I didn't say anything. And suddenly he was all appeal, full of kid hungers, his knees shaking. "Come *on*, man. I'm hungry. Okay, forget the double cheese. Just a burger."

"All right."

"Cool. A burger. And fries. You said fries, right? You won't believe this, man, but I got rich parents, too."

So began my time in Golden Gate Park. It turned out my new friend, Matt, wasn't lying about his parents. He was from the Main Line. His father was a divorce lawyer in Philadelphia. Matt was the fourth child, the youngest. Stocky, with a lug's jaw, a throaty, smoke-roughened voice, he had left home to follow the Grateful Dead the summer before but had never stopped. He sold tie-dyed T-shirts at their concerts, and dope or acid when he could. Deep in the park, where he led me, I found his cohorts.

"This is Cal," Matt told them. "He's going to crash here for a while."

"That's cool."

"You an undertaker, man?"

"I thought it was Abe Lincoln at first."

"Nah, these are just Cal's traveling clothes," Matt said. "He's got some others in that suitcase. Right?"

I nodded.

"You want to buy a shirt? I got some shirts."

"All right."

The camp was located in a grove of mimosa trees. The fuzzy red flowers on the branches were like pipe cleaners. Stretching over the dunes were huge evergreen bushes that formed natural huts. They were hollow inside, the soil dry underneath. The bushes kept the wind out and, most of the time, the rain. Inside, there was enough room to sit up. Each bush contained a few sleeping bags; you chose whichever one happened to be empty when you wanted to sleep. Communal ethics applied. Kids were always leaving the camp or showing up. It was equipped with all the stuff they abandoned: a camping stove, a pasta pot, miscellaneous silverware, jelly jar glasses, bedding, and a glow-in-the-dark Frisbee the guys tossed around, sometimes enlisting me to even out the sides. ("Jesus, Gator, you throw like a girl, man.") They were well stocked with gorp, bongs, pipes, vials of amyl nitrate, but understocked on towels, underwear, toothpaste. There was a ditch thirty or so yards distant that we employed as a latrine. The fountain by the aquarium was good for washing oneself, but you had to do it at night to avoid the police.

If one of the guys had a girlfriend there would be a girl around for a while. I stayed away from them, feeling they might guess my secret. I was like an immigrant, putting on airs, who runs into someone from the old country. I didn't want to be found out, so remained tight-lipped. But I would have been laconic in that company in any case. They were all Deadheads, and that was what the talk was. Who saw Jerry on which night. Who had a bootleg of which concert. Matt had flunked out of high school but had an impressive mind when it came to cataloguing Dead trivia. He carried the dates and cities of their tour in his head. He knew the lyrics of every song, when and where the Dead had played it, how many times, and what songs they had played only once. He lived in expectation of certain songs being performed as the faithful await the Messiah. Someday the Dead were going to play "Cosmic Charlie" and Matt Larson wanted to be there to see creation redeemed. He had once met Mountain Girl, Jerry's wife. "She was so fucking cool," he said. "I would fucking love a woman like that. If I found a lady as cool as Mountain Girl, I'd marry her and have kids and all that shit like that."

"Get a job, too?"

"We could follow the tour. Keep our babies in little sacks. Papoose style. And sell weed."

We weren't the only ones living in the park. Occupying some dunes on the other side of the field were homeless guys, with long beards, their faces brown from sun and dirt. They were known to ransack other people's camps, so we never left ours unattended. That was pretty much the only rule we had. Someone always had to stand guard.

I hung around the Deadheads because I was scared alone. My time on the road made me see the benefits of being in a pack. We had left home for different reasons. They weren't kids I would ever have been friends with in normal circumstances, but for that brief time I made do, because I had nowhere else to go. I was never at ease around them. But they weren't especially cruel. Fights broke out when kids had been drinking, but the ethos was non-violent. Everyone was reading *Siddhartha*. An old paperback got passed around the camp. I read it, too. It's one of the things I remember most about that time: Cal, sitting on a rock, reading Hermann Hesse and learning about the Buddha.

"I heard the Buddha dropped acid," said one Head. "That's what his enlightenment was."

"They didn't have acid back then, man."

"No, it was like, you know, a 'shroom."

"I think Jerry's the Buddha, man."

"Yeah!"

"Like when I fucking saw Jerry play that forty-five-minute space jam on 'Truckin' in Santa Fe,' I *knew* he was the Buddha."

In all these conversations I took no part. See Cal in the far underhang of the bushes, as all the Deadheads drift off to sleep.

I had run away without thinking what my life would be like. I had fled without having anywhere to run to. Now I was dirty, I was running out of money. Sooner or later I would have to call my parents. But for the first time in my life, I knew that there was nothing they could do to help me. Nothing anyone could do.

Every day I took the band to Ali Baba's and bought them veggie burgers for seventy-five cents each. I opted out on the begging and the dope dealing. Mostly I hung around the mimosa grove, in growing despair. A few times I walked out to the beach to sit by the sea, but after a while I stopped doing that, too. Nature brought no relief. Outside had ended. There was nowhere to go that wouldn't be me.

It was the opposite for my parents. Wherever they went, whatever they did, what greeted them was my absence. After the third week of my vanishing, friends and relatives stopped coming over to Middlesex in such numbers. The house got quieter. The phone didn't ring. Milton called Chapter Eleven, who was now living in the Upper Peninsula, and said, "Your mother's going through a rough period. We still don't know where your sister is. I'm sure your mother would feel a little better if she could see you. Why don't you come down for the weekend?" Milton didn't mention anything about my note. Throughout my time at the Clinic he had kept Chapter Eleven apprised of the situation in only the simplest terms. Chapter Eleven heard the seriousness in Milton's voice and agreed to start coming down on weekends and staying in his old bedroom. Gradually, he learned the details of my condition, reacting to them in a milder way than my parents had, which allowed them, or at least Tessie, to begin to accept the new reality. It was during those weekends that Milton, desperate to cement his restored relationship with his son, urged him once again to go into the family business. "You're not still going with that Meg, are you?"

"No."

"Well, you dropped out of your engineering studies. So what are you doing now? Your mother and I don't have a very clear idea of your life up there in Marquette."

"I work in a bar."

"You work in a bar? Doing what?"

"Short-order cook."

Milton paused only a moment. "What would you rather do, stay behind the grill or run Hercules Hot Dogs someday? You're the one that invented them anyway."

Chapter Eleven did not say yes. But he did not say no. He had once been a science geek, but the sixties had changed that. Under the imperatives of that decade, Chapter Eleven had become a lacto-vegetarian, a Transcendental Meditation student, a chewer of peyote buttons. Once, long ago, he had sawed golf balls in half, trying to find out what was inside; but at some point in his life my brother had become fascinated with the interior of the mind. Convinced of the essential uselessness of formalized education, he had retreated from civilization. Both of us had our moments of getting back to nature, Chapter Eleven in the U.P. and me in my bush in Golden Gate Park. By the time my father made his offer, however, Chapter Eleven had begun to tire of the woods.

"Come on," Milton said, "let's go have a Hercules right now."

"I don't eat meat," Chapter Eleven said. "How can I run the place if I don't eat meat?"

"I've been thinking about putting in salad bars," said Milton. "Lotta people eating a low-fat diet these days."

"Good idea."

"Yeah? You think so? That can be your department, then." Milton elbowed Chapter Eleven, kidding, "We'll start you off as vice president in charge of salad bars."

They drove to the Hercules downtown. It was busy when they arrived. Milton greeted the manager, Gus Zaras. *"Yahsou."*

Gus looked up and, a second late, began to smile broadly. "Hey there, Milt. How you doing?"

"Fine, fine. I brought the future boss down to see the place." He indicated Chapter Eleven.

"Welcome to the family dynasty," Gus

joked, spreading his arms. He laughed too loudly. Seeming to realize this, he stopped. There was an awkward silence. Then Gus asked, "So, Milt, what'll it be?"

"Two with everything. And what do we got that's vegetarian?"

"We got bean soup."

"Okay. Get my kid here a bowl of bean soup."

"You got it."

Milton and Chapter Eleven chose stools and waited to be served. After another long silence, Milton said, "You know how many of these places your old man owns right now?"

"How many?" said Chapter Eleven.

"Sixty-six. Got eight in Florida."

That was as far as the hard sell went. Milton ate his Hercules hot dogs in silence. He knew perfectly well why Gus was acting so overfriendly. It was because he was thinking what everyone thinks when a girl disappears. He was thinking the worst. There were moments when Milton did, too. He didn't admit it to anyone. He didn't admit it to himself. But whenever Tessie spoke about the umbilical cord, when she claimed that she could still feel me out there somewhere, Milton found himself wanting to believe her.

One Sunday as Tessie left for church, Milton handed her a large bill. "Light a candle for Callie. Get a bunch." He shrugged. "Couldn't hurt."

But after she was gone he shook his head. "What's the matter with me? Lighting candles! Christ!" He was furious at himself for giving in to such superstition. He vowed again that he would find me; he would get me back. Somehow or other. A chance would come his way, and when it did, Milton Stephanides wouldn't miss it.

The Dead came to Berkeley. Matt and the other kids trooped off to the concert. I was given the job to look after the camp.

It is midnight in the mimosa grove. I awaken, hearing noises. Lights are moving through the bushes. Voices are murmuring. The leaves over my head turn white and I can see the scaffolding of branches. Light speckles the ground, my body, my face. In the next second a flashlight comes blazing through the opening in my lair.

The men are on me at once. One shines his flashlight in my face as the other jumps onto my chest, pinning my arms.

"Rise and shine," says the one with the flashlight.

It is two homeless guys from the dunes opposite. While the one sits on top of me, the other begins searching the camp.

"What kind of goodies you little fuckers got in here?"

"Look at him," says the other. "Little fucker's gonna shit his pants."

I squeeze my legs together, the girlish fears still operating in me.

They are looking for drugs mainly. The one with the flashlight shakes out the sleeping bags and searches my suitcase. After a while he comes back and gets down on one knee.

"Where are all your friends, man? They go off and leave you all alone?"

He has begun to go through my pockets. Soon he finds my wallet and empties it. As he does, my school ID falls out. He shines the flashlight on it.

"What's this? Your girlfriend?"

He stares at the photo, grinning. "Your girlfriend like to suck cock? I bet she does." He picks up the ID and holds it over the front of his pants, thrusting his hips. "Oh yeah, she does!"

"Let me see that," says the one on top of me.

The guy with the flashlight tosses the ID onto my chest. The guy pinning me lowers his face close to mine and says in a deep voice, "Don't you move, motherfucker." He lets go of my arms and picks up the ID.

I can see his face now. Grizzled beard, bad teeth, nose askew, showing septum. He contemplates the snapshot. "Skinny bitch." He looks from me to the ID and his expression changes.

"It's a chick!"

"Quick on the uptake, man. I always say that about you."

"No, I mean *him*." He is pointing down at me. "It's her! He's a she." He holds up the ID for the other one to see. The flashlight is again trained on Calliope in her blazer and blouse.

At length the kneeling man grins. "You holding out on us? Huh? You got the goods stashed away under those pants? Hold her," he orders. The man astride me pins my arms again while the other one undoes my belt.

I tried to fight them off. I squirmed and kicked. But they were too strong. They got my pants down to my knees. The one aimed the flashlight and then sprang away.

"Jesus Christ!"

"What?"

"Fuck!"

"What?"

"It's a fucking freak."

"What?"

"I'm gonna puke, man. Look!"

No sooner had the other one done so than he let go of me as though I were contaminated. He stood up, enraged. By silent agreement, they then began to kick me. As they did, they uttered curses. The one who had pinned me drove his toe into my side. I grabbed his leg and hung on.

"Let go of me, you fucking freak!"

The other one was kicking me in the head. He did it three or four times before I blacked out.

When I came to, everything was quiet. I had the impression they had gone. Then somebody chuckled. "Cross swords," a voice said. The twin yellow streams, scintillant, intersected, soaking me.

"Crawl back into the hole you came out of, freak."

They left me there.

It was still dark out when I found the public fountain by the aquarium and bathed in it. I didn't seem to be bleeding anywhere. My right eye was swollen shut. My side hurt if I took a deep breath. I had my dad's Samsonite with me. I had seventy-five cents to my name. I wished more than anything that I could call home. Instead, I called Bob Presto. He said he would be right over to pick me up.

Hermaphroditus

❦

It's no surprise that Luce's theory of gender identity was popular in the early seventies. Back then, as my first barber put it, everybody wanted to go unisex. The consensus was that personality was primarily determined by environment, each child a blank slate to be written on. My own medical story was only a reflection of what was happening psychologically to everyone in those years. Women were becoming more like men and men were becoming more like women. For a little while during the seventies it seemed that sexual difference might pass away. But then another thing happened.

It was called evolutionary biology. Under its sway, the sexes were separated again, men into hunters and women into gatherers. Nurture no longer formed us; nature did. Impulses of hominids dating from 20,000 B.C. were still controlling us. And so today on television and in magazines you get the current simplifications. Why can't men communicate? (Because they

859

had to be quiet on the hunt.) Why do women communicate so well? (Because they had to call out to one another where the fruits and berries were.) Why can men never find things around the house? (Because they have a narrow field of vision, useful in tracking prey.) Why can women find things so easily? (Because in protecting the nest they were used to scanning a wide field.) Why can't women parallel-park? (Because low testosterone inhibits spatial ability.) Why won't men ask for directions? (Because asking for directions is a sign of weakness, and hunters never show weakness.) This is where we are today. Men and women, tired of being the same, want to be different again.

Therefore, it's also no surprise that Dr. Luce's theory had come under attack by the 1990s. The child was no longer a blank slate; every newborn had been inscribed by genetics and evolution. My life exists at the center of this debate. I am, in a sense, its solution. At first when I disappeared, Dr. Luce was desperate, feeling that he had lost his greatest find. But later, possibly realizing why I had run away, he came to the conclusion that I was not evidence in support of his theory but against it. He hoped I would stay quiet. He published his articles about me and prayed that I would never show up to refute them.

But it's not as simple as that. I don't fit into any of these theories. Not the evolutionary biologists' and not Luce's either. My psychological makeup doesn't accord with the essentialism popular in the intersex movement, either. Unlike other so-called male pseudo-hermaphrodites who have been written about in the press, I never felt out of place being a girl. I still don't feel entirely at home among men. Desire made me cross over to the other side, desire and the facticity of my body. In the twentieth century, genetics brought the Ancient Greek notion of fate into our very cells. This new century we've just begun has found something different. Contrary to all expectations, the code underlying our being is woefully inadequate. Instead of the expected 200,000 genes, we have only 30,000. Not many more than a mouse.

And so a strange new possibility is arising. Compromised, indefinite, sketchy, but not entirely obliterated: free will is making a comeback. Biology gives you a brain. Life turns it into a mind.

At any rate, in San Francisco in 1974, life was working hard to give me one.

There it is again: the chlorine smell. Under the nasally significant odor of the girl sitting astride his lap, distinct, even, from the buttery popcorn smell that still pervades the old movie seats, Mr. Go can detect the unmistakable scent of a swimming pool. In here? In Sixty-Niners? He sniffs. Flora, the girl on his lap, says, "Do you like my perfume?" But Mr. Go does not answer. Mr. Go has a way of ignoring the girls he pays to wiggle in his lap. What he likes best is to have one girl frog-kicking on top of him while he watches another girl dancing around the glittery firemen's pole on the stage. Mr. Go is multitasking. But tonight he is unable to divide his attentions. The swimming pool smell is distracting him. It has done so for over a week. Turning his head, which is gently bobbing under Flora's exertions, Mr. Go looks at the line forming before the velvet rope. The fifty or so theater seats here in the Show Room are almost entirely empty. In the blue light only a few men's heads are visible, some alone facing the stage, a few like Mr. Go with a companion riding them: those peroxide equestriennes.

Behind the velvet rope rises a flight of stairs edged with blinking lights. To climb these stairs you must pay a separate admission of five dollars. Upon reaching the club's second floor (Mr. Go has been told), your only option is to enter a booth, where it is then necessary to insert tokens, which you must buy downstairs for a quarter each. If you do all this, you will be afforded brief glimpses of something Mr. Go does not quite understand. Mr. Go's English is more than adequate. He has lived in America for fifty-two years. But the sign advertising the attractions upstairs doesn't make much sense to him. For that reason he is curious. The chlorine smell only makes him more so.

Despite the increased traffic going upstairs in recent weeks, Mr. Go has not yet gone himself. He has remained faithful to the first floor where, for the single admission price of ten dollars, he has a choice of activities. Mr. Go might, if he so desires, quit the Show Room and go into the Dark Room at the end of the hall. In the Dark Room there are flashlights with pinpoint beams. There are huddled men, wielding said flashlights. If you work your way in far enough, you will find a girl, or sometimes two, lying on a riser carpeted in foam rubber. Of course it is in some sense an act of faith to postulate the existence of an actual girl, or even two. You never see a complete girl in the Dark Room. You see only pieces. You see what your flashlight illuminates. A knee, for instance, or a nipple. Or, of particular interest to Mr. Go and his fellows, you see the source of life, the thing of things, purified as it were, without the clutter of a person attached.

Mr. Go might also venture into the Ball

Room. In the Ball Room there are girls who long to slow-dance with Mr. Go. He doesn't care for disco music, however, and at his age tires easily. It is too much effort to press the girls up against the padded walls of the Ball Room. Mr. Go much prefers to sit in the Show Room, in the stained Art Deco theater seats that originally belonged to a movie house in Oakland, now demolished.

Mr. Go is seventy-three years old. Every morning, to retain his virility, he drinks a tea containing rhinoceros horn. He also eats the gall bladders of bears when he can get them at the Chinese apothecary shop near his apartment. These aphrodisiacs appear to work. Mr. Go comes into Sixty-Niners nearly every night. He has a joke he likes to tell the girls who sit on his lap. "Mr. Go go for go-go." That is the only time he laughs or smiles, when he tells them that joke.

If the club is not crowded — which it rarely is downstairs anymore — Flora will sometimes give Mr. Go her company for three or four songs. For a dollar she will ride him for one song, but she will sit through one or two more songs for free. This is one of Flora's recommendations in Mr. Go's mind. She is not young, Flora, but she has nice, clear skin. Mr. Go feels she is healthy.

Tonight, however, after only two songs, Flora slides off Mr. Go, grumbling. "I'm not a credit bureau, you know." She stalks off. Mr. Go rises, adjusting his pants, and right then the swimming pool smell hits him again and his curiosity gets the better of him. He shuffles out of the Show Room and gazes up the stairs at the printed sign:

And now Mr. Go's curiosity has gotten the better of him. He buys a ticket and a handful of tokens and waits in line with the others. When the bouncer lets him through, he climbs up the blinking stairs. The booths on the second floor have no numbers, only lights indicating whether they are occupied. He finds an empty one, closes the door behind him, and puts a token in the slot. Immediately, the screen slides away to reveal a porthole looking onto underwater depths. Music plays from a speaker in the roof and a deep voice begins narrating a story:

"Once upon a time in ancient Greece, there was an enchanted pool. This pool was sacred to Salmacis, the water nymph. And one day Hermaphroditus, a beautiful boy, went swimming there." The voice continues, but Mr. Go is no longer paying attention. He is looking into the pool, which is blue and empty. He is wondering where the girls are. He is beginning to regret buying a ticket to Octopussy's Garden. But just then the voice intones:

"Ladies and Gentlemen, behold the god Hermaphroditus! Half woman, half man!"

There is a splash from above. The water in the pool goes white, then pink. Only inches away on the other side of the porthole's glass is a body, a living body. Mr. Go looks. He squints. He presses his face right up to the porthole. He has never seen anything like what he is seeing now. Not in all his years of visiting the Dark Room. He isn't sure he likes what he sees. But the sight makes him feel strange, lightheaded, weightless, and somehow younger. Suddenly the screen slides shut. Without hesitation Mr. Go drops another token in the slot.

San Francisco's Sixty-Niners, Bob Presto's

club: it stood in North Beach, within view of the skyscrapers downtown. It was a neighborhood of Italian cafés, pizza restaurants, and topless bars. In North Beach you had the glitzy strip palaces like Carol Doda's with her famous bust outlined on the marquee. Barkers on the sidewalks collared passersby: "Gentlemen! Come in and see the show! Just have a look. Doesn't cost anything to have a look." While the guy outside the next club was shouting, "Our girls are the best, right this way through the curtain!" And the next, "Live erotic show, gentlemen! Plus in our establishment you can watch the football game!" The barkers were all interesting guys, poets manqués, most of them, and spent their time off in City Lights Bookstore, leafing through New Directions paperbacks. They wore striped pants, loud ties, sideburns, goatees. They tended to resemble Tom Waits, or maybe it was the other way around. Like Mamet characters, they populated an America that had never existed, a kid's idea of sharpies and hucksters and underworld life.

It is said: San Francisco is where young people go to retire. And though it would certainly add color to my story to present a descent into a seamy underworld, I can't fail to mention that the North Beach Strip is only a few blocks long. The geography of San Francisco is too beautiful to allow seaminess to get much of a foothold, and so along with these barkers there were many tourists afoot, tourists carrying loaves of sourdough bread and Ghirardelli chocolates. In the daytime there were rollerskaters and hackey sack players in the parks. But at night things got a little seamy at last, and from 9 p.m. to three in the morning the men streamed into Sixty-Niners.

Which was where, obviously enough, I was now working. Five nights a week, six hours a day, for the next four months — and, fortunately, never again — I made my living by exhibiting the peculiar way I am formed. The Clinic had prepared me for it, benumbing my sense of shame, and besides, I was desperate for money. Sixty-Niners also had a perfect venue for me. I worked with two other girls, so called: Carmen and Zora.

Presto was an exploiter, a porn dog, a sex pig, but I could have done worse. Without him I might never have found myself. After he had picked me up in the park, bruised and battered, Presto took me back to his apartment. His Namibian girlfriend, Wilhelmina, dressed my wounds. At some point I passed out again and they undressed me to put me in bed. It was then that Presto realized the extent of his windfall.

I drifted in and out of consciousness, catching bits of what they said to each other.

"I knew it. I knew it when I saw him at the steak house."

"You didn't know a thing, Bob. You thought he was a sex-change."

"I knew he was a gold mine."

And later, Wilhelmina: "How old is he?"

"Eighteen."

"He doesn't look eighteen."

"He says he is."

"And you want to believe him, don't you, Bob? You want him to work in the club."

"He called *me*. So I made him an offer."

And later still: "Why don't you call his parents, Bob?"

"The kid ran away from home. He doesn't want to call his parents."

Octopussy's Garden predated me. Presto had come up with the idea six months earlier. Carmen and Zora had been working there from the beginning, as Ellie and Melanie respectively. But Presto was always on the lookout for ever-freakier performers and knew I'd give him an edge over his competitors on the Strip. There was nothing like me around.

The tank itself was not that large. Not much bigger than an above-ground swimming pool in someone's backyard. Fifteen feet in length, maybe ten feet wide. We climbed down a ladder into the warm water. From the booths, you looked directly into the tank; it was impossible to see above the surface. So we could keep our heads out of the water, if we wanted, and talk to one another while we worked. As long as we submerged ourselves from the waist down the customers were content. "They don't come here to see your pretty face," was how Presto put it to me. All this made it much easier. I don't think I could have performed in a regular peep show, face-to-face with the voyeurs. Their gaze would have sucked my soul out of me. But in the tank when I was underwater my eyes were closed. I undulated in the deep-sea silence. When I pressed myself against a porthole's glass, I lifted my face up out of the water and so was unaware of the eyes studying my mollusk. How did I say it before? The surface of the sea is a mirror, reflecting divergent evolutionary paths. Up above, the creatures of air; down below, those of water. One planet, containing two worlds. The customers were the sea creatures; Zora, Carmen, and I remained essentially creatures of air. In her mermaid costume, Zora lay on the wet strip of outdoor carpeting, waiting to go on after me. Sometimes she held a joint to my lips so that I could smoke while I grabbed the rim of the pool. After my ten minutes were elapsed I clambered up onto the carpet and dried off. Over the sound system Bob Presto was saying, "Let's hear it for Hermaphroditus, ladies and gentlemen! Only here at Octopussy's Garden, where gender is always on a bender! I'm telling you, folks, we put the glam rock in the rock lobsters, we put the AC/DC in the mahi mahi . . ."

Beached on her side, Zora with blue eyes and golden hair asked me, "Am I zipped?"

I checked.

"This tank is making me all congested. I'm always congested."

"You want something from the bar?"

"Get me a Negroni, Cal. Thanks."

"Ladies and gentlemen, it's time for our next attraction here at Octopussy's Garden. Yes, I see now that the boys from Steinhardt Aquarium are just bringing her in. Put those tokens in the boxes, ladies and gentlemen, this is something you won't want to miss. May I have a drum roll, please? On second thought, make that a *sushi roll.*"

Zora's music started. Her overture.

"Ladies and gentlemen, since time immemorial mariners have told stories of seeing incredible creatures, half woman, half fish, swimming in the seas. We here at

Sixty-Niners did not give credence to such stories. But a tuna fisherman of our acquaintance brought us an amazing catch the other day. And now we know those stories are true. Ladies and gentlemen," crooned Bob Presto, "does . . . anyone . . . smell . . . *fish?*"

At that cue, Zora in her rubber suit with the flashing green sequin scales would tumble into the tank. The suit came up to her waist and left her chest and shoulders bare. Into the aquatic light Zora streamed, opening her eyes underwater as I did not, smiling at the men and women in the booths, her long blond hair flowing behind her like seaweed, tiny air bubbles beading her breasts like pearls, as she kicked her glittering emerald fish tail. She performed no lewdness. Zora's beauty was so great that everyone was content merely to look at her, the white skin, the beautiful breasts, the taut belly with its winking navel, the magnificent curve of her swaying backside where flesh merged with scales. She swam with her arms at her sides, voluptuously fluctuating. Her face was serene, her eyes a light Caribbean blue. Downstairs a constant disco beat throbbed, but up here in Octopussy's Garden the music was ethereal, a kind of melodious bubbling itself.

Viewed from a certain angle, there was a kind of artistry to it. Sixty-Niners was a smut pavilion, but up in the Garden the atmosphere was exotic rather than raunchy. It was the sexual equivalent of Trader Vic's. Viewers got to see strange things, uncommon bodies, but much of the appeal was the transport involved. Looking through their portholes, the customers were watching real bodies do the things bodies sometimes did in dreams. There were male customers, married heterosexual men, who sometimes dreamed of making love to women who possessed penises, not male penises, but thin, tapering feminized stalks, like the stamens of flowers, clitorises that had elongated tremendously from abundant desire. There were gay customers who dreamed of boys who were almost female, smooth-skinned, hairless. There were lesbian customers who dreamed of women with penises, not male penises but womanly erections, possessing a sensitivity and aliveness no dildo ever had. There is no way to tell what percentage of the population dreams such dreams of sexual transmogrification. But they came to our underwater garden every night and filled the booths to watch us.

After Melanie the Mermaid came Ellie and Her Electrifying Eel. This eel was not at first apparent. What splashed down through the aquamarine depths appeared to be a slender Hawaiian girl, clad in a bikini of water lilies. As she swam, her top came off and she remained a girl. But when she stood on her head, in graceful water ballet, pulling her bikini bottom to her knees — ah, then it was the eel's moment to shock. For there it was on the slender girl's body, there it was where it should not have been, a thin brown ill-tempered-looking eel, an endangered species, and as Ellie rubbed against the glass the eel grew longer and longer; it stared at the customers with its cyclopean eye; and they looked back at her breasts, her slim waist, they looked back and forth from Ellie to eel, from eel to Ellie, and were electrified by the wedding of opposites.

Carmen was a pre-op, male-to-female transsexual. She was from the Bronx. Small, delicately boned, she was fastidious about eyeliner and lipstick. She was always dieting. She stayed away from beer, fearing a belly. I thought she overdid the femme routine. There was entirely too much hip swaying and hair flipping in Carmen's airspace. She had a pretty naiad's face, a girl on the surface with a boy holding his breath just beneath. Sometimes the hormones she took made her skin break out. Her doctor (the much-in-demand Dr. Mel of San Bruno) had to constantly adjust her dosage. The only features that gave Carmen away were her voice, which remained husky despite the estrogen and progestin, and her hands. But the men never noticed that. And they wanted Carmen to be impure. That was the whole turn-on, really.

Her story followed the traditional lines better than mine. From an early age Carmen had felt that she had been born into the wrong body. In the dressing room one day, she told me in her South Bronx voice: "I was like, yo! Who put this dick on me? I never asked for no dick." It was still there, however, for the time being. It was what the men came to see. Zora, given to analytical thought, felt that Carmen's admirers were motivated by latent homosexuality. But Carmen resisted this notion. "My boyfriends are all straight. They want a *woman*."

"Obviously not," said Zora.

"Soon as I save my money I'm having my bottom done. Then we'll see. I'll be more of a woman than you, Z."

"Fine with me," replied Zora. "I don't want to be anything in particular."

Zora had Androgen Insensitivity. Her body was immune to male hormones. Though XY like me, she had developed along female lines. But Zora had done it far better than I had. Aside from being blond, she was shapely and full-lipped. Her prominent cheekbones divided her face in

Arctic planes. When Zora spoke you were aware of the skin stretching over these cheekbones and hollowing out between her jaws, the tight mask it made, banshee-like, with her blue eyes piercing through above. And then there was her figure, the milk-maid breasts, the swim champ stomach, the legs of a sprinter or a Martha Graham dancer. Even unclothed, Zora appeared to be all woman. There was no visible sign that she possessed neither womb nor ovaries. Androgen Insensitivity Syndrome created the perfect woman, Zora told me. A number of top fashion models had it. "How many chicks are six two, skinny, but with big boobs? Not many. That's normal for someone like me."

Beautiful or not, Zora didn't want to be a woman. She preferred to identify herself as a hermaphrodite. She was the first one I met. The first person like me. Even back in 1974 she was using the term "intersexual," which was rare then. Stonewall was only five years in the past. The Gay Rights Movement was under way. It was paving a path for all the identity struggles that followed, including ours. The Intersex Society of North America wouldn't be founded until 1993, however. So I think of Zora Khyber as an early pioneer, a sort of John the Baptist crying in the wilderness. Writ large, that wilderness was America, even the globe itself, but more specifically it was the redwood bungalow Zora lived in in Noe Valley and where I was now living, too. After Bob Presto had satisfied himself on the details of my manufacture, he had called Zora and arranged for me to stay with her. Zora took in strays like me. It was part of her calling. The fog of San Francisco provided cover for hermaphrodites, too. It's no surprise that ISNA was founded in San Francisco and not somewhere else. Zora was part of all this at a very disorganized time. Before movements emerge there are centers of energy, and Zora was one of these. Mainly, her politics consisted of studying and writing. And, during the months I lived with her, in educating me, in bringing me out of what she saw as my great midwestern darkness.

"You don't have to work for Bob if you don't want," she told me. "I'm going to quit soon anyway. This is just temporary."

"I need the money. They stole all my money."

"What about your parents?"

"I don't want to ask them," I said. I looked down and admitted, "I can't call them."

"What happened, Cal? If you don't mind me asking. What are you doing here?"

"They took me to this doctor in New

York. He wanted me to have an operation."

"So you ran away."

I nodded.

"Consider yourself lucky. I didn't know
until I was twenty."

All this happened on my first day in
Zora's house. I hadn't started working at
the club yet. My bruises had to heal first. I
wasn't surprised to be where I was. When
you travel like I did, vague about destination and with an open-ended itinerary, a
holy-seeming openness takes over your
character. It's the reason the first philoso-
phers were peripatetic. Christ, too. I see
myself that first day, sitting cross-legged on
a batik floor pillow, drinking green tea out
of a fired raku cup, and looking up at Zora
with my big, hopeful, curious, attentive
eyes. With my hair short, my eyes looked
even bigger now, more than ever the eyes
of someone in a Byzantine icon, one of
those figures ascending the ladder to
heaven, upward-gazing, while his fellows
fall to the fiery demons below. After all my
troubles, wasn't it my right to expect some
reward in the form of knowledge or revelation? In Zora's rice-paper house, with
misty light coming in at the windows, I
was like a blank canvas waiting to be filled
with what she told me.

"There have been hermaphrodites around

forever, Cal. Forever. Plato said that the original human being was a hermaphrodite. Did you know that? The original person was two halves, one male, one female. Then these got separated. That's why everybody's always searching for their other half. Except for us. We've got both halves already."

I didn't say anything about the Object.

"Okay, in some cultures we're considered freaks," she went on. "But in others it's just the opposite. The Navajo have a category of person they call a berdache. What a berdache is, basically, is someone who adopts a gender other than their biological one. Remember, Cal. Sex is biological. Gender is cultural. The Navajo understand this. If a person wants to switch her gender, they let her. And they don't denigrate that person — they honor her. The berdaches are the shamans of the tribe. They're the healers, the great weavers, the artists."

I wasn't the only one! Listening to Zora, that was mainly what hit home with me. I knew right then that I had to stay in San Francisco for a while. Fate or luck had brought me here and I had to take from it what I needed. It didn't matter what I might be compelled to do to make money. I just wanted to stay with Zora, to learn from her, and to be less alone in the world. I was already stepping through the charmed door of those druggy, celebratory, youthful days. By that first afternoon the soreness in my ribs was already lessening. Even the air seemed on fire, subtly aflame with energy as it does when you are young, when the synapses are firing wildly and death is far away.

Zora was writing a book. She claimed it was going to be published by a small press in Berkeley. She showed me the publisher's catalogue. The selections were eclectic, books on Buddhism, on the mystery cult of Mithras, even a strange book (a hybrid itself) mixing genetics, cellular biology, and Hindu mysticism. What Zora was working on would certainly have fit this list. But I was never clear how actual her publishing plans were. In the years since, I've looked out for Zora's book, which was called *The Sacred Hermaphrodite*. I've never found it. If she never finished it, it wasn't a question of ability. I read most of the book myself. At my age then, I wasn't much of a judge of literary or academic quality, but Zora's learning was real. She had gone into her subject and had much of it by heart. Her bookshelves were full of anthropology texts and works by French structuralists and deconstructionists. She wrote nearly every day. She spread her papers and books out on her desk and took notes and typed.

"I've got one question," I asked Zora

one day. "Why did you ever tell anybody?"

"What do you mean?"

"Look at you. No one would ever know."

"I want people to know, Cal."

"How come?"

Zora folded her long legs under herself. With her fairy's eyes, paisley-shaped, blue and glacial looking into mine, she said, "Because we're what's next."

"Once upon a time in ancient Greece, there was an enchanted pool. This pool was sacred to Salmacis, the water nymph. And one day Hermaphroditus, a beautiful boy, went swimming there."

Here I lowered my feet into the pool. I lolled them back and forth as the narration continued. "Salmacis looked upon the handsome boy and her lust was kindled. She swam nearer to get a closer look." Now I began to lower my own body into the water inch by inch: shin, knees, thighs. If I paced it the way Presto had instructed me, the peepholes slid shut at this point. Some customers left, but many dropped more tokens into the slots. The screens lifted from the portholes.

"The water nymph tried to control herself. But the boy's beauty was too much for her. Looking was not enough. Salmacis swam nearer and nearer. And then, overpowered by desire, she caught the boy from behind, wrapping her arms around him." I began to kick my legs, churning up water so that it was hard for the customers to see. "Hermaphroditus struggled to free himself from the tenacious grip of the water nymph, ladies and gentlemen. But Salmacis was too strong. So unbridled was her lust that the two became one. Their bodies fused, male into female, female into male. Behold the god Hermaphroditus!" At which point I plunged into the pool entire, all of me exposed.

And the peepholes slid shut.

No one ever left a booth at this point. Everyone extended his or her membership to the Garden. Underwater I could hear the tokens clinking into the change boxes. It reminded me of being at home, submerging my head under bathwater and hearing the pinging in the pipes. I tried to think of things like that. It made everything seem far away. I pretended I was in the bathtub on Middlesex. Meanwhile faces filled the portholes, gazing with amazement, curiosity, disgust, desire.

We were always stoned for work. That was a prerequisite. As we got into our costumes Zora and I would fire up a joint to start the night. Zora brought a thermos of Averna and ice, which I drank like Kool-Aid. What you aimed for was a state of half oblivion, a private party mood. This made the men less real, less noticeable. If it hadn't been for Zora I don't know what I would have done. Our little bungalow in the mist and trees, neatly surrounded by low-lying California ground cover, the tiny koi pond full of pet-store goldfish, the out-door Buddhist shrine made of blue granite — it was a refuge for me, a halfway house where I stayed, getting ready to go back into the world. My life during those months was as divided as my body. Nights we spent at Sixty-Niners, waiting around the tank, bored, high, giggling, unhappy. But you got used to that. You learned to medicate yourself against it and put it out of your mind.

In the daytime Zora and I were always straight. She had one hundred and eighteen pages of her book written. These were typed on the thinnest onionskin paper I had ever seen. The manuscript was there-fore perishable. You had to be careful in handling it. Zora made me sit at the kitchen table while she brought it out like a librarian with a Shakespeare folio. Other-wise, Zora didn't treat me like a kid. She let me keep my own hours. She asked me to help with the rent. We spent most days padding around the house in our kimonos. Z. had a stern expression when she was working. I sat out on the deck and read books from her shelves, Kate Chopin, Jane Bowles, and the poetry of Gary Snyder. Though we looked nothing alike, Zora was always emphatic about our solidarity. We were up against the same prejudices and misunderstandings. I was gladdened by this, but I never felt sisterly around Zora. Not completely. I was always aware of her figure under the robe. I went around averting my eyes and trying not to stare. On the street people took me for a boy. Zora turned heads. Men whistled at her. She didn't like men, however. Only lesbians.

She had a dark side. She drank to extremes and sometimes acted ugly. She raged against football, male bonding, babies, breeders, politicians, and men in general. There was a violence in Zora at such times that set me on edge. She had been the high school beauty. She had submitted to caresses that had done nothing for her and to sessions of painful lovemaking. Like many beauties, Zora had attracted the worst guys. The varsity stooges. The herpetic section leaders. It was no surprise that she held a low opinion of men. Me she exempted. She thought I was okay. Not a real man at all. Which I felt was pretty much right.

Hermaphroditus's parents were Hermes

and Aphrodite. Ovid doesn't tell us how they felt after their child went missing. As for my own parents, they still kept the telephone nearby at all times, refusing to leave the house together. But now they were scared to answer the phone, fearing bad news. Ignorance seemed preferable to grief. Whenever the phone rang, they paused before answering it. They waited until the third or fourth peal.

Their agony was harmonious. During the months I was missing, Milton and Tessie experienced the same spikes of panic, the same mad hopes, the same sleeplessness. It had been years since their emotional life had been so in sync and this had the result of bringing back the times when they first fell in love.

They began to make love with a frequency they hadn't known for years. If Chapter Eleven was out, they didn't wait to go upstairs but used whatever room they happened to be in. They tried the red leather couch in the den; they spread out on the bluebirds and red berries of the living room sofa; and a few times they even lay down on the heavy-duty kitchen carpeting, which had a pattern of bricks. The only place they didn't use was the basement because there was no telephone there. Their lovemaking was not passionate but slow and elegiac, carried out to the magisterial rhythms of suffering. They were not young anymore; their bodies were no longer beautiful. Tessie sometimes wept afterward. Milton kept his eyes squeezed shut. Their exertions resulted in no flowering of sensation, no release, or only seldom.

Then one day, three months after I was gone, the signals coming over my mother's spiritual umbilical cord stopped. Tessie was lying in bed when the faint purring or tingling in her navel ceased. She sat up. She put her hand to her belly.

"I can't feel her anymore!" Tessie cried.

"What?"

"The cord's cut! Somebody cut the cord!"

Milton tried to reason with Tessie, but it was no use. From that moment, my mother became convinced that something terrible had happened to me.

And so: into the harmony of their suffering entered discord. While Milton fought to keep up a positive attitude, Tessie increasingly gave in to despair. They began to quarrel. Every now and then Milton's optimism would sway my mother and she would become cheerful for a day or two. She would tell herself that, after all, they didn't know anything definite. But such moods were temporary. When she was alone Tessie tried to feel something coming in over the umbilical cord, but there was nothing, not even a sign of distress.

I had been missing four months by this time. It was now January 1975. My fifteenth birthday had passed without my being found. On a Sunday morning while Tessie was at church, praying for my return, the phone rang. Milton answered.

"Hello?"

At first there was no response. Milton could hear music in the background, a radio playing in another room maybe. Then a muffled voice spoke.

"I bet you miss your daughter, Milton."

"Who is this?"

"A daughter is a special thing."

"Who is this?" Milton demanded again, and the line went dead.

He didn't tell Tessie about the call. He suspected it was a crank. Or a disgruntled employee. The economy was in recession in 1975 and Milton had been forced to close a few franchises. The following Sunday, however, the phone rang again. This time Milton answered on the first ring.

"Hello?"

"Good morning, Milton. I have a question for you this morning. Would you like to know the question, Milton?"

"You tell me who this is or I'm hanging up."

"I doubt you'll do that, Milton. I'm the only chance you have to get your daughter back."

Milton did a characteristic thing right then. He swallowed, squared his shoulders, and with a small nod prepared himself to meet whatever was coming.

"Okay," he said, "I'm listening."

And the caller hung up.

"Once upon a time in ancient Greece, there was an enchanted pool . . ." I could do it in my sleep now. I *was* asleep, considering our backstage festivities, the flowing Averna, the tranquilizing smoke. Halloween had come and gone. Thanksgiving, too, and then Christmas. On New Year's, Bob Presto threw a big party. Zora and I drank champagne. When it was time for my act, I plunged into the pool. I was high, drunk, and so that night did something I didn't normally do. I opened my eyes underwater. I saw the faces looking back at me and I saw that they were not appalled. I had fun in the tank that night. It was all beneficial in some way. It was *therapeutic*. Inside Hermaphroditus old tensions were roiling, trying to work themselves out. Traumas of the locker room were being released. Shame over having a body unlike other bodies was passing away. The monster feeling was fading. And along with shame and self-loathing another hurt was healing. Hermaphroditus was beginning to forget about the Obscure Object.

In my last weeks in San Francisco I read everything Zora gave me, trying to educate myself. I learned what varieties we hermaphrodites came in. I read about hyperadrenocorticism and feminizing testes and something called cryptorchidism, which applied to me. I read about Klinefelter's Syndrome, where an extra X chromosome renders a person tall, eunuchoid, and temperamentally unpleasant. I was more interested in historical than medical material. From Zora's manuscript I became acquainted with the hijras of India, the *kwolu-aatmwols* of the Sambia in Papua New Guinea, and the *guevedoche* of the Dominican Republic. Karl Heinrich Ulrichs, writing in Germany in 1860, spoke of *das dritte Geschlecht*, the third gender. He called himself a Uranist and believed that he had a female soul in a male body. Many cultures on earth operated not with two genders but with three. And the third was always special, exalted, endowed with mystical gifts.

One cold drizzly night I gave it a try. Zora was out. It was a Sunday and we were off work. I sat in a half-lotus position on the floor and closed my eyes. Concentrating, prayerful, I waited for my soul to leave my body. I tried to fall into a trance state or become an animal. I did my best, but nothing happened. As far as special powers went, I didn't seem to have any. A Tiresias I wasn't.

All of which brings me to a Friday night in late January. It was after midnight. Carmen was in the tank, doing her Esther Williams. Zora and I were in the dressing room, maintaining traditions (thermos, cannabis). In the mermaid suit, Z. was none too mobile and stretched out across the couch, a Piscean odalisque. Her tail hung over the arm bolsters, dripping. She wore a T-shirt over her top. It had Emily Dickinson on it.

Sounds from the tank were piped into the dressing room. Bob Presto was giving his spiel: "Ladies and gentlemen, are you ready for a truly electrifying experience?"

Zora and I mouthed along with the next line: "Are you ready for some high voltage?"

"I've had enough of this place," said Zora. "I really have."

"Should we quit?"

"We should."

"What would we do instead?"

"Mortgage banking."

There was a splash in the tank. "But where is Ellie's eel today? It seems to be hiding, ladies and gentlemen. Could it be extinct? Maybe a fisherman caught it. That's right, ladies and gentleman, maybe Ellie's eel is for sale out on Fisherman's Wharf."

"Bob thinks he's a witty person," said Zora.

"Banish such worries, ladies and gentlemen. Ellie wouldn't let us down. Here it is, folks. Have a look at Ellie's electric eel!"

A strange noise came over the speaker. A door banging. Bob Presto shouted: "Hey, what the hell? You're not allowed in here."

And then the sound system went dead.

Eight years earlier, policemen had raided a blind pig on Twelfth Street in Detroit. Now, at the start of 1975, they raided Sixty-Niners. The action provoked no riot. The patrons quickly emptied the booths, fanning out into the street and hurrying off. We were led downstairs and lined up with the other girls.

"Well, hello there," said the officer when he came to me. "And how old might you be?"

From the police station I was allowed one call. And so I finally broke down, gave in, and did it: I called home.

My brother answered. "It's me," I said. "Cal." Before Chapter Eleven had time to respond, it all rushed out of me. I told him where I was and what had happened. "Don't tell Mom and Dad," I said.

"I can't," said Chapter Eleven. "I can't tell Dad." And then in an interrogative tone that showed he could hardly believe it himself, my brother told me that there had been an accident and that Milton was dead.

Air-Ride

In my official capacity as assistant cultural attaché, but on an unofficial errand, I attended the Warhol opening at the Neue Nationalgalerie. Within the famous Mies van der Rohe building, I passed by the famous silk-screened faces of the famous pop artist. The Neue Nationalgalerie is a wonderful art museum except for one thing: there's nowhere to hang the art. I didn't care much. I stared out the glass walls at Berlin and felt stupid. Did I think there would be artists at an art opening? There were only patrons, journalists, critics, and socialites.

After accepting a glass of wine from a passing waiter, I sat down in one of the leather and chrome chairs that line the perimeter. The chairs are by Mies, too. You see knockoffs everywhere but these are original, worn-out by now, the black leather browning at the edges. I lit a cigar and smoked, trying to make myself feel better.

The crowd chattered, circulating among

the Maos and Marilyns. The high ceiling made the acoustics muddy. Thin men with shaved heads darted by. Gray-haired women draped in natural shawls showed their yellow teeth. Out the windows, the Staatsbibliotek was visible across the way. The new Potsdamer Platz looked like a mall in Vancouver. In the distance construction lights illuminated the skeletons of cranes. Traffic surged in the street below. I took a drag on my cigar, squinting, and caught sight of my reflection in the glass.

I said before I look like a Musketeer. But I also tend to resemble (especially in mirrors late at night) a faun. The arched eyebrows, the wicked grin, the flames in the eyes. The cigar jutting up from between my teeth didn't help.

A hand tapped me on the back. "Cigar faddist," said a woman's voice.

In Mies's black glass I recognized Julie Kikuchi.

"Hey, this is Europe," I countered, smiling. "Cigars aren't a fad here."

"I was into cigars way back in college."

"Oh yeah," I challenged her. "Smoke one, then."

She sat down in the chair next to mine and held out her hand. I took another cigar from my jacket and handed it to her along with the cigar cutter and matches. Julie held the cigar under her nose and sniffed.

She rolled it between her fingers to test its moistness. Clipping off the end, she put it in her mouth, struck a match, and got it going, puffing serially.

"Mies van der Rohe smoked cigars," I said, by way of promotion.

"Have you ever seen a picture of Mies van der Rohe?" said Julie.

"Point taken."

We sat side by side, not speaking, only smoking, facing the interior of the museum. Julie's right knee was jiggling. After a while I swiveled around so I was facing her. She turned her face toward me.

"Nice cigar," she allowed.

I leaned toward her. Julie leaned toward me. Our faces got closer until finally our foreheads were almost touching. We stayed like that for ten or so seconds. Then I said, "Let me tell you why I didn't call you."

I took a long breath and began: "There's something you should know about me."

My story began in 1922 and there were concerns about the flow of oil. In 1975, when my story ends, dwindling oil supplies again had people worried. Two years earlier the Organization of Arab Oil Exporting Countries had begun an embargo. There were brownouts in the U.S. and long lines at the pumps. The President announced that the lights on the White House

Christmas tree would not be lit, and the gas-tank lock was born.

Scarcity was weighing on everybody's mind in those days. The economy was in recession. Across the nation families were eating dinner in the dark, the way we used to do on Seminole under one lightbulb. My father, however, took a dim view of conservation policies. Milton had come a long way from the days when he counted kilowatts. And so, on the night he set out to ransom me, he remained at the wheel of an enormous, gas-guzzling Cadillac.

My father's last Cadillac: a 1975 Eldorado. Painted a midnight blue that looked nearly black, the car bore a strong resemblance to the Batmobile. Milton had all the doors locked. It was just past 2 a.m. The roads in this downriver neighborhood were full of potholes, the curbs choked with weeds and litter. The powerful high beams picked up sprays of broken glass in the street, as well as nails, shards of metal, old hubcaps, tin cans, a flattened pair of men's underpants. Beneath an overpass a car had been stripped, tires gone, windshield shattered, all the chrome detailing peeled away, and the engine missing. Milton stepped on the gas, ignoring the scarcity not only of petroleum but of many other things as well. There was, for instance, a scarcity of hope on Middlesex, where his wife no longer felt any stirrings in her spiritual umbilicus. There was a scarcity of food in the refrigerator, of snacks in the cupboards, and of freshly ironed shirts and clean socks in his dresser. There was a scarcity of social invitations and phone calls, as my parents' friends grew afraid to call a house that existed in a limbo between exhilaration and grief. Against the pressure of all this scarcity, Milton flooded the Eldorado's engine, and when that wasn't enough, he opened the briefcase on the seat beside him and stared in dashboard light at the twenty-five thousand dollars in cash bundled inside.

My mother had been awake when Milton slipped out of bed less than an hour earlier. Lying on her back, she heard him dressing in the dark. She hadn't asked him why he was getting up in the middle of the night. Once upon a time, she would have, but not anymore. Since my disappearance, daily routines had crumbled. Milton and Tessie often found themselves in the kitchen at four in the morning, drinking coffee. Only when Tessie heard the front door close had she become concerned. Next Milton's car started up and began backing down the drive. My mother listened until the engine faded away. She thought to herself with surprising calmness, "Maybe he's leaving for good." To her list of runaway father and runaway daughter she now added a further possibility: runaway husband.

Milton hadn't told Tessie where he was going for a number of reasons. First, he was afraid she would stop him. She would tell him to call the police, and he didn't want to call the police. The kidnapper had told him not to involve the law. Besides, Milton had had enough of cops and their blasé attitude. The only way to get something done was to do it yourself. On top of all that, this whole thing might be a wild-goose chase. If he told Tessie about it she would only worry. She might call Zoë and then he'd get an earful from his sister. In short, Milton was doing what he always did when it came to important decisions. Like the time he joined the Navy, or the time he moved us all to Grosse Pointe, Milton did whatever he wanted, confident that he knew best.

After the last mysterious phone call, Milton had waited for another. The following Sunday morning it came.

"Hello?"

"Good morning, Milton."

"Listen, whoever you are. I want some answers."

"I didn't call to hear what you want, Milton. What's important is what I want."

"I want my daughter. Where is she?"

"She's here with me."

The music, or singing, was still perceptible in the background. It reminded Milton of something long ago.

"How do I know you have her?"

"Why don't you ask me a question? She's told me a lot about her family. Quite a lot."

The rage surging through Milton at that moment was nearly unbearable. It was all he could do to keep from smashing the phone against the desk. At the same time, he was thinking, calculating.

"What's the name of the village her grandparents came from?"

"Just a minute." The phone was covered. Then the voice said, "Bithynios."

Milton's knees went weak. He sat down at the desk.

"Do you believe me yet, Milton?"

"We went to these caverns in Tennessee once. A real rip-off tourist trap. What were they called?"

Again the phone was covered. In a moment the voice replied, "The Mammothonics Caves."

At that Milton shot up out of his chair again. His face darkened and he tugged at his collar to help himself breathe.

"Now I have a question, Milton."

"What?"

"How much is it worth to you to get

your daughter back?"

"How much do you want?"

"Is this business, now? Are we negotiating a deal?"

"I'm ready to make a deal."

"How exciting."

"What do you want?"

"Twenty-five thousand dollars."

"All right."

"No, Milton," the voice corrected, "you don't understand. I want to bargain."

"What?"

"Haggle, Milton. This is business."

Milton was perplexed. He shook his head at the oddity of this request. But in the end he fulfilled it.

"Okay. Twenty-five's too much. I'll pay thirteen thousand."

"We're talking about your daughter, Milton. Not hot dogs."

"I haven't got that kind of cash."

"I might take twenty-two thousand."

"I'll give you fifteen."

"Twenty is as low as I can go."

"Seventeen is my final offer."

"How about nineteen?"

"Eighteen."

"Eighteen five."

"Deal."

The caller laughed. "Oh, that was fun, Milt." Then, in a gruff voice: "But I want twenty-five." And he hung up.

Back in 1933, a disembodied voice had spoken to my grandmother through the heating grate. Now, forty-two years later, a disguised voice spoke to my father over the phone.

"Good morning, Milton."

There was the music again, the faint singing.

"I've got the money," said Milton. "Now I want my girl."

"Tomorrow night," the kidnapper said. And then he told Milton where to leave the money, and where to wait for me to be released.

Across the lowland downriver plain Grand Trunk rose before Milton's Cadillac. The train station was still in use in 1975, though just barely. The once-opulent terminal was now only a shell. False Amtrak façades concealed the flaking, peeling walls. Most corridors were blocked off. Meanwhile, all around the operative core, the great old building continued to fall into ruin, the Guastavino tiles in the Palm Court falling, splintering on the ground, the immense barbershop now a junk room, the skylights caved in, heaped with filth. The office tower attached to the terminal was now a thirteen-story pigeon coop, all five hundred of its windows smashed, as if with diligence. At this same train station my grandparents had arrived a half century earlier. Lefty and Desdemona, one time only, had revealed their secret here to Sourmelina; and now their son, who never learned it, was pulling in behind the station, also secretly.

A scene like this, a ransom scene, calls for a noirish mood: shadows, sinister silhouettes. But the sky wasn't cooperating. We were having one of our pink nights. They happened every so often, depending on temperature and the level of chemicals in the air. When particulate matter in the atmosphere was sufficient, light from the ground got trapped and reflected back, and the entire Detroit sky would become the soft pink of cotton candy. It never got dark on pink nights, but the light was nothing like daytime. Our pink nights glowed with the raw luminescence of the night shift, of factories running around the clock. Sometimes the sky would become as bright as Pepto-Bismol, but more often it was a muted, a fabric-softener color. Nobody thought it was strange. Nobody said anything about it. We had all grown up with pink nights. They were not a natural phenomenon, but they were natural to us.

Under this strange nocturnal sky Milton pulled his car as close to the train platform as possible and stopped. He shut off the engine. Taking the briefcase, he got out into the still, crystalline winter air of Michigan. All the world was frozen, the distant trees, the telephone lines, the grass in the yards of the downriver houses, the ground itself. Out on the river a freighter bellowed. Here there were no sounds, the station completely deserted at night. Milton had on his tasseled black loafers. Dressing in the dark, he had decided they were the easiest to slip on. He was also wearing his car coat, beige and dingy, with a muff of fur at the collar. Against the cold he had worn a hat, a gray felt Borsalino, with a red feather in the black band. An old-timer's hat now in 1975. With hat, briefcase, and loafers, Milton might have been on his way to work. And certainly he was walking quickly. He climbed the metal steps to the train platform. He headed along it, looking for the trash can where he was supposed to drop the briefcase. The kidnapper said it would have an X chalked on the lid.

Milton hurried along the platform, the tassels on his loafers bouncing, the tiny feather in his hat rippling in the cold wind. It would not be strictly truthful to say that he was afraid. Milton Stephanides did not admit to being afraid. The physiological manifestations of fear, the racing heart, the torched armpits, went on in him without official acknowledgment. He wasn't alone among his generation in this. There were lots of fathers who shouted when they were afraid or scolded their children to deflect blame from themselves. It's possible that such qualities were indispensable in the generation that won the war. A lack of introspection was good for bolstering your courage, but in the last months and weeks it had done damage to Milton. Throughout my disappearance Milton had kept up a brave front while doubts worked invisibly inside him. He was like a statue being chiseled away from the inside, hollowed out. As more and more of his thoughts gave him pain, Milton had increasingly avoided them. Instead he concentrated on the few that made him feel better, the bromides about everything working out. Milton, quite simply, had ceased to think things through. What was he doing out there on the dark train platform? Why did he go out there alone? We would never be able to explain it adequately.

It didn't take him long to find the trash can marked with chalk. Swiftly Milton lifted its triangular green lid and laid the briefcase inside. But when he tried to pull his arm back out, something wouldn't let him: it was his hand. Since Milton had stopped thinking things through, his body was now doing the work for him. His hand seemed to be saying something. It was voicing reservations. "What if the kidnapper doesn't set Callie free?" the hand was saying. But Milton answered, "There's no time to think about that now." Again he tried to pull his arm out of the trash can, but his hand stubbornly resisted: "What if the kidnapper takes this money and then asks for more?" asked the hand. "That's the chance we'll have to take," Milton snapped back, and with all his strength pulled his arm out of the trash can. His hand lost its grip; the briefcase fell onto the refuse inside. Milton hurried back across the platform (dragging his hand with him) and got into the Cadillac.

He started the engine. He turned on the heat, warming the car up for me. He leaned forward staring through the windshield, expecting me to appear any minute. His hand was still smarting, muttering to itself. Milton thought about the briefcase lying out in the trash can. His mind filled with the image of the money inside. Twenty-five grand! He saw the individual stacks of hundred-dollar bills; the repeating face of Benjamin Franklin in the doubled mirrors of all that cash. Milton's throat went dry; a spasm of anxiety known to all Depression babies gripped his body; and in the next second he was jumping out of the car again, running back to the platform.

This guy wanted to do business? Then Milton would show him how to do business! He wanted to negotiate? How about this! (Milton was climbing the steps now, loafers ringing against the metal.) Instead of leaving twenty-five thousand bucks, why not leave twelve thousand five hundred? *This way I'll have some leverage. Half now, half later.* Why hadn't he thought of this before? What the hell was the matter with him? He was under too much strain . . . No sooner had he reached the platform, however, than my father stopped cold. Less than twenty yards away, a dark figure in a stocking cap was reaching into the trash can. Milton's blood froze. He didn't know whether to retreat or advance. The kidnapper tried to pull the briefcase out, but it wouldn't fit through the swinging door. He went behind the can and lifted up the entire metal lid. In the chemical brightness Milton saw the patriarchal beard, the pale, waxen cheeks, and — most tellingly — the tiny five-foot-four frame. Father Mike.

Father *Mike?* Father Mike was the kidnapper? Impossible. Incredible! But there was no doubt. Standing on the platform was the man who had once been engaged to my mother and who, at my father's hands, had had her stolen away. Taking the ransom was the former seminarian who had married Milton's sister, Zoë, instead, a choice that had sentenced him to a life of invidious comparisons, of Zoë always asking why he hadn't invested in the stock market when Milton had, or bought gold when Milton had, or stashed money away in the Cayman Islands as Milton had; a choice that had condemned Father Mike to being a poor relation, forced to endure Milton's lack of respect while accepting his hospitality, and compelling him to carry a dining room chair into the living room if he wanted to sit. Yes, it was a great shock for Milton to discover his brother-in-law on the train platform. But it also made sense. It was clear now why the kidnapper had wanted to haggle over the price, why he wanted to feel like a businessman for once, and, alas, how he had known about Bithynios. Explained, too, were why the telephone calls had come on Sundays, whenever Tessie was at church, and the music in the background, which Milton now identified as the priests chanting the liturgy. Long ago, my father had stolen Father's Mike's fiancée and married her himself. The child of the union, me, had poured salt in the wound by baptizing the priest in reverse. Now Father Mike was trying to get even.

But not if Milton could help it. "Hey!" he shouted, putting his hands on his hips. "Just what the hell are you trying to pull, Mike?" Father Mike didn't answer. He looked up and, out of priestly habit, smiled benignantly at Milton, his white teeth appearing in the great bush of black beard. But already he was backing away, stepping on crushed cups and other litter, hugging the briefcase to his chest like a packed parachute. Three or four steps backward, smiling that gentle smile, before he turned and fled in earnest. He was small but quick. Like a shot he disappeared down a set of stairs on the other side of the platform. In pink light Milton saw him crossing the train tracks to his car, a bright green ("Grecian green" according to the catalogue), fuel-efficient AMC Gremlin. And Milton ran back to the Cadillac to follow him.

It wasn't like a car chase in the movies. There was no swerving, no near collisions. It was, after all, a car chase between a Greek Orthodox priest and a middle-aged Republican. As they sped (relatively speaking) away from Grand Trunk, heading in the direction of the river, Father Mike and Milton never exceeded the limit by more than ten miles per hour. Father Mike didn't want to attract the police. Milton, realizing that his brother-in-law had nowhere to go, was content to follow him to the water. So they went along in their pokey fashion, the weirdly shaped Gremlin making rolling stops at traffic signs and the Eldorado, a little bit later, doing the same. Down nameless streets, past junk houses, across a dead-end piece of land created by the freeways and the river, Father Mike unwisely attempted to escape. It was just like always; Aunt Zo should have been there to holler at Father Mike, because only an idiot would have headed toward the river instead of the highway. Every street he could possibly take would go nowhere. "I got you now," Milton exulted. The Gremlin made a right. The Eldorado made a right. The Gremlin made a left, and so did the Cadillac. Milton's tank was full. He could track Father Mike all night if he had to.

Feeling confident, Milton adjusted the heat, which was a little too high. He turned on the radio. He let a little more space get between the Gremlin and the Eldorado. When he looked up again, the Gremlin was making another right. Thirty seconds later, when Milton turned the same corner, he saw the sweeping expanse of the Ambassador Bridge. And his confidence crumbled. This was not just like always. Tonight, his brother-in-law the priest, who spent his life in the fairy tale world of the Church, dressed up like Liberace, had figured things out for once. As soon as Milton saw the bridge strung like a giant, glittering harp over the river, panic seized his soul. With horror Milton understood

Father Mike's plan. As Chapter Eleven had intended when he threatened to dodge the draft, Father Mike was heading for Canada! Like Jimmy Zizmo the bootlegger, he was heading for the lawless, liberal hideaway to the north! He was planning to take the money out of the country. And he was no longer going slow.

Yes, despite its thimble-sized engine that sounded like a sewing machine, the Gremlin was managing to accelerate. Leaving the no-man's-land around Grand Trunk Station, it had now entered the bright, Customs-controlled, high-traffic area of the United States–Canada border. Tall, carbon-gas streetlights irradiated the Gremlin, whose bright green color now looked even more acid than ever. Putting distance between itself and the Eldorado (like the Joker's car getting away from the Batmobile), the Gremlin joined the trucks and cars converging around the entrance to the great suspension bridge. Milton stepped on it. The huge engine of the Cadillac roared; white smoke spumed from the tailpipe. At this point the two cars had become exactly what cars are supposed to be; they were extensions of their owners. The Gremlin was small and nimble, as Father Mike was; it disappeared and reappeared in traffic much as he did behind the icon screen at church. The Eldorado, substantial and boat-like — as was Milton — proved difficult to maneuver in the late-night bridge traffic. There were huge semis. There were passenger cars heading for the casinos and strip clubs in Windsor. In all this traffic Milton lost sight of the Gremlin. He pulled into a line and waited. Suddenly, six cars ahead, he saw Father Mike dart out of line, cutting off another car and slipping into a toll booth. Milton rolled down his automatic window. Sticking his head out into the cold, exhaust-clouded air, he shouted, "Stop that man! He's got my money!" The Customs officer didn't hear him, however. Milton could see the officer asking Father Mike a few questions and then — No! Stop! — he was waving Father Mike through. At that point Milton started hammering on his horn.

The blasts erupting from beneath the Eldorado's hood might have been emanating from Milton's own chest. His blood pressure was surging, and inside his car coat his body began to drip with sweat. He had been confident of bringing Father Mike to justice in the U.S. courts. But who knew what would happen once he got to Canada? Canada with its pacifism and its socialized medicine! Canada with its millions of French speakers! It was like . . . like . . . like a foreign country! Father Mike might become a fugitive over there, living it up in Quebec. He might disappear into Saskatchewan and roam with the moose. It wasn't only losing the money that enraged Milton. In addition to absconding with twenty-five thousand dollars and giving Milton false hopes of my return, Father Mike was abandoning his own family. Brotherly protectiveness mixed with financial and paternal pain in Milton's heaving breast. "You don't do this to my sister, you hear me?" Milton fruitlessly shouted from the driver's seat of his huge, boxed-in car. Next he called after Father Mike, "Hey, dumb-ass. Haven't you ever heard of commissions? Soon as you change that money you're going to lose five percent!" Fulminating at the wheel, his progress curtailed by semis in front and strip-clubbers behind, Milton squirmed and hollered, his fury unbearable.

My father's honking hadn't gone unnoticed, however. Customs agents were used to the horn-blowing of impatient drivers. They had a way of handling them. As soon as Milton pulled up to the booth, the official signaled him to pull over.

Through his open window Milton shouted, "There's a guy who just came through. He stole some money of mine. Can you have him stopped at the other end? He's driving a Gremlin."

"Pull your car over there, sir."

"He stole twenty-five thousand dollars!"

"We can talk about that as soon as you pull over and get out of your car, sir."

"He's trying to take it out of the country!" Milton explained one last time. But the Customs agent continued to direct him to the inspection area. Finally Milton gave up. Withdrawing his face from the open window, he took hold of the steering wheel and obediently began pulling over to the empty lane. As soon as he was clear of the Customs booth, however, he stomped a tasseled loafer down on the accelerator and the squealing Cadillac rocketed away.

Now it *was* something like a car chase. For out on the bridge, Father Mike, too, had stepped on the gas. Snaking between the cars and trucks, he was racing toward the international divide, while Milton pursued, flashing his brights to get people out of the way. The bridge rose up over the river in a graceful parabola, its steel cables strung with red lights. The Cadillac's tires hummed over its striated surface. Milton had his foot to the floor, engaging what he called the goose gear. And now the difference between a luxury automobile and a newfangled cartoon car began to show itself. The Cadillac engine roared with power. Its eight cylinders fired, the carburetor sucking in vast quantities of fuel. The pistons thumped and jumped and the drive wheel spun like mad, as the long, superhero car passed others as if they were standing still. Seeing the Eldorado coming so fast, other drivers moved aside. Milton cut straight through the traffic until he spotted the green Gremlin up ahead. "So much for your high gas mileage," Milton cried. "Sometimes you need a little power!"

By this time Father Mike saw the Eldorado looming, too. He floored the accelerator, but the Gremlin's engine was already working at capacity. The car vibrated wildly but picked up no speed. On and on came the Cadillac. Milton didn't take his foot off the pedal until his front bumper was nearly touching the Gremlin's rear. They were traveling now at seventy miles per hour. Father Mike looked up to see Milton's avenging eyes filling the rearview mirror. Milton, gazing ahead into the Gremlin's interior, saw a slice of Father Mike's face. The priest seemed to be asking for forgiveness, or explaining his actions. There was a strange sadness in his eyes, a weakness, which Milton could not interpret.

. . . And now I have to enter Father Mike's head, I'm afraid. I feel myself being sucked in and I can't resist. The front part of his mind is a whirl of fear, greed, and desperate thoughts of escape. All to be expected. But going deeper in, I discover things about him I never knew. There's no serenity, for instance, none at all, no closeness to God. The gentleness Father Mike had, his smiling silence at family meals, the way he would bend down to be face-to-face with children (not far for him, but still) — all these attributes existed apart from any communication with a transcendent realm. They were just a passive-aggressive method of survival, the result of having a wife with a voice as loud as Aunt Zo's. Yes, echoing inside Father Mike's head is all the shouting Aunt Zo has done over the years, ever since she was pregnant nonstop in Greece without a washer or dryer. I can hear: "Do you call this a life?" And: "If you've got the ear of God, tell Him to send me a check for the drapes." And: "Maybe the Catholics have the right idea. Priests shouldn't have families." At church Michael Antoniou is called Father. He is deferred to, catered to. At church he has the power to forgive sins and consecrate the host. But as soon as he steps through the front door of their duplex in Harper Woods, Father Mike suffers an immediate drop in status. At home he is nobody. At home he is bossed around, complained about, ignored. And so it was not so difficult to see why Father Mike decided to flee his marriage, and why he needed money . . .

. . . none of which, however, could Milton read in his brother-in-law's eyes. And in the next moment those eyes changed again. Father Mike had shifted his gaze back to the road, where they met a terrifying sight. The red brake lights of the car in front of him were flashing. Father Mike was going much too fast to stop in time. He stomped on his brakes, but it was too late: the Grecian green Gremlin slammed into the car ahead. The Eldorado came next. Milton braced himself for the impact. But it was then an amazing thing happened. He heard metal crunching and glass shattering, but this was coming from the cars ahead. As for the Cadillac itself, it never stopped moving forward. It climbed right up Father Mike's car. The weird, slanted back end of the Gremlin acted as a kind of ramp, and in the next second Milton realized he was airborne. The midnight blue Eldorado rose above the accident on the bridge. It sailed up over the guardrails, through the cables, plunging off the middle span of the Ambassador Bridge.

The Eldorado fell hood first, gathering speed. Through the tinted windshield Milton could see the Detroit River below; but only briefly. In those last seconds, as life prepared to leave his body, it withdrew its laws, too. Instead of falling into the river, the Cadillac swooped upward and leveled itself. Milton was surprised but very pleased. He didn't remember the salesman's having mentioned anything about a flight feature. Even better, Milton hadn't paid extra for it. As the car floated away from the bridge he was smiling. "Now, *this* is what I call an Air-Ride," he said to himself. The Eldorado was flying high above the river, wasting who knew how much gas. The sky outside was pink while the lights on the dashboard were green. There were all sorts of switches and gauges. Milton had never noticed most of them before. It looked more like an airplane cockpit than a car, and Milton was at the controls, Milton was flying his last Cadillac over the Detroit River. It didn't matter what eyewitnesses saw, or that the newspapers reported the next day that the Cadillac was part of the ten-car pileup on the bridge. Sitting back in the comfortable leather bucket seat, Milton Stephanides could see the downtown skyline approaching. Music was playing on the radio, an old Artie Shaw tune, why not, and Milton watched the red light on the Penobscot Building blinking on and off. After a certain amount of trial and error, he learned how to steer the flying car. It wasn't a matter of turning the wheel but of willing it, as in a lucid dream. Milton brought the car in over land. He passed above Cobo Hall. He circled the Top of the Pontch, where he had once taken me to lunch. For some reason Milton was no longer afraid of heights. He guessed that this was because his death was imminent; there was nothing left to fear. Without vertigo or perspiration, he gazed down at Grand Circus Park until he spotted what was left of the wheels of Detroit; and after that he headed for the West Side to look for the old Zebra Room. Back on the bridge, my father's head had been crushed against the steering wheel. The detective who later informed my mother of the accident, when asked about the condition of Milton's body, said only, "It was consistent with a crash of a vehicle going at seventy-plus miles an hour." Milton no longer had any brain waves, so it was understandable why, hovering in the Cadillac, he might have forgotten that the Zebra Room had burned down long ago. He was mystified at not being able to find it. All that was left of the old neighborhood was empty land. It seemed that most of the city was gone, as he gazed down. Empty lot followed empty lot. But Milton was wrong about this, too. Corn was sprouting up in some places, and grass was coming back. It looked like farmland down there. "Might as well give it back to the Indians," Milton thought. "Maybe the Potowatomies would want it. They could put up a casino." The sky had turned to cotton candy and the city had become a plain again. But another red light was blinking now. Not on the Penobscot Building; inside the car. It was one of the gauges Milton had never seen before. He knew what it indicated.

At that moment, Milton began to cry. All of a sudden his face was wet and he touched it, sniffling and weeping. He slumped back, and because no one was there to see, he opened his mouth to give outlet to his overpowering grief. He hadn't cried since he was a boy. The sound of his deep voice crying surprised him. It was the sound of a bear, wounded or dying. Milton bellowed in the Cadillac as the car began, once again, to descend. He was crying not because he was about to die but because I, Calliope, was still gone, because he had failed to save me, because he had done everything he could to get me back and still I was missing.

As the car tipped its nose down, the river appeared again. Milton Stephanides, an old navy man, prepared to meet it. Right at the end he was no longer thinking about me. I have to be honest and record Milton's thoughts as they occurred to him. At the very end he wasn't thinking about me or

Tessie or any of us. There was no time. As the car plunged, Milton only had time to be astonished by the way things had turned out. All his life he had lectured everybody about the right way to do things and now he had done this, the stupidest thing ever. He could hardly believe he had loused things up quite so badly. His last word, therefore, was spoken softly, without anger or fear, only with bewilderment and a measure of bravery. "Birdbrain," Milton said, to himself, in his last Cadillac. And then the water claimed him.

A real Greek might end on this tragic note. But an American is inclined to stay upbeat. These days, whenever we talk about Milton, my mother and I come to the conclusion that he got out just in time. He got out before Chapter Eleven, taking over the family business, ran it into the ground in less than five years. Before Chapter Eleven, in a reprise of Desdemona's gender prognostications, began wearing a tiny silver spoon around his neck. He got out before the draining of bank accounts and the jacking up of credit cards. Before Tessie was forced to sell Middlesex and move down to Florida with Aunt Zo. And he got out three months before Cadillac, in April 1975, introduced the Seville, a fuel-efficient model that looked as though it had lost its pants, after which Cadillacs were never the same. Milton got out before many of the things that I will not include in this story, because they are the common tragedies of American life, and as such do not fit into this singular and uncommon record. He got out before the Cold War ended, before missile shields and global warming and September 11 and a second President with only one vowel in his name.

Most important, Milton got out without ever seeing me again. That would not have been easy. I like to think that my father's love for me was strong enough that he could have accepted me. But in some ways it's better that we never had to work that out, he and I. With respect to my father I will always remain a girl. There's a kind of purity in that, the purity of childhood.

The Last Stop

❧

"It sort of still applies," said Julie Kikuchi.

"It does not," I said.

"It's in the same ballpark."

"What I told you about myself has nothing whatsoever to do with being gay or closeted. I've always liked girls. I liked girls when I was a girl."

"I wouldn't be some kind of last stop for you?"

"More like a first stop."

Julie laughed. She still had not made a decision. I waited. Then at last she said, "All right."

"All right?" I asked.

She nodded.

"All *right*," I said.

So we left the museum and went back to my apartment. We had another drink; we slow-danced in the living room. And then I led Julie into the bedroom, where I hadn't led anyone in quite a long time.

She switched off the lights.

"Wait a minute," I said. "Are you turning off the lights because of you or because of me?"

"Because of me."

"Why?"

"Because I'm a shy, modest Oriental lady. Just don't expect me to bathe you."

"No bathing?"

"Not unless you do a Zorba dance."

"Where did I put that bouzouki of mine, anyway?" I was trying to keep up the banter. I was also taking off my clothes. So was Julie. It was like jumping into cold water. You had to do it without thinking too much. We got under the covers and held each other, petrified, happy.

"I might be your last stop, too," I said, clinging to her. "Did you ever think of that?"

And Julie Kikuchi answered, "It crossed my mind."

***

Chapter Eleven flew to San Francisco to collect me from jail. My mother had to sign a letter requesting that the police release me into my brother's custody. A trial date would be set in the near future but, as a juvenile and first-time offender, I was likely to receive only probation. (The offense came off my record, never interfering with my subsequent job prospects at the State Department. Not that I concerned myself with these details at the time. I was too stunned, sick with grief poisons, and wanted to go home.)

When I came out into the outer police station, my brother was sitting alone on a long wooden bench. He looked up at me with no expression, blinking. That was Chapter Eleven's way. Everything went on in him internally. Inside his braincase sensations were being reviewed, evaluated, before any official reaction was given. I was used to this, of course. What is more natural than the tics and habits of one's close relatives? Years ago, Chapter Eleven had made me pull down my underpants so that he could look at me. Now his eyes were raised but no less riveted. He was taking in my deforested head. He was getting a load of the funereal suit. It was a lucky thing that my brother had taken as much LSD as he had. Chapter Eleven had gone in early for mind expansion. He contemplated the veil of Maya, the existence of various planes of being. For a personality thus prepared, it was somewhat easier to deal with your sister becoming your brother. There have been hermaphrodites like me since the world began. But as I came out from my holding pen it was possible that no generation other than my brother's was as well disposed to accept me. Still, it was not nothing to witness me so changed. Chapter Eleven's eyes widened.

We hadn't seen each other for over a

year. Chapter Eleven had changed, too. His hair was shorter. It had receded farther. His friend's girlfriend had given him a home perm. Chapter Eleven's previously lank hair was now leonine in back, while the front retreated. He didn't look like John Lennon anymore. Gone were his faded bell-bottoms, his granny glasses. Now he wore brown hip-huggers. His wide-lapel shirt shimmered under the fluorescent lights. The sixties have never really come to an end. They're still going on right now in Goa. But by 1975 the sixties had finally ended for my brother.

At any other time, we would have lingered over these details. But we didn't have the luxury for that. I came across the room. Chapter Eleven stood up and then we were hugging, swaying. "Dad's dead," my brother repeated in my ear. "He's dead."

I asked him what had happened and he told me. Milton had charged through customs. Father Mike had also been on the bridge. He was now in the hospital. Milton's old briefcase had been found in the wreckage of the Gremlin, full of money. Father Mike had confessed everything to the police, the kidnapping ruse, the ransom.

When this had sunk in, I asked, "How's Mom?"

"She's all right. She's holding up. She's pissed at Milt."

"Pissed?"

"For going out there. For not telling her. She's glad you're coming home. That's what she's focusing on. You coming back for the funeral. So that's good."

We were scheduled to take the red-eye out that night. The funeral was the next morning. Chapter Eleven had been dealing with the bureaucratic side of things, getting the death certificates and placing the obituaries. He asked me nothing about my time in San Francisco or at Sixty-Niners. Only when we were on the plane and Chapter Eleven had had a few beers did he allude to my condition. "So, I guess I can't call you Callie anymore."

"Call me whatever you want."

"How about 'bro'?"

"Fine with me."

He was quiet, blinking. There was the usual lag time while he thought. "I never heard much about what happened out there at that clinic. I was up in Marquette. I wasn't talking to Mom and Dad that much."

"I ran away."

"Why?"

"They were going to cut me up."

I could feel him staring at me, with that outer glaze that concealed considerable mental activity. "It's a little bit weird for me," he said.

"It's weird for me, too."

A moment later he let out a laugh. "Hah! Weird! Pretty fucking weird."

I was shaking my head in comic despair. "You can say that again. Bro."

Confronted with the impossible, there was no option but to treat it as normal. We didn't have an upper register, so to speak, but only the middle range of our shared experience and ways of behaving, of joking around. But it got us through.

"One good thing about this gene I have, though," I said.

"What?"

"I'll never go bald."

"Why not?"

"You have to have DHT to go bald."

"Huh," said Chapter Eleven, feeling his scalp. "I guess I'm a little heavy on the DHT. I guess I'm what they'd call DHT-rich."

We reached Detroit a little after six in the morning. The smashed-up Eldorado had been towed to a police yard. Waiting in the airport parking lot was our mother's car, the "Florida Special." The lemon-colored Cadillac was all we had left of Milton. It was already beginning to take on the attributes of a relic. The driver's seat was sunken from the weight of his body. You could see the impression of Milton's cloven backside in the leather upholstery. Tessie filled this hollow with throw pillows in order to see over the steering wheel. Chapter Eleven had tossed the pillows into the backseat.

In the unseasonal car, with its powerful air-conditioning switched off and sunroof closed, we started for home. We passed the giant Uniroyal tire and the thready woods of Inkster.

"What time's the funeral?" I asked.

"Eleven."

It was just getting light. The sun was rising from wherever it rose, behind the distant factories maybe, or over the blind river. The growing light was like a leakage or flood, seeping into the ground.

"Go through downtown," I told my brother.

"It'll take too long."

"We've got time. I want to see it."

Chapter Eleven obliged me. We took I-94 past River Rouge and Olympia Stadium and then curled in toward the river on the Lodge Freeway and entered the city from the north.

Grow up in Detroit and you understand the way of all things. Early on, you are put on close relations with entropy. As we rose out of the highway trough, we could see the condemned houses, many burned, as well as the stark beauty of all the vacant lots, gray and frozen. Once-elegant apartment buildings stood next to scrapyards, and where there had been furriers and movie palaces there were now blood banks and methadone clinics and Mother Waddles Perpetual Mission. Returning to Detroit from bright climes usually depressed me. But now I welcomed it. The blight eased the pain of my father's death, making it seem like a general state of affairs. At least the city didn't mock my grief by being sparkling or winsome.

Downtown looked the same, only emptier. You couldn't knock down the skyscrapers when the tenants left; so instead boards went over the windows and doors, and the great shells of commerce were put in cold storage. On the riverfront the Renaissance Center was being built, inaugurating a renaissance that has never arrived. "Let's go through Greektown," I said. Again my brother humored me. Soon we came down the block of restaurants and souvenir stores. Amid the ethnic kitsch, there were still a few authentic coffee houses, patronized by old men in their seventies and eighties. Some were already up this morning, drinking coffee, playing backgammon, and reading the Greek newspapers. When these old men died, the coffee houses would suffer and finally close. Little by little, the restaurants on the block would suffer, too, their awnings getting ripped, the big yellow lightbulbs on the Laikon marquee burning out, the Greek bakery on the corner being taken over by South Yemenis from Dearborn. But all that hadn't happened yet. On Monroe Street, we passed the Grecian Gardens, where we had held Lefty's *makaria*.

"Are we having a *makaria* for Dad?" I asked.

"Yeah. The whole deal."

"Where? At the Grecian Gardens?"

Chapter Eleven laughed. "You kidding? Nobody wanted to come down here."

"I like it here," I said. "I love Detroit."

"Yeah? Well, welcome home."

He had turned back onto Jefferson for the long miles through the blighted East Side. A wig shop. Vanity Dancing, the old club, now for rent. A used-record store with a hand-painted sign showing people grooving amid an explosion of musical notes. The old dime stores and sweet shops were closed, Kresge's, Woolworth's, Sanders Ice Cream. It was cold out. Not many people were on the streets. On one corner a man stood impervious, cutting a fine figure against the winter sky. His leather coat reached to his ankles. Space funk goggles wrapped around his dignified, long-jawed head, on top of which sat, or sailed really, the Spanish galleon of a velvet maroon hat. Not part of my suburban world, this figure; therefore exotic. But nevertheless familiar, and suggestive of the peculiar creative energies of my hometown. I was glad to see him anyway. I couldn't take my eyes away.

When I was little, street-corner dudes like that would sometimes lower their shades to wink, keen on getting a rise out of the white girl in the backseat passing by. But now the dude gave me a different look altogether. He didn't lower his sunglasses, but his mouth, his flared nostrils, and the tilt of his head communicated defiance and even hate. That was when I realized a shocking thing. I couldn't become a man without becoming The Man. Even if I didn't want to.

I made Chapter Eleven go through Indian Village, passing our old house. I wanted to take a nostalgia bath to calm my nerves before seeing my mother. The streets were still full of trees, bare in winter, so that we could see all the way to the frozen river. I was thinking how amazing it was that the world contained so many lives. Out in these streets people were embroiled in a thousand matters, money problems, love problems, school problems. People were falling in love, getting married, going to drug rehab, learning how to ice-skate, getting bifocals, studying for exams, trying on clothes, getting their hair cut, and getting born. And in some houses people were getting old and sick and were dying, leaving others to grieve. It was happening all the time, unnoticed, and it was the thing that really mattered. What really mattered in life, what gave it weight, was death. Seen this way, my bodily metamorphosis was a small event. Only the pimp might have been interested.

Soon we reached Grosse Pointe. The naked elms reached across our street from both sides, touching fingertips, and snow lay crusted in the flower beds before the warm, hibernatory houses. My body was reacting to the sight of home. Happy sparks were shooting off inside me. It was a canine feeling, full of eager love, and dumb to tragedy. Here was my home, Middlesex. Up there in that window, on the tiled window seat, I used to read for hours, eating mulberries off the tree outside.

The driveway hadn't been shoveled. Nobody had had time to think about that. Chapter Eleven took the driveway a little fast and we bounced in our seats, the tailpipe hitting. After we got out of the car, he opened the trunk and began carrying my suitcase to the house. But halfway there he stopped. "Hey, bro," he said. "You can carry this yourself." He was smiling with mischief. You could see he was enjoying the paradigm shift. He was taking my metamorphosis as a brain teaser, like the ones in the back of his sci-fi magazines.

"Let's not get carried away," I answered. "Feel free to carry my luggage anytime."

"Catch!" shouted Chapter Eleven, and hefted the suitcase. I caught it, staggering back. Right then the door of the house opened and my mother, in house slippers, stepped out into the frost-powdery air.

Tessie Stephanides, who in a different lifetime when space travel was new had decided to go along with her husband and create a girl by devious means, now saw before her, in the snowy driveway, the fruit of that scheme. Not a daughter at all anymore but, at least by looks, a son. She was tired and heartsick and had no energy to deal with this new event. It was not acceptable that I was now living as a male person. Tessie didn't think it should be up to me. She had given birth to me and nursed me and brought me up. She had known me before I knew myself and now she had no say in the matter. Life started out one thing and then suddenly turned a corner and became something else. Tessie didn't know how this had happened. Though she could still see Calliope in my face, each feature seemed changed, thickened, and there were whiskers on my chin and above my upper lip. There was a criminal aspect to my appearance, in Tessie's eyes. She couldn't help herself thinking that my arrival was part of some settling of accounts, that Milton had been punished and that her punishment was just beginning. For all these reasons she stood still, red-eyed, in the doorway.

"Hi, Mom," I said. "I'm home."

I went forward to meet her. I set down my suitcase, and when I looked up again, Tessie's face had altered. She had been preparing for this moment for months. Now her faint eyebrows lifted, the corners of her mouth rose, crinkling the wan cheeks. Her expression was that of a mother watching a doctor remove bandages from a severely burned child. An optimistic, dishonest, bedside face. Still, it told me all I needed to know. Tessie was going to try to accept things. She felt crushed by what had happened to me but she was going to endure it for my sake.

We embraced. Tall as I was, I laid my head on my mother's shoulder, and she stroked my hair while I sobbed.

"Why?" she kept crying softly, shaking her head. "Why?" I thought she was talking about Milton. But then she clarified: "Why did you run away, honey?"

"I had to."

"Don't you think it would have been easier just to stay the way you were?"

I lifted my face and looked into my mother's eyes. And I told her: "This is the way I was."

You will want to know: How did we get used to things? What happened to our memories? Did Calliope have to die in order to make room for Cal? To all these questions I offer the same truism: it's amazing what you can get used to. After I returned from San Francisco and started living as a male, my family found that, contrary to popular opinion, gender was not all that important. My change from girl to boy was far less dramatic than the distance anybody travels from infancy to adulthood. In most ways I remained the person I'd always been. Even now, though I live as a man, I remain in essential ways Tessie's daughter. I'm still the one who remembers to call her every Sunday. I'm the one she recounts her growing list of ailments to. Like any good daughter, I'll be the one to nurse her in her old age. We still discuss what's wrong with men; we still, on visits back home, have our hair done together. Bowing to the changing times, the Golden Fleece now cuts men's hair as well as women's. (And I've finally let dear old Sophie give me that short haircut she always wanted.)

But all that came later. Right then, we were in a hurry. It was almost ten. The limousine from the funeral parlor would be arriving in thirty-five minutes. "You better get cleaned up," Tessie said to me. The funeral did what funerals are supposed to do: it gave us no time to dwell on our feelings. Hooking her arm in mine, Tessie led me into the house. Middlesex, too, was in mourning. The mirror in the den was covered by a black cloth. There were black streamers on the sliding doors. All the old immigrant touches. Aside from that, the house seemed unnaturally still and dim. As always, the enormous windows brought the outdoors in, so that it was winter in the living room; snow lay all around us.

"I guess you can wear that suit," Chapter Eleven said to me. "It looks pretty appropriate."

"I doubt you even have a suit."

"I don't. I didn't go to a stuck-up private school. Where did you get that thing, anyway? It smells."

"At least it's a suit."

While my brother and I teased each other, Tessie watched closely. She was picking up the cue from my brother that this thing that had happened to me might be handled lightly. She wasn't sure she could do this herself, but she was watching how the younger generation pulled it off.

Suddenly there was a strange noise, like an eagle's cry. The intercom on the living room wall crackled. A voice shrieked, "Yoo-hoo! Tessie honey!"

The immigrant touches, of course, weren't around the house because of Tessie. The person shrieking over the intercom was none other than Desdemona.

Patient reader, you may have been wondering what happened to my grandmother. You may have noticed that, shortly after she climbed into bed forever, Desdemona began to fade away. But that was intentional. I allowed Desdemona to slip out of my narrative because, to be honest, in the dramatic years of my transformation, she slipped out of my attention most of the time. For the last five years she had remained bedridden in the guest house. During my time at Baker & Inglis, while I was falling in love with the Object, I had remained aware of my grandmother only in the vaguest of ways. I saw Tessie preparing her meals and carrying trays out to the guest house. Every evening I saw my father make a dutiful visit to her perpetual sickroom with its hot-water bottles and pharmaceutical supplies. At those times Milton spoke to his mother in Greek, with increasing difficulty. During the war Desdemona had failed to teach her son to write Greek. Now in her old age she recognized with horror that he was forgetting how to speak it as well. Occasionally, I brought Desdemona's food trays out and for a few minutes would reacquaint myself with her time-capsule life. The framed photograph of her burial plot still stood on her bedside table for reassurance.

Tessie went to the intercom. "Yes, *yia yia*," she said. "Did you need something?"

"My feet they are terrible today. Did you get the Epsom salts?"

"Yes. I'll bring them to you."

"Why God no let *yia yia* die, Tessie? Everybody's dead! Everybody but *yia yia*! *Yia yia* she is too old to live now. And what does God do? Nothing."

"Are you finished with your breakfast?"

"Yes, thank you, honey. But the prunes they were not good ones today."

"Those are the same prunes you always have."

"Something maybe it happen to them. Get a new box, please, Tessie. The Sunkist."

"I will."

"Okay, honey *mou*. Thank you, honey."

My mother silenced the intercom and turned back to me. "*Yia yia*'s not doing so good anymore. Her mind's going. Since you've been away she's really gone downhill. We told her about Milt." Tessie faltered, near tears. "About what happened.

938

Yia yia couldn't stop crying. I thought she was going to die right then and there. And then a few hours later she asked me where Milt was. She forgot the entire thing. Maybe it's better that way."

"Is she going to the funeral?"

"She can barely walk. Mrs. Papanikolas is coming to watch her. She doesn't know where she is half the time." Tessie smiled sadly, shaking her head. "Who would have thought she would outlive Milt?" She teared up again and forced the tears back.

"Can I go and see her?"

"You want to?"

"Yes."

Tessie looked apprehensive. "What will you tell her?"

"What should I tell her?"

For another few seconds my mother was silent, thinking. Then she shrugged. "It doesn't matter. Whatever you say she won't remember. Take this out to her. She wants to soak her feet."

Carrying the Epsom salts and a piece of the baklava wrapped in cellophane, I came out of the house and walked along the portico past the courtyard and bathhouse to the guest house behind. The door was unlocked. I opened it and stepped in. The only light in the room came from the television, which was turned up extremely loud. Facing me when I entered was the old portrait of Patriarch Athenagoras that Desdemona had saved from the yard sale years ago. In a birdcage by the window, a green parakeet, the last surviving member of my grandparents' former aviary, was moving back and forth on its balsa wood perch. Other familiar objects and furnishings were still in evidence, Lefty's rebetika records, the brass coffee table, and, of course, the silkworm box, sitting in the middle of the engraved circular top. The box was now so stuffed with mementos it wouldn't shut. Inside were snapshots, old letters, precious buttons, worry beads. Somewhere below all that, I knew, were two long braids of hair, tied with crumbling black ribbons, and a wedding crown made of ship's rope. I wanted to look at these things, but as I stepped farther into the room my attention was diverted by the grand spectacle on the bed.

Desdemona was propped up, regally, against a beige corduroy cushion known as a husband. The arms of this cushion encircled her. Protruding from the elastic pocket on the outside of one arm was an aspirator, along with two or three pill bottles. Desdemona was in a pale white nightgown, the bedcovers pulled up to her waist, and in her lap sat one of her Turkish atrocity fans. None of this was surprising. It was what Desdemona had done with her hair that shocked me. On hearing about Milton's death, she had removed her hairnet, tearing at the masses of hair that tumbled down. Her hair was completely gray but still very fine and, in the light coming from the television, it appeared to be almost blond. The hair fell over her shoulders and spread out over her body like the hair of Botticelli's Venus. The face framed by this astonishing cascade, however, was not that of a beautiful young woman but that of an old widow with a square head and dried-out mouth. In the unmoving air of the room and the smell of medicine and skin salves I could feel the weight of the time she had spent in this bed waiting and hoping to die. I'm not sure, with a grandmother like mine, if you can ever become a true American in the sense of believing that life is about the pursuit of happiness. The lesson of Desdemona's suffering and rejection of life insisted that old age would not continue the manifold pleasures of youth but would instead be a long trial that slowly robbed life of even its smallest, simplest joys. Everyone struggles against despair, but it always wins in the end. It has to. It's the thing that lets us say goodbye.

As I was standing there taking my grandmother in, Desdemona suddenly turned her head and noticed me. Her hand went up to her breast. With a frightened expression she reared back into her pillows and shouted, "Lefty!"

Now I was the one who was shocked. "No, *yia yia*. It's not *papou*. It's me. Cal."

"Who?"

"Cal." I paused. "Your grandson."

This wasn't fair, of course. Desdemona's memory was no longer sharp. But I wasn't helping her out any.

"Cal?"

"They called me Calliope when I was little."

"You look like my Lefty," she said.

"I do?"

"I thought you were my husband coming to take me to heaven." She laughed for the first time.

"I'm Milt and Tessie's kid."

As quickly as it had come, the humor left Desdemona's face and she looked sad and apologetic. "I'm sorry. I don't remember you, honey."

"I brought you these." I held out the Epsom salts and baklava.

"Why Tessie isn't coming?"

"She has to get dressed."

"Dressed for why?"

"For the funeral."

Desdemona gave a cry and clutched her breast again. "Who died?"

I didn't answer. Instead I turned down

the volume on the television. Then, pointing at the birdcage, I said, "I remember when you used to have about twenty birds."

She looked over at the cage but said nothing.

"You used to live in the attic. On Seminole. Remember? That's when you got all the birds. You said they reminded you of Bursa."

At the sound of the name, Desdemona smiled again. "In Bursa we have all kind of birds. Green, yellow, red. All kind. Little birds but very beautiful. Like made from glass."

"I want to go there. Remember that church there? I want to go and fix it up someday."

"Milton is going to fix it. I keep telling him."

"If he doesn't do it, I will."

Desdemona looked at me a moment as if measuring my ability to fulfill this promise. Then she said, "I don't remember you, honey, but please can you fix for *yia yia* the Epsom salts?"

I got the foot basin and filled it with warm water from the bathtub faucet. I sprinkled in the soaking salts and brought it back into the bedroom.

"Put it next the chair, dolly *mou*."

I did so.

"Now help *yia yia* to get out of bed."

Coming closer, I bent down. I slid each of her legs out of the covers, turning her. Putting her arm over my shoulder, I pulled her to her feet for the short walk to the chair.

"I can't do nothing anymore," she lamented on the way. "I'm too old, honey."

"You're doing okay."

"No, I can't remember nothing. I have aches and pains. My heart it is not good."

We had reached the chair now. I maneuvered around behind her to ease her down. Coming around to the front again, I lifted her swollen, blue-veined feet into the sudsy water. Desdemona murmured with pleasure. She closed her eyes.

For the next few minutes Desdemona was silent, luxuriating in the warm foot bath. Color returned to her ankles and rose up her legs. This rosiness disappeared under the hem of her nightgown but, a minute later, peeked out the collar. The flush spread up to her face, and when she opened her eyes there was a clarity in them that had been absent before. She stared straight at me. And then she shouted, "Calliope!"

She held her hand to her mouth. "*Mana!* What happen to you?"

"I grew up," was all I said. I hadn't intended to tell her but now it was out. I had an idea it wouldn't make any difference. She wouldn't remember this conversation.

She was still examining me, the lenses of her glasses magnifying her eyes. Had she had all her wits, Desdemona could not possibly have fathomed what I was saying. But in her senility she somehow accommodated the information. She lived now amid memories and dreams, and in this state the old village stories grew near again.

"You're a boy now, Calliope?"

"More or less."

She took this in. "My mother she use to tell me something funny," she said. "In the village, long time ago, they use to have sometimes babies who were looking like girls. Then — fifteen, sixteen — they are looking like boys! My mother tell me this but I never believe."

"It's a genetic thing. The doctor I went to says it happens in little villages. Where everyone marries each other."

"Dr. Phil he used to talk about this, too."

"He did?"

"It's all my fault." She shook her head grimly.

"What was? What was your fault?"

She was not crying exactly. Her tear ducts were dried up and no moisture rolled down her cheeks. But her face was going through the motions, her shoulders quaking.

"The priests say even first cousins never should marry," she said. "Second cousins is okay, but you have to ask first the archbishop." She was looking away now, trying to remember it all. "Even if you want to marry your godparents' son, you can't. I thought it was only something for the Church. I didn't know it was because what can happen to the babies. I was just stupid girl from village." She went on in that vein for a while, castigating herself. She had momentarily forgotten that I was there or that she was speaking aloud. "And then Dr. Phil he tell me terrible things. I was so scared I had an operation! No more babies. Then Milton he have children and again I was scared. But nothing happen. So I think, after so long time, everything was okay."

"What are you saying, *yia yia? Papou* was your cousin?"

"Third cousin."

"That's all right."

"Not third cousin only. Also brother."

My heart skipped. "*Papou* was your brother?"

"Yes, honey," Desdemona said with infinite weariness. "Long time ago. In another country."

Right then the intercom sounded:

"Callie?" Tessie coughed, correcting herself: "Cal?"

"Yeah."

"You better get cleaned up. The car's coming in ten minutes."

"I'm not going." I paused. "I'm going to stay here with *yia yia*."

"You need to be there, honey," said Tessie.

I crossed to the intercom and put my mouth against the speaker and said in a deep voice, "I'm not going into that church."

"Why not?"

"Have you seen what they charge for those goddamn candles?"

Tessie laughed. She needed to. So I kept going, lowering my voice to sound like my father's. "Two bucks for a candle? What a racket! Maybe you could convince somebody from the old country to shell out for that kind of thing, but not here in the U.S.A.!"

It was infectious to do Milton. Now Tessie lowered her voice in the speaker: "Total rip-off!" she said, and laughed again. We understood then that this was how we were going to do it. This was how we were going to keep Milton alive.

"Are you sure you don't want to go?" she asked me.

"It'll be too complicated, Mom. I don't want to have to explain everything to everybody. Not yet. It'll be too big of a distraction. It'll be better if I'm not there."

947

In her heart Tessie agreed, and so she soon relented. "I'll tell Mrs. Papanikolas she doesn't need to come stay with *yia yia.*"

Desdemona was still looking at me but her eyes had gone dreamy. She was smiling. And then she said, "My spoon was right."

"I guess so."

"I'm sorry, honey. I'm sorry this happen to you."

"It's all right."

"I'm sorry, honey *mou.*"

"I like my life," I told her. "I'm going to have a good life." She still looked pained, so I took her hand.

"Don't worry, *yia yia*. I won't tell anyone."

"Who's to tell? Everybody's dead now."

"You're not. I'll wait until you're gone."

"Okay. When I die, you can tell everything."

"I will."

"Bravo, honey *mou*. Bravo."

At Assumption Church, no doubt against his wishes, Milton Stephanides was given a full Orthodox funeral. Father Greg performed the service. As for Father Michael Antoniou, he was later convicted of attempted grand larceny and served two years in prison. Aunt Zo divorced him and moved to Florida with Desdemona. Where to exactly? New Smyrna Beach. Where else? A few years later, when my mother was forced to sell our house, she moved to Florida, too, and the three of them lived together as they once had on Hurlbut Street, until Desdemona's death in 1980. Tessie and Zoë are still in Florida today, two women living on their own.

Milton's casket remained closed during the funeral. Tessie had given Georgie Pappas, the undertaker, her husband's wedding crown, so that it could be buried along with him. When it came time to give the deceased the final kiss, the mourners filed past Milton's coffin and kissed its burnished lid. Fewer people came to my father's funeral than we expected. None of the Hercules franchise owners showed up, not one of the men Milton had socialized with for years and years; and so we realized that, despite his bonhomie, Milton had never had any friends, only business associates. Family members turned out instead. Peter Tatakis, the chiropractor, arrived in his wine-dark Buick, and Bart Skiotis paid his respects at the church whose foundation he had laid with substandard materials. Gus and Helen Panos were there and, because it was a funeral, Gus's tracheotomy made his voice sound even more like the voice of death. Aunt Zo and our cousins didn't sit in front. That pew was reserved for my mother and brother.

And so it was I who, upholding an old Greek custom no one remembered anymore, stayed behind on Middlesex, blocking the door, so that Milton's spirit wouldn't reenter the house. It was always a man who did this, and now I qualified. In my black suit, with my dirty Wallabees, I stood in the doorway, which was open to the winter wind. The weeping willows were bare but still massive and threw up their twisted arms like women in grief. The pastel yellow cube of our modern house sat cleanly on the white snow. Middlesex was now almost seventy years old. Though we had ruined it with our colonial furniture, it was still the beacon it was intended to be, a place with few interior walls, divested of the formalities of bourgeois life, a place designed for a new type of human being, who would inhabit a new world. I couldn't help feeling, of course, that that person was me, me and all the others like me.

After the funeral service, everyone got back into the cars for the drive to the cemetery. Purple pennants flew from the antennas as the procession drove slowly through the streets of the old East Side where my father had grown up, where he had once serenaded my mother from his bedroom window. The motorcade came down Mack Avenue and when they passed Hurlbut, Tessie looked out the limousine window to see the old house. But she couldn't find it. Bushes had grown up all around, the yards were littered, and the decrepit houses now all looked the same to her. A little later, the hearse and limousines encountered a line of motorcycles and my mother noticed that the drivers were all wearing fezzes. They were Shriners, in town for a convention. Respectfully, they pulled over to let the funeral procession pass.

On Middlesex, I remained in the front doorway. I took my duty seriously and didn't budge, despite the freezing wind. Milton, the child apostate, would have been confirmed in his skepticism, because his spirit never returned that day, trying to get past me. The mulberry tree had no leaves. The wind swept over the crusted snow into my Byzantine face, which was the face of my grandfather and of the American girl I had once been. I stood in the door for an hour, maybe two. I lost track after a while, happy to be home, weeping for my father, and thinking about what was next.

About the Author

⚜

Jeffrey Eugenides was born in Detroit, Michigan, in 1960, the third son of an American-born father whose Greek parents emigrated from Asia Minor and an American mother of Anglo-Irish descent. Mr. Eugenides was educated at public and private schools, graduated from Brown University, and received an M.A. in English and Creative Writing from Stanford University in 1986. Two years later, in 1988, he published his first short story.

Mr. Eugenides' first novel, *The Virgin Suicides* (FSG), was published in 1993. His fiction has appeared in *The New Yorker*, *The Paris Review*, *The Yale Review*, *Best American Short Stories*, *The Gettysburg Review*, and *Granta*. His many awards include fellowships from the Guggenheim Foundation and the National Endowment for the Arts, a Whiting Writers' Award, and the Harold D. Vursell Award from the American Academy of Arts and Letters. In the past few years he has been a Fellow of the Berliner Künstlerprogramm of the DAAD and of the American Academy in Berlin. Mr. Eugenides now lives in Berlin, Germany, with his wife and daughter.

The employees of Thorndike Press hope you have enjoyed this Large Print book. All our Thorndike and Wheeler Large Print titles are designed for easy reading, and all our books are made to last. Other Thorndike Press Large Print books are available at your library, through selected bookstores, or directly from us.

For information about titles, please call:

(800) 223-1244

or visit our Web site at:

www.gale.com/thorndike
www.gale.com/wheeler

To share your comments, please write:

Publisher
Thorndike Press
295 Kennedy Memorial Drive
Waterville, ME   04901